THE CAMBRIDGE EDITION
OF THE WORKS OF

JANE AUSTEN

JUVENILIA

Cambridge University Press and the General Editor
Janet Todd wish to express their gratitude to the
University of Glasgow and the University of Aberdeen for
providing funding towards the creation of this edition.
Their generosity made possible the employment of
Antje Blank as research assistant throughout the project.

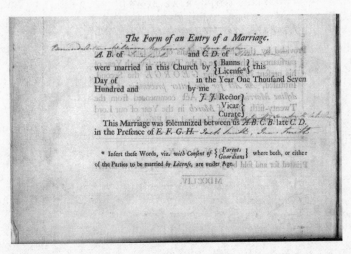

Frontispiece: Page from the Marriage Register of St Nicholas Church, Steventon, reproduced by permission of the Hampshire Record Office. Austen's insertions are indicated in italics:

The Banns of Marriage between *Henry Frederic Howard Fitzwilliam* of *London* and *Jane Austen* of *Steventon*
    Edmund Arthur William Mortimer of *Liverpool* and *Jane Austen* of *Steventon* were married in this Church
    This Marriage was solemnized between us *Jack Smith & Jane Smith late Austen*, in the Presence of *Jack Smith, Jane Smith*

JANE AUSTEN

JUVENILIA

Edited by
Peter Sabor

CAMBRIDGE
UNIVERSITY PRESS

CAMBRIDGE UNIVERSITY PRESS
Cambridge, New York, Melbourne, Madrid, Cape Town, Singapore, São Paulo

Cambridge University Press
The Edinburgh Building, Cambridge CB2 2RU, UK

Published in the United States of America by
Cambridge University Press, New York

www.cambridge.org
Information on this title: www.cambridge.org/9780521824200

© Cambridge University Press 2006

First published 2006

Printed in the United Kingdom at the University Press, Cambridge

A catalogue record for this publication is available from the British Library

ISBN-13   978-0-521-82420-0 hardback
ISBN-10   0-521-82420-6 hardback

CONTENTS

Volume the Second

Volume the Third

GENERAL EDITOR'S PREFACE

Jane Austen wrote to be read and reread. '[A]n artist cannot do anything slovenly,' she remarked to her sister Cassandra. Her subtle, crafted novels repay close and repeated attention to vocabulary, syntax and punctuation as much as to irony and allusion; yet the reader can take immediate and intense delight in their plots and characters. As a result Austen has a unique status among early English novelists – appreciated by the academy and the general public alike. What Henry Crawford remarks about Shakespeare in *Mansfield Park* has become equally true of its author: she 'is a part of an Englishman's constitution. [Her] thoughts and beauties are so spread abroad that one touches them every where, one is intimate with [her] by instinct.' This edition of the complete oeuvre of the published novels and manuscript works is testament to Austen's exceptional cultural and literary position. As well as attempting to establish an accurate and authoritative text, it provides a full contextual placing of the novels.

The editing of any canonical writer is a practice which has been guided by many conflicting ideologies. In the early twentieth century, editors, often working alone, largely agreed that they were producing definitive editions, although they used eclectic methods and often revised the text at will. Later in the century, fidelity to the author's creative intentions was paramount, and the emphasis switched to devising an edition that would as far as possible represent the final authorial wishes. By the 1980s, however, the pursuit of the single perfected text had given way to the recording of multiple intentions of equal interest. Authors were seen to have changed, revised or recanted, or indeed to have directed various versions of their work towards different audiences. Consequently all states had validity and the text became a process rather than a fixed entity. With this approach came emphasis on the print culture in which the text appeared as well as on the social implications of authorship. Rather than being stages in the evolution of a single work, the various versions existed in their own right, all having something to tell.

The Cambridge edition describes fully Austen's early publishing history and provides details of composition, publication and publishers as well as printers and compositors where known. It accepts that many of the decisions concerning spelling, punctuation, capitalizing, italicizing and paragraphing may well have been the compositors' rather than Austen's but that others may represent the author's own chosen style. For the novels published in Jane Austen's lifetime the edition takes as its copytext the latest edition to which she might plausibly have made some contribution: that is, the first editions of *Pride and Prejudice* and *Emma* and the second editions of *Sense and Sensibility* and *Mansfield Park*. Where a second edition is used, all substantive and accidental changes between editions are shown on the page so that the reader can reconstruct the first edition, and the dominance of either first or second editions is avoided. For the two novels published posthumously together, *Northanger Abbey* and *Persuasion*, the copytext is the first published edition.

Our texts as printed here remain as close to the copytexts as possible: spelling and punctuation have not been modernized and inconsistencies in presentation have not been regularized. The few corrections and emendations made to the texts – beyond replacing dropped or missing letters – occur only when an error is very obvious indeed, and/or where retention might interrupt reading or understanding: for example, missing quotation marks have been supplied, run-on words have been separated and repeated words excised. All changes to the texts, substantive and accidental, have been noted in the final apparatus. Four of the six novels appeared individually in three volumes; we have kept the volume divisions and numbering. In the case of *Persuasion,* which was first published as volumes 3 and 4 of a four-volume set including *Northanger Abbey,* the volume division has been retained but volumes 3 and 4 have been relabeled volumes 1 and 2.

For all these novels the copytext has been set against two other copies of the same edition. Where there have been any substantive differences, further copies have been examined; details of these copies are given in the initial textual notes within each volume, along with information about the printing and publishing context of this particular work. The two volumes of the edition devoted to manuscript writings divide the works between the three juvenile notebooks on the one hand and all the remaining manuscript writings on the other. The juvenile notebooks and *Lady Susan* have some resemblance to the published works, being fair copies and following some of the conventions of publishing. The other manuscript writings consist in part of fictional works in early drafts, burlesques and autograph and allograph copies of occasional verses and prayers. The possible dating of the manuscript work, as well as the method of editing, is considered in the introductions to the relevant volumes. The cancelled chapters of *Persuasion* are included in an appendix to the volume *Persuasion;* they appear both in a transliteration and in facsimile. For all the manuscript works, their features as manuscripts have been respected and all changes and erasures either reproduced or noted.

In all the volumes superscript numbers in the texts indicate endnotes. Throughout the edition we have provided full annotations to give clear and informative historical and cultural information to the modern reader while largely avoiding critical speculation; we have also indicated words which no longer have currency or have altered in meaning in some way. The introductions give information concerning the genesis and immediate public reception of the text; they also indicate the most significant stylistic and generic features. A chronology of Austen's life appears in each volume. More information about the life, Austen's reading, her relationship to publication, the print history of the novels and their critical reception through the centuries, as well as the historical, political, intellectual and religious context in which she wrote is available in the final volume of the edition: *Jane Austen in Context*.

I would like to thank Cambridge University Library for supplying the copytexts for the six novels. I am most grateful to Linda Bree at Cambridge University Press for her constant support and unflagging enthusiasm for the edition and to Maartje Scheltens and Alison Powell for their help at every stage of production. I owe the greatest debt to my research assistant Antje Blank for her rare combination of scholarly dedication, editorial skills and critical discernment.

Janet Todd
University of Aberdeen

ACKNOWLEDGEMENTS

For help and advice with various aspects of this edition, I am grateful to Gefen Bar-On, Stephen Clarke, Rosemary Culley, Margaret Anne Doody, Jocelyn Harris, Nicole Joy, Thomas Keymer, Shelley King, Maggie Lane, Deirdre Le Faye, Marie Legroulx, George Logan, Juliet McMaster, Alexis McQuigge, Kerry McSweeney, Lesley Peterson, Emilie Sabor, Philip Smallwood, Brian Southam, Catherine Spencer, Kathryn Sutherland and Lonnie Weatherby. Robert L. Mack, Anje Müller, Claude Rawson and Peter Wagner kindly invited me to present conference papers on Austen's juvenilia, which have helped formulate my ideas.

I am much indebted to Katharine Beaumont, who on two occasions made Austen's annotated copy of Oliver Goldsmith's *History of England* available to me for extended periods of study. I am likewise indebted to Tom Carpenter and Jean Bowden at Jane Austen's House, Chawton, for giving me access to Austen's copy of Vicesimus Knox's *Elegant Extracts*; Martin Kauffmann and B.C. Barker-Benfield at the Bodleian Library, for enabling me to study Austen's 'Volume the First'; and Sally Brown, Andrea Clarke, Michael Crump and Christopher Wright at the British Library, for aiding me with my examination of 'Volume the Second' and 'Volume the Third'. Copies of James Edward Austen-Leigh's handwriting at different stages of his life were kindly provided by Claire Skinner of the Hampshire Record Office.

Linda Bree at Cambridge University Press has been a superb editor and counsellor. I am grateful to her for making many valuable suggestions for the introduction and explanatory notes and for her advice on all aspects of the edition, as well as to others at the Press, including Helen Francis, Alison Powell and Maartje Scheltens. I have also benefited greatly from the assistance and support of the General Editor of the Cambridge Edition of the Works of Jane Austen, Janet Todd, and her research assistant, Antje Blank.

In preparing my explanatory notes, I have drawn on the work of previous editors: especially Brian Southam's edition of *Volume the Third*; Margaret Anne Doody and Douglas Murray's *Catharine and other Writings*; and the Juvenilia Press editions of individual items. My explanatory and textual notes on 'Frederic and Elfrida' and 'Evelyn' are informed by those in Juvenilia Press editions, commissioned by the general editor Juliet McMaster, that I prepared with groups of graduate students at Université Laval.

I began work on this edition as a Visiting Fellow at Christ's College, Cambridge, and thank the Master and Fellows for their hospitality during my stay. I am grateful for strong support at McGill University from the Chair of the Department of English, Paul Yachnin, and his predecessor, Maggie Kilgour, as well as from two former Deans of the Faculty of Arts: Carman Miller and John Hall. Several McGill graduate and postdoctoral students have provided valuable assistance. In the early stages, Jacqueline Reid-Walsh and Elise Moore undertook research for the explanatory notes, while Leslie Wickes contributed to the preparation of the text and the textual notes. In the redaction of the typescript, the editorial skills of Lindsay Holmgren and Laura Kopp were indispensable. For financial support, I am indebted to substantial grants from the Social Sciences and Research Council of Canada and the Canada Research Chairs programme. My father Rudolph, my late mother Emmi and my sister Monika have been a constant source of encouragement. I have shared love and friendship with my wife Marie, who has been living with Jane Austen for many years.

CHRONOLOGY

DEIRDRE LE FAYE

1764
26 April   Marriage of Revd George Austen, rector of
Steventon, and Cassandra Leigh; they go to live at
Deane, Hampshire, and their first three children –
James (1765), George (1766) and Edward (1767) –
are born here.

1768
Summer   The Austen family move to Steventon, Hampshire.
Five more children – Henry (1771), Cassandra
(1773), Francis (1774), Jane (1775), Charles (1779) –
are born here.

1773
23 March   Mr Austen becomes Rector of Deane as well as
Steventon, and takes pupils at Steventon from now
until 1796.

1775
16 December   Jane Austen born at Steventon.

1781
Winter   JA's cousin, Eliza Hancock, marries Jean-François
Capot de Feuillide, in France.

1782

First mention of JA in family tradition, and the first
of the family's amateur theatrical productions takes
place.

1783

JA's third brother, Edward, is adopted by Mr and
Mrs Thomas Knight II, and starts to spend time with
them at Godmersham in Kent.
JA, with her sister Cassandra and cousin

	Jane Cooper, stays for some months in Oxford and then Southampton, with kinswoman Mrs Cawley.
1785 Spring	JA and Cassandra go to the Abbey House School in Reading.
1786	Edward sets off for his Grand Tour of Europe, and does not return until autumn 1790.
April	JA's fifth brother, Francis, enters the Royal Naval Academy in Portsmouth.
December	JA and Cassandra have left school and are at home again in Steventon. Between now and 1793 JA writes her three volumes of *Juvenilia*.
1788 Summer	Mr and Mrs Austen take JA and Cassandra on a trip to Kent and London.
December	Francis leaves the RN Academy and sails to East Indies; does not return until winter 1793.
1791 July	JA's sixth and youngest brother, Charles, enters the Royal Naval Academy in Portsmouth.
27 December	Edward Austen marries Elizabeth Bridges, and they live at Rowling in Kent.
1792 27 March	JA's eldest brother, James, marries Anne Mathew; they live at Deane.
?Winter	Cassandra becomes engaged to Revd Tom Fowle.
1793 23 January	Edward Austen's first child, Fanny, is born at Rowling.
1 February	Republican France declares war on Great Britain and Holland.
8 April	JA's fourth brother, Henry, becomes a lieutenant in the Oxfordshire Militia.

15 April	James Austen's first child, Anna, born at Deane.
3 June	JA writes the last item of her *J.*

1794

22 February	M de Feuillide guillotined in Paris.
September	Charles leaves the RN Academy and goes to sea.
?Autumn	JA possibly writes the novella *Lady Susan* this year.

1795

	JA probably writes 'Elinor and Marianne' this year.
3 May	James's wife Anne dies, and infant Anna is sent to live at Steventon.
Autumn	Revd Tom Fowle joins Lord Craven as his private chaplain for the West Indian campaign.
December	Tom Lefroy visits Ashe Rectory – he and JA have a flirtation over the Christmas holiday period.

1796

October	JA starts writing 'First Impressions'.

1797

17 January	James Austen marries Mary Lloyd, and infant Anna returns to live at Deane.
February	Revd Tom Fowle dies of fever at San Domingo and is buried at sea.
August	JA finishes 'First Impressions' and Mr Austen offers it for publication to Thomas Cadell – rejected sight unseen.
November	JA starts converting 'Elinor and Marianne' into *Sense and Sensibility*. Mrs Austen takes her daughters for a visit to Bath. Edward Austen and his young family move from Rowling to Godmersham.
31 December	Henry Austen marries his cousin, the widowed Eliza de Feuillide, in London.

1798

	JA probably starts writing 'Susan' (later to become *Northanger Abbey*).

| 17 November | James Austen's son James Edward born at Deane. |

1799

| Summer | JA probably finishes 'Susan' (*NA*) about now. |

1800

| | Mr Austen decides to retire and move to Bath. |

1801

| 24 January | Henry Austen resigns his commission in the Oxfordshire Militia and sets up as a banker and army agent in London. |
| May | The Austen family leave Steventon for Bath, and then go for a seaside holiday in the West Country. JA's traditional West Country romance presumably occurs between now and the autumn of 1804. |

1802

25 March	Peace of Amiens appears to bring the war with France to a close.
Summer	Charles Austen joins his family for a seaside holiday in Wales and the West Country.
December	JA and Cassandra visit James and Mary at Steventon; while there, Harris Bigg-Wither proposes to JA and she accepts him, only to withdraw her consent the following day.
Winter	JA revises 'Susan' (*NA*).

1803

Spring	JA sells 'Susan' (*NA*) to Benjamin Crosby; he promises to publish it by 1804, but does not do so.
18 May	Napoleon breaks the Peace of Amiens, and war with France recommences.
Summer	The Austens visit Ramsgate in Kent, and possibly also go to the West Country again.
November	The Austens visit Lyme Regis.

1804

| | JA probably starts writing *The Watsons* this year, but leaves it unfinished. |

Summer	The Austens visit Lyme Regis again.

1805

21 January	Mr Austen dies and is buried in Bath.
Summer	Martha Lloyd joins forces with Mrs Austen and her daughters.
18 June	James Austen's younger daughter, Caroline, born at Steventon.
21 October	Battle of Trafalgar.

1806

2 July	Mrs Austen and her daughters finally leave Bath; they visit Clifton, Adlestrop, Stoneleigh and Hamstall Ridware, before settling in Southampton in the autumn.
24 July	Francis Austen marries Mary Gibson.

1807

19 May	Charles Austen marries Fanny Palmer, in Bermuda.

1808

10 October	Edward Austen's wife Elizabeth dies at Godmersham.

1809

5 April	JA makes an unsuccessful attempt to secure the publication of 'Susan' (*NA*).
7 July	Mrs Austen and her daughters, and Martha Lloyd, move to Chawton, Hants.

1810

Winter	*S&S* is accepted for publication by Thomas Egerton.

1811

February	JA starts planning *Mansfield Park*.
30 October	*S&S* published.
?Winter	JA starts revising 'First Impressions' into *Pride and Prejudice*.

1812

17 June	America declares war on Great Britain.

| 14 October | Mrs Thomas Knight II dies, and Edward Austen now officially takes surname of Knight. |
| Autumn | JA sells copyright of *P&P* to Egerton. |

1813

28 January	*P&P* published; JA half-way through *MP*.
?July	JA finishes *MP*.
?November	*MP* accepted for publication by Egerton about now.

1814

21 January	JA commences *Emma*.
5 April	Napoleon abdicates and is exiled to Elba.
9 May	*MP* published.
24 December	Treaty of Ghent officially ends war with America.

1815

March	Napoleon escapes and resumes power in France; hostilities recommence.
29 March	*E* finished.
18 June	Battle of Waterloo finally ends war with France.
8 August	JA starts *Persuasion*.
4 October	Henry Austen takes JA to London; he falls ill, and she stays longer than anticipated.
13 November	JA visits Carlton House, and receives an invitation to dedicate a future work to the Prince Regent.
December	*E* published by John Murray, dedicated to the Prince Regent (title page 1816).

1816

19 February	2nd edition of *MP* published.
Spring	JA's health starts to fail. Henry Austen buys back manuscript of 'Susan' (*NA*), which JA revises and intends to offer again for publication.
18 July	First draft of *P* finished.
6 August	*P* finally completed.

1817

27 January   JA starts *Sanditon*.

18 March   JA now too ill to work, and has to leave *S* unfinished.

24 May   Cassandra takes JA to Winchester for medical attention.

18 July   JA dies in the early morning.

24 July   JA buried in Winchester Cathedral.

December   *NA* and *P* published together, by Murray, with a 'Biographical Notice' added by Henry Austen (title page 1818).

1869

16 December   JA's nephew, the Revd James Edward Austen-Leigh (JEAL), publishes his *Memoir of Jane Austen*, from which all subsequent biographies have stemmed (title page 1870).

1871

JEAL publishes a second and enlarged edition of his *Memoir*, including in this the novella *LS*, the cancelled chapters of *P*, the unfinished *W*, a précis of *S*, and 'The Mystery' from the *J*.

1884

JA's great-nephew, Lord Brabourne, publishes *Letters of Jane Austen*, the first attempt to collect her surviving correspondence.

1922

Volume the Second of the *J* published.

1925

The manuscript of the unfinished *S* edited by R. W. Chapman and published as *Fragment of a Novel by Jane Austen*.

1932

R. W. Chapman publishes *Jane Austen's Letters to her sister Cassandra and others*, giving letters unknown to Lord Brabourne.

1933

Volume the First of the *J* published.

1951

Volume the Third of the *J* published.

1952

Second edition of R. W. Chapman's *Jane Austen's Letters* published, with additional items.

1954

R. W. Chapman publishes *Jane Austen's Minor Works*, which includes the three volumes of the *J* and other smaller items.

1980

B. C. Southam publishes *Jane Austen's 'Sir Charles Grandison'*, a small manuscript discovered in 1977.

1995

Deirdre Le Faye publishes the third (new) edition of *Jane Austen's Letters*, containing further additions to the Chapman collections.

INTRODUCTION

In a letter to her sister Cassandra of 23 August 1814, Jane Austen refers to some odd travelling arrangements that 'put me in mind of my own Coach between Edinburgh & Sterling'.[1] The allusion is to the ending of 'Love and Freindship', perhaps the most brilliant of all her youthful productions and the one most appreciated by critics since the rediscovery of her early writings began in the 1920s. Astonishingly sophisticated and inventive, these writings are now receiving the attention they deserve, after long being overshadowed by the six published novels. The present volume is the fourth collected edition of Austen's juvenilia, following those edited by R. W. Chapman in 1954, Margaret Anne Doody and Douglas Murray in 1993, and Janet Todd in 1998,[2] and the first to include the copious marginalia that she wrote on her copies of Oliver Goldsmith's four-volume *History of England* (1772) and Vicesimus Knox's *Elegant Extracts . . . in Prose*. Chapman, afraid that they might detract from Austen's stature as a novelist, presented the juvenilia diffidently, declaring that 'these immature or fragmentary fictions call for hardly any comment'.[3] Fifty years later, Austen's remarkable early fictions, fragmentary though some of them are, can no longer be dismissed as mere apprentice work, and rather than damaging Austen's reputation they have come to augment it. With what Doody has aptly termed their 'ruthless and exuberant style of comic

---

[1] Deirdre Le Faye (ed.), *Jane Austen's Letters*, 3rd edn (Oxford: Oxford University Press, 1995), p. 270.

[2] R. W. Chapman (ed.), *The Works of Jane Austen*, vol. VI: *Minor Works* (Oxford: Clarendon Press, 1954); Margaret Anne Doody and Douglas Murray (eds.), *Catharine and Other Writings* (Oxford: Oxford World's Classics, 1993); Janet Todd (ed.), *Love and Freindship and Other Stories by Jane Austen* (New York: Phoenix, 1998).

[3] Chapman (ed.), *Minor Works*, p. v.

vision',[4] they represent not an embryonic form of the later novels but a major achievement in their own right. Ruthlessness and exuberance also pervade Austen's letters, but these qualities are muted in her mature fiction until the last novel, *Sanditon*, on which she was working until the final months of her life and which has something of the wild abruptness of her earliest writings. Scattered allusions to the juvenilia in her letters, as well as occasional revisions made in 1811 or later, show that Austen continued to value her first productions. Unlike Frances Burney, who in 1767 destroyed all of her juvenilia – everything she wrote before *Evelina* – in a ceremonial bonfire on her fifteenth birthday, Austen preserved her early writings until her death in 1817.

COMPOSITION AND PUBLICATION

No original drafts of Austen's first writings survive. What remains are her transcriptions in three notebooks, containing a total of some 74,000 words.[5] She gave these notebooks the mock-solemn titles of 'Volume the First', 'Volume the Second' and 'Volume the Third', as though to form a three-volume novel. When her first novel, *Sense and Sensibility*, was published in 1811 it appeared in just such a format, as did the others that she published in her lifetime: *Pride and Prejudice* (1813), *Mansfield Park* (1814) and *Emma* (1816). The notebooks, however, gather together writings from a much earlier period of Austen's life: from 1787, when she was eleven, to June 1793, when she was seventeen. During these years, probably in 1792, Austen wrote the marginalia, hitherto largely unpublished, transcribed in Appendixes A and B below. Also during this period, possibly in 1793 or even later, she wrote mock entries in a page of the St Nicholas Church marriage register

---

[4] Margaret Anne Doody, 'Jane Austen, That Disconcerting "child"', in *The Child Writer from Austen to Woolf*, ed. Christine Alexander and Juliet McMaster (Cambridge: Cambridge University Press, 2005), p. 119.

[5] My computer-generated count differs from that of B. C. Southam, who estimated 'over 90,000 words' (*Jane Austen's Literary Manuscripts: A Study of the Novelist's Development through the Surviving Papers* (Oxford: Oxford University Press, 1964), p. 1).

(reproduced as the frontispiece to this edition), with the names of three imaginary husbands: Henry Frederic Howard Fitzwilliam of London, Edmund Arthur William Mortimer of Liverpool and, with deft comic bathos, plain Jack Smith.[6]

Austen's manuscript notebooks contain twenty-seven items in all: sixteen in 'Volume the First', nine in 'Volume the Second' and two in 'Volume the Third'. Most are short fictions, but the young Austen also wrote the opening of what could have become a full-length novel, 'Catharine', as well as dramatic sketches, verses and a few non-fictional pieces, including a condensed history of England that covers the events of some three hundred years in well under twenty pages. 'Volume the First', the shabbiest of the three notebooks, is a small quarto, bound in quarter calf and marbled boards. The leather on the spine is now largely worn away, and the boards are severely rubbed and faded. The front board has an ink inscription, 'Volume the First', written in large letters, possibly by Austen herself, while the front pastedown endpaper has a pencil inscription by her sister Cassandra, 'For my Brother Charles'. Pasted to this endpaper is a scrap of paper with an ink inscription, also by Cassandra: 'For my Brother Charles. I think I recollect that a few of the trifles in this Vol. were written expressly for his amusement. C. E. A.' The notebook has ninety-two leaves, the first two unnumbered and the others paginated 1–180 by Austen.[7]

'Volume the Second' is also a small quarto, bound in white vellum, now faded to yellow and heavily stained with ink. It was a gift from Austen's father, the Reverend George Austen; the contents page contains the phrase, in her hand, 'Ex dono mei Patris', one of the only Latin tags in her fiction or letters. Doody supposes

---

[6] Elizabeth Jenkins suggests that the hand is later than that of 'Love and Freindship', written in 1790 when Austen was fourteen ('The Marriage Registers at Steventon', *Jane Austen Society Collected Reports 1949–1965* (London: William Dawson, 1967), pp. 294–5).

[7] Page 167 is misnumbered 177, and page 175 is unnumbered. The first two unnumbered pages contain a list of contents, the third is blank, while the fourth contains the dedication of the first item, 'Frederic and Elfrida'.

that George Austen had been 'so pleased and entertained with the material already appearing in *Volume the First* that he supplied the finer notebook as an encouragement to further productions'.[8] The front board has an ink inscription, 'Volume the Second', in Austen's hand, while the spine contains what might be the same words, in barely legible lettering. The front pastedown endpaper has a pencil inscription by Cassandra, 'For my Brother Frank, C. E. A.', and the same words are inscribed in ink, on a scrap of paper pasted to the endpaper. 'Volume the Second' is the longest of the notebooks, with 264 pages paginated by Austen. The pagination was made after twelve leaves had been cut out with scissors, apparently by Austen herself, leaving stubs in each case.[9] Some of the missing pages, such as those at the end of the notebook, were probably blanks, thriftily recycled for use elsewhere; others, such as the leaves in 'Letter the second' and 'Letter the fourth', seem to have been removed because they were spoiled.[10] The contents page, in Austen's hand, shows that no pieces are missing, and there are no breaks in the text in any of the volume's nine items.

'Volume the Third', another small quarto, bound in vellum-covered boards, is the shortest of the notebooks, with 140 pages, the majority paginated by Austen. The contents page is signed 'Jane Austen – May 6th 1792'. On the inside front cover is a pencil note in the hand of Jane's father: 'Effusions of Fancy by a very Young Lady consisting of Tales in a Style entirely new'. The front board has an ink inscription, 'Volume the Third', in Jane Austen's hand, while

---

[8] Margaret Anne Doody, intro. to *Catharine*, p. xvi.

[9] The missing leaves are between pages 64 (the end of 'Love and Freindship') and 67 (the beginning of 'Lesley Castle': one leaf missing); 186 (the end of 'The History of England') and 187 (the dedication to 'A Collection of Letters': two leaves missing); 200 (near the end of 'Letter the second') and 201 (three leaves missing); 212 (the second page of 'Letter the fourth') and 213 (one leaf missing); and after 252 (five leaves removed from the end of the notebook).

[10] B. C. Southam notes that the stub between the second and third pages of 'Letter the fourth' 'shows the beginning of words' and believes that the missing sheet 'was certainly completely written on both sides' ('Note on the Missing Sheets', in *Volume the Second*, ed. Southam (Oxford: Clarendon Press, 1963), p. 210).

the spine bears the mysterious inscription 'aft. 18', possibly by her and possibly standing for 'after 18'. On the first page, in Cassandra's hand, is the inscription 'for James Edward Austen', son of Austen's brother James. The word 'Leigh' was later inserted after 'Austen' in a different hand, evidently not before 1837, when James Edward Austen added 'Leigh' to his surname. Both items in 'Volume the Third' – 'Evelyn' and 'Catharine' – are unfinished, and both have continuations by James Edward, who completed 'Evelyn' and twice attempted, unsuccessfully, to complete 'Catharine'; see Appendix E below.

As Austen's favourite nephew and a would-be novelist himself, James Edward Austen-Leigh used his knowledge of his aunt to produce a first-hand account, *A Memoir of Jane Austen*, published in December 1869. In a second edition of 1871, he attempted to date Austen's early writings, using clues provided by his sister Caroline Austen. According to Caroline, in Austen's final months, after her move to Winchester in May 1817, 'she sent me a message to this effect, that if I would take her advice I should cease writing till I was sixteen; that she had herself often wished she had read more, and written less in the corresponding years of her own life'.[11] Caroline, born on 18 June 1805, was eleven when Austen moved to Winchester and had just turned twelve at the time of Austen's death in July 1817. This suggests, as Austen-Leigh noted, that Austen began writing her juvenilia before her own twelfth birthday, in December 1787. From the spring of 1785, Austen, together with Cassandra and their cousin Jane Cooper, attended the Abbey House School, Reading, returning to her family home in Steventon before the end of 1786. The earliest of the juvenilia were probably written shortly after Austen left school, and subsequently copied into the first of the manuscript notebooks. The three volumes are not, however, ordered chronologically, and as Brian Southam conjectures,

---

[11] James Edward Austen-Leigh, *A Memoir of Jane Austen and Other Family Recollections*, ed. Kathryn Sutherland (Oxford: Oxford World's Classics, 2002), p. 42.

'it looks as if Jane Austen entered fresh material into whichever of the three notebooks was most conveniently to hand'.[12]

Each of the manuscript volumes contains dates provided by Austen herself. In 'Volume the First', three pieces dedicated to her niece Anna – 'A fragment—written to inculcate the practice of Virtue', 'A beautiful description of the different effects of sensibility on different minds' and 'The Generous Curate' – are dated 2 June 1793, and after the final item, 'Ode to Pity', Austen wrote 'End of the first Volume June 3d 1793'. Most of the other items in the volume can be dated at least conjecturally. All but one, 'The Three Sisters', are written in a relatively childish hand, and probably belong to the years 1787 to 1790. The following table provides tentative dates; for justifications, see the explanatory notes for each item:

'Volume the First'

1787	'Edgar and Emma', 'Amelia Webster', 'Frederic and Elfrida'
1788	'Sir William Mountague', 'Memoirs of Mr Clifford', 'The Mystery', 'The beautifull Cassandra' (after August), 'Henry and Eliza' (late December or early January 1789)
1789	'The Visit'
1790	'Jack and Alice', 'The adventures of Mr Harley'
1791	'The Three Sisters' (December?)
1793	'A fragment', 'A beautiful description', 'The Generous Curate' (all 2 June), 'Ode to Pity' (3 June)

Dating the contents of 'Volume the Second' is more straightforward. 'Love and Freindship' and 'The History of England' are both given precise dates by Austen: 13 June 1790 and 26 November 1791. 'Lesley Castle' can be conjecturally dated to spring 1792, while 'A Collection of Letters' probably dates from autumn of that year. The five short pieces dedicated to Fanny Catherine Austen

---

[12] Brian Southam, 'Juvenilia', in *The Jane Austen Handbook*, ed. J. David Grey (London: Athlone Press, 1986), p. 245.

that conclude the volume were probably written between January and June 1793. The following table provides tentative dates:

'Volume the Second'

1790	'Love and Freindship' (13 June)
1791	'The History of England' (26 November)
1792	'Lesley Castle' (spring), 'A Collection of Letters' (autumn)
1793	'The female philosopher', 'The first Act of a Comedy', 'A Letter from a Young Lady', 'A Tour through Wales', 'A Tale' (all between January and June)

In 'Volume the Third', Austen dated the contents page: 6 May 1792. The first item, however, 'Evelyn', was probably written in late 1791, before being transcribed in the notebook, while the dedication to 'Catharine' is dated August 1792. The following table provides tentative dates:

'Volume the Third'

1791	'Evelyn' (November–December)
1792	Contents page (6 May), 'Catharine, or the Bower' (August)

The three manuscript volumes do not contain all of Austen's early writings. In dedicating her dramatic sketch 'The Visit' to her brother James, Austen terms it 'inferior to those celebrated Comedies called "The school for Jealousy" and "The travelled Man"'. No comedies with these titles are recorded. They could be mock-titles or they could be plays written by James for the Austen family's private theatricals. But it is at least equally probable that Austen is referring jokingly to two of her own earlier comedies. She wrote, originally, that her aim was to 'afford some amusement' when 'they [the three plays] was first composed' (p. 61). She later changed the 'they' to 'it', referring to 'The Visit' alone, perhaps not wishing to reveal her authorship of earlier, now discarded comedies. Another dedication, that to 'Lesley Castle', also suggests the existence of lost writings. Here Austen tells her brother Henry: 'I am now availing myself of the Liberty you have frequently honoured me with of dedicating one of my Novels to you' (p. 142). The remark is again ambiguous, and could refer to fiction that Henry had dedicated to his sister. A more probable reading, however, is that Jane Austen had previously dedicated 'Novels' to Henry, without caring to preserve them in her notebooks. Henry was, after all, Austen's 'favourite brother',[13] and it seems unlikely that she would have waited until 1792 to dedicate one of her writings to him.[14]

Another possible early composition by Austen is a letter from 'Sophia Sentiment' in *The Loiterer*, a weekly periodical founded by her brother James at Oxford in January 1789 (see Appendix D below). First attributed to Austen on stylistic grounds in 1966, the letter, published in *The Loiterer* for 28 March 1789, has the characteristic verve and inventiveness of her youthful writings. The young Austen, who read contemporary fiction and drama voraciously, would have known *The Mausoleum* (1785), a comedy by William Hayley in which a character named Lady Sophia Sentiment appears.[15] The ninth number of *The Loiterer*, in which the letter was published, was the first to be sold in Reading and advertised in the *Reading Mercury*, the newspaper circulating in Austen's North Hampshire. None of these points is conclusive in itself, but the overall case for Austen's authorship of the letter is strong. Austen was certainly a close reader of *The Loiterer*, and some parallels between contributions to the magazine and her early writings are noted in the explanatory notes below.[16] Also possibly dating

---

[13] William and Richard Arthur Austen-Leigh, *Jane Austen: Her Life and Letters, A Family Record* (London: Smith, Elder, 1913), p. 48.

[14] See B. C. Southam, 'Jane Austen's Juvenilia: The Question of Completeness', *Notes and Queries*, 209 (1964), 180–1. The editors of the Pléiade edition of Jane Austen go further, contending that the notebooks are an anthology, containing only a small part of Austen's early writings (Pierre Goubert *et al.* (eds.), *Œuvres romanesques complètes* (Paris: Gallimard, 2000–), vol. I, p. 1093.

[15] Austen acquired her own set of Hayley's works in April 1791; see David Gilson, *A Bibliography of Jane Austen*, rev. edn (Winchester: St Paul's Bibliographies, 1997), p. 442.

[16] See also Walton Litz, '*The Loiterer*: A Reflection of Jane Austen's Early Environment', *Review of English Studies*, new series, 12 (1961), 251–61; and Li-Ping Geng, '*The Loiterer* and Jane Austen's Literary Identity', *Eighteenth-Century Fiction*, 13 (2001), 579–92.

from this period is the first act of a dramatic adaptation of scenes from Samuel Richardson's novel *Sir Charles Grandison*. The comedy was formerly attributed to Austen's niece Anna, daughter of her brother James, who was thought to have dictated it to her aunt in the early 1800s. Southam, however, believes that Austen wrote most of the play herself, completing the first act in the early 1790s when she 'was first trying her hand at *Grandison* jokes in the small prose satires'.[17] Another composition in Austen's hand excluded from the notebooks is a poem entitled 'This little bag', dated by the author: January 1792. The verses were written to accompany a sewing bag given to Mary Lloyd, and Austen presumably felt that they should not be divorced from the gift that occasioned them.[18]

While some of Austen's early writings are missing from her manuscript notebooks, the notebooks, conversely, contain material that is not by her. In 'Volume the Second', her brother Henry wrote a comic reply to Austen's dedication to 'Lesley Castle', purporting to order his bank ('Messrs Demand and Co') to pay her the sum of one hundred guineas. The next item in 'Volume the Second', 'The History of England', contains thirteen pen and watercolour medallion portraits, painted and signed by Cassandra Austen. These satirical illustrations work in close conjunction with Austen's text: 'The History of England' is a collaborative project between the two sisters. Austen also had collaborators for both of her unfinished writings in 'Volume the Third': 'Evelyn' and 'Catharine'. Having transcribed 'Evelyn' into the notebook in May 1792, she left ten blank pages in which the story could be completed. Almost twenty-five years later, in about 1815–16, her nephew James Edward wrote an ending and transcribed it into the vacant space in 'Volume the

---

[17] Brian Southam (ed.), *Jane Austen's 'Sir Charles Grandison'* (Oxford: Clarendon Press, 1980), p. 9. Paula Byrne suggests that the first act might be still earlier, dating 'from the 1780s, when the family was engaged in private theatricals' (*Jane Austen and the Theatre* (London: Hambledon, 2002), p. 90). Deirdre Le Faye, however, dates the whole play to c. 1800–5 (*Jane Austen: A Family Record*, 2nd edn (Cambridge: Cambridge University Press, 2004), p. 150).

[18] 'Sir Charles Grandison' and 'This Little Bag' are both included in the volume of Austen's *Later Manuscripts* in the Cambridge Edition.

Third', presumably with Austen's permission. Another attempted conclusion by Austen's niece Anna Lefroy, inserted into the volume on loose leaves of paper, was itself left incomplete and might not have been written until after Austen's death in 1817 (see Appendix E below). James Edward also made two attempts to complete 'Catharine': one in about 1815–16 and the other when he inherited 'Volume the Third' in 1845. This, however, was a much more demanding task than finishing 'Evelyn', and neither of his brief continuations does much to advance Austen's work.

The text of the notebooks is further complicated by Austen's extensive revisions, deletions and insertions, recorded here in the textual notes. Most of these alterations were made during the initial transcription, but others are clearly later additions. In 'Frederic and Elfrida', for example, the initial item in 'Volume the First', the dedication to Martha Lloyd, is written in a hand that seems considerably more mature than that in which the work itself is written and probably postdates the transcription of the story by several years. In 'Catharine', a reference to a 'Regency walking dress' could not have been inserted before 1811, when the Regency Act was proclaimed, while another late revision in 'Catharine' is a reference to Hannah More's didactic novel of 1809, *Coelebs in Search of a Wife*. Some of the pieces are very lightly altered while others contain copious revisions: about a hundred each for 'Love and Freindship' and 'Lesley Castle' and 115 for 'Catharine'. In 'Volume the First', the ten changes to 'Frederic and Elfrida' are almost all of single words. The revisions to 'The Three Sisters' in the same volume are much more extensive, including the deletion of three passages of several lines each. One of these concerns the desire of Mary, the eldest sister, to have new jewels on her marriage, including 'Pearls, Rubies, Emeralds, and Beads out of number' (p. 82). Mary's greed is risible as it stands, but originally Austen had made her far more extravagant, dreaming of 'Pearls as large as those of the Princess Badroulbadour, in the 4th Volume of the Arabian Nights and Rubies, Emeralds, Toppazes, Sapphires, Amythists, Turkey stones, Agate, Beads, Bugles and Garnets'.

The hand in which 'The Three Sisters' is written is later than that of the preceding eleven pieces in 'Volume the First', and Austen, at this later date, was more severe in editing her own writings. Another sign of this severity is the cancellation of an entire short piece, 'A Fragment written to inculcate the practice of Virtue': dedicated to Austen's niece Anna but then scored through with horizontal, vertical and diagonal lines. In 'Catharine', similarly, Austen deletes spirited retorts by the heroine to her aunt and to her friend Miss Stanley, thus softening her character somewhat, and also removes an especially offensive criticism of Catharine by Mrs Percival: 'Her intimacies with Young men are abominable; and it is all the same to her, who it is, no one comes amiss to her' (p. 282). In the third of 'A Collection of Letters', 'From A Young Lady in distress'd Circumstances', written at about the same time as 'Catharine', Austen makes similar revisions in Maria's exchanges with Lady Greville, subduing the tone of Maria's responses to aristocratic hauteur. These revisions, conversely, make Lady Greville still more insulting when she refers to the wind's exposing Maria's 'legs', rather than her 'ancles'.

In addition to revising the texts of the notebooks, Austen made occasional efforts to amend her idiosyncratic spellings. By the time she came to prepare the contents page for 'Volume the Second', probably in June 1793, she was spelling 'Friendship' in the conventional manner.[19] In all three notebooks, however, she uses 'freind', 'freindship', etc., with only one exception: in 'The female philosopher', one of the last items in 'Volume the Second', 'freind' is changed to 'friend' (p. 216). Austen also made occasional but not consistent corrections to spellings such as 'compleat' and 'extreamly', as well as to some uses of the 'full' suffix in words such as 'beautifull', 'wonderfull', etc. She was equally unsystematic in making changes to the names of her characters. In 'The Visit', Sir Arthur Hampton's name is first spelled 'Authar'; Austen changed

---

[19] For a useful account of Austen's spelling in the juvenilia and in 'Lady Susan', see Christine Alexander and David Owen, 'Spelling and Punctuation in *Lady Susan*', in *Lady Susan*, ed. Alexander and Owen (Sydney: Juvenilia Press, 2005) pp. 101–5.

this to 'Authur', before finally settling on 'Arthur'. In 'Lesley
Castle', the Lutterell sisters are spelled 'Luttrell' from letter the
fifth onwards, but in letter the ninth the name is changed back to
Lutterell. In the same story, Louisa runs away with 'Danvers and
dishonour', but when Austen added a playful footnote here, she used
a different spelling, 'Dishonor' (letter the first). In 'Catharine', the
heroine appears as Kitty on the contents page for 'Volume the Third'
and as Kitty, Catharine or Catherine in the text. Her aunt, originally Mrs Peterson, becomes Mrs Percival, but in some instances
'Peterson' is not corrected, or else scored through to become simply
'P'. As Southam observes, Austen's manuscript revision 'was not
a full-scale process, but an alteration of whatever discarded forms
happened to meet her eye, probably as she was reading the stories aloud'.[20] Occasionally too, Austen caught herself committing
factual errors. In 'Edgar and Emma', for example, she originally
has Mr Willmot inheriting the paternal estate, although he is 'a
younger representative' of his family; in her revision, he becomes
simply 'the representative' (p. 34).

Austen dedicated all but one of her early writings, 'Edgar and
Emma', to a family member or close friend, with several being
honoured on two or more occasions. Some of these dedications are
literary compositions in themselves, such as that to 'The Beautifull
Cassandra', in which Austen, addressing her sister as a 'Phoenix',
contrives to sound like a preposterously formal Elizabethan courtier
addressing the Queen. The following table lists the dedicatees in
descending order of frequency:

Fanny Austen (niece)	'The female philosopher', 'The first Act of a Comedy', 'A Letter from a Young Lady', 'A Tour Through Wales', 'A Tale' ['Scraps' in Austen's

---

[20] B. C. Southam, 'The Manuscript of Jane Austen's Volume the First', *The Library*, 5th
series, 17 (1962), 237. I disagree, however, with Southam's claim (p. 236) that Austen
twice uses the conventional spelling of 'friend' in the latter part of 'Volume the First';
in both of the instances he cites, the correct manuscript reading is 'freind'.

	contents page for 'Volume the Second'] (5)
Cassandra Austen (sister)	'The beautifull Cassandra', 'Ode to Pity', 'The History of England', 'Catharine, or the Bower' (4)
Anna Austen (niece)	'A fragment', 'A beautiful description', 'The Generous Curate' ['Detached pieces' in Austen's contents page for 'Volume the First'] (3)
Jane Cooper (cousin)	'Henry and Eliza', 'A Collection of Letters' (2)
Francis Austen (brother)	'Jack and Alice', 'The adventures of Mr Harley' (2)
Charles Austen (brother)	'Sir William Mountague', 'Memoirs of Mr Clifford' (2)
James Austen (brother)	'The Visit' (1)
Edward Austen (brother)	'The Three Sisters' (1)
Henry Austen (brother)	'Lesley Castle' (1)
Cassandra Leigh Austen (mother)	'Amelia Webster' (1)
George Austen (father)	'The Mystery' (1)
Eliza de Feuillide (cousin)	'Love and Freindship' (1)
Martha Lloyd (friend)	'Frederic and Elfrida' (1)
Mary Lloyd (friend)	'Evelyn' (1)

The links between writings and their dedicatees are carefully calibrated. The two nieces Anna and Fanny Austen, newborn babies when Austen wrote her dedications to 'Detached pieces' (for Anna) and 'Scraps' (for Fanny), receive eight items between them, almost a third of the total, but these are all brief and relatively simple pieces which the recipients could have enjoyed from a young age. Austen's beloved sister Cassandra appears as dedicatee in all three volumes and is the recipient of two of Austen's most ambitious early writings: the 'History of England' and 'Catharine'. To James Austen, writer of a series of prologues for the Austen family theatricals at Steventon, Austen dedicated 'The Visit', the best of her comic plays. Another brother, Edward, became engaged in 1791 to Elizabeth Bridges, whose two sisters became engaged in the same year; Austen naturally made him the dedicatee of 'The Three Sisters', in which the sisters vie for the attention of a single suitor. The outrageously inventive 'Love and Freindship' is dedicated to Austen's indomitable cousin, Eliza de Feuillide. 'Evelyn', in which the hero instantaneously acquires a new house and bride, was presented to Mary Lloyd, Austen's friend and neighbour, just before she left Deane parsonage. The new owner, James Austen, was also about to acquire a house and bride; Austen's black humour made the displaced Mary the obvious dedicatee.

During Austen's lifetime, the existence of her early writings was unknown outside her immediate circle of family and close friends. Cassandra and some of the other dedicatees, such as Austen's mother and father, probably read them all, or would at least have heard them read aloud by the author. In his 'Biographical Notice' prefixed to the posthumous edition of *Northanger Abbey* and *Persuasion* (1818), her brother Henry noted that Austen's works 'were never heard to so much advantage as from her own mouth; for she partook largely in all the best gifts of the comic muse'.[21] Presumably, these family readings began with the juvenilia; Southam suggests that 'the carelessness of some of the writing may . . . be attributed to the fact that Jane Austen intended these pieces to be heard, not read'.[22] Some nieces and nephews born too late to have pieces dedicated to them would also have heard or read the early writings. But the total number of readers was small, as Austen's mocking reference, in one of her dedications, to the presence of 'The beautifull Cassandra' and 'The History of England' in 'every library in the Kingdom' (p. 241) suggests. Even in the Steventon rectory, Austen's juvenilia would have been found in the drawing room, not the library, and far from having 'run through threescore

---

[21] Henry Austen, 'Biographical Notice of the Author', in James Edward Austen-Leigh, *A Memoir of Jane Austen*, ed. Sutherland, p. 140.

[22] Southam (ed.), *Volume the Second*, p. xi.

Editions' as the dedication boasts, they would remain in manuscript until well into the twentieth century.

On Austen's death in 1817, the three manuscript notebooks were preserved by Cassandra, and after Cassandra's death in 1845 they were passed down in different branches of the Austen family. 'Volume the First' went, as Cassandra intended, to her youngest brother Charles and remained in his family, descending to his eldest daughter, Cassandra Esten, and then to Cassandra Esten's nieces, the daughters of his son Charles John. Three of these daughters – Jane, Emma Florence and Blanche Frederica Austen – all impecunious spinsters, sold various Austen manuscripts in the 1920s, including 'Volume the First'. In November 1932 its whereabouts was discovered by R. W. Chapman, who arranged for it to be bought for the Bodleian Library, Oxford, by the Friends of the Bodleian, for £75. The sale was completed in January 1933 but Chapman retained possession of the notebook for several months, giving him time to edit the work for the Clarendon Press.[23]

'Volume the Second', also following Cassandra's wishes, went to her brother Frank (later Admiral of the Fleet, Sir Francis Austen), remaining in his family's possession until 1977, when it was put on sale at Sotheby's and listed in the catalogue for 6 July as 'the property of a descendant of Jane Austen'. The buyer was the British Library, which acquired it for £40,000.[24] Editions of 'Volume the Second' were published in 1922 and 1963, both prepared while the notebook was still in the hands of Francis Austen's descendants: first Janet R. Sanders, his granddaughter, and later Rosemary Mowll, his great-granddaughter.[25] 'Volume the Third', on Cassandra's death, went to her nephew James Edward Austen-Leigh and remained in the Austen-Leigh family until 1976. The last of the three notebooks

---

[23] See Gilson, *A Bibliography of Jane Austen*, p. 383, and R. W. Chapman's unpublished correspondence, Bodleian Library.

[24] See Gilson, *A Bibliography of Jane Austen*, p. 373, and Gilson, 'Notes on Auction Sales, 1975–July 1977', *Jane Austen Society Collected Reports 1976–1985* (Chippenham: The Jane Austen Society, 1989), p. 51.

[25] *Love & Freindship and Other Early Works*, pref. G. K. Chesterton (London: Chatto & Windus, 1922); Southam (ed.), *Volume the Second*.

to be published, it was first edited by Chapman in 1951, when it belonged to Austen-Leigh's grandson, Richard Arthur Austen-Leigh. In 1963 it was deposited on loan in the British Museum, before being put on sale at Sotheby's and listed in the catalogue for 14 December 1976. It was bought by the British Rail Pension Fund under the pseudonym of 'Maxwell' for £30,000, before being sold again by Sotheby's, on 27 September 1988, and bought by the British Library for £120,000.[26] Within the space of fifty-five years, from 1933 to 1988, the price fetched by an Austen notebook had thus increased dramatically, from £75 to £120,000. Even allowing for general inflation, this is a spectacular rise. In comparison, consumer prices in general rose by a factor of about 26 over the same period; Austen notebooks rose by a factor of 1,600.

No mention of Austen's early writings was made in her brother Henry's 'Biographical Notice of the Author' (1818), or in the expanded version, entitled 'Memoir of Miss Austen', prefixed to the first collected edition of Austen's novels, issued by Richard Bentley in 1833. According to Henry's account, Jane Austen's creative writing began with *Sense and Sensibility*. The first public notice of Austen's juvenilia came in December 1869, when James Edward Austen-Leigh published *A Memoir of Jane Austen*. Without printing any of the material, Austen-Leigh declared that 'there is extant an old copy-book containing several tales, some of which seem to have been composed while she was quite a girl'. The statement is disingenuous, since Austen-Leigh knew of the existence of all three of the manuscript notebooks: 'Volume the First', then owned by his cousin Cassandra Esten Austen; 'Volume the Second', owned by his cousin Frances Sophia Austen; and 'Volume the Third', in his own possession. After thus concealing the existence of two of the three volumes of juvenilia, he added that 'it would be as unfair to expose this preliminary process to the world, as it would be to display all that goes on behind the curtain of the theatre before

---

[26] See David Gilson, 'Notes on Auction Sales, 1988–89', *Jane Austen Society Collected Reports 1986–1995* (Alton: The Jane Austen Society, 1997), p. 149; and Gilson, *A Bibliography of Jane Austen*, pp. xli, 386.

it is drawn up'.[27] The simile is revealing. Like many of Austen's subsequent critics, Austen-Leigh regarded his aunt's early writings merely as stage rehearsals for the six published novels; rather than considering them in their own right, he dismissed them as the crude experiments of a child.

In the second edition of his *Memoir*, Austen-Leigh was somewhat more forthcoming about Austen's early writings. Here he states, more accurately, that 'there are copy books extant containing tales some of which must have been composed while she was a young girl, as they had amounted to a considerable number by the time she was sixteen'. In both versions of his account, Austen-Leigh declares that the stories are 'of a slight and flimsy texture, and are generally intended to be nonsensical', but in the second edition he provides a sample, described as 'one of her juvenile effusions', given 'as a specimen of the kind of transitory amusement which Jane was continually supplying to the family party'.[28] The item selected for publication, the first of Austen's juvenilia ever to be printed, was the slighter of two miniature comic dramas in 'Volume the First', 'The Mystery'. As one of Austen's earliest writings, the play is of considerable interest. It might have been performed as an afterpiece by the Austen family as part of what they termed a 'private Theatrical Exhibition' in 1788, together with a main play for which a prologue by Austen-Leigh's father, James Austen, survives.[29] Austen-Leigh, however, makes no mention of this. The play's principal merit for him was probably its extreme brevity: among the shortest of all the early writings and occupying less than two pages of his volume, it was in no danger of calling attention to the juvenilia as a substantial body of work and thus undermining the image of Austen as a mature writer of realistic fiction that his memoir sought to construct.[30]

---

[27] James Edward Austen-Leigh, *A Memoir of Jane Austen* (London: Richard Bentley, 1870), pp. 59, 62.

[28] Austen-Leigh, *A Memoir of Jane Austen*, ed. Sutherland, pp. 39–40.

[29] See Le Faye, *A Family Record*, p. 66.

[30] See Kathryn Sutherland, intro. to Austen-Leigh, *A Memoir of Jane Austen*, p. xvi.

While preparing his *Memoir*, Austen-Leigh had consulted his sister Caroline and other family members on the question of which Austen manuscripts he might choose for publication. Caroline's recommendation was 'Evelyn', the first item in 'Volume the Third'. Explaining her choice, she wrote:

I have thought that the story, I beleive in your possession, all nonsense, *might* be used. I don't mean Kitty's Bower, but the other—of the gentleman who wanders forth and is put in possession of a stranger's house, and married to his daughter Maria. I have always thought it remarkable that the early workings of her mind should have been in burlesque, and comic exaggeration, setting at nought all rules of probable or possible—when of all her finished and later writings, the exact contrary is the characteristic. The story I mean is clever nonsense but one knows not how it might be taken by the public, tho' *some*thing must *ever* be risked.[31]

By 'Kitty's Bower', Caroline Austen meant 'Catharine'. Her preference was for 'Evelyn', but her distinctly limited enthusiasm for this story, which although 'all nonsense, *might* be used', perhaps encouraged Austen-Leigh to print instead the much briefer comedy from 'Volume the First'.

Since none of the other early writings would be published until 1922, Austen-Leigh's decision to publish 'The Mystery' controlled the reception of Austen's juvenilia for over fifty years. His memoir of Austen, containing the play, was reprinted on numerous occasions, both on its own and prefixed to various editions of her collected works. In addition, 'The Mystery' was included in at least two early biographical studies of Austen.[32] As a result, when late nineteenth- and early twentieth-century readers thought of Austen's juvenilia, they conceived of her not as a writer of short fiction but as a

---

[31] Caroline Austen to James Edward Austen-Leigh, 1 April [1869?], in Austen-Leigh, *A Memoir of Jane Austen*, ed. Sutherland, pp. 185–6.

[32] S. F. Malden, *Jane Austen* (London: W. H. Allen, 1889), pp. 20–2; Oscar Fay Adams, *The Story of Jane Austen's Life* (Chicago: A. C. McClurg, 1891), pp. 37–42. These early reprintings are noted by David J. Gilson and J. David Grey, 'Jane Austen's Juvenilia and *Lady Susan*: An Annotated Bibliography', in *Jane Austen's Beginnings*, ed. Grey (Ann Arbor, MI: UMI Research Press, 1989), pp. 243–62.

dramatist, even though her dramatic sketches, 'The Mystery' and two others,[33] comprise only a small fraction of the manuscript notebooks.

In 1913, Austen-Leigh's son William and his grandson Richard Arthur (William's nephew) together published *Jane Austen: Her Life and Letters, A Family Record*. In their preface, the collaborators noted that since the publication of the *Memoir*, 'considerable additions have been made to the stock of information available for her biographers'. Their professed aim was not to supersede the earlier work, with its 'vivid personal recollections', but to supplement it.[34] In the case of Austen's early writings, they did provide significant new information. They revealed, for the first time, the names of the two stories in 'Volume the Third', described 'Evelyn' as 'pure extravaganza', and transcribed the dedications to each of them. They quoted the opening paragraph of 'Catharine' and briefly summarized the remainder of the story, observing that

Evelyn and *Kitty* seem to mark a second stage in [Austen's] literary education: when she was hesitating between burlesque and immature story-telling, and when indeed it seemed as if she were first taking note of all the faults to be avoided, and curiously considering how she ought *not* to write before she attempted to put forth her strength in the right direction.[35]

The Austen-Leighs make no mention of 'Volume the Second', to which they had no access,[36] but they do list the titles of four items from 'Volume the First', with the names of their respective dedicatees: 'Henry and Eliza', 'The Visit', 'Jack and Alice' and 'The adventures of Mr Harley'. The only piece they transcribe in full,

---

[33] 'The Visit' in 'Volume the First' and 'The First Act of a Comedy' in 'Volume the Second'.

[34] Austen-Leigh, *Jane Austen: Her Life and Letters*, pp. v–vi.

[35] *Ibid.*, pp. 55–7.

[36] The Austen-Leighs make an astute guess when they suggest that Austen's allusion to 'my own coach between Edinburgh and Stirling', in her September 1814 letter to Cassandra, might refer to 'some forgotten tale' (*Jane Austen: Her Life and Letters*, p. 305, n. 2). The allusion, as noted above, is to 'Love and Freindship', which would not be published until 1922.

however, is, yet again, 'The Mystery', reprinted from James Edward Austen-Leigh's *Memoir*.

Austen's marginal commentary on Goldsmith first became known in 1920, when Mary Augusta Austen-Leigh, then aged eighty-two, published a memoir entitled *Personal Aspects of Jane Austen*, dedicated 'to all true lovers of Jane Austen and her Works'. The elder sister of William and the aunt of Richard Austen-Leigh, Mary Augusta was certainly a true lover herself, and her book contains some significant material. Aged seven when Cassandra Austen died in 1845, Mary Augusta provides some vivid recollections of Austen's sister, as well as some Austen family charades. She also provides ten examples of Austen's marginal commentary; see Appendix B below. She did not, however, print or even quote any of the juvenilia, which she dismissed as 'childish absurdities' and 'as the kind of productions naturally to be expected from a droll and merry little sister'.[37] And she was probably unaware of the existence of Austen's still unpublished 'History of England', despite its obvious connection with the Goldsmith marginalia in her memoir.

It would take another forty years before the full range of Austen's early writings was brought into print with the publication, in 1954, of the *Minor Works*, the long-awaited sixth and final volume of R. W. Chapman's edition of the Works of Jane Austen, of which the first five volumes were published in 1923.[38] Chapman's *Minor Works* formed the basis for a French translation of the complete juvenilia in 1984, and for an Italian selection in 1989.[39] Another collected edition of the early writings was published in 1993, edited by Margaret Anne Doody and Douglas Murray, with valuable explanatory and textual notes. This edition made Austen's complete early writings available for the first time in an inexpensive paperback edition.

[37] Mary Augusta Austen-Leigh, *Personal Aspects of Jane Austen* (London: John Murray, 1920), pp. 52–3.

[38] A prospectus announcing the 'Minor Works' volume was first issued in 1926; see Gilson, *A Bibliography of Jane Austen*, p. 495. In his preface, Chapman writes that the project has been 'long entertained' (*Minor Works*, p. v).

[39] *Juvenilia et autres textes*, trans. Josette Salesse-Lavergne (Paris: Christian Bourgois, 1984); *Amore & amicizia e altri romanzi*, trans. Letizia Ciotti Miller (Milan: Edizioni La Tartaruga, 1989).

Its title, however, *Catharine and other Writings*, is somewhat mis-leading in privileging one of the items, just as the 1922 edition of 'Volume the Second' had privileged 'Love and Freindship'. Janet Todd's collected edition of 1998, *Love and Friendship and Other Stories*, gives prominence to the same piece. Austen's own titles for the manuscript notebooks, in contrast, are studiedly neutral: no work is singled out for particular attention.

In addition to the collected editions by Chapman, Doody and Murray, and Todd, various selections from Austen's early writings have been published. The first was *Shorter Works by Jane Austen*, an edition issued by the Folio Society in 1963, with illustrations by Joan Hassall and an introduction by Richard Church. It contains the most substantial of the early writings, but in a notably odd arrangement. 'Love and Freindship' is coupled with Austen's epistolary novella 'Lady Susan', probably begun in about 1794, in a section entitled 'Complete Novels'; 'Catharine' is placed with the two unfinished novels, 'The Watsons' and 'Sanditon', in a second section entitled, 'Major Fragments'; while 'The History of England' gets a section to itself. A final section includes seven of the remaining early writings, under the rubric 'Minor Novels', in apparently random order: 'Lesley Castle', 'Evelyn', 'Frederic and Elfrida', 'Jack and Alice', 'Edgar and Emma', 'Henry and Eliza' and 'The Three Sisters'. A briefer selection, entitled *Love and Freindship and other Early Works*, was published by the Women's Press in 1978, with illustrations by Suzanne Perkins and an introduction by Geraldine Killalea. This edition contains the four principal contributions to 'Volume the Second' – 'Love and Freindship', 'Lesley Castle', 'The History of England' and 'A Collection of Letters' – together with 'The Three Sisters', the most mature piece in 'Volume the First', but nothing at all from 'Volume the Third'. A Penguin selection of 1986, *The Juvenilia of Jane Austen and Charlotte Brontë*, edited by Frances Beer, contains more material, but the omissions are surprising. This edition includes seventeen of the twenty-seven items, but excludes three of the most significant ones: 'Lesley Castle' and 'The History of England' in 'Volume the Second', and 'Evelyn' in

'Volume the Third'. The editor, Frances Beer, justifies her selection on the grounds that 'Lesley Castle' and 'Evelyn' are dull and thus 'abandoned without regret', while 'The History of England' 'does not reflect, as the other entries do, on Austen's novelistic development'.[40] In 1995, Penguin seemed to have second thoughts on the importance of two of these three omissions, issuing 'The History of England' and 'Evelyn' together in a single slim volume, with no introduction or editorial material.[41]

Further brief selections from Austen's juvenilia continue to appear. In 2000, the first of a two-volume collected edition of Austen's works in French translation was published in Gallimard's Pléiade series. Only two early writings were included, however: 'Love and Freindship' and 'The History of England'. In a prefatory note, the editor, Pierre Goubert, declares that these are the most important items among Austen's juvenilia and discusses them at some length, but without mentioning even the titles of the remainder.[42] Still more recently, two selections from the juvenilia have been published by Hesperus Press.[43] The first, with a foreword by Fay Weldon, contains the inevitable 'Love and Freindship', accompanied by two less obvious choices: 'The Three Sisters' and 'A Collection of Letters'. The collection, however, is entitled simply *Love and Friendship* (spelled thus), with no mention of the accompanying pieces. The second Hesperus volume, with a foreword by Zoë Heller, contains 'Lesley Castle', together with 'The History of England' and 'Catharine'. The title page, once again, makes no mention of the accompanying items, and the star-billing given to 'Lesley Castle' is surprising; the work written off as dull in the first Penguin selection is here acclaimed by Heller as 'a rambunctious parody of the epistolary novel'.[44]

---

[40] Frances Beer (ed.), *The Juvenilia of Jane Austen and Charlotte Brontë* (London: Penguin Classics, 1986), p. 32.

[41] *The History of England and Evelyn* (London: Penguin 60s Classics, 1995).

[42] Goubert (ed.), *Œuvres romanesques*, vol. I, pp. 1093–7.

[43] *Love and Friendship* (London: Hesperus Press, 2003); *Lesley Castle* (London: Hesperus Press, 2005).

[44] Zoë Heller, foreword to *Lesley Castle*, p. vii.

In addition to these selections from Austen's early writings, editions of individual items are being published with increasing frequency. The most popular has been 'The History of England', with at least five separate editions since 1962.[45] Various presses have produced single editions of other Austen juvenilia, including 'Edgar and Emma' (1967), 'Henry & Eliza' (1984), 'Frederic & Elfrida' (1987), 'The beautifull Cassandra' (1993) and 'Catharine' (1996).[46] The most developed of her three comedies, 'The Visit', forms part of an appendix, entitled 'Jane Austen, Dramatist', in Michael Caines' anthology of eighteenth-century women playwrights.[47] By far the most important producer and promoter of Austen's early writings, however, has been the Juvenilia Press, which since 1992 has produced individual editions of eleven items, including all of the established favourites, with further Austen publications in progress. These editions, equipped with introductions, illustrations and commentaries, have become increasingly ambitious, and in two cases – *Jack & Alice* and *The Three Sisters* – the original Juvenilia Press edition has been re-edited.[48] The more scholarly nature of the recent

---

[45] These editions are published by the Keepsake Press (London, 1962); the Aliquando Press (Toronto, 1966); J. L. Carr (Kettering, 1977); the British Library and Algonquin Books (London and Chapel Hill, NC, 1993); and the Juvenilia Press (Edmonton, Alberta, 1995).

[46] *Edgar and Emma* (Hunton Bridge: Kit-Cat Press, 1967); *Henry and Eliza* (Hunton Bridge: Kit-Cat Press, 1984); *Frederic & Elfrida* (Hunton Bridge: Kit-Cat Press, 1987); *The Beautifull Cassandra* (Victoria, British Columbia: Sono Nis Press, 1993); *Catharine* (London: Phoenix Books, 1996).

[47] *Major Voices: 18th Century Women Playwrights* (London: Toby Press, 2004).

[48] Juvenilia Press editions of Austen to date are *Jack & Alice*, ed. Juliet McMaster, 1992; *Amelia Webster and The Three Sisters*, ed. McMaster, 1993; *The History of England*, ed. Jan Fergus, 1995; *Love & Freindship*, ed. McMaster, 1995; *Catharine, or The Bower*, ed. McMaster, 1996; *Henry and Eliza*, ed. Karen L. Hartric, 1996; *A Collection of Letters*, ed. McMaster, 1998; *Lesley Castle*, ed. Fergus, 1998; *Evelyn*, ed. Peter Sabor, 1999; *Jack & Alice*, ed. Joseph Wiesenfarth, 2001; *Frederic & Elfrida*, ed. Sabor, 2002; *The Three Sisters*, ed. Wiesenfarth, 2004; *Lady Susan*, ed. Christine Alexander and David Owen, 2005. Each volume contains contributions by student collaborators. The volumes were published in Edmonton, Alberta, under the general editorship of McMaster, until 2004; subsequent volumes are published under the general editorship of Christine Alexander, in Sydney, Australia. A volume containing Austen's three plays, edited by McMaster and Lesley Peterson, is forthcoming.

Juvenilia Press editions reflects the increasing academic, as well as popular, interest in Austen's early writings.

While 'The History of England' has received the lion's share of individual editions, 'Love and Freindship' is becoming a favourite among anthologizers looking for a brief, self-contained example of Austen's famous irony and wit. It was printed in part (letters 3–8) in a 1961 anthology of parodies, edited by Dwight Macdonald; Sandra Gilbert and Susan Gubar included it in their best-selling *Norton Anthology of Literature by Women* (1985); and it was excerpted again in the *Macmillan Anthologies of English Literature* (1989).[49] The most influential of all teaching anthologies, at least in North America, the two-volume *Norton Anthology of English Literature*, went through seven editions without printing anything by Austen. The eighth edition of 2005 still has nothing from the published novels, but it does, for the first time contain 'Love and Freindship', as well as the parodic 'Plan of a Novel' (1816).[50] The inclusion of 'Love and Freindship' in the *Norton Anthology*, as well as in the *Norton Anthology of Literature by Women*, should increase its prominence (together with 'The History of England' and 'Catharine') among Austen's early writings, and further establish the juvenilia as a substantial part of her œuvre.

RECEPTION

When 'Volume the Second' first appeared in 1922, under the title of *Love & Freindship*, not even the titles of the various items had yet been made public. Unknown writings by a major English novelist were a tantalizing prospect, and the small, attractively printed volume proved to be something of a publishing sensation. Cassandra's watercolour portraits for 'The History of England' were

---

[49] 'Love and Freindship', excerpted in *Parodies: An Anthology from Chaucer to Beerbohm – and After*, ed. Dwight Macdonald (London: Faber, 1961), pp. 40–51; excerpted in *The Norton Anthology of Literature by Women*, ed. Sandra M. Gilbert and Susan Gubar (New York: Norton, 1985), pp. 206–32; excerpted in the *Macmillan Anthologies of English Literature*, vol. III, *The Restoration and the Eighteenth Century*, ed. Ian McGowan (London: Macmillan, 1989), pp. 571–5.

[50] 'Love and Freindship', in *The Norton Anthology of English Literature*, ed. Stephen Greenblatt *et al.*, 8th edn (New York: Norton, 2005), vol. II, pp. 515–35.

reproduced in colour on the endpapers,[51] followed by a facsimile of the title page, and an important preface by G. K. Chesterton made some striking claims for the significance of Austen's early writings. Chesterton compares 'Love and Freindship', written by Austen at the age of fourteen, to 'the great burlesques of Peacock or Max Beerbohm', and contends that the source of her inspiration was that 'of Gargantua and of Pickwick; it was the gigantic inspiration of laughter'.[52] Placing Austen in a comic tradition running from Rabelais to Dickens was a bold move on Chesterton's part, and it paid off. The London edition went through four impressions within seven months, while a New York edition went through four impressions still more rapidly.[53]

Love & Freindship appeared shortly after *The Young Visiters*, a novel written by the nine-year-old Daisy Ashford in 1890. Chatto and Windus published Ashford's manuscript in 1919, with a preface by Sir James Barrie, and sold an astonishing 230,000 copies within two years.[54] These sales were probably responsible for the same publisher's decision to bring out *Love & Freindship*. In the wake of *The Young Visiters*, juvenile writing had become a marketable item: Opal Whiteley's childhood journal, *The Story of Opal: The Journal of an Understanding Heart* (1920), was published shortly after Daisy Ashford's novel, and the success of both smoothed the way for Austen's youthful work. Several reviewers compared *Love & Freindship* with *The Young Visiters*, written at an interval of one hundred years but published just three years apart. A front-page review in the *New York Times Book Review* by Zona Gale, entitled 'Jane Austen Outdoes Daisy Ashford', made its preference clear. Gale also insisted on the intrinsic significance of the juvenilia, declaring at the outset: 'Henceforth it is a part of literary experience to

---

[51] Twelve of the thirteen portraits are reproduced, but that of Richard III is omitted without explanation. The text was prepared not by Chesterton but by an unknown editor.

[52] *Love & Freindship*, pp. xi, xiv.

[53] See Gilson, *A Bibliography of Jane Austen*, pp. 372–3. The London printing also appeared in a 'Special Edition de Luxe'.

[54] See Juliet McMaster, 'What Daisy Knew: the Epistemology of the Child Writer', in *The Child Writer from Austen to Woolf*, p. 53.

have read Jane Austen's "Love and Freindship" '. Remarkably, Gale contrasts the juvenilia favourably with the adult fiction: 'here she is – this Jane Austen of library shelves and bookcases – here she is, human, laughing, alive, taken unaware, as she must so often have longed to be taken. Never before has she quite escaped from the rectory'.[55] An extensive review in *The Times* of London by Augustine Birrell also gave high praise to both 'Love and Freindship' and 'The History of England': 'we found ourselves simply revelling in the revelation . . . made to us of the "Elementary Jane" and entirely in agreement with Mr Chesterton'.[56] Other reviewers, more conventionally, portrayed the volume merely as a prelude to the novels to come. One such was Virginia Woolf, whose review in the *New Statesman* is entitled 'Jane Austen Practising'. Woolf's Austen is 'only humming a tune beneath her breath, trying over a few bars of the music for *Pride and Prejudice* and *Emma*'. Woolf, however, adds: 'there is no one else who can sing like that. She need not raise her voice.'[57] And Woolf's praise was influential. Her signed review was soon reprinted, with considerable revisions, as part of a piece on Austen in the first of her two celebrated essay collections, *The Common Reader*, 1st series (1925). Here, but not in the original review, Woolf describes 'Love and Freindship' as 'an astonishing and unchildish story . . . which, incredible though it appears, was written at the age of fifteen'.[58]

In addition to newspaper and magazine reviewers, 'Volume the Second' was of considerable interest to academic critics. A particular enthusiast was R. Brimley Johnson, an Austen critic and editor of long standing, who in 1924 published an extended essay with the surprising title *A New Study of Jane Austen (interpreted through*

---

[55] Zona Gale, 'Jane Austen Outdoes Daisy Ashford', *New York Times Book Review*, 17 September 1922, pp. 1, 24.

[56] Augustine Birrell, 'Elementary Jane', *The Times*, 12 June 1922, p. 15.

[57] Virginia Woolf, 'Jane Austen Practising', *New Statesman*, 15 July 1922, p. 420, rpt. in *The Essays of Virginia Woolf*, vol. III, *1919–1924*, ed. Andrew McNeillie (London: Chatto & Windus, 1988), p. 334.

[58] Woolf, 'Jane Austen', *The Essays of Virginia Woolf*, vol. IV, *1925-1928*, ed. Andrew McNeillie (London: Hogarth, 1994), p. 147.

'Love and Freindship').[59] A subsequent book on Austen by Johnson, published in 1930, contains a chapter on the juvenilia entitled 'Folly Burlesqued'.[60] Both Johnson and Annette Hopkins, in a 1925 article on 'Volume the Second', attempt to locate the targets of Austen's satire, pointing to novels of sensibility such as Henry Mackenzie's *The Man of Feeling* (1771) and Goethe's *The Sorrows of Young Werther* (1774).[61] Also of notable interest are two lectures given by the philosopher and historian R. G. Collingwood at Oxford colleges in 1921 and 1934 (but first published only in 2005). Collingwood's insights into Austen's early writings are remarkably astute. In his first lecture, written before the publication of *Love & Freindship*, he declared that Austen 'wrote great quantities of stories in her childhood', consisting 'largely of parody or burlesque of the popular literary styles'.[62] Contrasting Austen and Ashford, he found *The Young Visiters* conventional next to Austen's parodies, which are not imitative but profoundly reflective. Collingwood was clearly handicapped by his lack of access, in 1921, to the juvenilia; his remarks rest on 'The Mystery', available since 1871, and the brief, tantalizing excerpts in the Austen-Leighs' *Jane Austen: Her Life and Letters* (1913). In the second lecture, however, Collingwood could draw on 'Love and Freindship', which, he declared, parodied 'the whole apparatus of the romantic novel – the innocent country-bred heroine, the interesting stranger arriving by night, the elopement, the accident to the coach, the swoon'.[63]

---

[59] Johnson's essay has gone largely unnoticed, prefixed to an English translation of a French study of Austen: Léonie Villard, *Jane Austen: A French Appreciation* (London: George Routledge, 1924); see Gilson, *A Bibliography of Jane Austen*, p. 526.

[60] R. Brimley Johnson, *Jane Austen: Her Life, Her Work, Her Family, and Her Critics* (London: Dent, 1930).

[61] Annette B. Hopkins, 'Jane Austen's "Love and Freindship": A Study in Literary Relations', *South Atlantic Quarterly*, 24 (1925), 34–49.

[62] R. G. Collingwood, 'Jane Austen (1921)', in *The Philosophy of Enchantment: Studies in Folktale, Cultural Criticism, and Anthropology*, ed. David Boucher, Wendy James, and Philip Smallwood (Oxford: Clarendon Press, 2005), p. 28. This and Collingwood's second Austen lecture are dated by Smallwood, pp. xlvii, n. 83, and pp. 47–8, n. 23. See also Smallwood, 'From Illusion to Reality: R. G. Collingwood and the Fictional Art of Jane Austen', *Collingwood Studies*, 4 (1998), *Themes from the Manuscripts*, 71–100.

[63] Collingwood, 'Jane Austen (?1934)', in *The Philosophy of Enchantment*, p. 39.

Given the brisk sales and critical success of *Love & Freindship*, editions of Austen's other two notebooks might have been expected to follow in quick succession, but for the time being they remained in private hands, inaccessible to editors. Chapman's remarkable, and remarkably long-lived, edition of the novels appeared a year later, in 1923, without any of the early writings or even a mention of them in the general preface.[64] With its elaborate apparatus, copious appendixes, indexes and illustrations it was, as contemporary reviewers such as Wilbur Cross observed, the first critical edition of any of the major English novelists.[65] For Chapman, however, at least in the 1920s, the early writings represented a potential embarrassment to his massive enterprise. He had been among the reviewers of *Love and Freindship*, and under the *Times Literary Supplement*'s cloak of anonymity he depicted the volume as an 'act of espionage or exhumation', adding that 'we should be sorry to have been responsible for this publication'.[66] Following the generally enthusiastic reception of the early writings, however, Chapman could not continue to adopt this stance. In the preface to his 1926 edition of Austen-Leigh's *Memoir of Jane Austen*, he gave a brief account of the manuscript notebooks.[67] And after discovering the whereabouts of 'Volume the First' in 1933, he duly produced his own edition. A delay of almost twenty years followed

---

[64] Hopkins regrets the omission from Chapman's edition of 'the highly interesting, recently published volume, *Love and Freindship*' ('Jane Austen's "Love and Freindship"', p. 34).

[65] Wilbur Cross, 'An Austen Scholar', *Yale Review*, 17 (1928), 380–2.

[66] [R. W. Chapman], 'Love and Freindship', *Times Literary Supplement*, 15 June 1922, p. 393.

[67] James Edward Austen-Leigh, *A Memoir of Jane Austen*, ed. R. W. Chapman (Oxford: Clarendon Press, 1926), p. xiv. Chapman notes the existence of a collection of transcripts, 'written in a later generation, of pieces "from Miss Austen's writings"'; see also Chapman, 'A Jane Austen Collection', *Times Literary Supplement*, 14 January 1926, p. 27. At least one such collection, transcribed by several hands, is extant, housed in the Austen-Leigh Archive at the Hampshire Record Office; see Kathryn Sutherland, *Jane Austen's Textual Lives: From Aeschylus to Bollywood* (Oxford: Oxford University Press, 2005), pp. 202–3. Another collection, transcribed by Mary Augusta Austen-Leigh, was still extant in 1930; see Johnson, *Jane Austen: Her Life*, pp. 270–1.

before Chapman edited 'Volume the Third' in 1951, making all of Austen's early writings available at last.

In his editions of *Volume the First* and *Volume the Third*, Chapman recorded some of the many manuscript revisions, so that scholars could now study, for the first time, how Austen reworked her early writings. But while he clearly felt compelled, as Austen's editor, to publish all that she was known to have written, his minimalist prefaces reveal his disdain for her earliest writings. Echoing his precursors, the Austen-Leighs, Chapman claims, in his edition of *Volume the First*, that 'it will always be disputed whether such effusions as these ought to be published; and it may be that we have enough already of Jane Austen's early scraps'.[68] The word 'effusions', tellingly, is the patronizing term used by Austen's father in his inscription in 'Volume the Third' (a volume that Chapman had seen but not yet published). George Austen employed it in the eighteenth-century sense of 'outpourings', and Austen herself seems to have found the term apt, alluding to it in her famous passage on novel-writing in *Northanger Abbey*: 'Let us leave it to the Reviewers to abuse such effusions of fancy' (vol. 1, ch. 5). For Chapman, however, the term held the modern sense of 'effusiveness'; he thus turns a compliment by Austen's father into a patronizing jibe. This is a far cry from Chesterton, with his comparisons to Rabelais and Dickens, and several reviewers of *Volume the First* suggested that a more positive approach was called for. John Sparrow declared that Austen's juvenilia 'thoroughly deserve to be published on their own account', while David Garnett compared Austen's depictions of unintelligence with 'Flaubert collecting his *Sottisier*' and with 'Shakespeare's portraits of Polonius and Shallow'.[69] In his preface to *Volume the Third*, Chapman ventured at least one critical comment,

---

[68] R. W. Chapman (ed.), *Volume the First* (Oxford: Clarendon Press, 1933), p. ix. Over fifty years later, Chapman's misgivings were echoed by Joan Austen-Leigh, great-granddaughter of James Edward Austen-Leigh, who declared that her ancestor was right to suppress Austen's 'earliest scraps', many of which 'would never have seen the light of day if they had been by another hand' ('The Juvenilia: A Family "Veiw"', in *Jane Austen's Beginnings*, p. 177).

[69] John Sparrow, review of *Volume the First*, *Bodleian Quarterly Record*, 7 (1932–4), 298; David Garnett, 'Books in General', *New Statesman*, 1 July 1933, p. 16.

noting that despite its 'absurd dedication', 'Catharine' is Austen's 'first essay in serious fiction'.[70] Reviewers were quick to develop this remark. Mary Lascelles contended that with its 'agreeable tartness', 'Catharine' promised 'comic rather than satiric development', while Marghanita Laski noted that 'the writing is already imbued with dignified and balanced irony, and Catherine herself, and possibly her aunt, are already characters who are something more than butts for the author's wit'.[71]

Criticism of Austen's early writings between the early 1950s and the late 1970s struggled to find ways to approach these still unfamiliar works. Marvin Mudrick's fine chapter on the juvenilia in his critical monograph of 1952 sets them in the context of eighteenth-century sentimental fiction,[72] an approach first developed by R. Brimley Johnson and Annette Hopkins in their pioneering studies of the 1920s. Mudrick draws extensive comparisons between 'Love and Freindship' and the anonymously published *Laura and Augustus* (1784), an epistolary novel now known to be by Eliza Nugent Bromley, which was the particular focus of Austen's mockery of sentimental excesses. A more common strategy, however, was to depict the early writings as novels in training, as though Austen in her youth was simply practising skills she would put to better use as an adult. The chief exponent of this approach was Q. D. Leavis, whose influential 'Critical Theory of Jane Austen's Writings' was published as a series of articles in *Scrutiny* between 1941 and 1945, well before 'Volume the Third' had yet appeared. Despite this impediment, Leavis set out to show that Austen's novels were 'palimpsests through whose surface portions of earlier versions, or of other and earlier compositions quite unrelated, constantly protrude'. These 'earlier compositions', in Leavis's view, included the later unpublished fiction, 'Lady Susan' and 'The Watsons', as well

---

[70] R. W. Chapman (ed.), *Volume the Third* (Oxford: Clarendon Press, 1951), p. vii.

[71] Mary Lascelles, review of *Volume the Third*, *Review of English Studies*, new series, 3 (1952), 184; Marghanita Laski, review of *Volume the Third*, *Spectator*, 8 June 1951, p. 762.

[72] Marvin Mudrick, *Jane Austen: Irony as Defense and Discovery* (Princeton: Princeton University Press, 1952).

as the juvenilia. Focusing on 'A Collection of Letters' in 'Volume the Second', she claims that one of its letters lies behind various episodes in *Pride and Prejudice*, *Mansfield Park* and *Northanger Abbey*. For Leavis, the 'Collection of Letters' has no intrinsic worth; it is merely a series of 'jottings' that Austen the novelist would subsequently transform. Significantly, while regretting that 'Volume the Third' was still unavailable to readers, Leavis claims that 'a sufficient description of it can be found in the *Life and Letters* published by W. and R. A. Austen-Leigh':[73] a description that contains not a line from 'Evelyn' and no more than the opening paragraph of 'Catharine'.

Leavis's approach to the juvenilia retained its hold on Austen criticism for several decades. In the 1950s and 1960s it became increasingly common for books on Austen to contain a section on the early writings, often coupled with 'Lady Susan', but they were seldom studied for characteristics of their own. A. Walton Litz's *Jane Austen: A Study of Her Artistic Development* (1965), for example, devotes a substantial chapter to the juvenilia, but, as his title suggests, he regards them in developmental terms: the earliest, which he terms 'high-spirited burlesques', being the most primitive, and even the latest showing us, above all, 'the world of the major novels taking shape'. Litz warns us that 'in considering these early productions we must bear in mind that they are chiefly important in relation to the major novels, and that an assessment of their place in Jane Austen's artistic career should take precedence over any search for "sources"'. In Litz's view, the juvenilia constitute a steady progression towards 'Catharine', which is Austen's 'first full-scale attempt to place a heroine in a completely realistic social situation'.[74] The key words are 'full-scale' and 'realistic': fantastic miniatures are merely, in this reading, something that Austen would have to outgrow. And 'Catharine', in its turn, is significant primarily

---

[73] Q. D. Leavis, *Collected Essays*, vol. I, *The Englishness of the English Novel*, ed. G. Singh (Cambridge: Cambridge University Press, 1983), pp. 65, 67–8, 63.
[74] A. Walton Litz, *Jane Austen: A Study of Her Artistic Development* (New York: Oxford University Press, 1965), pp. 17–18, 37.

as a precursor of *Northanger Abbey*: Litz regards the earlier heroine as a sketch for her namesake, Catherine Morland.

Among the few critics of this period to study Austen's early writings at length is Brian Southam, who produced a valuable new edition of *Volume the Second* (1963) and devoted a series of articles to textual issues in the juvenilia, as well as writing a monograph, *Jane Austen's Literary Manuscripts* (1964), on the writings left unpublished at the time of her death. Southam's book is subtitled 'A study of the novelist's development through the surviving papers', and like Litz he is concerned primarily with discovering marks of the mature novelist in the writings of her childhood and youth. Repeated comparisons are made between stories such as 'Catharine' and novels such as *Pride and Prejudice*, and, not surprisingly, the early writings fare badly. In 1792, declares Southam, when Austen was sixteen, her 'attitude was sometimes hard, with the simplicity and impatience of youth',[75] and such an attitude was inimical to the production of social comedy.

A turning-point in the reception of Austen's juvenilia came in the late 1970s, when the early writings were taken up by feminist critics. Geraldine Killalea, in her introduction to the Women's Press edition of 1978, found 'a feminist view' in Austen's depiction of Charlotte Lutterell in 'Lesley Castle', a 'fully-realised woman of independent mind'.[76] This rather crude formulation was shortly followed, in 1979, by Sandra Gilbert and Susan Gubar's wide-ranging and innovative study, *The Madwoman in the Attic*, which contains a substantial chapter on Austen's early writings. Here, almost for the first time since Chesterfield's seminal essay, the unrestrained energy of the juvenilia was made a cause for celebration, not regret. For Gilbert and Gubar, the heroines of 'Love and Freindship', Laura and Sophia, are 'really quite attractive in their exuberant assertiveness, their exploration and exploitation of the world, their curiously honest expression of their needs, their rebellious rejection of their

---

[75] B. C. Southam, *Jane Austen's Literary Manuscripts*, p. 43.
[76] Geraldine Killalea, intro. to *Love and Freindship* (London: The Women's Press, 1978), pp. ix–x.

fathers' advice . . . their gullible delight in playing out the plots they have admired'. Even a character such as the anonymous heroine of the 'Letter from a Young Lady', with her brisk declaration that 'I murdered my Father at a very early period of my Life, I have since murdered my Mother, and I am now going to murder my Sister', meets with Gilbert and Gubar's approval: her matricides and patricides, they contend, make 'such characters seem much more exuberantly alive than their sensible, slow-witted, dying parents'.[77] In a work that takes Charlotte Brontë's homicidal Bertha Mason as the archetype for female creativity, Austen's juvenilia had at last found their natural home. After publishing *The Madwoman in the Attic*, Gilbert and Gubar went on to edit the *Norton Anthology of Literature by Women* (1985), in which Austen's writings are represented by 'Love and Freindship' alone. While Gilbert and Gubar here acknowledge the power of Austen's published novels, they reserve their fullest praise for her early writings, in which she 'began to define herself as a writer by self-consciously satirizing not only the female tradition in literature but also its effects on the growth and development of the female imagination'.[78]

Once Austen's juvenilia had thus been reinvented as proto-feminist fiction, critics had a new vocabulary with which to describe the young author at work. In the stream of publications on Austen that followed *The Madwoman in the Attic*, the early writings are often accorded an important place in her œuvre: not as mere proto-types for the novels but rather as a crucial indicator of Austen's aims and achievement. In her contribution to a volume of essays on teaching *Pride and Prejudice*, for example, Susan Fraiman contends that Austen's 'critique of marriage, male authority, and proper femininity' is 'closer to the surface in works written before 1794'. Teaching stories such as 'Love and Freindship' and 'The Three Sisters' can thus 'help to excavate those feminist paradigms present

---

[77] Sandra M. Gilbert and Susan Gubar, *The Madwoman in the Attic: The Woman Writer and the Nineteenth-Century Literary Imagination* (New Haven: Yale University Press, 1979), pp 115–16.

[78] Gilbert and Gubar (eds.), *The Norton Anthology of Literature by Women*, p. 207.

but more deeply buried in *Pride and Prejudice*.[79] In readings such as this, the old approach to the juvenilia is inverted: rather than their being pale foreshadowings of the novels, the novels instead are subdued afterwords to the early writings.

By the end of the 1980s, far from being an embarrassment for her critics, Austen's early writings were seen as a fruitful field of enquiry. The publication, in 1989, of *Jane Austen's Beginnings*, the first collection of essays on the juvenilia and 'Lady Susan' marked the distance travelled since Austen-Leigh's first tentative step 120 years earlier. In a spirited foreword, Margaret Drabble contends that Austen's 'burlesques, her *History* and her tales and sketches and proto-novels constitute one of the most remarkable collections ever discovered from so young a pen'. Following the lead of Gilbert and Gubar, Drabble perceives 'in some of the shorter fragments . . . hints of another Jane Austen, a fiercer, wilder, more outspoken, more ruthless writer, with a dark vision of human motivation . . . and a breathless, almost manic energy'.[80] Some of the essays in this fine collection, including those by Claudia Johnson on Austen's politics, Christopher Kent on 'The History of England' (his second publication on the 'History') and Juliet McMaster on 'Love and Freindship', are among the most incisive interpretations to date of the juvenilia.[81] Kent's two essays form part of a flurry of writings on Austen's 'History', which began in 1963 with a pioneering piece by Brigid Brophy. More recently, feminist critics such as Jacqueline Reid-Walsh, A. S. Byatt, Jan Fergus, Antoinette Burton and Devoney Looser have emphasized the high proportion of women featured in the 'History' and considered both Jane

---

[79] Susan Fraiman, 'Peevish Accents in the Juvenilia: A Feminist Key to *Pride and Prejudice*', in *Approaches to Teaching Austen's Pride and Prejudice*, ed. Marcia McClintock Folsom (New York: Modern Language Association, 1993), p. 75.

[80] Margaret Drabble, 'Foreword', in *Jane Austen's Beginnings*, xiii, xiv.

[81] Claudia L. Johnson, ' "The Kingdom at Sixes and Sevens": Politics and the Juvenilia', Christopher Kent, 'Learning History with, and from, Jane Austen', Juliet McMaster, 'Teaching "Love and Freindship" ', in *Jane Austen's Beginnings*, pp. 45–58, 59–72, 135–51; Kent, ' "Real Solemn History" and Social History', in *Jane Austen in a Social Context* (London: Macmillan, 1981), pp. 86–104.

and Cassandra Austen's methods of reducing historical distance through their comic treatment of historical personages.[82]

McMaster's essay on 'Love and Freindship' in *Jane Austen's Beginnings* includes a chart revealing the extraordinary care that Austen took in constructing the elaborate genealogies of her story.[83] Since 1989, McMaster has been by far the most prolific writer on Austen's juvenilia, presenting her findings in the form of essays, journal articles and introductions, commentaries and illustrations in the Juvenilia Press editions. Her attention to 'Love and Freindship', in particular, has helped make it the most discussed of all the juvenilia, ahead even of 'The History of England'. These are also the two early writings that Brian Southam singles out, in his edition of Austen's *Sir Charles Grandison*, as falling into 'the "minor masterpiece" category'.[84] No monograph on Austen's early writings has yet appeared, but books on Austen are increasingly likely to devote a chapter or a substantial section to the juvenilia. The tendency is exemplified by two works of 2002 on very different topics: Paula Byrne's *Jane Austen and the Theatre* and Clara Tuite's *Romantic Austen*. Byrne's chapters 'Private Theatricals' and 'Early Works' explore Austen's three miniature comedies, usefully relating them to the tradition of eighteenth-century stage burlesque, and in particular to comedies such as Fielding's *Tragedy of Tom Thumb* acted by the Austen family at Steventon.[85] For Tuite, the key early work is 'Catharine', which she depicts as one of Austen's 'betweenities',

---

[82] Brigid Brophy, 'Jane Austen and the Stuarts', in *Critical Essays on Jane Austen*, ed. B. C. Southam (London: Routledge, 1968), pp. 21–38; Jacqueline Reid-Walsh, 'A Female Interrogative Reader: The Adolescent Jane Austen Reads and Rewrites (His)tory', *English Quarterly*, 24 (1992), 8–19; A. S. Byatt, intro., and Deirdre Le Faye, 'Note on the Text', in *The History of England* (Chapel Hill, NC: Algonquin Books, 1993); Jan Fergus, intro. to *The History of England* (Edmonton, Alberta: Juvenilia Press, 1995), pp. i–xii; Antoinette Burton, ' "Invention Is What Delights Me": Jane Austen's Remaking of "English" History', in *Jane Austen and Discourses of Feminism*, ed. Devoney Looser (New York: St Martin's Press, 1995), pp. 35–50; Devoney Looser, *British Women Writers and the Writing of History, 1670–1820* (Baltimore: Johns Hopkins University Press, 2000).

[83] McMaster, 'Teaching "Love and Freindship"', p. 146.

[84] Brian Southam, intro. to *Sir Charles Grandison*, p. 3.

[85] Paula Byrne, *Jane Austen and the Theatre*, pp. 3–28, 71–87.

presenting a challenge to 'the construction of the Austen *œuvre* as the six "finished" novels'.[86]

Unlike the published novels, none of Austen's early writings has yet been filmed or televised, but several have been adapted in various forms. A dramatization by May Wood Wigginton, 'Love and Friendship', in five acts and with sixteen characters, was published as early as 1925, but no record of a performance has been found.[87] 'Love and Freindship' was, however, produced by the BBC as a radio play on two occasions: in 1936, dramatized by M. H. Allen, and in 1953, dramatized by Terence Tiller.[88] 'The History of England' was surely an inspiration for Sellar and Yeatman's 1930 bestselling parody, *1066 And All That*, with its famous dictum: 'History is not what you thought. *It is what you can remember.* All other history defeats itself.'[89] Excerpts from Austen's history form part of John Barton's highly successful historical drama *The Hollow Crown*,[90] first produced by the Royal Shakespeare Company at Stratford in 1961 and since performed on numerous occasions. Another, more recent refashioning creates unexpected links between several of Austen's early writings and *Mansfield Park*. In her 1999 film of the novel, the director Patricia Rozema turns Austen's heroine, Fanny Price, into a youthful author, busily writing several of the early works, including

---

[86] Clara Tuite, *Romantic Austen: Sexual Politics and the Literary Canon* (Cambridge: Cambridge University Press, 2002), p. 25. Tuite takes the term 'betweenities' from a letter of 1 April [1869?] by Caroline Austen, first printed in Austen-Leigh, *Memoir*. She supposes that Caroline had 'Catharine' in mind here; Caroline's principal reference, however, was to 'Lady Susan'. For Caroline's letter, see Austen-Leigh, *A Memoir of Jane Austen*, pp. 185–7, and Sutherland's note, pp. 218–19.

[87] May Wood Wigginton, *Love and Friendship* (London: Samuel French, 1925); see Gilson, *A Bibliography of Jane Austen*, p. 417.

[88] *Love and Freindship*, produced and adapted by M. H. Allen, BBC Regional Service, 17 August 1936; dramatized and produced by Terence Tiller, BBC Third Programme, 4 November 1953; see Andrew Wright, 'Jane Austen Adapted', *Nineteenth-Century Fiction*, 30 (1975), 451.

[89] W. C. Sellar and R. J. Yeatman, *1066 And All That* (London: Methuen, 1930), p. vii. Deirdre Le Faye finds Austen's work 'uncannily prophetic' of Sellar and Yeatman ('Note on the Text', in *The History of England* (1993), p. xi). The resemblance is, I believe, not uncanny but the result of Sellar and Yeatman's careful study of Austen's history.

[90] John Barton, *The Hollow Crown: An Entertainment By and About the Kings and Queens of England* (London: Samuel French, 1962), rev. edn (London: Hamish Hamilton, 1971).

'Henry and Eliza', 'The History of England', 'Love and Freindship' and 'Frederic and Elfrida'. Rozema's Fanny emphasizes, in particular, Sophia's memorable dying words in 'Love and Freindship': 'Run mad as often as you chuse; but do not faint' (p. 133). By making the timid heroine of Austen's novel the precocious, feisty author of the juvenilia, Rozena uses the early writings to transform a much later Austen work: deftly reversing the familiar process in which the juvenilia are judged by the standards of the mature novels and, inevitably, found wanting. 'Catharine' does not appear in Rozema's film, but it received an adaptation of its own in September 2005: performed by the Regency Duo as 'The Bower: A Youthful Romance in Words and Music' at Quebec House, Chartwell.[91]

Surprisingly, no stage performances of two of Austen's three plays, 'The Mystery' and 'The First Act of a Comedy', have been recorded. 'The Visit', however, at last received its premiere on 2 November 2005, when it was performed on two occasions at Branksome Hall, an independent girls' school in Rosedale, Toronto. The youthful, all-female cast, directed by Lesley Peterson, included two actresses playing Jane Austen and together performing her elaborate dedication of 'The Visit' to her brother James. The production highlighted Austen's skill in bringing Sir Arthur Hampton to life on stage, despite his never saying a word; his not eating tripe, liver and crow, or suet pudding, as well as not drinking gooseberry wine, were all memorable non-events. In her programme notes, Lesley Peterson points out that the multiple marriage proposals with which the play concludes grow out of Miss Fitzgerald's careful planning of her guest list, 'composed of just the right number of single young men and equally single young women, along with an older couple to lend the gathering status and propriety'.[92] Professional performances of this and the other Austen plays will surely follow.

---

[91] 'The Bower: A Youthful Romance in Word and Music' was performed twice at Quebec House on 29 September 2005. Ruth Gomme, a soprano, was accompanied by Jean Phillips playing a 1788 Broadwood Square Piano.

[92] Lesley Peterson, Director's Notes for 'The Visit', Branksome Hall, Rosedale, Toronto, 2 November 2005.

LITERARY SIGNIFICANCE

When R. G. Collingwood wrote his first lecture on Jane Austen in 1921, he had read her play 'The Mystery' but not 'The Visit', or any of her other juvenilia beyond brief excerpts. He speculated, however, that 'Jane's earliest efforts were not wholly unlike *The Young Visiters*' by Daisy Ashford before deleting the sentence: perhaps because the miniature play could hardly form the basis of a comparison.[93] He might also have been reluctant to impute a quality of sexual knowingness to Austen: a quality that had shocked several of the nine-year-old Ashford's early reviewers.[94] The knowingness appears in passages such as the following, in which the heroine, Ethel Monticue, is taken on an excursion to London's Crystal Palace: 'She looked a dainty vishen with her fair hair waving in the breeze and Bernard bit his lips rarther hard for he could hardly contain himself and felt he must marry Ethel soon'.[95] It is obvious that Ashford, with her lip-biting hero, is aware of the force of sexual attraction, but a similar awareness in Austen is too often overlooked. It is, however, present from the outset: beginning with 'Frederic and Elfrida', the first piece transcribed in 'Volume the First' and possibly written when Austen was eleven. A running joke here concerns Elfrida's pathological fear of the wedding night. Although engaged to her first cousin Frederic, she cannot bring herself to name a day for the ceremony, and her parents, 'knowing the delicate frame of her mind could ill bear the least excertion . . . forebore to press her on the subject' (p. 11). A further joke occurs when Elfrida yields at last, after an engagement of over eighteen years, and no clergyman is present as Frederic 'flew to her and . . . was united to her Forever' (p. 12).

Frederic and Elfrida are the second in a long line of couples in the juvenilia united without benefit of clergy, following the lead of Miss Fitzroy in the same story who 'ran off with the Coachman' (p. 7).

---

[93] R. G. Collingwood, 'Jane Austen (1921)', in *The Philosophy of Enchantment*, p. 28, n. 15.

[94] See Juliet McMaster, 'What Daisy Knew', p. 55.

[95] Daisy Ashford, *The Young Visiters* (London: Chatto & Windus, 1919), p. 65.

Others include Henry and Eliza, illegally united in a 'private union' by a domestic chaplain (p. 40); Sir William Mountague and Emma Stanhope, 'privately married' without a license and also under the age of consent (p. 48); Louisa Lesley, who leaves her husband for two male companions, Danvers and Rakehelly Dishonor (p. 143); Miss Jane and Captain Dashwood in 'A Collection of Letters', supposedly married without parental consent but also without Jane's taking her husband's name or acknowledging her children as her own (pp. 195–97); and Frederick Gower and Maria Webb in 'Evelyn', whose nuptials are 'celebrated' the day after they meet, without a marriage having taken place (p. 234). In 'Love and Freindship', Edward asks the 'Adorable Laura' for her hand in marriage, using the stale language of the conventional despairing lover: 'when may I hope to receive that reward of all the painfull sufferings I have undergone during the course of my Attachment to you, to which I have ever aspired? Oh! When will you reward me with Yourself?'. Laura's reply is startlingly abrupt: 'This instant, Dear and Amiable Edward.' And her father, far from blocking the marriage in traditional paternal fashion, at once conducts the ceremony, despite lacking the necessary qualifications: 'We were immediately united by my Father, who tho' he had never taken orders had been bred to the Church' (p. 109). 'Love and Freindship' is a hotbed of illicit unions: Lord St Clair has four illegitimate children by his mistress Laurina, an Italian opera girl; his two youngest daughters, Bertha and Agatha, have illegitimate children – Philander and Gustavus respectively – by their lovers, Philip Jones and Gregory Staves; while Janetta Macdonald elopes with M'Kenzie. As the daughter of a clergyman who performed marriages, Austen could readily draw on her knowledge of the legalities involved in creating her fictive unions, just as she does in filling out names and witnesses in her father's marriage register.

The young Austen was equally knowing on the subject of homosexual desire. In her later years, she expected women authors to respect sexual decorum, and in 1807, when she was in her early thirties, she was quick to censure a novel such as *Alphonsine* by

Mme de Genlis, telling Cassandra that she was 'disgusted' by 'indel-
icacies which disgrace a pen hitherto so pure'.[96] John Wiltshire,
commenting on Mary Crawford's notorious '*Rears, and Vices*' pun
in *Mansfield Park* (vol. 1, ch. 6), contends that 'it is inconceiv-
able, given the proprieties of the period' that Austen would con-
sciously introduce the subject of sodomy in the navy into her text.[97]
But in her teenage years, Austen was not writing for publication
and was much readier to experiment with her characters' sexual
conduct. When Edward and Augustus, in 'Love and Freindship',
fly 'into each other's arms', exclaiming 'My Life! My Soul!' and
'My Adorable Angel!' (p. 114), they go far beyond conventional
eighteenth-century expressions of male friendship. In 'The History of England', Austen creates a bizarre homosexual fantasy in
her account of Richard III, declaring: 'it may also be affirmed that
he did not kill his Wife, for if Perkin Warbeck was really the Duke
of York, why might not Lambert Simnel be the Widow of Richard'
(p. 179). There are also homosexual jokes swirling through the
chapter on James I, such as a remark that Henry Percy's 'Attentions'
were 'entirely Confined to Lord Mounteagle' and a pun on James'
'keener penetration' in his male friendships (pp. 186–7).[98] There is
likewise nothing innocent about Austen's charade on James' Scottish favourite Sir Robert Carr, likened to a carpet and derided as a
'pet' by the tag, 'you tread on my whole'.

The reluctance of Austen's Victorian descendants, the Austen-
Leighs, to publish her juvenilia is understandable; they are, after
all, writings in which murder, suicide, violence, theft, verbal abuse,
gluttony and drunkenness all play a prominent part. Austen's mur-
derers include Sukey Simpson in 'Jack and Alice', who after endeavouring to cut Lucy's throat poisons her instead and is 'speedily
raised to the Gallows' (p. 32); Sir William Mountague, who shoots

---

[96] Letter of 7–8 January 1807, Le Faye (ed.), *Letters*, p. 115.

[97] John Wiltshire (ed.), *Mansfield Park* (Cambridge: Cambridge University Press, 2005),
p. 657.

[98] Christopher Kent observes that Austen 'cannot resist going farther than either
Goldsmith or Hume in discussing James I's partiality for handsome young men', and
notes the play on 'penetration' ('Learning History', in *Jane Austen's Beginnings*, p. 67).

his rival Mr Stanhope but escapes unpunished (p. 48); and Anna Parker, who ends a letter to her friend Elinor by mentioning casually, 'I am now going to murder my Sister' (p. 223). Only one character in the juvenilia commits suicide: Charlotte in 'Frederic and Elfrida', who drowns herself in the 'deep stream which ran thro' her Aunts pleasure Grounds in Portland Place' (p. 9). In addition, however, various young women die of grief, in the manner of Richardson's Clarissa. Emma in 'Edgar and Emma', with her beloved Edgar absent at college, retires to her room in despair and 'continued in tears the remainder of her Life' (p. 37); Melissa in 'A beautiful description' is bedridden, mysteriously wasting away (p. 92); Sophia in 'Love and Freindship' dies 'a Martyr to [her] greif for the loss of Augustus' (p. 132); and in 'Evelyn' two young women die for love of Frederick Gower: his sister Rosa and, at least in the continuation by James Edward Austen, his wife Maria (pp. 237, 356).

Acts of violence in the juvenilia include kicking others out of the window 'on the slightest provocation' in 'Frederic and Elfrida' (p. 6); the maiming of Lucy's leg by one of Charles Adams' steel traps in 'Jack and Alice' (p. 24); Sir George and Lady Harcourt's cudgelling their haymakers in 'Henry and Eliza' and Eliza's children's biting off two of her fingers (p. 43); Cassandra's knocking down a pastry cook in 'The beautifull Cassandra' (p. 54); Williams' flinging stones at a duck in 'The Generous Curate' (p. 95); the death of Edward and Augustus, 'weltering in their blood', in a carriage accident in 'Love and Freindship' (p. 129); and the death of Henry Hervey, thrown from a horse and dying of a fractured skull in 'Lesley Castle' (p. 146). Theft is still more common, and often accompanied by preening self-congratulation, combined with contempt for the victim. Eliza, in 'Henry and Eliza', steals fifty pounds from Sir George and Lady Harcourt, her 'inhuman Benefactors', but remains 'happy in the conscious knowledge of her own Excellence' (pp. 38–39); the beautiful Cassandra steals a bonnet and six ices, and bilks a coachman of his fare (pp. 54–55). In 'Love and Freindship' Augustus steals 'a considerable Sum of Money' from 'his Unworthy father's Escritoire' (p. 116); Philander and Gustavus steal first nine hundred pounds from their mothers, Bertha and Agatha, and then one hundred pounds from their cousins, Laura and Sophia (pp. 138, 121); and Sophia in turn steals five banknotes from her cousin Macdonald, while demanding 'in a haughty tone of voice "Wherefore her retirement was thus insolently broken in on?"' (p. 126). In 'The First Act of a Comedy', Strephon declares that his only means of support is 'a bad guinea', a counterfeit gold coin (p. 221); and in 'A Tale', Wilhelminus goes to Wales to 'take possession' of a desirable cottage, but omits to rent or purchase it (p. 225).

Not surprisingly, the creator of Lady Catherine de Bourgh in *Pride and Prejudice* excels in creating characters given to verbal abuse, but abuse in Austen's juvenilia has a rawness and vulgarity that she eschews in the novels. Frederic and Elfrida, together with their friend Charlotte, declare to the 'amiable Rebecca': 'your forbidding Squint, your greazy tresses and your swelling Back . . . are more frightfull than imagination can paint or pen describe' (p. 6). In 'Jack and Alice', Lady Williams tells the alcoholic heroine that 'when a person is in Liquor, there is no answering for what they may do', while Charles Adams calls Alice's father, Mr Johnson, 'a drunken old Dog' (pp. 21, 28). Lady Greville in Letter the third of 'A Collection of Letters' takes pleasure in tormenting the impoverished Maria Williams, asking her 'was not your Father as poor as a Rat' and enquiring whether he had been in debtor's prison (pp. 200–1). In 'The female philosopher', Arabella Smythe tells her visitors about her friend and correspondent Louisa Clarke, who 'is in general a very pleasant Girl, yet sometimes her good humour is clouded by Peevishness, Envy and Spite' (p. 217). And in 'Catharine', Mrs Percival tells Mr Stanley that her niece is 'one of the most impudent Girls that ever existed', using 'impudent' in the sense of sexually profligate (p. 282).

Heroic feats of eating and drinking take place in several of the early writings. In 'Frederic and Elfrida', Charlotte and her aunt 'sat down to Supper on a young Leveret, a brace of Partridges, a leash of [three] Pheasants and a Dozen Pigeons' (p. 9). At a masquerade in 'Jack and Alice', 'the whole party not excepting even Virtue [one of the masqueraders] were carried home, Dead Drunk' (p. 16). In 'Lesley Castle', Charlotte Luttrell prepares astonishing quantities of food while regretting the inability of her guests to consume what she prepares. And in 'Evelyn', Mr Gower has no sooner eaten his way through 'The Chocolate, The Sandwiches, the Jellies, the Cakes, the Ice, and the Soup' than, not forgetting to pocket the rest, he enjoys 'a most excellent Dinner and partook of the most exquisite Wines' (pp. 232–33).

Where the young Jane Austen differs most obviously from the still younger Daisy Ashford is in her extraordinary ability to undermine while mimicking the literary conventions of her age. In a famous letter of 1816, Austen tells the Prince Regent's Librarian, James Stanier Clarke: 'I could no more write a Romance than an Epic Poem. – I could not sit seriously down to write a serious Romance under any other motive than to save my Life.' Austen dated the letter, with some malice, 1 April; Clarke had been urging her to write 'an Historical Romance, founded on the House of Saxe Cobourg'[99] and the April Fool's date suggests what she thought of the idea. What the young Austen could do supremely well was to write mock-romances, such as 'Frederic and Elfrida'; mock-libertine fiction, such as 'Sir William Mountague'; mock-travel fiction, such as 'Memoirs of Mr Clifford', 'A Tour through Wales' or 'A Tale'; mock-epistolary fiction, such as 'The Three Sisters' or 'A Collection of Letters'; mock-moral tales, such as 'The Generous Curate'; mock-odes, such as 'Ode to Pity'; mock-sentimental fiction, such as 'Love and Freindship'; and mock-histories, such as 'The History of England'. She could, it seems, create mock-anything, including, of course, mock-husbands for herself, with names ranging from Edmund to Jack and from Mortimer to Smith.

Only one of Austen's juvenilia goes entirely against the grain: 'A fragment written to inculcate the practice of Virtue'. Here it is hard to judge Austen's intentions. Is the fragment, briefer than any

---

[99] Letter of 1 April 1816, Le Faye (ed.), *Letters*, p. 312.

other item in the three notebooks, a parody of didactic treatises that she mocks elsewhere, or is it, alone among the juvenilia, to be taken at face value? Or, a third possibility, should the phrase 'To seek them out to study their wants, and to leave them unsupplied' (p. 91), be read ironically, as advice to leave the wants of the poor unfulfilled? Austen herself, perhaps finding the tone uncertain, resolved the problem by deleting the entire piece. Richardson's *Pamela* announces on its title page that it will 'cultivate the Principles of Virtue', but Austen would allow nothing in her early writings to do so, at least in so explicit a fashion. Instead, she presents us with characters like the beautiful Cassandra who, after carrying out a series of minor crimes, 'smiled and whispered to herself "This is a day well spent"' (p. 56).

The cancelled 'fragment' is followed by a piece with what seems to be an equally portentous title, 'A beautiful description of the different effects of Sensibility on different Minds'. Sensibility is, of course, a key term for Austen and for eighteenth-century thought in general, as the title of her first published novel, *Sense and Sensibility*, suggests. It is a double-edged term, implying a capacity to be moved by and sympathize with others, as well as an acute sensitivity that could quickly become ridiculous. Marianne in the novel possesses sensibility in both senses and is thus at once sympathetic and absurd, an object of pity as well as a target of Austen's satire. In 'A beautiful description', in contrast, Melissa, ostensibly an 'affecting' object, seems merely ridiculous, 'wrapped in a book muslin bedgown, a chambray gauze shift, and a french net nightcap'. Her lover Sir William, with his lugubrious interjections 'Oh! Melissa, Ah! Melissa', spoils the melancholy effect by repeatedly scratching his head. The first-person narrator is always busy 'cooking some little delicacy for the unhappy invalid', such as 'hashing up the remains of an old Duck, toasting some cheese or making a Curry' (p. 92). The effects of sensibility on these two minds are clearly risible. The hero of the story, and a heroic figure in the juvenilia, is Dr Dowkins, who deals with Melissa's illness with a series of excruciating but bracing puns.

In July 1817, three days before her death, Austen wrote 'When Winchester races', her comic verses on downpours plaguing the horse-races in the town where she was about to die. Melissa in the latest of her juvenilia, dated June 1793, also seems close to death. And the best way to deal with death, here and elsewhere in Austen's early writings, is suggested by the black humour in the dialogue between the punning doctor and the narrator that concludes the 'beautiful description': ' "Does she think of dieing?" "She has not strength to think at all." "Nay then she cannot think to have Strength" ' (p. 93). Austen's father rightly noted that her juvenilia were written 'in a Style entirely new'. Having read what seems to have been much of the fiction and drama published in the eighteenth century, she was able, before the age of eighteen, to create a body of writings which drew heavily on her reading but which was as original as her father claimed, manipulating and subverting while giving the appearance of replicating existing literary forms. Austen was, as her father indicated, a 'very Young Lady' when she completed her three manuscript notebooks, but, with their anarchic energy, violence and irreverence, there was nothing ladylike about them. The 'Style entirely new', which presented a barrier to their critical appreciation for too long, can now be seen as one of the most appealing features of Austen's early writings, which are quite unlike the work of any of her contemporaries, and equally unlike her own mature novels.

NOTE ON THE TEXT

The text of this edition of Jane Austen's juvenilia has been prepared from the surviving holograph manuscripts: 'Volume the First' in the Bodleian Library and 'Volume the Second' and 'Volume the Third' in the British Library. It follows the manuscript notebooks closely, while recognizing that a printed transcription must diverge from a handwritten source in certain ways. No changes have been made to Austen's spelling, capitalization, paragraphing or punctuation. Her idiosyncrasies and inconsistencies, which form part of the texture of her prose and which can help establish the date of a particular item, have been carefully preserved.

Limited changes have been undertaken to other features of the manuscripts. Austen occasionally uses the long 's'; this has been regularized throughout to the modern 's'. She generally uses the ampersand (&) in place of 'and'; this too has been regularized. Her other contractions and abbreviations are retained, but the raised letters that she uses for abbreviations are lowered. Words and phrases underlined for emphasis are printed in italics. No attempt has been made to represent graphic features of the manuscripts, such as lines drawn above or below titles or chapter numbers. Catch-words, ornamental letters, different sizes of capitals and other such features of the manuscripts have not been reproduced. In the special case of 'The History of England', illustrated by Cassandra Austen, a facsimile is provided in Appendix A (p. 297). On occasion, Austen places commas directly beneath exclamation marks or question marks; in this edition, they are placed before or after these marks. Austen's use of quotation marks in direct speech differs from modern usage, and changes from item to item within the notebooks. Her various systems are followed here, but when opening or closing quotation marks are accidentally omitted they have been inserted. When Austen uses running quotation marks at the beginning of lines, they have been deleted.

Some ambiguous elements in the manuscripts cause difficulties in transcription. Since Austen's indentations are often extremely slight, it is not always clear where a new paragraph begins. Some of her letters, similarly, waver between upper and lower cases, while her commas cannot always be distinguished from her periods, nor her exclamation marks from her question marks. In such cases I have used my best editorial judgement, taking the context and Austen's practice elsewhere in the notebooks into account.

All of Austen's extensive revisions, deletions and additions are recorded in textual notes at the foot of the page. The great majority of her alterations, amounting to some 550 in all, can be readily deciphered, but on occasion Austen obliterated heavily. There are thus some conjectural readings, indicated by question marks, and on a few occasions a deleted word or phrase cannot be recovered, even after prolonged and repeated study of the manuscript. On thirteen occasions, I have corrected obvious errors, such as the accidental omission or repetition of a word. These editorial changes are recorded in the textual notes and in a separate list of 'Corrections and Emendations'. In most cases, the intended reading is obvious; when the emendation is conjectural, the issue is considered in an explanatory note.

Volume the First

VOLUME THE FIRST

CONTENTS

To Miss Lloyd[1]

My dear Martha

As a small testimony of the gratitude I feel for your late generosity to me in finishing my muslin Cloak,[2] I beg leave to offer you this little production of your sincere Freind[3]

The Author

line 4: 'muslin' inserted above line.

Frederic and Elfrida
a novel.[4]

The Uncle of Elfrida[5] was the Father of Frederic; in other words, they were first cousins by the Father's side.[6]

Being both born in one day and both brought up at one school,[7] it was not wonderfull[8] that they should look on each other with something more than bare politeness.[9] They loved with mutual sincerity but were both determined not to transgress the rules of Propriety by owning their attachment, either to the object beloved, or to any one else.[10]

They were exceedingly handsome and so much alike,[11] that it was not every one who knew them apart. Nay even their most intimate freinds had nothing to distinguish them by, but the shape of the face, the colour of the Eye, the length of the Nose and the difference of the complexion.

Elfrida had an intimate freind to whom, being on a visit to an Aunt, she wrote the following Letter.

To Miss Drummond

"Dear Charlotte"[12]

"I should be obliged to you, if you would buy me, during your stay with Mrs Williamson, a new and fashionable Bonnet, to suit the Complexion[13] of your

E. Falknor."

line 2: 'Mother' deleted; 'Father' inserted above line.   //   line 6: 'politenness' changed to 'politeness'.   //   line 9: 'either to the object beloved, or' inserted above line.

Charlotte, whose character was a willingness to oblige every one, when she returned into the Country, brought her Freind the wished-for Bonnet, and so ended this little adventure, much to the satisfaction of all parties.

On her return to Crankhumdunberry (of which sweet village[14] her father was Rector) Charlotte was received with the greatest Joy by Frederic and Elfrida, who, after pressing her alternately to their Bosoms, proposed to her to take a walk in a Grove of Poplars which led from the Parsonage to a verdant Lawn enamelled with a variety of variegated flowers[15] and watered by a purling Stream, brought from the Valley of Tempé[16] by a passage under ground.

In this Grove they had scarcely remained above 9 hours, when they were suddenly agreably surprized by hearing a most delightfull voice warble the following stanza.

Song.
That Damon[17] was in love with me
I once thought and beleiv'd
But now that he is not I see,
I fear I was deceiv'd.

No sooner were the lines finished than they beheld by a turning in the Grove 2 elegant young women leaning on each other's arm, who immediately on perceiving them, took a different path and disappeared from their sight.

CHAPTER THE SECOND

As Elfrida and her companions, had seen enough of them to know that they were neither the 2 Miss Greens, nor Mrs Jackson and her Daughter, they could not help expressing their surprise at their appearance; till at length recollecting, that a new family had lately taken a House not far from the Grove, they hastened home, determined to lose no time in forming an acquaintance with 2 such amiable and worthy Girls, of which family they rightly imagined them to be a part.

Agreable to such a determination, they went that very evening to pay their respects to Mrs Fitzroy and her two Daughters. On being shewn into an elegant dressing room, ornamented with festoons of artificial flowers,[18] they were struck with the engaging Exterior and beautifull outside of Jezalinda[19] the eldest of the young Ladies; but e'er they had been many minutes seated, the Wit and Charms which shone resplendant in the conversation of the amiable Rebecca,[20] enchanted them so much that they all with one accord jumped up and exclaimed.

"Lovely and too charming Fair one,[21] notwithstanding your forbidding Squint, your greazy tresses and your swelling Back,[22] which are more frightfull than imagination can paint or pen describe, I cannot refrain from expressing my raptures, at the engaging Qualities of your Mind, which so amply atone for the Horror, with which your first appearance must ever inspire the unwary visitor."

"Your Sentiments so nobly expressed on the different excellencies of Indian and English Muslins,[23] and the judicious preference you give the former, have excited in me an admiration of which I can alone give an adequate idea, by assuring you it is nearly equal to what I feel for myself."

Then making a profound Curtesy[24] to the amiable and abashed Rebecca, they left the room and hurried home.

From this period, the intimacy between the Families of Fitzroy, Drummond, and Falknor, daily increased till at length it grew to such a pitch, that they did not scruple to kick one another out of the window on the slightest provocation.[25]

line 2: 'them' inserted above line.

During this happy state of Harmony, the eldest Miss Fitzroy ran off with the Coachman[26] and the amiable Rebecca was asked in marriage by Captain Roger of Buckinghamshire.[27]

Mrs Fitzroy did not approve of the match on account of the tender years of the young couple, Rebecca being but 36 and Captain Roger little more than 63.[28] To remedy this objection, it was agreed that they should wait a little while till they were a good deal older.

CHAPTER THE THIRD

In the mean time the parents of Frederic proposed to those of Elfrida, an union between them,[29] which being accepted with pleasure, the wedding cloathes were bought and nothing remained to be settled but the naming of the Day.[30]

As to the lovely Charlotte, being importuned with eagerness to pay another visit to her Aunt, she determined to accept the invitation and in consequence of it walked to Mrs Fitzroys to take leave of the amiable Rebecca, whom she found surrounded by Patches, Powder, Pomatum and Paint[31] with which she was vainly endeavouring to remedy the natural plainness of her face.

"I am come my amiable Rebecca, to take my leave of you for the fortnight I am destined to spend with my Aunt. Beleive me this separation is painfull to me, but it is as necessary as the labour which now engages you."

"Why to tell you the truth my Love, replied Rebecca, I have lately taken it into my head to think (perhaps with little reason) that my complexion is by no means equal to the rest of my face and have therefore taken, as you see, to white and

line 19: 'Rouge' deleted; 'Patches' inserted above line.

red paint which I would scorn to use on any other occasion as I hate Art."

Charlotte, who perfectly understood the meaning of her freind's speech, was too goodtemper'd and obliging to refuse her, what she knew she wished,—a compliment; and they parted the best freinds in the world.

With a heavy heart and streaming Eyes did she ascend the lovely vehicle[a][32] which bore her from her freinds and home; but greived as she was, she little thought in what a strange and different manner she should return to it.

On her entrance into the city of London which was the place of Mrs Williamson's abode, the postilion,[33] whose stupidity was amazing, declared and declared even without the least shame or Compunction, that having never been informed he was totally ignorant of what part of the Town, he was to drive to.

Charlotte, whose nature we have before intimated, was an earnest desire to oblige every one, with the greatest Condescension[34] and Good humour informed him that he was to drive to Portland Place,[35] which he accordingly did and Charlotte soon found herself in the arms of a fond Aunt.

Scarcely were they seated as usual, in the most affectionate manner in one chair,[36] than the Door suddenly opened and an aged gentleman with a sallow face and old pink Coat,[37] partly by intention and partly thro' weakness was at the feet of the lovely Charlotte, declaring his attachment to her and beseeching her pity in the most moving manner.

Not being able to resolve to make any one miserable, she consented to become his wife; where upon the Gentleman left the room and all was quiet.

[a] a post chaise [JA's note].
line 10: 'would' deleted; 'should' inserted above line.   //   line 20: 'did' inserted above line.

Their quiet however continued but a short time, for on a second opening of the door a young and Handsome Gentleman with a new blue coat,[38] entered and intreated from the lovely Charlotte, permission to pay to her, his addresses.

There was a something in the appearance of the second Stranger, that influenced Charlotte in his favour, to the full as much as the appearance of the first: she could not account for it,[39] but so it was.

Having therefore agreable to that and the natural turn of her mind to make every one happy, promised to become his Wife the next morning, he took his leave and the two Ladies sat down to Supper on a young Leveret,[40] a brace of Partridges, a leash of Pheasants[41] and a Dozen of Pigeons.

CHAPTER THE FOURTH

It was not till the next morning that Charlotte recollected the double engagement[42] she had entered into; but when she did, the reflection of her past folly, operated so strongly on her mind, that she resolved to be guilty of a greater, and to that end threw herself into a deep stream which ran thro' her Aunts pleasure Grounds in Portland Place.[43]

She floated to Crankhumdunberry where she was picked up and buried; the following epitaph, composed by Frederic Elfrida and Rebecca, was placed on her tomb.

Epitaph
Here lies our freind who having promis-ed
That unto two she would be marri-ed
Threw her sweet Body and her lovely face
Into the Stream that runs thro' Portland Place

These sweet lines, as pathetic as beautifull[44] were never read by any one who passed that way, without a shower of

line 3: ampersand deleted after 'coat'.

tears, which if they should fail of exciting in you, Reader, your mind must be unworthy to peruse them.[45]

Having performed the last sad office to their departed freind, Frederic and Elfrida together with Captain Roger and Rebecca returned to Mrs Fitzroy's at whose feet they threw themselves with one accord and addressed her in the following Manner.

"Madam"

"When the sweet Captain Roger first addressed the amiable Rebecca, you alone objected to their union on account of the tender years of the Parties. That plea can be no more, seven days being now expired, together with the lovely Charlotte,[46] since the Captain first spoke to you on the subject."

"Consent then Madam to their union and as a reward, this smelling Bottle which I enclose in my right hand, shall be yours and yours forever; I never will claim it again. But if you refuse to join their hands in 3 days time, this dagger[47] which I enclose in my left shall be steeped in your hearts blood."

"Speak then Madam and decide their fate and yours."

Such gentle and sweet persuasion could not fail of having the desired effect. The answer they received, was this.

"My dear young freinds"

"The arguments you have used are too just and too eloquent to be withstood; Rebecca in 3 days time, you shall be united to the Captain."

This speech, than which nothing could be more satisfactory, was received with Joy by all; and peace being once more restored on all sides, Captain Roger intreated Rebecca to favour them with a Song, in compliance with which request

line 9: 'must'(?) deleted; 'first' inserted above line.

having first assured them that she had a terrible cold,[48] she sung as follows.

Song

When Corydon[49] went to the fair
He bought a red ribbon for Bess,
With which she encircled her hair
And made herself look very fess.[50]

CHAPTER THE FIFTH

At the end of 3 days Captain Roger and Rebecca were united and immediately after the Ceremony set off in the Stage Waggon[51] for the Captains seat in Buckinghamshire.

The parents of Elfrida, alltho' they earnestly wished to see her married to Frederic before they died, yet knowing the delicate frame of her mind could ill bear the least excertion and rightly judging that naming her wedding day would be too great a one, forebore to press her on the subject.[52]

Weeks and Fortnights flew away without gaining the least ground; the Cloathes grew out of fashion and at length Capt. Roger and his Lady arrived to pay a visit to their Mother and introduce to her their beautifull Daughter of eighteen.

Elfrida, who had found her former acquaintance were growing too old and too ugly to be any longer agreable, was rejoiced to hear of the arrival of so pretty a girl as Eleanor[53] with whom she determined to form the strictest freindship.

But the Happiness she had expected from an acquaintance with Eleanor, she soon found was not to be received, for she had not only the mortification of finding herself treated by her as little less than an old woman, but had actually the horror of perceiving a growing passion in the Bosom of Frederic for the Daughter of the amiable Rebecca.

The instant she had the first idea of such an attachment, she flew to Frederic and in a manner truly heroick, spluttered[54] out to him her intention of being married the next Day.

To one in his predicament who possessed less personal Courage than Frederic was master of, such a speech would have been Death; but he not being the least terrified boldly replied,

"Damme Elfrida—*you* may be married tomorrow but *I* won't."

This answer distressed her too much for her delicate Constitution. She accordingly fainted and was in such a hurry to have a succession of fainting fits, that she had scarcely patience enough to recover from one before she fell into another.[55]

Tho', in any threatening Danger to his Life or Liberty, Frederic was as bold as brass yet in other respects his heart was as soft as cotton[56] and immediately on hearing of the dangerous way Elfrida was in,[57] he flew to her and finding her better than he had been taught to expect, was united to her Forever—.

FINIS.

Jack and Alice
a novel.

Is respectfully inscribed to Francis William Austen Esqr
Midshipman on board his Majesty's Ship the Perseverance[1]
by his obedient humble
Servant The Author

CHAPTER THE FIRST

Mr Johnson[2] was once upon atime about 53; in a twelvemonth afterwards he was 54, which so much delighted him
that he was determined to celebrate his next Birth day by
giving a Masquerade[3] to his Children and Freinds. Accordingly on the Day he attained his 55th year tickets[4] were dispatched to all his Neighbours to that purpose. His acquaintance indeed in that part of the World were not very numerous
as they consisted only of Lady Williams, Mr and Mrs Jones,
Charles Adams[5] and the 3 Miss Simpsons,[6] who composed
the neighbourhood of Pammydiddle[7] and formed the Masquerade.

Before I proceed to give an account of the Evening, it will
be proper to describe to my reader, the persons and Characters
of the party introduced to his acquaintance.

Mr and Mrs Jones were both rather tall[8] and very
passionate,[9] but were in other respects, good tempered,

line 8: 'up' inserted above line. // line 7–8: 's' deleted at the end of
'twelvemonth'. // line 20: 'of the party' inserted above line. // line 21:
'both' inserted above line.

wellbehaved People. Charles Adams was an amiable,[10] accomplished and bewitching[11] young Man; of so dazzling a Beauty that none but Eagles could look him in the Face.[12]

Miss Simpson was pleasing in her person, in her Manners and in her Disposition; an unbounded ambition was her only fault. Her second sister Sukey[13] was Envious, Spitefull and Malicious. Her person was short, fat and disagreable. Cecilia[14] (the youngest) was perfectly handsome but too affected to be pleasing.

In Lady Williams every virtue met. She was a widow with a handsome Jointure[15] and the remains of a very handsome face. Tho' Benevolent and Candid, she was Generous and sincere; Tho' Pious and Good, she was Religious and amiable, and Tho' Elegant and Agreable, she was Polished and Entertaining.[16]

The Johnsons were a family of Love,[17] and though a little addicted to the Bottle and the Dice,[18] had many good Qualities.

Such was the party assembled in the elegant Drawing Room[19] of Johnson Court, amongst which the pleasing figure of a Sultana was the most remarkable of the female Masks.[20] Of the Males a Mask representing the Sun, was the most universally admired. The Beams that darted from his Eyes were like those of that glorious Luminary[21] tho' infinitely Superior. So strong were they that no one dared venture within half a mile of them; he had therefore the best part of the Room to himself, its size not amounting to more than 3 quarters of a mile in length and half a one in breadth.[22] The Gentleman at last finding the feirceness of his beams to be very inconvenient

line 9: 'agreable' deleted; 'pleasing' inserted above line.   //   line 16: 'Such was' deleted before 'The Johnsons'.   //   line 29: 'inconvenience' deleted; 'feirceness' inserted above line.

to the concourse²³ by obliging them to croud together in one corner of the room, half shut his eyes by which means, the Company discovered him to be Charles Adams in his plain green Coat,²⁴ without any mask at all.

When their astonishment was a little subsided their attention was attracted by 2 Domino's²⁵ who advanced in a horrible Passion;²⁶ they were both very tall, but seemed in other respects to have many good qualities. "These said the witty Charles, these are Mr and Mrs Jones." and so indeed they were.

No one could imagine who was the Sultana! Till at length on her addressing a beautifull Flora²⁷ who was reclining in a studied attitude²⁸ on a couch, with "Oh Cecilia, I wish I was really what I pretend to be", she was discovered by the never failing genius of Charles Adams, to be the elegant but ambitious Caroline²⁹ Simpson, and the person to whom she addressed herself, he rightly imagined to be her lovely but affected sister Cecilia.

The Company now advanced to a Gaming Table where sat 3 Dominos³⁰ (each with a bottle in their hand) deeply engaged, but a female in the character of Virtue³¹ fled with hasty footsteps from the shocking scene, whilst a little fat woman representing Envy, sate alternately on the foreheads of the 3 Gamesters.³² Charles Adams was still as bright as ever; he soon discovered the party at play to be the 3 Johnsons, Envy to be Sukey Simpson and Virtue to be Lady Williams.

The Masks were then all removed and the Company retired to another room, to partake of elegant and well managed Entertainment,³³ after which the Bottle being pretty briskly

line 1: 'of masks' deleted after 'concourse'. // line 13: 'attidude' corrected to 'attitude'. // line 20: 'by his side' deleted; 'in their hand' inserted above line.

pushed about by the 3 Johnsons, the whole party not excepting even Virtue were carried home, Dead Drunk.

CHAPTER THE SECOND

For three months did the Masquerade afford ample subject for conversation to the inhabitants of Pammydiddle;[34] but no character at it was so fully expatiated on as Charles Adams. The singularity of his appearance, the beams which darted from his eyes, the brightness of his Wit, and the whole *tout ensemble*[35] of his person had subdued the hearts of so many of the young Ladies, that of the six present at the Masquerade but five had returned uncaptivated. Alice[36] Johnson was the unhappy sixth whose heart had not been able to withstand the power of his Charms. But as it may appear strange to my Readers, that so much worth and Excellence as he possessed should have conquered only hers, it will be necessary to inform them that the Miss Simpsons were defended from his Power by Ambition, Envy, and Self-admiration.

Every wish of Caroline was centered in a titled Husband; whilst in Sukey such superior excellence could only raise her Envy not her Love, and Cecilia was too tenderly attached to herself to be pleased with any one besides. As for Lady Williams and Mrs Jones, the former of them was too sensible, to fall in love with one so much her Junior[37] and the latter, tho' very tall and very passionate was too fond of her Husband to think of such a thing.

Yet in spite of every endeavour on the part of Miss Johnson to discover any attachment to her in him; the cold and indifferent heart of Charles Adams still to all appearance, preserved its native freedom; polite to all but partial to none,[38] he

line 23: 'inferior' deleted; 'Junior' inserted above line.

still remained the lovely, the lively, but insensible[39] Charles Adams.

One evening, Alice finding herself somewhat heated by wine (no very uncommon case) determined to seek a releif for her disordered Head and Love-sick Heart in the Conversation of the intelligent Lady Williams.

She found her Ladyship at home as was in general the Case, for she was not fond of going out, and like the great Sir Charles Grandison scorned to deny herself when at Home,[40] as she looked on that fashionable method of shutting out disagreable Visitors, as little less than downright Bigamy.

In spite of the wine she had been drinking, poor Alice was uncommonly out of spirits;[41] she could think of nothing but Charles Adams, she could talk of nothing but him, and in short spoke so openly that Lady Williams soon discovered the unreturned affection she bore him, which excited her Pity and Compassion so strongly that she addressed her in the following Manner.

"I perceive but too plainly my dear Miss Johnson, that your Heart has not been able to withstand the fascinating Charms of this young Man and I pity you sincerely. Is it a first Love?"

"It is."

"I am still more greived to hear *that*; I am myself a sad example of the Miseries, in general attendant on a first Love and I am determined for the future to avoid the like Misfortune. I wish it may not be too late for you to do the same; if it is not endeavour my dear Girl to secure yourself from so great a Danger. A second attachment is seldom attended with any serious consequences;[42] against *that* therefore I have nothing

---

line 16: 'discovered' written over 'perceived'. // line 17: 'unreturned' inserted above line.

to say. Preserve yourself from a first Love and you need not fear a second."

"You mentioned Madam something of your having yourself been a sufferer by the misfortune you are so good as to wish me to avoid. Will you favour me with your Life and Adventures?"[43]

"Willingly my Love."

CHAPTER THE THIRD

"My Father was a gentleman of considerable Fortune in Berkshire;[44] myself and a few more his only Children. I was but six years old when I had the misfortune of losing my Mother and being at that time young and Tender, my father instead of sending me to School, procured an able handed Governess to superintend my Education at Home.[45] My Brothers were placed at Schools suitable to their Ages and my Sisters being all younger than myself, remained still under the Care of their Nurse."

"Miss Dickins was an excellent Governess. She instructed me in the Paths of Virtue; under her tuition I daily became more amiable, and might perhaps by this time have nearly attained perfection, had not my worthy Preceptoress been torn from my arms e'er I had attained my seventeenth year. I never shall forget her last words. 'My dear Kitty'[46] she said 'Good night t'ye.'[47] I never saw her afterwards" continued Lady Williams wiping her eyes, "She eloped with the Butler the same night."

"I was invited the following year by a distant relation of my Father's to spend the Winter with her in town.[48]

line 20: 'had not' deleted after 'and'. // line 27: 'Xmas' deleted; 'year' inserted above line.

Mrs Watkins was a Lady of Fashion, Family and fortune; she was in general esteemed a pretty Woman, but I never thought her very handsome, for my part. She had too high a forehead, Her eyes were too small and she had too much colour."[49]

"How can *that* be?" interrupted Miss Johnson reddening with anger; "Do you think that any one can have too much colour?"

"Indeed I do, and I'll tell you why I do my dear Alice; when a person has too great a degree of red in their Complexion, it gives their face in my opinion, too red a look."[50]

"But can a face my Lady have too red a look."?

"Certainly my dear Miss Johnson and I'll tell you why. When a face has too red a look it does not appear to so much advantage as it would were it paler."

"Pray Ma'am proceed in your story."

"Well, as I said before, I was invited by this Lady to spend some weeks with her in town. Many Gentlemen thought her Handsome but in my opinion, Her forehead was too high, her eyes too small and she had too much colour."

"In that Madam as I said before your Ladyship must have been mistaken. Mrs Watkins could not have too much colour since no one can have too much."

"Excuse me my Love if I do not agree with you in that particular. Let me explain myself clearly; my idea of the case is this. When a Woman has too great a proportion of red in her Cheeks, she must have too much colour."

"But Madam I deny that it is possible for any one to have too great a proportion of red in their Cheeks."

line 10: 'much colour' deleted; 'red a look' inserted above line.   //   line 12: 'tell' is a conjectural editorial insertion.   //   line 24: 's' deleted at the end of 'idea'.   //   line 25: 'are' deleted; 'is' inserted above line.   //   line 25: 'these' corrected to 'this'.

"What my Love not if they have too much colour?"

Miss Johnson was now out of all patience, the more so perhaps as Lady Williams still remained so inflexibly cool. It must be remembered however that her Ladyship had in one respect by far the advantage of Alice; I mean in not being drunk, for heated with wine and raised by Passion, she could have little command of her Temper.

The Dispute at length grew so hot on the part of Alice that "From Words she almost came to Blows"[51]

When Mr Johnson luckily entered and with some difficulty forced her away from Lady Williams, Mrs Watkins and her red cheeks.

CHAPTER THE FOURTH

My Readers may perhaps imagine that after such a fracas,[52] no intimacy could longer subsist between the Johnsons and Lady Williams, but in that they are mistaken for her Ladyship was too sensible to be angry at a conduct which she could not help perceiving to be the natural consequence of inebriety and Alice had too sincere a respect for Lady Williams and too great a relish for her Claret,[53] not to make every concession in her power.

A few days after their reconciliation Lady Williams called on Miss Johnson to propose a walk in a Citron Grove[54] which led from her Ladyship's pigstye to Charles Adams's Horsepond.[55] Alice was too sensible[56] of Lady Williams's kindness in proposing such a walk and too much pleased with the prospect of seeing at the end of it, a Horsepond of Charles's, not to accept it with visible delight. They had not

line 8: 'that' deleted after 'hot'. // line 9: 'they' deleted; 'she' inserted above line. // line 11: first 'her' inserted above line. // line 11: 'his Daughter' deleted. // line 22: 'her ladyship' deleted; 'Lady Williams' inserted above line.

proceeded far before she was roused from the reflection of the happiness she was going to enjoy, by Lady Williams's thus addressing her.

"I have as yet forborn my dear Alice to continue the narrative of my Life from an unwillingness of recalling to your Memory a scene which (since it reflects on you rather disgrace than credit) had better be forgot than remembered."

Alice had already begun to colour up and was beginning to speak, when her Ladyship perceiving her displeasure, continued thus.

"I am afraid my dear Girl that I have offended you by what I have just said; I assure you I do not mean to distress you by a retrospection of what cannot now be helped; considering all things I do not think you so much to blame as many People do; for when a person is in Liquor, there is no answering for what they may do."[57]

"Madam, this is not to be borne, I insist—"

"My dear Girl dont vex yourself about the matter; I assure you I have entirely forgiven every thing respecting it; indeed I was not angry at the time, because as I saw all along, you were nearly dead drunk. I knew you could not help saying the strange things you did. But I see I distress you; so I will change the subject and desire it may never again be mentioned; remember it is all forgot—I will now pursue my story; but I must insist upon not giving you any description of Mrs. Watkins; it would only be reviving old stories and as you never saw her, it can be nothing to you, if her forehead was too high, her eyes were too small, or if she had too much colour."

---

line 1: 'a' deleted after 'from'; 'the' inserted above line.   //   line 16: three and a half lines heavily deleted after 'do': '; a young woman (?) in *such* a situation is particularly off her guard because her head is not strong enough to support intoxication.'   //   line 20: 'because' inserted above line.

"Again! Lady Williams: this is too much"—

So provoked was poor Alice at this renewal of the old story, that I know not what might have been the consequence of it, had not their attention been engaged by another object. A lovely young Woman lying apparently in great pain beneath a Citron tree, was an object too interesting not to attract their notice. Forgetting their own dispute they both with simpathizing Tenderness advanced towards her and accosted her in these terms.

"You seem fair Nymph to be labouring under some misfortune which we shall be happy to releive if you will inform us what it is. Will you favour us with your Life and adventures?"[58]

"Willingly Ladies, if you will be so kind as to be seated." They took their places and she thus began.

CHAPTER THE FIFTH

"I am a native of North Wales and my Father is one of the most capital Taylors[59] in it. Having a numerous family, he was easily prevailed on by a sister of my Mother's who is a widow in good circumstances and keeps an alehouse in the next Village to ours, to let her take me and breed me up at her own expence.[60] Accordingly I have lived with her for the last 8 years of my Life, during which time she provided me with some of the first rate Masters, who taught me all the accomplishments requisite for one of my sex and rank. Under their instructions I learned Dancing, Music, Drawing and various Languages,[61] by which means I became more accomplished than any other Taylor's Daughter in Wales. Never was there a happier Creature than I was, till within

line 19: 'was' deleted; 'is' inserted above line. // line 22: 'have' inserted above line. // line 23: 'some' deleted by 'time'.

the last half year—but I should have told you before that the principal Estate in our Neighbourhood belongs to Charles Adams, the owner of the brick House, you see yonder."

"Charles Adams!" exclaimed the astonished Alice; "are you acquainted with Charles Adams?"

"To my sorrow madam I am. He came about half a year ago to receive the rents of the Estate[62] I have just mentioned. At that time I first saw him; as you seem ma'am acquainted with him, I need not describe to you how charming he is. I could not resist his attractions;"—

"Ah! who can," said Alice with a deep sigh.

"My Aunt being in terms of the greatest intimacy with his cook, determined, at my request, to try whether she could discover, by means of her freind if there were any chance of his returning my affection. For this purpose she went one evening to drink tea with Mrs Susan,[63] who in the course of Conversation mentioned the goodness of her Place[64] and the Goodness of her Master; upon which my Aunt began pumping[65] her with so much dexterity that in a short time Susan owned, that she did not think her Master would ever marry, 'for (said she) he has often and often declared to me that his wife, whoever she might be, must possess, Youth, Beauty, Birth, Wit, Merit, and Money.[66] I have many a time (she continued) endeavoured to reason him out of his resolution and to convince him of the improbability of his ever meeting with such a Lady; but my arguments have had no effect and he continues as firm in his determination as ever.' You may imagine Ladies my distress on hearing this; for I was fearfull that tho' possessed of Youth, Beauty, Wit and Merit, and tho' the probable Heiress of my Aunts House and business, he might think me deficient in Rank, and in being so, unworthy of his hand."

"However I was determined to make a bold push and therefore wrote him a very kind letter, offering him with great tenderness my hand and heart.[67] To this I received an angry and peremptory refusal, but thinking it might be rather the effect of his modesty than any thing else, I pressed him again on the subject.[68] But he never answered any more of my Letters and very soon afterwards left the Country. As soon as I heard of his departure I wrote to him here, informing him that I should shortly do myself the honour of waiting on him at Pammydiddle, to which I received no answer; therefore choosing to take, Silence for Consent, I left Wales, unknown to my Aunt, and arrived here after a tedious Journey this Morning. On enquiring for his House I was directed thro' this Wood, to the one you there see. With a heart elated by the expected happiness of beholding him I entered it and had proceeded thus far in my progress thro' it, when I found myself suddenly seized by the leg and on examining the cause of it, found that I was caught in one of the steel traps so common in gentlemen's grounds."[69]

"Ah cried Lady Williams, how fortunate we are to meet with you; since we might otherwise perhaps have shared the like misfortune"—

"It is indeed happy for you Ladies, that I should have been a short time before you. I screamed as you may easily imagine till the woods resounded again and till one of the inhuman Wretch's servants came to my assistance and released me from my dreadfull prison, but not before one of my legs was entirely broken."

line 5: 'other reason' deleted; 'thing else' inserted above line.   //   line 9: 'soon' deleted; 'shortly' inserted above line.   //   line 21: 'or' deleted; 'since' inserted above line.   //   line 21: 'otherwise' inserted above line.   //   line 24: 'may' inserted above line.

CHAPTER THE SIXTH

At this melancholy recital the fair eyes of Lady Williams, were suffused in tears and Alice could not help exclaiming,

"Oh! cruel Charles to wound the hearts and legs[70] of all the fair."

Lady Williams now interposed and observed that the young Lady's leg ought to be set without farther delay. After examining the fracture therefore, she immediately began and performed the operation with great skill which was the more wonderfull on account of her having never performed such a one before.[71] Lucy,[72] then arose from the ground and finding that she could walk with the greatest ease, accompanied them to Lady Williams's House at her Ladyship's particular request.

The perfect form, the beautifull face, and elegant manners of Lucy so won on the affections of Alice that when they parted, which was not till after Supper, she assured her that except her Father, Brother, Uncles, Aunts, Cousins and other relations, Lady Williams, Charles Adams and a few dozen more of particular freinds, she loved her better than almost any other person in the world.

Such a flattering assurance of her regard would justly have given much pleasure to the object of it, had she not plainly perceived that the amiable Alice had partaken too freely of Lady Williams's claret.

Her Ladyship (whose discernment was great) read in the intelligent countenance of Lucy her thoughts on the subject and as soon as Miss Johnson had taken her leave, thus addressed her.

line 27: 'on' deleted; 'her' inserted above line.   //   line 28: 'when' deleted; 'as soon as' inserted above line.

"When you are more intimately acquainted with my Alice you will not be surprised, Lucy, to see the dear Creature drink a little too much; for such things happen every day. She has many rare and charming qualities, but Sobriety is not one of them. The whole Family are indeed a sad drunken set. I am sorry to say too that I never knew three such thorough Gamesters as they are, more particularly Alice. But she is a charming girl. I fancy not one of the sweetest tempers in the world; to be sure I have seen her in such passions! However she is a sweet young Woman. I am sure you'll like her. I scarcely know any one so amiable.—Oh! that you could but have seen her the other Evening! How she raved! and on such a trifle too! She is indeed a most pleasing Girl! I shall always love her!"

"She appears by your ladyship's account to have many good qualities," replied Lucy. "Oh! a thousand," answered Lady Williams; "tho' I am very partial to her, and perhaps am blinded by my affection, to her real defects."[73]

CHAPTER THE SEVENTH

The next morning brought the three Miss Simpsons to wait on Lady Williams; who received them with the utmost politeness and introduced to their acquaintance Lucy, with whom the eldest was so much pleased that at parting she declared her sole *ambition* was to have her accompany them the next morning to Bath,[74] whither they were going for some weeks.

"Lucy, said Lady Williams, is quite at her own disposal and if she chooses to accept so kind an invitation, I hope she will not hesitate, from any motives of delicacy on my account. I

line 8: 'that' (?) heavily deleted after 'fancy'.   //   line 12: 'yesterday' deleted; 'the other' inserted above line.   //   line 17–18: 'I may be partial; indeed I believe I am; yes I am very partial to her.' deleted; 'I am very . . . her real defects' inserted above line.

know not indeed how I shall ever be able to part with her.
She never was at Bath and I should think that it would be
a most agreable Jaunt[75] to her. Speak my Love," continued
she, turning to Lucy, "what say you to accompanying these
Ladies? I shall be miserable without you—t'will be a most
pleasant tour to you—I hope you'll go; if you do I am sure
t'will be the Death of me—pray be persuaded"—

Lucy begged leave to decline the honour of accompanying
them, with many expressions of gratitude for the extream
politeness of Miss Simpson in inviting her.

Miss Simpson appeared much disappointed by her refusal.
Lady Williams insisted on her going—declared that she
would never forgive her if she did not, and that she should
never survive it if she did, and inshort used such persuasive
arguments that it was at length resolved she was to go. The
Miss Simpsons called for her at ten o'clock the next morning and Lady Williams had soon the satisfaction of receiving
from her young freind, the pleasing intelligence of their safe
arrival in Bath.

It may now be proper to return to the Hero of this Novel,[76]
the brother of Alice, of whom I beleive I have scarcely ever
had occasion to speak; which may perhaps be partly oweing
to his unfortunate propensity to Liquor, which so compleatly
deprived him of the use of those faculties Nature had endowed
him with, that he never did anything worth mentioning. His
Death happened a short time after Lucy's departure and was
the natural Consequence of this pernicious practice. By his
decease, his sister became the sole inheritress of a very large
fortune, which as it gave her fresh Hopes of rendering herself
acceptable as a wife to Charles Adams could not fail of being

line 6: 'I'll' corrected to 'I' before 'hope'.

most pleasing to her—and as the effect was Joyfull the Cause could scarcely be lamented.

Finding the violence of her attachment to him daily augment, she at length disclosed it to her Father and desired him to propose a union between them to Charles. Her father consented and set out one morning to open the affair to the young Man. Mr Johnson being a man of few words his part was soon performed and the answer he received was as follows—

"Sir, I may perhaps be expected to appear pleased at and gratefull for the offer you have made me: but let me tell you that I consider it as an affront. I look upon myself to be Sir a perfect Beauty—where would you see a finer figure or a more charming face. Then, sir I imagine my Manners and Address to be of the most polished kind; there is a certain elegance a peculiar sweetness in them that I never saw equalled and cannot describe—. Partiality aside, I am certainly more accomplished in every Language, every Science, every Art and every thing than any other person in Europe. My temper is even, my virtues innumerable, my self unparalelled.[77] Since such Sir is my character, what do you mean by wishing me to marry your Daughter? Let me give you a short sketch of yourself and of her. I look upon you Sir to be a very good sort of Man in the main; a drunken old Dog to be sure, but that's nothing to me. Your daughter sir, is neither sufficiently beautifull, sufficiently amiable, sufficiently witty, nor sufficiently rich for me—. I expect nothing more in my wife than my wife will find in me—Perfection. These sir, are my sentiments and I honour myself for having such. One freind I have[78] and glory in having but one—. She is at present preparing my Dinner, but if you choose to see her, she shall

line 9: 'appeared' in ms.   //   line 9: 'at' inserted above line.   //   line 10: 'me:' inserted above line.   //   line 22: 'of' inserted above line after 'and'.

come and she will inform you that these have ever been my sentiments."

Mr Johnson was satisfied; and expressing himself to be much obliged to Mr. Adams for the characters he had favoured him with of himself and his Daughter, took his leave.

The unfortunate Alice on receiving from her father the sad account of the ill success his visit had been attended with, could scarcely support the disappointment—She flew to her Bottle and it was soon forgot.

CHAPTER THE EIGHTH

While these affairs were transacting at Pammydiddle, Lucy was conquering every Heart at Bath. A fortnight's residence there had nearly effaced from her remembrance the captivating form of Charles—The recollection of what her Heart had formerly suffered by his charms and her Leg by his trap, enabled her to forget him with tolerable Ease, which was what she determined to do; and for that purpose dedicated five minutes in every day to the employment of driving him from her remembrance.

Her second Letter to Lady Williams contained the pleasing intelligence of her having accomplished her undertaking to her entire satisfaction; she mentioned in it also an offer of marriage she had received from the Duke of —— an elderly Man of noble fortune whose ill health was the cheif inducement of his Journey to Bath. "I am distressed (she continued) to know whether I mean to accept him or not. There are a thousand advantages to be derived from a marriage with the Duke, for besides those more inferior ones of Rank

line 4: 'him' deleted; 'Mr. Adams' inserted above line.   //   line 13: 'ever' is 'every' in ms.   //   line 18: 'to do' inserted above line.   //   line 22: 'having' inserted above line.

and Fortune it will procure me a home, which of all other things is what I most desire. Your Ladyship's kind wish of my always remaining with you, is noble and generous but I cannot think of becoming so great a burden on one I so much love and esteem. That One should receive obligations only from those we despise, is a sentiment instilled into my mind by my worthy Aunt, in my early years, and cannot in my opinion be too strictly adhered to. The excellent woman of whom I now speak, is I hear too much incensed by my imprudent departure from Wales, to receive me again—. I most earnestly wish to leave the Ladies I am now with. Miss Simpson is indeed (setting aside ambition) very amiable, but her 2d Sister the envious and malvolent Sukey is too disagreable to live with.—. I have reason to think that the admiration I have met with in the circles of the Great at this Place, has raised her Hatred and Envy; for often has she threatened, and sometimes endeavoured to cutt my throat.—Your Ladyship will therefore allow that I am not wrong in wishing to leave Bath, and in wishing to have a home to receive me, when I do. I shall expect with impatience your advice concerning the Duke and am your most obliged

&c &c—Lucy."

Lady Williams sent her, her opinion on the subject in the following Manner.

"Why do you hesitate my dearest Lucy, a moment with respect to the Duke? I have enquired into his Character and find him to be an unprincipaled, illiterate Man. Never shall my Lucy be united to such a one! He has a princely fortune, which is every day encreasing.[79] How nobly will you spend it!, what credit will you give him in the eyes of all!, How

---

line 4: 'That' inserted above line. // line 6: 'mind' inserted above line. //
line 7: 'is' corrected to first 'in'. // line 28: repetition of 'be united' deleted.

much will he be respected on his Wife's account![80] But why my dearest Lucy, why will you not at once decide this affair by returning to me and never leaving me again? Altho' I admire your noble sentiments with respect to obligations, yet let me beg that they may not prevent your making me happy. It will to be sure be a great expence to me, to have you always with me—I shall not be able to support it—but what is that in comparison with the happiness I shall enjoy in your society?—t'will ruin me I know—you will not therefore surely, withstand these arguments, or refuse to return to yours most affectionately—&c &c

C. Williams"

CHAPTER THE NINTH

What might have been the effect of her Ladyship's advice, had it ever been received by Lucy, is uncertain, as it reached Bath a few Hours after she had breathed her last. She fell a sacrifice to the Envy and Malice of Sukey who jealous of her superior charms took her by poison from an admiring World at the age of seventeen.[81]

Thus fell the amiable and lovely Lucy whose Life had been marked by no crime, and stained by no blemish but her imprudent departure from her Aunts, and whose death was sincerely lamented by every one who knew her. Among the most afflicted of her freinds were Lady Williams, Miss Johnson and the Duke; the 2 last[82] of whom had a most sincere regard for her, more particularly Alice, who had spent a

line 4: 'the' deleted; 'your' inserted above line.   //   line 5: 'less deeply felt for Want of sufficient time, preventing you from' heavily deleted; 'yet let me . . . prevent your' inserted above line. After 'prevent', 'charming dear (?) Lucy' was originally inserted, then deleted.   //   line 10: 'and' deleted; 'or' inserted above line.   //   line 21: 'plot, but' deleted; 'blemish but' inserted above line.   //   line 25: 'last' written over 'first'.   //   line 25: 'having' deleted; 'of whom had' inserted above line.

whole evening in her company and had never thought of her since. His Grace's affliction may likewise be easily accounted for, since he lost one for whom he had experienced during the last ten days, a tender affection and sincere regard. He mourned her loss with unshaken constancy for the next fortnight at the end of which time, he gratified the ambition of Caroline Simpson by raising her to the rank of a Dutchess. Thus was she at length rendered compleatly happy in the gratification of her favourite passion. Her sister the perfidious Sukey, was likewise shortly after exalted in a manner she truly deserved, and by her actions appeared to have always desired. Her barbarous Murder was discovered and in spite of every interceding freind she was speedily raised to the Gallows[83]—. The beautifull but affected Cecilia was too sensible of her own superior charms, not to imagine that if Caroline could engage a Duke, she might without censure aspire to the affections of some Prince—and knowing that those of her native Country were cheifly engaged,[84] she left England and I have since heard is at present the favourite Sultana of the great Mogul[85]—.

In the mean time the inhabitants of Pammydiddle were in a state of the greatest astonishment and Wonder, a report being circulated of the intended marriage of Charles Adams. The Lady's name was still a secret. Mr and Mrs Jones imagined it to be, Miss Johnson; but *she* knew better; all *her* fears were centered in his Cook, when to the astonishment of every one, he was publicly united to Lady Williams—

FINIS.

line 19: 'at present' inserted above line.

Edgar and Emma
a tale.[1]

CHAPTER THE FIRST

"I cannot imagine," said Sir Godfrey[2] to his Lady, "why we continue in such deplorable Lodgings as these, in a paltry Market-town,[3] while we have 3 good Houses of our own situated in some of the finest parts of England, and perfectly ready to receive us!"

"I'm sure Sir Godfrey," replied Lady Marlow, "it has been much against my inclination that we have staid here so long; or why we should ever have come at all indeed, has been to me a wonder, as none of our Houses have been in the least want of repair."

"Nay my dear," answered Sir Godfrey, "you are the last person who ought to be displeased with what was always meant as a compliment to you; for you cannot but be sensible of the very great inconvenience your Daughters and I have been put to during the 2 years we have remained crowded in these Lodgings in order to give you pleasure."

"My dear," replied Lady Marlow, "How can you stand and tell such lies, when you very well know that it was merely to oblige the Girls and you, that I left a most commodious House situated in a most delightfull Country and surrounded by a most agreable Neighbourhood, to live 2 years cramped

line 9: 'is' deleted; 'indeed, has been' inserted above line.

up in Lodgings three pair of stairs high,[4] in a smokey and unwholesome town, which has given me a continual fever and almost thrown me into a Consumption."[5]

As, after a few more speeches on both sides they could not determine which was the most to blame, they prudently laid aside the debate, and having packed up their Cloathes and paid their rent, they set out the next morning with their 2 Daughters for their seat in Sussex.[6]

Sir Godfrey and Lady Marlow were indeed very sensible people and tho' (as in this instance) like many other sensible People, they sometimes did a foolish thing, yet in general their actions were guided by Prudence and regulated by discretion.

After a Journey of two Days and a half they arrived at Marlhurst[7] in good health and high spirits; so overjoyed were they all to inhabit again a place, they had left with mutual regret for two years, that they ordered the bells to be rung and distributed ninepence among the Ringers.[8]

CHAPTER THE SECOND

The news of their arrival being quickly spread throughout the Country, brought them in a few Days visits of congratulation from every family in it.

Amongst the rest came the inhabitants of Willmot Lodge a beautifull Villa[9] not far from Marlhurst. Mr Willmot was the representative[10] of a very ancient Family and possessed besides his paternal Estate, a considerable share in a Lead mine and a ticket in the Lottery.[11] His Lady was an agreable Woman. Their Children were too numerous to be particularly described;[12] it is sufficient to say that in general they

---

line 23: 'a younger' deleted after 'was'.   //   line 27: 'too' inserted above line.

were virtuously inclined and not given to any wicked ways. Their family being too large to accompany them in every visit, they took nine with them alternately. When their Coach[13] stopped at Sir Godfrey's door, the Miss Marlow's Hearts throbbed in the eager expectation of once more beholding a family so dear to them. Emma[14] the youngest (who was more particularly interested in their arrival, being attached to their eldest Son) continued at her Dressing-room window in anxious Hopes of seeing young Edgar[15] descend from the Carriage.

Mr and Mrs Willmot with their three eldest Daughters first appeared—Emma began to tremble[16]—. Robert, Richard, Ralph, and Rodolphus[17] followed—Emma turned pale—. Their two youngest Girls were lifted from the Coach—Emma sunk breathless on a Sopha.[18] A footman came to announce to her the arrival of Company; her heart was too full to contain its afflictions. A confidante[19] was necessary—In Thomas she hoped to experience a faithfull one—for one she must have and Thomas was the only one at Hand. To him she unbosomed herself without restraint and after owning her passion for young Willmot, requested his advice in what manner she should conduct herself in the melancholy Disappointment under which she laboured.

Thomas, who would gladly have been excused from listening to her complaint, begged leave to decline giving any advice concerning it, which much against her will, she was obliged to comply with.

Having dispatched him therefore with many injunctions of secrecy, she descended with a heavy heart into the Parlour,

line 6: 'a' inserted above line.   //   line 12: 'fear' heavily deleted; 'tremble' inserted above line.   //   line 26: 'must' deleted; 'much' inserted above line.

where she found the good Party seated in a social Manner[20] round a blazing fire.

CHAPTER THE THIRD

Emma had continued in the Parlour some time before she could summon up sufficient courage to ask Mrs Willmot after the rest of her family; and when she did, it was in so low, so faltering a voice that no one knew she spoke. Dejected by the ill success of her first attempt she made no other, till on Mrs Willmots desiring one of the little Girls to ring the bell for their Carriage, she stepped across the room and seizing the string said in a resolute manner.

"Mrs Willmot, you do not stir from this House till you let me know how all the rest of your family do, particularly your eldest son."

They were all greatly surprised by such an unexpected address and the more so, on account of the manner in which it was spoken; but Emma, who would not be again disappointed, requesting an answer, Mrs Willmot made the following eloquent oration.

"Our children are all extremely well but at present most of them from home. Amy[21] is with my sister Clayton. Sam at Eton.[22] David with his Uncle John. Jem and Will at Winchester.[23] Kitty at Queens Square.[24] Ned with his Grandmother. Hetty and Patty[25] in a convent at Brussells.[26] Edgar at college,[27] Peter at Nurse,[28] and all the rest (except the nine here) at home."

It was with difficulty that Emma could refrain from tears on hearing of the absence of Edgar; she remained however

line 7: 'faultering' changed to 'faltering'; 'faltering a manner' deleted; 'faltering a voice' inserted above line. // line 20: 'extremely' written over 'extreamly'.

tolerably composed till the Willmot's were gone when having no check to the overflowings of her greif, she gave free vent to them, and retiring to her own room, continued in tears the remainder of her Life.[29]

FINIS.

Henry and Eliza[1]
a novel.

Is humbly dedicated to Miss Cooper[2] by her obedient
Humble Servant
                                                    The Author

As Sir George and Lady Harcourt were superintending the
Labours of their Haymakers, rewarding the industry of some
by smiles of approbation,[3] and punishing the idleness of
others, by a cudgel, they perceived lying closely concealed
beneath the thick foliage of a Haycock,[4] a beautifull little
Girl not more than 3 months old.

Touched with the enchanting Graces of her face and
delighted with the infantine tho' sprightly answers she
returned to their many questions, they resolved to take her
home and, having no Children of their own, to educate her
with care and cost.

Being good People themselves, their first and principal care
was to incite in her a Love of Virtue and a Hatred of Vice,
in which they so well succeeded (Eliza having a natural turn
that way herself) that when she grew up, she was the delight
of all who knew her.

Beloved by Lady Harcourt, adored by Sir George and
admired by all the World, she lived in a continued course
of uninterrupted Happiness, till she had attained her eighteenth year; when happening one day to be detected in stealing a banknote of 50£, she was turned out of doors by her
inhuman Benefactors.[5] Such a transition to one who did not

possess so noble and exalted a mind as Eliza, would have been Death, but she, happy in the conscious knowledge of her own Excellence, amused herself, as she sate beneath a tree with making and singing the following Lines.

Song.

Though misfortunes my footsteps may ever attend
I hope I shall never have need of a Freind
as an innocent Heart I will ever preserve
and will never from Virtue's dear boundaries swerve.

Having amused herself some hours, with this song and her own pleasing reflections, she arose and took the road to M.[6] a small market town of which place her most intimate freind kept the red Lion.[7]

To this freind she immediately went, to whom having recounted her late misfortune, she communicated her wish of getting into some family in the capacity of Humble Companion.[8]

Mrs Willson,[9] who was the most amiable creature on earth, was no sooner acquainted with her Desire, than she sate down in the Bar and wrote the following Letter to the Dutchess of F, the woman whom of all others, she most Esteemed.

"To the Dutchess of F."
"Receive into your Family, at my request a young woman of unexceptionable Character, who is so good as to choose your Society in preference to going to Service. Hasten, and take her from the arms of your"

"Sarah[10] Wilson."

The Dutchess, whose freindship for Mrs Wilson would have carried her any lengths, was overjoyed at such an

line 10: 'with' deleted after 'herself'.   //   line 18: 'Jones' deleted; 'Willson' inserted above line.   //   line 19: 'had' deleted; 'was' inserted above line.   //   line 28: 'Jones' deleted; 'Wilson' inserted above line.

opportunity of obliging her and accordingly sate out immediately on the receipt of her letter for the red Lion, which she reached the same Evening.[11] The Dutchess of F. was about 45 and a half; Her passions were strong, her freindships firm and her Enmities, unconquerable.[12] She was a widow and had only one Daughter who was on the point of marriage with a young Man of considerable fortune.

The Dutchess no sooner beheld our Heroine than throwing her arms around her neck, she declared herself so much pleased with her, that she was resolved they never more should part. Eliza was delighted with such a protestation of freindship, and after taking a most affecting leave of her dear Mrs Wilson, accompanied her Grace the next morning to her seat in Surry.[13]

With every expression of regard did the Dutchess introduce her to Lady Hariet, who was so much pleased with her appearance that she besought her, to consider her as her Sister, which Eliza with the greatest Condescension promised to do.

Mr Cecil, the Lover of Lady Harriet, being often with the family was often with Eliza. A mutual Love took place and Cecil having declared his first, prevailed on Eliza to consent to a private union,[14] which was easy to be effected, as the dutchess's chaplain[15] being very much in love with Eliza himself, would they were certain do anything to oblige her.

The Dutchess and Lady Harriet being engaged one evening to an assembly,[16] they took the opportunity of their absence and were united by the enamoured Chaplain.

lines 1–2: 'of expressing the Love she bore her' deleted; 'accordingly sate out immediately on the' inserted above line.   //   line 16: 'by' deleted; 'with' inserted.   //   line 17: 'his' changed to 'her' before 'Sister'.   //   line 20: 'often' written over 'with' (?).   //   line 23: an illegible word deleted before 'a'.   //   line 23: 'as' inserted above line.   //   line 24: 'likewise' deleted after 'being'.

When the Ladies returned, their amazement was great at finding instead of Eliza the following Note.

"Madam"
  "We are married and gone."
        "Henry and Eliza Cecil."

Her Grace as soon as she had read the letter, which sufficiently explained the whole affair, flew into the most violent passion and after having spent an agreable half hour, in calling them by all the shocking Names her rage could suggest to her, sent out after them 300 armed Men, with orders not to return without their Bodies, dead or alive; intending that if they should be brought to her in the latter condition to have them put to Death in some torturelike manner, after a few years Confinement.[17]

In the mean time Cecil and Eliza continued their flight to the Continent,[18] which they judged to be more secure than their native Land, from the dreadfull effects of the Dutchess's vengeance, which they had so much reason to apprehend.

In France they remained 3 years, during which time they became the parents of two Boys, and at the end of it Eliza became a widow without any thing to support either her or her Children. They had lived since their Marriage at the rate of 12,000£ a year,[19] of which Mr Cecil's estate being rather less than the twentieth part,[20] they had been able to save but a trifle, having lived to the utmost extent of their Income.

Eliza, being perfectly conscious of the derangement in their affairs, immediately on her Husband's death set sail

line 6: 'after having read it' deleted; 'as soon as she had read' inserted above line. // line 10: repetition of 'after' deleted. // line 11: 'out' inserted above line, thus changing 'with' to 'without'. // line 23: '2' written over '0', changing '10,000' to '12,000'. // line 24: 'secure' deleted; 'save' inserted above line.

for England, in a man of War of 55 Guns,[21] which they had built in their more prosperous Days. But no sooner had she stepped on Shore at Dover,[22] with a Child in each hand, than she was seized by the officers of the Dutchess, and conducted by them to a snug little Newgate[23] of their Lady's, which she had erected for the reception of her own private Prisoners.

No sooner had Eliza entered her Dungeon than the first thought which occurred to her, was how to get out of it again.

She went to the Door; but it was locked. She looked at the Window; but it was barred with iron; disappointed in both her expectations, she dispaired of effecting her Escape, when she fortunately perceived in a Corner of her Cell, a small saw and a Ladder of ropes. With the saw she instantly went to work and in a few weeks had displaced every Bar but one to which she fastened the Ladder.

A difficulty then occurred which for some time, she knew not how to obviate. Her Children were too small to get down the Ladder by themselves, nor would it be possible for her to take them in her arms, when *she* did. At last she determined to fling down all her Cloathes, of which she had a large Quantity, and then having given them strict Charge not to hurt themselves, threw her Children after them.[24] She herself with ease descended by the Ladder, at the bottom of which she had the pleasure of finding Her little boys in perfect Health and fast asleep.

Her wardrobe she now saw a fatal necessity of selling, both for the preservation of her Children and herself. With tears in her eyes, she parted with these last reliques of her former Glory, and with the money she got for them, bought others more usefull, some playthings for her Boys and a gold Watch for herself.[25]

---

line 18: 'be' inserted above line.   //   line 24: 'little' inserted above line.

But scarcely was she provided with the above-mentioned necessaries, than she began to find herself rather hungry, and had reason to think, by their biting off two of her fingers, that her Children were much in the same situation.

To remedy these unavoidable misfortunes, she determined to return to her old freinds, Sir George and Lady Harcourt, whose generosity she had so often experienced and hoped to experience as often again.

She had about 40 miles to travel before she could reach their hospitable Mansion, of which having walked 30 without stopping,[26] she found herself at the Entrance of a Town, where often in happier times, she had accompanied Sir George and Lady Harcourt to regale themselves with a cold collation[27] at one of the Inns.

The reflections that her adventures since the last time she had partaken of these happy *Junketings*,[28] afforded her, occupied her mind, for some time, as she sate on the steps at the door of a Gentleman's house. As soon as these reflections were ended, she arose and determined to take her station at the very inn, she remembered with so much delight, from the Company of which, as they went in and out, she hoped to receive some Charitable Gratuity.[29]

She had but just taken her post at the Innyard before a Carriage drove out of it, and on turning the Corner at which she was stationed, stopped to give the Postilion an opportunity of admiring the beauty of the prospect.[30] Eliza then advanced to the carriage and was going to request their Charity, when on fixing her Eyes on the Lady within it, she exclaimed,

"Lady Harcourt!"

To which the lady replied:

"Eliza!"

line 17: 'of' deleted; 'at' inserted above line.

"Yes Madam it is the wretched Eliza herself."

Sir George, who was also in the Carriage, but too much amazed to speek, was proceeding to demand an explanation from Eliza of the Situation she was then in, when Lady Harcourt in transports of Joy, exclaimed.

"Sir George, Sir George, she is not only Eliza our adopted Daughter, but our real Child."[31]

"Our real Child! What Lady Harcourt, do you mean? You know you never even was with child. Explain yourself, I beseech you."

"You must remember Sir George that when you sailed for America, you left me breeding."

"I do, I do, go on dear Polly."[32]

"Four months after you were gone, I was delivered of this Girl, but dreading your just resentment at her not proving the Boy you wished, I took her to a Haycock and laid her down. A few weeks afterwards, you returned, and fortunately for me, made no enquiries on the subject. Satisfied within myself of the wellfare of my Child, I soon forgot I had one, insomuch that when, we shortly after found her in the very Haycock, I had placed her, I had no more idea of her being my own, than you had, and nothing I will venture to say could have recalled the circumstance to my remembrance, but my thus accidentally hearing her voice which now strikes me as being the very counterpart of my own Child's."

"The rational and convincing Account you have given of the whole affair, said Sir George, leaves no doubt of her being our Daughter and as such I freely forgive the robbery she was guilty of."

line 22: 'do' deleted; 'had' inserted above line.   //   line 24: 'never before struck me with' deleted; 'now strikes me as' inserted above line.

A mutual Reconciliation then took place, and Eliza, ascending the Carriage with her two Children returned to that home from which she had been absent nearly four years.

No sooner was she reinstated in her accustomed power at Harcourt Hall, than she raised an Army,[33] with which she entirely demolished the Dutchess's Newgate, snug as it was, and by that act, gained the Blessings of thousands, and the Applause of her own Heart.

FINIS.

line 5: 'she' inserted above line after 'which'.

The adventures of Mr Harley

a short, but interesting Tale, is with all imaginable Respect inscribed to Mr Francis William Austen Midshipman on board his Majestys Ship the Perseverance[1] by his Obedient Servant

The Author.

Mr Harley[2] was one of many Children. Destined by his father for the Church and by his Mother for the Sea,[3] desirous of pleasing both, he prevailed on Sir John to obtain for him a Chaplaincy on board a Man of War. He accordingly, cut his Hair and sailed.

In half a year[4] he returned and sat-off[5] in the Stage Coach[6] for Hogsworth Green,[7] the seat of Emma. His fellow travellers were, A man without a Hat, Another with two, An old maid and a young Wife.

This last appeared about 17 with fine dark Eyes[8] and an elegant Shape; inshort Mr Harley soon found out, that she was his Emma and recollected he had married her a few weeks before he left England.

FINIS.

Sir William Mountague
an unfinished performance[1]

is humbly dedicated to Charles John Austen Esqre,[2] by his
most obedient humble Servant
>The Author.

Sir William Mountague was the son of Sir Henry Mountague, who was the son of Sir John Mountague, a descendant
of Sir Christopher Mountague, who was the nephew of Sir
Edward Mountague, whose ancestor was Sir James Mountague a near relation of Sir Robert Mountague, who inherited
the Title and Estate from Sir Frederic Mountague.[3]

Sir William was about 17 when his Father died, and left
him a handsome fortune, an ancient House and a Park well
stocked with Deer.[4] Sir William had not been long in the
possession of his Estate before he fell in Love with the 3 Miss
Cliftons[5] of Kilhoobery Park.[6] These young Ladies were all
equally young, equally handsome, equally rich and equally
amiable—Sir William was equally in Love with them all,
and knowing not which to prefer, he left the Country and
took Lodgings in a small Village near Dover.[7]

In this retreat, to which he had retired in the hope of finding a shelter from the Pangs of Love, he became enamoured
of a young Widow of Quality, who came for change of air to
the same Village, after the death of a Husband, whom she

line 22: 'with' deleted; 'of' inserted above line.   //   line 23: 'whom' inserted
above line.

had always tenderly loved and now sincerely lamented. Lady Percival was young, accomplished and lovely. Sir William adored her and she consented to become his Wife. Vehemently pressed by Sir William to name the Day in which he might conduct her to the Altar, she at length fixed on the following Monday, which was the first of September.[8] Sir William was a Shot[9] and could not support the idea of losing such a Day, even for such a Cause.[10] He begged her to delay the Wedding a short time. Lady Percival was enraged and returned to London the next Morning.

Sir William was sorry to lose her, but as he knew that he should have been much more greived by the Loss of the 1st of September, his Sorrow was not without a mixture of Happiness, and his Affliction was considerably lessened by his Joy.

After staying at the Village a few weeks longer, he left it and went to a freind's House in Surry. Mr Brudenell was a sensible Man, and had a beautifull Neice with whom Sir William soon fell in love. But Miss Arundel was cruel; she preferred a Mr Stanhope:[11] Sir William shot Mr Stanhope; the lady had then no reason to refuse him; she accepted him, and they were to be married on the 27th of October. But on the 25th Sir William received a visit from Emma Stanhope the sister of the unfortunate Victim of his rage. She begged some recompence, some atonement for the cruel Murder of her Brother. Sir William bade her name her price. She fixed on 14s.[12] Sir William offered her himself and Fortune. They went to London the next day and were there privately married.[13] For a fortnight Sir William was compleatly happy, but chancing

line 11–12: 'I would' deleted; 'as he knew that he should' inserted above line. // line 12: 'at' deleted; 'by' inserted above line.   // line 16: 'a' deleted; 'the' inserted above line.

one day to see a charming young Woman entering a Chariot[14] in Brook Street,[15] he became again most violently in love. On enquiring the name of this fair Unknown, he found that she was the Sister of his old freind Lady Percival, at which he was much rejoiced, as he hoped to have, by his acquaintance with her Ladyship, free access[16] to Miss Wentworth. . . . .

FINIS.

line 1: repetition of first 'a' deleted.   //   line 4: 'with' deleted; 'at' inserted above line.

To Charles John Austen Esqre

Sir,

Your generous patronage[1] of the unfinished tale, I have already taken the Liberty of dedicating to you, encourages me to dedicate to you a second, as unfinished as the first.

I am Sir with every expression
of regard for you and yr noble
Family,[2] your most obedt
&c &c . . . .
The Author

line 3: 'Permit' deleted before 'Your'.

Memoirs of Mr Clifford
an unfinished tale—

Mr Clifford lived at Bath; and having never seen London, set off one monday morning determined to feast his eyes with a sight of that great Metropolis.[3] He travelled in his Coach and Four,[4] for he was a very rich young Man and kept a great many Carriages of which I do not recollect half. I can only remember that he had a Coach, a Chariot, a Chaise,[5] a Landeau,[6] a Landeaulet,[7] a Phaeton,[8] a Gig,[9] a Whisky,[10] an italian Chair,[11] a Buggy,[12] a Curricle[13] and a wheelbarrow.[14] He had likewise an amazing fine stud[15] of Horses. To my knowledge he had six Greys, 4 Bays,[16] eight Blacks and a poney.[17]

In his Coach and 4 Bays Mr Clifford sate forward about 5 o'clock on Monday Morning the 1st of May for London. He always travelled remarkably expeditiously and contrived therefore to get to Devizes[18] from Bath, which is no less than nineteen miles, the first Day. To be sure he did not get in till eleven at night and pretty tight work it was as you may imagine.

However when he was once got to Devizes he was determined to comfort himself with a good hot Supper and therefore ordered a whole Egg to be boiled for him and his Servants. The next morning he pursued his Journey and in the course of 3 days hard labour reached Overton,[19] where he was seized with a dangerous fever the Consequence of too violent Exercise.

line 23: 'violent' deleted; 'dangerous' inserted above line.

Five months did our Hero remain in this celebrated City under the care of its no less celebrated Physician,[20] who at length compleatly cured him of his troublesome Desease.

As Mr Clifford still continued very weak, his first Day's Journey carried him only to Dean Gate,[21] where he remained a few Days and found himself much benefited by the change of Air.

In easy Stages he proceeded to Basingstoke.[22] One day Carrying him to Clarkengreen,[23] the next to Worting,[24] the 3d to the bottom of Basingstoke Hill, and the fourth, to Mr Robins's[25]. . . .

FINIS.

The beautifull Cassandra.
a novel in twelve Chapters.
dedicated by permission to Miss Austen.[1]
Dedication.

Madam

You are a Phoenix.[2] Your taste is refined, Your Sentiments are noble, and your Virtues innumerable. Your Person
is lovely, your Figure, elegant, and your Form, magestic. Your
Manners, are polished, your Conversation is rational and
your appearance singular. If therefore the following Tale will
afford one moment's amusement to you, every wish will be
gratified of

your most obediant
humble Servant
The Author.

line 9: 'are' inserted above line.

The beautifull Cassandra.
a novel, in twelve Chapters.

CHAPTER THE FIRST

Cassandra[3] was the Daughter and the only Daughter of a celebrated Millener in Bond Street.[4] Her father was of noble Birth, being the near relation of the Dutchess of——'s Butler.

CHAPTER THE 2D

When Cassandra had attained her 16th year,[5] she was lovely and amiable and chancing to fall in love with an elegant Bonnet,[6] her Mother had just compleated bespoke by the Countess of—— she placed it on her gentle Head and walked from her Mother's shop to make her Fortune.

CHAPTER THE 3RD

The first person she met, was the Viscount of —— a young man, no less celebrated for his Accomplishments and Virtues, than for his Elegance and Beauty.[7] She curtseyed and walked on.

CHAPTER THE 4TH

She then proceeded to a Pastry-cooks where she devoured six ices,[8] refused to pay for them, knocked down the Pastry Cook and walked away.

line 10: 'shop' inserted above line.

CHAPTER THE 5TH

She next ascended a Hackney Coach[9] and ordered it to Hampstead,[10] where she was no sooner arrived than she ordered the Coachman to turn round and drive her back again.

CHAPTER THE 6TH

Being returned to the same spot of the same Street she had sate out from, the Coachman demanded his Pay.[11]

CHAPTER THE 7TH

She searched her pockets over again and again; but every search was unsuccessfull. No money could she find. The man grew peremptory. She placed her bonnet on his head[12] and ran away.

CHAPTER THE 8TH

Thro' many a Street she then proceeded and met in none the least Adventure till on turning a Corner of Bloomsbury Square,[13] she met Maria.

CHAPTER THE 9TH

Cassandra started and Maria seemed surprised; they trembled, blushed, turned pale[14] and passed each other in a mutual Silence.

CHAPTER THE 10TH

Cassandra was next accosted by her freind the Widow, who squeezing out her little Head thro' her less window,[15] asked her how she did? Cassandra curtseyed and went on.

line 12: 'arrogant' deleted; 'peremptory' inserted above line.   //   line 23: 'the' written over 'a'.

CHAPTER THE 11TH

A quarter of a mile brought her to her paternal roof in Bond Street from which she had now been absent nearly 7 hours.

CHAPTER THE 12TH

She entered it and was pressed to her Mother's bosom by that worthy Woman. Cassandra smiled and whispered to herself "This is a day well spent."

FINIS.

Amelia Webster.

an interesting and well written Tale
is dedicated by Permission
to
Mrs Austen[1]
by
Her humble Servant
The Author.

To Miss Webster

My dear Amelia[3]

You will rejoice to hear of the return of my amiable Brother from abroad. He arrived on thursday, and never did I see a finer form, save that of your sincere freind

Matilda[4] Hervey

LETTER THE 2D

To H. Beverley[5] Esqre

Dear Beverley

I arrived here last thursday and met with a hearty reception from my Father, Mother and Sisters. The latter are both fine Girls—particularly Maud,[6] who I think would suit you as a Wife well enough. What say you to this? She will have two thousand Pounds[7] and as much more as you can get. If you don't marry her you will mortally offend

George Hervey

LETTER THE 3D

To Miss Hervey

Dear Maud

Beleive me I'm happy to hear of your Brother's arrival. I have a thousand things to tell you,[8] but my paper will only permit me to add[9] that I am yr affect. Freind

Amelia Webster

LETTER THE 4TH
To Miss S. Hervey[10]

Dear Sally[11]

I have found a very convenient old hollow oak[12] to put our Letters in; for you know we have long maintained a private Correspondence.[13] It is about a mile from my House and seven from Yours. You may perhaps imagine that I might have made choice of a tree which would have divided the Distance more equally—I was sensible of this at the time, but as I considered that the walk would be of benefit to you in your weak and uncertain state of Health, I preferred it to one nearer your House, and am yr faithfull

Benjamin Bar

LETTER THE 5TH
To Miss Hervey

Dear Maud

I write now to inform you that I did not stop at your house in my way to Bath last Monday.—. I have many things to inform you of, besides; but my Paper reminds me of concluding;[14] and beleive me yours ever &c.

Amelia Webster.

LETTER THE 6TH
To Miss Webster

Madam   Saturday

An humble Admirer now addresses you—I saw you lovely Fair one as you passed on Monday last, before our House in your way to Bath. I saw you thro' a telescope,[15] and was so

line 19: 'besides;' inserted above line.

struck by your Charms that from that time to this I have not tasted human food.

George Hervey.

LETTER THE 7TH
To Jack

As I was this morning at Breakfast the Newspaper was brought me, and in the list of Marriages I read the following.

"George Hervey Esqre to Miss Amelia Webster"
"Henry Beverley Esqre to Miss Hervey"
and
"Benjamin Bar Esqre to Miss Sarah Hervey."

yours, Tom.[16]

FINIS—

The Visit
a comedy in 2 acts

Dedication.
To the Revd James Austen[1]

Sir,

The following Drama, which I humbly recommend to your
Protection and Patronage, tho' inferior to those celebrated
Comedies called "The school for Jealousy" and "The travelled
Man,"[2] will I hope afford some amusement to so respectable
a *Curate*[3] as yourself; which was the end in veiw when it was
first composed[4] by your Humble Servant the Author.

line 6: 'c' inserted above line in 'school'.
line 8: 'they' deleted; 'it' inserted above line.

Dramatis Personae

Sir Arthur[5] Hampton
Lord Fitzgerald
Stanly[6]
Willoughby, Sir Arthur's nephew

Lady Hampton
Miss Fitzgerald
Sophy[7] Hampton
Cloe[8] Willoughby

The scenes are laid in
Lord Fitzgerald's House.

line 2: 'Authar' changed to 'Arthur' here and below.

Act the First
Scene the first a Parlour—
enter Lord Fitzgerald and Stanly

Stanly. Cousin your Servant.

Fitzgerald. Stanly, good morning to you. I hope you slept well last night.

Stanly. Remarkably well; I thank you.

Fitzgerald. I am afraid you found your Bed too short. It was bought in my Grandmother's time, who was herself a very short woman and made a point of suiting all her Beds to her own length,[9] as she never wished to have any company in the House, on account of an unfortunate impediment in her speech, which she was sensible of being very disagreable to her inmates.

Stanly. Make no more excuses dear Fitzgerald.

Fitzgerald. I will not distress you by too much civility—I only beg you will consider yourself as much at home as in your Father's house. Remember, "The more free, the more Wellcome."[10]

(exit Fitzgerald)

Stanly. Amiable Youth!
 Your virtues could he imitate
 How happy would be Stanly's fate!

(exit Stanly.)

Scene the 2nd
Stanly and Miss Fitzgerald, discovered.[11]

Stanly. What Company is it you expect to dine with you to Day, Cousin?

Miss F. Sir Arthur and Lady Hampton; their Daughter, Nephew and Neice.

Stanly. Miss Hampton and her Cousin are both Handsome, are they not?

Miss F. Miss Willoughby is extreamly so. Miss Hampton is a fine Girl, but not equal to her.

Stanly. Is not your Brother attached to the Latter?

Miss F. He admires her I know, but I beleive nothing more. Indeed I have heard him say that she was the most beautifull, pleasing, and amiable Girl in the world, and that of all others he should prefer her for his Wife. But it never went any farther I'm certain.

Stanly. And yet my Cousin never says a thing he does not mean.

Miss F. Never. From his Cradle he has always been a strict adherent to Truth.[12]

(Exeunt Severally)[13]
End of the First Act.

Act the Second.
Scene the first. The Drawing Room.
Chairs set round in a row.[14] Lord Fitzgerald, Miss Fitzgerald and Stanly seated.
Enter a Servant.

---

line 16: 'any' inserted above line.   //   line 19: 'ever' deleted; 'always' inserted above line.   //   line 20: three and a half lines deleted after 'Truth': 'He never told a Lie but once, and that was merely to oblige me. Indeed I may truly say there never was such a Brother!'

Servant. Sir Arthur and Lady Hampton. Miss Hampton, Mr and Miss Willoughby.

(exit Servant)

Enter the Company.

Miss F. I hope I have the pleasure of seeing your Ladyship well. Sir Arthur your servant. Yours Mr Willoughby. Dear Sophy, Dear Cloe,—

(They pay their Compliments alternately.)

Miss F.—Pray be seated.

(They sit)

Bless me! there ought to be 8 Chairs and these are but 6. However, if your Ladyship will but take Sir Arthur in your Lap, and Sophy, my Brother in hers, I beleive we shall do pretty well.[15]

Lady H. Oh! with pleasure. . . .

Sophy. I beg his Lordship would be seated.

Miss F. I am really shocked at crouding you in such a manner, but my Grandmother (who bought all the furniture of this room) as she had never a very large Party, did not think it necessary to buy more Chairs than were sufficient for her own family and two of her particular freinds.

Sophy. I beg you will make no apologies. Your Brother is very light.[16]

Stanly, aside) What a cherub is Cloe!

Cloe, aside) What a seraph[17] is Stanly!

Enter a Servant.

Servant. Dinner is on table.

They all rise.

Miss F. Lady Hampton, Miss Hampton, Miss Willoughby.

---

line 1: 'Authur' changed to 'Arthur' here and for the remainder of the ms.
lines 12–13: 'take' inserted above line and deleted after 'Sophy'.

Stanly. hands[18] Cloe, Lord Fitzgerald, Sophy Willoughby,
Miss Fitzgerald, and Sir Arthur, Lady Hampton.

(Exeunt.)

Scene the 2nd
The Dining Parlour.

Miss Fitzgerald at top. Lord Fitzgerald at bottom.[19] Company ranged on each side.

Servants waiting.

Cloe. I shall trouble Mr Stanly for a Little of the fried
Cowheel and Onion.[20]

Stanly. Oh Madam, there is a secret pleasure in helping so
amiable a Lady—.

Lady H. I assure you my Lord, Sir Arthur never touches wine;
but Sophy will toss off a bumper[21] I am sure to oblige your
Lordship.

Lord F. Elder wine or Mead,[22] Miss Hampton?

Sophy. If it is equal to you Sir, I should prefer some warm ale
with a toast and nutmeg.[23]

Lord F. Two glasses of warmed ale with a toast and nutmeg.

Miss F. I am afraid Mr Willoughby you take no care of yourself. I fear you dont meet with any thing to your liking.

Willoughby. Oh! Madam, I can want for nothing while there
are red herrings[24] on table.

Lord F. Sir Arthur taste that Tripe. I think you will not find
it amiss.

Lady H. Sir Arthur never eats Tripe; 'tis too savoury for him,
you know my Lord.

Miss F. Take away the Liver and Crow[25] and bring in the
Suet pudding.[26]

---

line 14: 'however' deleted by 'but'.   //   line 18: 'a' deleted; 'a toast and'
inserted above line.   //   line 19: 'toast and' inserted.   //   line 26: one or
two illegible words heavily deleted; 'him' inserted above line.

(a short Pause.)

Miss F. Sir Arthur shant I send you a bit of pudding?

Lady H. Sir Arthur never eats suet pudding Ma'am. It is too high a Dish for him.

Miss F. Will no one allow me the honour of helping them? Then John take away the Pudding, and bring the Wine.
(Servants take away the things and bring in the Bottles and Glasses.)

Lord F. I wish we had any Desert[27] to offer you. But my Grandmother in her Lifetime, destroyed the Hothouse[28] in order to build a receptacle for the Turkies with its' materials; and we have never been able to raise another tolerable one.

Lady H. I beg you will make no apologies my Lord.

Willoughby. Come Girls, let us circulate the Bottle.[29]

Sophy. A very good motion Cousin; and I will second it with all my Heart. Stanly you dont drink.

Stanly. Madam, I am drinking draughts of Love from Cloe's eyes.

Sophy. That's poor nourishment truly. Come, drink to her better acquaintance.

(Miss Fitzgerald goes to a Closet and brings out a bottle)

Miss F. This, Ladies and Gentlemen is some of my dear Grandmother's own manufacture. She excelled in Gooseberry Wine.[30] Pray taste it Lady Hampton?

Lady H. How refreshing it is!

Miss F. I should think with your Ladyship's permission, that Sir Arthur might taste a little of it.

Lady H. Not for Worlds. Sir Arthur never drinks anything so high.

---

line 3: 'suet' inserted above line.   //   line 6: 'suet' inserted above line before 'Pudding' and deleted.

Lord F. And now my amiable Sophia condescend to marry me.

(He takes her hand and leads her to the front)

Stanly. Oh! Cloe could I but hope you would make me blessed—

Cloe. I will.

(They advance.)

Miss F. Since you Willoughby are the only one left, I cannot refuse your earnest solicitations—There is my Hand.—

Lady H. And may you all be Happy!

FINIS.

The Mystery
An unfinished Comedy.

Dedication
To the Revd George Austen[1]

Sir,
I humbly solicit your Patronage to the following Comedy,
which tho' an unfinished one, is I flatter myself as *complete* a
Mystery as any of its kind.

I am Sir your most Humle
Servant
The Author

line 6: 'of hair' deleted; 'to' inserted above line.   //   line 7: '*complete*'
changed to '*compleat*' but then original spelling restored.

The Mystery
a Comedy

Dramatis Personae
      Men.
Colonel Elliott
Sir Edward Spangle[2]
Old Humbug[3]
Young Humbug
      and
Corydon.[4]

      Women.
Fanny[5] Elliott
Mrs Humbug
      and
Daphne[6]

Act the First
Scene the 1st

A Garden.

Enter Corydon.

Cory.) But Hush! I am interrupted.

(Exit Corydon.)

Enter Old Humbug and his Son, talking.

Old Hum:) It is for that reason I wish you to follow my advice. Are you convinced of its propriety?

Young Hum:) I am Sir, and will certainly act in the manner you have pointed out to me.

Old Hum:) Then let us return to the House.

(Exeunt)

Scene the 2nd

A Parlour in Humbug's house.
Mrs Humbug and Fanny, discovered at work.[7]

Mrs Hum:) You understand me my Love?

Fanny) Perfectly ma'am. Pray continue your narration.

Mrs. Hum:) Alas! It is nearly concluded, for I have nothing more to say on the Subject.

Fanny) Ah! here's Daphne.

Enter Daphne.

Daphne) My dear Mrs Humbug how d'ye do? Oh! Fanny 'tis all over.

Fanny) Is it indeed!

Mrs Hum:) I'm very sorry to hear it.

Fanny) Then t'was to no purpose that I. . . .

Daphne) None upon Earth.

Mrs Hum:) And what is to become of?. . . .

Daphne) Oh! that's all settled. (whispers[8] Mrs Humbug)

Fanny) And how is it determined?

Daphne) I'll tell you. (whispers Fanny)

Mrs Hum:) And is he to?. . . .

Daphne) I'll tell you all I know of the matter.

(whispers Mrs Humbug and Fanny)

Fanny) Well! now I know everything about it, I'll go away.

Mrs Hum:

And so will I

Daphne

(Exeunt)

Scene the 3d

The Curtain rises and discovers Sir Edward Spangle reclined in an elegant Attitude[9] on a Sofa, fast asleep.[10]

Enter Colonel Elliott.

Colonel) My Daughter is not here I see . . . there lies Sir Edward . . . Shall I tell him the secret? . . . No, he'll certainly blab it . . . But he is asleep and wont hear me . . . So I'll e'en venture.

(Goes up to Sir Edward, whispers him, and Exit)

End of the 1st Act.

FINIS.

line 1: 'l' written over '?'. // line 12: 'and dress' deleted; 'away' inserted above line.

To Edward Austen Esqre[1]
The following unfinished Novel
is respectfully inscribed
by
His obedient Humle Servt
The Author

line 5: 'ant' in 'obedient' deleted; 'ent' inserted above line.

The Three Sisters
a novel.

Miss Stanhope to Mrs——

My dear Fanny

I am the happiest creature in the World, for I have just received an offer of marriage from Mr Watts. It is the first I have ever had and I hardly know how to value it enough.[2] How I will triumph over the Duttons! I do not intend to accept it, at least I beleive not, but as I am not quite certain I gave him an equivocal answer and left him. And now my dear Fanny I want your Advice whether I should accept his offer or not, but that you may be able to judge of his merits and the situation of affairs I will give you an account of them. He is quite an old Man, about two and thirty,[3] very plain *so* plain that I cannot bear to look at him. He is extremely disagreable and I hate him more than any body else in the world. He has a large fortune and will make great Settlements[4] on me, but then he is very healthy. In short I do not know what to do. If I refuse him he as good as told me that he should offer himself to Sophia and if *she* refused him to Georgiana,[5] and I could not bear to have either of them married before me. If I accept him I know I shall be miserable all the rest of my Life, for he is very illtempered and peevish extremely jealous, and so stingy that there is no living in the house with him. He told me he should mention the affair to Mama, but I insisted upon it that he did not for very likely she would make me marry him whether I would or no; however probably he *has* before now, for he never does anything he is desired to do. I believe I shall have him. It will be such a triumph to be married before Sophy, Georgiana and the Duttons; And he promised to have a new Carriage on the occasion, but we almost quarrelled about the colour, for I insisted upon its being blue spotted with silver,[6] and he declared it should be a plain Chocolate; and to provoke me more said it should be just as low as his old one.[7] I wont have him I declare. He said he should come again tomorrow and take my final Answer, so I believe I must get him while I can. I know the Duttons will envy me and I shall be able to chaprone[8] Sophy and Georgiana to all the Winter Balls.[9] But then what will be the use of that when very likely he wont let me go myself, for I know he hates dancing and what he hates himself he has no idea of any other person's liking; and besides he talks a great deal of Women's always Staying at home[10] and such stuff. I believe I shant have him; I would refuse him at once if I were certain that neither of my Sisters would accept him, and that if they did not, he would not offer to the Duttons. I cannot run such a risk, so, if he will promise to have the Carriage ordered as I like, I will have him, if not he may ride in it by himself for me. I hope you like my determination; I can think of nothing better;

And am your ever affecte.
Mary Stanhope.[11]

---

line 16: one line heavily deleted after 'and': 'has a great idea of Womens never going from home' and 'never' (inserted above line).   //   lines 17–18: 'has a great idea' deleted; 'talks a great deal' inserted above line.

From the Same to the Same

Dear Fanny

I had but just sealed my last letter to you when my Mother came up and told me she wanted to speak to me on a very particular subject.

"Ah! I know what you mean; (said I) That old fool Mr Watts has told you all about it, tho' I bid him not. However you shant force me to have him if I don't like it."

"I am not going to force you Child, but only want to know what your resolution is with regard to his Proposals, and to insist upon your making up your mind one way or t'other, that if *you* don't accept him *Sophy* may."

"Indeed (replied I hastily) Sophy need not trouble herself for I shall certainly marry him myself."

"If that is your resolution (said my Mother) why should you be afraid of my forcing your inclinations?"

"Why, because I have not settled whether I shall have him or not."

"You are the strangest Girl in the World Mary. What you say one moment, you unsay the next. Do tell me once for all, whether you intend to marry Mr Watts or not?"

"Law[12] Mama how can I tell you what I dont know myself?"

"Then I desire you will know, and quickly too, for Mr Watts says he wont be kept in suspense."

"That depends upon me."

"No it does not, for if you do not give him your final Answer tomorrow when he drinks Tea[13] with us, he intends to pay his Addresses to Sophy."

"Then I shall tell all the World that he behaved very ill to me."

line 8: 'him' deleted; 'it' inserted above line.   //   line 9: 'not' inserted above line.

"What good will that do? Mr Watts has been too long abused by all the World to mind it now."

"I wish I had a Father or a Brother because then they should fight him."[14]

"They would be cunning if they did, for Mr Watts would run away first; and therefore you must and shall resolve either to accept or refuse him before tomorrow evening."

"But why if I don't have him, must he offer to my Sisters?"

"Why! Because he wishes to be allied to the Family and because they are as pretty as you are."

"But will Sophy marry him Mama if he offers to her?"

"Most likely. Why should not she? If however she does not choose it, then Georgiana must, for I am determined not to let such an opportunity escape of settling one of my Daughters so advantageously. So, make the most of your time; I leave you to settle the Matter with yourself." And then she went away. The only thing I can think of my dear Fanny is to ask Sophy and Georgiana whether they would have him were he to make proposals to them, and if they say they would not I am resolved to refuse him too, for I hate him more than you can imagine. As for the Duttons if he marries one of *them* I shall still have the triumph of having refused him first. So, adeiu my dear Freind

—Yrs ever M.S.

Miss Georgiana Stanhope to Miss x x x
Wednesday

My dear Anne

Sophy and I have just been practising a little deceit on our eldest Sister, to which we are not perfectly reconciled, and yet the circumstances were such that if any thing will excuse it, they must. Our neighbour Mr Watts has made proposals to Mary; Proposals which she knew not how to receive, for tho' she has a particular Dislike to him (in which she is not singular) yet she would willingly marry him sooner than risk his offering to Sophy or me which in case of a refusal from herself, he told her he should do, for you must know that the poor Girl considers our marrying before her as one of the greatest misfortunes that can possibly befall her, and to prevent it would willingly ensure herself everlasting Misery by a Marriage with Mr Watts. An hour ago she came to us to sound our inclinations respecting the affair which were to determine hers. A little before she came my Mother had given us an account of it, telling us that she certainly would not let him go farther than our family for a Wife. "And therefore (said she) If Mary wont have him Sophy must, and if Sophy wont Georgiana *shall*." Poor Georgiana!—We neither of us attempted to alter my Mother's resolution, which I am sorry to say is generally more strictly kept than rationally formed. As soon as she was gone however I broke silence to assure Sophy that if Mary should refuse Mr Watts I should not expect her to sacrifice *her* happiness by becoming his Wife from a motive of Generosity to me, which I was afraid her Good nature and Sisterly affection might induce her to do.

"Let us flatter ourselves (replied She) that Mary will not refuse him. Yet how can I hope that my Sister may accept a Man who cannot make her happy."

"*He* cannot it is true but his Fortune his Name, his House, his Carriage will and I have no doubt but that Mary will marry him; indeed why should she not? He is not more than two and thirty; a very proper age for a Man to marry at; He

---

line 5: 'herself' written over 'refusal'. // line 5: 'should be the result' (?) heavily deleted; 'he should do,' inserted above line. // line 14: 'him' inserted above line. // line 17: 'most' changed to 'more'.

is rather plain to be sure, but then what is Beauty in a Man; if he has but a genteel figure and a sensible looking Face it is quite sufficient."

"This is all very true Georgiana but Mr Watts's figure is unfortunately extremely vulgar and his Countenance is very heavy.[15]

"And then as to his temper; it has been reckoned bad, but may not the World be deceived in their Judgement of it. There is an open Frankness in his Disposition which becomes a Man; They say he is stingy; We'll call that Prudence. They say he is suspicious. That proceeds from a warmth of Heart always excusable in Youth, and inshort I see no reason why he should not make a very good Husband, or why Mary should not be very happy with him."

Sophy laughed; I continued,

"However whether Mary accepts him or not I am resolved. My determination is made. I never would marry Mr Watts were Beggary the only alternative. So deficient in every respect! Hideous in his person and without one good Quality to make amends for it. His fortune to be sure is good. Yet not so very large! Three thousand a year.[16] What is three thousand a year? It is but six times as much as my Mother's income. It will not tempt me."

"Yet it will be a noble fortune for Mary" said Sophy laughing again.

"For Mary! Yes indeed it will give me pleasure to see *her* in such affluence."

Thus I ran on to the great Entertainment of my Sister till Mary came into the room to appearance in great agitation. She sate down. We made room for her at the fire. She seemed at a loss how to begin and at last said in some confusion

"Pray Sophy have you any mind to be married?"

"To be married! None in the least. But why do you ask me? Are you acquainted with any one who means to make me proposals?"

"I—no, how should I? But may'nt I ask a common question?"

"Not a very common one Mary surely." (said I) She paused and after some moments silence went on—

"How should you like to marry Mr Watts Sophy?"

I winked at Sophy and replied for her. "Who is there but must rejoice to marry a man of three thousand a year?"[17]

"Very true (she replied) That's very true. So you would have him if he would offer, Georgiana. And would *you* Sophy?"

Sophy did not like the idea of telling a lie and deceiving her Sister; she prevented the first and saved half her conscience by equivocation.

"I should certainly act just as Georgiana would do."

"Well then said Mary with triumph in her Eyes, *I* have had an offer from Mr Watts." We were of course very much surprised; "Oh! do not accept him said I, and then perhaps he may have me."

In short my scheme took and Mary is resolved to do *that* to prevent our supposed happiness which she would not have done to ensure it in reality. Yet after all my Heart cannot acquit me and Sophy is even more scrupulous. Quiet our Minds my dear Anne by writing and telling us you approve our conduct. Consider it well over. Mary will have real plea-sure in being a married Woman, and able to chaprone us, which she certainly shall do, for I think myself bound to Contribute as much as possible to her happiness in a State I

line 10: two and a half lines heavily deleted after 'year': '; who keeps a post-chaise and pair, with silver Harness a boot before and a window to look out at behind'.   //   line 23: 'have made us really so' deleted; 'ensure it in reality' inserted above line.

have made her choose. They will probably have a new Carriage, which will be paradise to her, and if we can prevail on Mr W. to set up his Phaeton she will be too happy. These things however would be no consolation to Sophy or me for domestic Misery. Remember all this and do not condemn us.

Friday.

Last night Mr Watts by appointment drank tea with us. As soon as his Carriage stopped at the Door, Mary went to the Window.

"Would you beleive it Sophy (said she) the old Fool wants to have his new Chaise just the colour of the old one, and hung as low too. But it shant—I *will* carry my point. And if he wont let it be as high as the Duttons, and blue spotted with Silver, I wont have him. Yes I will too. Here he comes. I know he'll be rude; I know he'll be illtempered and wont say one civil thing to me! nor behave at all like a Lover." She then sate down and Mr Watts entered.

"Ladies your most obedient."[18] We paid our Compliments and he seated himself.

"Fine Weather Ladies." Then turning to Mary, "Well Miss Stanhope I hope you have *at last* settled the Matter in your own mind; and will be so good as to let me know whether you will *condescend* to marry me or not."

"I think Sir (said Mary) you might have asked in a genteeler way than that. I do not know whether I *shall* have you if you behave so odd."

"Mary!" (said my Mother) "Well Mama if he will be so cross. . . . ."

"Hush, hush, Mary, you shall not be rude to Mr Watts."

"Pray Madam do not lay any restraint on Miss Stanhope by obliging her to be civil. If she does not choose to accept

line 27: 'so angry and' (?) after 'be' heavily deleted.

my hand, I can offer it else where, for as I am by no means guided by a particular preference to you above your Sisters it is equally the Same to me which I marry of the three." Was there ever such a Wretch! Sophy reddened with Anger, and I felt *so* spiteful!

"Well then (said Mary in a peevish Accent) I *will* have you if I *must*."

"I should have thought Miss Stanhope that when such Settlements are offered as I have offered to you there can be no great violence done to the inclinations in accepting of them."

Mary mumbled out something, which I who sate close to her could just distinguish to be "What's the use of a great Jointure if Men live forever?" And then audibly "Remember the pin money;[19] two hundred a year."

"A hundred and seventy five Madam."

"Two hundred indeed Sir" said my Mother.

"And Remember I am to have a new Carriage hung as high as the Duttons', and blue spotted with silver; and I shall expect a new Saddle horse,[20] a suit of fine lace,[21] and an infinite number of the most valuable Jewels. Diamonds such as never were seen! And Pearls, Rubies, Emeralds, and Beads out of number.[22] You must set up your Phaeton which must be cream coloured with a wreath of silver flowers round it, You must buy 4 of the finest Bays in the Kingdom and you must drive me in it every day. This is not all; You must entirely new furnish your House after my Taste, You must hire two new Footmen to attend me, two Women to wait on

line 23: four lines heavily deleted: 'Pearls as large as those of the Princess Badroulbadour, in the 4th Volume of the Arabian Nights and Rubies, Emeralds, Toppazes, Sapphires, Amythists, Turkey stones, Agate, Beads, Bugles and Garnets'; 'And Pearls, Rubies, Emeralds, and Beads' inserted above line.

me, must always let me do just as I please and make a very good husband."

Here she stopped, I beleive rather out of breath.

"This is all very reasonable Mr Watts for my Daughter to expect."

"And it is very reasonable Mrs Stanhope that your daughter should be disappointed." He was going on but Mary interrupted him.

"You must build me an elegant Greenhouse[23] and stock it with plants. You must let me spend every Winter in Bath, every Spring in Town,[24] Every Summer in taking some Tour,[25] And every Autumn at a Watering Place,[26] And if we are at home the rest of the year" (Sophy and I laughed) "You must do nothing but give Balls and Masquerades. You must build a room on purpose and a Theatre to act Plays in.[27] The first Play we have shall be *Which is the Man*[28] and I will do Lady Bell Bloomer."

"And pray Miss Stanhope (said Mr Watts) What am I to expect from you in return for all this."

"Expect? why you may expect to have me pleased."

"It would be odd if I did not. Your expectations Madam are too high for me, and I must apply to Miss Sophy who perhaps, may not have raised her's so much."

"You are mistaken Sir in supposing so, (said Sophy) for tho' they may not be exactly in the same Line, yet my expectations are to the full as high as my Sister's; for I expect my Husband to be good tempered and Chearful; to consult my Happiness in all his Actions, and to love me with Constancy and Sincerity."

Mr Watts stared. "These are very odd Ideas truly Young Lady. You had better discard them before you marry, or you will be obliged to do it afterwards."

My Mother in the meantime was lecturing Mary who was sensible that she had gone too far, and when Mr Watts was just turning towards me in order I beleive to address me, she spoke to him in a voice half humble, half sulky.

"You are mistaken Mr Watts if you think I was in earnest when I said I expected so much. However I must have a new Chaise."

"Yes Sir, you must allow that Mary has a right to expect that."

"Mrs Stanhope, I *mean* and have always meant to have a new one on my Marriage. But it shall be the colour of my present one."

"I think Mr Watts you should pay my Girl the compliment of consulting her Taste on such Matters."

Mr Watts would not agree to this, and for some time insisted upon its being a Chocolate colour, while Mary was as eager for having it blue with silver Spots. At length however Sophy proposed that to please Mr W. it should be a dark brown and to please Mary it should be hung rather high and have a silver Border.[29] This was at length agreed to, tho' reluctantly on both sides, as each had intended to carry their point entire. We then proceeded to other Matters, and it was settled that they should be married as soon as the Writings[30] could be completed. Mary was very eager for a Special Licence and Mr Watts talked of Banns.[31] A common Licence[32] was at last agreed on. Mary is to have all the Family Jewels which are very inconsiderable I beleive and Mr W. promised to buy her a Saddle horse; but in return she is not to expect to go to Town or any other public place for these three Years. She is to have neither Greenhouse, Theatre or Phaeton; to be contented with one Maid without an additional Footman. It engrossed the whole Evening to settle these affairs; Mr W. supped with us and did not go till twelve. As soon as he was gone Mary exclaimed "Thank Heaven! he's off at last; how I do hate him!" It was in vain that Mama represented to her the impropriety she was guilty of in disliking him who was to be her Husband, for she persisted in declaring her Aversion to him and hoping she might never see him again. What a Wedding will this be! Adeiu my dear Anne

—Yr faithfully Sincere
Georgiana Stanhope

From the Same to the Same

Dear Anne   Saturday

Mary eager to have every one know of her approaching Wedding and more particularly desirous of triumphing as she called it over the Duttons, desired us to walk with her this Morning to Stoneham.[33] As we had nothing else to do we readily agreed, and had as pleasant a walk as we could have with Mary whose conversation entirely consisted in abusing the Man she is so soon to marry and in longing for a blue Chaise spotted with Silver. When we reached the Duttons we found the two Girls in the dressing-room with a very handsome Young Man, who was of course introduced to us. He is the son of Sir Henry Brudenell of Leicestershire.[34] Mr Brudenell is the handsomest Man I ever saw in my Life; we are all three very much pleased with him. Mary, who from the moment of our reaching the Dressing-room had been swelling with the knowledge of her own importance and with the Desire of making it known, could not remain long silent on the Subject after we were seated, and soon addressing herself to Kitty said,

line 16: 'with' inserted above line.   //   line 21: four lines heavily deleted before 'Mr Brudenell': 'Not related to the Family and even but distantly connected with it. His Sister is married to John Dutton's Wife's Brother. When you have puzzled over this account a little you will understand it.'

"Dont you think it will be necessary to have all the Jewels new set?"

"Necessary for what?"

"For What! Why for my appearance."[35]

"I beg your pardon but I really do not understand you. What Jewels do you speak of, and where is your appearance to be made?"

"At the next Ball to be sure after I am married."

You may imagine their Surprise. They were at first incredulous, but on our joining in the Story they at last beleived it. "And who is it to" was of course the first Question. Mary pretended Bashfulness, and answered in Confusion her Eyes cast down "to Mr Watts." This also required Confirmation from us, for that anyone who had the Beauty and fortune (tho' small yet a provision[36]) of Mary would willingly marry Mr Watts, could by them scarcely be credited. The subject being now fairly introduced and she found herself the object of every one's attention in company, she lost all her confusion and became perfectly unreserved and communicative.

"I wonder you should never have heard of it before for in general things of this Nature are very well known in the Neighbourhood."

"I assure you said Jemima[37] I never had the least suspicion of such an affair. Has it been in agitation long?"

"Oh! Yes, ever since Wednesday."

They all smiled particularly Mr Brudenell.

"You must know Mr Watts is very much in love with me, so that it is quite a match of Affection on his side."

"Not on his only, I suppose" said Kitty.

line 18: 'general' heavily deleted; 'every one's' inserted above line.

"Oh! when there is so much Love on one side there is no occasion for it on the other.[38] However I do not much dislike him tho' he is very plain to be sure."

Mr Brudenell stared, the Miss Duttons laughed and Sophy and I were heartily ashamed of our Sister. She went on.

"We are to have a new Postchaise and very likely may set up our Phaeton."

This we knew to be false but the poor Girl was pleased at the idea of persuading the company that such a thing was to be and I would not deprive her of so harmless an Enjoyment. She continued.

"Mr Watts is to present me with the family Jewels which I fancy are very considerable." I could not help whispering Sophy "I fancy not."

"These Jewels are what I suppose must be new set before they can be worn. I shall not wear them till the first Ball I go to after my Marriage. If Mrs Dutton should not go to it, I hope you will let me chaprone you; I shall certainly take Sophy and Georgiana."

"You are very good (said Kitty) and since you are inclined to undertake the Care of young Ladies, I should advise you to prevail on Mrs Edgecumbe to let you chaprone her six Daughters[39] which with your two Sisters and ourselves will make your Entrée[40] very respectable."

Kitty made us all smile except Mary who did not understand her Meaning and coolly said, that she should not like to chaperone so many.

Sophy and I now endeavoured to change the conversation but succeeded only for a few Minutes, for Mary took care to bring back their attention to her and her approaching Wedding.

I was sorry for my Sister's sake to see that Mr Brudenell seemed to take pleasure in listening to her account of it, and even encouraged her by his Questions and Remarks, for it was evident that his only Aim was to laugh at her. I am afraid he found her very ridiculous. He kept his Countenance extremely well, yet it was easy to see that it was with difficulty he kept it. At length however he seemed fatigued and Disgusted with her ridiculous Conversation, as he turned from her to us, and spoke but little to her for about half an hour before we left Stoneham. As soon as we were out of the House we all joined in praising the Person and Manners of Mr Brudenell.

We found Mr Watts at home.

"So, Miss Stanhope (said he) you see I am come a courting in a true Lover like Manner."

"Well you need not have *told* me that. I knew why you came very well."

Sophy and I then left the room, imagining of course that we must be in the way, if a Scene of Courtship were to begin. We were surprised at being followed almost immediately by Mary.

"And is your Courting so soon over?" said Sophy.

"Courting! (replied Mary) we have been quarrelling. Watts is such a Fool! I hope I shall never see him again."

"I am afraid you will, (said I) as he dines here to day. But what has been your dispute?"

"Why only because I told him that I had seen a Man much handsomer than he was this Morning, he flew into a great Passion and called me a Vixen,[41] so I only stayed to tell him I thought him a Blackguard[42] and came away."

line 3: 'in doing so' deleted after 'her'.

"Short and sweet,[43] (said Sophy) but pray Mary how will this be made up?"

"He ought to ask my pardon; but if he did, I would not forgive him."

"His Submission then would not be very useful." When we were dressed[44] we returned to the Parlour where Mama and Mr Watts were in close Conversation. It seems that he had been complaining to her of her Daughter's behaviour, and she had persuaded him to think no more of it. He therefore met Mary with all his accustomed Civility, and except one touch at the Phaeton and another at the Greenhouse, the Evening went off with great Harmony and Cordiality. Watts is going to Town to hasten the preparations for the Wedding. I am your affecte Freind. G. S.

line 1: 'be' deleted after 'will' in ms.

To Miss Jane Anna Elizabeth Austen[1]

My Dear Neice

Though you are at this period not many degrees removed from Infancy, Yet trusting that you will in time be older,[2] and that through the care of your excellent Parents,[3] You will one day or another be able to read written hand, I dedicate to You the following Miscellanious Morsels, convinced that if you seriously attend to them, You will derive from them very important Instructions, with regard to your Conduct in Life.—If such my hopes should hereafter be realized, never shall I regret the Days and Nights that have been spent in composing these Treatises for your Benefit.[4] I am my dear Neice

> Your very Affectionate
> Aunt.
> The Author.

June 2d
  1793–

A fragment—written to inculcate the practise of Virtue.[1]

We all know that many are unfortunate in their progress through the world, but we do not know all that are so. To seek them out to study their wants, and to leave them unsupplied[2] is the duty, and ought to be the Business of Man. But few have time, fewer still have inclination, and no one has either the one or the other for such employments. Who amidst those that perspire away their Evenings in crouded assemblies can have leisure to bestow a thought on such as sweat under the fatigue of their daily Labour.

Title: the title is scored through with horizontal lines and the remainder scored through with a combination of horizontal, diagonal and vertical lines.

A beautiful description of the different effects of Sensibility on different Minds.

I am but just returned from Melissa's[1] Bedside, and in my Life tho' it has been a pretty long one, and I have during the course of it been at many Bedsides, I never saw so affecting an object as she exhibits. She lies wrapped in a book muslin bedgown,[2] a chambray gauze shift,[3] and a french net nightcap.[4] Sir William is constantly at her bedside. The only repose he takes is on the Sopha in the Drawing room, where for five minutes every fortnight he remains in an imperfect Slumber,[5] starting up every Moment and exclaiming "Oh! Melissa, Ah! Melissa," then sinking down again, raises his left arm and scratches his head. Poor Mrs Burnaby is beyond measure afflicted. She sighs every now and then, that is about once a week; while the melancholy Charles says every Moment, "Melissa, how are you?" The lovely Sisters are much to be pitied. Julia is ever lamenting the situation of her freind, while lying behind her pillow and supporting her head—Maria more mild in her greif talks of going to Town[6] next week, and Anna is always recurring to the pleasures we once enjoyed when Melissa was well.—I am usually at the fire cooking some little delicacy for the unhappy invalid— Perhaps hashing up the remains of an old Duck,[7] toasting some cheese[8] or making a Curry[9] which are the favourite Dishes of our poor freind.—In these situations we were this morning surprised by receiving a visit from Dr Dowkins; "I am come to see Melissa," said he. "How is She?" "Very weak indeed," said the fainting Melissa—. "Very weak, replied the punning Doctor,[10] aye indeed it is more than a very *week* since you have taken to your bed—How is your appetite?" "Bad, very bad, said Julia." "That *is* very bad—replied he. Are her spirits good Madam?" "So poorly Sir that we are obliged to strengthen her with cordials[11] every Minute."— "Well then she receives *Spirits* from your being with her. Does she sleep?" "Scarcely ever—." "And Ever Scarcely I suppose when she does. Poor thing! Does she think of dieing?" "She has not strength to think at all." "Nay then she cannot think to have Strength."

line 10: 'of' deleted; 'to' inserted above line.

The Generous Curate—

a moral Tale,[1] setting forth the Advantages of being
Generous and a Curate.

In a part little known of the County of Warwick,[2] a very worthy Clergyman[3] lately resided. The income of his living which
amounted to about two hundred pound,[4] and the interest of
his Wife's fortune which was nothing at all, was entirely sufficient for the Wants and Wishes of a Family who neither
wanted or wished for anything beyond what their income
afforded them. Mr Williams had been in possession of his
living above twenty Years, when this history commences, and
his Marriage which had taken place soon after his presentation to it, had made him the father of six very fine Children.
The eldest had been placed at the Royal Academy for Seamen at Portsmouth[5] when about thirteen years old, and from
thence had been discharged on board of one of the Vessels of
a small fleet destined for Newfoundland,[6] where his promising and amiable disposition had procured him many freinds
among the Natives, and from whence he regularly sent home
a large Newfoundland Dog[7] every Month[8] to his family. The
second, who was also a Son had been adopted by a neighbouring Clergyman[9] with the intention of educating him at
his own expence, which would have been a very desirable

line 3: 'shire' deleted at the end of 'Warwick'.   //   line 19: 'Month' written
over 'Year' (?).

Circumstance had the Gentleman's fortune been equal to his generosity, but as he had nothing to support himself and a very large family but a Curacy of fifty pound a year,[10] Young Williams knew nothing more at the age of 18 than what a twopenny Dame's School[11] in the village could teach him. His Character however was perfectly amiable though his genius[12] might be cramped, and he was addicted to no vice, or ever guilty of any fault beyond what his age and situation rendered perfectly excusable. He had indeed sometimes been detected in flinging Stones at a Duck or putting brickbats[13] into his Benefactor's bed; but these innocent efforts of wit were considered by that good Man rather as the effects of a lively imagination, than of anything bad in his Nature, and if any punishment were decreed for the offence it was in general no greater than that the Culprit should pick up the Stones or take the brickbats away.—

FINIS.

To Miss Austen,[1] the following Ode to Pity[2] is dedicated, from a thorough knowledge of her pitiful[3] Nature, by her obedt humle Servt

The Author

Ode to Pity

I

Ever musing I delight to tread
    The Paths of honour and the Myrtle[4] Grove
Whilst the pale Moon her beams doth shed
    On disappointed Love.
While Philomel[5] on airy hawthorn Bush
    Sings sweet and Melancholy, And the Thrush
Converses with the Dove.

2.

Gently brawling[6] down the turnpike road,[7]
    Sweetly noisy[8] falls the Silent Stream[9]—
The Moon emerges from behind a Cloud
    And darts upon the Myrtle Grove her beam.
Ah! then what Lovely Scenes[10] appear,
    The hut,[11] the Cot, the Grot,[12] and Chapel queer,
And eke[13] the Abbey too a mouldering heap,[14]
    Conceal'd by aged pines[15] her head doth rear
And quite invisible doth take a peep.

End of the first volume.
        June 3d 1793[16]—

Volume the Second

VOLUME THE SECOND
Ex dono mei Patris[1]

CONTENTS

line 2: 'Freindship' changed to 'Friendship'

To Madame La Comtesse De Feuillide[1]
This Novel is inscribed
by
Her obliged Humble Servant
The Author

Love and Freindship[2]
a novel
in a series of Letters[3]—.

"Deceived in Freindship and Betrayed in Love."[4]

LETTER THE FIRST

From Isabel[5] to Laura[6]

How often, in answer to my repeated intreaties that you would give my Daughter a regular detail of the Misfortunes and Adventures of your Life,[7] have you said "No, my freind never will I comply with your request till I may be no longer in Danger of again experiencing such dreadful ones."

Surely that time is now at hand. You are this Day 55. If a woman may ever be said to be in safety from the determined Perseverance of disagreable Lovers and the cruel Persecutions of obstinate Fathers,[8] surely it must be at such a time of Life.

Isabel.

LETTER 2D

Laura to Isabel

Altho' I cannot agree with you in supposing that I shall never again be exposed to Misfortunes as unmerited as those I have already experienced, yet to avoid the imputation of Obstinacy or ill-nature, I will gratify the curiosity of your daughter; and may the fortitude with which I have suffered the many Afflictions of my past Life, prove to her a useful

---

line 7: 'cruel' deleted; 'dreadful' inserted above line. // line 10: 'reiterated' (?) heavily deleted; 'cruel' inserted above line. // line 21: 'that' replaced by 'my past'.

Lesson for the support of those which may befall her in her own.

Laura

LETTER 3RD

Laura to Marianne[9]

As the Daughter of my most intimate freind I think you entitled to that knowledge of my unhappy Story, which your Mother has so often solicited me to give you.

My Father was a native of Ireland and an inhabitant of Wales; my Mother was the natural[10] Daughter of a Scotch Peer by an italian Opera-girl[11]—I was born in Spain and received my Education at a Convent in France.[12]

When I had reached my eighteenth Year I was recalled by my Parents to my paternal roof in Wales. Our mansion was situated in one of the most romantic[13] parts of the Vale of Uske.[14] Tho' my Charms are now considerably softened and somewhat impaired by the Misfortunes I have undergone, I was once beautiful. But lovely as I was the Graces of my Person were the least of my Perfections. Of every accomplishment accustomary to my sex, I was Mistress.—When in the Convent, my progress had always exceeded my instructions; my Acquirements had been wonderfull for my Age, and I had shortly surpassed my Masters.[15]

In my Mind, every Virtue that could adorn it was centered; it was the Rendez-vous[16] of every good Quality and of every noble sentiment.

A sensibility too tremblingly alive[17] to every affliction of my Freinds, my Acquaintance and particularly to every affliction of my own, was my only fault, if a fault it could be called.

---

line 22: 'were' deleted; 'had been' inserted above line. // line 23: 'had' inserted above line. // line 24: 'adorn' inserted above line. // line 25: 'the place of appointment' deleted after 'and'.

Alas! how altered now! Tho' indeed my own Misfortunes do not make less impression on me, than they ever did, yet now I never feel for those of an other. My accomplishments too, begin to fade—I can neither sing so well nor Dance so grace-fully as I once did—and I have entirely forgot the *Minuet Dela Cour*[18]—

Adeiu.
Laura

LETTER 4TH

Laura to Marianne

Our neighbourhood was small, for it consisted only of your Mother. She may probably have already told you that being left by her Parents in indigent Circumstances she had retired into Wales on eoconomical motives.[19] There it was, our freindship first commenced—. Isabel was then one and twenty—Tho' pleasing both in her Person and Manners (between ourselves) she never possessed the hundredth part of my Beauty or Accomplishments. Isabel had seen the World. She had passed 2 Years at one of the first Boarding-schools in London;[20] had spent a fortnight in Bath and had supped one night in Southampton.[21]

"Beware my Laura (she would often say) Beware of the insipid Vanities and idle Dissipations of the Metropolis of England;[22] Beware of the unmeaning Luxuries of Bath and of the Stinking fish of Southampton."[23]

"Alas! (exclaimed I) how am I to avoid those evils I shall never be exposed to? What probability is there of my ever tasting the Dissipations of London, the Luxuries of Bath, or the stinking Fish of Southampton? I who am doomed to

line 18: 'I' deleted before 'Isabel'.   //   line 20: 'slept' deleted; 'supped' inserted above line.

waste my Days of Youth and Beauty in an humble Cottage in the Vale of Uske."

Ah! little did I then think I was ordained so soon to quit that humble Cottage for the Deceitfull Pleasures of the World.

adeiu

Laura—

LETTER 5TH

Laura to Marianne

One Evening in December as my Father, my Mother and myself, were arranged in social converse round our Fireside, we were on a sudden, greatly astonished, by hearing a violent knocking on the outward Door of our rustic Cot.[24]

My Father started—"What noise is that," (said he.) "It sounds like a loud rapping at the Door"—(replied my Mother.) "it does indeed." (cried I.) "I am of your opinion; (said my Father) it certainly does appear to proceed from some uncommon violence exerted against our unoffending Door." "Yes (exclaimed I) I cannot help thinking it must be somebody who knocks for Admittance."

"That is another point (replied he;) We must not pretend to determine on what motive the person may knock—tho' that someone *does* rap at the Door, I am partly convinced."[25]

Here, a 2d tremendous rap interrupted my Father in his speech and somewhat alarmed my Mother and me.

"Had we not better go and see who it is? (said she) the servants are out." "I think we had." (replied I.) "Certainly, (added my Father) by all means." "Shall we go now?" (said

line 12: one line deleted after 'astonished': 'considerably amazed and somewhat surprised'.   //   line 23: three lines deleted: 'I cannot pretend to assert that any one knocks, tho' for my own part, I own I rather imagine it is a knock at the Door that somebody does. Yet as we have no ocular Demonstration. . .'; 'We must not . . . partly convinced' inserted above line.

my Mother). "The sooner the better." (answered he.) "Oh! Let no time be lost." (cried I.)

A third more violent Rap than ever again assaulted our ears. "I am certain there is somebody knocking at the Door." (said my Mother.) "I think there must," (replied my Father) "I fancy the Servants are returned; (said I) I think I hear Mary[26] going to the Door." "I'm glad of it" (cried my Father) "for I long to know who it is."[27]

I was right in my Conjecture, for Mary instantly entering the Room, informed us that a young Gentleman and his Servant were at the Door, who had lossed their way, were very cold and begged leave to warm themselves by our fire.

"Wont you admit them?" (said I) "You have no objection, my Dear?" (said my Father.) "None in the World." (replied my Mother.)

Mary, without waiting for any further commands immediately left the room and quietly returned introducing the most beauteous and amiable Youth, I had ever beheld.[28] The servant, She kept to herself.[29]

My natural Sensibility had already been greatly affected by the sufferings of the unfortunate Stranger and no sooner did I first behold him, than I felt that on him the happiness or Misery of my future Life must depend.[30]—

adeiu
Laura

LETTER 6TH

Laura to Marianne

The noble Youth informed us that his name was Lindsay—. for particular reasons however I shall conceal it under that

---

line 2: 'us go immediately.' deleted; 'no time be lost.' inserted above line.   //
line 3: 'A' written over 'a'.   //   line 23: one line heavily deleted: 'myself
instantaneously in Love with him'; 'that on him the happiness or Misery of
my future Life must depend' inserted above and below line.

of Talbot.[31] He told us that he was the son of an English Baronet, that his Mother had been many years no more and that he had a Sister of the middle size. "My Father (he continued) is a mean and mercenary wretch—it is only to such particular freinds as this Dear Party that I would thus betray his failings—. Your Virtues my amiable Polydore (addressing himself to my father) yours Dear Claudia[32] and yours my Charming Laura call on me to repose in you my Confidence." We bowed. "My Father, seduced by the false glare of Fortune and the Deluding Pomp of Title, insisted on my giving my hand to Lady Dorothea.[33] No never exclaimed I. Lady Dorothea is lovely and Engaging; I prefer no woman to her; but Know Sir, that I scorn to marry her in compliance with your Wishes. No! Never shall it be said that I obliged my Father."[34]

We all admired the noble Manliness of his reply. He continued.

"Sir Edward was surprised; he had perhaps little expected to meet with so spirited an opposition to his will. 'Where Edward in the name of Wonder (said he) did you pick up this unmeaning Gibberish?[35] You have been studying Novels I suspect.'[36] I scorned to answer: it would have been beneath my Dignity. I mounted my Horse and followed by my faithful William set forwards for my Aunts.

"My Father's house is situated in Bedfordshire, my Aunt's in Middlesex,[37] and tho' I flatter myself with being a tolerable proficient in Geography, I know not how it happened, but I found myself entering this beautifull Vale which I find is

lines 13–14: 'if you wish I should' deleted; 'in compliance with your Wishes' inserted above line.   //   line 18: 'perhaps' inserted above line.   //   line 19: 'have met' deleted; 'meet' inserted above line.   //   line 21: 'this' written over 'these'.

in South Wales, when I had expected to have reached my Aunts.

"After having wandered some time on the Banks of the Uske without knowing which way to go, I began to lament my cruel Destiny in the bitterest and most pathetic Manner. It was now perfectly Dark, not a single Star was there to direct my steps, and I know not what might have befallen me had I not at length discerned thro' the solemn Gloom that surrounded me a distant Light, which as I approached it, I discovered to be the chearfull Blaze of your fire. Impelled by the combination of Misfortunes under which I laboured, namely Fear, Cold and Hunger I hesitated not to ask admittance which at length I have gained; and now my Adorable Laura (continued he taking my Hand) when may I hope to receive that reward of all the painfull sufferings I have undergone during the course of my Attachment to you, to which I have ever aspired? Oh! when will you reward me with Yourself?"

"This instant, Dear and Amiable Edward." (replied I.). We were immediately united by my Father, who tho' he had never taken orders had been bred to the Church.[38]

adeiu

Laura.

LETTER 7TH

Laura to Marianne

We remained but a few Days after our Marriage, in the Vale of Uske—. After taking an affecting Farewell of my Father, my Mother and my Isabel, I accompanied Edward to his Aunt's in Middlesex. Philippa[39] received us both with every expression of affectionate Love. My arrival was indeed a

line 7: 'me' inserted above line.

most agreable surprize to her as she had not only been totally
ignorant of my Marriage with her Nephew, but had never
even had the slightest idea of there being such a person in
the World.

Augusta,[40] the sister of Edward was on a visit to her
when we arrived. I found her exactly what her Brother had
described her to be—of the middle size. She received me with
equal surprise though not with equal Cordiality, as Philippa.
There was a Disagreable Coldness and Forbidding Reserve
in her reception of me which was equally Distressing and
Unexpected. None of that interesting Sensibility or amiable
Simpathy in her Manners and Address to me, when we first
met which should have Distinguished our introduction to
each other—. Her Language was neither warm, nor affectionate, her expressions of regard were neither animated nor
cordial; her arms were not opened to receive me to her Heart,
tho' my own were extended to press her to mine.

A short Conversation between Augusta and her Brother,
which I accidentally overheard encreased my Dislike to her,
and convinced me that her Heart was no more formed for
the soft ties of Love than for the endearing intercourse of
Freindship.

"But do you think that my Father will ever be reconciled
to this imprudent connection?" (said Augusta.)

"Augusta (replied the noble Youth) I thought you had a
better opinion of me, than to imagine I would so abjectly
degrade myself as to consider my Father's Concurrence in
any of my Affairs, either of Consequence or concern to me—.
Tell me Augusta tell me with sincerity; did you ever know

lines 2–3: 'not even the' deleted; 'never even had the' inserted above line.   //
line 7: 'Her', originally beginning the sentence, deleted.

me consult his inclinations or follow his Advice in the least
trifling Particular since the age of fifteen?"

"Edward (replied she) you are surely too diffident in
your own praise—. Since you were fifteen only!—My Dear
Brother since you were five years old, I entirely acquit you
of ever having willingly contributed to the Satisfaction of
your Father. But still I am not without apprehensions of your
being shortly obliged to degrade yourself in your own eyes
by seeking a Support for your Wife in the Generosity of Sir
Edward."

"Never, never Augusta will I so demean myself. (said
Edward). Support! What support will Laura want which she
can receive from him?"

"Only those very insignificant ones of Victuals and Drink."
(answered she.)

"Victuals and Drink! (replied my Husband in a most nobly
contemptuous Manner) and dost thou then imagine that
there is no other support for an exalted Mind (such as is
my Laura's) than the mean and indelicate employment of
Eating and Drinking?"

"None that I know of, so efficacious." (returned Augusta)

"And did you then never feel the pleasing Pangs of Love,
Augusta? (replied my Edward). Does it appear impossible to
your vile and corrupted Palate, to exist on Love? Can you not
conceive the Luxury of living in every Distress that Poverty
can inflict, with the object of your tenderest affection?"

"You are too ridiculous (said Augusta) to argue with;[41]
perhaps however you may in time be convinced that. . . ."

---

line 6: 'ever' inserted above line.   //   lines 11–12: '(said Edward).' inserted
above line.   //   line 21: 'replied' deleted; 'returned' inserted above line.   //
line 23: 'Did' deleted; 'Does' inserted above line.   //   line 24: 'Vulgar'
deleted; 'corrupted' inserted above line.   //   line 25: 't' written over 'n' in
'that'.

Here I was prevented from hearing the remainder of her Speech, by the appearance of a very Handsome young Woman, who was ushured into the Room at the Door of which I had been listening. On hearing her announced by the Name of "Lady Dorothea", I instantly quitted my Post and followed her into the Parlour, for I well remembered that she was the Lady, proposed as a Wife for my Edward by the Cruel and Unrelenting Baronet.

Altho' Lady Dorothea's visit was nominally to Philippa and Augusta, yet I have some reason to imagine that (acquainted with the Marriage and arrival of Edward) to see me was a principal motive to it.

I soon perceived that tho' Lovely and Elegant in her Person and tho' Easy and Polite in her Address, she was of that inferior order of Beings with regard to Delicate Feeling, tender Sentiments, and refined Sensibility, of which Augusta was one.[42]

She staid but half an hour and neither in the Course of her Visit, confided to me any of her Secret thoughts, nor requested me to confide in her, any of Mine. You will easily imagine therefore my Dear Marianne that I could not feel any ardent Affection or very sincere Attachment for Lady Dorothea.

Adeiu

Laura.

LETTER 8TH

Laura to Marianne, in continuation

Lady Dorothea had not left us long before another visitor as unexpected a one as her Ladyship, was announced. It was Sir

line 1: 'interrupted' deleted; 'prevented' inserted above line. // line 17: 'once' in ms.

Edward, who informed by Augusta of her Brother's marriage, came doubtless to reproach him for having dared to unite himself to me without his Knowledge. But Edward foreseeing his design, approached him with heroic fortitude as soon as he entered the Room, and addressed him in the following Manner.

"Sir Edward, I know the motive of your Journey here— You come with the base Design of reproaching me for having entered into an indissoluble engagement with my Laura without your Consent—But Sir, I glory in the Act—. It is my greatest boast that I have incurred the Displeasure of my Father!"

So saying, he took my hand and whilst Sir Edward, Philippa, and Augusta were doubtless reflecting with Admiration on his undaunted Bravery, led me from the Parlour to his Father's Carriage which yet remained at the Door and in which we were instantly conveyed from the pursuit of Sir Edward.

The Postilions had at first received orders only to take the London road; as soon as we had sufficiently reflected However, we ordered them to Drive to M——.the seat of Edward's most particular freind, which was but a few miles distant.

At M——. we arrived in a few hours; and on sending in our names were immediately admitted to Sophia,[43] the Wife of Edward's freind. After having been deprived during the course of 3 weeks of a real freind (for such I term your Mother) imagine my transports at beholding one, most truly worthy of the Name. Sophia was rather above the middle size;[44] most elegantly formed. A soft Languor spread over her lovely features, but increased their Beauty—. It was

---

line 2: first 'to' inserted above line.   //   line 22: 'freind' inserted above line.
//   line 23: 'less than an hour;' deleted; 'a few hours;' inserted above line.

the Charectaristic of her Mind—. She was all Sensibility and Feeling. We flew into each others arms and after having exchanged vows of mutual Freindship for the rest of our Lives, instantly unfolded to each other the most inward Secrets of our Hearts[45]—. We were interrupted in this Delightfull Employment by the entrance of Augustus, (Edward's freind) who was just returned from a solitary ramble.

Never did I see such an affecting Scene as was the meeting of Edward and Augustus.

"My Life! my Soul!" (exclaimed the former). "My Adorable Angel!" (replied the latter) as they flew into each other's arms.[46]—It was too pathetic[47] for the feelings of Sophia and myself—We fainted Alternately on a Sofa.[48]

Adeiu

Laura

LETTER THE 9TH—FROM THE SAME TO THE SAME[49]

Towards the close of the Day we received the following Letter from Philippa.

"Sir Edward is greatly incensed by your abrupt departure; he has taken back Augusta with him to Bedfordshire. Much as I wish to enjoy again your charming Society, I cannot determine to Snatch you from that, of such dear and deserving Freinds—When your Visit to them is terminated, I trust you will return to the arms of your

Philippa."

We returned a suitable answer to this affectionate Note and after thanking her for her kind invitation assured her that we

---

line 1: 'Charecteristic' changed to 'Charectaristic'.   //   line 18: two lines deleted: 'When we were somewhat recovered from the overpowering effusions of our'. These are the opening lines of Letter 10th below.   //   line 22: 'yet' deleted after 'Society'.

would certainly avail ourselves of it, whenever we might have no other place to go to. Tho' certainly nothing could to any reasonable Being, have appeared more satisfactory, than so gratefull a reply to her invitation, yet I know not how it was, but she was certainly capricious enough to be displeased with our behaviour and in a few weeks after, either to revenge our Conduct, or releive her own solitude, married a young and illiterate[50] Fortune-hunter. This imprudent Step (tho' we were sensible that it would probably deprive us of that fortune which Philippa had ever taught us to expect) could not on our own accounts, excite from our exalted Minds a single sigh; yet fearfull lest it might prove a source of endless misery to the deluded Bride, our trembling Sensibility was greatly affected when we were first informed of the Event. The affectionate Entreaties of Augustus and Sophia that we would for ever consider their House as our Home, easily prevailed on us to determine never more to leave them—. In the Society of my Edward and this Amiable Pair, I passed the happiest moments of my Life; Our time was most delightfully spent, in mutual Protestations of Freindship, and in vows of unalterable Love, in which we were secure from being interrupted, by intruding and disagreable Visitors, as Augustus and Sophia had on their first Entrance in the Neighbourhood, taken due care to inform the surrounding Families, that as their Happiness centered wholly in themselves, they wished for no other society. But alas! my Dear Marianne such Happiness as I then enjoyed was too perfect to be lasting. A most severe and unexpected Blow at once destroyed every Sensation of Pleasure. Convinced as you must be from what I have already told you concerning Augustus and Sophia,

line 6: 'it' changed to 'our'.   //   line 10: 'which' inserted above line.   //   line 12: 'endless' written over 'needless'.   //   line 27: 'then' inserted above line.

that there never were a happier Couple, I need not I imagine
inform you that their union had been contrary to the inclinations of their Cruel and Mercenary Parents; who had vainly
endeavoured with obstinate Perseverance to force them into
a Marriage with those whom they had ever abhorred; but
with an Heroic Fortitude worthy to be related and Admired,
they had both, constantly refused to submit to such despotic
Power.

After having so nobly disentangled themselves from the
Shackles of Parental Authority, by a Clandestine Marriage,[51]
they were determined never to forfeit the good opinion they
had gained in the World, in so doing, by accepting any proposals of reconciliation that might be offered them by their
Fathers—to this farther tryal of their noble independence
however they never were exposed.

They had been married but a few months when our visit
to them commenced during which time they had been amply
supported by a considerable Sum of Money which Augustus had gracefully purloined[52] from his Unworthy father's
Escritoire,[53] a few days before his union with Sophia.

By our arrival their Expenses were considerably encreased
tho' their means for supplying them were then nearly
exhausted. But they, Exalted Creatures!, scorned to reflect
a moment on their pecuniary Distresses and would have
blushed at the idea of paying their Debts.[54]—Alas! what was
their Reward for such disinterested Behaviour! The beautifull
Augustus was arrested and we were all undone. Such perfidious Treachery in the merciless perpetrators of the Deed will

line 1: 'was' deleted; 'were' (originally 'where') inserted above line.   //   line
2: 'inform' inserted above line.   //   line 5: 'whom' inserted above line.   //
line 7: 'their'(?) deleted; 'such' inserted above line.   //   line 7: 'will'(?)
deleted after 'despotic'.   //   line 11: 'good' inserted above line.   //   line
12: 'by' deleted; second 'in' inserted above line.

shock your gentle nature Dearest Marianne as much as it then affected the Delicate Sensibility of Edward, Sophia, your Laura, and of Augustus himself. To compleat such unparalelled Barbarity we were informed that an Execution in the House[55] would shortly take place. Ah! what could we do but what we did! We sighed and fainted on the Sofa.

Adeiu
Laura

LETTER 10TH

Laura in continuation

When we were somewhat recovered from the overpowering Effusions of our Greif, Edward desired that we would consider what was the most prudent step to be taken in our unhappy situation while he repaired to his imprisoned freind to lament over his misfortunes. We promised that we would, and he set forwards on his Journey to Town. During his Absence we faithfully complied with his Desire and after the most mature Deliberation, at length agreed that the best thing we could do was to leave the House; of which we every moment expected the Officers of Justice[56] to take possession. We waited therefore with the greatest impatience, for the return of Edward in order to impart to him the result of our Deliberations—. But no Edward appeared—. In vain did we count the tedious Moments of his Absence—in vain did we weep—in vain even did we sigh—no Edward returned—. This was too cruel, too unexpected a Blow to our Gentle Sensibility—. we could not support it—we could only faint—. At length collecting all the Resolution I was Mistress of, I arose and after packing up some necessary Apparel

line 2: 'Augus' deleted before 'Edward'.   //   line 15: 'he' deleted; 'we' inserted above line.

for Sophia and myself, I dragged her to a Carriage I had ordered and we instantly set out for London. As the Habitation of Augustus was within twelve miles of Town, it was not long e'er we arrived there, and no sooner had we entered Holbourn[57] than letting down one of the Front Glasses[58] I enquired of every decent-looking Person that we passed "If they had seen my Edward"?

But as we drove too rapidly to allow them to answer my repeated Enquiries, I gained little, or indeed, no information concerning him. "Where am I to Drive?" said the Postilion. "To Newgate[59] Gentle Youth (replied I), to see Augustus." "Oh! no, no, (exclaimed Sophia) I cannot go to Newgate; I shall not be able to support the sight of my Augustus in so cruel a confinement—my feelings are sufficiently shocked by the *recital*, of his Distress, but to behold it will overpower my Sensibility."[60] As I perfectly agreed with her in the Justice of her Sentiments the Postilion was instantly directed to return into the Country. You may perhaps have been somewhat surprised my Dearest Marianne, that in the Distress I then endured, destitute of any Support, and unprovided with any Habitation, I should never once have remembered my Father and Mother or my paternal Cottage in the Vale of Uske. To account for this seeming forgetfullness I must inform you of a trifling Circumstance concerning them which I have as yet never mentioned—. The death of my Parents a few weeks after my Departure, is the circumstance I allude to. By their decease I became the lawfull Inheritress of their House and Fortune. But alas! the House had never been their own and their Fortune had only been an Annuity on their

---

line 3: 'six' deleted; 'twelve' inserted above line.   //   line 5: 'Piccadilly' deleted; 'Holbourn' inserted above line.   //   line 20: 'un' in 'unprovided' inserted above line.

own Lives.[61]—Such is the Depravity of the World! To your Mother I should have returned with Pleasure, should have been happy to have introduced to her, my Charming Sophia and should with Chearfullness have passed the remainder of my Life in their dear Society in the Vale of Uske, had not one obstacle to the execution of so agreable a Scheme, intervened; which was the Marriage and Removal of your Mother to a Distant part of Ireland.[62] Adeiu.

Laura.

LETTER 11TH

Laura in continuation

"I have a Relation in Scotland (said Sophia to me as we left London) who I am certain would not hesitate in receiving me." "Shall I order the Boy to drive there?" said I—but instantly recollecting myself, exclaimed, "Alas I fear it will be too long a Journey for the Horses."[63] Unwilling however to act only from my own inadequate Knowledge of the Strength and Abilities of Horses, I consulted the Postilion, who was entirely of my Opinion concerning the Affair. We therefore determined to change Horses at the next Town and to travel Post[64] the remainder of the Journey.—. When we arrived at the last Inn we were to stop at, which was but a few miles from the House of Sophia's Relation, unwilling to intrude our Society on him unexpected and unthought of, we wrote a very elegant and well-penned Note to him containing an Account of our Destitute and melancholy Situation, and of our intention to spend some months with him in Scotland. As soon as we had dispatched this Letter, we immediately prepared to follow it in person and were stepping into the Carriage for that Purpose when our Attention was attracted by the Entrance of

line 29: 'her' deleted; 'it' inserted above line.

a coroneted Coach and 4[65] into the Inn-yard. A Gentleman considerably advanced in years, descended from it—. At his first Appearance my Sensibility was wonderfully affected and e'er I had gazed at him a 2d time, an instinctive Sympathy whispered to my Heart, that he was my Grandfather.

Convinced that I could not be mistaken in my conjecture I instantly sprang from the Carriage I had just entered, and following the Venerable Stranger into the Room he had been shewn to, I threw myself on my knees before him and besought him to acknowledge me as his Grand-Child.—He started, and after having attentively examined my features, raised me from the Ground and throwing his Grand-fatherly arms around my Neck, exclaimed, "Acknowledge thee![66] Yes dear resemblance of my Laurina[67] and my Laurina's Daughter, sweet image of my Claudia and my Claudia's Mother, I do acknowledge thee as the Daughter of the one and the Grandaughter of the other." While he was thus tenderly embracing me, Sophia astonished at my precipitate Departure, entered the Room in search of me—. No sooner had she caught the eye of the venerable Peer, than he exclaimed with every mark of Astonishment—"Another Grandaughter! Yes, yes, I see you are the Daughter of my Laurina's eldest Girl; Your resemblance to the beauteous Matilda sufficiently proclaims it." "Oh!" replied Sophia, "when I first beheld you the instinct of Nature whispered me[68] that we were in some degree related—But whether Grandfathers, or Grandmothers, I could not pretend to determine." He folded her in his arms, and whilst they were tenderly embracing, the Door of the Apartment opened and a most beautifull Young Man appeared. On perceiving him Lord St Clair started and retreating back a few paces, with uplifted Hands, said,

line 20: 'cau' (beginning of 'caught'(?)) deleted after first 'the'.

"Another Grand-child! What an unexpected Happiness is this! to discover in the space of 3 minutes, as many of my Descendants! This, I am certain is Philander the son of my Laurina's 3d Girl the amiable Bertha; there wants now but the presence of Gustavus to compleat the Union of my Laurina's Grand-Children."

"And here he is; (said a Gracefull Youth who that instant entered the room) here is the Gustavus you desire to see. I am the son of Agatha your Laurina's 4th and Youngest Daughter."[69] "I see you are indeed; replied Lord St. Clair— But tell me (continued he looking fearfully towards the Door) tell me, have I any other Grand-Children in the House."[70] "None my Lord." "Then I will provide for you all without farther delay—Here are 4 Banknotes of 50£ each—Take them and remember I have done the Duty of a Grandfather—." He instantly left the Room and immediately afterwards the House.

Adeiu.

Laura.

LETTER THE 12TH

Laura in continuation

You may imagine how greatly we were surprized by the sudden departure of Lord St. Clair—. "Ignoble Grandsire!" exclaimed Sophia. "Unworthy Grand-father!" said I, and instantly fainted in each other's arms. How long we remained in this situation I know not; but when we recovered we found ourselves alone, without either Gustavus, Philander, or the Bank-notes. As we were deploring our unhappy fate, the Door of the Apartment opened and "Macdonald" was announced. He was Sophia's cousin. The haste with which he came to our releif so soon after the receipt of our Note, spoke so greatly in his favour that I hesitated not to pronounce

him at first sight, a tender and simpathetic Freind. Alas! he
little deserved the name—for though he told us that he was
much concerned at our Misfortunes, yet by his own account
it appeared that the perusal of them, had neither drawn from
him a single sigh, nor induced him to bestow one curse on
our vindictive Stars.—. He told Sophia that his Daughter
depended on her returning with him to Macdonald-Hall,
and that as his Cousin's freind he should be happy to see
me there also. To Macdonald-Hall, therefore we went, and
were received with great kindness by Janetta the daughter of
Macdonald,[71] and the Mistress of the Mansion. Janetta was
then only fifteen; naturally well disposed, endowed with a susceptible Heart, and a simpathetic Disposition, she might, had
these amiable Qualities been properly encouraged, have been
an ornament to human Nature; but unfortunately her Father
possessed not a soul sufficiently exalted to admire so promising a Disposition, and had endeavoured by every means in
his power to prevent its encreasing with her Years. He had
actually so far extinguished the natural noble Sensibility of
her Heart, as to prevail on her to accept an offer from a young
Man of his Recommendation. They were to be married in
a few Months, and Graham, was in the House when we
arrived. *We* soon saw through his Character—. He was just
such a Man as one might have expected to be the choice of
Macdonald. They said he was Sensible, well-informed, and
Agreable; we did not pretend to Judge of such trifles, but as
we were convinced he had no soul, that he had never read
the Sorrows of Werter,[72] and that his Hair bore not the least
resemblance to auburn,[73] we were certain that Janetta could
feel no affection for him, or at least that she ought to feel
none. The very circumstance of his being her father's choice

line 19: 'noble' inserted above line.

too, was so much in his disfavour, that had he been deserving
her, in every other respect yet *that* of itself ought to have been
a sufficient reason in the Eyes of Janetta for rejecting him.
These considerations we were determined to represent to her
in their proper light and doubted not of meeting with the
desired Success from one naturally so well disposed, whose
errors in the Affair had only arisen from a want of proper
confidence in her own opinion, and a suitable contempt of
her father's. We found her indeed all that our warmest wishes
could have hoped for; we had no difficulty to convince her
that it was impossible she could love Graham, or that it was
her Duty to disobey her Father; the only thing at which she
rather seemed to hesitate was our assertion that she must be
attached to some other Person. For some time, she persevered in declaring that she knew no other young Man for
whom she had the smallest Affection; but upon explaining
the impossibility of such a thing she said that she beleived
she *did like* Captain M'Kenzie better than any one she knew
besides. This confession satisfied us and after having enumer-
ated the good Qualites of M'Kenzie and assured her that she
was violently in love with him, we desired to know whether
he had ever in anywise declared his Affection to her.

"So far from having ever declared it, I have no reason
to imagine that he has ever felt any for me." said Janetta.
"That he certainly adores you (replied Sophia) there can be
no doubt—. The Attachment must be reciprocal—. Did
he never gaze on you with Admiration—tenderly press
your hand—drop an involantary tear—and leave the room
abruptly?" "Never (replied She) that I remember—he has
always left the room indeed when his visit has been ended, but

line 15: 'young' written over 'person'.   //   line 20: 'that' inserted above
line.   //   line 24: 'that' inserted above line.

has never gone away particularly abruptly or without making a bow." "Indeed my Love (said I) you must be mistaken—: for it is absolutely impossible that he should ever have left you but with, Confusion, Despair, and Precipitation—. Consider but for a moment Janetta, and you must be convinced how absurd it is to suppose that he could ever make a Bow, or behave like any other Person." Having settled this Point to our satisfaction, the next we took into consideration was, to determine in what manner we should inform M'Kenzie of the favourable Opinion Janetta entertained of him.—. We at length agreed to acquaint him with it by an anonymous Letter which Sophia drew up in the following Manner.

"Oh! happy Lover of the beautifull Janetta, oh! enviable Possessor of *her* Heart whose hand is destined to another, why do you thus delay a confession of your Attachment to the amiable Object of it? Oh! consider that a few weeks will at once put an end to every flattering Hope that you may now entertain, by uniting the unfortunate Victim of her father's Cruelty to the execrable and detested Graham.

"Alas! why do you thus so cruelly connive at the projected Misery of her and of yourself by delaying to communicate that scheme which has doubtless long possessed your imagination? A secret Union will at once secure the felicity of both."

The amiable M'Kenzie, whose modesty as he afterwards assured us had been the only reason of his having so long concealed the violence of his affection for Janetta, on receiving this Billet[74] flew on the wings of Love to Macdonald-Hall, and so powerfully pleaded his Attachment to her who inspired it, that after a few more private interviews, Sophia

line 4: repetition of 'with' deleted.   //   line 7: 'other People' deleted; 'any other Person' inserted above line.

and I experienced the Satisfaction of seeing them depart for Gretna-Green,[75] which they chose for the celebration of their Nuptials, in preference to any other place although it was at a considerable distance[76] from Macdonald-Hall.

Adeiu—

Laura—

LETTER THE 13TH

Laura in Continuation

They had been gone nearly a couple of Hours, before either Macdonald or Graham had entertained any suspicion of the affair—. And they might not even then have suspected it, but for the following little Accident. Sophia happening one Day to open a private Drawer in Macdonald's Library with one of her own keys, discovered that it was the Place where he kept his Papers of consequence and amongst them some bank notes of considerable amount. This discovery she imparted to me; and having agreed together that it would be a proper treatment of so vile a Wretch as Macdonald to deprive him of Money, perhaps dishonestly gained, it was determined that the next time we should either of us happen to go that way, we would take one or more of the Bank notes from the drawer. This well-meant Plan we had often successfully put in Execution; but alas! on the very day of Janetta's Escape, as Sophia was majestically removing the 5th Bank-note from the Drawer to her own purse, she was suddenly most impertinently interrupted in her employment by the entrance of

lines 4–5: 'as it was a most agreable Drive' deleted; 'from its wonderful Celebrity,' inserted above line and then deleted'; 'although it was at a considerable distance' inserted above line; 'a' inserted further above line before 'considerable'. // line 11: 'had it not' deleted before 'but'. // line 15: 'with' deleted; 'amongst' inserted above line. // line 24: 'j' written over 'g' in 'majestically'.

Macdonald himself, in a most abrupt and precipitate Manner. Sophia (who though naturally all winning sweetness could when occasions demanded it call forth the Dignity of her Sex) instantly put on a most forbiding look, and darting an angry frown on the undaunted Culprit, demanded in a haughty tone of voice "Wherefore her retirement was thus insolently broken in on?" The unblushing Macdonald without even endeavouring to exculpate himself from the crime he was charged with, meanly endeavoured to reproach Sophia with ignobly defrauding him of his Money . . . The dignity of Sophia was wounded; "Wretch (exclaimed she, hastily replacing the Bank-note in the Drawer) how darest thou to accuse me of an Act, of which the bare idea makes me blush?" The base wretch was still unconvinced and continued to upbraid the justly-offended Sophia in such opprobious Language, that at length he so greatly provoked the gentle sweetness of her Nature, as to induce her to revenge herself on him by informing him of Janetta's Elopement, and of the active Part we had both taken in the Affair. At this period of their Quarrel I entered the Library and was as you may imagine equally offended as Sophia at the ill-grounded Accusations of the malevolent and contemptible Macdonald. "Base Miscreant! (cried I) how canst thou thus undauntedly endeavour to sully the spotless reputation of such bright Excellence? Why dost thou not suspect *my* innocence as soon?"

"Be satisfied Madam" (replied he) "I *do* suspect it, and therefore must desire that you will both leave this House in less than half an hour."

"We shall go willingly; (answered Sophia) our hearts have long detested thee, and nothing but our freindship for thy

line 28: 'that' inserted above line.

126

Daughter could have induced us to remain so long beneath thy roof."

"Your Freindship for my Daughter has indeed been most powerfully exerted by throwing her into the arms of an unprincipled Fortune-hunter." (replied he)

"Yes, (exclaimed I) amidst every misfortune, it will afford us some consolation to reflect that by this one act of Freindship to Janetta, we have amply discharged every obligation that we have received from her father."

"It must indeed be a most gratefull reflection, to your exalted minds." (said he.)

As soon as we had packed up our wardrobe and valuables, we left Macdonald Hall, and after having walked about a mile and a half we sate down by the side of a clear limpid stream[77] to refresh our exhausted limbs. The place was suited to meditation—. A Grove of full-grown Elms sheltered us from the East—. A Bed of full-grown Nettles from the West—. Before us ran the murmuring brook and behind us ran the turn-pike road.[78] We were in a mood for contemplation and in a Disposition to enjoy so beautifull a spot. A mutual Silence which had for some time reigned between us, was at length broke by my exclaiming—"What a lovely Scene! Alas why are not Edward and Augustus here to enjoy its Beauties with us?"

"Ah! my beloved Laura (cried Sophia) for pity's sake forbear recalling to my remembrance the unhappy situation of my imprisoned Husband. Alas, what would I not give to learn the fate of my Augustus!—to know if he is still in Newgate, or if he is yet hung.[79]—But never shall I be able so far to conquer my tender sensibility as to enquire after him. Oh! do not I beseech you ever let me again hear you repeat his beloved Name—. It affects me too deeply—. I cannot bear to hear him mentioned, it wounds my feelings."

"Excuse me my Sophia for having thus unwillingly offended you—" replied I—and then changing the conversation, desired her to admire the Noble Grandeur of the Elms which Sheltered us from the Eastern Zephyr.[80] "Alas! my Laura (returned she) avoid so melancholy a subject, I intreat you—Do not again wound my Sensibility by Observations on those elms—. They remind me of Augustus—. He was like them, tall, magestic[81]—he possessed that noble grandeur which you admire in them."

I was silent, fearfull lest I might any more unwillingly distress her by fixing on any other subject of conversation which might again remind her of Augustus.

"Why do you not speak my Laura? (said she after a short pause) I cannot support this silence—you must not leave me to my own reflections; they ever recur to Augustus."

"What a beautifull Sky! (said I) How charmingly is the azure varied by those delicate streaks of white!"

"Oh! my Laura (replied she hastily withdrawing her Eyes from a momentary glance at the sky) do not thus distress me by calling my Attention to an object which so cruelly reminds me of my Augustus's blue Sattin Waistcoat striped with white![82] In pity to your unhappy freind avoid a subject so distressing." What could I do? The feelings of Sophia were at that time so exquisite, and the tenderness she felt for Augustus so poignant that I had not power to start any other topic, justly fearing that it might in some unforseen manner again awaken all her sensibility by directing her thoughts to her Husband.—Yet to be silent would be cruel; She had intreated me to talk.

From this Dilemma I was most fortunately releived by an accident truly apropos;[83] it was the lucky overturning of

line 28: 'cruel' deleted, then inserted above line.

a Gentleman's Phaeton, on the road which ran murmuring behind us.[84] It was a most fortunate Accident as it diverted the Attention of Sophia from the melancholy reflections which she had been before indulging. We instantly quitted our seats and ran to the rescue of those who but a few moments before had been in so elevated a situation as a fashionably high Phaeton,[85] but who were now laid low and sprawling in the Dust—. "What an ample subject for reflection on the uncertain Enjoyments of this World, would not that Phaeton and the Life of Cardinal Wolsey afford a thinking Mind"![86] said I to Sophia as we were hastening to the field of Action.

She had not time to answer me, for every thought was now engaged by the horrid[87] Spectacle before us. Two Gentlemen most elegantly attired but weltering in their blood[88] was what first struck our Eyes—we approached—they were Edward and Augustus—Yes dearest Marianne they were our Husbands. Sophia shreiked and fainted on the Ground—I screamed and instantly ran mad—. We remained thus mutually deprived of our Senses, some minutes, and on regaining them were deprived of them again—. For an Hour and a Quarter did we continue in this unfortunate Situation— Sophia fainting every moment and I running Mad as often—. At length a Groan from the hapless Edward (who alone retained any share of Life) restored us to ourselves—. Had we indeed before imagined that either of them lived, we should have been more sparing of our Greif—but as we had supposed when we first beheld them that they were no more, we knew that nothing could remain to be done but what we were about—. No sooner therefore did we hear my Edward's groan than postponing our Lamentations for the present, we

line 3: 'of Augustus' deleted after 'reflections'.

hastily ran to the Dear Youth and kneeling on each side of him implored him not to die—. "Laura (said He fixing his now languid Eyes on me) I fear I have been overturned."

I was overjoyed to find him yet sensible[89]—.

"Oh! tell me Edward (said I) tell me I beseech you before you die, what has befallen you since that unhappy Day in which Augustus was arrested and we were separated—"

"I will" (said he) and instantly fetching a Deep sigh, Expired—. Sophia immediately sunk again into a swoon—. *My* Greif was more audible. My Voice faltered, My Eyes assumed a vacant Stare, My face became as pale as Death, and my Senses were considerably impaired—.

"Talk not to me of Phaetons (said I, raving in a frantic, incoherent manner)—Give me a violin—. I'll play to him and sooth him in his melancholy Hours—Beware ye gentle Nymphs of Cupid's Thunderbolts, avoid the piercing Shafts of Jupiter[90]—Look at that Grove of Firs—I see a Leg of Mutton—They told me Edward was not Dead; but they deceived me—they took him for a Cucumber[91]—" Thus I continued wildly exclaiming on my Edward's Death—. For two Hours did I rave[92] thus madly and should not then have left off, as I was not in the least fatigued, had not Sophia who was just recovered from her swoon, intreated me to consider that Night was now approaching and that the Damps began to fall. "And whither shall we go (said I) to shelter us from either"? "To that white Cottage." (replied she pointing to a neat Building which rose up amidst the Grove of Elms and which I had not before observed—) I agreed and we instantly walked to it—we knocked at the door—it was opened by an old Woman; on being requested to afford us a Night's Lodging, she informed us that her House was but small, that she

line 20: 'Edward's' inserted above line.

had only two Bedrooms, but that However we should be wellcome to one of them. We were satisfied and followed the good Woman into the House where we were greatly cheered by the Sight of a comfortable fire—. She was a Widow and had only one Daughter, who was then just Seventeen—One of the best of ages;[93] but alas! she was very plain and her name was Bridget[94]. . . . Nothing therefore could be expected from her . . . she could not be supposed to possess either exalted Ideas, Delicate Feelings or refined Sensibilities—She was nothing more than a mere good-tempered, civil and obliging Young Woman; as such we could scarcely dislike her—she was only an Object of Contempt—.

Adeiu

Laura—

LETTER THE 14TH

Laura in continuation

Arm yourself my amiable Young Freind with all the philosophy you are Mistress of; Summon up all the fortitude you possess, for Alas! in the perusal of the following Pages your sensibility will be most severely tried. Ah! what were the Misfortunes I had before experienced and which I have already related to you, to the one I am now going to inform you of! The Death of my Father my Mother, and my Husband though almost more than my gentle Nature could support, were trifles in comparison to the misfortune I am now proceeding to relate. The morning after our arrival at the Cottage, Sophia complained of a violent pain in her delicate limbs, accompanied with a disagreable Head-ake. She attributed it to a cold caught by her continual faintings in the open Air as the Dew was falling the Evening before. This I

line 9: 'Sensibility' changed to 'Sensibilities'.

feared was but too probably the case; since how could it be otherwise accounted for that I should have escaped the same indisposition, but by supposing that the bodily Exertions I had undergone in my repeated fits of frenzy had so effectually circulated and warmed my Blood[95] as to make me proof against the chilling Damps of Night, whereas, Sophia lying totally inactive on the Ground must have been exposed to all their Severity. I was most seriously alarmed by her illness which trifling as it may appear to you, a certain instinctive Sensibility whispered me, would in the End be fatal to her.

Alas! my fears were but too fully justified; she grew gradually worse—and I daily became more alarmed for her.—At length she was obliged to confine herself solely to the Bed allotted us by our worthy Landlady—. Her disorder turned to a galloping Consumption[96] and in a few Days carried her off. Amidst all my Lamentations for her (and violent you may suppose they were) I yet received some consolation in the reflection of my having paid every Attention to her, that could be offered, in her illness. I had wept over her every Day—had bathed her sweet face with my tears and had pressed her fair Hands continually in mine—. "My beloved Laura (said she to me a few Hours before she died) take warning from my unhappy End and avoid the imprudent conduct which has occasioned it . . . Beware of fainting-fits . . . Though at the time they may be refreshing and Agreable yet beleive me they will in the end, if too often repeated and at improper seasons, prove destructive to your Constitution . . . My fate will teach you this . . . I die a Martyr to my greif for the loss of Augustus . . . One fatal swoon has cost me my Life . . . Beware of swoons Dear Laura. . . . A frenzy fit is not one quarter so

line 14: 'her' deleted after 'allotted'.   //   line 20: 'fair' deleted; 'sweet' inserted above line.

pernicious; it is an exercise to the Body and if not too violent, is I dare say conducive to Health in its consequences—Run mad as often as you chuse; but do not faint—".

These were the last words she ever addressed to me . . . It was her dieing Advice to her afflicted Laura, who has ever most faithfully adhered to it.

After having attended my lamented freind to her Early Grave, I immediately (tho' late at night) left the detested Village in which she died, and near which had expired my Husband and Augustus. I had not walked many yards from it before I was overtaken by a Stage-Coach, in which I instantly took a place, determined to proceed in it to Edinburgh, where I hoped to find some kind some pitying Freind who would receive and comfort me in my Afflictions.

It was so dark when I entered the Coach that I could not distinguish the Number of my Fellow-travellers;[97] I could only perceive that they were Many. Regardless however of any thing concerning them, I gave myself up to my own sad Reflections. A general Silence prevailed—A Silence, which was by nothing interrupted but by the loud and repeated Snores of one of the Party.

"What an illiterate villain must that Man be! (thought I to myself) What a total Want of delicate refinement must he have, who can thus shock our senses by such a brutal Noise! He must I am certain be capable of every bad Action! There is no crime too black for such a Character!" Thus reasoned I within myself, and doubtless such were the reflections of my fellow travellers.

At length, returning Day enabled me to behold the unprincipled Scoundrel who had so violently disturbed my feelings.

line 4: 'words' inserted above line.   //   line 9: 'where' deleted; 'in which' inserted above line.   //   line 19: 'mutual' deleted; 'general' inserted above line.   //   line 19: 'amongst us all' deleted after 'prevailed'.

It was Sir Edward the father of my Deceased Husband. By his side, sate Augusta, and on the same seat with me were your Mother and Lady Dorothea. Imagine my Surprize at finding myself thus seated amongst my old Acquaintance. Great as was my astonishment, it was yet increased, when on looking out of Windows, I beheld the Husband of Philippa, with Philippa by his side, on the Coach-box,[98] and when on looking behind I beheld, Philander and Gustavus in the Basket.[99] "Oh! Heavens, (exclaimed I) is it possible that I should so unexpectedly be surrounded by my nearest Relations and Connections"? These words rouzed the rest of the Party, and every eye was directed to the corner in which I sat. "Oh! my Isabel (continued I throwing myself, across Lady Dorothea into her arms) receive once more to your Bosom the unfortunate Laura. Alas! when we last parted in the Vale of Usk, I was happy in being united to the best of Edwards; I had then a Father and a Mother, and had never known misfortunes—But now deprived of every freind but you—"

"What! (interrupted Augusta) is my Brother dead then? Tell us I intreat you what is become of him?"

"Yes, cold and insensible Nymph, (replied I) that luckless Swain[100] your Brother, is no more, and you may now glory in being the Heiress of Sir Edward's fortune."

Although I had always despised her from the Day I had overheard her conversation with my Edward, yet in civility I complied with hers and Sir Edward's intreaties that I would inform them of the whole melancholy Affair. They were greatly shocked—Even the obdurate Heart of Sir Edward and the insensible one of Augusta, were touched with Sorrow, by the unhappy tale. At the request of your Mother I

line 8: 'on' inserted above line.　//　line 30: 'and' inserted above line.

related to them every other misfortune which had befallen me since we parted. Of the imprisonment of Augustus and the Absence of Edward—of our arrival in Scotland—of our unexpected Meeting with our Grand-father and our cousins—of our visit to Macdonald-Hall—of the singular Service we there performed towards Janetta—of her Fathers ingratitude for it. . . . of his inhuman Behaviour, unaccountable suspicions, and barbarous treatment of us, in obliging us to leave the House. . . . of our Lamentations on the loss of Edward and Augustus and finally of the melancholy Death of my beloved Companion.

Pity and Surprise were strongly depictured in your Mother's Countenance, during the whole of my narration, but I am sorry to say, that to the eternal reproach of her Sensibility, the latter infinitely predominated. Nay, faultless as my Conduct had certainly been during the whole Course of my late Misfortunes and Adventures, she pretended to find fault with my Behaviour in many of the situations in which I had been placed. As I was sensible myself, that I had always behaved in a manner which reflected Honour on my Feelings and Refinement, I paid little attention to what she said, and desired her to satisfy my Curiosity by informing me how she came there, instead of wounding my spotless reputation with unjustifiable Reproaches. As soon as she had complied with my wishes in this particular and had given me an accurate detail of every thing that had befallen her since our separation (the particulars of which if you are not already acquainted with, your Mother will give you) I applied to Augusta for the same information respecting herself, Sir Edward and Lady Dorothea.

line 5: 'Service' inserted above line.   //   line 20: 'Honour' inserted above line.   //   line 24: 'unmanly' deleted; 'unjustifiable' inserted above line.

She told me that having a considerable taste for the Beauties of Nature, her curiosity to behold the delightful scenes it exhibited in that part of the World had been so much raised by Gilpin's Tour to the Highlands,[101] that she had prevailed on her Father to undertake a Tour to Scotland and had persuaded Lady Dorothea to accompany them. That they had arrived at Edinburgh a few Days before and from thence had made daily Excursions into the Country around in the Stage Coach they were then in, from one of which Excursions they were at that time returning. My next enquiries were concerning Philippa and her Husband, the latter of whom I learned having spent all her fortune, had recourse for subsistance to the talent in which, he had always most excelled, namely, Driving, and that having sold every thing which belonged to them except their Coach, had converted it into a Stage and in order to be removed from any of his former Acquaintance,[102] had driven it to Edinburgh from whence he went to Sterling[103] every other Day; That Philippa still retaining her affection for her ungratefull Husband, had followed him to Scotland and generally accompanied him in his little Excursions to Sterling. "It has only been to throw a little money into their Pockets (continued Augusta) that my Father has always travelled in their Coach to veiw the beauties of the Country since our arrival in Scotland—for it would certainly have been much more agreable to us, to visit the Highlands in a Postchaise[104] than merely to travel from Edinburgh to Sterling and from Sterling to Edinburgh every other Day in a crouded and uncomfortable Stage." I perfectly agreed with

line 2: 'Beautifull' deleted; 'delightful' inserted above line.   //   line 8: 'many' deleted; 'made' inserted above line.   //   line 13: 'ence' in 'subsistence' deleted and 'ance' inserted above line.   //   line 20: 'always' deleted; 'generally' inserted above line.

her in her sentiments on the Affair, and secretly blamed Sir
Edward for thus sacrificing his Daughter's Pleasure for the
sake of a ridiculous old Woman whose folly in marrying so
young a Man ought to be punished. His Behaviour however
was entirely of a peice with his general Character; for what
could be expected from a Man who possessed not the smallest atom of Sensibility, who scarcely knew the meaning of
Simpathy, and who actually snored—.

Adeiu
Laura.

LETTER THE 15TH

Laura in continuation.

When we arrived at the town where we were to Breakfast,
I was determined to speak with Philander and Gustavus,
and to that purpose as soon as I left the Carriage, I went to
the Basket and tenderly enquired after their Health, expressing my fears of the uneasiness of their Situation. At first
they seemed rather confused at my Appearance dreading no
doubt that I might call them to account for the money which
our Grandfather had left me and which they had unjustly
deprived me of, but finding that I mentioned nothing of
the Matter, they desired me to step into the Basket[105] as we
might there converse with greater ease. Accordingly I entered
and whilst the rest of the party were devouring Green tea[106]
and buttered toast, we feasted ourselves in a more refined
and Sentimental[107] Manner by a confidential Conversation.
I informed them of every thing which had befallen me during
the course of my Life, and at my request they related to me
every incident of theirs.

line 17: 'for' deleted; first 'of' inserted above line. // line 27: 'them'
deleted; 'me' inserted above line.

"We are the sons as you already know, of the two youngest Daughters which Lord St. Clair had by Laurina an italian Opera-girl. Our mothers could neither of them exactly ascertain who were our Fathers; though it is generally beleived that Philander, is the son of one Philip Jones a Bricklayer and that my Father was Gregory Staves a Staymaker[108] of Edinburgh. This is however of little consequence, for as our Mothers were certainly never married to either of them, it reflects no Dishonour on our Blood, which is of a most ancient and unpolluted kind. Bertha (the Mother of Philander) and Agatha (my own Mother) always lived together. They were neither of them very rich; their united fortunes had originally amounted to nine thousand Pounds, but as they had always lived upon the principal of it,[109] when we were fifteen it was diminished to nine Hundred. This nine Hundred, they always kept in a Drawer in one of the Tables which stood in our common sitting Parlour,[110] for the Convenience of having it always at Hand. Whether it was from this circumstance, of its being easily taken, or from a wish of being independent, or from an excess of Sensibility (for which we were always remarkable) I cannot now determine, but certain it is that when we had reached our 15th Year, we took the Nine Hundred Pounds and ran away. Having obtained this prize we were determined to manage it with eoconomy and not to spend it either with folly or Extravagance. To this purpose we therefore divided it into nine parcels, one of which we devoted to Victuals, the 2d to Drink, the 3d to House-keeping, the 4th to Carriages, the 5th to Horses, the 6th to Servants, the 7th to Amusements the 8th to Cloathes and the 9th to Silver Buckles.[111] Having thus arranged our Expences for two

line 11: 'Mother' inserted above line.

Months (for we expected to make the nine Hundred Pounds last as long) we hastened to London and had the good luck to spend it in 7 weeks and a Day which was 6 Days sooner than we had intended. As soon as we had thus happily disencumbered ourselves from the weight of so much Money, we began to think of returning to our Mothers, but accidentally hearing that they were both starved to Death, we gave over the design and determined to engage ourselves to some strolling Company of Players,[112] as we had always a turn for the Stage.[113] Accordingly we offered our Services to one and were accepted; our Company was indeed rather small, as it consisted only of the Manager his Wife and ourselves, but there were fewer to pay and the only inconvenience attending it was the Scarcity of Plays which for want of People to fill the Characters, we could perform.—. We did not mind trifles however—. One of our most admired Performances was *Macbeth*, in which we were truly great. The Manager always played *Banquo* himself, his Wife my *Lady Macbeth*, I did the *Three Witches* and Philander acted *all the rest*.[114] To say the truth this tragedy was not only the Best, but the only Play we ever performed; and after having acted it all over England, and Wales, we came to Scotland to exhibit it over the remainder of Great Britain. We happened to be quartered in that very Town, where you came and met your Grandfather—. We were in the Inn-yard when his Carriage entered and perceiving by the Arms to whom it belonged, and knowing that Lord St. Clair was our Grand-father, we agreed to endeavour to get something from him by discovering the Relationship—. You know how well it succeeded—. Having obtained the two Hundred Pounds, we instantly left

line 1: 'were determined' deleted; 'expected' inserted above line. // line 7: 'dead,' deleted; 'starved to Death,' inserted above line. // line 22: 'Ireland,' deleted after 'England'. // line 23: 'quit' deleted after 'to'.

the Town, leaving our Manager and his Wife to act *Macbeth* by themselves, and took the road to Sterling, where we spent our little fortunes with great *eclat*.[115] We are now returning to Edinburgh in order to get some preferment[116] in the Acting way; and such my Dear Cousin is our History."

I thanked the amiable Youth for his entertaining Narration, and after expressing my Wishes for their Welfare and Happiness, left them in their little Habitation[117] and returned to my other Freinds who impatiently expected me.

My Adventures are now drawing to a close my dearest Marianne; at least for the present.

When we arrived at Edinburgh Sir Edward told me that as the Widow of his Son, he desired I would accept from his Hands of four Hundred a year. I graciously promised that I would, but could not help observing that the unsimpathetic Baronet offered it more on account of my being the Widow of Edward than in being the refined and Amiable Laura.

I took up my Residence in a romantic Village in the Highlands of Scotland, where I have ever since continued, and where I can uninterrupted by unmeaning Visits, indulge in a melancholy Solitude, my unceasing Lamentations for the Death of my Father, my Mother, my Husband and my Freind.

Augusta has been for several Years united to Graham the Man of all others most suited to her; she became acquainted with him during her stay in Scotland.

Sir Edward in hopes of gaining an Heir to his Title and Estate, at the same time married Lady Dorothea—. His wishes have been answered.

---

line 1: 'room' deleted; 'Town' inserted above line.   //   line 10: 'drawing' deleted, then inserted above line.   //   line 18: 'Lodging' deleted after 'my'. //   line 23: 'Graham' inserted at end of line.   //   line 24: 'Graham' deleted after 'her'.

Philander and Gustavus, after having raised their reputation by their Performances in the Theatrical Line at Edinburgh, removed to Covent Garden, where they still Exhibit under the assumed names of *Lewis* and *Quick*.[118]

Philippa has long paid the Debt of Nature,[119] Her Husband however still continues to drive the Stage-Coach from Edinburgh to Sterling:—

Adeiu my Dearest Marianne—.

Laura—

FINIS

June 13th 1790[120]

line 3: 'continue to' deleted after 'still'.   //   line 11: 'Sunday,' deleted before 'June'.

To Henry Thomas Austen Esqre[1]—.

Sir

    I am now availing myself of the Liberty you have frequently honoured me with[2] of dedicating one of my Novels to you. That it is unfinished, I greive; yet fear that from me, it will always remain so; that as far as it is carried, it Should be so trifling and so unworthy of you, is

    another concern to your obliged humble

Servant

The Author

Messrs Demand and Co—please to pay Jane Austen Spinster the sum of one hundred guineas on account of your Humbl. Servant.

H. T. Austen.

£ 105.0.0[3]

---

line 6: 'always' inserted above line.   //   line 6: 'is' inserted above line.

Lesley Castle
an unfinished Novel in Letters.

LETTER THE FIRST IS FROM

Miss Margaret Lesley to Miss Charlotte Lutterell.

Lesley-Castle Janry. 3d—1792.

My Brother[4] has just left us. "Matilda (said he at parting) you and Margaret[5] will I am certain take all the care of my dear little one, that she might have received from an indulgent, an affectionate an amiable Mother." Tears rolled down his Cheeks as he spoke these words—the remembrance of her, who had so wantonly disgraced the Maternal character and so openly violated the conjugal Duties, prevented his adding anything farther; he embraced his sweet Child and after saluting Matilda and Me hastily broke from us—and seating himself in his Chaise, pursued the road to Aberdeen.[6] Never was there a better young Man! Ah! how little did he deserve the misfortunes he has experienced in the Marriage State. So good a Husband to so bad a Wife!, for you know my dear Charlotte that the Worthless Louisa[7] left him, her Child and reputation a few weeks ago in company with Danvers and dishonour.[a] Never was there a sweeter face, a finer form, or a less amiable Heart than Louisa owned! Her child already possesses the personal Charms of her unhappy Mother! May she inherit from her Father all his mental ones! Lesley is at present but five and twenty, and has already given himself up to melancholy and Despair; what a difference between him

[a] Rakehelly Dishonor Esqre. [JA's note][8]

143

and his Father!, Sir George is 57 and still remains the Beau, the flighty stripling,[9] the gay Lad, and sprightly Youngster, that his Son was really about five years back, and that *he* has affected to appear ever since my remembrance. While our father is fluttering about the Streets of London, gay, dissipated, and Thoughtless at the age of 57, Matilda and I continue secluded from Mankind in our old and Mouldering Castle, which is situated two miles from Perth[10] on a bold projecting Rock,[11] and commands an extensive veiw of the Town and its delightful Environs. But tho' retired from almost all the World,[12] (for we visit no one but the M'Leods, The M'Kenzies, the M'Phersons, the M'Cartneys, the M'donalds, The M'kinnons, the M'lellans, the M'kays, the Macbeths and the Macduffs)[13] we are neither dull nor unhappy; on the contrary there never were two more lively, more agreable or more witty Girls, than we are; not an hour in the Day hangs heavy on our hands. We read, we work, we walk, and when fatigued with these Employments releive our spirits, either by a lively song, a graceful Dance, or by some smart bon-mot, and witty repartée.[14] We are handsome my dear Charlotte, very handsome and the greatest of our Perfections is, that we are entirely insensible of them ourselves. But why do I thus dwell on myself? Let me rather repeat the praise of our dear little Neice the innocent Louisa, who is at present sweetly smiling in a gentle Nap, as she reposes on the Sofa. The dear Creature is just turned of two years old; as handsome as tho' 2 and 20, as sensible as tho' 2 and 30, and as prudent as tho' 2 and 40. To convince you of this, I must inform you that she has a very fine complexion and very pretty features, that she already knows the two first Letters in the

---

line 4: 'for' deleted, thus changing 'forever' to 'ever'.   //   line 8: 'two' written over 'a' and 's' added to 'mile'.

Alphabet,[15] and that she never tears her frocks—. If I have not now convinced you of her Beauty, Sense and Prudence, I have nothing more to urge in support of my assertion, and you will therefore have no way of deciding the Affair but by coming to Lesley-castle, and by a personal acquaintance with Louisa, determine for yourself. Ah! my dear Freind, how happy should I be to see you within these venerable Walls! It is now four years since my removal from School has separated me from you; that two such tender Hearts, so closely linked together by the ties of simpathy and Freindship, should be so widely removed from each other, is vastly moving. I live in Perthshire, You in Sussex.[16] We might meet in London, were my Father disposed to carry me there, and were your Mother to be there at the same time. We might meet at Bath, at Tunbridge,[17] or any where else indeed, could we but be at the same place together. We have only to hope that such a period may arrive. My Father does not return to us till Autumn; my Brother will leave Scotland in a few Days; he is impatient to travel. Mistaken Youth! He vainly flatters himself that change of Air will heal the Wounds of a broken Heart! You will join with me I am certain my dear Charlotte, in prayers for the recovery of the unhappy Lesley's peace of Mind, which must ever be essential to that of your sincere freind

M. Lesley.

LETTER THE SECOND

From Miss C. Lutterell to Miss M. Lesley in answer
Glenford[18] Febry. 12

I have a thousand excuses to beg for having so long delayed thanking you my dear Peggy[19] for your agreable Letter,

---

line 9: 'too' deleted; 'two' inserted above line.   //   line 15: 'else' inserted above line.   //   line 16: 'I' deleted; 'We' inserted above line.   //   line 16: 'to' inserted above line.

which beleive me I should not have deferred doing, had not
every moment of my time during the last five weeks been so
fully employed in the necessary arrangements for my sisters
Wedding, as to allow me no time to devote either to you or
myself. And now what provokes me more than any thing else
is that the Match is broke off, and all my Labour thrown
away. Imagine how great the Dissapointment must be to me,
when you consider that after having laboured both by Night
and by Day, in order to get the Wedding dinner ready by the
time appointed, after having roasted Beef, Broiled Mutton,
and Stewed Soup[20] enough to last the new-married Couple
through the Honey-moon, I had the mortification of finding
that I had been Roasting, Broiling and Stewing both the Meat
and Myself to no purpose. Indeed my dear Freind, I never
remember suffering any vexation equal to what I experienced
on last Monday when my Sister came running to me in the
Store-room with her face as White as a Whipt syllabub,[21]
and told me that Hervey had been thrown from his Horse,
had fractured his Scull and was pronounced by his Surgeon
to be in the most emminent Danger.

"Good God! (said I) you dont say so? why what in the
name of Heaven will become of all the Victuals! We shall
never be able to eat it while it is good. However, we'll call
in the Surgeon to help us—. I shall be able to manage the
Sir-loin myself; my Mother will eat the Soup, and You and
the Doctor must finish the rest." Here I was interrupted,
by seeing my poor Sister fall down to appearance Lifeless
upon one of the Chests, where we keep our Table linen. I
immediately called my Mother and the Maids, and at last we
brought her to herself again; as soon as ever she was sensible,

line 12: 'to find that' deleted; 'I had the' inserted above line.   //   line 30: 's'
at the end of 'her' deleted.

she expressed a determination of going instantly to Henry, and was so wildly bent on this Scheme, that we had the greatest Difficulty in the World to prevent her putting it in execution; at last however more by Force than Entreaty we prevailed on her to go into her room; we laid her upon the Bed, and she continued for some Hours in the most dreadful Convulsions. My Mother and I continued in the room with her, and when any intervals of tolerable Composure in Eloisa[22] would allow us, we joined in heartfelt lamentations on the dreadful Waste in our provisions which this Event must occasion, and in concerting some plan for getting rid of them. We agreed that the best thing we could do was to begin eating them immediately, and accordingly we ordered up the cold Ham and Fowls, and instantly began our Devouring Plan on them with great Alacrity. We would have persuaded Eloisa to have taken a Wing of a Chicken, but she would not be persuaded. She was however much quieter than she had been; the Convulsions she had before suffered having given way to an almost perfect Insensibility. We endeavoured to rouse her by every means in our power, but to no purpose. I talked to her of Henry. "Dear Eloisa (said I) there's no occasion for your crying so much about such a trifle. (for I was willing to make light of it in order to comfort her) I beg you would not mind it—. You see it does not vex me in the least; though perhaps *I* may suffer most from it after all; for I shall not only be obliged to eat up all the Victuals I have dressed[23] already, but must if Hervey should recover (which however

line 1: 'instantly' inserted above line.   //   line 2: 'wildly' written over 'very'.   //   line 5: 'where' deleted after 'room'.   //   line 6: 'the' inserted above line.   //   line 10: 'in our provisions' inserted above line.   //   line 11: 'scheme' written above 'plan' and deleted.   //   line 12: 'best' written over 'only'.   //   line 20: 'to' inserted above line.   //   line 25: 'for' deleted; 'from' inserted above line.

is not very likely) dress as much for you again; or should he die (as I suppose he will) I shall still have to prepare a Dinner for you whenever you marry any one else. So you see that tho' perhaps for the present it may afflict you to think of Henry's sufferings, Yet I dare say he'll die soon, and then his pain will be over and you will be easy, whereas my Trouble will last much longer for work as hard as I may, I am certain that the pantry cannot be cleared in less than a fortnight." Thus I did all in my power to console her, but without any effect, and at last as I saw that she did not seem to listen to me, I said no more, but leaving her with my Mother I took down the remains of The Ham and Chicken, and sent William to ask how Hervey did. He was not expected to live many Hours; he died the same day. We took all possible Care to break the Melancholy Event to Eloisa in the tenderest manner; yet in spite of every precaution, her Sufferings on hearing it were too violent for her reason, and she continued for many hours in a high Delirium. She is still extremely ill, and her Physicians[24] are greatly afraid of her going into a Decline.[25] We are therefore preparing for Bristol,[26] where we mean to be in the course of the next Week. And now my dear Margaret let me talk a little of your affairs; and in the first place I must inform you that it is confidently reported, your Father is going to be married; I am very unwilling to beleive so unpleasing a report, and at the same time cannot wholly discredit it. I have written to my freind Susan Fitzgerald, for information concerning it, which as she is at present in Town, she will be very able to give me. I know not who is the Lady. I think your Brother is extremely right in the resolution he has

line 11: 'I left' deleted; 'but leaving' inserted above line. // line 11–12: 'and taking' deleted; 'I took' inserted above line. // line 15: 'Account' deleted; 'Event' inserted above line. // line 19: 's' added at the end of 'Physicians' and 'are' written over 'is'. // line 19: 'going into' written over 'being in'.

taken of travelling, as it will perhaps contribute to obliterate from his remembrance, those disagreable Events, which have lately so much afflicted him—I am happy to find that tho' secluded from all the World, neither You nor Matilda are dull or unhappy—that you may never know what it is to be either is the Wish of your Sincerely Affectionate

C. L.

P.S. I have this instant received an answer from my freind Susan, which I enclose to you, and on which you will make your own reflections.

The enclosed Letter

My dear Charlotte

You could not have applied for information concerning the report of Sir George Lesleys Marriage, to any one better able to give it you than I am. Sir George is certainly married; I was myself present at the Ceremony, which you will not be surprised at when I subscribe myself your

Affectionate Susan Lesley

LETTER THE THIRD

From Miss Margaret Lesley to Miss C. Lutterell
Lesley Castle February the 16th

I *have* made my own reflections on the letter you enclosed to me, my Dear Charlotte and I will now tell you what those reflections were. I reflected that if by this second Marriage Sir George should have a second family, our fortunes must be considerably diminished—that if his Wife should be of an extravagant turn, she would encourage him to persevere in that Gay and Dissipated way of Life to which little encouragement would be necessary, and which has I fear already

---

line 4: 'n' added in 'nor'. // line 24: 'were' written over 'are'.

proved but too detrimental to his health and fortune—that
she would now become Mistress of those Jewels which once
adorned our Mother, and which Sir George had always
promised us—that if they did not come into Perthshire I
should not be able to gratify my curiosity of beholding my
Mother-in-law,[27] and that if they did, Matilda would no
longer sit at the head of her Father's table[28]—. These my dear
Charlotte were the melancholy reflections which crouded
into my imagination after perusing Susan's letter to you, and
which instantly occurred to Matilda when she had perused it
likewise. The same ideas, the same fears, immediately occupied her Mind, and I know not which reflection distressed
her most, whether the probable Diminution of our Fortunes,
or her own Consequence. We both wish very much to know
whether Lady Lesley is handsome and what is your opinion
of her; as you honour her with the appellation of your freind,
we flatter ourselves that she must be amiable. My Brother is
already in Paris. He intends to quit it in a few Days, and to
begin his route to Italy.[29] He writes in a most chearfull Manner, says that the air of France has greatly recovered both
his Health and Spirits; that he has now entirely ceased to
think of Louisa with any degree either of Pity or Affection,
that he even feels himself obliged to her for her Elopement,
as he thinks it very good fun to be single again. By this,
you may perceive that he has entirely regained that chearful
Gaiety, and sprightly Wit, for which he was once so remarkable. When he first became acquainted with Louisa which
was little more than three years ago, he was one of the most
lively, the most agreable young Men of the age—. I beleive
you never yet heard the particulars of his first acquaintance

line 13: 'us' deleted; 'her' inserted above line.   //   line 19: 'lively' deleted;
'chearfull' inserted above line.   //   line 26: 'e' inserted above line in 'Gaiety'.
//   line 29: 'e' written over 'a' in 'Men'.

with her. It commenced at our cousin Colonel Drummond's; at whose house in Cumberland[30] he spent the Christmas, in which he attained the age of two and twenty. Louisa Burton was the Daughter of a distant Relation of Mrs. Drummond, who dieing a few Months before in extreme poverty, left his only Child then about eighteen to the protection of any of his Relations who would protect her. Mrs. Drummond was the only one who found herself so disposed—Louisa was therefore removed from a miserable Cottage in Yorkshire[31] to an elegant Mansion in Cumberland, and from every pecuniary Distress that Poverty could inflict, to every elegant Enjoyment that Money could purchase—. Louisa was naturally ill-tempered and Cunning; but she had been taught to disguise her real Disposition, under the appearance of insinuating Sweetness, by a father who but too well knew, that to be married, would be the only chance she would have of not being starved, and who flattered himself that with such an extroidinary share of personal beauty, joined to a gentleness of Manners, and an engaging address, she might stand a good chance of pleasing some young Man who might afford to marry a Girl without a Shilling. Louisa perfectly entered into her father's schemes and was determined to forward them with all her care and attention. By dint of Perseverance and Application, she had at length so thoroughly disguised her natural disposition under the mask of Innocence and Softness, as to impose upon every one who had not by a long and constant intimacy with her discovered her real Character. Such was Louisa when the hapless Lesley first beheld her at Drummond-house. His heart which (to use your favourite comparison) was as delicate as sweet and

line 6: 's' deleted at the end of 'protection'.   //   line 9: 'from a miserable' written over 'to an elegant'.

as tender as a Whipt-syllabub, could not resist her attractions.
In a very few Days, he was falling in love, shortly after actually
fell, and before he had known her a Month, he had married
her. My Father was at first highly displeased at so hasty and
imprudent a connection; but when he found that they did not
mind it, he soon became perfectly reconciled to the match.
The Estate near Aberdeen[32] which my brother possesses by
the bounty of his great Uncle independant of Sir George, was
entirely sufficient to support him and my Sister in Elegance
and Ease. For the first twelvemonth, no one could be happier
than Lesley, and no one more amiable to appearance than
Louisa, and so plausibly did she act and so cautiously behave
that tho' Matilda and I often spent several weeks together
with them, yet we neither of us had any suspicion of her real
Disposition. After the birth of Louisa however, which one
would have thought would have strengthened her regard for
Lesley, the mask she had so long supported was by degrees
thrown aside, and as probably she then thought herself secure
in the affection of her Husband (which did indeed appear if
possible augmented by the birth of his Child) she seemed to
take no pains to prevent that affection from ever diminishing.
Our visits therefore to Dunbeath,[33] were now less frequent
and by far less agreable than they used to be. Our absence
was however never either mentioned or lamented by Louisa
who in the society of young Danvers with whom she became
acquainted at Aberdeen (he was at one of the Universities
there,[34]) felt infinitely happier than in that of Matilda and
your freind, tho' there certainly never were pleasanter Girls
than we are. You know the sad end of all Lesleys connubial

---

line 3: 'felled' deleted; 'fell' inserted above line.   //   line 21: 'n' deleted at
the end of 'take'.   //   line 22: 'Dunbeath' written over an illegible word
line 28: 'never' inserted at end of line.

happiness; I will not repeat it—. Adeiu my dear Charlotte; although I have not yet mentioned any thing of the matter, I hope you will do me the justice to beleive that I *think* and *feel*,[35] a great deal for your Sisters affliction. I do not doubt but that the healthy air of the Bristol-downs[36] will intirely remove it, by erasing from her Mind the remembrance of Henry. I am my dear Charlotte yrs ever

ML—

LETTER THE FOURTH

From Miss C. Lutterell to Miss M. Lesley

Bristol February 27th

My dear Peggy

I have but just received your letter, which being directed to Sussex while I was at Bristol was obliged to be forwarded to me here, and from some unaccountable Delay, has but this instant reached me—. I return you many thanks for the account it contains of Lesley's acquaintance, Love and Marriage with Louisa, which has not the less entertained me for having often been repeated to me before.

I have the satisfaction of informing you that we have every reason to imagine our pantry is by this time nearly cleared, as we left particular orders with the Servants to eat as hard as they possibly could, and to call in a couple of Chairwomen[37] to assist them. We brought a cold Pigeon-pye, a cold turkey, a cold tongue, and half a dozen Jellies[38] with us, which we were lucky enough with the help of our Landlady, her husband, and their three children, to get rid of, in less than two days after our arrival. Poor Eloisa is still so very indifferent both in Health and Spirits, that I very much fear, the air of the

line 10: 'Lesley' written over 'Lutterell'.

Bristol-downs, healthy as it is, has not been able to drive poor
Henry from her remembrance—.

You ask me whether your new Mother in law is handsome
and amiable—I will now give you an exact description of her
bodily and Mental charms. She is short, and extremely well-
made; is naturally pale, but rouges a good deal;[39] has fine eyes,
and fine teeth, as she will take care to let you know as soon as
she sees you, and is altogether very pretty. She is remarkably
good-tempered when she has her own way, and very lively
when she is not out of humour. She is naturally extravagant
and not very affected; she never reads any thing but the letters she receives from me, and never writes anything but her
answers to them. She plays, sings and Dances, but has no
taste for either, and excells in none, tho' she says she is passionately fond of all. Perhaps you may flatter me so far as to
be surprised that one of whom I speak with so little affection
should be my particular freind; but to tell you the truth, our
freindship arose rather from Caprice on her side, than Esteem
on mine. We spent two or three days together with a Lady in
Berkshire with whom we both happened to be connected—.
During our visit, the Weather being remarkably bad, and our
party particularly stupid, she was so good as to conceive a violent partiality for me, which very soon settled in a downright
Freindship, and ended in an established correspondence. She
is probably by this time as tired of me, as I am of her; but as she
is too polite and I am too civil to say so, our letters are still as
frequent and affectionate as ever, and our Attachment as firm
and Sincere as when it first commenced.—As she has a great

---

line 9: 'tempered' written over 'humoured'.   //   line 18: 'herself' deleted;
'her side' inserted above line.   //   line 23: 'freindship' deleted; 'partiality'
inserted above line.   //   line 23: 'settled in' written over 'turned to'.   //
line 28: 'was' deleted after 'it'.

taste for the pleasures of London, and of Brighthelmstone,[40] he will I dare say find some difficulty in prevailing on herself ever to satisfy the curiosity I dare say she feels of behold-ing you, at the expence of quitting those favourite haunts of Dissipation, for the melancholy tho' venerable gloom of the castle you inhabit. Perhaps however if she finds her health impaired by too much amusement, she may acquire fortitude sufficient to undertake a Journey to Scotland in the hope of its proving at least beneficial to her health, if not conducive to her happiness. Your fears I am sorry to say, concerning your father's extravagance, your own fortunes, your Mothers Jewels and your Sister's consequence, I should suppose are but too well founded. My freind herself has four thousand pounds, and will probably spend nearly as much every year in Dress and Public places,[41] if she can get it—she will cer-tainly not endeavour to reclaim Sir George from the manner of living to which he has been so long accustomed, and there is therefore some reason to fear that you will be very well off, if you get any fortune at all. The Jewels I should imagine too will undoubtedly be hers, and there is too much reason to think that she will preside[42] at her Husbands table in pref-erence to his Daughter. But as so melancholy a subject must necessarily extremely distress you, I will no longer dwell on it—.

Eloisa's indisposition has brought us to Bristol at so unfashionable a season of the year,[43] that we have actually seen but one genteel family since we came. Mr and Mrs Mar-lowe are very agreable people; the ill health of their little boy occasioned their arrival here; you may imagine that being the only family with whom we can converse, we are of course on

---

line 1: 'the Amusements' deleted after 'and'.   //   line 3: 'certainty' deleted; 'curiosity' inserted above line.   //   line 16: 'from' written over 'but'(?).

a footing of intimacy with them; we see them indeed almost every day, and dined with them yesterday. We spent a very pleasant Day, and had a very good Dinner, tho' to be sure the Veal was terribly underdone, and the Curry had no seasoning. I could not help wishing all dinner-time that I had been at the dressing it—. A brother of Mrs Marlowe, Mr Cleveland is with them at present; he is a good-looking young Man and seems to have a good deal to say for himself. I tell Eloisa that she should set her cap at him,[44] but she does not at all seem to relish the proposal. I should like to see the girl married and Cleveland has a very good estate. Perhaps you may wonder that I do not consider *myself* as well as my Sister in my matrimonial Projects; but to tell you the truth I never wish to act a more principal part at a Wedding than the superintending and directing the Dinner, and therefore while I can get any of my acquaintance to marry for me, I shall never think of doing it myself, as I very much suspect that I should not have so much time for dressing my own Wedding-dinner, as for dressing that of my freinds. Yrs sincerely

CL.

LETTER THE FIFTH

Miss Margaret Lesley to Miss Charlotte Luttrell

Lesley-Castle March 18th

On the same day that I received your last kind letter, Matilda received one from Sir George which was dated from Edinburgh, and informed us that he should do himself the pleasure of introducing Lady Lesley to us on the following Evening. This as you may suppose considerably surprised us, particularly as your account of her Ladyship had given

---

line 16: 'freinds' deleted; 'acquaintance' inserted above line.   //   line 22: 'and' deleted; 'to' inserted above line.

us reason to imagine there was little chance of her visiting Scotland at a time that London must be so gay.[45] As it was our business however to be delighted at such a mark of condescension as a visit from Sir George and Lady Lesley, we prepared to return them an answer expressive of the happiness we enjoyed in expectation of such a Blessing, when luckily recollecting that as they were to reach the Castle the next Evening, it would be impossible for my father to receive it before he left Edinburgh, We contented ourselves with leaving them to suppose that we were as happy as we ought to be. At nine in the Evening on the following day, they came, accompanied by one of Lady Lesleys brothers. Her Ladyship perfectly answers the description you sent me of her, except that I do not think her so pretty as you seem to consider her. She has not a bad face, but there is something so extremely unmajestic in her little diminutive figure, as to render her in comparison with the elegant height of Matilda and Myself, an insignificant Dwarf. Her curiosity to see us (which must have been great to bring her more than four hundred miles[46]) being now perfectly gratified, she already begins to mention their return to town, and has desired us to accompany her—. We cannot refuse her request since it is seconded by the commands of our Father, and thirded by the entreaties of Mr Fitzgerald who is certainly one of the most pleasing young Men, I ever beheld. It is not yet determined when we are to go, but when we do we shall certainly take our little Louisa with us. Adeiu my dear Charlotte; Matilda unites in best wishes to You and Eloisa, with yours ever

ML

line 1: 'that' deleted after 'imagine'.   //   line 2: 'gay' written over 'giddy'(?).   //   line 9: 'therefore' deleted after 'We'.   //   line 16: 'j' written over 'g' in 'majestic'.   //   line 17: 'to' deleted; 'with' inserted above line.   //   line 19: 'have brought us' deleted; 'bring her' inserted above line.

LETTER THE SIXTH

Lady Lesley to Miss Charlotte Luttrell

Lesley-Castle March 20th

We arrived here my sweet Freind about a fortnight ago, and I already heartily repent that I ever left our charming House in Portman-Square[47] for such a dismal old Weather-beaten Castle[48] as this. You can form no idea sufficiently hideous, of its dungeon-like form. It is actually perched upon a Rock to appearance so totally inaccessible, that I expected to have been pulled up by a rope; and sincerely repented having gratified my curiosity to behold my Daughters at the expence of being obliged to enter their prison in so dangerous and ridiculous a Manner. But as soon as I once found myself safely arrived in the inside of this tremendous building, I comforted myself with the hope of having my spirits revived, by the sight of two beautifull Girls, such as the Miss Lesleys had been represented to me, at Edinburgh. But here again, I met with nothing but Disapointment and Surprise. Matilda and Margaret Lesley are two great, tall, out of the way, over-grown, Girls, just of a proper size to inhabit a Castle almost as Large in comparison as themselves. I wish my dear Charlotte that you could but behold these Scotch Giants; I am sure they would frighten you out of your wits. They will do very well as foils to myself, so I have invited them to accompany me to London where I hope to be in the course of a fortnight. Besides these two fair Damsels, I found a little humoured Brat here who I beleive is some relation to them; they told me who she was, and gave me a long rigmerole[49] Story of her father and a Miss *Somebody*[50] which I have entirely forgot.

---

line 8: 'appearance' deleted; 'form' inserted above line. // line 9: 'to appearance' inserted above line. // line 16: 'such' inserted above line.

I hate Scandal and detest Children.—. I have been plagued ever since I came here with tiresome visits from a parcel of Scotch wretches, with terrible hard-names; they were so civil, gave me so many invitations, and talked of coming again so soon, that I could not help affronting them. I suppose I shall not see them any more, and yet as a family party we are so stupid, that I do not know what to do with myself. These girls have no Music, but Scotch Airs, no Drawings but Scotch Mountains, and no Books but Scotch Poems—And I hate everything Scotch.[51] In general I can spend half the Day at my toilett[52] with a great deal of pleasure, but why should I dress here, since there is not a creature in the House whom I have any wish to please.—. I have just had a conversation with my Brother in which he has greatly offended me, and which as I have nothing more entertaining to send you I will give you the particulars of. You must know that I have for these 4 or 5 Days past strongly suspected William of entertaining a partiality for my eldest Daughter. I own indeed that had *I* been inclined to fall in love with any woman, I should not have made choice of Matilda Lesley for the object of my passion; for there is nothing I hate so much as a tall Woman: but however there is no accounting for some men's taste and as William is himself nearly six feet high, it is not wonderful that he should be partial to that height. Now as I have very great affection for my Brother and should be extremely sorry to see him unhappy, which I suppose he means to be if he cannot marry Matilda, as moreover I know that his Circumstances will not allow him to marry any one without a fortune, and that Matilda's is entirely dependent on her Father, who will neither have his own inclination nor my permission to give her anything at present, I thought it would be doing a good-natured action by my Brother to let him know as much, in order that he might choose for himself, whether to conquer his passion, or Love and Despair. Accordingly finding myself this Morning alone with him in one of the horrid old rooms of this Castle, I opened the cause to him in the following Manner.

"Well my dear William what do you think of these girls? for my part, I do not find them so plain as I expected: but perhaps you may think me partial to the Daughters of my Husband and perhaps you are right—They are indeed so very like Sir George that it is natural to think. . . . ."

"My Dear Susan (cried he in a tone of the greatest amazement) You do not really think they bear the least resemblance to their Father! He is so very plain!—but I beg your pardon—I had entirely forgotten to whom I was speaking—"

"Oh! pray don't mind me; (replied I) every one knows Sir George is horribly ugly, and I assure you I always thought him a fright."

"You surprise me extremely (answered William) by what you say both with respect to Sir George and his Daughters. You cannot think Your Husband so deficient in personal Charms as you speak of, nor can you surely see any resemblance between him and the Miss Lesleys who are in my opinion perfectly unlike him and perfectly Handsome."

"If that is your opinion with regard to the girls it certainly is no proof of their Father's beauty, for if they are perfectly unlike him and very handsome at the same time, it is natural to suppose that he is very plain."

"By no means, (said he) for what may be pretty in a Woman, may be very unpleasing in a Man."

line 2: 'her' deleted; 'his' inserted above line.   //   line 7: 'expected' written over 'suspected'.   //   line 22: 'with' deleted; 'between' inserted above line.

"But, you yourself (replied I) but a few Minutes ago allowed him to be very plain."

"Men are no Judges of Beauty in their own Sex." (said he)

"Neither Men nor Women can think Sir George tolerable."

"Well, well, (said he) we will not dispute about *his* Beauty, but your opinion of his *Daughters* is surely very singular, for if I understood you right, you said you did not find them so plain as you expected to do."!

"Why, do *you* find them plainer then?" (said I)

"I can scarcely beleive you to be serious (returned he) when you speak of their persons in so extroidinary a Manner. Do not you not think the Miss Lesleys are two very handsome Young Women?"

"Lord! No! (cried I) I think them terribly plain!"

"Plain! (replied He) My dear Susan, you cannot really think so! Why what single Feature in the face of either of them, can you possibly find fault with?"

"Oh! trust me for that; (replied I). Come I will begin with the eldest—with Matilda. Shall I, William?" (I looked as cunning as I could when I said it, in order to shame him.)

"They are so much alike (said he) that I should suppose the faults of one, would be the faults of both."

"Well, then, in the first place, they are both so horribly tall!"

"They are *taller* than you are indeed." (said he with a saucy smile.)

"Nay, (said I) I know nothing of that."

"Well, but (he continued) tho' they may be above the common size, their figures are perfectly elegant; and as to their faces, their Eyes are beautifull—."

line 7: 'that' deleted after 'said'. // line 12: 'that' deleted after 'think'.

"I never can think such tremendous, knock-me-down figures in the least degree elegant, and as for their eyes, they are so tall that I never could strain my neck enough to look at them."

"Nay, (replied he) I know not whether you may not be in the right in not attempting it, for perhaps they might dazzle you with their Lustre."

"Oh! Certainly. (said I, with the greatest Complacency, for I assure you my dearest Charlotte I was not in the least offended tho' by what followed, one would suppose that William was conscious of having given me just cause to be so, for coming up to me and taking my hand, he said) "You must not look so grave Susan; you will make me fear I have offended you!"

"Offended me! Dear Brother, how came such a thought in your head! (returned I) No really! I assure you that I am not in the least surprised at your being so warm an advocate for the Beauty of these Girls—"

"Well, but (interrupted William) remember that we have not yet concluded our dispute concerning them. What fault do you find with their complexion?"

"They are so horridly pale."

"They have always a little colour, and after any exercise it is considerably heightened."

"Yes, but if there should ever happen to be any rain in this part of the world, they will never be able to raise more than their common stock—except indeed they amuse themselves with running up and Down these horrid old Galleries and Antichambers[53]—"

---

line 9: 'that' deleted after 'Charlotte'.   //   line 21: 's' deleted at the end of 'complexion'.   //   line 26: 'able raise' in ms.

"Well, (replied my Brother in a tone of vexation, and glancing an impertinent look at me) if they *have* but little colour, at least, it is all their own."

This was too much my dear Charlotte, for I am certain that he had the impudence by that look, of pretending to suspect the reality of mine. But you I am sure will vindicate my character whenever you may hear it so cruelly aspersed, for you can witness how often I have protested against wearing Rouge, and how much I always told you I disliked it. And I assure you that my opinions are still the same.—. Well, not bearing to be so suspected by my Brother, I left the room immediately, and have been ever since in my own Dressing-room writing to you. What a long Letter have I made of it. But you must not expect to receive such from me when I get to Town; for it is only at Lesley castle, that one has time to write even to a Charlotte Luttrell.—. I was so much vexed by William's Glance, that I could not summon Patience enough, to stay and give him that Advice respecting his Attachment to Matilda which had first induced me from pure Love to him to begin the conversation; and I am now so thoroughly convinced by it, of his violent passion for her, that I am certain he would never hear reason on the Subject, and I shall therefore give myself no more trouble either about him or his favourite. Adeiu my dear Girl—

Yrs affectionately Susan L.

LETTER THE SEVENTH

From Miss C. Luttrell to Miss M. Lesley

Bristol the 27th of March

I have received Letters from You and your Mother-in-law within this week which have greatly entertained me, as

line 11: 'so' inserted above line. // line 14: 'expect' written over 'suspect'.

I find by them that you are both downright jealous of each others Beauty. It is very odd that two pretty Women tho' actually Mother and Daughter cannot be in the same House without falling out about their faces. Do be convinced that you are both perfectly handsome and say no more of the Matter. I suppose this Letter must be directed to Portman Square where probably (great as is your affection for Lesley Castle) you will not be sorry to find yourself. In spite of all that People may say about Green fields and the Country I was always of opinion that London and its Amusements must be very agreable for a while, and should be very happy could my Mother's income allow her to jockey us into its Public-places,[54] during Winter. I always longed particularly to go to Vaux-hall,[55] to see whether the cold Beef there is cut so thin[56] as it is reported, for I have a sly suspicion that few people understand the act of cutting a slice of cold Beef so well as I do: nay it would be hard of I did not know something of the Matter, for it was a part of my Education that I took by far the most pains with. Mama always found me *her* best Scholar, tho' when Papa was alive Eloisa was *his*. Never to be sure were there two more different Dispositions in the World. We both loved Reading. *She* preferred Histories, and *I* Receipts.[57] She loved drawing Pictures, and I drawing Pullets.[58] No one could sing a better Song than She, and no one make a better Pye than I.—And so it has always continued since we have been no longer Children. The only difference is that all disputes on the superior excellence of our Employments *then* so frequent are now no more. We have for many years entered into an agreement always to admire each other's works; I never fail listening to *her* Music, and she is as

line 6: 'that' deleted after 'suppose'. // line 12: 'her' deleted; 'its' inserted above line. // line 19: 'I always took' deleted; 'that I took by far the' inserted above line. // line 25: 'has' inserted above line.

constant in eating *my* pies. Such at least was the case till Henry Hervey made his appearance in Sussex. Before the arrival of his Aunt in our neighbourhood where she established herself you know about a twelvemonth ago, his visits to her had been at stated times, and of equal and settled Duration; but on her removal to the Hall which is within a walk from our House, they became both more frequent and longer. This as you may suppose could not be pleasing to Mrs Diana who is a professed Enemy to everything which is not directed by Decorum and Formality, or which bears the least resemblance to Ease and Good-breeding. Nay so great was her aversion to her Nephews behaviour that I have often heard her give such hints of it before his face that had not Henry at such times been engaged in conversation with Eloisa, they must have caught his Attention and have very much distressed him. The alteration in my Sister's behaviour which I have before hinted at, now took place. The Agreement we had entered into of admiring each others productions she no longer seemed to regard, and tho' I constantly applauded even every Country-dance, She play'd,[59] yet not even a pidgeon-pye of my making could obtain from her a single word of Approbation. This was certainly enough to put any one in a Passion; however, I was as cool as a Cream-cheese and having formed my plan and concerted a scheme of Revenge, I was determined to let her have her own way and not even to make her a single reproach. My Scheme was to treat her as she treated me, and tho' she might even draw my own Picture or play Malbrook[60] (which is the only tune I ever really liked) not to say so much as "Thank you Eloisa"; tho' I had for many years constantly

line 5: 'of' deleted; second 'and' inserted above line.   //   line 17: originally 'Agreament'; 'e' inserted above line in place of 'a'.   //   line 21: 'Praise' deleted; 'Approbation' inserted above line.   //   line 28: 'was' deleted; 'is' inserted above line.

hollowed whenever she played, *Bravo, Bravissimo, Encora, Da Capro, allegretto, con espressioné*, and *Poco presto*[61] with many other such outlandish words, all of them as Eloisa told me expressive of my Admiration; and so indeed I suppose they are, as I see some of them in every Page of every Music-book, being the Sentiments I imagine of the Composer.

I executed my Plan with great Punctuality, I can not say success, for Alas! my silence while she played seemed not in the least to displease her; on the contrary she actually said to me one day "Well Charlotte, I am very glad to find that you have at last left off that ridiculous custom of applauding my Execution[62] on the Harpsichord[63] till you made *my* head ake, and yourself hoarse. I feel very much obliged to you for keeping your Admiration to yourself." I never shall forget the very witty answer I made to this speech.

"Eloisa (said I) I beg you would be quite at your Ease with respect to all such fears in future, for be assured that I shall always keep my Admiration to myself and my own pursuits and never extend it to yours." This was the only very severe thing I ever said in my Life; not but that I have often felt myself extremely satirical[64] but it was the only time I ever made my feelings public.

I suppose there never were two young people who had a greater affection for each other than Henry and Eloisa; no, the Love of your Brother for Miss Burton could not be so strong tho' it might be more violent. You may imagine therefore how provoked my Sister must have been to have him play her such a trick. Poor Girl! She still laments his Death, with undiminished Constancy, notwithstanding he has been dead more than six weeks; but some people mind such things more

line 2: first 's' written over 'x' in 'espressioné'.   //   line 11: 'last' written over 'least'.   //   line 19: 'speech' deleted after 'severe'.

than others. The ill state of Health into which his Loss has thrown her makes her so weak, and so unable to support the least exertion, that she has been in tears all this morning merely from having taken leave of Mrs Marlowe who with her Husband, Brother and Child are to leave Bristol this Morning. I am sorry to have them go because they are the only family with whom we have here any acquaintance, but I never thought of crying; to be sure Eloisa and Mrs Marlowe have always been more together than with me, and have therefore contracted a kind of affection for each other, which does not make Tears so inexcusable in them as they would be in me. The Marlowes are going to Town, Cleveland accompanies them; as neither Eloisa nor I could catch him I hope You or Matilda may have better Luck. I know not when we shall leave Bristol, Eloisa's Spirits are so low that she is very averse to moving, and yet is certainly by no means mended by her residence here. A week or two will I hope determine our Measures—in the mean time beleive me

etc—etc—Charlotte Luttrell

LETTER THE EIGHTH

Miss Luttrell to Mrs Marlowe.

Bristol April 4th

I feel myself greatly obliged to you my dear Emma for such a mark of your affection as I flatter myself was conveyed in the proposal you made me of our Corresponding; I assure you that it will be a great releif to me to write to you and as long as my Health and Spirits will allow me, you will find me a very constant Correspondent; I will not say an entertaining one, for you know my situation sufficiently not to be

---

line 10: 'an' deleted; 'a kind of' inserted above line.   //   line 13: 'that' deleted after 'hope'.

ignorant that in me Mirth would be improper and I know my own Heart too well not to be sensible that it would be unnatural. You must not expect News for we see no one with whom we are in the least acquainted, or in whose proceedings we have any Interest. You must not expect Scandal for by the same rule we are equally debarred either from hearing or inventing it.—You must expect from me nothing but the melancholy effusions of a broken Heart which is ever reverting to the Happiness it once enjoyed and which ill supports its present Wretchedness. The Possibility of being able to write, to speak, to you of my losst Henry will be a Luxury to me, and your Goodness will not I know refuse to read what it will so much releive my Heart to write. I once thought that to have what is in general called a Freind (I mean one of my own Sex to whom I might speak with less reserve than to any other person) independant of my Sister would never be an object of my wishes, but how much was I mistaken! Charlotte is too much engrossed by two confidential Correspondents of that sort, to supply the place of one to me, and I hope you will not think me girlishly romantic, when I say that to have some kind and compassionate Freind who might listen to my Sorrows without endeavouring to console me was what I had for some time wished for, when our acquaintance with you, the intimacy which followed it and the particular affectionate Attention you paid me almost from the first, caused me to entertain the flattering Idea of those attentions being improved on a closer acquaintance into a Freindship which, if you were what my wishes formed you would be the greatest Happiness I could be capable of enjoying. To find that such Hopes are realized is a satisfaction indeed, a satisfaction

line 1: 'that' is 'than' in ms.   //   line 2: 'well enough' deleted; 'too well not' inserted above line.   //   line 11: 'to speak,' inserted above line.

which is now almost the only one I can ever experience.—I feel myself so languid[65] that I am sure were you with me you would oblige me to leave off writing, and I can not give you a greater proof of my Affection for you than by acting, as I know you would wish me to do, whether Absent or Present. I am my dear Emmas sincere freind

E. L.

LETTER THE NINTH

Mrs Marlowe to Miss Lutterell

Grosvenor Street,[66] April 10th

Need I say my dear Eloisa how wellcome your Letter was to me? I cannot give a greater proof of the pleasure I received from it, or of the Desire I feel that our Correspondence may be regular and frequent than by setting you so good an example as I now do in answering it before the end of the week—. But do not imagine that I claim any merit in being so punctual; on the contrary I assure you, that it is a far greater Gratification to me to write to you, than to spend the Evening either at a Concert or a Ball. Mr Marlowe is so desirous of my appearing at some of the Public places every evening that I do not like to refuse him, but at the same time so much wish to remain at Home, that independant of the Pleasure I experience in devoting any portion of my Time to my Dear Eloisa, yet the Liberty I claim from having a Letter to write of spending an Evening at home with my little Boy, You know me well enough to be sensible, will of itself be a sufficient Inducement (if one is necessary) to my maintaining with Pleasure a Correspondence with you. As to the Subjects of your Letters to me, whether Grave or Merry, if they concern you they

---

line 9: first 'e' inserted in 'Lutterell'.   //   line 18: third 'to' inserted above line.

must be equally interesting to me; Not but that I think the Melancholy Indulgence of your own Sorrows by repeating them and dwelling on them to me, will only encourage and increase them, and that it will be more prudent in you to avoid so sad a subject; but yet knowing as I do what a soothing and Melancholy Pleasure it must afford you, I cannot prevail on myself to deny you so great an Indulgence, and will only insist on your not expecting me to encourage you in it, by my own Letters; on the contrary I intend to fill them with such lively Wit and entertaining Humour as shall even provoke a Smile in the sweet but Sorrowfull Countenance of my Eloisa.

In the first place you are to learn that I have met your Sisters three freinds Lady Lesley and her Daughters, twice in Public since I have been here. I know you will be impatient to hear my opinion of the Beauty of three Ladies of whom You have heard so much. Now, as you are too ill and too unhappy to be vain, I think I may venture to inform you that I like none of their faces so well as I do your own. Yet they are all handsome—Lady Lesley indeed I have seen before; her Daughters I beleive would in general be said to have a finer face than her Ladyship, and Yet what with the charms of a Blooming Complexion,[67] a little Affectation and a great deal of Small-talk, (in each of which She is superior to the Young Ladies) she will I dare say gain herself as many Admirers as the more regular features of Matilda, and Margaret. I am sure you will agree with me in saying that they can none of them be of a proper size for real Beauty,[68] when you know that two of them are taller and the other shorter than ourselves. In spite of this Defect (or rather by reason of it) there is something very noble and majestic in the figures of the Miss Lesleys, and something agreably Lively in the Appearance of their pretty

line 1: 'you' deleted after 'to'. // line 25: 'that' deleted after 'sure'.

little Mother-in-law. But tho' one may be majestic and the other Lively, yet the faces of neither possess that Bewitching Sweetness of my Eloisas, which her present Languor is so far from diminushing. What would my Husband and Brother say of us, if they knew all the fine things I have been saying to you in this Letter. It is very hard that a pretty Woman is never to be told she is so by any one of her own Sex, without that person's being suspected to be either her determined Enemy, or her professed Toad-eater.[69] How much more amiable are women in that particular! one Man may say forty civil things to another without our supposing that he is ever paid for it, and provided he does his Duty by our Sex, we care not how Polite he is to his own.

Mrs Luttrell will be so good as to accept my Compliments, Charlotte, my Love, and Eloisa the best wishes for the recovery of her Health and Spirits that can be offered by her Affectionate Freind E. Marlowe.

I am afraid this Letter will be but a poor Specimen of my Powers in the Witty Way; and your opinion of them will not be greatly increased when I assure you that I have been as entertaining as I possibly could—.

LETTER THE TENTH

From Miss Margaret Lesley to Miss Charlotte Luttrell

Portman Square April 13th

My dear Charlotte

We left Lesley-Castle on the 28th of Last Month, and arrived safely in London after a Journey of seven Days;[70] I had the pleasure of finding your Letter here waiting my

---

line 7: 'one' inserted above line. // line 10: 'one' inserted above line and 'Men' changed to 'Man'. // line 14–15: 'best' deleted after 'Compliments'. // line 16: 'her' written over 'his'. // line 18: 'that' deleted after 'afraid'. // line 20: 'as' deleted after 'have'. // line 27: 'ly' inserted after 'safe'.

Arrival, for which you have my grateful Thanks. Ah! my dear Freind I every day more regret the serene and tranquil Pleasures of the Castle we have left, in exchange for the uncertain and unequal Amusements of this vaunted City. Not that I will pretend to assert that these uncertain and unequal Amusements are in the least Degree unpleasing to me; on the contrary I enjoy them extremely and should enjoy them even more, were I not certain that every appearance I make in Public but rivetts the Chains of those unhappy Beings whose Passion it is impossible not to pity, tho' it is out of my power to return. In short my Dear Charlotte it is my sensibility for the sufferings of so many amiable Young Men, my Dislike of the extreme Admiration I meet with, and my Aversion to being so celebrated both in Public, in Private, in Papers, and in Printshops,[71] that are the reasons why I cannot more fully enjoy, the Amusements so various and pleasing of London. How often have I wished that I possessed as little personal Beauty as you do; that my figure were as inelegant; my face as unlovely; and my Appearance as unpleasing as yours! But Ah! what little chance is there of so desirable an Event; I have had the Small-pox,[72] and must therefore submit to my unhappy fate.

I am now going to intrust you my dear Charlotte with a secret which has long disturbed the tranquility of my days, and which is of a kind to require the most inviolable Secrecy from you. Last Monday se'night[73] Matilda and I accompanied Lady Lesley to a Rout[74] at the Honourable Mrs Kickabout's;[75] we were escorted by Mr Fitzgerald who is a very amiable Young Man in the main, tho' perhaps a little Singular in his Taste—He is in love with Matilda—. We had

line 15: 'why' inserted above line.   //   line 26: 'On' deleted before 'Last' and 'L' written over 'I'.   //   line 26: 'sen'nit' deleted; 'se'night' inserted above line.

scarcely paid our Compliments to the Lady of the House and curtseyed to half a Score different people when my Attention was attracted by the appearance of a Young Man the most lovely of his Sex, who at that Moment entered the Room with another Gentleman and Lady. From the first moment I beheld him, I was certain that on him depended the future Happiness of my Life.[76] Imagine my surprise when he was introduced to me by the name of Cleveland—I instantly recognized him as the Brother of Mrs Marlowe, and the acquaintance of my Charlotte at Bristol. Mr and Mrs M. were the Gentleman and Lady who accompanied him. (You do not think Mrs Marlowe handsome?) The elegant address of Mr Cleveland, his polished Manners and Delightful Bow, at once confirmed my attachment. He did not speak; but I can imagine every thing he would have said, had he opened his Mouth. I can picture to myself the cultivated Understanding, the Noble Sentiments, and elegant Language which would have shone so conspicuous in the conversation of Mr Cleveland. The approach of Sir James Gower (one of my too numerous Admirers) prevented the Discovery of any such Powers, by putting an end to a Conversation we had never commenced,[77] and by attracting my attention to himself. But Oh! how inferior are the accomplishments of Sir James to those of his so greatly envied Rival! Sir James is one of the most frequent of our Visitors, and is almost always of our Parties. We have since often met Mr and Mrs Marlowe but no Cleveland—he is always engaged some where else. Mrs Marlowe fatigues me to Death every time I see her by her tiresome Conversations about You and Eloisa. She is so Stupid! I live in the hope of seeing her irrisistable Brother to night, as we are going to

line 21: 'never' inserted above line.   //   line 24: 'frequent' inserted above line.   //   line 25: 'most' deleted after first 'our'.

Lady Flambeau's,[78] who is I know intimate with the Marlowes. Our party will be Lady Lesley, Matilda, Fitzgerald, Sir James Gower, and myself. We see little of Sir George, who is almost always at the Gaming-table. Ah! my poor Fortune where art thou by this time? We see more of Lady L. who always makes her appearance (highly rouged) at Dinnertime. Alas! what Delightful Jewels will she be decked in this evening at Lady Flambeau's! Yet I wonder how she can herself delight in wearing them; surely she must be sensible of the ridiculous impropriety of loading her little diminutive figure with such superfluous ornaments; is it possible that she can not know how greatly superior an elegant simplicity is to the most studied apparel? Would she but present them to Matilda and me, how greatly should we be obliged to her. How becoming would Diamonds be on our fine majestic figures! And how surprising it is that such an Idea should never have occurred to *her*: I am sure if I have reflected in this Manner once, I have fifty times. Whenever I see Lady Lesley dressed in them such reflections immediately come across me. My own Mother's Jewels too! But I will say no more on so melancholy a Subject—Let me entertain you with something more pleasing—Matilda had a letter this Morning from Lesley, by which we have the pleasure of finding that he is at Naples has turned Roman-catholic, obtained one of the Pope's Bulls[79] for annulling his 1st Marriage and has since actually married a Neapolitan Lady of great Rank and Fortune. He tells us moreover that much the same sort of affair has befallen his first Wife the worthless Louisa who is likewise at Naples has turned Roman-catholic, and is soon to be married[80] to a

line 13: 'Matilda' written over 'Margaret'.   //   line 25: '1st' inserted above line.   //   line 29: 'obtained another of the Pope's Bulls for annulling' deleted; 'turned Roman-catholic, and is soon to be married' inserted above line.

Neapolitan Nobleman of great and Distinguished Merit. He says, that they are at present very good Freinds, have quite forgiven all past errors and intend in future to be very good Neighbours. He invites Matilda and me to pay him a visit in Italy and to bring him his little Louisa whom both her Mother, Step-Mother, and himself are equally desirous of beholding. As to our accepting his invitation, it is at present very uncertain; Lady Lesley advises us to go without loss of time; Fitzgerald offers to escort us there, but Matilda has some doubts of the Propriety of such a Scheme—She owns it would be very agreable. I am certain she likes the Fellow. My Father desires us not to be in a hurry, as perhaps if we wait a few months both he and Lady Lesley will do themselves the pleasure of attending us. Lady Lesley says no, that nothing will ever tempt her to forego the Amusements of Brighthelmstone for a Journey to Italy merely to see our Brother. "No (says the disagreable Woman) I have once in my Life been fool enough to travel I dont know how many hundred Miles to see two of the Family, and I found it did not answer, so Deuce take me, if ever I am so foolish again." So says her Ladyship, but Sir George still perseveres in saying that perhaps in a Month or two, they may accompany us.

Adeiu my Dear Charlotte—

Yr faithful Margaret Lesley

line 10: 'me to' deleted after 'owns'.

The History of England

from the reign of
Henry the 4th
to the death of
Charles the 1st.[1]

By a partial, prejudiced, and ignorant Historian[2]

To Miss Austen[3] eldest daughter of the Revd George Austen,[4] this Work is inscribed with all due respect by

The Author

N. B. There will be very few Dates in this History.[5]

HENRY THE 4TH

Henry the 4th ascended the throne of England much to his own satisfaction in the year 1399, after having prevailed on his cousin and predecessor Richard the 2d, to resign it to him, and to retire for the rest of his Life to Pomfret Castle,[6] where he happened to be murdered. It is to be supposed that Henry was Married, since he had certainly four sons, but it is not in my power to inform the Reader who was his Wife.[7] Be this as it may, he did not live for ever, but falling ill, his son the Prince of Wales came and took away the crown; whereupon the King made a long speech, for which I must refer the Reader to Shakespear's Plays, and the Prince made a still longer.[8] Things being thus settled between them the King died, and was succeeded by his Son Henry[9] who had previously beat Sir William Gascoigne.[10]

HENRY THE 5TH[11]

This Prince after he succeeded to the throne grew quite reformed and Amiable, forsaking all his dissipated Companions,[12] and never thrashing Sir William again. During his reign, Lord Cobham was burnt alive,[13] but I forget what for. His Majesty then turned his thoughts to France,[14] where he went and fought the famous Battle of Agincourt.[15] He afterwards married the King's daughter Catherine, a very agreable Woman by Shakespear's account.[16] Inspite of all this however he died, and was succeeded by his son Henry.[17]

HENRY THE 6TH

I cannot say much for this Monarch's Sense[18]—Nor would I if I could, for he was a Lancastrian. I suppose you know all about the Wars between him and the Duke of York who was of the right side;[19] if you do not, you had better read some other History, for I shall not be very diffuse in this, meaning by it only to vent my Spleen[20] *against*, and shew my Hatred *to* all those people whose parties or principles do not suit with mine, and not to give information. This King married Margaret of Anjou, a Woman whose distresses and Misfortunes were so great as almost to make me who hate her, pity her.[21] It was in this reign that Joan of Arc[22] lived and made such a *row*[23] among the English. They should not have burnt her— but they did. There were several Battles between the Yorkists and Lancastrians, in which the former (as they ought) usually conquered. At length they were entirely over come; The King was murdered[24]—The Queen was sent home—and Edward the 4th Ascended the Throne.[25]

EDWARD THE 4TH.[26]

This Monarch was famous only for his Beauty and his Courage, of which the Picture we have here given of him, and his undaunted Behaviour in marrying one Woman while he was engaged to another,[27] are sufficient proofs. His Wife was Elizabeth Woodville, a Widow who, poor Woman!, was afterwards confined in a Convent by that Monster of Iniquity and Avarice Henry the 7th.[28] One of Edward's Mistresses was

line 15: 'have' inserted above line.   //   line 23: 'here' inserted above line.   //   line 27: 'C' written over 'c' in 'Convent'.

Jane Shore, who has had a play written about her,[29] but it is a tragedy and therefore not worth reading. Having performed all these noble actions, his Majesty died, and was succeeded by his son.[30]

EDWARD THE 5TH

This unfortunate Prince lived so little a while that no body had time to draw his picture.[31] He was murdered by his Uncle's Contrivance, whose name was Richard the 3d.

RICHARD THE 3D

The Character of this Prince has been in general very severely treated by Historians, but as he was a *York*, I am rather inclined to suppose him a very respectable Man.[32] It has indeed been confidently asserted that he killed his two Nephews and his Wife, but it has also been declared the he did *not* kill his two Nephews, which I am inclined to beleive true;[33] and if this is the case, it may also be affirmed that he did not kill his Wife,[34] for if Perkin Warbeck[35] was really the Duke of York, why might not Lambert Simnel[36] be the Widow of Richard. Whether innocent or guilty, he did not reign long in peace, for Henry Tudor E. of Richmond as great a Villain as ever lived, made a great fuss about getting the Crown[37] and having killed the King at the battle of Bosworth,[38] he succeeded to it.[39]

HENRY THE 7TH[40]

This Monarch soon after his accession married the Princess Elizabeth of York;[41] by which alliance he plainly proved that he thought his own right inferior to hers, tho' he pretended to the contrary. By this Marriage he had two sons and two

line 15: 'two' inserted above line.   //   line 20: 'long' written over 'for ever'(?).

daughters, the elder of which Daughters was married to the King of Scotland and had the happiness of being grandmother to one of the first Characters in the World.[42] But of *her*, I shall have occasion to speak more at large in future. The Youngest, Mary, married first the King of France and secondly the D. of Suffolk, by whom she had one daughter, afterwards the Mother of Lady Jane Grey, who tho' inferior to her lovely Cousin the Queen of Scots, was yet an amiable young Woman and famous for reading Greek while other people were hunting.[43] It was in the reign of Henry the 7th that Perkin Warbeck and Lambert Simnel before mentioned made their appearance, the former of whom was set in the Stocks, took shelter in Beaulieu Abbey, and was beheaded with the Earl of Warwick, and the latter was taken into the King's Kitchen.[44] His Majesty died and was succeeded by his son Henry[45] whose only merit was his not being *quite* so bad as his daughter Elizabeth.

HENRY THE 8TH[46] —

It would be an affront to my Readers were I to suppose that they were not as well acquainted with the particulars of this King's reign as I am myself. It will therefore be saving *them* the task of reading again what they have read before, and *myself* the trouble of writing what I do not perfectly recollect, by giving only a slight sketch of the principal Events which marked his reign. Among these may be ranked Cardinal Wolsey's telling the father Abbott of Leicester Abbey that "he was come to lay his bones among them,"[47] the reformation in Religion, and the King's riding through the Streets of

line 12: 'which' deleted; 'whom' inserted above line.   //   line 17: 'Gran' deleted before 'daughter'.   //   line 19: 'It would be an' was originally written without leaving sufficient space for the portrait. JA then began the paragraph again a line below.   //   line 24: 'only' inserted above line.

London with Anna Bullen.[48] It is however but Justice, and my Duty to declare that this amiable Woman was entirely innocent of the Crimes with which she was accused,[49] of which her Beauty, her Elegance, and her Sprightliness were sufficient proofs, not to mention her solemn protestations of Innocence, the weakness of the Charges against her, and the King's Character; all of which add some confirmation, tho' perhaps slight ones when in comparison with those before alledged in her favour. Tho' I do not profess giving many dates, yet as I think it proper to give some and shall of course Make choice of those which it is most necessary for the Reader to know, I think it right to inform him that her letter to the King was dated on the 6th of May.[50] The Crimes and Cruelties of this Prince, were too numerous to be mentioned,[51] (as this history I trust has fully shewn;) and nothing can be said in his vindication, but that his abolishing Religious Houses[52] and leaving them to the ruinous depredations of time has been of infinite use to the landscape of England in general,[53] which probably was a principal motive for his doing it, since otherwise why should a Man who was of no Religion himself be at so much trouble to abolish one which had for Ages been established in the Kingdom. His Majesty's 5th Wife was the Duke of Norfolk's Neice who, tho' universally acquitted of the crimes for which she was beheaded, has been by many people supposed to have led an abandoned Life before her Marriage[54]—Of this however I have many doubts, since she was a relation of that noble Duke of Norfolk[55] who was so warm in the Queen of Scotland's cause, and who at last fell a victim to it. The King's last wife[56]

line 3: 'with which' inserted above line.   //   line 3: 'with' deleted after 'accused'; 'of' inserted above line and then deleted.   //   line 9: 'before' inserted above line.   //   line 23: '5' written over '4'.

contrived to survive him, but with difficulty effected it. He was succeeded by his only son Edward.

EDWARD THE 6TH

As this prince was only nine years old at the time of his Father's death, he was considered by many people as too young to govern, and the late King happening to be of the same opinion, his mother's Brother the Duke of Somerset[57] was chosen Protector of the realm during his minority. This Man was on the whole of a very amiable Character, and is somewhat of a favourite with me, tho' I would by no means pretend to affirm that he was equal to those first of Men Robert Earl of Essex, Delamere, or Gilpin.[58] He was beheaded, of which he might with reason have been proud, had he known that such was the death of Mary Queen of Scotland; but as it was impossible that he should be conscious of what had never happened, it does not appear that he felt particularly delighted with the manner of it. After his decease the Duke of Northumberland[59] had the care of the King and the Kingdom, and performed his trust of both so well that the King died[60] and the Kingdom was left to his daughter in law the Lady Jane Grey, who has been already mentioned as reading Greek. Whether she really understood that language or whether such a Study proceeded only from an excess of vanity[61] for which I beleive she was always rather remarkable, is uncertain. Whatever might be the cause, she preserved the same appearance of Knowledge, and contempt of what was generally esteemed pleasure, during the whole of her Life, for she declared herself displeased with being appointed Queen, and while conducting to the Scaffold, she

line 17: 'his death.' deleted; 'it.' inserted above line. // line 24: 'Cockylorum' deleted; 'vanity' inserted above line.

wrote a Sentence in Latin and another in Greek on seeing the dead Body of her Husband accidentally passing that
way.[62]

MARY

This Woman had the good luck of being advanced to the
throne of England, inspite of the Superior pretensions, Merit,
and *Beauty* of her Cousins Mary Queen of Scotland and Jane
Grey. Nor can I pity the Kingdom for the misfortunes they
experienced during her Reign, since they fully deserved them,
for having allowed her to succeed her Brother[63]—which was
a double peice of folly, since they might have foreseen that as
she died without Children, she would be succeeded by that
disgrace to humanity, that pest of society, Elizabeth. Many
were the people who fell Martyrs to the protestant Religion
during her reign; I suppose not fewer than a dozen.[64] She
married Philip King of Spain who in her Sister's reign was
famous for building Armadas.[65] She died without issue, and
then the dreadful moment came in which the destroyer of all
comfort, the deceitful Betrayer of trust reposed in her, and
the Murderess of her Cousin succeeded to the Throne.[66]—

ELIZABETH[67]—

It was the peculiar Misfortune of this Woman to have bad
Ministers—Since wicked as she herself was, she could not
have committed such extensive Mischeif, had not these vile
and abandoned Men connived at, and encouraged her in her
Crimes. I know that it has by many people been asserted
and beleived that Lord Burleigh, Sir Francis Walsingham,[68]
and the rest of those who filled the cheif Offices of State
were deserving, experienced, and able Ministers. But Oh!

line 17: 'was' is 'for' in ms.

how blinded such Writers and such Readers must be to true Merit, to Merit despised, neglected and defamed, if they can persist in such opinions when they reflect that these Men, these boasted Men were such Scandals to their Country and their Sex as to allow and assist their Queen in confining for the space of nineteen years, a *Woman* who if the claims of Relationship and Merit were of no avail, yet as a Queen and as one who condescended to place confidence in her, had every reason to expect Assistance and protection; and at length in allowing Elizabeth to bring this amiable Woman to an untimely, unmerited, and scandalous Death. Can any one if he reflects but for a moment on this blot, this ever-lasting blot upon their Understanding and their Character, allow any praise to Lord Burleigh or Sir Francis Walsingham? Oh! what must this bewitching Princess whose only freind was then the Duke of Norfolk, and whose only ones are now Mr Whitaker, Mrs Lefroy, Mrs Knight[69] and myself, who was abandoned by her Son,[70] confined by her Cousin, Abused, reproached and vilified by all, what must not her most noble Mind have suffered when informed that Eliza-beth had given orders for her Death! Yet she bore it with a most unshaken fortitude; firm in her Mind; Constant in her Religion; and prepared herself to meet the cruel fate to which she was doomed, with a magnanimity that could alone pro-ceed from conscious Innocence. And Yet could you Reader have beleived it possible that some hardened and zealous Protestants have even abused her for that Steadfastness in the Catholic Religion which reflected on her so much credit? But this is a striking proof of *their* narrow Souls and prejudiced Judgements who accuse her. She was executed in the Great

line 6: repetition of 'the' before 'claims' deleted.   //   line 30: 'She' written over 'I'.

Hall at Fotheringay Castle! (sacred Place!) on Wednesday the 8th of February—1586[71]—to the everlasting Reproach of Elizabeth, her Ministers, and of England in general. It may not be unnecessary before I entirely conclude my account of this ill-fated Queen, to observe that she had been accused of several crimes during the time of her reigning in Scotland, of which I now most seriously do assure my Reader that she was entirely innocent; having never been guilty of anything more than Imprudencies into which she was betrayed by the openness of her Heart, her Youth, and her Education. Having I trust by this assurance entirely done away every Suspicion and every doubt which might have arisen in the Reader's mind, from what other Historians have written of her, I shall proceed to mention the remaining Events, that marked Elizabeth's reign. It was about this time that Sir Francis Drake the first English Navigator who sailed round the World,[72] lived, to be the ornament of his Country and his profession. Yet great as he was, and justly celebrated as a Sailor, I cannot help foreseeing that he will be equalled in this or the next Century by one who tho' now but young,[73] already promises to answer all the ardent and sanguine expectations of his Relations and Freinds, amongst whom I may class the amiable Lady to whom this work is dedicated, and my no less amiable Self.

Though of a different profession, and shining in a different Sphere of Life, yet equally conspicuous in the Character of an *Earl*, as Drake was in that of a *Sailor*, was Robert Devereux Lord Essex. This unfortunate young Man was not unlike in Character to that equally unfortunate one *Frederic Delamere*.[74] The simile may be carried still farther, and

---

line 1: 'on Wednesday' written over two or three illegible words.   //   line 20: 'the' inserted above line.   //   line 20: 'now' inserted above line.

Elizabeth the torment of Essex may be compared to the Emmeline of Delamere. It would be endless to recount the misfortunes of this noble and gallant Earl. It is sufficient to say that he was beheaded on the 25th of Febry,[75] after having been Lord Leuitenant of Ireland, after having clapped his hand on his Sword,[76] and after performing many other services to his Country. Elizabeth did not long survive his loss,[77] and died *so* miserable that were it not an injury to the memory of Mary I should pity her.

JAMES THE IST

Though this King had some faults, among which and as the most principal, was his allowing his Mother's death,[78] yet considered on the whole I cannot help liking him. He married Anne of Denmark,[79] and had several Children; fortunately for him his eldest son Prince Henry died before his father[80] or he might have experienced the evils which befell his unfortunate Brother.

As I am myself partial to the roman catholic religion,[81] it is with infinite regret that I am obliged to blame the Behaviour of any Member of it; yet Truth being I think very excusable in an Historian, I am necessitated to say that in this reign the roman Catholics of England did not behave like Gentlemen to the protestants. Their Behaviour indeed to the Royal Family and both Houses of Parliament might justly be considered by them as very uncivil, and even Sir Henry Percy tho' certainly the best bred Man of the party, had none of that general politeness which is so universally pleasing, as his Attentions were entirely Confined to Lord Mounteagle.[82]

Sir Walter Raleigh flourished in this and the preceding reign, and is by many people held in great veneration and respect—But as he was an enemy of the noble Essex, I have nothing to say in praise of him, and must refer all those who may wish to be acquainted with the particulars of his Life, to Mr Sheridan's play of the Critic, where they will find many interesting Anecdotes as well of him as of his freind Sir Christopher Hatton.[83]—His Majesty was of that amiable disposition which inclines to Freindships, and in such points was possessed of a keener penetration[84] in Discovering Merit than many other people. I once heard an excellent Sharade[85] on a Carpet, of which the subject I am now on reminds me, and as I think it may afford my Readers some Amusement to *find it out*, I shall here take the liberty of presenting it to them.

Sharade

My first is what my second was to King James the 1st, and you tread on my whole.

The principal favourites of his Majesty were Car, who was afterwards created Earl of Somerset and whose name perhaps may have some share in the above-mentioned Sharade,[86] and George Villiers afterwards Duke of Buckingham.[87] On his Majesty's death he was succeeded by his son Charles.

CHARLES THE IST[88]

This amiable Monarch seems born to have suffered Misfortunes equal to those of his lovely Grandmother;[89] Misfortunes which he could not deserve since he was her descendant. Never certainly were there before so many detestable Characters at one time in England as in this period of its History; Never were amiable Men so Scarce. The number of them throughout the whole Kingdom amounting only to *five*, besides the inhabitants of Oxford who were always loyal to their King and faithful to his interests. The names of this noble five who never forgot the duty of the Subject, or swerved from their attachment to his Majesty, were as follows—The King himself, ever stedfast in his own support—Archbishop Laud, Earl of Strafford, Viscount Faulkland and Duke of Ormond,[90] who were scarcely less strenuous or zealous in the cause. While the *Villains* of the time would make too long a list to be written or read; I shall therefore content myself with mentioning the leaders of the Gang. Cromwell, Fairfax, Hampden, and Pym[91] may be considered as the original Causers of all the disturbances, Distresses, and Civil Wars in which England for many years was embroiled. In this reign as well as in that of Elizabeth, I am obliged in spite of my Attachment to the Scotch,[92] to consider them as equally guilty with the generality of the English, since they dared to think differently from their Sovereign, to forget the Adoration which as *Stuarts* it was their Duty to pay them, to rebel against, dethrone and imprison the unfortunate Mary; to oppose, to deceive, and to sell the no less unfortunate Charles. The Events of this Monarch's reign are too numerous for my pen, and indeed the recital of any Events (except what I make myself) is uninteresting to me; my principal reason for undertaking the History of England being to prove the innocence of the Queen of Scotland, which I flatter myself with having effectually done, and to abuse Elizabeth, tho' I am rather fearful of having fallen short in the latter part of my Scheme.—. As therefore it is not my intention to give any particular account of the distresses into which this King was involved through the misconduct and Cruelty of his Parliament, I shall satisfy myself with vindicating him from the Reproach of Arbitrary and tyrannical Government with which he has often been Charged. This, I feel, is not difficult to be done, for with one argument I am certain of satisfying

line 8: 'all' deleted after 'be'.   //   line 19: 'tedious' deleted; 'uninteresting' inserted above line.

every sensible and well disposed person whose opinions have been properly guided by a good Education—and this Argument is that he was a **Stuart**.

FINIS
Saturday Nov. 26th 1791

To Miss Cooper[1]—

Cousin

Conscious of the Charming Character which in every Country, and every Clime[2] in Christendom is Cried, Concerning you, With Caution and Care I Commend to your Charitable Criticism this Clever Collection of Curious[3] Comments, which have been Carefully Culled, Collected and Classed by your Comical Cousin[4]

The Author.

line 2: 'Cousin' written over an illegible word.   //   line 4: 'ry' written over 'y' in 'Country'.   //   line 6: 'Criticism' written over 'Critics' (?).   //   line 6: 'Clever' written over 'Short'.

A Collection of Letters—

From a Mother to her freind.

My Children begin now to claim all my attention in a different Manner from that in which they have been used to receive it, as they are now arrived at that age when it is necessary for them in some measure to become conversant with the World. My Augusta is 17 and her Sister scarcely a twelvemonth younger. I flatter myself that their education has been such as will not disgrace their appearance in the World,[5] and that *they* will not disgrace their Education I have every reason to beleive. Indeed they are sweet Girls—. Sensible yet unaffected—Accomplished yet Easy—. Lively yet Gentle—. As their progress in every thing they have learnt has been always the same, I am willing to forget the difference of age, and to introduce them together into Public.[6] This very Evening is fixed on as their first entrée into Life, as we are to drink tea with Mrs Cope and her Daughter. I am glad that we are to meet no one for my Girls sake, as it would be awkward for them to enter too wide a Circle on the very first day. But we shall proceed by degrees—. Tomorrow Mr Stanly's family will drink tea with us, and perhaps the Miss Phillips's will meet them. On Tuesday we shall pay Morning-Visits[7]—On

line 4: 'to' deleted; 'from' inserted above line.   //   line 21: 'tea' inserted above line.

Wednesday we are to dine at Westbrook.[8] On Thursday we have Company at home. On Friday we are to be at a private Concert at Sir John Wynne's—and on Saturday we expect Miss Dawson to call in the Morning—which will complete my Daughters Introduction into Life. How they will bear so much dissipation I cannot imagine; of their Spirits I have no fear, I only dread their health.

———

This mighty affair is now happily over, and my Girls *are out*.[9]—As the moment approached for our departure, you can have no idea how the sweet Creatures trembled with fear and Expectation. Before the Carriage drove to the door, I called them into my dressing-room, and as soon as they were seated thus addressed them. "My dear Girls the moment is now arrived when I am to reap the rewards of all my Anxieties and Labours towards you during your Education. You are this Evening to enter a World in which you will meet with many wonderfull Things; Yet let me warn you against suffering yourselves to be meanly swayed by the Follies and Vices of others, for believe me my beloved Children that if you do——I shall be very sorry for it." They both assured me that they would ever remember my Advice with Gratitude, and follow it with Attention; That they were prepared to find a World full of things to amaze and to shock them: but that they trusted their behaviour would never give me reason to repent the Watchful Care with which I had presided over their infancy[10] and formed their Minds—"With such expectations and such intentions (cried I) I can have nothing to fear from you—and can chearfully conduct you to Mrs Cope's without a fear of your being

line 12: 'Expectation' written over 'Apprehension'. // line 23: 'at' deleted after 'with'.

seduced by her Example, or contaminated by her Follies. Come, then my Children (added I) the Carriage is driving to the door, and I will not a moment delay the happiness you are so impatient to enjoy." When we arrived at Warleigh,[11] poor Augusta could scarcely breathe, while Margaret was all Life and Rapture. "The long-expected Moment is now arrived (said she) and we shall soon be in the World."—In a few Moments we were in Mrs Cope's parlour—, where with her daughter she sate ready to receive us. I observed with delight the impression my Children made on them—. They were indeed two sweet, elegant-looking Girls, and tho' somewhat abashed from the peculiarity of their Situation, Yet there was an ease in their Manners and Address which could not fail of pleasing—. Imagine my dear Madam how delighted I must have been in beholding as I did, how attentively they observed every object they saw, how disgusted with some Things, how enchanted with others, how astonished at all! On the whole however they returned in raptures with the World, its Inhabitants, and Manners.

Yrs Ever—A—F—.

LETTER THE SECOND

From a Young Lady crossed in Love to her freind—

Why should this last disappointment hang so heavily on my Spirits? Why should I feel it more, why should it wound me deeper than those I have experienced before? Can it be that I have a greater affection for Willoughby[12] than I had for his amiable predecessors—? Or is it that our feelings become more acute from being often wounded? I must suppose my

---

line 1: 'contaminated' deleted; 'seduced' inserted above line.   //   line 1: 'contaminated by' inserted above line.   //   line 14: 'must' written over 'have'.   //   line 23: 'heavy' changed to 'heavily'.

dear Belle[13] that this is the Case, since I am not conscious of being more sincerely attached to Willoughby than I was to Neville, Fitzowen, or either of the Crawfords, for all of whom I once felt the most lasting affection that ever warmed a Woman's heart. Tell me then dear Belle why I still sigh when I think of the faithless Edward, or why I weep when I behold his Bride?, for too surely this is the case—. My Freinds are all alarmed for me; They fear my declining health; they lament my want of Spirits; they dread the effects of both. In hopes of releiving my Melancholy,[14] by directing my thoughts to other objects, they have invited several of their freinds to spend the Christmas with us. Lady Bridget Dashwood and her Sister-in-Law Miss Jane are expected on Friday; and Colonel Seaton's family will be with us next week. This is all most kindly meant by my Uncle and Cousins; but what can the presence of a dozen indifferent people do to me; but weary and distress me—. I will not finish my Letter till some of our Visitors are arrived.

———————

Friday Evening—

Lady Bridget came this Morning, and with her, her sweet Sister[15] Miss Jane—. Although I have been acquainted with this charming Woman above fifteen Years, Yet I never before observed how lovely she is. She is now about 35, and in spite of sickness, Sorrow and Time is more blooming than I ever saw a Girl of 17. I was delighted with her, the moment she entered the house, and she appeared equally pleased with me, attaching herself to me during the remainder of the day. There is something so sweet, so mild in her Countenance, that she seems more than Mortal. Her Conversation is as bewitching as her appearance—; I could not help telling her how much

line 15: 'by' written over 'in'.

she engaged my Admiration—. "Oh! Miss Jane (said I)—and stopped from an inability at the moment of expressing myself as I could wish—"Oh! Miss Jane—(I repeated)—I could not think of words to suit my feelings—. She seemed waiting for my Speech—. I was confused—distressed—My thoughts were bewildered—and I could only add—"How do you do?" She saw and felt for my Embarrassment and with admirable presence of mind releived me from it by saying—"My dear Sophia be not uneasy at having exposed Yourself—I will turn the Conversation without appearing to notice it." Oh! how I loved her for her kindness! "Do you ride as much as you used to do?" said she—. "I am advised to ride by my Physician,[16] We have delightful Rides round us, I have a Charming horse, am uncommonly fond of the Amusement," replied I quite recovered from my Confusion, "and in short I ride a great deal." "You are in the right my Love," said She, Then repeating the following Line which was an extempore and equally adapted to recommend both Riding and Candour—

"Ride where you may, Be Candid where You can,"[17] She added, "*I* rode once, but it is many years ago"—She spoke this in so Low and tremulous a Voice, that I was silent— Struck with her Manner of Speaking I could make no reply. "I have not ridden, continued she fixing her Eyes on my face, since I was married."

I was never so surprised—"Married, Ma'am!" I repeated. "You may well wear that look of astonishment, said she, since what I have said must appear improbable to you—Yet nothing is more true than that I once was married."

"Then why are you called Miss Jane?"

"I married, my Sophia without the consent or knowledge of my father the late Admiral Annesley. It was therefore

line 16–17: 'repeating' written over 'repeated'.   //   line 30: 'or knowledge' written over 'of my'.

necessary to keep the Secret from him and from every one, till some fortunate opportunity might offer of revealing it—. Such an opportunity alas! was but too soon given in the death of my dear Capt. Dashwood—Pardon these tears, continued Miss Jane wiping her Eyes, I owe them to my Husband's Memory. He fell my Sophia, while fighting for his Country in America[18] after a most happy Union of seven Years—. My Children, two sweet Boys and a Girl, who had constantly resided with my Father and me, passing with him and with every one as the Children of a Brother (tho' I had ever been an only Child) had as yet been the Comforts of my Life. But no sooner had I lossed my Henry, than these sweet Creatures fell sick and died—. Conceive dear Sophia what my feelings must have been when as an Aunt I attended my Children to their early Grave—. My Father did not survive them many weeks—He died, poor Good old Man, happily ignorant to his last hour of my Marriage."

"But did not you own it, and assume his name at your husband's death?"

"No; I could not bring myself to do it; more especially when in my Children I lost all inducement for doing it. Lady Bridget, and Yourself are the only persons who are in the knowledge of my having ever been either Wife or Mother. As I could not prevail on myself to take the name of Dashwood (a name which after my Henry's death I could never hear without emotion) and as I was conscious of having no right to that of Annesley, I dropt all thoughts of either,[19] and have made it a point of bearing only my Christian one since my Father's death." She paused—"Oh! my dear Miss Jane (said I) how infinitely am I obliged to you for so entertaining a

line 5: 'my' deleted; 'her' inserted above line.   //   line 27: 'have' inserted above line.

Story! You cannot think how it has diverted me! But have you quite done?"

"I have only to add my dear Sophia, that my Henry's elder Brother dieing about the same time, Lady Bridget became a Widow like myself,[20] and as we had always loved each other in idea from the high Character in which we had ever been spoken of, though we had never met, we determined to live together.[21] We wrote to one another on the same subject by the same post, so exactly did our feelings and our Actions coincide! We both eagerly embraced the proposals we gave and received of becoming one family, and have from that time lived together in the greatest affection."

"And is this all?" said I, "I hope you have not done."

"Indeed I have; and did you ever hear a Story more pathetic?"

"I never did—and it is for that reason it pleases me so much, for when one is unhappy nothing is so delightful to one's Sensations as to hear of equal Misery."

"Ah! but my Sophia why *are you* unhappy?"

"Have you not heard Madam of Willoughby's Marriage?" "But my Love why lament *his* perfidy, when you bore so well that of many young Men before?" "Ah! Madam, I was used to it then, but when Willoughby broke his Engagements I had not been dissapointed for half a year." "Poor Girl!" said Miss Jane.

LETTER THE THIRD

From A young Lady in distress'd Circumstances to her freind.

A few days ago I was at a private Ball given by Mr Ashburnham. As my Mother never goes out she entrusted me to the care of Lady Greville who did me the honour of calling for me in her way[22] and of allowing me to sit forwards,[23]

which is a favour about which I am very indifferent especially as I know it is considered as confering a great obligation on me. "So Miss Maria (said her Ladyship as she
saw me advancing to the door of the Carriage) you seem
very smart to night—*My* poor Girls will appear quite to disadvantage by *you*—I only hope your Mother may not have
distressed herself to set *you* off. Have you got a new Gown
on?"

"Yes Ma'am." replied I, with as much indifference as I
could assume.

"Aye, and a fine one too I think—(feeling it, as by her permission I seated myself by her) I dare say it is all very smart—
But I must own, for you know I always speak my mind, that
I think it was quite a needless peice of expence—Why could
not you have worn your old striped one?[24] It is not my way to
find fault with people because they are poor, for I always think
that they are more to be despised and pitied than blamed for
it, especially if they cannot help it, but at the same time I
must say that in my opinion your old striped Gown would
have been quite fine enough for its wearer—for to tell you the
truth (I always speak my mind) I am very much afraid that one
half of the people in the room will not know whether you have
a Gown on or not—But I suppose you intend to make your
fortune tonight—: Well, the sooner the better; and I wish you
success."

"Indeed Ma'am I have no such intention—"

"Who ever heard a Young Lady own that she was a
Fortune-hunter?" Miss Greville laughed, but I am sure Ellen
felt for me.[25]

---

line 1: 'for' deleted; 'about' inserted above line. // line 7: 'herself' written
over 'yourself'. // line 15: 'you' inserted above line. // line 16:
'because' deleted; 'for' inserted above line. // line 28: 'Ellen' written over
'Fanny' here and throughout the ms.

"Was your Mother gone to bed before you left her?" said her Ladyship—

"Dear Ma'am," said Ellen "it is but nine o'clock."

"True Ellen, but Candles cost money,[26] and Mrs Williams is too wise to be extravagant."

"She was just sitting down to supper Ma'am—"

"And what had she got for Supper?" "I did not observe." "Bread and Cheese[27] I suppose." "I should never wish for a better supper." said Ellen. "You have never any reason" replied her Mother, "as a better is always provided for you." Miss Greville laughed excessively, as she constantly does at her Mother's wit.

Such is the humiliating Situation in which I am forced to appear while riding in her Ladyship's Coach—I dare not be impertinent, as my Mother is always admonishing me to be humble and patient if I wish to make my way in the world. She insists on my accepting every invitation of Lady Greville, or you may be certain that I would never enter either her House, or her Coach, with the disagreable certainty I always have of being abused for my Poverty while I am in them.—When we arrived at Ashburnham,[28] it was nearly ten o'clock, which was an hour and a half later than we were desired to be there; but Lady Greville is too fashionable (or fancies herself to be so) to be punctual.[29] The Dancing however was not begun as they waited for Miss Greville. I had not been long in the room before I was engaged to dance by Mr Bernard, but just as we were going to stand up, he recollected that his Servant had got his white Gloves;[30] and immediately ran out to fetch them. In the mean time the Dancing began and Lady Greville in passing to another room went exactly before me—She saw me and instantly stopping, said to me though there were several people close to us;

"Hey day, Miss Maria! What cannot you get a partner?[31] Poor Young Lady! I am afraid your new Gown was put on for nothing. But do not despair; perhaps you may get a hop[32] before the Evening is over." So saying, she passed on without hearing my repeated assurance of being engaged, and leaving me very much provoked at being so exposed before every one—Mr Bernard however soon returned and by coming to me the moment he entered the room, and leading me to the Dancers my Character I hope was cleared from the imputation Lady Greville had thrown on it, in the eyes of all the old Ladies who had heard her speech. I soon forgot all my vexations in the pleasure of dancing and of having the most agreable partner in the room. As he is moreover heir to a very large Estate I could see that Lady Greville did not look very well pleased when she found who had been his Choice— She was determined to mortify me, and accordingly when we were sitting down between the dances, she came to me with *more* than her usual insulting importance attended by Miss Mason and said loud enough to be heard by half the people in the room, "Pray Miss Maria in what way of business was your Grandfather? for Miss Mason and I cannot agree whether he was a Grocer or a Bookbinder."[33] I saw that she wanted to mortify me, and was resolved if I possibly could to prevent her seeing that her scheme succeeded. "Neither Madam; he was a Wine Merchant."[34] "Aye, I knew he was in some such low way—He broke[35] did not he?" "I beleive not Ma'am." "Did not he abscond?" "I never heard that he did." "At least he died insolvent?" "I was never told so before." "Why, was not your Father as poor as a Rat?"[36] "I fancy not," "Was not he in

---

line 12: 'having' inserted above line.   //   line 28: 'Why, was' written over two or three illegible words.   //   line 29: 'but your Ladyship knows best' deleted after first 'not'.

the Kings Bench[37] once?" "I never saw him there." She gave me *such* a look, and turned away in a great passion; while I was half delighted with myself for my impertinence, and half afraid of being thought too saucy.[38] As Lady Greville was extremely angry with me, she took no further notice of me all the Evening, and indeed had I been in favour I should have been equally neglected, as she was got into a party of great folks and she never speaks to me when she can to anyone else. Miss Greville was with her Mother's party at Supper, but Ellen preferred staying with the Bernards and me. We had a very pleasant Dance and as Lady G— slept all the way home, I had a very comfortable ride.

The next day while we were at dinner Lady Greville's Coach stopped at the door, for that is the time of day she generally contrives it should. She sent in a message by the Servant to say that "she should not get out but that Miss Maria must come to the Coach-door, as she wanted to speak to her, and that she must make haste and come immediately—" "What an impertinent Message Mama!" said I—"Go Maria—" replied She—Accordingly I went and was obliged to stand there at her Ladyships pleasure though the Wind was extremely high and very cold.[39]

"Why I think Miss Maria you are not quite so smart as you were last night—But I did not come to examine your dress, but to tell you that you may dine with us the day after tomorrow—Not tomorrow, remember, do not come tomorrow, for we expect Lord and Lady Clermont and Sir Thomas Stanley's family—There will be no occasion for your being very fine for I shant send the Carriage—If it rains you may

line 1: one line heavily deleted: 'Just as your Ladyship pleases—it is the same to me.'; 'I never saw him there.' inserted above line. // line 4: 'having' deleted after 'of'. // line 4: 'saucy' written over 'much so'.

take an umbrella[40]—"I could hardly help laughing at hearing her give me leave to keep myself dry—"And pray remember to be in time, for I shant wait—I hate my Victuals over-done—But you need not come *before* the time—How does your Mother do—? She is at dinner is not she?" "Yes Ma'am we were in the middle of dinner when your Ladyship came." "I am afraid you find it very cold Maria." said Ellen. "Yes, it is an horrible East wind—said her Mother—I assure you I can hardly bear the window down—But you are used to be blown about by the wind Miss Maria and that is what has made your Complexion so ruddy and coarse.[41] You young Ladies who cannot often ride in a Carriage never mind what weather you trudge in, or how the wind shews your legs.[42] I would not have *my* Girls stand out of doors as you do in such a day as this. But some sort of people have no feelings either of cold or Delicacy—Well, remember that we shall expect you on Thursday at 5 o'clock—You must tell your Maid to come for you at night—There will be no Moon[43]—and You will have an horrid walk home—My Comps to your Mother—I am afraid your dinner will be cold—Drive on—"And away she went, leaving me in a great passion with her as she always does.

Maria Williams

LETTER THE FOURTH

From a young Lady rather impertinent to her freind.

We dined yesterday with Mr Evelyn where we were intro-duced to a very agreable looking Girl his Cousin. I was extremely pleased with her appearance, for added to the charms of an engaging face, her manner and voice had

line 11: 'u' changed to 'a' in 'coarse'.   //   line 13: 'legs' written over 'Ancles'.   //   line 15: a triple revision: 'your sort' changed to 'low', then 'odd'(?), and then 'some sort'.   //   line 19–20: 'I am afraid' written over 'Drive on' (?)

something peculiarly interesting in them. So much so, that they inspired me with a great curiosity to know the history of her Life, who were her Parents, where she came from, and what had befallen her,[44] for it was then only known that she was a relation of Mr Evelyn, and that her name was Grenville. In the evening a favourable opportunity offered to me of attempting at least to know what I wished to know, for every one played at Cards but Mrs Evelyn, My Mother, Dr Drayton, Miss Grenville and myself, and as the two former were engaged in a whispering Conversation,[45] and the Doctor fell asleep, we were of necessity obliged to entertain each other. This was what I wished and being determined not to remain in ignorance for want of asking, I began the Conversation in the following Manner.

"Have you been long in Essex Ma'am?"

"I arrived on Tuesday."

"You came from Derbyshire?"

"No Ma'am—! appearing surprised at my question, from Suffolk."[46] You will think this a good dash[47] of mine my dear Mary, but you know that I am not wanting for Impudence when I have any end in veiw. "Are you pleased with the Country Miss Grenville? Do you find it equal to the one you have left?"

"Much Superior Ma'am in point of Beauty." She sighed. I longed to know for why.

"But the face of any Country however beautiful said I, can be but a poor consolation for the loss of one's dearest Freinds." She shook her head, as if she felt the truth of what I said. My Curiosity was so much raised, that I was resolved at any rate to satisfy it.

"You regret having left Suffolk then Miss Grenville?" "Indeed I do." "You were born there I suppose?" "Yes Ma'am I was and passed many happy years there—"

"That is a great comfort—" said I—"I hope Ma'am that you never spent any *un*happy one's there?"

"Perfect Felicity is not the property of Mortals, and no one has a right to expect uninterrupted Happiness.—*Some* Misfortunes I have certainly met with—"

"*What* Misfortunes dear Ma'am? replied I, burning with impatience to know every thing. "*None* Ma'am I hope that have been the effect of any wilfull fault in me." "I dare say not Ma'am, and have no doubt but that any sufferings you may have experienced could arise only from the cruelties of Relations or the Errors of Freinds." She sighed—"You seem unhappy my dear Miss Grenville—Is it in my power to soften your Misfortunes?" "*Your* power Ma'am replied she extremely surprised; it is in *no ones* power to make me happy." She pronounced these words in so mournfull and Solemn an accent, that for some time I had not courage to reply—I was actually silenced. I recovered myself however in a few moments and looking at her with all the affection I could, "My dear Miss Grenville said I you appear extremely young—and may probably stand in need of some one's advice whose regard for you, joined to superior Age, perhaps superior Judgement might authorise her to give it—. I am that person, and I now challenge you to accept the offer I make you of my Confidence and Freindship, in return to which I shall only ask for yours—"

"You are extremely obliging Ma'am—said She—and I am highly flattered by your attention to me—. But I am in no difficulty, no doubt, no uncertainty of situation in which any Advice can be wanted. Whenever I am however continued

line 4: 'Felicity' deleted; 'Happiness.' inserted above line. // line 10: 'arise' written over 'arrise'. // line 17: 'Could you have beleived it Mary?' deleted after 'silenced'.

she brightening into a complaisant Smile, I shall know where to apply."

I bowed, but felt a good deal mortified by such a repulse; Still however I had not given up my point. I found that by the appearance of Sentiment and Freindship nothing was to be gained and determined therefore to renew my Attacks by Questions and Suppositions.

"Do you intend staying long in this part of England Miss Grenville?"

"Yes Ma'am, some time I beleive."

"But how will Mr and Mrs Grenville bear your Absence?"

"They are neither of them alive Ma'am."

This was an answer I did not expect—I was quite silenced, and never felt so awkward in my Life—.

LETTER THE FIFTH

From a Young Lady very much in love to her Freind.

My Uncle gets more Stingy,[48] my Aunt more particular,[49] and I more in love every day. What shall we all be at this rate by the end of the year! I had this morning the happiness of receiving the following Letter from my dear Musgrove.

Sackville St.[50] Janry. 7th

It is a month to day since I first beheld my lovely Henrietta, and the sacred anniversary must and shall be kept in a manner becoming the day—by writing to her. Never shall I forget the moment when her Beauties first broke on my sight—No time as you well know[51] can erase it from my Memory. It was at Lady Scudamores. Happy Lady Scudamore to live within a mile of the divine Henrietta! When the lovely Creature first entered the room, Oh! what were

line 11: 'during a long stay in Essex' deleted after 'Absence'. // line 29: 'were' inserted above line.

my sensations? The sight of you was like the sight of a wonderful fine Thing. I started—I gazed at her with Admiration—She appeared every moment more Charming, and the unfortunate Musgrove became a Captive to your Charms before I had time to look about me. Yes Madam, I had the happiness of adoring you, an happiness for which I cannot be too grateful. "What said he to himself is Musgrove allowed to die for Henrietta,? Enviable Mortal,! and may he pine for her who is the object of universal Admiration, who is adored by a Colonel, and toasted[52] by a Baronet!—Adorable Henrietta how beautiful you are! I declare you are quite divine! You are more than Mortal. You are an Angel. You are Venus herself. Inshort Madam you are the prettiest Girl I ever saw in my Life—and her Beauty is encreased in her Musgrove's Eyes, by permitting him to love her and allowing me to hope. And Ah! Angelic Miss Henrietta Heaven is my Witness how ardently I do hope for the death of your villanous Uncle and his Abandoned[53] Wife, Since my fair one, will not consent to be mine till their decease has placed her in affluence above what my fortune can procure—. Though it is an improvable Estate[54]—. Cruel Henrietta to persist in such a resolution! I am at present with my Sister where I mean to continue till my own house which tho' an excellent one is at present somewhat out of repair, is ready to receive me. Amiable princess of my Heart farewell—Of that Heart which trembles while it signs itself your most ardent Admirer

and devoted humble Servt.[55]

T. Musgrove [56]

line 18: 'one,' inserted above line.   //   line 23: 'House' deleted; 'one' inserted above line.   //   line 25: Repetition of 'Of' deleted.   //   line 28: three and a half lines following signature deleted: 'May I hope to receive an answer to this e'er many days have tortured me with Suspence! Any Letter (post paid) will be most welcome.'

There is a pattern for a Love-letter[57] Matilda! Did you ever read such a masterpeice of Writing? Such Sense, Such Sentiment, Such purity of Thought, Such flow of Language and such unfeigned Love in one Sheet? No, never I can answer for it, since a Musgrove is not to be met with by every Girl. Oh! how I long to be with him! I intend to send him the following in answer to his Letter tomorrow.

My dearest Musgrove—. Words cannot express how happy your Letter made me; I thought I should have cried for Joy, for I love you better than any body in the World. I think you the most amiable, and the handsomest Man in England, and so to be sure you are. I never read so sweet a Letter in my Life. Do write me another just like it, and tell me you are in love with me in every other line. I quite die to see you. How shall we manage to see one another—? for we are so much in love that we cannot live asunder. Oh! my dear Musgrove you cannot think how impatiently I wait for the death of my Uncle and Aunt—If they will not die soon, I beleive I shall run mad,[58] for I get more in love with you every day of my Life.[59] How happy your Sister is to enjoy the pleasure of your Company in her house, and how happy every body in London must be because you are there. I hope you will be so kind as to write to me again soon, for I never read such sweet Letters as yours. I am my dearest Musgrove most truly and faithfully Yours for ever and ever

Henrietta Halton—

I hope he will like my answer; it is as good a one as I can write though nothing to his; Indeed I had always heard what a dab[60] he was at a Love-letter. I saw him you know for the first time at Lady Scudamore's—And when I saw her

line 20: two and a half lines heavily deleted after 'Life': 'How fond we shall be of one another when we are married! oh, do not you long for the time?' (?).

Ladyship afterwards she asked me how I liked her Cousin Musgrove?

"Why upon my word said I, I think he is a very handsome young Man."

"I am glad you think so replied she, for he is distractedly in love with you."

"Law! Lady Scudamore said I, how can you talk so ridiculously?"

"Nay, 'tis very true answered She, I assure you, for he was in love with you from the first moment he beheld you."

"I wish it may be true said I, for that is the only kind of love I would give a farthing for[61]—There is some Sense in being in love at first sight."[62]

"Well, I give you Joy of your conquest, replied Lady Scudamore, "and I beleive it to have been a very complete one; I am sure it is not a contemptible one, for my Cousin is a charming young fellow, has seen a great deal of the World, and writes the best Love-letters I ever read."

This made me very happy, and I was excessively pleased with my conquest. However I thought it was proper to give myself a few Airs—. So I said to her—

"This is all very pretty Lady Scudamore, but you know that we young Ladies who are Heiresses must not throw ourselves away upon Men who have no fortune at all."

"My dear Miss Halton said She, I am as much convinced of that as you can be, and I do assure you that I should be the last person to encourage your marrying any one who had not some pretensions to expect a fortune with you. Mr Musgrove is so far from being poor that he has an estate of Several hundreds an year[63] which is capable of great Improvement,

line 21: 'proper' written over 'best'.

and an excellent House, though at present it is not quite in repair."

"If that is the case replied I, I have nothing more to say against him, and if as you say he is an informed young Man and can write good Love-letters, I am sure I have no reason to find fault with him for admiring me, tho' perhaps I may not marry him for all that Lady Scudamore."

"You are certainly under no obligation to marry him answered her Ladyship, except that which love himself will dictate to you, for if I am not greatly mistaken You are at this very moment unknown to yourself, cherishing a most tender affection for him."

"Law, Lady Scudamore replied I blushing how can you think of such a thing?"

"Because every look, every word betrays it, answered She; "Come my dear Henrietta, consider me as a freind, and be sincere with me—Do not you prefer Mr Musgrove to any man of your acquaintance?"

"Pray do not ask me such questions Lady Scudamore, said I turning away my head, for it is not fit for me to answer them."

"Nay my Love replied she, now you confirm my suspicions. But why Henrietta should you be ashamed to own a well-placed Love, or why refuse to confide in me?"

"I am not ashamed to own it; said I taking Courage. I do not refuse to confide in you or blush to say that I do love your cousin Mr Musgrove, that I am sincerely attached to him, for it is no disgrace to love a handsome Man. If he were plain indeed I might have had reason to be ashamed of a passion which must have been mean since the Object would have been unworthy. But with such a figure and face, and

line 5: 'a' deleted after 'write'.

such beautiful hair as your Cousin has, why should I blush to own that such Superior Merit has made an impression on me."

"My Sweet Girl (said Lady Scudamore embracing me with great Affection) what a delicate way of thinking you have in these Matters, and what a quick discernment for one of your years! Oh! how I honour you for such Noble Sentiments!"

"Do you Ma'am,? said I; You are vastly obliging. But pray Lady Scudamore did your Cousin himself tell you of his Affection for me? I shall like him the better if he did, for what is a Lover without a Confidante?"

"Oh! my Love replied She, you were born for each other. Every word you say more deeply convinces me that your Minds are actuated by the invisible power of simpathy, for your opinions and Sentiments so exactly coincide. Nay, the colour of your Hair is not very different. Yes my dear Girl, the poor despairing Musgrove did reveal to me the story of his Love—. Nor was I surprised at it—I know not how it was, but I had a kind of presentiment that he *would* be in love with you."

"Well, but how did he break it to you?"

"It was not till after Supper. We were sitting round the fire together talking on indifferent Subjects, though to say the truth the Conversation was cheifly on my side for he was thoughtful and silent, when on a Sudden he interrupted me in the midst of something I was saying, by exclaiming in a most Theatrical tone—

Yes I'm in love I feel it now

And Henrietta Halton has undone me[64]—"

"Oh! What a sweet Way replied I, of declaring his Passion! To make such a couple of charming Lines about me! What a pity it is that they are not in rhime!"[65]

"I am very glad you like it answered She; To be sure there was a great deal of Taste in it. And are you in love with her, Cousin?, said I, I am very sorry for it, for unexceptionable as you are in every respect, with a pretty Estate capable of Great improvements, and an excellent House tho' somewhat out of repair, Yet who can hope to aspire with Success to the adorable Henrietta who has had an offer from a Colonel and been toasted by a Baronet—" "*That* I have—" cried I. Lady Scudamore continued. "Ah dear Cousin replied he, I am so well convinced of the little Chance I can have of winning her who is adored by thousands, that I need no assurances of yours to make me more thoroughly so. Yet surely neither you or the fair Henrietta herself will deny me the exquisite Gratification of dieing for her, of falling a victim to her Charms. And when I am dead"—continued he—

"Oh Lady Scudamore, said I wiping my eyes, that such a sweet Creature should talk of dieing!"

"It is an affecting Circumstance indeed," replied Lady Scudamore. "When I am dead said he, Let me be carried and lain at her feet, and perhaps she may not disdain to drop a pitying tear on my poor remains."

"Dear Lady Scudamore interrupted I, say no more on this affecting Subject. I cannot bear it."

"Oh! how I admire the sweet Sensibility of your Soul, and as I would not for Worlds wound it too deeply, I will be silent."

"Pray go on." said I. She did so.

"And then added he, Ah! Cousin imagine what my transports will be when I feel the dear precious drops trickle o'er

line 1: 'Indeed' deleted; 'To be sure' inserted above line.   //   line 4: 'in' inserted above line.

my face! Who would not die to taste such extacy! And when I am interred, may the divine Henrietta bless some happier Youth with her affection, May he be as tenderly attached to her as the hapless Musgrove and while *he* crumbles to dust, May they live an example of Felicity in the Conjugal state!"

Did you ever hear any thing so pathetic? What a charming Wish, to be lain at my feet when he was dead! Oh! What an exalted mind he must have to be capable of Such a wish! Lady Scudamore went on.

"Ah! my dear Cousin replied I to him, Such noble behaviour as this, must melt the heart of any Woman however obdurate it may naturally be; and could the divine Henrietta but hear your generous wishes for her happiness, all gentle as is her Mind, I have not a doubt but that she would pity your affection and endeavour to return it." "Oh! Cousin answered he, do not endeavour to raise my hopes by such flattering Assurances. No, I cannot hope to please this angel of a Woman, and the only thing which remains for me to do, is to die." "True Love is ever desponding replied I, but *I* my dear Tom[66] will give you even greater hopes of conquering this fair one's heart, than I have yet given you, by assuring you that I watched her with the strictest attention during the whole day, and could plainly discover that she cherishes in her bosom though unknown to herself, a most tender affection for you."

"Dear Lady Scudamore cried I, This is more than I ever knew!"

"Did not I say that it was unknown to yourself? I did not, continued I to him, encourage you by saying this at first,

line 5: 'Felicity' written over 'conjugal'.   //   line 20: 'Tom' written over 'Cousin'.   //   line 26: 'n' deleted at the beginning of 'ever'.

that Surprise might render the pleasure Still Greater." "No Cousin replied he in a languid voice, nothing will convince me that *I* can have touched the heart of Henrietta Halton, and if you are deceived yourself, do not attempt deceiving me." "Inshort my Love it was the work of some hours for me to persuade the poor despairing Youth that you had really a preference for him; but when at last he could no longer deny the force of my arguments, or discredit what I told him, his transports, his Raptures, his Extacies are beyond my power to describe."

"Oh! the dear Creature, cried I, how passionately he loves me! But dear Lady Scudamore did you tell him that I was totally dependant on my Uncle and Aunt?"

"Yes, I told him every thing."

"And what did he say."

"He exclaimed with virulence against Uncles and Aunts; Accused the Laws of England for allowing them to possess their Estates when wanted by their Nephews or Neices, and wished *he* were in the House of Commons, that he might reform the Legislature, and rectify all its abuses."

"Oh! the sweet Man! What a spirit he has!" said I.

"He could not flatter himself he added, that the adorable Henrietta would condescend for his Sake to resign those Luxuries and that Splendor to which She had been used, and accept only in exchange the Comforts and Elegancies which his limited Income could afford her, even supposing that his house were in Readiness to receive her. I told him that it could not be expected that she would; it would be doing her an injustice to suppose her capable of giving up the power she now possesses and so nobly uses of doing such extensive Good to the poorer part of her fellow Creatures, merely for the gratification of you and herself."

"To be sure said I, I *am* very Charitable every now and then.[67] And what did Mr Musgrove say to this?"

"He replied that he was under a melancholy Necessity of owning the truth of what I said, and that therefore if he should be the happy Creature destined to be the Husband of the Beautiful Henrietta he must bring himself to wait, however impatiently, for the fortunate day, when she might be freed from the power of worthless Relations and able to bestow herself on him."

What a noble Creature he is! Oh! Matilda what a fortunate one *I am*, who am to be his Wife! My Aunt is calling me to come and make the pies.[68] So adieu my dear freind.

and beleive me yours etc.—H. Halton.

FINIS.

line 2: 'I gave away twopence this Morning.' deleted after 'then'.   //   line 3: 'said' deleted; 'replied' inserted above line.   //   line 5: 'as' deleted; 'to be' inserted above line.

To Miss Fanny Catherine Austen[1]

My dear Neice

 As I am prevented by the great distance between Rowling and Steventon[2] from superintending Your Education Myself, the care of which will probably on that account devolve on your Father and Mother, I think it is my particular Duty to prevent your feeling as much as possible the want of my personal instructions, by addressing to You on paper my Opinions and Admonitions on the conduct of Young Women,[3] which you will find expressed in the following pages. I am my dear Neice

Your affectionate Aunt
The Author.

The female philosopher[1]—
a Letter.

My dear Louisa

Your freind Mr Millar called upon us yesterday in his way to Bath, whither he is going for his health; two of his daughters were with him, but the oldest and the three Boys are with their Mother in Sussex. Though you have often told me that Miss Millar was remarkably handsome, You never mentioned anything of her Sisters' beauty; yet they are certainly extremely pretty. I'll give you their description.—Julia is eighteen; with a countenance in which Modesty, Sense and Dignity are happily blended, she has a form which at once presents you with Grace, Elegance and Symmetry. Charlotte who is just Sixteen is shorter than her Sister, and though her figure cannot boast the easy dignity of Julia's, yet it has a pleasing plumpness which is in a different way as estimable. She is fair and her face is expressive sometimes of softness the most bewitching, and at others of Vivacity the most striking. She appears to have infinite Wit and a good humour unalterable; her conversation during the half hour they set with us, was replete with humourous Sallies,[2] Bonmots and repartées, while the sensible, the amiable Julia uttered Sentiments of Morality worthy of a heart like her own.

Mr Millar appeared to answer the character I had always received of him. My Father met him with that look of Love, that social Shake, and Cordial Kiss[3] which marked his

line 14: 'pleasing' deleted; 'estimable' inserted above line.

gladness at beholding an old and valued friend from whom thro' various circumstances he had been separated nearly twenty Years. Mr Millar observed (and very justly too) that many events had befallen each during that interval of time, which gave occasion to the lovely Julia for making most sensible reflections on the many changes in their situation which so long a period had occasioned, on the advantages of some, and the disadvantages of others. From this subject she made a short digression to the instability of human pleasures and the uncertainty of their duration, which led her to observe that all earthly Joys must be imperfect. She was proceeding to illustrate this doctrine by examples from the Lives of great Men when the Carriage came to the Door and the amiable Moralist[4] with her Father and Sister was obliged to depart, but not without a promise of spending five or six months with us[5] on their return. We of course mentioned You, and I assure you that ample Justice was done to your Merits by all. "Louisa Clarke (said I) is in general a very pleasant Girl, yet sometimes her good humour is clouded by Peevishness, Envy and Spite. She neither wants Understanding nor is without some pretensions to Beauty, but these are so very trifling, that the value she sets on her personal charms, and the adoration she expects them to be offered are at once a striking example of her vanity, her pride, and her folly."[6] So said I, and to my opinion every one added weight by the concurrence of their own.

your affecte. Arabella[7] Smythe

line 1: 'ie' written over 'ei' in 'friend'.   //   line 20: 'or' changed to 'nor' and 'is' inserted above line.

The first Act of a Comedy—

Characters
Popgun
Charles
Postilion
Chorus of ploughboys
and
Strephon

Maria
Pistoletta
Hostess
Cook
and
Chloe

Scene—an Inn—
Enter Hostess, Charles, Maria, and Cook.

Hostss. to Maria) If the gentry in the Lion[1] should want
beds, shew them number 9.—

Maria) Yes Mistress.   exit Maria—

Hostss. to Cook) If their Honours[2] in the Moon ask for
the bill of fare,[3] give it to them.

Cook)—I wull,[4] I wull.   exit Cook.

Hostss. to Charles) If their Ladyships[5] in the Sun ring
their Bell—answer it.

Charles) Yes Ma'am.—   Exeunt Severally—

Scene changes to the Moon, and discovers
Popgun and Pistoletta.[6]

Pistoltta.) Pray papa how far is it to London?

Popgun) My Girl, my Darling, my favourite of all my
Children, who art the picture of thy poor Mother who
died two months ago, with whom I am going to Town to
marry to Strephon,[7] and to whom I mean to bequeath
my whole Estate, it wants seven Miles.[8]

line 18: 'to' written over 'you to' before 'Strephon'.

219

Scene changes to the Sun—
Enter Chloe and a chorus of ploughboys.[9]

Chloe) Where am I? At Hounslow.[10]—Where go I? To
London—What to do? To be married—. Unto whom?
Unto Strephon. Who is he? A Youth. Then I will sing a
Song.

Song
I go to Town
And when I come down,
I shall be married to Stree-phon[11]
And that to me will be fun.
Chorus) Be fun, be fun, be fun,
And that to me will be fun,
Enter Cook
Cook) Here is the bill of fare.
Chloe reads) 2 Ducks, a leg of beef, a stinking partridge,[12]
and a tart.—I will have the leg of beef and the partridge.
exit Cook.

And now I will sing another Song.
Song—
I am going to have my dinner,
After which I shan't be thinner,
I wish I had here Strephon
For he would carve the partridge if it should be
a tough one
Chorus)   Tough one, tough one, tough one,
For he would carve the partridge if it should be
a tough one.
Exit Chloe and Chorus—.

Scene changes to the inside of the Lion.
Enter Strephon and Postilion

Streph.) You drove me from Staines[13] to this place, from whence I mean to go to Town to marry Chloe.[14] How much is your due?

Post.) Eighteen pence.

Streph.) Alas, my freind, I have but a bad guinea[15] with which I mean to support myself in Town. But I will pawn to you an undirected Letter[16] that I received from Chloe.

Post.) Sir, I accept your offer.

End of the first Act.—

A Letter from a Young Lady, whose feelings being too Strong for her Judgement led her into the commission of Errors which her Heart disapproved.—

Many have been the cares and vicissitudes of my past life, my beloved Ellinor, and the only consolation I feel for their bitterness is that on a close examination of my conduct, I am convinced that I have strictly deserved them. I murdered my father at a very early period of my Life, I have since murdered my Mother, and I am now going to murder my Sister. I have changed my religion so often that at present I have not an idea of any left. I have been a perjured witness in every public tryal for these last twelve Years,[1] and I have forged my own Will.[2] In short there is scarcely a crime that I have not committed—But I am now going to reform. Colonel Martin of the Horseguards[3] has paid his Addresses to me, and we are to be married in a few days. As there is something Singular in our Courtship, I will give you an account of it. Col. Martin is the second Son of the late Sir John Martin who died immensely rich, but bequeathing only one hundred thousand pound apeice to his three younger Children, left the bulk of his fortune, about eight Million[4] to the present Sir Thomas. Upon his Small pittance[5] the Colonel lived tolerably contented for nearly four months when he took it into his head to determine on getting the whole of his eldest Brother's

---

Title: 'several faults' deleted; 'Errors' inserted above line.   //   line 9: 'Years' written over 'months'.   //   line 11: 'now' inserted above line.

Estate. A new will was forged and the Colonel produced it in Court—but nobody would swear to it's being the right Will except himself, and he had sworn so much that Nobody believed him. At that moment I happened to be passing by the door of the Court, and was beckoned in by the Judge who told the Colonel that I was a Lady ready to witness anything for the cause of Justice, and advised him to apply to me. In short the Affair was soon adjusted. The Colonel and I swore to its' being the right will, and Sir Thomas has been obliged to resign all his illgotten Wealth.[6] The Colonel in gratitude waited on me the next day with an offer of his hand—. I am now going to murder my Sister.

Yours Ever,

Anna Parker.

line 4: repetition of 'to' deleted.

A Tour through Wales—
in a Letter from a young Lady—

My dear Clara

I have been so long on the ramble[1] that I have not till now had it in my power to thank you for your Letter—. We left our dear home on last Monday Month;[2] and proceeded on our tour through Wales,[3] which is a principality contiguous to England[4] and gives the title to the Prince of Wales.[5] We travelled on horseback[6] by preference. My Mother rode upon our little poney and Fanny and I walked by her side or rather ran, for my Mother is so fond of riding fast that She galloped all the way. You may be sure that we were in a fine perspiration when we came to our place of resting. Fanny has taken a great Many Drawings of the Country,[7] which are very beautiful, tho' perhaps not such exact resemblances as might be wished, from their being taken as she ran along. It would astonish you to see all the Shoes we wore out in our Tour. We determined to take a good Stock with us and therefore each took a pair of our own besides those we set off in. However we were obliged to have them both capped and heelpeiced[8] at Carmarthen,[9] and at last when they were quite gone, Mama was so kind as to lend us a pair of blue Sattin Slippers,[10] of which we each took one and hopped home from Hereford[11] delightfully—

> I am your ever affectionate
> Elizabeth Johnson.

line 5: 'which' is 'with' in ms.

A Tale.

A Gentleman whose family name I shall conceal,[1] bought a small Cottage in Pembrokeshire[2] about two Years ago. This daring Action was suggested to him by his elder Brother who promised to furnish two rooms and a Closet[3] for him, provided he would take a small house near the borders of an extensive Forest and about three Miles from the Sea. Wilhelminus[4] gladly accepted the Offer and Continued for some time searching after such a retreat when he was one morning agreably releived from his Suspence by reading this advertisement in a Newspaper.[5]

To be Lett

A Neat Cottage on the borders of an extensive forest and about three Miles from the Sea. It is ready furnished except two rooms and a Closet.

The delighted Wilhelminus posted away immediately to his brother, and shewed him the advertisement. Robertus[6] congratulated him and sent him in his Carriage to take possession of the Cottage. After travelling for three days and Six Nights without Stopping,[7] they arrived at the Forest and following a track which led by it's side down a steep Hill over which ten Rivulets meandered, they reached the Cottage in half an hour. Wilhelminus alighted, and after knocking for some time without receiving any answer or hearing anyone stir within, he opened the door which was fastened only by a

line 20: 'it' deleted after 'by'.   //   line 24: 'by' inserted above line.

wooden latch and entered a small room, which he immediately perceived to be one of the two that were unfurnished—From thence he proceeded into a Closet equally bare. A pair of Stairs[8] that went out of it led him into a room above, no less destitute, and these apartments he found composed the whole of the House. He was by no means displeased with this discovery, as he had the comfort of reflecting that he should not be obliged to lay out any thing on furniture himself—. He returned immediately to his Brother, who took him the next day to every Shop in Town, and bought what ever was requisite to furnish the two rooms and the Closet. In a few days everything was completed, and Wilhelminus returned to take possession of his Cottage. Robertus accompanied him, with his Lady the amiable Cecilia and her two lovely Sisters Arabella and Marina[9] to whom Wilhelminus was tenderly attached,[10] and a large number of Attendants.—An ordinary Genius[11] might probably have been embarrassed in endeavouring to accommodate so large a party, but Wilhelminus with admirable presence of Mind, gave orders for the immediate erection of two noble Tents[12] in an open Spot in the Forest adjoining to the house. Their Construction was both simple and elegant—A Couple of old blankets, each supported by four Sticks, gave a striking proof of that Taste for Architecture and that happy ease in overcoming difficulties which were some of Wilhelminus's most striking Virtues.

FINIS

End of the Second Volume.

line 8: 'im' written over 'er' in 'himself'.

Volume the Third

VOLUME THE THIRD
Jane Austen—May 6th 1792.[1]

CONTENTS

To Miss Mary Lloyd,[1]
The following Novel is by permission
Dedicated,
    by her Obedt. humble Servt.
            The Author

Evelyn

In a retired part of the County of Sussex there is a village (for what I know to the Contrary) called Evelyn,[2] perhaps one of the most beautiful Spots in the south of England. A Gentleman passing through it on horseback about twenty years ago,[3] was so entirely of my opinion in this respect, that he put up at the little Alehouse[4] in it and enquired with great earnestness whether there were any house to be lett[5] in the Parish.[6] The Landlady,[7] who as well as every one else in Evelyn was remarkably amiable, shook her head at this question, but seemed unwilling to give him any answer. He could not bear this uncertainty—yet knew not how to obtain the information he desired. To repeat a question which had already appear'd to make the good woman uneasy was impossible—. He turned from her in visible agitation. "What a situation am I in!" said he to himself as he walked to the window and threw up the sash.[8] He found himself revived by the Air, which he felt to a much greater degree when he had opened the window than he had done before. Yet it was but for a moment—. The agonizing pain of Doubt and Suspence again weighed down his Spirits. The good woman who had watched in eager silence every turn of his Countenance with that benevolence which characterizes the inhabitants of Evelyn, intreated him to tell her the cause of his uneasiness. "Is there anything Sir in my power to do that may releive Your Greifs—Tell me in what

line 19: 'idea' deleted; 'pain' inserted above line.

Manner I can sooth them, and beleive me that the freindly balm of Comfort and Assistance shall not be wanting; for indeed Sir I have a simpathetic Soul."

"Amiable Woman (said Mr Gower, affected almost to tears by this generous offer) This Greatness of mind in one to whom I am almost a Stranger, serves but to make me the more warmly wish for a house in this sweet village—. What would I not give to be your Neighbour, to be blessed with your Acquaintance, and with the farther knowledge of your virtues! Oh! with what pleasure would I form myself by such an example! Tell me then, best of Women, is there no possibility?—I cannot speak—you know my meaning—"

"Alas! Sir, replied Mrs Willis, there is *none*. Every house in this village, from the sweetness of the Situation, and the purity of the Air, in which neither Misery, Illhealth, or Vice are ever wafted, is inhabited. And yet, (after a short pause) there is a Family, who tho' warmly attached to the spot, yet from a peculiar Generosity of Disposition would perhaps be willing to oblige you with their house."[9] He eagerly caught at this idea, and having gained a direction to the place, he set off immediately on his walk to it. As he approached the House, he was delighted with its situation. It was in the exact center of a small circular paddock,[10] which was enclosed by a regular paling,[11] and bordered with a plantation of Lombardy poplars,[12] and Spruce firs alternately placed in three rows.[13] A gravel walk ran through this beautiful Shrubbery,[14] and as the remainder of the paddock was unincumbered with any other Timber, the surface of it perfectly even and smooth, and grazed by four white Cows which were disposed at equal

line 1: 'the' inserted above line.   //   line 19: 'the remainder of their Lease' deleted; 'their house' inserted above line.   //   line 20: 'House' deleted; 'place' inserted above line.   //   line 27: 'by' deleted after 'unincumbered'.

distances from each other,[15] the whole appearance of the place as Mr Gower entered the Paddock was uncommonly striking. A beautifully-rounded, gravel road without any turn or interruption[16] led immediately to the house. Mr Gower rang—the Door was soon opened. "Are Mr and Mrs Webb[17] at home?" "My Good Sir they are—" replied the Servant; And leading the way, conducted Mr Gower up stairs into a very elegant Dressing room, where a Lady rising from her seat, welcomed him with all the Generosity which Mrs Willis had attributed to the Family.

"Welcome best of Men[18]—Welcome to this House, and to every thing it contains. William, tell your Master of the happiness I enjoy—invite him to partake of it—. Bring up some Chocolate[19] immediately; Spread a Cloth in the dining Parlour, and carry in the venison pasty[20]—. In the mean time let the Gentleman have some sandwiches, and bring in a Basket of Fruit—Send up some Ices and a bason of Soup, and do not forget some Jellies and Cakes."[21] Then turning to Mr Gower, and taking out her purse, "Accept this my good Sir,—. Beleive me you are welcome to everything that is in my power to bestow.—I wish my purse were weightier, but Mr Webb must make up my deficiences—. I know he has cash in the house to the amount of an hundred pounds, which he shall bring you immediately." Mr Gower felt overpowered by her generosity as he put the purse in his pocket, and from the excess of his Gratitude, could scarcely express himself intelligibly when he accepted her offer of the hundred pounds. Mr Webb soon entered the room, and repeated every protestation of Freindship and Cordiality which his Lady had already made—. The Chocolate, The Sandwiches,

line 19: 'her' written over 'a'.   //   line 26: 'effusions' deleted; 'excess' inserted above line.   //   line 27: 'the' written over 'an'.   //   line 30: 'before expressed' deleted; 'already made' inserted above line.

the Jellies, the Cakes, the Ice, and the Soup soon made their appearance, and Mr Gower having tasted something of all, and pocketted the rest, was conducted into the dining parlour, where he eat a most excellent Dinner and partook of the most exquisite Wines, while Mr and Mrs Webb stood by him still pressing him to eat and drink a little more. "And now my good Sir, said Mr Webb, when Mr Gower's repast was concluded, what else can we do to contribute to your happiness and express the Affection we bear you. Tell us what you wish more to receive, and depend upon our gratitude for the communication of your wishes." "Give me then your house and Grounds; I ask for nothing else." "It is yours, exclaimed both at once; from this moment it is yours." This Agreement concluded on and the present accepted by Mr Gower, Mr Webb rang to have the Carriage ordered, telling William at the same time to call the Young Ladies.

"Best of Men, said Mrs Webb, we will not long intrude upon your Time."

"Make no Apologies dear Madam, replied Mr Gower, You are welcome to stay this half hour if you like it."

They both burst forth into raptures of Admiration at his politeness, which they agreed served only to make their Conduct appear more inexcusable in trespassing on his time.

The Young Ladies soon entered the room. The eldest of them was about seventeen, the other, several years younger. Mr Gower had no sooner fixed his Eyes on Miss Webb than he felt that something more was necessary to his happiness than the house he had just received—Mrs Webb introduced him to her daughter. "Our dear freind Mr Gower my Love— He has been so good as to accept of this house, small as it

line 9: 'for' deleted after 'bear'.

is, and to promise to keep it for ever." "Give me leave to assure you Sir, said Miss Webb, that I am highly sensible of your kindness in this respect, which from the shortness of my Father's and Mother's acquaintance with You, is more than usually flattering." Mr Gower bowed—"You are too obliging Ma'am—I assure you that I like the house extremely—and if they would complete their generosity by giving me their elder daughter in marriage with a handsome portion,[22] I should have nothing more to wish for." This compliment brought a blush into the cheeks of the lovely Miss Webb, who seemed however to refer herself to her father and Mother. *They* looked delighted at each other—At length Mrs Webb breaking silence, said—"We bend under a weight of obligations to you which we can never repay. Take our girl, take our Maria, and on her must the difficult task fall, of endeavouring to make some return to so much Beneficence." Mr Webb added, "Her fortune is but ten thousand pounds,[23] which is almost too small a sum to be offered." This objection however being instantly removed by the generosity of Mr Gower, who declared himself satisfied with the sum mentioned, Mr and Mrs Webb, with their youngest daughter took their leave, and on the next day, the nuptials of their eldest with Mr Gower were celebrated.[24]—This amiable Man now found himself perfectly happy; united to a very lovely and deserving young woman, with an handsome fortune, an elegant house, settled in the village of Evelyn, and by that means enabled to cultivate his acquaintance with Mrs Willis,[25] could he have a wish ungratified?—For some months he found that he could *not*, till one day as he was walking in the Shrubbery with Maria leaning on his arm, they observed a rose full-blown

line 1: 'promise to' inserted above line.

lying on the gravel; it had fallen from a rose tree which with three others had been planted by Mr Webb to give a pleasing variety[26] to the walk. These four Rose trees served also to mark the quarters of the Shrubbery, by which means the Traveller might always know how far in his progress round the Paddock he was got—. Maria stooped to pick up the beautiful flower, and with all her Family Generosity presented it to her Husband. "My dear Frederic, said she, pray take this charming rose." "Rose! exclaimed Mr Gower—. Oh! Maria, of what does not that remind me! Alas my poor Sister, how have I neglected you!" The truth was that Mr Gower was the only son of a very large Family, of which Miss Rose Gower was the thirteenth daughter. This Young Lady whose merits deserved a better fate than she met with, was the darling of her relations—From the clearness of her skin and the Brilliancy of her Eyes, she was fully entitled to all their partial affection. Another circumstance contributed to the general Love they bore her, and that was one of the finest heads of hair in the world. A few Months before her Brother's marriage, her heart had been engaged by the attentions and charms of a young Man whose high rank and expectations seemed to foretell objections from his Family to a match which would be highly desirable to theirs.[27] Proposals were made on the young Man's part, and proper objections on his Father's—He was desired to return from Carlisle[28] where he was with his beloved Rose, to the family seat in Sussex. He was obliged to comply, and the angry father then finding from his Conversation how determined he was to marry no other woman, sent him for a fortnight to the Isle of Wight under the care of the Family Chaplain,[29] with the hope of overcoming his Constancy by Time and Absence in a foreign Country.[30] They accordingly prepared to bid a long adeiu to England—The young Nobleman was not allowed to see his Rosa.[31] They set sail—A storm arose which baffled the arts of the Seamen. The Vessel was wrecked on the coast of Calshot[32] and every Soul on board perished. This sad Event soon reached Carlisle, and the beautiful Rose was affected by it, beyond the power of Expression. It was to soften her affliction by obtaining a picture of her unfortunate Lover that her brother undertook a Journey into Sussex, where he hoped that his petition would not be rejected, by the severe yet afflicted Father. When he reached Evelyn he was not many miles from——Castle, but the pleasing events which befell him in that place had for a while made him totally forget the object of his Journey and his unhappy Sister. The little incident of the rose however brought everything concerning her to his recollection again, and he bitterly repented his neglect. He returned to the house immediately and agitated by Greif, Apprehension and Shame wrote the following Letter to Rosa.

July 14th——.Evelyn

My dearest Sister

As it is now four months since I left Carlisle, during which period I have not once written to you, You will perhaps unjustly accuse me of Neglect and Forgetfulness. Alas! I blush when I own the truth of your accusation.—Yet if you are still alive, do not think too harshly of me, or suppose that I could for a moment forget the situation of my Rose. Beleive me I will forget you no longer, but will hasten as soon as possible to——Castle if I find by your answer that you are still alive. Maria joins me in every dutiful and affectionate wish, and I am yours sincerely

Fr. Gower.

line 16: 'with' deleted; 'by' inserted above line.   //   line 26: first 'will' inserted above line.

He waited in the most anxious expectation for an answer to his Letter, which arrived as soon as the great distance from Carlisle would admit of.[33]—But alas, it came not from Rosa.

Carlisle July 17th—

Dear Brother

My Mother has taken the liberty of opening your Letter to poor Rose, as she has been dead these six weeks.[34] Your long absence and continued Silence gave us all great uneasiness and hastened her to her Grave. Your Journey to——Castle therefore may be spared. You do not tell us where you have been since the time of your quitting Carlisle, nor in any way account for your tedious absence, which gives us some surprise. We all unite in Compts. to Maria, and beg to know who she is——.

Your affecte. Sister
M. Gower.

This Letter, by which Mr Gower was obliged to attribute to his own conduct, his Sister's death, was so violent a shock to his feelings, that in spite of his living at Evelyn where Illness was scarcely ever heard of, he was attacked by a fit of the gout,[35] which confining him to his own room afforded an opportunity to Maria of shining in that favourite character of Sir Charles Grandison's, a nurse.[36] No woman could ever appear more amiable than Maria did under such circumstances, and at last by her unremitting attentions had the pleasure of seeing him gradually recover the use of his feet. It was a blessing by no means lost on him, for he was no sooner in a condition to leave the house, than he mounted his horse, and rode to——Castle, wishing to find whether

---

line 3: 'for' deleted; second 'from' inserted below line in pencil in a different hand.

his Lordship softened by his Son's death, might have been brought to consent to the match, had both *he* and Rosa been alive. His amiable Maria followed him with her Eyes till she could see him no longer, and then sinking into her chair overwhelmed with Greif, found that in his absence she could enjoy no comfort.

Mr Gower arrived late in the evening at the castle, which was situated on a woody Eminence commanding a beautiful prospect of the Sea. Mr Gower did not dislike the situation, tho' it was certainly greatly inferior to that of his own house. There was an irregularity in the fall of the ground, and a profusion of old Timber which appeared to him illsuited to the stile of the Castle, for it being a building of a very ancient date, he thought it required the Paddock of Evelyn lodge to form a Contrast, and enliven the structure.[37] The gloomy appearance of the old Castle frowning on him as he followed its' winding approach,[38] struck him with terror. Nor did he think himself safe, till he was introduced into the Drawing room where the Family were assembled to tea. Mr Gower was a perfect stranger to every one in the Circle but tho' he was always timid in the Dark and easily terrified when alone, he did not want that more necessary and more noble courage which enabled him without a Blush to enter a large party of superior Rank, whom he had never seen before, and to take his Seat amongst them with perfect Indifference. The name of Gower was not unknown to Lord——. He felt distressed and astonished; yet rose and received him with all the politeness of a well-bred Man. Lady——who felt a deeper sorrow at the loss of her son, than his Lordships harder heart was capable of, could hardly keep her Seat when she found

line 10: 'superior' deleted; 'inferior' inserted above line.   //   line 13: 'old' deleted; 'ancient' inserted above line.

that he was the Brother of her lamented Henry's Rosa. "My Lord said Mr Gower as soon as he was seated, You are perhaps surprised at receiving a visit from a Man whom you could not have the least expectation of seeing here. But my Sister my unfortunate Sister is the real cause of my thus troubling you: That luckless Girl is now no more—and tho' *she* can receive no pleasure from the intelligence, yet for the satisfaction of her Family I wish to know whether the Death of this unhappy Pair has made an impression on your heart sufficiently strong to obtain that consent to their Marriage which in happier circumstances you would not be persuaded to give supposing that they now were both alive." His Lordship seemed lossed in astonishment. Lady——could not support the mention of her Son, and left the room in tears; the rest of the Family remained attentively listening, almost persuaded that Mr Gower was distracted. "Mr Gower, replied his Lordship This is a very odd question—It appears to me that you are supposing an impossibility—No one can more sincerely regret the death of my Son than I have always done, and it gives me great concern to know that Miss Gower's was hastened by his—. Yet to suppose them alive is destroying at once the Motive for a change in my sentiments concerning the affair." "My Lord, replied Mr Gower in anger, I see that you are a most inflexible Man, and that not even the death of your Son can make you wish his future Life happy. I will no longer detain your Lordship. I see, I plainly see that you are a very vile Man—And now I have the honour of wishing all your Lordships, and Ladyships a good Night." He immediately left the room, forgetting in the heat of his Anger the lateness of the hour, which at any other time would have made him tremble, and leaving the whole Company unanimous in their

line 1: 'Sister' heavily deleted; 'Henry's' inserted above line.

opinion of his being Mad. When however he had mounted his horse and the great Gates of the Castle had shut him out, he felt an universal tremor through out his whole frame.[39] If we consider his Situation indeed, alone, on horseback, as late in the year as August, and in the day, as nine o'clock,[40] with no light to direct him but that of the Moon almost full, and the Stars which alarmed him by their twinkling, who can refrain from pitying him?—No house within a quarter of a mile, and a Gloomy Castle blackened by the deep shade of Walnuts and Pines, behind him.—He felt indeed almost distracted with his fears, and shutting his Eyes till he arrived at the Village to prevent his seeing either Gipsies[41] or Ghosts, he rode on a full gallop all the way.[42]

To Miss Austen[1]

Madam

Encouraged by your warm patronage of The beautiful Cassandra, and The History of England, which through your generous support, have obtained a place in every library in the Kingdom, and run through threescore Editions,[2] I take the liberty of begging the same Exertions in favour of the following Novel, which I humbly flatter myself, possesses Merit beyond any already published, or any that will ever in future appear, except such as may proceed from the pen of Your Most Grateful Humble Servt.

The Author

Steventon August 1792—

Catharine, or the Bower

Catharine[3] had the misfortune, as many heroines have had before her, of losing her Parents when she was very young, and of being brought up under the care of a Maiden Aunt, who while she tenderly loved her, watched over her conduct with so scrutinizing a severity, as to make it very doubtful to many people, and to Catharine amongst the rest, whether she loved her or not. She had frequently been deprived of a real pleasure through this jealous Caution, had been sometimes obliged to relinquish a Ball because an Officer was to be there, or to dance with a Partner of her Aunt's introduction in preference to one of her own Choice. But her Spirits were naturally good, and not easily depressed, and she possessed such a fund of vivacity and good humour as could only be damped by some very serious vexation.—Besides these antidotes against every disappointment, and consolations under them, she had another, which afforded her constant releif in all her misfortunes, and that was a fine shady Bower,[4] the work of her own infantine[5] Labours assisted by those of two young Companions who had resided in the same village—. To this Bower, which terminated a very pleasant and retired walk in her Aunt's Garden, she always wandered whenever anything disturbed her, and it possessed such a charm over her

Title: 'Kitty' deleted; 'Catharine' inserted above line.   //   line 1: 'Kitty' deleted; 'Catharine' inserted above line.   //   line 6: 'Kitty' deleted; 'Catharine' inserted above line.   //   line 20: 'Garden' deleted; 'Bower' inserted above line.

senses, as constantly to tranquillize her mind and quiet her spirits—Solitude and reflection might perhaps have had the same effect in her Bed Chamber, yet Habit had so strengthened the idea which Fancy had first suggested, that such a thought never occurred to Kitty who was firmly persuaded that her Bower alone could restore her to herself. Her imagination was warm, and in her Freindships, as well as in the whole tenure[6] of her Mind, she was enthousiastic.[7] This beloved Bower had been the united work of herself and two amiable Girls, for whom since her earliest Years, she had felt the tenderest regard. They were the daughters of the Clergyman of the Parish with whose Family, while it had continued there, her Aunt had been on the most intimate terms, and the little Girls tho' separated for the greatest part of the Year by the different Modes of their Education, were constantly together during the holidays of the Miss Wynnes.[8] In those days of happy Childhood, now so often regretted by Kitty this arbour had been formed, and separated perhaps for ever from these dear freinds, it encouraged more than any other place the tender and Melancholly recollections, of hours rendered pleasant by *them*, at once so sorrowful, yet so soothing! It was now two years since the death of Mr Wynne, and the consequent dispersion of his Family who had been left by it in great distress. They had been reduced to a state of absolute dependance on some relations, who though very opulent, and very nearly connected with them, had with difficulty been prevailed on to contribute anything towards their Support. Mrs Wynne was fortunately spared the knowledge and

line 16: five and a half lines deleted after 'Wynnes': '; they were companions in their walks, their Schemes and Amusements, and while the sweetness of their dispositions had [inserted above line] prevented any serious Quarrels, the trifling disputes which it was impossible wholly to avoid, had been far from lessening their affection'.   //   line 21: 'once' is 'one' in ms.

participation of their distress, by her release from a painful illness a few months before the death of her husband.—. The eldest daughter had been obliged to accept the offer of one of her cousins to equip her for the East Indies,[9] and tho' infinitely against her inclinations had been necessitated to embrace the only possibility that was offered to her, of a Maintenance; Yet it was *one*, so opposite to all her ideas of Propriety, so contrary to her Wishes, so repugnant to her feelings, that she would almost have preferred Servitude to it, had Choice been allowed her—. Her personal Attractions had gained her a husband as soon as she had arrived at Bengal[10] and she had now been married nearly a twelvemonth. Splendidly, yet unhappily married. United to a Man of double her own age, whose disposition was not amiable, and whose Manners were unpleasing, though his Character was respectable.[11] Kitty had heard twice from her freind since her marriage, but her Letters were always unsatisfactory, and though she did not openly avow her feelings, yet every line proved her to be Unhappy. She spoke with pleasure of nothing, but of those Amusements which they had shared together and which could return no more, and seemed to have no happiness in veiw but that of returning to England again. Her sister had been taken by another relation the Dowager[12] Lady Halifax as a companion[13] to her Daughters, and had accompanied her family into Scotland about the same time of Cecilia's leaving England. From Mary therefore Kitty had the power of hearing more frequently, but her Letters were scarcely more comfortable—. There was not indeed that hopelessness of sorrow in her situation as in her sisters; she was not married, and could yet look forward to a change in her circumstances; but situated for the present without

line 11: 'a' inserted above line.

any immediate hope of it, in a family where, tho' all were her relations she had no freind, she wrote usually in depressed Spirits, which her separation from her Sister and her Sister's Marriage had greatly contributed to make so.—Divided thus from the two she loved best on Earth, while Cecilia and Mary were still more endeared to her by their loss, everything that brought a remembrance of them was doubly cherished, and the Shrubs they had planted, and the keepsakes they had given were rendered sacred—. The living of Chetwynde[14] was now in the possession of a Mr Dudley, whose Family unlike the Wynnes, were productive only of vexation and trouble to Mrs Percival,[15] and her Neice. Mr Dudley, who was the younger Son of a very noble Family,[16] of a Family more famed for their Pride than their opulence, tenacious of his Dignity, and jealous of his rights, was forever quarrelling, if not with Mrs P herself, with her Steward and Tenants concerning tythes,[17] and with the principal Neighbours themselves concerning the respect and parade,[18] he exacted. His Wife, an ill-educated, untaught Woman of ancient family, was proud of that family almost without knowing why, and like him too was haughty and quarrelsome, without considering for what. Their only daughter, who inherited the ignorance, the insolence, and pride of her parents, was from that Beauty of which she was unreasonably vain, considered by them as an irresistable Creature, and looked up to as the future restorer, by a Splendid Marriage, of the dignity which their reduced Situation and Mr Dudley's being obliged to take orders for a Country Living had so much lessened. They at once despised the Percivals as people of mean family, and envied them as

line 12: 'Peterson' deleted; 'Percival' inserted above line.   //   line 16: 'eterson' deleted, leaving 'P'.   //   line 18: 'His' written over 'This'.   //   line 23: 'her' inserted above line.   //   line 29: 'Petersons' deleted; 'Percivals' inserted above line.   //   line 29: 'no' deleted; 'mean' inserted above line.

people of fortune. They were jealous of their being more respected that themselves and while they affected to consider them as of no Consequence, were continually seeking to lessen them in the opinion of the Neighbourhood by Scandalous and Malicious reports. Such a family as this, was ill calculated to console Kitty for the loss of the Wynnes, or to fill up by their society, those occasionally irksome hours which in so retired a Situation would sometimes occur for want of a Companion. Her aunt was most excessively fond of her, and miserable if she saw her for a moment out of spirits; Yet she lived in such constant apprehension of her marrying imprudently if she were allowed the opportunity of Choosing, and was so dissatisfied with her behaviour when she saw her with Young Men, for it was, from her natural disposition remarkably open and unreserved, that though she frequently wished for her Neice's sake, that the Neighbourhood were larger, and that She had used herself to mix more with it, yet the recollection of there being young Men in almost every Family in it, always conquered the Wish. The same fears that prevented Mrs Peterson's joining much in the Society of her Neighbours, led her equally to avoid inviting her relations to spend any time in her House—She had therefore constantly repelled the Annual attempt of a distant relation to visit her at Chetwynde, as there was a young Man in the Family of whom she had heard many traits that alarmed her. This Son was however now on his travels,[19] and the repeated solicitations of Kitty, joined to a consciousness of having declined with too little Ceremony the frequent overtures, of her Freinds to be admitted, and a real wish to see them herself, easily prevailed on her to press with

line 8: 'to her'(?) inserted above line and heavily deleted after 'occur'. //
line 13: 'was' inserted above line. // line 29: 'endeavours' deleted;
'overtures' inserted above line.

great Earnestness the pleasure of a visit from them during the Summer. Mr and Mrs Stanley[20] were accordingly to come, and Catharine, in having an object to look forward to, a something to expect that must inevitably releive the dullness of a constant tete-a tete with her Aunt, was so delighted, and her spirits so elevated, that for the three or four days immediately preceding their Arrival, she could scarcely fix herself to any employment. In this point Mrs Percival always thought her defective, and frequently complained of a want of Steadiness and perseverance in her occupations, which were by no means congenial to the eagerness of Kitty's Disposition, and perhaps not often met with in any young person. The tediousness too of her Aunt's conversation and the want of agreable Companions greatly encreased this desire of Change in her Employments, for Kitty found herself much sooner tired of Reading, Working,[21] or Drawing, in Mrs Peterson's parlour than in her own Arbour, where Mrs Peterson for fear of its being damp never accompanied her.

As her Aunt prided herself on the exact propriety and Neatness with which everything in her Family was conducted, and had no higher Satisfaction than that of knowing her house to be always in complete Order, as her fortune was good, and her Establishment[22] Ample, few were the preparations Necessary for the reception of her Visitors. The day of their arrival so long expected, at length came, and the Noise of the Coach and 4 as it drove round the sweep,[23] was to Catherine a more interesting sound, than the Music of an Italian Opera, which to most Heroines is the hight of Enjoyment.[24] Mr and Mrs Stanley were people

line 3: 'Kitty' deleted; 'Catharine' inserted above line.   //   line 8: 'Percival' written over 'Peterson'.   //   line 13: 'Aunt's' written over 'aunt's'.   //   line 25: 'arrived' deleted; 'came' inserted above line.   //   line 28: 'is' inserted above line.

of Large Fortune and high Fashion. He was a Member of the house of Commons, and they were therefore most agreably necessitated to reside half the Year in Town;[25] where Miss Stanley had been attended by the most capital Masters from the time of her being six years old to the last Spring, which comprehending a period of twelve Years had been dedicated to the acquirement of Accomplishments which were now to be displayed and in a few Years entirely neglected. She was[26] elegant in her appearance, rather handsome, and naturally not deficient in Abilities; but those Years which ought to have been spent in the attainment of useful knowledge and Mental Improvement, had been all bestowed in learning Drawing, Italian and Music, more especially the latter, and she now united to these Accomplishments, an Understanding unimproved by reading and a Mind totally devoid either of Taste or Judgement. Her temper was by Nature good, but unassisted by reflection, she had neither patience under Disappointment, nor could sacrifice her own inclinations to promote the happiness of others. All her Ideas were towards the Elegance of her appearance, the fashion of her dress, and the Admiration she wished them to excite. She professed a love of Books without Reading, was Lively without Wit, and generally Good humoured without Merit. Such was Camilla Stanley; and Catherine, who was prejudiced by her appearance, and who from her solitary Situation was ready to like anyone, tho' her Understanding and Judgement would not otherwise have been easily satisfied, felt almost convinced when she saw her, that Miss Stanley would be the very companion She wanted, and in some degree make amends for the loss of Cecilia and Mary Wynne. She therefore attached

line 2: 'and' deleted after 'house'.   //   line 9: 'about Kitty's age,' deleted; 'not in' inserted above line (to form the phrase 'not inelegant') but then deleted. //   line 28: 'when she saw her,' inserted above line.

herself to Camilla from the first day of her arrival, and from
being the only young People in the house, they were by inclination constant Companions. Kitty was herself a great reader,
tho' perhaps not a very deep one,[27] and felt therefore highly
delighted to find that Miss Stanley was equally fond of it.
Eager to know that their sentiments as to Books were similar, she very soon began questioning her new Acquaintance
on the subject; but though She was well read in Modern
history[28] herself, she Chose rather to speak first of Books of
a lighter kind, of Books universally read and Admired.

"You have read Mrs Smith's Novels,[29] I suppose?" said she
to her Companion—. "Oh! Yes, replied the other, and I am
quite delighted with them—They are the sweetest things in
the world—" "And which do you prefer of them?" "Oh! dear,
I think there is no comparison between them—Emmeline[30]
is *so much* better than any of the others—"

"Many people think so, I know; but there does not appear
so great a disproportion in their Merits to *me*; do you think
it is better written?"

"Oh! I do not know anything about *that*—but it is better
in *everything*—Besides, Ethelinde is so long[31]—" "That is a
very common Objection I beleive, said Kitty, but for my own
part, if a book is well written, I always find it too short."

"So do I, only I get tired of it before it is finished." "But did
not you find the story of Ethelinde very interesting? And the
Descriptions of Grasmere,[32] are not they Beautiful?" "Oh! I
missed them all, because I was in such a hurry to know the
end of it—Then from an easy transition she added, We are
going to the Lakes[33] this Autumn, and I am quite Mad with

line 6: second 'to' inserted above line, in pencil, in a different hand.   //
line 10: two lines deleted after 'Admired': 'and that have given rise perhaps to
more frequent Arguments than any other of the same sort.'   //   line 21: 'in
everything' written over 'all together'.   //   line 26: 'they' is 'the' in ms.

Joy; Sir Henry Devereux[34] has promised to go with us, and that will make it so pleasant, you know—"

"I dare say it will; but I think it is a pity that Sir Henry's powers of pleasing were not reserved for an occasion where they might be more wanted.—However I quite envy you the pleasure of such a Scheme." "Oh! I am quite delighted with the thoughts of it; I can think of nothing else. I assure you I have done nothing for this last Month but plan what Cloathes I should take with me, and I have at last determined to take very few indeed besides my travelling Dress,[35] and so I advise you to do, when ever you go; for I intend in case we should fall in with any races,[36] or stop at Matlock or Scarborough, to have some Things made for the occasion."

"You intend then to go into Yorkshire?"

"I beleive not—indeed I know nothing of the Route, for I never trouble myself about such things—. I only know that we are to go from Derbyshire to Matlock[37] and Scarborough,[38] but to which of them first, I neither know nor care[39]—I am in hopes of meeting some particular freinds of mine at Scarborough—Augusta told me in her last Letter that Sir Peter talked of going; but then you know that is so uncertain. I cannot bear Sir Peter, he is such a horrid Creature—"

"He *is*, is he?" said Kitty, not knowing what else to say. "Oh! he is quite Shocking." Here the Conversation was interrupted, and Kitty was left in a painful Uncertainty, as to the particulars of Sir Peter's Character; She knew only that he was Horrid and Shocking, but why, and in what, yet remained to be discovered. She could scarcely resolve what to think of her

line 5: 'However' inserted above line.   //   line 7: 'assure' written over illegible word.   //   line 8: 'done' inserted above line.   //   line 8: 'what' written over 'what Cloathes'; 'Cloathes' had been too cramped at the end of a line.   //   line 16: 'never' written over 'scarce'(?).

new Acquaintance; She appeared to be shamefully ignorant as to the Geography of England, if she had understood her right, and equally devoid of Taste and Information. Kitty was however unwilling to decide hastily; she was at once desirous of doing Miss Stanley justice, and of having her own Wishes in her answered; she determined therefore to suspend all Judgement for some time. After Supper, the Conversation turning on the State of Affairs in the political World, Mrs P, who was firmly of opinion that the whole race of Mankind were degenerating, said that for her part, Everything she beleived was going to rack and ruin, all order was destroyed over the face of the World, The house of Commons she heard did not break up sometimes till five in the Morning,[40] and Depravity never was so general before; concluding with a wish that she might live to see the Manners of the People in Queen Elizabeth's reign, restored again. "Well Ma'am, said her Neice,[41] but I hope you do not mean with the times to restore Queen Elizth. herself."

"Queen Elizth., said Mrs Stanley who never hazarded a remark on History that was not well founded, lived to a good old Age, and was a very Clever Woman."[42]

"True Ma'am, said Kitty; but I do not consider either of those Circumstances as meritorious in herself, and they are very far from making me wish her return, for if she were to come again with the same Abilities and the same good Constitution She might do as much Mischeif and last as long as she did before—then turning to Camilla who had been sitting very silent for some time, she added What do *you* think of Elizabeth Miss Stanley? I hope you will not defend her."

line 8: 'eterson' deleted, leaving 'P'.   //   line 16: 'I beleive you have as good a chance of it as any one else' deleted after 'Neice'.

"Oh! dear, said Miss Stanley, I know nothing of Politics, and cannot bear to hear them mentioned." Kitty started at this repulse, but made no answer; that Miss Stanley must be ignorant of what she could not distinguish from Politics,[43] she felt perfectly convinced.—She retired to her own room, perplexed in her opinion about her new Acquaintance, and fearful of her being very unlike Cecilia and Mary. She arose the next morning to experience a fuller conviction of this, and every future day encreased it—. She found no variety in her conversation; She received no information from her but in fashions, and no Amusement but in her performance on the Harpsichord;[44] and after repeated endeavours to find her what she wished, she was obliged to give up the attempt and to consider it as fruitless. There had occasionally appeared a something like humour in Camilla which had inspired her with hopes, that she might at least have a natural Genius, tho' not an improved one, but these Sparklings of Wit happened so seldom, and were so ill-supported that she was at last convinced of their being merely accidental. All her stock of knowledge was exhausted in a very few Days, and when Kitty had learnt from her, how large their house in Town was, when the fashionable Amusements began, who were the celebrated Beauties and who the best Millener, Camilla had nothing further to teach, except the Characters of any of her Acquaintance as they occurred in Conversation, which was done with equal Ease and Brevity, by saying that the person was either the sweetest Creature in the world,[45] and one of whom she was doatingly fond, or horrid, Shocking and not fit to be seen.

As Catherine was very desirous of gaining every possible information as to the Characters of the Halifax Family, and

line 4: 'History' deleted; 'Politics' inserted above line.   //   line 22: 'began' written over 'again'.

concluded that Miss Stanley must be acquainted with them, as she seemed to be so with every one of any Consequence, she took an opportunity as Camilla was one day enumerating all the people of rank that her Mother visited, of asking her whether Lady Halifax were among the number.

"Oh! Thank you for reminding me of her, She is the sweetest Woman in the world, and one of our most intimate Acquaintance; I do not suppose there is a day passes during the six Months that we are in Town, but what we see each other in the course of it—. And I correspond with all the Girls."

"They *are* then a very pleasant Family? said Kitty. They ought to be so indeed, to allow of such frequent Meetings, or all Conversation must be at end."

"Oh! dear, not at all, said Miss Stanley, for sometimes we do not speak to each other for a month together. We meet perhaps only in Public,[46] and then you know we are often not able to get near enough; but in that case we always nod and smile."

"Which does just as well—. But I was going to ask you whether you have ever seen a Miss Wynne with them?"

"I know who you mean perfectly—she wears a blue hat[47]—. I have frequently seen her in Brook Street,[48] when I have been at Lady Halifax's Balls—She gives one every Month during the Winter—. But only think how good it is in her to take care of Miss Wynne, for she is a very distant relation, and so poor that, as Miss Halifax told me, her Mother was obliged to find her in Cloathes.[49] Is not it shameful?"

"That she should be so poor;? it is indeed, with such wealthy connexions as the Family have."

---

lines 17–18: 'not always' deleted; 'often not' inserted above line. // line 21: 'ever' inserted above line.

"Oh! no; I mean, was not it shameful in Mr Wynne to leave his Children so distressed, when he had actually the Living of Chetwynde and two or three Curacies,[50] and only four Children to provide for—. What would he have done if he had had ten, as many people have?"

"He would have given them all a good Education and have left them all equally poor."

"Well I do think there never was so lucky a Family. Sir George Fitzgibbon you know sent the eldest Girl to India entirely at his own Expence, where they say she is most nobly married and the happiest Creature in the World—Lady Halifax you see has taken care of the youngest and treats her as if she were her Daughter; She does not go out into Public with her to be sure; but then she is always present when her Ladyship gives her Balls, and nothing can be kinder to her than Lady Halifax is; she would have taken her to Cheltenham[51] last year, if there had been room enough at the Lodgings, and therefore I dont think that *she* can have anything to complain of. Then there are the two Sons; one of them the Bishop of M——has got into the Army[52] as a Leiutenant I suppose; and the other is extremely well off I know, for I have a notion that somebody puts him to School somewhere in Wales.[53] Perhaps you knew them when they lived here?"

"Very well, We met as often as your Family and the Halifaxes do in Town, but as we seldom had any difficulty in getting near enough to speak, we seldom parted with merely a Nod and a Smile. They were indeed a most charming Family, and I beleive have scarcely their Equals in the World; The Neighbours we now have at the Parsonage, appear to more disadvantage in coming after them."

line 13: 'into' written over 'with'. // line 20: 'sent to Sea' deleted; 'got into the Army' inserted above line. // line 21: 'a' inserted above line. // line 24: 'Slightly:' deleted; 'Very well,' inserted above line.

"Oh! horrid Wretches! I wonder You can endure them."

"Why, what would you have one do?"

"Oh! Lord, If I were in your place, I should abuse them all day long."

"So I do, but it does no good."

"Well, I declare it is quite a pity that they should be suffered to live. I wish my Father would propose knocking all their Brains out, some day or other when he is in the House. So abominably proud of their Family! And I dare say after all, that there is nothing particular in it."

"Why Yes, I beleive they *have* reason to value themselves on it, if any body has; for you know he is Lord Amyatt's Brother."

"Oh! I know all that very well, but it is no reason for their being so horrid. I remember I met Miss Dudley last Spring with Lady Amyatt at Ranelagh,[54] and she had such a frightful Cap on, that I have never been able to bear any of them since.—And so you used to think the Wynnes very pleasant?"

"You speak as if their being so were doubtful! Pleasant! Oh! they were every thing that could interest and Attach. It is not in my power to do Justice to their Merits, tho' not to feel them, I think must be impossible. They have unfitted me for any Society but their own!"

"Well, That is just what I think of the Miss Halifaxes; by the bye, I must write to Caroline tomorrow, and I do not know what to say to her. The Barlows too are just such other sweet Girls; but I wish Augusta's hair was not so dark. I cannot bear Sir Peter—Horrid Wretch! He is *always* laid up with the Gout, which is exceedingly disagreable to the Family."

line 17: 'b' written over 'w' in 'bear'. // line 26: 'Barkers' deleted; 'Barlows' inserted above line.

"And perhaps not very pleasant to *himself*—. But as to the Wynnes; do you really think them very fortunate?"

"Do I? Why, does not every body? Miss Halifax and Caroline and Maria all say that they are the luckiest Creatures in the World. So does Sir George Fitzgibbon and so do Everybody."

"That is, Every body who have themselves conferred an obligation on them. But do you call it lucky, for a Girl of Genius and Feeling to be sent in quest of a Husband to Bengal, to be married there to a Man of whose Disposition she has no opportunity of judging till her Judgement is of no use to her, who may be a Tyrant, or a Fool or both for what she knows to the Contrary. Do you call *that* fortunate?"

"I know nothing of all that; I only know that it was extremely good in Sir George to fit her out and pay for her Passage, and that she would not have found Many who would have done the same."

"I wish she had not found *one*, said Kitty with great Eagerness, she might then have remained in England and been happy."

"Well, I cannot conceive the hardship of going out in a very agreable Manner with two or three sweet Girls for Companions, having a delightful voyage to Bengal or Barbadoes[55] or wherever it is, and being married soon after one's arrival to a very charming Man immensely rich—. I see no hardship in all that."

"Your representation of the Affair, said Kitty laughing, certainly gives a very different idea of it from Mine. But supposing all this to be true, still, as it was by no means certain that she would be so fortunate either in her voyage, her Companions, or her husband; in being obliged to run the risk

line 19: 'then' inserted above line.

of their proving very different, she undoubtedly experienced a great hardship—. Besides, to a Girl of any Delicacy, the voyage in itself, since the object of it is so universally known, is a punishment that needs no other to make it very severe."

"I do not see that at all. She is not the first Girl who has gone to the East Indies for a Husband, and I declare I should think it very good fun if I were as poor."

"I beleive you would think very differently *then*. But at least you will not defend her Sister's situation? Dependant even for her Cloathes on the bounty of others, who of course do not pity her, as by your own account, they consider her as very fortunate."

"You are extremely nice[56] upon my word; Lady Halifax is a delightful Woman, and one of the sweetest tempered Creatures in the World; I am sure I have every reason to speak well of her, for we are under most amazing Obligations to her. She has frequently chaperoned me when my Mother has been indisposed, and last Spring she lent me her own horse three times, which was a prodigious favour, for it is the most beautiful Creature that ever was seen, and I am the only person she ever lent it to.[57]

And then, continued she, the Miss Halifaxes are quite delightful—. Maria is one of the cleverest Girls that ever were known—Draws in Oils,[58] and plays anything by sight. She promised me one of her Drawings before I left Town, but I entirely forgot to ask her for it—. I would give any thing to have one."[59]

---

line 21: Catharine's reply deleted after 'to': 'If so, *Mary Wynne* can receive very little advantage from *her* having it.' // line 22: 'continued she,' inserted above line. // line 27: first four lines of Catharine's reply deleted after 'one': 'Why indeed, if Maria will give my Freind a drawing, she can have nothing to complain of, but as she does not write in Spirits, I suppose she has not yet been fortunate enough to be so distinguished.'

"But was not it very odd, said Kitty, that the Bishop should send Charles Wynne to sea,[60] when he must have had a much better chance of providing for him in the Church, which was the profession that Charles liked best, and the one for which his Father had intended him? The Bishop I know had often promised Mr Wynne a living, and as he never gave him one, I think it was incumbant on him to transfer the promise to his Son."

"I beleive you think he ought to have resigned his Bishopric to him; you seem determined to be dissatisfied with every thing that has been done for them."

"Well, said Kitty, this is a subject on which we shall never agree, and therefore it will be useless to continue it farther, or to mention it again—" She then left the room, and running out of the House was soon in her dear Bower where she could indulge in peace all her affectionate Anger against the relations of the Wynnes, which was greatly heightened by finding from Camilla that they were in general considered as having acted particularly well by them—. She amused herself for some time in Abusing, and Hating them all, with great Spirit, and when this tribute to her regard for the Wynnes, was paid, and the Bower began to have its usual influence over her Spirits, she contributed towards settling them, by taking out a book, for she had always one about her, and reading—. She had been so employed for nearly an hour, when Camilla came running towards her with great Eagerness, and apparently great Pleasure—. "Oh! my Dear Catherine, said she, half out of Breath—I have such delightful News for You—But you shall guess what it is—We are all the happiest Creatures in the World; would you beleive it,

line 1: 'said Kitty,' inserted above line.   //   line 21: 'the' deleted; 'her' inserted above line.   //   line 26: 'her' inserted above line.

the Dudleys have sent us an invitation to a Ball at their own House—. What Charming People they are! I had no idea of there being so much Sense in the whole Family—I declare I quite doat upon them—. And it happens so fortunately too, for I expect a new Cap from Town tomorrow which will just do for a Ball—Gold Net.[61]—It will be a most angelic thing—Every Body will be longing for the pattern[62]—" The expectation of a Ball was indeed very agreable intelligence to Kitty, who fond of Dancing and seldom able to enjoy it, had reason to feel even greater pleasure in it than her Freind; for to *her*, it was now no novelty—. Camilla's delight however was by no means inferior to Kitty's, and she rather expressed the most of the two. The Cap came and every other preparation was soon completed; while these were in agitation the Days passed gaily away, but when Directions were no longer necessary, Taste could no longer be displayed, and Difficulties no longer overcome, the short period that intervened before the day of the Ball hung heavily on their hands, and every hour was too long. The very few Times that Kitty had ever enjoyed the Amusement of Dancing was an excuse for *her* impatience, and an apology for the Idleness it occasioned to a Mind naturally very Active; but her Freind without such a plea was infinitely worse than herself. She could do nothing but wander from the house to the Garden, and from the Garden to the avenue, wondering when Thursday would come, which she might easily have ascertained, and counting the hours as they passed which served only to lengthen them.—. They retired to their rooms in high Spirits on Wednesday night, but Kitty awoke the next Morning with a violent Toothake. It was in vain that she endeavoured at first to deceive herself; her feelings were witnesses too acute of it's reality; with as

line 6: 'Gold Net.' inserted above line.

little success did she try to sleep it off, for the pain she suffered prevented her closing her Eyes—. She then summoned her Maid and with the Assistance of the Housekeeper, every remedy that the receipt book[63] or the head of the latter contained, was tried, but ineffectually; for though for a short time releived by them, the pain still returned. She was now obliged to give up the endeavour, and to reconcile herself not only to the pain of a Toothake, but to the loss of a Ball; and though she had with so much eagerness looked forward to the day of its arrival, had received such pleasure in the necessary preparations, and promised herself so much delight in it, Yet she was not so totally void of philosophy as many Girls of her age, might have been in her situation. She considered that there were Misfortunes of a much greater magnitude than the loss of a Ball, experienced every day by somepart of Mortality, and that the time might come when She would herself look back with Wonder and perhaps with Envy on her having known no greater vexation. By such reflections as these, she soon reasoned herself into as much Resignation and Patience as the pain she suffered, would allow of, which after all was the greatest Misfortune of the two, and told the sad Story when she entered the Breakfast room, with tolerable Composure. Mrs Percival more greived for her toothake than her Disappointment, as she feared that it would not be possible to prevent her Dancing with a *Man* if she went, was eager to try everything that had already been applied to alleviate the pain, while at the same time She declared it was impossible for her to leave the House. Miss Stanley who joined to her concern for her Freind, felt a mixture of Dread lest her Mother's proposal that they should all remain at home, might be accepted,

line 16: 'that' inserted above line.   //   line 23: 'Peterson' deleted; 'Percival' inserted above line.

was very violent in her sorrow on the occasion, and though her apprehensions on the subject were soon quieted by Kitty's protesting that sooner than allow any one to stay with her, she would herself go, she continued to lament it with such unceasing vehemence as at last drove Kitty to her own room. Her Fears for herself being now entirely dissipated left her more than ever at leisure to pity and persecute her Freind who tho' safe when in her own room, was frequently removing from it to some other in hopes of being more free from pain, and then had no opportunity of escaping her—.

"To be sure, there never was anything so shocking, said Camilla; To come on such a day too! For one would not have minded it you know had it been at *any other* time. But it always is so. I never was at a Ball in my Life, but what something happened to prevent somebody from going! I wish there were no such things as Teeth in the World; they are nothing but plagues to one, and I dare say that People might easily invent something to eat with instead of them; Poor Thing! what pain you are in! I declare it is quite Shocking to look at you. But you w'ont have it out, will you? For Heaven's sake do'nt; for there is nothing I dread so much. I declare I had rather undergo the greatest Tortures in the World than have a tooth drawn.[64] Well! how patiently you do bear it! how can you be so quiet? Lord, if I were in your place I should make such a fuss, there would be no bearing me. I should torment you to Death."

"So you do, as it is." thought Kitty.

"For my own part, Catherine said Mrs Percival I have not a doubt but that you caught this toothake by sitting so much in that Arbour, for it is always damp. I know it has ruined your Constitution entirely; and indeed I do not beleive it has been of much service to mine; I sate down in it last May to rest myself, and I have never been quite well since—. I shall order John to pull it all down[65] I assure you."

"I know you will not do that Ma'am, said Kitty, as you must be convinced how unhappy it would make me."

"You talk very ridiculously Child; it is all whim and Nonsense. Why cannot you fancy this room an Arbour?"

"Had this room been built by Cecilia and Mary, I should have valued it equally Ma'am, for it is not merely the name of an Arbour, which charms me."

"Why indeed Mrs Percival, said Mrs Stanley, I must think that Catherine's affection for her Bower is the effect of a Sensibility that does her Credit. I love to see a Freindship between young Persons and always consider it as a sure mark of an amiable affectionate disposition. I have from Camilla's infancy taught her to think the same, and have taken great pains to introduce her to young people of her own age who were likely to be worthy of her regard. nothing forms the taste more than sensible and Elegant Letters—. Lady Halifax thinks just like me—. Camilla corresponds with her Daughters, and I believe I may venture to say that they are none of them *the worse* for it." These ideas were too modern to suit Mrs Percival who considered a correspondence between Girls as productive of no good, and as the frequent origin of imprudence and Error by the effect of pernicious advice and bad Example. She could not therefore refrain from saying that for her part, she had lived fifty Years in the world without

line 12: 'Peterson' deleted; 'Percival' inserted above line.   //   line 15: 'Ladies' deleted; 'Persons' inserted above line.   //   line 16: 'of their being disposed to like one another' deleted; 'of an amiable affectionate disposition' inserted above line.   //   line 19: 'There is something mighty pretty I think in young Ladies corresponding with each other, and' deleted after 'regard'. //   line 24: 'Peterson' deleted; 'Percival' inserted above line.

having ever had a correspondent, and did not find herself at all the less respectable for it—. Mrs Stanley could say nothing in answer to this, but her Daughter who was less governed by Propriety said in her thoughtless way, "But who knows what you might have been Ma'am, if you *had* had a Correspondent; perhaps it would have made you quite a different Creature. I declare I would not be without those I have for all the World. It is the greatest delight of my Life, and you cannot think how much their Letters have formed my taste as Mama says, for I hear from them generally every week."

"You received a Letter from Augusta Barlow to day, did not you my Love? said her Mother—. She writes remarkably well I know."

"Oh! Yes Ma'am, the most delightful Letter you ever heard of. She sends me a long account of the new Regency walking dress[66] Lady Susan has given her, and it is so beautiful that I am quite dieing with envy for it."

"Well, I am prodigiously happy to hear such pleasing news of my young freind; I have a high regard for Augusta, and most sincerely partake in the general Joy on the occasion. But does she say nothing else? it seemed to be a long Letter—Are they to be at Scarborough?"

"Oh! Lord, she never once mentions it, now I recollect it; and I entirely forgot to ask her when I wrote last. She says nothing indeed except about the Regency." "She *must* write well thought Kitty, to make a long Letter upon a Bonnet and Pelisse."[67] She then left the room tired of listening to a conversation which tho' it might have diverted her had she been

line 11: 'Barlow' inserted above line.   //   line 15–16: 'Bonnet'(?) deleted; 'Regency walking dress' inserted above line.   //   line 25: 'Bonnet'(?) deleted; 'Regency' inserted above line.   //   line 26–27: 'Jacket and petticoat' deleted; 'Bonnet and Pelisse' inserted above line.   //   line 27: 'the' inserted above line.

well, served only to fatigue and depress her, while in pain. Happy was it for *her*, when the hour of dressing came, for Camilla satisfied with being surrounded by her Mother and half the Maids in the House did not want her assistance, and was too agreably employed to want her Society. She remained therefore alone in the parlour, till joined by Mr Stanley and her Aunt, who however after a few enquiries, allowed her to continue undisturbed and began their usual conversation on Politics. This was a Subject on which they could never agree, for Mr Stanley who considered himself as perfectly qualified by his Seat in the House, to decide on it without hesitation, resolutely maintained that the Kingdom had not for ages been in so flourishing and prosperous a state,[68] and Mrs Percival with equal warmth, tho' perhaps less argument, as vehemently asserted that the whole Nation would speedily be ruined, and everything as she expressed herself be at sixes and sevens.[69] It was not however unamusing to Kitty to listen to the Dispute, especially as she began then to be more free from pain, and without taking any share in it herself, she found it very entertaining to observe the eagerness with which they both defended their opinions, and could not help thinking that Mr Stanley would not feel more disappointed if her Aunt's expectations were fulfilled, than her Aunt would be mortified by their failure. After waiting a considerable time Mrs Stanley and her daughter appeared, and Camilla in high Spirits, and perfect good humour with her own looks, was more violent than ever in her lamentations over her Freind as she practised her scotch Steps[70] about the room—. At length they departed, and Kitty better able to amuse herself than she had been the whole Day before, wrote a long account

line 1: 'her,' inserted above line.   //   line 8: 'remain' deleted; 'continue' inserted above line.   //   line 14: 'Peterson' deleted; 'Percival' inserted above line.

of her Misfortunes to Mary Wynne. When her Letter was concluded she had an opportunity of witnessing the truth of that assertion which says that Sorrows are lightened by Communication, for her toothake was then so much releived that she began to entertain an idea of following her Freinds to Mr Dudley's. They had been gone an hour, and as every thing relative to her Dress was in complete readiness, She considered that in another hour[71] since there was so little a way to go, She might be there—. They were gone in Mr Stanley's Carriage and therefore She might follow in her Aunt's. . As the plan seemed so very easy to be executed, and promising so much pleasure, it was after a few Minutes deliberation finally adopted, and running up stairs, She rang in great haste for her Maid. The Bustle and Hurry which then ensued for nearly an hour was at last happily concluded by her finding herself very well-dressed and in high Beauty. Anne was then dispatched in the same haste to order the Carriage, while her Mistress was putting on her gloves, and arranging the folds of her dress.[72] In a few Minutes she heard the Carriage drive up to the Door, and tho' at first surprised at the expedition with which it had been got ready, she concluded after a little reflection that the Men had received some hint of her intentions beforehand, and was hastening out of the room, when Anne came running into it in the greatest hurry and agitation, exclaiming "Lord Ma'am! Here's a Gentleman in a Chaise and four[73] come, and I cannot for my Life conceive who it is! I happened to be crossing the hall when the Carriage drove

line 6: 'but half' deleted after 'gone'.   //   line 6: 'thing' inserted above line.   //   line 8: 'an hour and a half' deleted; 'another hour' inserted above line.   //   line 12: 'in itself' deleted after 'pleasure'.   //   line 15: 'about' deleted; 'nearly' inserted above line.   //   line 16: 'Nanny' deleted; 'Anne' inserted above line.   //   line 18: ampersand inserted above line.   //   line 19: 'and providing herself with Lavender water' deleted after 'dress'.   //   line 24: 'Nanny' deleted; 'Anne' inserted above line.

up, and I knew nobody would be in the way to let him in but
Tom, and he looks so awkward you know Ma'am, now his
hair is just done up,[74] that I was not willing the gentleman
should see him, and so I went to the door myself. And he is
one of the handsomest young Men you would wish to see; I
was almost ashamed of being seen in my Apron[75] Ma'am, but
however he is vastly handsome and did not seem to mind it
at all.—And he asked me whether the Family were at home;
and so I said everybody was gone out but you Ma'am, for I
would not deny you because I was sure you would like to see
him. And then he asked me whether Mr and Mrs Stanley
were not here, and so I said Yes, and then—

"Good Heavens! said Kitty, what can all this mean! And
who can it possibly be! Did you never see him before? And
Did not he tell you his Name?"

"No Ma'am, he never said anything about it—So then I
asked him to walk into the parlour, and he was prodigious
agreable, and—"

"Whoever he is, said her Mistress, he has made a great
impression upon you Nanny—But where did he come from?
and what does he want here?"

"Oh! Ma'am, I was going to tell you, that I fancy his business is with You; for he asked me whether you were at leisure
to see anybody, and desired I would give his Compliments
to you, and say he should be very happy to wait on you—
However I thought he had better not come up into your
Dressing room, especially as everything is in such a litter,[76]
so I told him if he would be so obliging as to stay in the
parlour, I would run up Stairs and tell you he was come, and
I dared to say that you would wait upon *him*. Lord Ma'am,

line 1: 'as' deleted after 'and'.   //   line 6: 'because you know Ma'am I am all
over powder' deleted; 'in my Apron Ma'am' inserted above line.

I'd lay anything that he is come to ask you to dance with him tonight, and has got his Chaise ready to take you to Mr Dudley's."

Kitty could not help laughing at this idea, and only wished it might be true, as it was very likely that she would be too late for any other partner—"But what in the name of wonder, can he have to say to me? Perhaps he is come to rob the house—. he comes in stile at least; and it will be some consolation for our losses to be robbed by a Gentleman in a Chaise and 4—. What Livery[77] has his Servants?"

"Why that is the most wonderful thing about him Ma'am, for he has not a single servant with him, and came with hack horses;[78] But he is as handsome as a Prince for all that, and has quite the look of one—. Do dear Ma'am, go down, for I am sure you will be delighted with him—"

"Well, I beleive I must go; but it is very odd! What can he have to say to me." Then giving one look at herself in the Glass,[79] she walked with great impatience, tho' trembling all the while from not knowing what to expect, down Stairs, and after pausing a moment at the door to gather Courage for opening it, she resolutely entered the room.

The Stranger, whose appearance did not disgrace the account she had received of it from her Maid, rose up on her entrance, and laying aside the Newspaper he had been reading, advanced towards her with an air of the most perfect Ease and Vivacity, and said to her, "It is certainly a very awkward circumstance to be thus obliged to introduce myself, but I trust that the necessity of the case will plead my Excuse, and prevent your being prejudiced by it against me—. *Your* name, I need not ask Ma'am—. Miss Percival is too well known to me by description to need any information of that." Kitty,

line 30: 'Miss Peterson' deleted; 'Miss Percival' inserted above line.

who had been expecting him to tell his own name, instead of hers, and who from having been little in company, and never before in such a situation, felt herself unable to ask it, tho' she had been planning her speech all the way down stairs, was so confused and distressed by this unexpected addess that she could only return a slight curtesy to it and accepted the chair he reached her, without knowing what she did. The gentleman then continued. "You are, I dare say, surprised to see me returned from France so soon, and nothing indeed but business would have brought me to England; a very Melancholy affair has now occasioned it, and I was unwilling to leave it without paying my respects to the Family in Devonshire[80] whom I have so long wished to be acquainted with—."

Kitty, who felt much more surprised at his supposing her *to be so*, than at seeing a person in England, whose having ever left it was perfectly unknown to her, still continued silent from Wonder and Perplexity, and her visitor still continued to talk. "You will suppose Madam that I was not the *less* desirous of waiting on you, from your having Mr and Mrs Stanley with You—. I hope they are well? And Mrs Percival how does *she* do?" Then without waiting for an answer he gaily added, "But my dear Miss Percival you are going out I am sure; and I am detaining you from your appointment. How can I ever expect to be forgiven for such injustice! Yet how can I, so circumstanced, forbear to offend! You seem dressed for a Ball? But this is the Land of gaiety I know; I have for many years been desirous of visiting it. You have Dances I suppose at least every week—But where are the rest of your party gone, and what kind Angel in compassion to me, has excluded *you* from it?"

line 20: 'Peterson' deleted; 'Percival' inserted above line.   //   line 22: 'eterson' deleted; 'ercival' inserted above line.

"Perhaps Sir, said Kitty extremely confused by his manner of speaking to her, and highly displeased with the freedom of his Conversation towards one who had never seen him before and did not *now* know his name, perhaps Sir, you are acquainted with Mr and Mrs Stanley; and your business may be with *them*?"

"You do me too much honour Ma'am, replied he laughing, in supposing me to be acquainted with Mr and Mrs Stanley; I merely know them by sight; very distant relations; only my Father and Mother; Nothing more. I assure you."

"Gracious Heaven! said Kitty, are *you* Mr Stanley then?—I beg a thousand pardons—Though really upon recollection I do not know for what—for you never told me your name—"

"I beg your pardon—I made a very fine Speech when you entered the room, all about introducing myself; I assure you it was very great for *me*."

"The speech had certainly great Merit, said Kitty smiling; I thought so at the time; but since you never mentioned your name in it, as an *introductory one* it might have been better."

There was such an air of good humour and Gaiety in Stanley, that Kitty, tho' perhaps not authorized to address him with so much familiarity on so short an acquaintance, could not forbear indulging the natural Unreserve and Vivacity of her own Disposition, in speaking to him, as he spoke to her. She was intimately acquainted too with his Family who were her relations, and she chose to consider herself entitled by the connexion to forget how little a while they had known each other. "Mr and Mrs Stanley and your Sister are extremely well, said She, and will I dare say be very much surprised to

line 18: 'as' deleted; 'since' inserted above line.   //   line 21: 'e' in 'Gaiety' inserted above line.

see you—But I am sorry to hear that your return to England has been occasioned by any unpleasant circumstance."

"Oh! Do'nt talk of it, said he, it is a most confounded shocking[81] affair, and makes me miserable to think of it; But where are my Father and Mother, and your Aunt gone? Oh! Do you know that I met the prettiest little waiting maid in the World, when I came here; she let me into the house; I took her for you at first."

"You did me a great deal of honour, and give me more credit for good nature than I deserve, for I *never* go to the door when any one comes."[82]

"Nay do not be angry; I mean no offence. But tell me, where are you going to so smart?[83] Your carriage is just coming round."

"I am going to a Dance at a Neighbour's, where your Family and my Aunt are already gone."

"Gone, without you! what's the meaning of *that*? But I suppose you are like myself, rather long in dressing."

"I must have been so indeed, if that were the case for they have been gone nearly these two hours; The reason how-ever was not what you suppose—I was prevented going by a pain—"

"By a pain! interrupted Stanley, Oh! heavens, that is dread-ful indeed! No Matter where the pain was. But my dear Miss Percival, what do you say to my accompanying you? And sup-pose you were to dance with me too? *I* think it would be very pleasant."

"I can have no objection to either I am sure, said Kitty laughing to find how near the truth her Maid's conjecture had been; on the contrary I shall be highly honoured by both,

line 14: 'round' written over 'to fetch'(?). // line 15: 'of ours' deleted after 'Neighbours'. // line 25: 'Peterson' deleted; 'Percival' inserted above line.

and I can answer for Your being extremely welcome to the Family who give the Ball."

"Oh! hang them; who cares for that; they cannot turn me out of the house. But I am afraid I shall cut a sad figure among all your Devonshire Beaux[84] in this dusty, travelling apparel,[85] and I have not wherewithal to change it. You can procure me some powder[86] perhaps, and I must get a pair of Shoes[87] from one of the Men, for I was in such a devil of a hurry to leave Lyons[88] that I had not time to have anything pack'd up but some linen."[89] Kitty very readily undertook to procure for him everything he wanted, and telling the footman to shew him into Mr Stanley's dressing room,[90] gave Nanny orders to send in some powder and pomatum, which orders Nanny chose to execute in person. As Stanley's preparations in dressing were confined to such very trifling articles, Kitty of course expected him in about ten minutes; but she found that it had not been merely a boast of vanity in saying that he was dilatory in that respect, as he kept her waiting for him above half an hour, so that the Clock had struck ten before he entered the room and the rest of the party had gone by eight.[91]

"Well, said he as he came in, have not I been very quick? I never hurried so much in my Life before."

"In that case you certainly have, replied Kitty, for all Merit you know is comparative."

"Oh! I knew you would be delighted with me for making so much haste—. But come, the Carriage is ready; so, do not keep me waiting." And so saying he took her by the hand, and led her out of the room. "Why, my dear Cousin, said he

line 6: 'lend' deleted; 'procure' inserted above line. // line 9: 'pack up anything' deleted; 'have anything pack'd up' inserted above line. // line 20: 'by' written over 'before'. // line 27: 'much' is 'must' in ms. // line 30: 'her' inserted above line.

when they were seated, this will be a most agreable surprize to every body to see you enter the room with such a smart Young Fellow as I am—I hope your Aunt w'ont be alarmed."

"To tell you the truth, replied Kitty, I think the best way to prevent it, will be to send for her, or your Mother before we go into the room, especially as you are a perfect stranger, and must of course be introduced to Mr and Mrs Dudley—"

"Oh! Nonsense, said he; I did not expect *you* to stand upon such Ceremony; Our acquaintance with each other renders all such Prudery, ridiculous; Besides, if we go in together, we shall be the whole talk of the Country—"

"To *me* replied Kitty, that would certainly be a most powerful inducement; but I scarcely know whether my Aunt would consider it as such—. Women at her time of life, have odd ideas of propriety you know."

"Which is the very thing that you ought to break them of; and why should you object to entering a room with me where all our relations are, when you have done me the honour to admit me without any chaprone into your Carriage? Do not you think your Aunt will be as much offended with you for one, as for the other of these mighty crimes."

"Why really said Catherine, I do not know but that she may; however, it is no reason that I should offend against Decorum a second time, because I have already done it once."

"On the contrary, that is the very reason which makes it impossible for you to prevent it, since you cannot offend for the *first time* again."

"You are very ridiculous, said she laughing, but I am afraid your arguments divert me too much to convince me."

"At least they will convince you that I am very agreable, which after all, is the happiest conviction for me, and as to the affair of Propriety we will let that rest till we arrive at our

Journey's end—. This is a monthly Ball[92] I suppose. Nothing but Dancing here—."

"I thought I had told you that it was given by a Mr Dudley—"

"Oh! aye so you did; but why should not Mr Dudley give one every month? By the bye who *is that* Man? Every body gives Balls now I think; I beleive I must give one myself soon—. Well, but how do you like my Father and Mother? And poor little Camilla too, has not she plagued you to death with the Halifaxes?" Here the Carriage fortunately stopped at Mr Dudley's, and Stanley was too much engaged in handing her out of it, to wait for an answer, or to remember that what he had said required one. They entered the small vestibule which Mr Dudley had raised to the Dignity of a Hall,[93] and Kitty immediately desired the footman who was leading the way upstairs, to inform either Mrs Peterson, or Mrs Stanley of her arrival, and beg them to come to her, but Stanley unused to any contradiction and impatient to be amongst them, would neither allow her to wait, or listen to what she said, and forcibly seizing her arm within his, overpowered her voice with the rapidity of his own, and Kitty half angry, and half laughing was obliged to go with him up stairs, and could even with difficulty prevail on him to relinquish her hand before they entered the room. Mrs Percival was at that very moment engaged in conversation with a Lady at the upper end of the room,[94] to whom she had been giving a long account of her Neice's unlucky disappointment, and the dreadful pain that she had with so much fortitude, endured the whole Day—"I left her however, said She, thank heaven!, a little better, and I hope she has been able to amuse herself

line 24: 'Peterson' deleted; 'Percival' inserted above line.

with a book, poor thing! for she must otherwise be very dull. She is probably in bed by this time, which while she is so poorly, is the best place for her you know Ma'am." The Lady was going to give her assent to this opinion, when the Noise of voices on the stairs, and the footman's opening the door as if for the entrance of Company, attracted the attention of every body in the room; and as it was in one of those Intervals between the Dances when every one seemed glad to sit down, Mrs Peterson had a most unfortunate opportunity of seeing her Neice whom she had supposed in bed, or amusing herself as the height of gaity with a book, enter the room most elegantly dressed, with a smile on her Countenance, and a glow of mingled Chearfulness and Confusion on her Cheeks, attended by a young Man uncommonly handsome, and who without any of her Confusion, appeared to have all her vivacity. Mrs Percival, colouring with anger and Astonishment, rose from her Seat, and Kitty walked eagerly towards her, impatient to account for what she saw appeared wonderful to every body, and extremely offensive to *her*, while Camilla on seeing her Brother ran instantly towards him, and very soon explained who he was by her words and her actions. Mr Stanley, who so fondly doated on his Son, that the pleasure of seeing him again after an absence of three Months prevented his feeling for the time any anger against him for returning to England without his knowledge, received him with equal surprise and delight; and soon comprehending the cause of his Journey, forbore any further conversation with him, as he was eager to see his Mother, and it was necessary that he should be introduced to Mr Dudley's family. This introduction to any one but Stanley would have been highly unpleasant, for they considered their dignity injured by his

line 16: 'Peterson' deleted; 'Percival' inserted above line.

coming uninvited to their house, and received him with more than their usual haughtiness; But Stanley who with a vivacity of temper seldom subdued, and a contempt of censure not to be overcome, possessed an opinion of his own Consequence, and a perseverance in his own schemes which were not to be damped by the conduct of others, appeared not to perceive it. The Civilities therefore which they coldly offered, he received with a gaiety and ease peculiar to himself, and then attended by his Father and Sister walked into another room where his Mother was playing at Cards,[95] to experience another Meeting, and undergo a repetition of pleasure, Surprise, and Explanations. While these were passing, Camilla eager to communicate all she felt to some one who would attend to her, returned to Catherine, and seating herself by her, immediately began—"Well, did you ever know anything so delightful as this? But it always is so; I never go to a Ball in my Life but what something or other happens unexpectedly that is quite charming!"

"A Ball replied Kitty, seems to be a most eventful thing to You—".

"Oh! Lord, it is indeed—But only think of my brother's returning so suddenly—And how shocking a thing it is that has brought him over! I never heard anything so dreadful—!"

"What is it pray that has occasioned his leaving France? I am sorry to find that it is a melancholy event."

"Oh! it is beyond anything you can conceive! His favourite Hunter[96] who was turned out in the park on his going abroad, somehow or other fell ill—No, I beleive it was an accident, but however it was something or other, or else it was something else, and so they sent an Express[97] immediately to Lyons

line 2: 'joined to' deleted; 'with' inserted above line. // line 8: 'e' in 'gaiety' inserted above line.

where my Brother was, for they knew that he valued this Mare more than anything else in the World besides; and so my Brother set off directly for England, and without packing up another Coat; I am quite angry with him about it; it was so shocking you know to come away without a change of Cloathes—"

"Why indeed said Kitty, it seems to have been a very shocking affair from beginning to end."

"Oh! it is beyond anything You can conceive! I would rather have had *anything* happen than that he should have lossed that mare."

"Except his coming away without an other coat."

"Oh! yes, that has vexed me more than you can imagine—. Well, and so Edward got to Brampton[98] just as the poor Thing was dead,—but as he could not bear to remain there *then*, he came off directly to Chetwynde on purpose to see us—. I hope he may not go abroad again."

"Do you think he will not?"

"Oh! dear, to be sure he must, but I wish he may not with all my heart—. You cannot think how fond I am of him! By the bye are not you in love with him yourself?"

"To be sure I am replied Kitty laughing, I am in love with every handsome Man I see."

"That is just like me—*I* am always in love with every handsome Man in the World."

"There you outdo me replied Catherine for I am only in love with those I *do* see." Mrs Percival who was sitting on the other side of her, and who began now to distinguish the words, *Love* and *handsome Man*, turned hastily towards them, and said "What are you talking of Catherine?" To

line 12: 'your Brother's' deleted; 'his' inserted above line. // line 27: 'Peterson' deleted; 'Percival' inserted above line.

which Catherine immediately answered with the simple arti-
fice of a Child, "Nothing Ma'am." She had already received
a very severe lecture from her Aunt on the imprudence of
her behaviour during the whole evening; She blamed her for
coming to the Ball, for coming in the same Carriage with
Edward Stanley, and still more for entering the room with
him. For the last-mentioned offence Catherine knew not
what apology to give, and tho' she longed in answer to the
second to say that she had not thought it would be civil to
make Mr Stanley *walk*, she dared not so to trifle with her
aunt, who would have been but the more offended by it.
The first accusation however she considered as very unreasonable, as she thought herself perfectly justified in coming.
This conversation continued till Edward Stanley entering the
room came instantly towards her, and telling her that every
one waited for *her* to begin the next Dance led her to the top
of the room,[99] for Kitty impatient to escape from so unpleasant a Companion, without the least hesitation, or one civil
scruple at being so distinguished, immediately gave him her
hand, and joyfully left her Seat. This Conduct however was
highly resented by several young Ladies present, and among
the rest by Miss Stanley whose regard for her brother tho'
excessive, and whose affection for Kitty tho' *prodigious*, were
not proof against such an injury to her importance and her
peace. Edward had however only consulted his own inclinations in desiring Miss Peterson to begin the Dance, nor had
he any reason to know that it was either wished or expected
by anyone else in the Party. As an heiress she was certainly
of consequence, but her Birth gave her no other claim to it,
for her Father had been a Merchant. It was this very circumstance which rendered this unfortunate affair so offensive to
Camilla, for tho' she would sometimes boast in the pride of
her heart, and her eagerness to be admired that she did not

know who her grandfather had been, and was as ignorant of everything relative to Genealogy as to Astronomy, (and she might have added, Geography) yet she was really proud of her family and Connexions, and easily offended if they were treated with Neglect. "I should not have minded it, said she to her Mother, if she had been *anybody* else's daughter; but to see her pretend to be above *me*, when her Father was only a tradesman,[100] is too bad! It is such an affront to our whole Family! I declare I think Papa ought to interfere in it, but he never cares about anything but Politics. If I were Mr Pitt or the Lord Chancellor,[101] he would take care I should not be insulted, but he never thinks about *me*; And it is so provoking that *Edward* should let her stand there. I wish with all my heart that he had never come to England! I hope she may fall down and break her neck, or sprain her Ancle." Mrs Stanley perfectly agreed with her daughter concerning the affair, and tho' with less violence, expressed almost equal resentment at the indignity. Kitty in the meantime remained insensible of having given any one Offence, and therefore unable either to offer an apology, or make a reparation; her whole attention was occupied by the happiness she enjoyed in dancing with the most elegant young Man in the room, and every one else was equally unregarded. The Evening indeed to *her*, passed off delightfully; he was her partner during the greatest part of it,[102] and the united attractions that he possessed of Person, Address[103] and vivacity, had easily gained that preference from Kitty which they seldom fail of obtaining from every one. She was too happy to care either for her Aunt's illhumour which she could not help remarking, or for the Alteration in Camilla's behaviour which forced itself at

line 24: 'to' written over 'with'.   //   line 25: 'that' inserted above line.   //
line 29: 'observing' deleted; 'remarking' inserted above line.

last on her observation. Her Spirits were elevated above the influence of Displeasure in any one, and she was equally indifferent as to the Cause of Camilla's, or the continuance of her Aunt's. Though Mr Stanley could never be really offended by any imprudence or folly in his Son that had given him the pleasure of seeing him, he was yet perfectly convinced that Edward ought not to remain in England, and was resolved to hasten his leaving it as soon as possible; but when he talked to Edward about it, he found him much less disposed towards returning to France, than to accompany them in their projected tour, which he assured his Father would be infinitely more pleasant to him, and that as to the affair of travelling he considered it of no importance, and what might be pursued at any little odd time, when he had nothing better to do. He advanced these objections in a manner which plainly shewed that he had scarcely a doubt of their being complied with, and appeared to consider his father's arguments in opposition to them, as merely given with a veiw to keep up his authority, and such as he should find little difficulty in combating. He concluded at last by saying, as the chaise in which they returned together from Mr Dudley's reached Mrs Percivals, "Well Sir, we will settle this point some other time, and fortunately it is of so little consequence, that an immediate discussion of it is unnecessary." He then got out of the chaise and entered the house without waiting for his Father's reply. It was not till their return that Kitty could account for that coldness in Camilla's behaviour to her, which had been so pointed as to render it impossible to be entirely unnoticed. When however they were seated in the Coach with the two other Ladies,

line 5: 'in his Son' inserted above line.   //   line 6: 'his' changed to 'him'; 'Son' deleted, thus changing 'his Son' to 'him'.   //   line 9: 'he found him' inserted above line.   //   line 21: 'Petersons' deleted; 'Percivals' inserted above line.

Miss Stanley's indignation was no longer to be suppressed from breaking out into words, and found the following vent.

"Well, I must say *this*, that I never was at a stupider Ball in my Life! But it always is so; I am always disappointed in them for some reason or other. I wish there were no such things."

"I am sorry Miss Stanley, said Mrs Percival drawing herself up, that you have not been amused; every thing was meant for the best I am sure, and it is a poor encouragement for your Mama to take you to another if you are so hard to be satisfied."

"I do not know what you mean Ma'am about Mama's *taking* me to another. You know I am come out."[104]

"Oh! dear Mrs Percival, said Mrs Stanley, you must not beleive every thing that my lively Camilla says, for her Spirits are prodigiously high sometimes, and she frequently speaks without thinking. I am sure it is impossible for *any one* to have been at a more elegant or agreable dance, and so she wishes to express herself I am certain."

"To be sure I do, said Camilla very sulkily, only I must say that it is not very pleasant to have any body behave so rude to one as to be quite shocking! I am sure I am not at all offended, and should not care if all the World were to stand above me, but still it is extremely abominable, and what I cannot put up with. It is not that I mind it in the least, for I had just as soon stand at the bottom as at the top all night long, if it was not so very disagreeable—. But to have a person come in the middle of the Evening and take everybody's place is what I am not used to, and tho' I do not care a pin about it myself, I assure you I shall not easily forgive or forget it."

line 7: 'Peterson' deleted; 'Percival' inserted above line.   //   line 9: 'it is' is 'it it' in ms.   //   line 14: 'Peterson' deleted; 'Percival' inserted above line.

This speech which perfectly explained the whole affair to
Kitty, was shortly followed on her side by a very submis-
sive apology, for she had too much good Sense to be proud
of her family, and too much good Nature to live at vari-
ance with any one. The Excuses she made, were delivered
with so much real concern for the Offence, and such unaffected Sweetness, that it was almost impossible for Camilla
to retain that anger which had occasioned them; She felt
indeed most highly gratified to find that no insult had been
intended and that Catherine was very far from forgetting
the difference in their birth for which she could *now* only
pity her, and her good humour being restored with the same
Ease in which it had been affected, she spoke with the highest delight of the Evening, and declared that she had never
before been at so pleasant a Ball. The same endeavours that
had procured the forgiveness of Miss Stanley ensured to her
the cordiality of her Mother, and nothing was wanting but
Mrs P's good humour to render the happiness of the others
complete; but She, offended with Camilla for her affected
Superiority, Still more so with her brother for coming to
Chetwynde, and dissatisfied with the whole Evening, continued silent and Gloomy and was a restraint on the vivacity
of her Companions. She eagerly seized the very first opportunity which the next Morning offered to her of speaking
to Mr Stanley on the subject of his Son's return, and after
having expressed her opinion of its being a very silly affair
that he came at all, concluded with desiring him to inform
Mr Edward Stanley that it was a rule with her never to admit
a young Man into her house as a visitor for any length of
time.

line 18: 'eterson' deleted, leaving 'P's'.   //   line 24: 'offered' deleted after
'which'.   //   line 24: 'offered to her' inserted above line.

"I do not speak Sir, she continued, out of any disrespect to You, but I could not answer it to myself to allow of his stay; there is no knowing what might be the consequence of it, if he were to continue here, for girls nowadays will always give a handsome young Man the preference before any other, tho' for why, I never could discover, for what after all is Youth and Beauty?—It is but a poor substitute for real worth and Merit; Beleive me Cousin that, what ever people may say to the contrary, there is certainly nothing like Virtue for making us what we ought to be, and as to a young Man's, being Young and handsome and having an agreable person, it is nothing at all to the purpose for he had much better be respectable. I always *did* think so, and I always *shall*, and therefore you will oblige me very much by desiring your Son to leave Chetwynde, or I cannot be answerable for what may happen between him and my Neice. You will be surprised to hear *me* say it, she continued, lowering her voice, but truth will out, and I must own that Kitty is one of the most impudent[105] Girls that ever existed.[106] I assure you Sir, that I have seen her sit and laugh and whisper with a young Man whom she has not seen above half a dozen times. Her behaviour indeed is scandalous, and therefore I beg you will send your Son away immediately, or everything will be at sixes and sevens." Mr Stanley who from one part of her Speech had scarcely known to what length her insinuations of Kitty's impudence were meant to extend, now endeavoured to quiet her fears on the occasion, by assuring her, that on every account he meant to allow only of his Son's continuing that day with them, and that she might depend

line 7: 'Why in fact, it is nothing more than being Young and Handsome—and that' deleted; 'It' inserted above line.   //   line 10: 'handsome' deleted after 'a'.   //   line 19: two lines deleted: 'Her intimacies with Young Men are abominable; and it is all the same to her, who it is, no one comes amiss to her—.' after 'existed'.

on his being more earnest in the affair from a wish of obliging her. He added also that he knew Edward to be very desirous himself of returning to France, as he wisely considered all time lost that did not forward the plans in which he was at present engaged, tho' he was but too well convinced of the contrary himself. His assurance in some degree quieted Mrs P, and left her tolerably relieved of her Cares and Alarms, and better disposed to behave with civility towards his Son during the short remainder of his Stay at Chetwynde. Mr Stanley went immediately to Edward, to whom he repeated the Conversation that had passed between Mrs P and himself, and strongly pointed out the necessity of his leaving Chetwynde the next day, since his word was already engaged for it. His son however appeared struck only by the ridiculous apprehensions of Mrs Peterson; and highly delighted at having occasioned them himself, seemed engrossed alone in thinking how he might encrease them, without attending to any other part of his Father's Conversation. Mr Stanley could get no determinate Answer from him, and tho' he still hoped for the best, they parted almost in anger on his side.

His Son though by no means disposed to marry, or any otherwise attached to Miss Percival than as a good-natured lively Girl who seemed pleased with him, took infinite pleasure in alarming the jealous fears of her Aunt by his attentions to her, without considering what effect they might have on the Lady herself. He would always sit by her when she was in the room, appeared dissatisfied if she left it, and was the first to enquire whether she meant soon to return. He was delighted with her Drawings, and enchanted with her performance on the Harpsichord; Everything that she said, appeared to

line 7: 'eterson' deleted, leaving 'P'. // line 11: 'eterson' deleted, leaving 'P'. // line 19: 'from him' inserted above line. // line 22: 'Peterson' deleted; 'Percival' inserted above line.

interest him; his Conversation was addressed to her alone, and she seemed to be the sole object of his attention. That such efforts should succeed with one so tremblingly alive[107] to every alarm of the kind as Mrs Percival, is by no means unnatural, and that they should have equal influence with her Neice whose imagination was lively, and whose Disposition romantic, who was already extremely pleased with him, and of course desirous that he might be so with her, is as little to be wondered at. Every moment as it added to the conviction of his liking her, made him still more pleasing, and strengthened in her Mind a wish of knowing him better. As for Mrs Percival, she was in tortures the whole Day; Nothing that she had ever felt before on a similar occasion was to be compared to the sensations which then distracted her; her fears had never been so strongly, or indeed so reasonably excited.—Her dislike of Stanly, her anger at her Neice, her impatience to have them separated conquered every idea of propriety and Goodbreeding, and though he had never mentioned any intention of leaving them the next day, she could not help asking him after Dinner, in her eagerness to have him gone, at what time he meant to set out.

"Oh! Ma'am, replied he, if I am off by twelve at night, you may think yourself lucky; and if I am not, you can only blame yourself for having left so much as the *hour* of my departure to my own disposal." Mrs Percival coloured very highly at this speech, and without addressing herself to any one in particular, immediately began a long harangue on the shocking behaviour of modern Young Men, and the wonderful Alteration that had taken place in them, since her time, which she illustrated with many instructive anecdotes of the

line 4: 'Peterson' deleted; 'Percival' inserted above line.   //   line 12: 'eterson' deleted; 'ercival' inserted above line.   //   line 16: 'before' deleted after 'excited'.   //   line 25: 'Peterson' deleted; 'Percival' inserted above line.

Decorum and Modesty which had marked the Characters of those whom she had known, when she had been young. This however did not prevent his walking in the Garden with her Neice, without any other companion for nearly an hour in the course of the Evening. They had left the room for that purpose with Camilla at a time when Mrs Peterson had been out of it, nor was it for some time after her return to it, that she could discover where they were. Camilla had taken two or three turns with them in the walk which led to the Arbour, but soon growing tired of listening to a Conversation in which she was seldom invited to join, and from its turning occasionally on Books, very little able to do it, she left them together in the arbour, to wander alone to some other part of the Garden, to eat the fruit, and examine Mrs Peterson's Greenhouse. Her absence was so far from being regretted, that it was scarcely noticed by them, and they continued conversing together on almost every subject, for Stanley seldom dwelt long on any, and had something to say on all, till they were interrupted by her Aunt.

Kitty was by this time perfectly convinced that both in Natural Abilities, and acquired information, Edward Stanley was infinitely superior to his Sister. Her desire of knowing that he was so, had induced her to take every opportunity of turning the Conversation on History and they were very soon engaged in an historical dispute, for which no one was more calculated[108] than Stanley who was so far from being really of any party, that he had scarcely a fixed opinion on the Subject. He could therefore always take either side, and always argue with temper.[109] In his indifference on all such topics he was very unlike his Companion, whose judgement

---

lines 12–13: 'together in the arbour,' inserted above line.   //   line 26: 'was' inserted above line.

being guided by her feelings which were eager and warm, was easily decided, and though it was not always infallible, she defended it with a Spirit and Enthouisasm which marked her own reliance on it. They had continued therefore for some-time conversing in this manner on the character of Richard the 3d, which he was warmly defending[110] when he suddenly seized hold of her hand, and exclaiming with great emotion, "Upon my honour you are entirely mistaken," pressed it passionately to his lips,[111] and ran out of the arbour. Astonished at this behaviour, for which she was wholly unable to account, she continued for a few Moments motionless on the Seat where he had left her, and was then on the point of following him up the narrow walk through which he had passed, when on looking up the one that lay immediately before the arbour, she saw her Aunt walking towards her with more than her usual quickness. This explained at once the reason of his leaving her, but his leaving her in such Manner was rendered still more inexplicable by it. She felt a considerable degree of confusion at having been seen by her in such a place with Edward, and at having that part of his conduct, for which she could not herself account, witnessed by one to whom all gallantry was odious. She remained therefore confused distressed and irresolute, and suffered her Aunt to approach her, without leaving the Arbour. Mrs Percival's looks were by no means calculated to animate the spirits of her Neice, who in silence awaited her accusation, and in silence meditated her Defence. After a few Moments suspence, for Mrs Peterson was too much fatigued to speak immediately, she began with great Anger and Asperity, the following harangue. "Well; *this* is beyond anything I could have supposed. *Profligate*[112] as I *knew* you to be, I was not prepared for such a sight. This

line 24: 'Peterson's' deleted; 'Percival's' inserted above line.

is beyond any thing you ever did *before*; beyond any thing I ever heard of in my Life! Such Impudence, I never witnessed before in such a Girl! And this is the reward for all the cares I have taken in your Education; for all my troubles and Anxieties, and Heaven knows how many they have been! All I wished for, was to breed you up virtuously; I never wanted you to play upon the Harpsichord, or draw better than any one else; but I had hoped to see you respectable and good; to see you able and willing to give an example of Modesty and Virtue to the Young people here abouts. I bought you Blair's Sermons,[113] and Coelebs in Search of a Wife,[114] I gave you the key to my own Library,[115] and borrowed a great many good books of my Neighbours for you, all to this purpose. But I might have spared myself the trouble—Oh! Catherine, you are an abandoned Creature, and I do not know what will become of you. I am glad however, she continued softening into some degree of Mildness, to see that you have some shame for what you have done, and if you are really sorry for it, and your future life is a life of penitence and reformation perhaps you may be forgiven. But I plainly see that every thing is going to sixes and sevens and all order will soon be at an end throughout the Kingdom."

"Not however Ma'am the sooner, I hope, from any conduct of mine, said Catherine in a tone of great humility, for upon my honour I have done nothing this evening that can contribute to overthrow the establishment of the kingdom."[116]

"You are mistaken Child, replied she; the welfare of every Nation depends upon the virtue of it's individuals, and any one who offends in so gross a manner against decorum and propriety, is certainly hastening it's ruin. You have been giving

line 11: 'Seccar's explanation of the Catechism' deleted; 'Coelebs in Search of a Wife' inserted above line.

a bad example to the World, and the World is but too well disposed to receive such."

"Pardon me Madam, said her Neice; but I *can* have given an Example only to *You*, for You alone have seen the offence. Upon my word however, there is no danger to fear from what I have done; Mr Stanley's behaviour has given me as much surprise, as it has done to You, and I can only suppose that it was the effect of his high spirits, authorized in his opinion by our relationship. But do you consider Madam that it is growing very late? Indeed You had better return to the house." This speech as she well knew, would be unanswerable with her Aunt, who instantly rose, and hurried away under so many apprehensions for her health, as banished for the time all anxiety about her Neice, who walked quietly by her side, revolving within her own Mind the occurrence that had given her Aunt so much alarm. "I am astonished at my own imprudence, said Mrs Percival; How could I be so forgetful as to sit down out of doors at such a time of night? I shall certainly have a return of my rheumatism after it—I begin to feel very chill already. I must have caught a dreadful cold by this time—I am sure of being lain-up all the winter after it—" Then reckoning with her fingers, "Let me see; This is July; the cold Weather will soon be coming in— August—September—October—November—December— January—February—March—April—Very likely I may not be tolerable again before May. I must and will have that arbour pulled down—it will be the death of me; who knows *now*, but what I may never recover—Such things *have* happened—My particular freind Miss Sarah Hutchinson's death was occasioned by nothing more—She staid out late one Evening in April, and got wet through for it rained

line 17: 'Peterson' deleted; 'Percival' inserted above line.

very hard, and never changed her Cloathes when she came home—It is unknown how many people have died in consequence of catching Cold! I do not beleive there is a disorder in the World except the Smallpox which does not spring from it." It was in vain that Kitty endeavoured to convince her that her fears on the occasion were groundless; that it was not yet late enough to catch cold, and that even if it were, she might hope to escape any other complaint, and to recover in less than ten Months. Mrs Percival only replied that she hoped she knew more of Ill health than to be convinced in such a point by a Girl who had always been perfectly well, and hurried up stairs leaving Kitty to make her apologies to Mr and Mrs Stanley for going to bed—. Tho' Mrs Percival seemed perfectly satisfied with the goodness of the Apology herself, Yet Kitty felt somewhat embarrassed to find that the only one she could offer to their Visitors was that her Aunt had *perhaps* caught cold, for Mrs Peterson charged her to make light of it, for fear of alarming them. Mr and Mrs Stanley however who well knew that their Cousin was easily terrified on that Score, received the account of it with very little surprise, and all proper concern. Edward and his Sister soon came in, and Kitty had no difficulty in gaining an explanation of his Conduct from him, for he was too warm on the subject himself, and too eager to learn its success, to refrain from making immediate Enquiries about it; and She could not help feeling both surprised and offended at the ease and Indifference with which he owned that all his intentions had been to frighten

line 9: 'Peterson' deleted; 'Percival only' inserted above line. 'Percival' is written over 'Peterson'; JA apparently first inserted 'Peterson' in error.   //
line 14: 'Peterson' deleted; 'Percival' inserted above line, in pencil, in a different hand.   //   line 23: 'of' deleted; 'in' inserted above line.   //   line 23: 'an explanation' inserted above line.

her Aunt by pretending an affection for *her*; a design so very incompatible with that partiality which she had at one time been almost convinced of his feeling for her. It is true that she had not yet seen enough of him to be actually in love with him, yet she felt greatly disappointed that so handsome, so elegant, so lively a young Man should be so perfectly free from any such Sentiment as to make it his principal Sport. There was a Novelty in his character which to *her* was extremely pleasing; his person was uncommonly fine, his Spirits and Vivacity suited to her own, and his Manners at once so animated and insinuating, that she thought it must be impossible for him to be otherwise than amiable, and was ready to give him Credit for being perfectly so. He knew the powers of them himself; to them he had often been endebted for his father's forgiveness of faults which had he been awkward and inelegant would have appeared very serious; to them, even more than to his person or his fortune, he owed the regard which almost every one was disposed to feel for him, and which Young Women in particular were inclined to entertain. Their influence was acknowledged on the present occasion by Kitty, whose Anger they entirely dispelled, and whose Chearfulness they had power not only to restore, but to raise—. The Evening passed off as agreably as the one that had preceded it; they continued talking to each other, during the cheif part of it, And such was the power of his Address, and the Brilliancy of his Eyes, that when they parted for the Night, tho' Catherine had but a few hours before totally given up the idea, yet she felt almost convinced again that he was really in love with her. She reflected on their past Conversation, and tho' it had

line 11: 'insinuating' written over 'gentle'.   //   line 12: 'than' inserted above line.   //   line 13: 'completely' deleted; 'perfectly' inserted above line.   //   line 20: 'disposed to feel' deleted; 'inclined to entertain' inserted above line.

been on various and indifferent subjects, and she could not
exactly recollect any Speech on his side expressive of such a
partiality, she was still however nearly certain of it's being
so; But fearful of being vain enough to suppose such a thing
without sufficient reason, she resolved to suspend her final
determination on it, till the next day, and more especially till
their parting which she thought would infallibly explain his
regard if any he had—. The more she had seen of him, the
more inclined was she to like him, and the more desirous
that he should like *her*. She was convinced of his being
naturally very clever and very well disposed, and that his
thoughtlessness and negligence, which tho' they appeared to
her as very becoming in *him*, she was aware would by many
people be considered as defects in his Character, merely
proceeded from a vivacity always pleasing in Young Men,
and were far from testifying a weak or vacant Understanding.
Having settled this point within herself, and being perfectly
convinced by her own arguments of it's truth, she went to
bed in high Spirits, determined to study his Character, and
watch his Behaviour still more the next day. She got up with
the same good resolutions and would probably have put
them in execution, had not Anne informed her as soon as
she entered the room that Mr Edward Stanley was already
gone. At first she refused to credit the information, but when
her Maid assured her that he had ordered a Carriage the
evening before to be there at seven o'clock in the Morning
and that she herself had actually seen him depart in it a
little after eight, she could no longer deny her beleif to it.
"And this, thought she to herself blushing with anger at
her own folly, this is the affection for me of which I was so
certain. Oh! what a silly Thing is Woman! How vain, how

line 22: 'Nanny' deleted; 'Anne' inserted above line.

unreasonable![117] To suppose that a young Man would be seriously attached in the course of four and twenty hours, to a Girl who has nothing to recommend her but a good pair of eyes! And he is really gone! Gone perhaps without bestowing a thought on me! Oh! why was not I up by eight o'clock? But it is a proper punishment for my Lazyness and Folly, and I am heartily glad of it. I deserve it all, and ten times more for such insufferable vanity. It will at least be of service to me in that respect; it will teach me in future *not* to think Every Body is in love with me. Yet I *should* like to have seen him before he went, for perhaps it may be many Years before we meet again. By his Manner of leaving us however, he seems to have been perfectly indifferent about it. How very odd, that he should go without giving us notice of it, or taking leave of any one! But it is just like a Young Man, governed by the whim of the Moment, or actuated merely by the love of doing anything oddly! Unaccountable Beings indeed! And Young Women are equally ridiculous! I shall soon begin to think like my Aunt that everything is going to Sixes and Sevens, and that the whole race of Mankind are degenerating." She was just dressed, and on the point of leaving her room to make her personal enquiries after Mrs Peterson, when Miss Stanley knocked at her door, and on her being admitted began in her Usual Strain a long harangue upon her Father's being so shocking as to make Edward go at all, and upon Edward's being so horrid as to leave them at such an hour in the Morning. "You have no idea, said she, how surprised I was, when he came into my Room to bid me good bye—"

"Have you seen him then, this Morning?" said Kitty.

"Oh Yes! And I was so sleepy that I could not open my eyes. And so he said, Camilla, goodbye to you for I am going away—. I have not time to take leave of any body else, and I dare not trust myself to see Kitty, for then you know I should never get away—"

"Nonsense, said Kitty; he did not say that, or he was in joke if he did."

"Oh! no I assure You he was as much in earnest as he ever was in his life; he was too much out of Spirits to joke *then*. And he desired me when we all met at Breakfast to give his Compts. to your Aunt, and his Love to You, for you was a nice Girl[118] he said, and he only wished it were in his power to be more with You. You were just the Girl to suit him, because you were so lively and good-natured, and he wished with all his heart that you might not be married before he came back, for there was nothing he liked better than being here. Oh! You have no idea what fine things he said about You, till at last I fell a sleep and he went away. But he certainly is in love with you—I am sure he is—I have thought so a great while I assure You."

"How can You be so ridiculous? said Kitty smiling with pleasure; I do not beleive him to be so easily affected. But he *did* desire his Love to me then? And wished I might not be married before his return? And said I was a nice Girl, did he?"

"Oh! dear, Yes, And I assure You it is the greatest praise in his opinion, that he can bestow on any body; I can hardly ever persuade him to call *me* one, tho' I beg him sometimes for an hour together."

"And do You really think that he was sorry to go?"

"Oh! You can have no idea how wretched it made him. He would not have gone this Month, if my Father had not insisted on it; Edward told me so himself yesterday. He said

line 7: 'me' written over 'us'(?).   //   line 12: 'be' inserted above line.   //
line 24: 'body' written over 'one'(?)

that he wished with all his heart he had never promised to go abroad, for that he repented it more and more every day; that it interfered with all his other schemes, and that since Papa had spoke to him about it, he was more unwilling to leave Chetwynde than ever."

"Did he really say all this? And why would your father insist upon his going? 'His leaving England interfered with all his other plans, and his Conversation with Mr Stanley had made him still more averse to it.' What can this Mean?"

"Why that he is excessively in love with You to be sure; what other plans can he have? And I suppose my father said that if he had not been going abroad, he should have wished him to marry you immediately.—But I must go and see your Aunt's plants—There is one of them that I quite doat on— and two or three more besides—"

"Can Camilla's explanation be true? said Catherine to her-self, when her freind had left the room. And after all my doubts and Uncertainties, can Stanley really be averse to leaving England for *my sake* only? 'His plans interrupted.' And what indeed can his plans be, but towards Marriage? Yet *so soon* to be in love with me!—But it is the effect perhaps only of a warmth of heart which to *me* is the highest recommendation in any one. A Heart disposed to love—And such under the appearance of so much Gaity and Inattention, is Stanley's! Oh! how much does it endear him to me! But he is gone—Gone perhaps for Years—Obliged to tear himself from what he most loves, his happiness is sacrificed to the vanity of his Father! In what anguish he must have left the house! Unable to see me, or to bid me adeiu, while I, senseless wretch, was daring to sleep. This, then explains his leaving us at such a time of day—. He could not trust himself to see me—. Charming Young Man! How much must you have suffered! I *knew* that it was impossible for one so elegant, and so well bred, to leave any Family in such a Manner, but for a Motive like this unanswerable." Satisfied, beyond the power of Change, of this, She went in high spirits to her Aunt's apartment, without giving a Moment's recollection on the vanity of Young Women, or the unaccountable conduct of Young Men.——

CORRECTIONS AND EMENDATIONS

Austen's revisions and corrections to her manuscripts are recorded in the textual notes. My editorial corrections and emendations are both recorded in the textual notes and listed here.

VOLUME THE FIRST

	manuscript	corrected to
p. 19, l. 8	I'll you why	I'll tell you why
p. 28, l. 9	appeared	appear
p. 29, l. 13	ever	every
p. 89, l. 1–2	will be this be	will this be

VOLUME THE SECOND

p. 112, l. 17	once	one
p. 162, l. 26	able raise	able to raise
p. 168, l. 1	ignorant than	ignorant that
p. 183, l. 17–18	for famous for	was famous for
p. 224, l. 5	with is	which is

VOLUME THE THIRD

p. 243, l. 21	one	once
p. 249, l. 27	the	they
p. 271, l. 27	must	much
p. 280, l. 9	it it	it

APPENDIX E

p. 361, l. 16	paneguge (?)	panegyric
p. 361, l. 20–21	her her own	her own

The History of England: facsimile

This appendix contains a facsimile reproduction of the manuscript of *The History of England*, showing Cassandra Austen's illustrations (see 'Introduction', pp. xxxi and 'Note on the text', pp. lxviii for more information about the manuscript). This facsimile is reproduced by kind permission of the British Library.

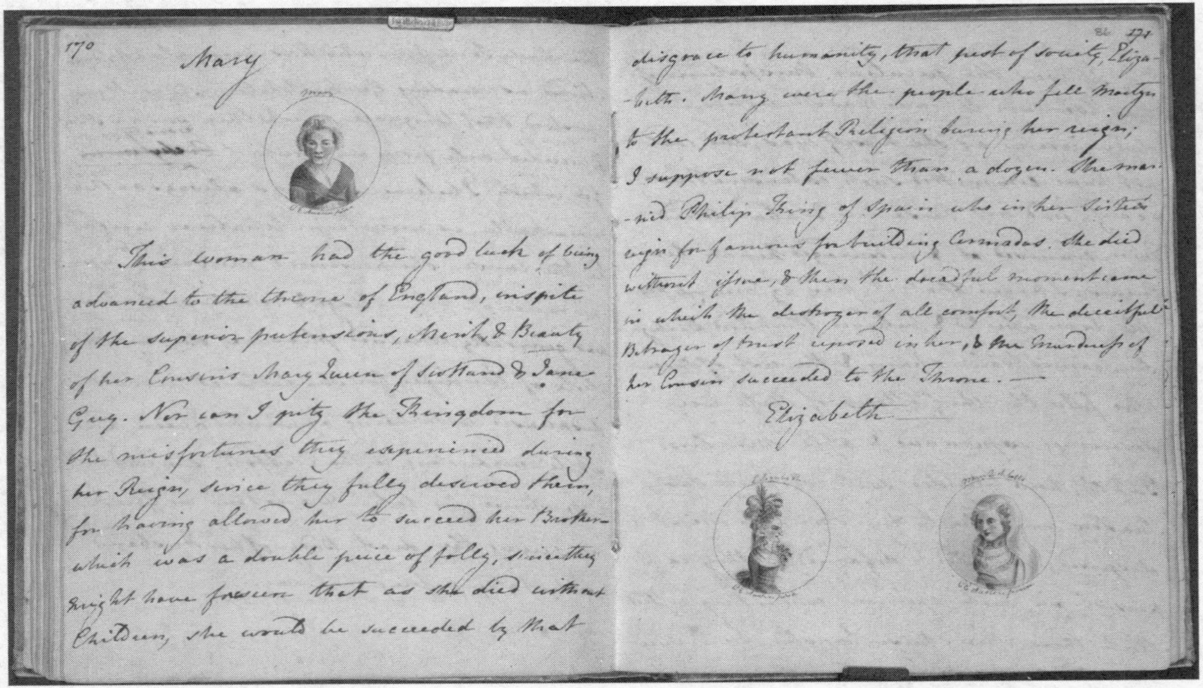

170

Mary

This woman had the good luck of being advanced to the throne of England, inspite of the superior pretensions, Merit, & Beauty of her Cousins Mary Queen of Scotland & Jane Grey. Nor can I pity the Kingdom for the misfortunes they experienced during her Reign, since they fully deserved them, for having allowed her to succeed her Brother—which was a double peice of folly, since they might have foreseen that as she died without Children, she would be succeeded by that

86 171

disgrace to humanity, that pest of society, Eliza-beth. Many were the people who fell Martyrs to the protestant Religion during her reign; I suppose not fewer than a dozen. She mar-ried Philip King of Spain who in her Sister's reign was famous for building Armadas. She died without issue, & then the dreadful moment came in which the destroyer of all comfort, the deceitful Betrayer of trust reposed in her, & the Murderess of her Cousin succeeded to the Throne.—

Elizabeth

1

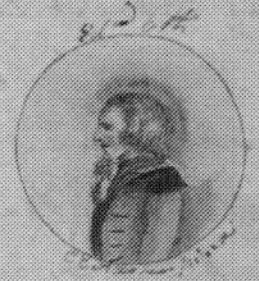

182

The principal favourite of his Majesty
was Carr, who was afterwards created Earl
of Somerset and whose name perhaps may
have some share in the above-mentioned affair,
& gave rise to his (or George Villiers afterwards Duke of Buckingham
on his Majesty's death having succeeded to
his own favour.

Charles the 1st

This amiable monarch scarce knew how to have
refused satisfaction equal to those of his

lucky grandmother's misfortunes which he and
her divorce since he was her discarded. But
never existing were there before so many
notable characters at one time in England
as in the period of its history; ... ...
... in them to share. The number of
them throughout the whole kingdom among
them only the faire, ... that the inhabitants
of ... who was always loyal to their
King, & faithful to his interests. He received
of this noble race, who emerging from their attack
of the subject, ... from their attachment to his majesty, were as follows:
The King's himself, were different ... in his
... me support, Archbishop Laud, Earl of
Stafford, Viscount Faulkland & Wellington

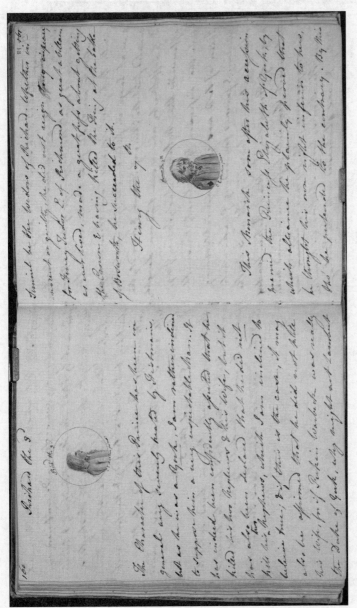

Richard the 3.

The Character of this Prince has been in general very variously treated of by Historians, but as he was a York, I am rather inclined to suppose him a very respectable Man. It has indeed been confidently asserted that he killed his two Nephews & his Wife, but it has also been declared that he did not kill his two Nephews, which I am inclined to believe true; & if this is the case, it may also be affirmed that he did not kill his Wife, for if Perkin Warbeck was really the Duke of York, why might not Lambert

...amiuel be the widow of Richard. Whether...
...guilty, he did not reign long enough...
...Duke of Richmond as great a villain...
...more... as great fools about...
...Queen & having killed the King at the battle
of Bosworth, he succeeded to it.

Henry the 7.

This Monarch soon after his accession
married the Princess Elizabeth of York,
which alliance he is famed to have...
brought his own...

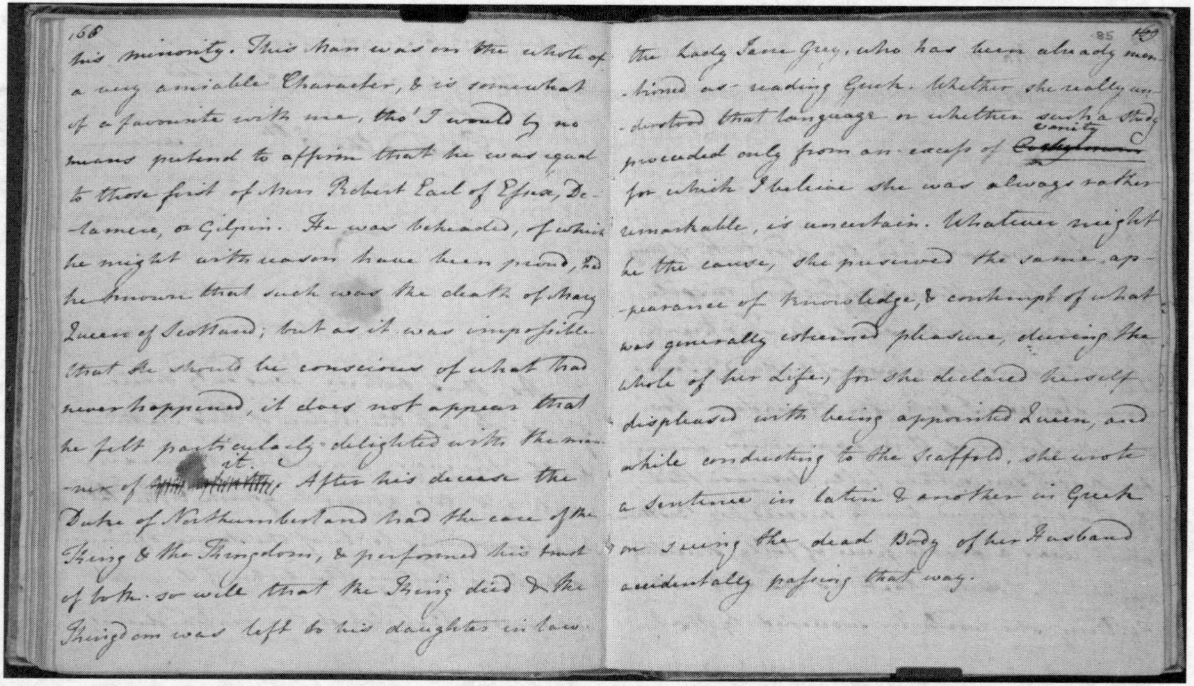

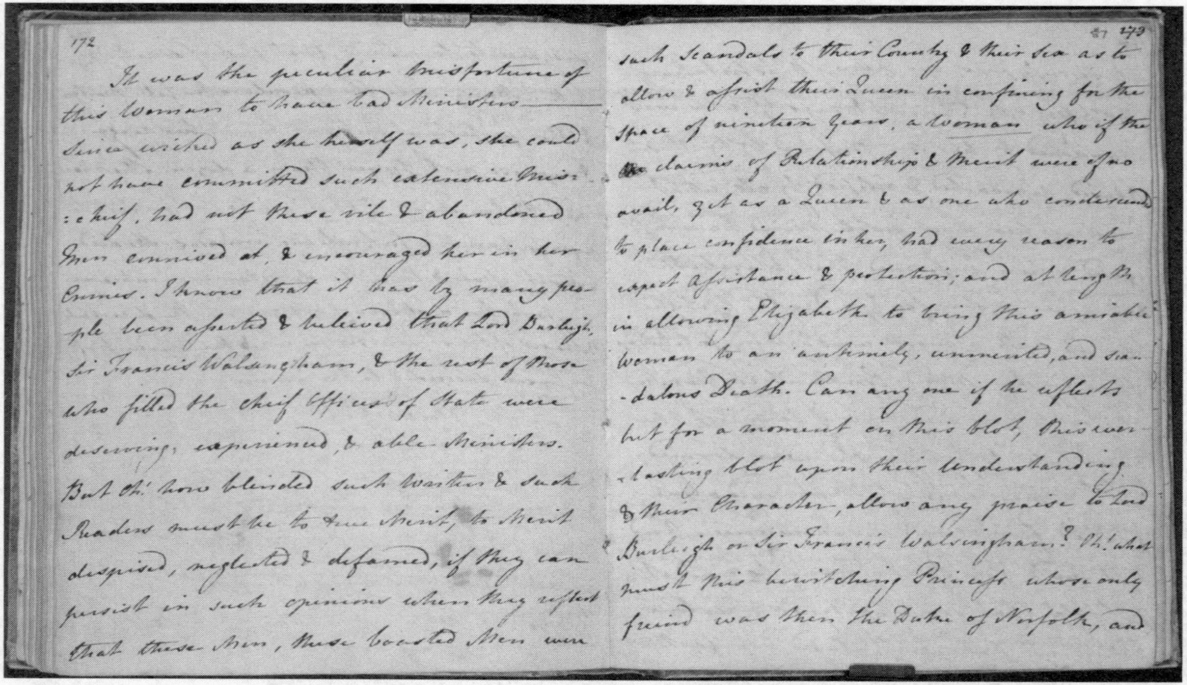

172

It was the peculiar misfortune of
this Woman to have bad Ministers———
Since wicked as she herself was, she could
not have committed such extensive mis-
:chief, had not these vile & abandoned
Men connived at, & encouraged her in her
Crimes. I know that it has by many people been asserted & beleived that Lord Burleigh,
Sir Francis Walsingham, & the rest of those
who filled the chief offices of State were
deserving, experienced, & able Ministers.
But oh! how blinded such Writers & such
Readers must be to true Merit, to Merit
despised, neglected & defamed, if they can
persist in such opinions when they reflect
that these Men, these boasted Men were

87 173

such Scandals to their Country & their sex as to
allow & assist their Queen in confining for the
space of nineteen Years, a Woman who if the
claims of Relationship & Merit were of no
avail, yet as a Queen & as one who condescended
to place confidence in her, had every reason to
expect Assistance & protection; and at length
in allowing Elizabeth to bring this amiable
Woman to an untimely, unmerited, and scan-
-dalous Death. Can any one if he reflects
but for a moment on this blot, this ever-
-lasting blot upon their Understanding
& their Character, allow any praise to Lord
Burleigh or Sir Francis Walsingham? Oh! what
must this bewitching Princess whose only
friend was then the Duke of Norfolk, and

11

174

whose only ones are now Mr Whitaker,
Mrs Lefroy, Mrs Knight & myself, who was
abandoned by her Son, confined by her Cousin,
Abused, reproached & vilified by all, what
must not her most noble Mind have suf-
:fered when informed that Elizabeth
had given orders for her Death! Yet she
bore it with a most unshaken fortitude;
firm in her Mind; Constant in her Re-
-ligion; & prepared herself to meet the
cruel fate to which she was doomed,
with a magnanimity that could alone
proceed from conscious Innocence. And
yet could you Reader have believed it
possible that some hardened & zealous
Protestants have even abused her for that

88 175

Steadfastness in the Catholic Religion which
reflected on her so much credit? But this
is a striking proof of their narrow Souls
& prejudiced Judgements who accuse her.
She was executed in the Great Hall at
Fotheringay Castle (sacred Place!) on Wednesday
the 8th of February - 1586 — to the everlasting
Reproach of Elizabeth, her Ministers, and of
England in general. It may not be unne-
-cessary before I entirely conclude my account
of this ill-fated Queen, to observe that she
had been accused of several crimes during
the time of her reigning in Scotland, of
which I now most seriously do assure my
Reader that she was entirely innocent; ha-
-ving never been guilty of anything more

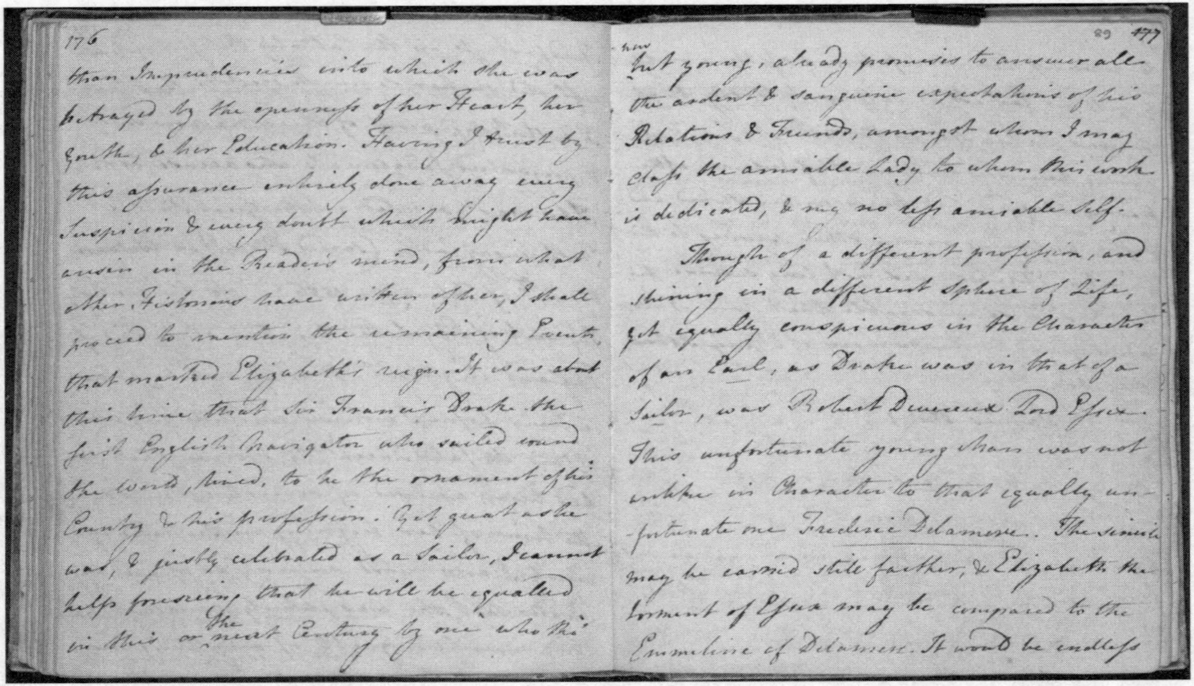

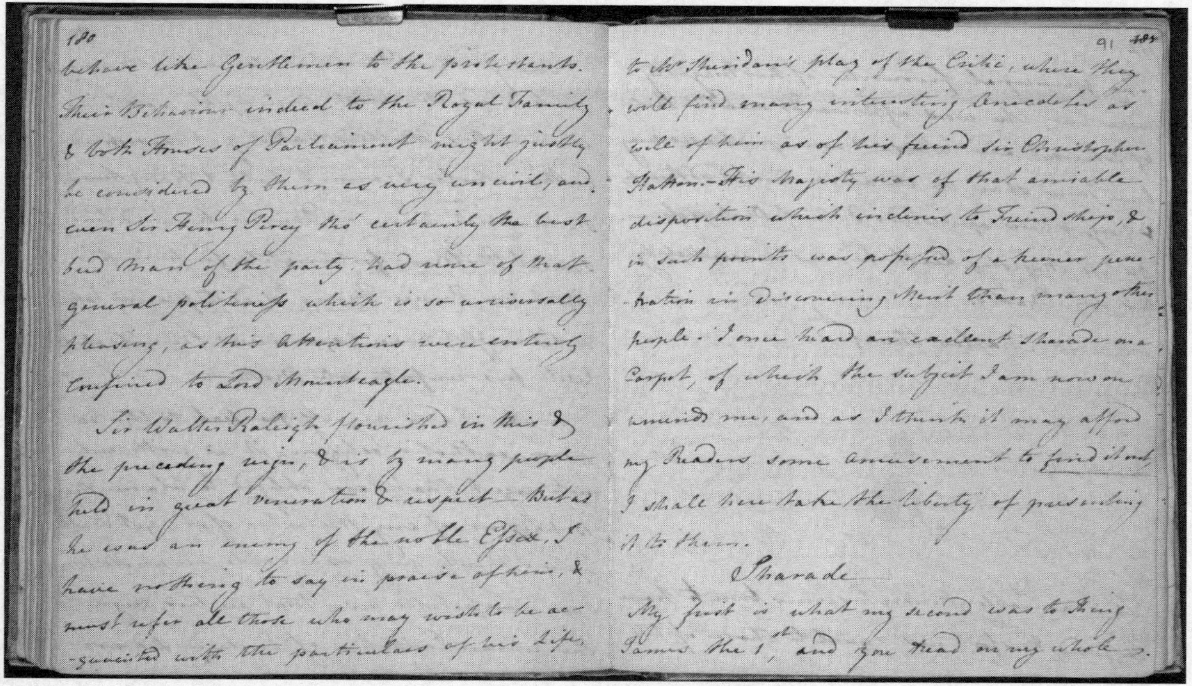

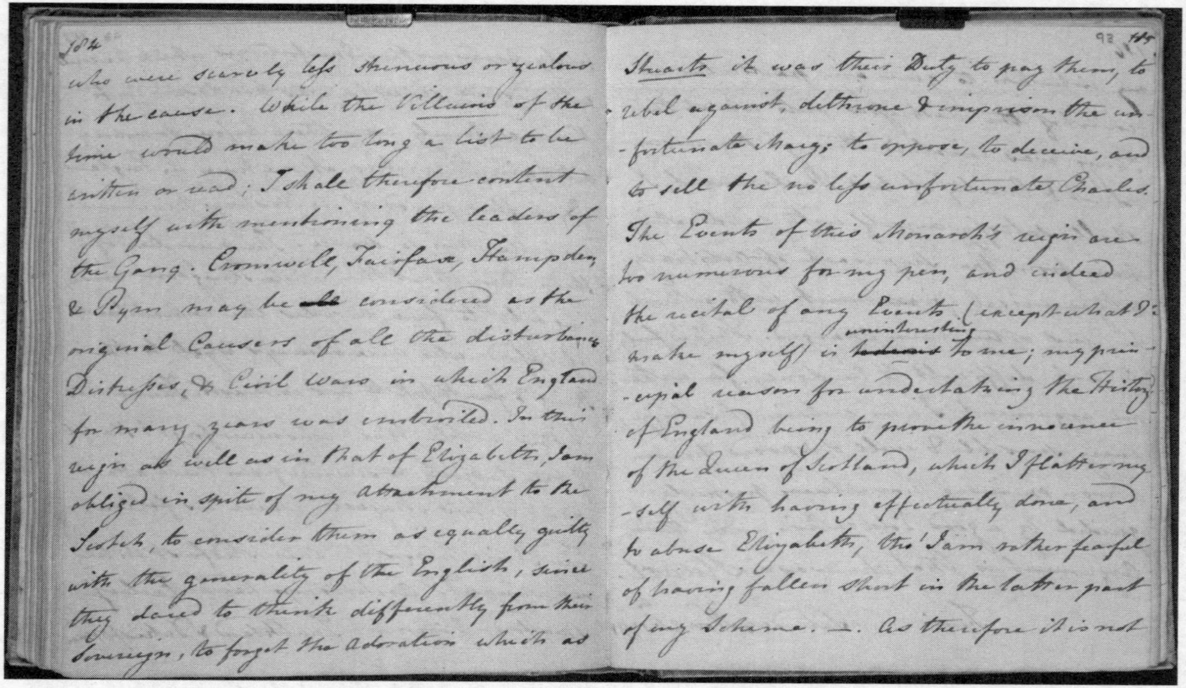

Henry the 4th

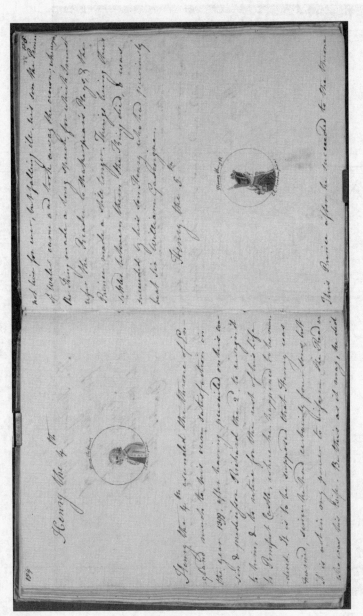

Henry the 4th succeeded the throne of England much to his own satisfaction in
the year 1399, after having prevailed on his uncle & predecessor Richard the 2d to resign it
to him, & to retire for the rest of his life
to Pomfret Castle, where he happened to be murdered. It is to be supposed that Henry was
concerned, during the Reign, for being left
It is not in any power to disprove the Red Ones
who were his best. But this was not any, he did

This Prince after he ascended to the Throne

nd him for ever, but putting the ... on the Prin-
of Water came & took away the crown, whereupon
the King made a long march for which himself
over the Ranks & Shakespeare Plays & the
Prince made a stole longer Things being Poor
which between them the King did, & was
murdered by his own King, who did ... procuring
had its Vartuam Gallopan.

Henry the 5th

The History of England
from the reign of
Henry the 4th
to the death of
Charles the 1st

By a partial, prejudiced, & ignorant Historian —

To Miss Austen, eldest daughter of the Rev.d
George Austen, this work is inscribed with
all due respect by

The Author

N.B. There will be very few Dates in
this History.

Ladyship, but Sir George still perseveres in
saying that perhaps in a Week or two My
accompany us —
Believe me, Dear Charlotte
Yr faithful humble servt

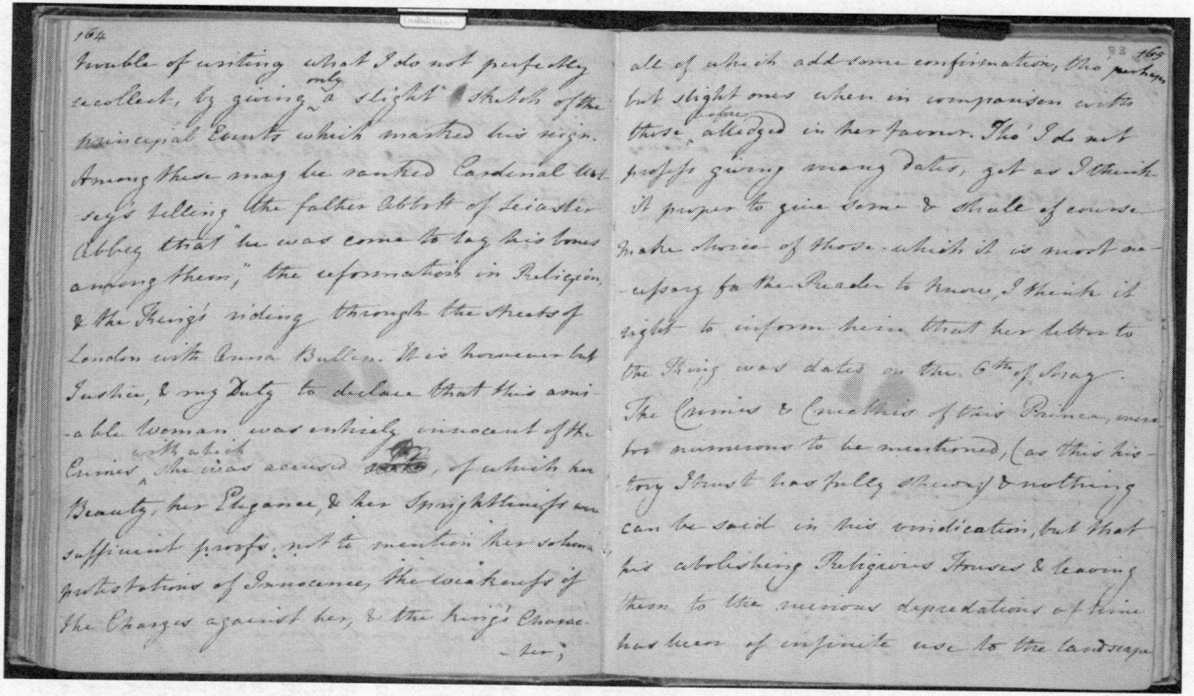
164
trouble of writing what I do not perfectly
recollect, by giving only a slight sketch of the
principal Events which marked his reign.
Among these may be ranked Cardinal Wolsey's telling the father Abbott of Leicester
Abbey that "he was come to lay his bones
among them," the reformation in Religion,
& the King's riding through the streets of
London with Anna Bullen. It is however but
Justice, & my Duty to declare that this ami-
-able Woman was entirely innocent of the
Crimes with which she was accused, of which her
Beauty, her Elegance, & her Sprightliness were
sufficient proofs, not to mention her solemn
protestations of Innocence, the weakness of
the Charges against her, & the King's Charac-
-ter;

83 165
all of which add some confirmation, tho' perhaps
but slight ones when in comparison with
those before alledged in her favour. Tho' I do not
profess giving many dates, yet as I think
it proper to give some & shall of course
make choice of those which it is most ne-
-cessary for the Reader to know, I think it
right to inform him that her letter to
the King was dated on the 6th of May.
The Crimes & Cruelties of this Prince, were
too numerous to be mentioned, (as this his-
-tory I trust has fully shewn) & nothing
can be said in his vindication, but that
his abolishing Religious Houses & leaving
them to the ruinous depredations of time
has been of infinite use to the landscape

18

Marginalia in Oliver Goldsmith's
The History of England, from the Earliest Times to the Death of George II

London, 4 vols., 1771

On 26 November 1791, Jane Austen dedicated her 'History of England' to her sister Cassandra. Before then, in all likelihood, and probably earlier in 1791, she wrote over a hundred marginal comments on a copy of Oliver Goldsmith's four-volume *History of England*. All four volumes bear the signature of her brother, 'James Austen Steventon', on the paste-down or front free endpaper, although that in volume three, seen by David Gilson, has since been covered during rebinding.[1] None of the volumes is signed by Austen, but Gilson notes that the front free endpaper of volume four has been roughly removed: perhaps because it contained a signature desired by an autograph collector.

Either during Austen's lifetime or after her death, the volumes were bequeathed to the son of the first owner, James Edward Austen-Leigh (1798–1874). In 1919, they were in the possession of Mary Augusta Austen-Leigh (1838–1922), James Edward's daughter, who inserted a note to this effect in the final volume and imperfectly transcribed ten of JA's marginal comments. A year later, she included these transcriptions in her *Personal Aspects of Jane Austen* (1920). After her death in 1922, the volumes were passed down in the Austen-Leigh family, from Laurence Impey (nephew of Richard Arthur Austen-Leigh) to his daughter Evelyn Fowle, and his granddaughter Katharine Beaumont, the present owner.

Austen's marginalia are concentrated almost entirely in the third and fourth volumes of Goldsmith's *History*. The first volume contains a summary of events in her hand but no marginal comments,

[1] See David Gilson, *A Bibliography of Jane Austen* (rev. edn., Winchester: St Paul's Bibliographies, 1997), p. 441.

while her only contribution to the second volume is the single word 'wretches' for the young princes murdered in the Tower. Her commentary begins midway through the third volume, with the outbreak of civil war in 1642, and continues to the end of the fourth volume, which concludes with the death of George II in 1760. Most of Austen's comments are in pencil, which is sometimes faded to the point of illegibility, a few are in ink and some have been written over in ink by another hand, leaving traces of her pencil clearly visible beneath.

In addition to the annotations in Austen's hand, there are various comments by other Austen family members. One of these, commending his aunt, is by James Edward Austen-Leigh, and other remarks are probably also by James Edward. In the first volume a series of dates appears, beginning with 8 August 1845, presumably indicating the day on which a particular passage was read. There are sketches—including a horse, birds and petals—and medallion portraits of all of the English monarchs have been garishly coloured in watercolour, possibly by Austen herself or by her sister Cassandra. The same watercolour has been used to highlight certain letters, words and phrases. Misprints and other minor errors are also corrected on occasion, and markings such as crosses and other symbols are scattered throughout the four volumes.

All previous transcriptions of Austen's marginalia, including those in recent scholarly biographies, derive from the faulty versions in Mary Augusta Austen-Leigh's volume of 1920. Austen-Leigh conjectured that Austen was 'twelve or thirteen' when she wrote her remarks,[2] but fifteen, Austen's age when she completed her 'History of England', seems more probable. One of the comments that Mary Augusta transcribes, 'Oh! Oh! The Wretches', a misreading of 'Horrible Wretches', is not in Austen's hand. She also errs in her interpretation of another remark, 'Nobly said! Spoken like a Tory!', regarding it as 'slightly ironical' because, she believes, the speaker is the Whig politician Robert Walpole.[3] The speaker, however, is

---

[2] Mary Augusta Austen-Leigh, *Personal Aspects of Jane Austen* (London: John Murray, 1920), p. 26.

[3] Goldsmith, *History*, vol. 3, p. 281, Austen-Leigh, *Personal Aspects*, p. 26; Goldsmith, *History*, vol. 4, p. 207, Austen-Leigh, *Personal Aspects*, p. 27.

a Tory, the Earl of Oxford: Austen's point is that Oxford is being true to himself.

Although Mary Augusta Austen-Leigh's transcriptions are inaccurate and fragmentary and form only a small part of her book, they caught the eye of two reviewers in 1920: Virginia Woolf and Katherine Mansfield. For Woolf, in fact, the marginalia are the only valuable item in Austen-Leigh's volume, refuting the idea that Austen is 'unemotional, unsentimental and passionless', and enabling us 'to hear Jane Austen saying nothing in her natural voice'.[4] For Mansfield, similarly, Austen's 'fiery outpourings' on Goldsmith's *History* are much the pleasantest part of *Personal Aspects*, and 'revive Jane Austen's own voice'.[5]

The present edition marks the first publication of Austen's complete marginalia on Goldsmith's *History*; some 90 per cent of the material is previously unpublished. Austen's comments are printed below the passages in Goldsmith's *History* to which they respond. Letters indicate the word or phrase with which the marginalia are most closely concerned. Editorial headnotes provide a brief context for each passage. Many of the marginalia are written in pencil and a few are faded to the point of illegibility; conjectural readings are placed within angle brackets (< >). The various comments, corrections and markings in hands other than Austen's are not reproduced here, with the exception of two (pp. 328, 335) that respond to Austen's own marginalia.

Vol. I, front free endpaper. Beneath James Austen's signature is a chronology by JA of significant events in Goldsmith's first volume.

Caesar landed	*Ante Christ*	*8*
Caractacus conquered by Ostorius Scupula		*50*
Romans left England		*488*
Alfred beat out the Danes		*876*

---

[4] Virginia Woolf, 'Jane Austen and the Geese', *Times Literary Supplement*, 28 October 1920, p. 699; rpt. in *The Essays of Virginia Woolf*, vol. III, *1919–1924*, ed. Andrew McNeillie (London: Chatto & Windus, 1988), pp. 269–70.

[5] Katherine Mansfield, 'Friends and Foes', *The Athenaeum*, 3 December 1920; rpt. in Mansfield, *Novels and Novelists*, ed. J. Middleton Murry (London: Constable, 1930), p. 304.

Battle of Hastings	*1066*
William Rufus came to the Throne	*1067*
Henry 1st came to the <Throne>	*1100*
Stephen ditto	*1135*

Vol. II, 264 Sir James Tyrrel is thought to have murdered the two young princes, Edward V and Richard, Duke of York in 1483. They had been imprisoned in the Tower of London by Richard III, and were never seen alive again. In her own 'History of England', JA writes that Edward 'was murdered by his Uncle's Contrivance', but continues, paradoxically, that 'it has also been declared that he did *not* kill his two Nephews, which I am inclined to beleive true' (p. 179).

Tyrrel chusing three associates, Slater, Deighton, and Forest, came in the night-time to the door of the chamber, where the princes were lodged; and sending in the assassins, he bid them execute their commission, while he himself staid without. They found the young princes in bed, and fallen into a sound sleep: after suffocating them with the bolster and pillows, they shewed their naked bodies to Tyrrel; who ordered them to be buried at the stair-foot, deep in the ground, under an heap of stones.[a]

[a] wretches

Vol. III, 260–1 In January 1642, Charles I failed in his attempt to arrest five members of Parliament for treason. Civil war broke out in August, the period described here.

Never was contest more unequal than seemed at first between the contending parties; the king being entirely destitute of every advantage. His revenue had been seized by parliament; all the sea-port towns were in their hands, except Newcastle, and thus they were possessed of the customs, which these could supply; the fleet was at their disposal; all magazines of arms and ammunition were seized for their use; and they had the wishes of all the most active members[a] of the nation.

[a] Shame to such Members

III, 267–8 Charles I won several victories in the first campaign of the Civil War, in which both the Parliamentarian John Hampden and the royalist Lucius Cary, Viscount Falkland, were killed. JA's sympathies are with the latter. In her 'History of England' she also praises Falkland, while naming Hampden as one of 'the original Causers of all the disturbances, Distresses, and Civil Wars in which England for many years was embroiled' (p. 188).

But in this campaign, the two bravest and greatest men of their respective parties were killed; as if it was intended, by the kindness of Providence, that they should be exempted from seeing the miseries and the slaughter which were shortly to ensue. These were John Hampden, and Lucius Cary, lord Falkland.[a]

In an incursion made by prince Rupert to within about two miles of the enemies quarters, a great booty was obtained. This the parliamentarians attempted to rescue; and Hampden at their head, overtook the royalists on Chalgrave Field. As he was ever the first to enter into the thickest of the battle, he was shot in the shoulder with a brace of bullets, and the bone broke . . . Hampden, whom we have seen in the beginning of these troubles refuse to pay ship-money, gained, by his inflexible integrity, the esteem even of his enemies. To these he added affability in conversation, temper, art, eloquence in debate, and penetration in counsel.[b]

[a] The *last* was indeed a great & noble Man
[b] What a pity that such virtues shd be clouded by Republicanism!

III, 270–1 Parliament had negotiated a treaty with the Scots in 1643, as a result of which the Scottish army joined Cromwell's forces. In her 'History of England', JA regrets that the Scots forgot their duty to the Stuarts and dared instead 'to oppose, to deceive, and to sell the no less unfortunate Charles' (p. 188).

[T]he Scotch, who considered their claims as similar, led a strong army to their assistance. They levied an army of fourteen thousand men in the east, under the earl of Manchester; they had an army of ten thousand men under Essex, another of nearly the same force, under Sir William Waller. These were superior to any force the king could bring into the field; and were well appointed with ammunition, provisions, and pay.[a]

[a] What a pity!

III, 288 Goldsmith provides a characteristically balanced portrait of Oliver Cromwell: too balanced to please JA.

Oliver Cromwell, whose talents now began to appear in full lustre, was the son of a private gentleman of Huntingdon; but being the son of a second brother, he inherited a very small paternal fortune.[a] He had been sent to Cambridge; but his inclinations not at that time turning to the calm occupations of elegant literature, he was remarkable only for the profligacy of his conduct, and the wasting his paternal fortune. It was, perhaps, his poverty that induced him to fall into the opposite extreme shortly after; for, from being one of the most debauched men in the kingdom, he became the most rigid and abstemious.

[a] And that was more than he deserved.

III, 308 Goldsmith has cited two remarks made by Lady Fairfax during the trial of Charles I in the Great Hall at Westminster in January 1649. JA's pencilled comment is written over in ink by another hand.

Axtel, the officer who guarded the court, giving orders to fire into the box from whence the voice proceeded, it was discovered that these bold answers came from the lady Fairfax, who alone had courage to condemn their proceedings.[a]

[a] Charming Woman!

III, 311 An account of Charles I's conduct at the end of his trial.

A soldier more compassionate than the rest, could not help imploring a blessing upon his royal head. An officer overhearing him, struck the honest centinel to the ground before the king, who could not help saying, that the punishment exceeded the offence.[a]

[a] Such was the fortitude of the Stuarts when oppressed and accused!

III, 314 Charles I's execution at Whitehall took place on 30 January 1649. JA's pencilled comment is written over in ink by another hand.

Charles having taken off his cloak delivered his George to the prelate, pronouncing the word "Remember." Then he laid his neck on the block, and stretching out his hands as a signal, one of the executioners severed his head from his body at a blow, while the other, holding it up, exclaimed, "This is the head of a traitor."[a] The spectators testified their horror at that sad spectacle in sighs, tears, and lamentations; the tide of their duty and affection began to return, and each blamed himself either with active disloyalty to his king, or a passive compliance with his destroyers.

[a] or rather the hand of a traitor who held it

III, 319 JA's comment on Goldsmith's portrait of the exiled Charles Stuart in Paris is in very faint pencil; only some of the words can be recovered.

Charles, after the death of his father, having passed some time at Paris, and finding no likelihood of assistance from that quarter, was glad to accept of any conditions. He possessed neither the virtues nor the constancy of his father;[a] and being attached to no religion as yet, he agreed to all their proposals, being satisfied with even the formalities of royalty.

[a] He was not indeed equal to his father <4–5 **illegible words**> since he was a Stuart.

III, 321–2 Charles Stuart, having landed in Scotland from France in June 1650, had pledged himself to Presbyterianism but was in the power of the clergy. Cromwell's army, meanwhile, was waging war in Ireland. The second of JA's comments here, on Cromwell's Irish campaign, is so faint as to be illegible. Above her third comment, 'Detesbaly' is written (and thus misspelled) in another, childish hand; the same hand has apparently inked over her pencilled remark.

Charles for a while bore all their insolence with hypocritical tranquility, and even pretended to be highly edified by their instructions. He once, indeed, attempted to escape from among them; but being brought back, he owned the greatness of his error, he testified repentance for what he had done,[a] and looked about for another opportunity of escaping.

In the mean time, Cromwell, who had been appointed to the command of the army in Ireland, prosecuted the war in that kingdom with his usual success.[b] He had to combat against the Royalists, commanded by the duke of Ormond, and the native Irish, led on by O'Neal. But such ill connected and barbarous troops could give very little opposition to Cromwell's more numerous forces, conducted by such a general, and emboldened by long success . . . In order to intimidate the natives from defending their towns, he, with a barbarous policy, put every garrison that made any resistance to the sword. He entered the city of Drogheda by storm, and indiscriminately butchered men, women, and children,[c] so that only one escaped the dreadful carnage to give an account of the massacre.

[a] was he to blame?
[b] < illegible comment >
[c] Detestable Monster!

III, 324 In 1650, the Scots 'espoused the royal cause' and 'raised a considerable army to support it' (III, 322). Cromwell prepared to engage the Scottish army in battle.

When he was told that the Scotch army were coming down to engage, he assured his Soldiers that the Lord had delivered his enemy into his hands; and he ordered his army to sing psalms, as already possessed of a certain victory. The Scotch, though double the number of the English, were soon put to flight, and pursued with great slaughter, while Cromwell did not lose above forty men in all.[a]

[a] It is a pity there were not forty *one!*

III, 325–6 **Charles Stuart, crowned king of Scots at Scone on 1 January 1651, advanced into England to wage war with Cromwell's forces. The running-head on pages 323 and 325, 'The Commonwealth', has been deleted in pencil, possibly by JA.**

But Charles soon found himself disappointed in the expectation of encreasing his army. The Scotch, terrified at the prospect of so hazardous an enterprize, fell from him in great numbers. The English, affrighted at the name of his opponent, dreaded to join him; but his mortifications were still more encreased as he arrived at Worcester, when informed, that Cromwell was marching with hasty strides[a] from Scotland, with an army encreased to forty thousand men.

[a] with his 7 league boots on—

III, 329 **Charles Stuart, having been defeated by Cromwell in a battle at Worcester, escaped to France in October 1751.**

At Shoreham, in Sussex, a vessel was at last found, in which he embarked. He was known to so many, that if he had not set sail in that critical moment, it had been impossible for him to escape. After one and forty days concealment, he arrived safely at Feschamp in Normandy. No less than forty men and women had, at different times, been privy to his escape.[a]

[a] God bless them.

III, 333–5 In 1653, Cromwell persuaded his army officers 'to present a petition for payment of arrears and redress of grievances, which he knew would be rejected with disdain' (III, 333). On 20 April, his forces entered the House of Commons and Parliament was dissolved. JA 's three pencilled comments here have all been inked over by another hand.

The petition was soon drawn up and presented, in which the officers, after demanding their arrears, desired the parliament to consider how many years they had sat; and what professions they had formerly made of their intentions to new model the house, and establish freedom on the broadest basis. They alledged, that it was now full time to give place to others; and however meritorious their actions might have been, yet the rest of the nation had some right, in turn, to shew their patriotism in the service of their country.[a]

The house was highly offended at the presumption of the army . . . To this the officers made a very warm remonstrance, and the parliament as angry a reply; while the breach between them every moment grew wider. This was what Cromwell had long wished, and had well foreseen. He was sitting in council with his officers, when informed of the subject on which the house was deliberating; upon which he rose up in the most seeming fury, and turning to major Vernon, cried out, "That he was compelled to do a thing that made the very hair of his head stand on end."[b] Then hastening to the house with three hundred soldiers, and with the marks of violent indignation on his countenance he entered, took his place, and attended to the debates for some time . . . "It is you, continued he to the members, that have forced me upon this. I have sought the Lord night and day that he would rather slay me than put me upon this work." Then pointing to the mace, "Take away, cried he, that bauble." After which, turning out all the members, and clearing the hall, he ordered the doors to be locked, and putting the key in his pocket, returned to Whitehall.[c]

[a] Impudent fellows
[b] Poor man.
[c] The Parliament deserved it all

III, 338 The legislature known as the 'Barebones' Parliament, convened by Cromwell after the expulsion of the former parliament, lasted for less than six months.

The very vulgar began now to exclaim against so foolish a legislature; and they themselves seemed not insensible of the ridicule which every day was thrown out against them. Cromwell was probably well enough pleased to find that his power was likely to receive no diminution from their endeavours; but began to be ashamed of their complicated absurdities.[a]

[a] As well he might

III, 357 After the death of Cromwell in September 1658, his son Richard succeeded him briefly as Protector before resigning his office in August 1659. A dispute between parliament and the army, led by John Lambert, ensued.

In this exigence, the officers held several conferences together, with a design to continue their power. They at length came to a resolution, usual enough in these times, to dissolve that assembly, by which they were so vehemently opposed. Accordingly Lambert, one of the general officers, drew up a chosen body of troops; and placing them in the streets which led to Westminster-hall, when the speaker Lenthall proceeded in his carriage to the house, he ordered the horses to be turned, and very civilly conducted him home.[a]

[a] A well-bred Man.

III, 399 In 1670, Charles II signed a treaty with France, committing both countries to a war against the Dutch. The war began in 1672.

Night parted the combatants; the Dutch retired, and were not followed by the English. The loss sustained by the two maritime powers was nearly equal; but the French suffered very little, not having entered into the heat of the engagement.[a]

[a] what cowards.

III, 416 In August 1678, Titus Oates claimed to have uncovered a threat against Charles II by a group of Catholics, the 'Popish Plot'. JA's contribution here is a correction, rather than a comment; the logic of Goldsmith's sentence requires the word 'guilt', not 'innocence'.

But the parliament testified greater credulity than even the vulgar. The cry of plot was immediately echoed from one house to the other; the country party would not let slip such an opportunity of managing the passions of the people; the courtiers were afraid of being thought disloyal, if they should doubt the innocence[a] of the pretended assassins of their king.

[a] 'innocence' deleted; '*Guilt*' written above.

III, 420–1 Titus Oates succeeded in arousing anti-Catholic hysteria. Charles II, who kept his own Catholic faith concealed until his deathbed, opposed Oates only when his queen, Catherine of Braganza, was accused of being a conspirator. The passages annotated by JA are underlined, presumably by JA herself.

The papists were thus become so obnoxious, that vote after vote passed against them in the house of commons. They were called idolaters; and such as did not concur in acknowledging the truth of the epithet, were expelled the house without ceremony. Even the duke of York was permitted to keep his place in the house by a majority of only two. "*I would not, said one of the lords, have so much as a popish man or a popish woman to remain here, not so much as a popish dog, or a popish bitch, not so much as a popish cat to mew, or pur about our king.*"[a] This was wretched eloquence; but it was admirably suited to the times.

Encouraged by the general voice in their favour, the witnesses, who all along had enlarged their narratives, in proportion as they were greedily received, went a step farther, and ventured to accuse the queen. The commons, in an address to the king, gave countenance to this scandalous accusation; the lords rejected it with becoming disdain. The king received the news of it with his usual good humour. *"They think, said he, that I have a mind to a new wife; but for all that I will not suffer an innocent woman to be abused."*[b]

[a] elegant creature what charming eloquence!
[b] that's right.

III, 446 The politician John Hampden, one of several conspirators against Charles II in 1683, was arrested as a conspirator in the Rye House plot. JA had previously expressed her disdain for his more famous grandfather, the statesman John Hampden (see p. 311 above). Here she drew a box, in pencil, around the word 'great' and wrote a pencilled comment, inked over by another hand.

The loss of Shaftesbury, though it retarded the views of the conspirators, did not suppress them. A council of six was erected, consisting of Monmouth, Russell, Essex, Howard, Algernon Sidney, and John Hambden, grandson to the ⬚great⬚[a] man of that name. These corresponded with Argyle and the malcontents in Scotland, and resolved to prosecute the scheme of the insurrection, though they widely differed in principles from each other.

[a] for great read vile

III, 448 William Howard was also accused of taking part in the Rye House plot. The passage annotated by JA is underlined, presumably by JA herself.

Sheppard, another conspirator, being apprehended, confessed all he knew, and general orders were soon issued out for apprehending the rest of the leaders of the conspiracy. Monmouth absconded; Russel was sent to the Tower; Grey escaped; *Howard*[a] *was taken concealed in a chimney;* Essex, Sidney, and Hamdben, were soon after arrested, and had the mortification to find lord Howard an evidence against them.

[a] how dirty he must have been.

Vol. IV, 1 JA's comment is written directly beneath the medallion portrait of James II, on the opening page of Goldsmith's final volume.[a]

[a] Poor Man!

IV, 10 James Scott, Duke of Monmouth, an illegitimate son of Charles II, invaded England in 1685 in an attempt to seize the throne. He was swiftly captured and beheaded.

. . . the executioner struck him again and again to no purpose. He at last threw the ax down; but the sheriff compelled him to resume the attempt, and at two blows more the head was severed from the body. Such was the end of James, duke of Monmouth, the darling of the English people. He was brave, sincere, and good natured, open to flattery and by that seduced into an enterprize, which exceded his capacity.[a]

[a] Sweet Man!

IV, 13 The object of Goldsmith's censure is the hanging judge, George Jeffreys, who condemned over three hundred of Monmouth's followers to death. JA's two pencilled comments are too faint to be legible.

The work of slaughter went forward.[a] One Cornish, a sheriff, who had been long obnoxious to the court, was accused by Goodenough, now turned a common informer, and in the space of a week was tried, condemned, and executed. After his death, the perjury of the witnesses appeared so flagrant, that the king himself expressed some regret, granted his estate to the family, and condemned the witnesses to perpetual imprisonment. Jefferies, on his return was immediately created a peer, and was soon after vested with the dignity of chancellor. This shewed the people that all the former cruelties were pleasing to the king, and that he was resolved to fix his throne upon severity.[b]

[a] <c. 8 illegible words>
[b] <c. 12 illegible words>

IV, 22–3 In 1687, James II dismissed the fellows of Magdalen College, Oxford, for refusing to accept the Bishop of Oxford as their new President. Bishop Parker, James's appointment, was 'a man of prostitute character; but who atoned for all his vices, by his willingness to embrace the catholic religion' (IV, 22). JA's pencilled comment is too faint to be legible.

Another refusal on their side served still more to exasperate him; and finding them resolute in the defence of their privileges, he ejected them all, except two, from their benefices, and Parker was put in possession of the place. Upon this, the college was filled with catholics; and Charnock, who was one of the two that remained, was made vice-president.[a]

[a] <c. 12 illegible words>

IV, 23–5 In April 1688, James II reissued a Declaration of Indulgence, suspending laws against Roman Catholics and Nonconformists, and in May gave orders for it to be read twice in every church. Several Anglican bishops, named by Goldsmith, drew up a petition, asking James to withdraw the order.

The first champions on this service of danger were Loyde, bishop of St. Asaph, Ken of Bath and Wells, Turner of Ely, Lake of Chichester, White of Peterborow, and Trelawney of Bristol; these, together with Sancroft the primate, concerted an address, in the form of a petition, to the king, which, with the warmest expressions of zeal and submission, remonstrated that they could not read his declaration consistent with their consciences, or the respect they owed the protestant religion. This modest[a] address only served still more to enflame the king's resentment . . .

The king's measures were now become so odious to the people, that although the bishops of Durham and Rochester, who were members of the ecclesiastical court, ordered the declaration to be read in the churches of their respective districts, the audience could not hear them with any patience. One minister told his congregation, that though he had positive orders to read the declaration, they had none to hear it, and therefore they might leave the church;[b] an hint which the congregation quickly obeyed.

[a] *Modest*! It would have been *impudent* had it been from Catholics I suppose.

[b] that's right, clever man!

IV, 27 **The petitioning bishops were prosecuted for libel, but acquitted on 30 June.**

If the bishops testified the readiness of martyrs in support of their religion, James shewed no less ardour in his attempts toward the establishment of his own. Grown odious to every class of his subject, he still resolved to persist; for it was a part of his character, that those measures he once embraced he always persevered in pursuing.[a]

[a] And if he thought those measures right, he could not be blamed for persevering in them.

IV, 28–9 **The birth of a son to James on 10 June 1688, just before the acquittal of the bishops, reduced the prospects of a Protestant succession by his daughter Mary, and thus further increased his unpopularity.**

A few days before the acquittal of the bishops, the queen was brought to bed of a son, who was baptised by the name of James. This would, if any thing could at that time, have served to establish him on the throne; but so great was the animosity against him, that a story was propagated that the child was suppositious, and brought to the queen's apartment in a warming-pan. But so great was this monarch's pride, that he scorned to take any precautions to refute the calumny.[a] Indeed all his measures were marked with the characters of pride, cruelty, bigotry, and weakness. In these he was chiefly supported by Father Peters, his confessor, an ambitious, ignorant, and intriguing priest, whom some scruple not to call a concealed creature belonging to the prince of Orange.[b]

[a] It would have been beneath him to refute such nonsense.
[b] Not unlikely

IV, 30 JA's comment is on the first sentence of a chapter introducing William of Orange, the future monarch William III.

William, prince of Orange,[a] had married Mary, the eldest daughter of king James.

[a] A Villain.

IV, 32 Algernon Sidney, part of JA's 'bad breed', was one of the conspirators against Charles II in the Rye House plot. His brother Henry Sidney was among William's first supporters.

The prince soon found that every rank was ripe for defection, and received invitations from some of the most considerable persons in the kingdom. Admiral Herbert, and admiral Russel, assured him in person of their own and the national attachment. Henry Sidney, brother to Algernon, and uncle to the earl of Sunderland,[a] came over to him with assurances of an universal combination against the king.

[a] Bad Breed

IV, 34 James II, who rejected offers of aid from Louis XIV of France, was slow to see the dangers posed by his son-in-law, William of Orange, who was planning an invasion from Holland.

Every place was in motion; all Europe saw and expected the descent, except the unfortunate James himself, who, secure in the piety of his intentions, thought nothing could injure his schemes calculated to promote the cause of heaven.[a]

[a] Since he acted upon *such* motives, he ought to be praised.

IV, 36 James II had first reinstated the expelled president and fellows of Magdalen College, Oxford and then dismissed them again. Appointing the Pope as one of the godfathers at the baptism of his infant son was also an imprudent move.

But all his concessions were now too late. They were regarded as the symptoms of fear, and not of repentance; as the cowardice of guilt, and not the conviction of error. Indeed he soon shewed the people the insincerity of his reformation; for hearing that the Dutch fleet was dispersed, he recalled those concessions which he had made in favour of Magdalen College; and to shew his attachment to the Romish church, at the baptism of his newborn son, he appointed the pope one of the sponsors.[a]

[a] I wonder whether his Holiness gave the Nurse the accustomed fee.

IV, 39 Henry, Lord Delamere, was among the first of the nobility to embrace William's cause after he landed at Torbay, Devon, on 5 November 1688. JA here compares him, tongue in cheek, with his namesake Frederic Delamere, the impetuous suitor of the heroine of Charlotte Smith's *Emmeline* (1788). Engaged to Delamere, Emmeline eventually marries a calmer, more reflective suitor, Godolphin, whom JA cannot envisage acting rapidly.

She also draws *Emmeline* into her own 'History of England' (p. 186).

England was in commotion. Lord Delamere took arms in Cheshire;[a] the earl of Danby seized York; the earl of Bath, governor of Plymouth, declared for the prince; the earl of Devonshire made a like declaration in Derby; the nobility and gentry of Nottingham embraced the same cause; and every day there appeared some effect of that universal combination into which the nation had entered against the measures of the king.

[a] I should have expected *Delamere* to have done so, for it was an action unsuited to *Godolphin*.

IV, 41 James's younger daughter Anne, who would succeed to the throne in 1702, and her husband George, Prince of Denmark, also gave their support to William.

It was no small addition to his present distress that the prince of Denmark, and Anne, his favourite daughter, perceiving the desperation of his circumstances, resolved to leave him, and take part with the prevailing side.[a] When he was told that the prince and princess had followed the rest of his favourites, he was stung with the most bitter anguish.

[a] Anne should not have done so—indeed I do not believe she *did*.

IV, 46–7 James II fled to France at the end of 1688; William acceded to the throne in January 1689. Although the House of Commons voted strongly in favour of a motion that James's flight had left the throne vacant, the House of Lords passed the motion only narrowly.

After this manner, the courage and abilities[a] of the prince of Orange, seconded by surprising fortune, effected the delivery of the kingdom . . .

This vote readily passed the house of commons; but it met with some opposition in the house of lords, and was at length carried by a majority of two voices only.[b]

[a] 'courage and abilities' changed to 'courage, abilities, *& insolence*'.
[b] And those two deserved to have no voices at all.

IV, 49 A declaration by William that he would not serve as regent, nor 'accept of the crown under the princess his wife' (IV, 49), was followed by a second vote in parliament, in William's favour.

This declaration produced the intended effect. After a long debate in both houses, a new sovereign was preferred to a regent, by a majority of two voices.[a] It was agreed that the prince and princess of Orange should reign jointly as king and queen of England, while the administration of government should be placed in the hands of the prince only.

[a] Two Voices are always in the way.

IV, 168 In the last years of her reign, 1712–14, Anne dismissed the Whig government, and the Treaty of Utrecht (1713) was negotiated by a Tory ministry, favoured by JA.

Through the course of the English history, France seems to have been the peculiar object of the hatred of the Whigs;[a] and a constitutional war with that country, seems to have been their aim.

[a] & without any reason.

IV, 172 Prince Eugene of Savoy, commander of the Austrian army during the War of Spanish Succession, played a part in negotiations between the Emperor Charles VI and Queen Anne. JA

commends the queen for rejecting his initial proposals, which preceded the Treaty of Utrecht.

But the confederates took a step from which they hoped success from the greatness of the agent whom they employed. Prince Eugene, who had been long famous for his talents in the cabinet and in the field, was sent over with a letter from the emperor to the queen. But his intrigues and his arts were unable to prevail; he found at court, indeed, a polite reception, such as was due to his merits and his fame; but at the same time such a repulse, as the private proposals he carried seemed to deserve.[a]

[a] This proves Anne to have been a sensible & a well-bred woman.

IV, 174 **The Dutch were among the many signatories of the Treaty of Utrecht, as were the French under Louis XIV.**

The Dutch . . . practiced a thousand little arts to intimidate the queen, to excite a jealousy of Lewis, to blacken the characters of her ministry, and to keep up a dangerous ferment among the people.[a]

[a] Charming Creatures!

IV, 185 **Richard Steele became a member of parliament in 1713. He was expelled in 1714, shortly before the death of Queen Anne, as a result of his pro-Hanoverian, anti-Jacobite pamphlet *The Crisis*, which was considered seditious.**

The house of lords seemed to share in the general apprehension . . . Mr. Steele, afterwards known as the celebrated Sir Richard Steele, was not a little active in raising and spreading these reports. In a pamphlet written by him, called the Crisis, he bitterly exclaimed against the ministry, and the immediate danger of their bringing in the pretender.[a]

[a] It is a pity that he had not been better employed.

IV, 191 Goldsmith's summation on Queen Anne and the house of Stuart elicited JA's own verdict on the Stuarts, while her remark in turn drew an approving comment from her nephew, James Edward Austen-Leigh.

In her ended the line of the Stuarts; a family whose misfortunes and misconducts are not to be paralleled in history.[a] A family, who less than men themselves, seemed to expect from their followers more than manhood in their defence;[b] a family that never rewarded their friends, and never avenged them of their enemies.[c]

[a] a lie

[b] another

[c] A Family, who were always illused, Betrayed or Neglected Whose Virtues are seldom allowed while their Errors are never forgotten.[†]

[†]Bravo Aunt Jane just my opinion of the Case.

IV, 193 At the beginning of his chapters on George I, Goldsmith summarizes the character of the Old Pretender, James Edward, son of James II, then living in France.

The Jacobites had long been flattered with the hopes of seeing the succession altered by the new ministry . . . Upon recollection, they saw nothing so eligible in the present crisis, as silence and submission; they hoped much from the assistance of France, and still more from the popularity and councils of the pretender. This unfortunate man, seemed to possess all the qualities of his father; his pride, his want of perseverance, and his attachment to the catholic religion. He was but a poor leader, therefore, to conduct so desperate a cause; and in fact, all the sensible[a] part of the kingdom had forsaken it as irretrievable.

[a] Sensible! Oh! Dr. Goldsmith Thou art as partial an Historian as myself!

IV, 195 **The Tory politician Henry St John, Lord Bolingbroke, was the principal architect of the Treaty of Utrecht. His government fell with George I's accession to the throne in September 1714.**

To mortify the late ministry the more, lord Bolingbroke was obliged to wait every morning in the passage, among the servants,[a] with his bag of papers, where there were persons purposely placed to insult and deride him. No tumult appeared, no commotion arose against the accession of the new king, and this gave a strong proof that no rational measures were ever taken to obstruct his exaltation.[b]

[a] Mean revenge!
[b] Oh no certainly no *rational* Measure *could* be taken by *Tories*!

IV, 197 **On their return to power under George I, the first Hanoverian king, the Whigs acted vindictively towards their Tory predecessors.**

An instantaneous and total change was made in all the offices of trust, honour, or advantage. The Whigs governed the senate and the court; whom they would, they oppressed; bound the lower orders of people with severe laws, and kept them at a distance by vile distinctions; and then taught them to call this—Liberty.[a]

[a] Yes, This is always the Liberty of Whigs & Republicans.

IV, 203 **Facing charges of treason, Bolingbroke fled to France, where he would remain in exile for ten years.**

Bolingbroke had hitherto appeared and spoke in the house as usual. However, his fears now prevailed over his desire to vindicate his character; finding an impeachment was likely to be made, he withdrew to the continent, leaving a letter, in which he declared, that if there had been any hopes of a fair and open trial, he would not have declined it; but being already prejudged in the minds of the majority, he thought fit, by flight, to consult their honour and his own safety.[a]

[a] Well done my Lord.

IV, 204 Robert Harley, Earl of Oxford and Mortimer, led the Tory ministry, together with Bolingbroke, from 1710 to 1714. He too was accused of treason by the new Whig government, but successfully resisted the charges.

. . . lord Coningsby, rising up, was heard to say, "The worthy chairman has impeached the hand, but I impeach the head; he has impeached the scholar; and I the master. I impeach Robert earl of Oxford, and earl of Mortimer, of high treason, and other crimes and misdemeanors."[a]

[a] More shame for you.

IV, 207 The last words of Oxford's speech in his own defence, spoken 'with great tranquillity' (IV, 206).

"My lords, I am now to take my leave of your lordships, and of this honourable house, perhaps, for ever. I shall lay down my life with pleasure, in a cause favoured by my late dear royal mistress. And when I consider that I am to be judged by the justice, honour, and virtue of my peers, I shall acquiesce, and retire with great content. And, my lords, God's will be done."[a]

[a] Nobly said! Spoken like a Tory!

IV, 209 **Goldsmith's reflections on the Whigs during the trial of Oxford. JA had lived for only some fifteen years when she wrote of having 'lived long enough in the World'.**

It is, indeed, very remarkable, that all the severe and most restrictive laws were enacted by that party that are continually stunning mankind with a cry of freedom.[a]

[a] My dear Dr G—I have lived long enough in the World to know that it is always so!

IV, 213 **Like Bolingbroke, James Butler, Duke of Ormonde fled from England and joined James Edward, the Old Pretender, the 'master unworthy of his services'.**

The night he [the Duke of Ormonde] took leave of England, it is said he paid a visit to lord Oxford, who dissuaded him from flying with as much earnestness as the duke entreated Oxford to fly. He bid his friend the last adieu, with these words, "Farewell Oxford, without an head." To which the other replied, "Farewell duke, without a duchy." He afterwards continued to reside chiefly in Spain, an illustrious exile, and fruitlessly attached to a master unworthy of his services.[a]

[a] Unworthy because he was a Stuart, I suppose. Unhappy Family.

IV, 214 **JA here corrects what is presumably a printer's error.**

The malcontents of that country [Scotland] had all along maintained a correspondence with their friends in England, who were now driven by resentment and apprehension into a system of politics they would not otherwise had[a] dreamt of.

[a] 'had' deleted; '*have*' written above line.

IV, 217 The Earl of Mar led a Jacobite rebellion in Scotland in September 1715. His army engaged with government troops under the Duke of Argyle at Sheriffmuir; the battle was indecisive.

At evening, both sides drew off, and both sides claimed the victory. Though the possession of the field was kept by neither, yet certainly all the honour, and all the advantages of the day, belonged only to the duke of Argyle.[a] It was sufficient for him to have interrupted the progress of the enemy.

[a] Oh! to be sure!

IV, 218 Many politicians and others were arrested in England and charged with supporting the Jacobite rebellion. Lords Landsdown and Duplin are among those named by Goldsmith.

Upon the first rumour, therefore, of an insurrection, they imprisoned several lords and gentlemen, of whom they had a suspicion ... The lords Landsdown and Duplin were taken into custody.[a]

[a] very kind!

IV, 225 JA's comment on the 'deluded wretches', arrested for their part in the 1715 rebellion, is in very faint pencil; the reading is conjectural. The word 'deluded' has been underlined, presumably by JA.

The law was now put in force with all its terrors; and the prisons of London were crowded with those *deluded*[a] wretches, whom the ministry seemed resolved not to pardon.

[a] They <were not> Deluded.

IV, 238–9 In 1719–20, a complex series of financial arrangements between the South Sea Company and the government culminated in a stock-market crash, known as the South Sea Bubble. Robert

Walpole's proposals for dealing with the crisis brought him to power; JA's comment reluctantly concedes the merit of one of his schemes.

Sir Robert Walpole conceived a design of lessening these national debts, by giving the several companies an alternative either of accepting a lower interest, namely, five per cent. or of being paid the principal . . . In the same manner, the governors and company of the bank, and other companies, were contented to receive a diminished annual interest for their respective loans, all which greatly lessened the debts of the nation.[a]

[a] It is a pity that a *Whig* should have been of such use to his Country.

IV, 244–5 Bishop Atterbury, a leading Tory, was accused in 1722 of planning a Jacobite invasion and banished from England for life. The Earl of Bathurst was among those who spoke in his defence.

Lord Bathurst also spoke in the bishop's favour, observing, that if such extraordinary proceedings were countenanced, he saw nothing remaining for him and others, but to retire to their country houses, and there, if possible, quietly to enjoy their estates within their own families, since the most trifling correspondence, or any intercepted letter, might be made criminal.[a]

[a] Very True.

IV, 246 Christopher Layer suffered a worse fate than Bishop Atterbury; found guilty of treason, he was hanged, drawn and quartered.

It is said, that the intention of the conspirators was, by introducing a number of foreign officers and soldiers into England unobserved, to prepare a junction with the duke of Ormond, who was to have landed in the river with a great quantity of arms provided for that purpose. However this be, Mr. Layer was reprieved from time to time, and many methods tried to make him discover his accomplices; but he continued stedfast in his trust, so that he suffered death at Tyburn, and his head was fixed on Temple-bar.[a]

[a] Poor Man! Alas Poor Man.

IV, 252 To Goldsmith's summation on the reign of George I, who died in 1727, JA adds her view of the 'always' corrupt Whig government.

Whatever was good or great in the reign of this monarch ought to be ascribed chiefly to himself; wherever he deviated he might have been misled by a ministry, always partial, sometimes[a] corrupt.

[a] 'sometimes' deleted; '*always*' written above.

IV, 256 The 'Country' party was led by Bolingbroke, who had been pardoned in 1723 and returned to join in the opposition to Walpole, leader of the 'Court' party.

The other side, who went by the name of the Country party, were entirely averse to continental connexions.[a] They complained that immense sums were lavished on subsidies which could never be useful; and that alliances were bought with money from nations that should rather contribute to England for her protection.

[a] Very Sensibly.

IV, 263 Among the examples of corruption in 1731–2 listed here, JA takes note of the fraudulent sale of the forfeited estate of the Earl of Derwentwater by Denis Bond and Serjeant Birch, two of the estate's commissioners. Derwentwater, a grandson of Charles II and thus of special interest to JA, had been impeached as a traitor after the 1715 Jacobite invasion and executed.

A spirit of avarice and rapacity had infected every rank of life about this time; no less than six members of parliament were expelled for the most sordid acts of knavery. Sir Robet Sutton, Sir Archibald Grant, and George Robinson, for their frauds in the management of the charitable corporation scheme; Dennis Bond, and Serjeant Burch, for a fraudulent sale of the late unfortunate[a] earl of Derwenwater's[b] large estate; and lastly, John Ward, of Hackney, for forgery.

[a] Unfortunate indeed.

[b] 'Derwenwater's' corrected to 'Derwentwater's' by the insertion of a 't'.

IV, 264 Goldsmith's remark follows his account of an impoverished couple, who in desperation cut their child's throat and then hanged themselves. JA's compassionate response is followed by a reply, possibly by James Edward Austen-Leigh, in very faint pencil; the reading is conjectural.

Suicide is often imputed to frenzy. We have here an instance of self-murder concerted with composure, and borrowing the aids of reason for its vindication.[a]

[a] How much are the Poor to be pitied, & the Rich to be blamed![†]

[†] Here I think you *should* say <both should be forgiven far from deserving to be blamed.>

IV, 269 Fielding's satirical comedy *Pasquin* opened at the Little Haymarket theatre in March 1736. It was among the last of his comedies to be produced before the passing of the Stage Licensing Act in 1737, which placed strict controls on the London stage. JA's comment is in very faint pencil; the reading is conjectural.

At a little theatre in the Hay-market the ministry was every night ridiculed, and their dress and manner exactly imitated. The ingenious Mr. Henry Fielding finding that the public had no taste for new pieces of real humour, was willing to gratify their appetite for scandal,[a] and brought on a theatrical thing, which he called Pasquin.

[a] <a dangerous experiment.>

IV, 270 JA's comment on the Stage Licensing Act is in very faint pencil and the reading is again conjectural. She is apparently referring to Goldsmith's divided loyalties, as a moralist and a dramatist. The last four words have been underlined, presumably by JA.

This bill, while it confined genius on the one hand, turned it to proper objects of pursuit on the other, and the stage is at present free from the scandalous licence which infects the press; but perhaps rendered more dull from the *abridgement of unlimited abuse.*[a]

[a] conflict <over his loyalties>

IV, 274 JA also expresses her approval of the Treaty of Utrecht above (pp. 326–9).

Ever since the treaty of Utrecht,[a] the Spaniards in America had insulted and distressed the commerce of Great Britain, and the British merchants had attempted to carry on an illicit trade into their dominions.

[a] That was a good treaty.

IV, 278–9 In 1740, a fleet commanded by George, Lord Anson, sailed round Cape Horn in a celebrated attack on Spanish possessions in South America and the Pacific. JA provides the names of Anson's flagship the Centurion, together with the remainder of his squadron, revealing her pride in the British navy.

The delays and mistakes of the ministry frustrated that part of the scheme, which was originally well laid. When it was too late in the season, the commodore set out with five ships of the line, a frigate, and two store-ships,[a] with about fourteen hundred men.

[a] The Centurion Gloucester, Severn; Pearl; Tryal & Wager

IV, 280 After several successful raids on the South American coast, three of Anson's ships were destroyed by storms and many of his crew died of scurvy. The survivors, loaded into the flagship the Centurion, were fortunate to land on the fertile island of Tinian: dear to JA for saving the life of a naval hero.

In this exigence having brought all his men into one vessel, and set fire to the other, he steered for the island of Tinian, which lies about half way between the new world and the old.[a] In this charming abode he continued for some time, till his men recovered their health, and his ship was refitted for sailing.

[a] Dear Tinian!

IV, 293 JA's first insertion here is a playful acknowledgement of the might of Peter I (Peter the Great), first emperor of Russia (1682–1725). She also underlined the word 'emperor' and identified him as Charles VI, Holy Roman Emperor (1711–40).

Peter the Great[a] had already civilized Russia, and this new created extensive empire began to influence the councils of other nations, and to give laws to the North ... All these states, however, continued to enjoy a profound peace, until the death of Augustus, king of Poland, by which a general flame was once more kindled in Europe. The *emperor*,[b] assisted by the arms of Russia, declared for the elector of Saxony, son to the deceased king.

[a] 'Great' changed to 'Greatest' by the insertion of 'est'.
[b] Charles 6th

IV, 301–2 The 'family' refers to the Old Pretender, James Edward Stuart, and his son, Charles Edward Stuart, the Young Pretender, 'Bonnie Prince Charlie'. In 1744, Sir John Norris led an English fleet that turned back an attempted French invasion in support of Charles Edward; the French fleet was then wrecked by a storm at Dunkirk.

An invasion was therefore actually projected; and Charles, the son of the old pretender, departed from Rome in the disguise of a Spanish courier, for Paris where he had an audience of the French king.

This family had long been the dupes of France;[a] but it was thought at present there were serious resolutions formed in their favour. The troops destined for the expedition amounted to fifteen thousand men . . . But the whole project was disconcerted by the appearance of Sir John Norris, who, with a superior fleet, made up to attack them.[b]

[a] Not only ill used by the french but by everyone.
[b] Sir John seems always to have been sailing about.

IV, 308–9 Goldsmith recounts the events of the Jacobite rebellion of 1745, while JA expresses her sympathy for Charles Edward Stuart and his cause.

Thus, for the conquest of the whole British empire, he only brought with him seven officers, and arms for two thousand men. Fortune, which ever persecuted his family,[a] seemed no way more favourable to him; for his convoy, a ship of sixty guns, was so disabled in an engagement with an Englishman of war, named the Lion, that it was obliged to return to Brest, while he continued his course to the Western parts of Scotland . . .

The boldness of this enterprize astonished all Europe. It awakened the fears of the pusilanimous, the ardour of the brave, and the pity of the wise.[b] The whole kingdom seemed unanimously bent upon opposing an enterprize, which they were sensible, as being supported by papists, would be instrumental in restoring popery.

[a] Too true!
[b] And the good wishes of the Just.

IV, 310 Charles Edward's defeat of General John Cope's forces at Prestonpans, Scotland, in September 1745 was the highpoint of his campaign.

In the mean time, Sir John Cope, who had pursued the rebels throughout the Highlands, but had declined meeting them in their descent, being now reinforced by two regiments of dragoons, resolved to march towards Edinburgh, and give the enemy battle. The young adventurer, whose forces were rather superior, though undisciplined, attacked him near Preston Pans, about twelve miles from the capital, and in a few minutes put him and his troops to flight.[a]

[a] Delightful

IV, 315 'Fiddlededia' or 'fiddlededee', meaning 'nonsense', was a term newly coined in the late eighteenth century. *OED* gives 1784 as the earliest use: Samuel Johnson, quoted in Boswell's *Life of Johnson* (1791). JA uses the word to express her view of an implausible scheme for lawyers and judges to take part in the defence of London against an expected Jacobite invasion.

In the mean time the king resolved to take the field in person. The volunteers of the city were incorporated into a regiment; the practitioners of the law agreed to take the field, with the judges at their head;[a] and even the managers of the theatre offered to raise a body of their dependents for the service of their country.

[a] Fiddlededia.

IV, 320–4 In April 1746, the Jacobite army under Charles Edward was routed at the Battle of Culloden by the Hanoverian forces, led by the Duke of Cumberland. Goldsmith's account of the battle and its aftermath elicited a series of comments by JA. The dash in her first remark on the 'conquerors' might stand for 'accursed'; that in her sixth remark might signify a 'blessed' cause. The third remark alludes to the playwright and politician Richard Brinsley Sheridan, whose speeches for the prosecution in the trial of Warren Hastings (1788–95) were offensive to JA. Arthur Elphinstone, 6th Baron Balmerino, the Jacobite named in JA's final remark, was one of the captured rebels brought to trial in London and executed at the Tower of London.

But little mercy was shewn here; the conquerors were seen to refuse quarter to the wounded, the unarmed, and the defenceless;[a] some were slain who were only excited by curiosity to become spectators of the combat, and soldiers were seen to anticipate the base employment of the executioner . . .

In this manner were blasted all the hopes, and all the ambition of the young adventurer; one short hour deprived him of imaginary thrones and scepters, and reduced him from a nominal king, to a distressed forlorn outcast, shunned by all mankind, except such as sought his destruction. To the good and the brave, subsequent distress often atones for former guilt; and while reason would speak for punishment, our hearts plead for mercy.[b] Immediately after the engagement, he fled away with a captain of Fitzjames's cavalry, and when their horses were fatigued, they both alighted, and separately sought for safety . . .

Sometimes he lay in forests, with one or two companions of his distress, continually pursued by the troops of the conqueror, as there was a reward of thirty thousand pounds offered for taking him, dead or alive. Sheridan, an Irish adventurer,[c] was the person who kept most faithfully by him, and inspired him with courage to support such incredible hardships. He had occasion in the course of his concealments, to trust his life to the fidelity of above fifty individuals, whose veneration for his family prevailed above their avarice.[d]

One day, having walked from morning till night, he ventured to enter a house, the owner of which he well knew was attached to the opposite party. As he entered, he addressed the master of the house in the following manner. "The son of your king comes to beg a little bread and a few cloaths. I know your present attachment to my adversaries, but I believe you have sufficient honour not to abuse my confidence, or to take advantage of my distressed situation."[e] . . .

In the mean time, while the pretender was thus pursued, the scaffolds and the gibbets were preparing for his adherents. Seventeen officers of the rebel army were hanged, drawn and quartered, at Kennington-common, in the neighbourhood of London. Their constancy in death gained more proselytes to their cause than even perhaps their victories would have obtained[f] . . .

But very different was the behaviour of Balmerino, who gloried in the cause for which he fell. When his fellow-sufferer was commanded to bid God bless king George, which he did with a faint voice, Balmerino still avowed his principles, and cried out aloud, "God bless king James!"[g]

[a] Horrid wretches in an — cause.
[b] But with the Just, Reason would not *have* plead for punishment.
[c] It is a pity that his namesake is not equally praiseworthy.
[d] A Just Veneration.
[e] Who but a Stuart could have so spoken?
[f] Fortitude will always attend a — cause.
[g] Dear Balmerino! I cannot express what I feel for you.

IV, 325 **The Highland chieftains, who had generally supported the rebellion, were punished by being forbidden to wear their distinctive tartans or to bear arms.**

The Highlanders had till this time continued to wear the old military dress of their ancestors, and never went without arms. In consequence of this, they considered themselves as a body of people distinct from the rest of the nation, and were ready, upon the shortest notice, to second the insurrections of their chiefs. But their habits were now reformed by an act of the legislature, and they were compelled to wear cloaths of the common fashion.[a]

[a] I do not like This—Every ancient custom ought to be sacred unless prejudicial to Happiness.

IV, 331–2 The Treaty of Aix-la-Chapelle (1748), which ended the War of Austrian Succession (1740–8), was intended to make peace between England and France. JA's comment reflects on the fact that the treaty largely restored the pre-war status quo; hence eight years of bloodshed had been in vain.

[T]he treaty of Utrecht was branded with universal contempt, and the treaty of Aix-la-Chapelle was extolled with the highest strains of praise. But the people were wearied with repeated disgrace, and only expecting an accumulation of misfortunes by continuing the war, they were glad of any peace that promised a pause to their disappointments.[a]

[a] It is very stupid.

IV, 404 After describing the astonishing force of the Prussian army, led by Frederick the Great, during the Seven Years War (1756–63), Goldsmith concludes his history on a reflective note. His remark on the human calamity resulting from advances in the art of warfare for once meets with JA's approval.

At no time since the days of heroism, were such numbers destroyed, so many towns taken, so many skirmishes fought, such stratagems practiced, or such intrepidity discovered. Armies were, by the German discipline, considered as composing one great machine, directed by one commander, and animated by a single will. From the commentary of these campaigns, succeeding generals will take their lessons of devastation, and improve upon the arts encreasing human calamity.[a]

[a] The best Thing in the Book.

Marginalia in Vicesimus Knox's *Elegant Extracts . . . in Prose*

London, n.d.

In her childhood, Jane Austen owned a copy of the popular anthology *Elegant Extracts: or useful and entertaining Passages in Prose Selected for the Improvement of Scholars*, compiled by the Christian philosopher Vicesimus Knox (1752–1821). Like its companion, Knox's *Elegant Extracts from the Most Eminent British Poets*, this anthology, first published in *c.* 1770, went through numerous editions, with later ones running to six small volumes. Austen's copy is a single-volume edition, of uncertain date. In 1801, she presented it to her then eight-year-old niece Anna, possibly on the child's birthday on 15 April. On the inside front cover, Austen inscribed her niece's full name, 'Jane Anna Elizth. Austen', and the date. Anna also recorded her own ownership, writing '1801' beside JA's '1801', and 'the gift of her Aunt Jane' below. The next owner, Anna's eldest daughter (1815–55), also recorded her name below her mother's, writing, in an adult hand, 'Anna Jemima Lefroy'. The book remained in the possession of the Lefroy family until the 1980s, when it was presented to the Jane Austen Memorial Trust; it is now on display at Jane Austen's House, Chawton.

Among the excerpts in *Elegant Extracts* is a passage entitled 'The Character of Mary Queen of Scots', taken from William Robertson's *The History of Scotland, during the reigns of Queen Mary and of King James VI* (London, 2nd edn, 1759) and one entitled 'The Character of Queen Elizabeth', taken from David Hume's *The History of England, from the Invasion of Julius Caesar to the Revolution in 1688* (London, 1763). Austen seems to have read these extracts at about the same time that she was reading Goldsmith's *History of England,* in 1791, annotating them, in black ink, in a hand similar to that in her copy of Goldsmith. Her marginalia on the excerpt from Robertson concern his depiction of Mary Queen of Scots; those on the excerpt from Hume concern his depiction of Queen Elizabeth. There are also pencil notes on pages 544–5 of the volume and on the inside back cover, in a different hand from the black-ink marginalia. Since they refer to 'Todds Johnson's dictionary', an edition by the Reverend Henry J. Todd, first published in 1818 and popular in the early nineteenth century, they are clearly not by Austen but probably by Anna Lefroy.[1]

The excerpts from Robertson and Hume are printed below, with Austen's commentary below the passage, with letters showing the point in the text to which each marginal comment refers.

---

[1] In 'New Marginalia in Jane Austen's Books' (*Book Collector*, 49 (2000), 222–6), Deirdre Le Faye transcribed JA's marginalia in *Elegant Extracts* for the first time. She suggests that the pencilled comments are also in JA's hand, although the references to 'Todds Johnson's dictionary' make this impossible.

ELEGANT EXTRACTS, PP. 361–2

The Character of MARY *Queen of* SCOTS.

To all the charms of beauty, and the utmost elegance of external form, Mary added those accomplishments which render their impression irresistible. Polite, affable, insinuating, sprightly, and capable of speaking and of writing with equal ease and dignity. Sudden, however, and violent in all her attachments;[a] because her heart was warm and unsuspicious. Impatient of contradiction,[b] because she had been accustomed from her infancy to be treated as a queen. No stranger, on some occasions, to dissimulation,[c] which in that perfidious court where she received her education, was reckoned among the necessary arts of government. Not insensible to flattery, or unconscious of that pleasure, with which almost every woman beholds the influence of her own beauty. Formed with the qualities that we love, not with the talents that we admire;[d] she was an

[a] No.
[b] No.
[c] Yes.
[d] A lie.

agreeable woman rather than an illustrious queen. The vivacity of her spirit, not sufficiently tempered with sound judgment, and the warmth of her heart, which was not at all times under the restraint of direction, betrayed her both into errors and into crimes.[e] To say that she was always unfortunate, will not account for that long and almost uninterrupted succession of calamities which befel her; we must likewise add, that she was often imprudent.[f] Her passion for Darnley was rash, youthful, and excessive. And though the sudden transition to the opposite extreme, was the natural effect of her ill-requited love, and of his ingratitude, insolence, and brutality; yet neither these, nor Bothwell's artful address and important services, can justify her attachments to that nobleman.[g] Even the manners of the age, licentious as they were, are no apology for this unhappy passion;[h] nor can they induce us to look on that tragical and infamous scene which followed upon it with less abhorrence.[i] Humanity will draw a veil over this part of her character which it cannot approve,[j] and may, perhaps, prompt some to impute her actions to her situation, more than to her dispositions; and to lament the unhappiness of the former, rather than accuse the perverseness of the latter. Mary's sufferings exceed, both in degree and in duration, those tragical distresses which fancy has feigned to excite sorrow and commiseration; and while we survey them, we are apt altogether to forget her frailties, we think of her faults with less indignation, and approve of our tears, as if they were shed for a person who had attained much nearer to pure virtue.[k]

. . . No man, says Brantome, ever beheld her person without admiration and love, or will read her history without sorrow.[l]

[e] another lie.

[f] a third.

[g] She was not attached to him.

[h] more than sufficient.

[i] They do.

[j] It more than approves, it admires.

[k] That was impossible.

[l] No one *ought*, but I fear that Mr Brantome has too favourable an opinion of Human Nature, if he makes no exception.

ELEGANT EXTRACTS, PP. 368–9

The Character of Queen ELIZABETH

There are few personages in history who have been more exposed to the calumny of enemies,[m] and the adulation of friends, than Queen Elizabeth, and yet there scarce is any whose reputation has been more certainly determined by the unanimous consent of posterity. The unusual length of her administration and the strong features of her character, were able to overcome all prejudices; and obliging her detractors to abate much of their invectives and her admirers somewhat of their panegyrics, have at last, in spite of political factions, and what is more, of religious animosities, produced an uniform judgment with regard to her conduct.[n]

... We may find it difficult to reconcile our fancy to her as a wife or a mistress; but her qualities as a sovereign, though with some considerable exceptions, are the object of undisputed applause and approbation.[o]

[m] None deserve it more.
[n] a lie.
[o] A Lie—an entire lie from beginning to end.

Sophia Sentiment's letter in *The Loiterer*, 28 March 1789

The Loiterer, a weekly periodical, was launched on Saturday, 31 January 1789 by Jane Austen's eldest brother James, then a Fellow of St John's College, Oxford. Its aim, according to James's first editorial, was to supply 'a regular succession of moral lectures, critical remarks, and elegant humour' (no. 1, p. 3). It continued to appear every Saturday for almost fourteen months, until the sixtieth and final number was published on 20 March 1790. A few weeks later, the weekly issues were collected into two substantial volumes, giving *The Loiterer* a wider circulation than its original, primarily Oxford readership. The contributions are unsigned, but in the final number James Austen provided a key to their authorship. Of the sixty essays, twenty-nine are by James himself; nine are by his brother Henry, then a Scholar at St John's; two are by the Revd Benjamin Portal, with a third by Portal and Henry in collaboration; and the others are by various Oxonians, most of them unidentified.[1]

Among James's contributions to *The Loiterer* is issue number nine, published on 28 March 1789, which begins by introducing a letter 'brought us the last week . . . and as it is the first favour of the kind we have ever received from the fair sex (I mean in our capacity of authors) we take the earliest opportunity of laying it before our readers' (pp. 3–4). The letter itself follows, above the pseudonym 'Sophia Sentiment', complaining that *The Loiterer* had hitherto neglected its female readers; unless this is rectified, Sophia will 'soon drop your acquaintance'. James's reply is a mock-solemn defence of *The Loiterer* against the letter-writer's various charges. It is possible that James Austen wrote the letter as well as the response. His key to authorship says nothing about 'Sophia Sentiment', and

---

[1] See Li-Ping Geng, Introduction to *The Loiterer* (Ann Arbor, MI: Scholars' Facsimiles & Reprints, 2000), pp. 11–12.

the letter is nowhere mentioned in his surviving papers or in any Austen family documents. It is, however, more probable that Sophia was a female writer known to James, and his sister Jane Austen, then aged thirteen, is much the most likely candidate.

In a pioneering article of 1961, Walton Litz explored various parallels between *The Loiterer* and Austen's juvenilia, noting that some numbers 'may have been planned and executed at Steventon' during Oxford vacations and suggesting that 'there is always the possibility that Jane herself exerted an influence on a few of the essays'.[2] Three years later B. C. Southam concurred, stating that Austen 'would have heard or read her brothers' contributions, perhaps even making suggestions at the time of writing'.[3] The letter by 'Sophia Sentiment' was first attributed to Jane Austen by Zachary Cope, in an article of 1966. Cope contends that neither James nor Henry Austen is likely to have written Sophia's witty contribution: 'James had a serious style that never descended to the light bantering and in places conversational writing that makes the letter sparkling and vivacious', while Henry 'had a lighter touch, but even his lightest manner was stilted in comparison with that of the letter'. Cope believes that the author was a 'very young woman, probably in her teens', and finds several remarks in the letter linking it to Jane Austen: the author's voracious reading of essays, novels and plays; the author's having once visited Oxford herself, as Jane Austen had as a child; the impertinent tone, which would have been offensive from a stranger, but not from a 'young and irrepressible sister'; and the pseudonym 'Sophia', the same as that of the excessively sentimental Sophia in 'Love and Freindship'. Cope even believes that 'the offer to help the editor, contained in the letter, may have been a genuine offer from the ambitious Jane'.[4]

Cope's attribution of the 'Sophia Sentiment' letter to Jane Austen was at once endorsed in the *Jane Austen Society Report* for 1966 by

---

[2] Walton Litz, '*The Loiterer*: A Reflection of Jane Austen's Early Environment', *Review of English Studies*, new series, 12 (1961), 252.

[3] B. C. Southam, *Jane Austen's Literary Manuscripts: A Study of the Novelist's Development through the Surviving Papers* (Oxford: Oxford University Press, 1964), p. 12.

[4] Zachary Cope, 'Who Was Sophia Sentiment? Was She Jane Austen?', *Book Collector*, 15 (1966), 143–51.

John Gore and, briefly, by Elizabeth Jenkins.[5] Gore's paper contains a summary of Cope's argument, together with a new suggestion by Cope: that since the Sophia Sentiment letter criticizes a previous contribution by Henry Austen, Jane might have written it with Henry 'in collusion'. Gore thinks that the letter was written at Steventon during the Christmas vacation, 1788, 'in deference to chaffing criticism of the paper's "dullness" ',[6] but this theory ignores chronology: the first number of *The Loiterer* would be published only a month later, so no such criticism could yet have been made.

Most recent students of *The Loiterer* have found the attribution to Austen suggestive but far from conclusive. Larry Bronson, in a 1983 essay on the periodical, describes the Sophia Sentiment letter as 'a parody by Jane Austen herself?',[7] the question mark acknowledging that the matter was not yet resolved. Li-Ping Geng, editor of a 2000 facsimile edition of *The Loiterer*, finds the letter 'full of young Jane's tone and voice'. Its 'crude irony', he acknowledges, 'resembles very much that seen in Henry Austen's essays, but the charming exuberance and feminine tone seem to suggest that it was the hand of Jane Austen'.[8] And Robert L. Mack, editor of a 2006 edition of *The Loiterer*, believes that while the letter might have been written by James's 'precocious thirteen-year-old sister', the attribution is open to question.[9]

Austen's recent biographers have reached no consensus on the issue. George Holbert Tucker finds the attribution 'highly plausible', terming Cope's article 'a fascinating bit of literary detection'.[10] Park Honan believes that Austen wrote the letter and that it made her brothers change their plans for *The Loiterer*: 'They wrote less

[5] John Gore, ' "Sophia Sentiment": Jane Austen?'; Elizabeth Jenkins, 'A Footnote to "Sophia Sentiment" ', *Jane Austen Society Report for the Year, 1966* (Winchester: Jane Austen Society, 1966), pp. 9–13.

[6] Gore, 'Sophia Sentiment', pp. 11, 12.

[7] Larry Bronson, 'The Loiterer', in *British Literary Magazines: The Romantic Age, 1789–1836*, ed. Alvin Sullivan (Westport, CT: Greenwood Press, 1983), p. 285.

[8] Geng, Introduction to *The Loiterer*, p. 17. Geng repeats these remarks in his article 'The *Loiterer* and Jane Austen's Literary Identity', *Eighteenth-Century Fiction*, 13 (2001), 587.

[9] Robert L. Mack, Introduction to *The Austen Family's* The Loiterer (Lewiston, NY: Edwin Mellen Press, 2006).

[10] George Holbert Tucker, *A Goodly Heritage: A History of Jane Austen's Family* (Manchester: Carcanet New Press, 1983), p. 105.

and less about Oxford, and more and more about love and the blisses and torments of marriage—which they knew rather little about'.[11] David Nokes concedes that the attribution 'cannot be asserted as a certainty', but finds that 'the tone of the piece is consistent with [Austen's] many juvenile essays in the style of literary parody'.[12] Jon Spence observes that 'the voice does sound like hers, and the quickness and inventiveness of the letter are characteristic of Jane'.[13] Spence also believes that the letter-writer is drawing on her knowledge of Eliza de Feuillide, and of Henry Austen's romantic interest in his cousin.

Other Austen biographers and critics, however, are sceptical. John McAleer floats the idea, unconvincingly, that 'if female authorship is insisted upon', the letter 'might just as well have been written by . . . her sister Cassandra'.[14] Jan Fergus finds the letter 'discursive, lacking the incisiveness of Austen's juvenilia'; 'nothing in its style is inconsistent with James's burlesque writing in *The Loiterer*, and much is inconsistent with Austen's'.[15] Claire Tomalin, who believes that Sophia 'is more likely to have been a transvestite, Henry or James', states that 'the letter is not an encouragement to *The Loiterer* to address women readers so much as a mockery of women's poor taste in literature'[16]—although mocking women's poor taste is very much within the young Jane Austen's range. And Peter Knox-Shaw finds the attribution 'attractive but questionable', since the letter 'is not easily read as a consistent burlesque', while its contents 'run clean contrary to the stance taken towards sentimental fiction and marvellous tales in the juvenilia'.[17]

The most impressive case for Austen's putative authorship of the letter has been made by Deirdre Le Faye. In an article of 1987, Le

[11] Park Honan, *Jane Austen: Her Life* (London: Weidenfeld & Nicolson, 1987), p. 61.
[12] David Nokes, *Jane Austen: A Life* (London: Fourth Estate, 1997), p. 536.
[13] Jon Spence, *Becoming Jane Austen: A Life* (London: Hambledon, 2003), p. 53.
[14] John McAleer, 'What a Biographer Can Learn about Jane Austen', in *Jane Austen's Beginnings: The Juvenilia and Lady Susan*, ed. J. David Grey (Ann Arbor, MI: UMI Research Press, 1989), p. 14.
[15] Jan Fergus, *Jane Austen: A Literary Life* (New York: St Martin's Press, 1991), p. 61.
[16] Claire Tomalin, *Jane Austen: A Life* (London: Viking, 1997), p. 63. Tomalin does, however, concede that the letter might have been co-authored by Henry and Jane Austen (pp. 303–4).
[17] Peter Knox-Shaw, *Jane Austen and the Enlightenment* (Cambridge: Cambridge University Press, 2004), p. 19.

Faye was the first to trace the name 'Sophia Sentiment' to a character in *The Mausoleum* (1785), a rhyming comedy by William Hayley in which 'one of the main characters is a lovely silly young widow whose name is "Lady Sophia Sentiment" '.[18] Austen acquired her own set of Hayley's works in April 1791, but could, of course, have read the comedy before creating her own Sophia Sentiment in 1789. Le Faye's findings were developed by Paula Byrne, who believes it 'highly probable that Jane Austen wrote this burlesque letter to her brother', a letter which is 'very close in spirit to her juvenilia of the same period'. Byrne also speculates that *The Mausoleum* might have been 'among the comedies considered for performance by the Austens when they were looking at material for home theatricals in 1788'.[19]

Le Faye's biographical studies strengthen the case for the attribution. In her life of Austen of 1998, she reprints a part of Sophia's letter closely resembling 'Love and Freindship' ('as for his mistress, she will of course go mad; or if you will, you may kill the lady, and let the lover run mad'), contending that 'the tone of this burlesque letter is so much in keeping with Jane's own jokes and essays in her *Juvenilia* as to make it seem entirely likely that she also wrote this offering for her brother's magazine'.[20] And in the second edition of her *Jane Austen: A Family Record*, Le Faye provides another argument in favour of Austen's authorship, drawing on a rare piece of external evidence. The ninth number of *The Loiterer*, Le Faye observes, which contains the Sophia Sentiment letter, was the only one 'advertised in the *Reading Mercury*, the local newspaper which circulated in North Hampshire'. James Austen, she suggests, could have 'arranged for the advertisement to be placed where he knew his little sister would read it and so enhance the pleasure she must have felt on seeing her first words in print'.[21]

---

[18] Deirdre Le Faye, 'Jane Austen and William Hayley', *Notes and Queries*, 232 (1987), 26.

[19] Paula Byrne, *Jane Austen and the Theatre* (London: Hambledon, 2002), p. 17.

[20] Le Faye, *The British Library Writers' Lives: Jane Austen* (London: British Library, 1998), p. 31.

[21] Le Faye, *Jane Austen: A Family Record* (Cambridge: Cambridge University Press, 2004), p. 68. See also Robin Vick, 'More on "Sophia Sentiment" ', *Jane Austen Society Report for the Year, 1999* (Winchester: Jane Austen Society, 1999), pp. 15–17. Vick notes that the *Reading Mercury* was the local paper for north Hampshire, and was 'certainly seen by Jane Austen' (p. 15), who alludes to it in a letter of 8 January 1799.

The ninth number of *The Loiterer* was the first to be sold by booksellers at Bath and Reading; numbers from five onwards had also been sold in London and Birmingham. It is possible that the expansion to Reading, like the advertisement in the *Reading Mercury*, was timed to coincide with the appearance of the 'Sophia Sentiment' letter, enabling Austen, if she were the author, to boast of the simultaneous appearance of her first publication in five English towns.

To *the* AUTHOR *of the* LOITERER

SIR,

I write this to inform you that you are very much out of my good graces, and that, if you do not mend your manners, I shall soon drop your acquaintance. You must know, Sir, I am a great reader, and not to mention some hundred volumes of Novels and Plays, have, in the two last summers, actually got through all the entertaining papers of our most celebrated periodical writers, from the Tatler and Spectator to the Microcosm and the Olla Podrida. Indeed I love a periodical work beyond any thing, especially those in which one meets with a great many stories, and where the papers are not too long. I assure you my heart beat with joy when I first heard of your publication, which I immediately sent for, and have taken in ever since.

I am sorry, however, to say it, but really, Sir, I think it the stupidest work of the kind I ever saw: not but that some of the papers are well written; but then your subjects are so badly chosen, that they never interest one.—Only conceive, in eight papers, not one sentimental story about love and honour, and all that.—Not one Eastern Tale full of Bashas and Hermits, Pyramids and Mosques—no, not even an allegory or dream have yet made their appearance in the Loiterer. Why, my dear Sir—what do you think we care about the way in which Oxford men spend their time and money—we, who have enough to do to spend our own. For my part, I never, but once, was at Oxford in my life, and I am sure I never wish to go there again— They dragged me through so many dismal chapels, dusty libraries, and greasy halls, that it gave me the vapours for two days afterwards.

As for your last paper, indeed, the story was good enough, but there was no love, and no lady in it, at least no young lady; and I wonder how you could be guilty of such an omission, especially when it could have been so easily avoided. Instead of retiring to Yorkshire, he might have fled into France, and there, you know, you might have made him fall in love with a French *Paysanne*, who might have turned out to be some great person. Or you might have let him set fire to a convent, and carry off a nun, whom he might afterwards have converted, or any thing of that kind, just to have created a little bustle, and made the story more interesting.

In short, you have never yet dedicated any one number to the amusement of our sex, and have taken no more notice of us, than if you thought, like the Turks, we had no souls. From all which I do conclude, that you are neither more nor less than some old Fellow of a College, who never saw any thing of the world beyond the limits of the University, and never conversed with a female, except your bed-maker and laundress. I therefore give you this advice, which you will follow as you value our favour, or your own reputation.—Let us hear no more of your Oxford Journals, your Homelys and Cockney: but send them about their business, and get a new set of correspondents, from among the young of both sexes, but particularly ours; and let us see some nice affecting stories, relating the misfortunes of two lovers, who died suddenly, just as they were going to church. Let the lover be killed in a duel, or lost at sea, or you may make him shoot himself, just as you please; and as for his mistress, she will of course go mad; or if you will, you may kill the lady, and let the lover run mad; only remember, whatever you do, that your hero and heroine must possess a great deal of feeling, and have very pretty names. If you think fit to comply with this my injunction, you may expect to hear from me again, and perhaps I may even give you a little assistance;—but, if not—may your work be condemned to the pastry-cook's shop, and may you always continue a bachelor, and be plagued with a maiden sister to keep house for you.

> Your's, as you behave,
> SOPHIA SENTIMENT.

Continuations of 'Evelyn' and 'Catharine' by James Edward Austen and Anna Lefroy

The two items in 'Volume the Third', 'Evelyn' and 'Catharine', written in 1792, were both left unfinished at that time. Jane Austen provided page numbers for 'Evelyn' up to 21, ending near the top of that page with the words 'full gallop all the way'. She began paginating again with number 31, the second page of 'Catharine', thus leaving nine blank pages in which 'Evelyn' could be completed. It was eventually finished, but not by Austen herself: the last few pages, written with a different pen and ink (number 1 below), are in the hand of James Edward Austen (1798–1874), the son of Austen's brother James, who changed his name to Austen-Leigh in 1837. He filled the rest of page 21 and pages 22 to 27 (without numbering them): pages 28 and 29 remained blank. 'Catharine', which occupies pages 30 to 127 of 'Volume the Third', was also left incomplete by its author. Austen's text ends at the foot of her page 124, with the words 'conduct of Young Men'. The story is continued on pages 125–7, also by James Edward Austen, but this continuation is in itself incomplete.

Further complicating the textual issues of 'Volume the Third' is a four-page continuation of 'Evelyn', written on separate leaves of paper loosely inserted in the volume. This continuation (number 2 below), in the hand of Jane's niece Anna (1793–1872), also the daughter of James Austen and the half-sister of James Edward Austen, is initialled 'JAEL', the letters standing for her married name, Jane Anna Elizabeth Lefroy. Since Anna married Benjamin Lefroy in November 1814, she must have initialled her continuation either at the end of that year or later. On 25 December 1814, Anna's grandmother, Cassandra Austen (Jane's mother), wrote her a letter, expressing concern that the young writer 'must be quite bewildered by composing two works at the same time'.[1] As Kathryn Sutherland contends, the two works are probably Anna's novel-in-progress, 'Which is the Heroine?' (never completed and later destroyed), and her continuation-in-progress, 'Evelyn', which breaks off abruptly without much advancing the story.[2] The parody of the Gothic in Anna's attempted completion of 'Evelyn' seems indebted to that in *Northanger Abbey*, which Austen was revising at the end of her life and which she could have discussed with her literary niece at that time.

James Edward Austen probably wrote his completion of 'Evelyn' in about 1815–16, when he was writing the novel to which Austen refers in several of her letters of that period. The hand of the completion closely resembles that of the unpublished novel, now in the Hampshire Record Office. In 1815–16, aged seventeen to eighteen, he visited Jane Austen and her family at Chawton quite frequently and could have received his aunt's permission to make additions to 'Volume the Third', completing stories that she too had written when she was about seventeen.[3]

The beginning of the abortive continuation to 'Catharine' (number 3 below) is in the same hand as that of the completion of 'Evelyn', and was probably also written by James Edward Austen in 1815–16. But the remainder of this continuation (number 4 below), while also by James Edward, is in his mature hand. He probably wrote it after 1845, when he inherited 'Volume the Third' from Cassandra Austen. After 1845, he would have had time to study the inherited volume, and attempt, unsuccessfully, to complete 'Catharine' once again.

One of the letters by Mr Gower in James Edward Austen's completion of 'Evelyn' is dated 19 August 1809. B. C. Southam has conjectured that the completion might itself have been written

---

[1] Mrs Austen's letter to Anna Lefroy, held in the Princeton University Library, is transcribed by Deirdre Le Faye, 'Anna Lefroy and Her Austen Family Letters', *Princeton University Library Chronicle*, 62 (2001), 530–2.

[2] Kathryn Sutherland, *Jane Austen's Textual Lives: From Aeschylus to Bollywood* (Oxford: Oxford University Press, 2005), p. 248.

[3] Deirdre Le Faye, *Jane Austen: A Family Record*, 2nd edn (Cambridge: Cambridge University Press, 2004), p. 240.

in that year, and perhaps on that very date.[4] In the last paragraph of her 'Evelyn', however, Austen tells us that Frederic Gower returned from Carlisle to Evelyn in August. In his completion, James Edward mentions not one but three dates in that month (12, 19 and 22 August), none of which need have any particular significance: he chose the month of August because that is when the latter part of the story is set. As for the year, 1809, he might first have seen his aunt's juvenilia in that year, when he was eleven, and commemorated the event later by inserting it in the text.[5]

[4] B. C. Southam, 'Interpolations to Jane Austen's "Volume the Third" ', *Notes and Queries*, 207 (1962), 185–7.

[5] I have drawn here on material in my 'James Edward Austen, Anna Lefroy, and the Interpolations to Jane Austen's "Volume the Third" ', *Notes and Queries*, 245 (2000), 304–6.

1. JAMES EDWARD AUSTEN, CONTINUATION OF 'EVELYN', C. 1815–16

On his return home, he rang the housebell, but no one appeared, a second time he rang, but the door was not opened, a third and a fourth with as little success, when observing the dining parlour window open he leapt in, and persued his way through the house till he reached Marias' Dressingroom, where he found all the servants assembled at tea. Surprized at so very unusual a sight, he fainted, on his recovery he found himself on the Sofa, with his wife's maid kneeling by him, chafing his temples with Hungary water—. From her he learned that his beloved Maria had been so much grieved at his departure that she died of a broken heart about 3 hours after his departure.

He then became sufficiently composed to give necessary orders for her funeral which took place the Monday following this being the Saturday—When Mr Gower had settled the order of the procession he set out himself to Carlisle, to give vent to his sorrow in the bosom of his family—He arrived there in high health and spirits, after a delightful journey of 3 days and a 1/2—What was his

line 17: 'On his' lightly deleted; 'stet' inserted in a different hand. // line 20: 'ed' deleted at the end of 'open'.

surprize on entering the Breakfast parlour to see Rosa his beloved Rosa seated on a Sofa; at the sight of him she fainted and would have fallen had not a Gentleman sitting with his back to the door, started up and saved her from sinking to the ground—She very soon came to herself and then introduced this gentleman to her Brother as her Husband a Mr Davenport—

But my dearest Rosa said the astonished Gower, I thought you were dead and buried. Why my dr Frederick replied Rosa I wished you to think so, hoping that you would spread the report about the country and it would thus by some means reach —— Castle—By this I hoped some how or other to touch the hearts of its inhabitants. It was not till the day before yesterday that I heard of the death of my beloved Henry which I learned from Mr D—— who concluded by offering me his hand. I accepted it with transport, and was married yesterday—Mr Gower, embraced his sister and shook hands with Mr Davenport, he then took a stroll into the town—As he passed by a public house he called for a pot of beer, which was brought him immediately by his old friend Mrs Willis—

Great was his astonishment at seeing Mrs Willis in Carlisle. But not forgetful of the respect he owed her, he dropped on one knee, and received the frothy cup from her, more grateful to *him* than Nectar—He instantly made her an offer of his hand and heart, which she graciously condescended to accept, telling him that she was only on a visit to her cousin, who kept the *Anchor* and should be ready to return to Evelyn, whenever he chose—The next morning they were married and immediately proceeded to Evelyn—When he reached home, he recollected that he had never written to Mr and Mrs Webb to inform them of the death of their daughter, which he rightly supposed they knew nothing of, as they never took in any newspapers—He immediately dispatched the following Letter—

Evelyn—Augst 19th—1809—

Dearest Madam,

How can words express the poignancy of my feelings! Our Maria, our beloved Maria is no more, she breathed her last, on Saturday

line 2: 'chaise-long' deleted before 'Sofa'.　//　line 20: 'ful' deleted at the end of 'respect'.

the 12th of Augst—I see you now in an agony of grief lamenting not your own, but my loss—Rest satisfied I am happy, possessed of my lovely Sarah what more can I wish for?—

I remain

respectfully Yours

Fr. Gower—

Westgate Builgs Augst 22d

Generous, best of Men

how truly we rejoice to hear of your present welfare and happiness! and how truly grateful are we for your unexampled generosity in writing to condole with us on the late unlucky accident which befel our Maria—I have enclosed a draught on our banker for 30 pounds, which Mr Webb joins with me in entreating you and the amiable Sarah to accept—

Your most grateful

Anne Augusta Webb

Mr and Mrs Gower resided many years at Evelyn enjoying perfect happiness the just reward of their virtues. The only alteration which took place at Evelyn was that Mr and Mrs Davenport settled there in Mrs Willis's former abode and were for many years the proprietors of the White horse Inn—

2. ANNA LEFROY, CONTINUATION OF 'EVELYN', *c.* 1814–15

On re entering his circular domain, his round-Robin of perpetual peace; where enjoyment had no End; and calamity no commencement, his spirits became wonderfully composed, and a delicious calm extended itself through every nerve—With his pocket hankerchief (once hemmed by the genius of the too susceptible Rosa) he wiped the morbid moisture from his brow;—then flew to the Boudoir of his Maria—And, did *she* not fly to meet her Frederick?

line 27: a draft of the first sentence is written on the reverse of the final page: 'But what found he on reentering that circle of peace, that round Robin of perpetual peace'; 'circle' inserted above line, replacing the deleted 'abode'.

Did she not dart from the Couch on which she had so gracefully reclined, and, bounding like an agile Fawn over the intervening Foot stool, precipitate herself into his arms? Does she not, though fainting between every syllable, breathe forth as it were by installments her Frederick's adored name? Who is there of perception so obtuse as not to realize the touching scene? Who, of ear so dull as not to catch the soft murmur of Maria's voice? Ah! Who? The heart of every sympathetic reader repeats, Ah, Who? Vain Echo! Vain sympathy! There is no Meeting—no Murmur—No Maria— It is not in the power of language however potent; nor in that of style, however diffuse to render justice to the astonishment of Mr. Gower—Arming himself with a mahogany ruler which some fatality had placed on Maria's writing table, and calling repeatedly on her beloved Name, he rushed forward to examine the adjacent apartments—In the Dressing room of his lost one he had the melancholy satisfaction of picking up a curl paper, and a gust of wind, as he re entered the Boudoir, swept from the table, and placed at his feet a skein of black sewing silk—These were the only traces of Maria!! Carefully locking the doors of these now desolate rooms, burying the key deep in his Waistcoat pocket, and the mystery of Maria's disappearance yet deeper in his heart of hearts, Mr. Gower left his once happy home, and sought a supper, and a Bed, at the house of the hospitable Mrs Willis—There was an oppression on his chest which made him extremely uncomfortable; he regretted that instead of the skein of silk carefully wrapped up in the curl paper and placed beneath his pillow, he had not rather swallowed Laudanum—It would have been, in all probability, more efficacious—At last, Mr Gower slept a troubled sleep, and in due course of time he dreamt a troubled dream—He dreamed of Maria, as how could he less? She stood by his Bed side, in her Dressing Gown—one hand held an open book, with the forefinger of the other she pointed to this ominous passage—"Tantôt c'est un vide; qui nous ennuie; tantôt c'est un poids qui nous oppresse"— The unfortunate Frederick uttered a deep groan—and as the vision closed the volume he observed these characters strangely imprinted

line 10: 'language' deleted before 'power'.   //   line 13: 'and' written over an illegible word.   //   line 26: 'which' deleted; 'and' inserted above line.   //   line 33: 'Tantôt' deleted before first 'qui'.

on the Cover—Rolandi—Berners Street. *Who* was this dangerous Rolandi? Doubtless a Bravo or a Monk—possibly both—and what was he to Maria? Vainly he would have dared the worst, and put the fatal question—the semblance of Maria raised her monitory finger, and interdicted speech—Yet, some words she spoke, or seemed to speak her self; Mr. Gower could distinguish only these—Search—Cupboard—Top shelf—Once more he essayed to speak, but it was all bewilderment—He heard strange Demon-like Sounds; hissing and spitting—he smelt an unearthly smell the agony became unbearable, and he awoke—Maria had vanished; the Rush light was expiring in the Socket; and the benevolent Mrs. Willis entering his room, threw open the shutters, and in accordance with her own warmth of heart admitted the full blaze of a Summer morning's Sun—

JAEL

3. JAMES EDWARD AUSTEN, FIRST CONTINUATION OF 'CATHARINE', C. 1815–16

Kitty continued in this state of satisfaction during the remainder of the Stanley's visit—Who took their leave with many pressing invitations to visit them in London, when as Camilla said, she might have an opportunity of becoming acquainted with that sweet girl Augusta Hallifax—Or Rather (thought Kitty,) of seeing my dr Mary Wynn again—Mrs Percival in answer to Mrs Stanley's invitation replied—That she looked upon London as the hot house of Vice where virtue had long been banished from Society and wickedness of every description was daily gaining ground—that Kitty was of herself sufficiently inclined to give way to, and indulge in vicious inclinations—and therefore was the last girl in the world to be trusted in London, as she would be totally unable to withstand temptation—

After the departure of the Stanleys Kitty returned to her usual occupations, but Alas! they had lost their power of pleasing. Her bower alone retained its interest in her feelings, and perhaps that

line 1: 'mysterious' deleted; 'dangerous' inserted above line. // line 22: 'Or' inserted above line. // line 23: 'Peterson' deleted; 'Percival' inserted above line.

was oweing to the particular remembrance it brought to her mind of Edwd Stanley.

4. JAMES EDWARD AUSTEN-LEIGH, SECOND CONTINUATION OF 'CATHARINE', POST-1845

The Summer passed away unmarked by any incident worth narrating, or any pleasure to Catharine save one, which arose from the receipt of a letter from her friend Cecilia now Mrs Lascelles, announcing the Speedy return of herself and Husband to England.

A correspondance productive indeed of little pleasure to either party had been established between Camilla and Catharine. The latter had now lost the only Satisfaction she had ever received from the letters of Miss Stanley, as that young Lady having informed her Friend of the departure of her Brother to Lyons now never mentioned his name—Her letters seldom contained any Intelligence except a description of some new Article of Dress, an enumeration of various engagements, a panegyric on Augusta Halifax and perhaps a little abuse of the unfortunate Sir Peter—

The Grove, for so was the Mansion of Mrs. Percival at Chetwynde denominated was situated wthin. five miles from Exeter, but though that Lady possessed a carriage and horses of her own, it was seldom that Catharine could prevail on her to visit that town for the purpose of shopping, on account of the many officers perpetually Quartered there and infested the principal Streets—A company of strolling players in their way from some Neighbouring Races having opened a temporary Theatre there, Mrs. Percival was prevailed on by her Niece to indulge her by attending the performance once during their stay—Mrs. Percival insisted on paying Miss Dudley the compliment of inviting her to join the party, when a new difficulty arose, from the necessity of having Some Gentleman to attend them—

line 1: 'it brought to her mind' inserted above line. // line 6: 'or any' written over 'save one'(?). // line 8: 'the' written over 'her'(?) // line 15: 'the account' deleted; 'a description' inserted above line. // line 16: 'paneguge'(?) in ms. // line 20: 'the town' deleted before 'Exeter'. // line 20: 'of her' is 'her her' in ms. // line 27: 'and an' deleted before 'once'. // line 30: 'of their party' deleted; 'to attend them' inserted above line.

ABBREVIATIONS

All Things Austen	Kirstin Olsen, *All Things Austen: An Encyclopaedia of Austen's World*, 2 vols. (Westport, CT: Greenwood Press, 2005).
Catharine	Margaret Anne Doody and Douglas Murray (eds.), *Catharine and Other Writings* (Oxford: Oxford University Press, 1993).
E	*Emma*
Father's Legacy	John Gregory, *A Father's Legacy to his Daughters*, in *The Young Lady's Pocket Library, or Parental Monitor* (1790) intro. Vivien Jones (Bristol: Thoemmes Press, 1995).
FR	Deirdre Le Faye (ed.), *Jane Austen: A Family Record*, 2nd edn (Cambridge: Cambridge University Press, 2004).
JA	Jane Austen
Johnson	Samuel Johnson, *A Dictionary of the English Language*, 4th edn (1773).
L	*Jane Austen's Letters*, 3rd edn, ed. Deirdre Le Faye (Oxford: Oxford University Press, 1995).
Loiterer	James Austen (ed.), *The Loiterer* (1790), intro. Li-Ping Geng (Ann Arbor, MI: Scholars' Facsimiles & Reprints, 2000).
LS	*Lady Susan*
'Manuscript'	B. C. Southam, 'The Manuscript of Jane Austen's Volume the First', *The Library*, 5th series, 17 (1962), 231–7.

Memoir	James Edward Austen-Leigh, *A Memoir of Jane Austen and Other Family Recollections*, ed. Kathryn Sutherland (Oxford: Oxford University Press, 2002).
MP	*Mansfield Park*
MW	*The Works of Jane Austen, Volume VI, Minor Works*, ed. R. W. Chapman, rev. B. C Southam (London: Oxford University Press, 1975).
NA	*Northanger Abbey*
Names	Maggie Lane, *Jane Austen and Names* (Bristol: Blaise Books, 2002).
OED	*Oxford English Dictionary*
P	*Persuasion*
P&P	*Pride and Prejudice*
S	*Sanditon*
S&S	*Sense and Sensibility*
VS	*Volume the Second*, ed. B. C. Southam (Oxford: Clarendon Press, 1963).
W	*The Watsons*

EXPLANATORY NOTES

VOLUME THE FIRST

FREDERIC AND ELFRIDA

1 **To Miss Lloyd:** Martha Lloyd (1765–1843), with her younger sisters Eliza and Mary, was a friend and neighbour of JA at Steventon. Martha, Mary and their newly widowed mother rented Deane parsonage from JA's father in Spring 1789. In 1828, at the age of 63, Martha would become the second wife of JA's brother Francis; her sister Mary became the second wife of JA's brother James in 1797. The dedication might have been added some years after 'Frederic and Elfrida' was transcribed into 'Volume the First': Southam notes that it is 'remarkable for being in a later hand than that in which the rest of the piece is written' ('Manuscript', p. 232, n. 4). The story itself might date from as early as 1787, when JA (in December) reached the age of twelve.

2 **muslin Cloak:** cloaks made of muslin, a finely woven cotton, were fashionable in the late 1780s and early 1790s. Rebecca, in 'Frederic and Elfrida', is an expert on the material; in adding the word 'muslin' to the manuscript, JA links her to the dedicatee. JA's interest in muslin, the successor to heavier silks previously in fashion, also appears in *NA*, where Henry Tilney displays considerable knowledge of the material (vol. 1, ch. 3), and in several of her letters, such as that to her sister Cassandra of 25 January 1801 (*L*, p. 77).

3 **Freind:** in most of her juvenilia JA uses this spelling, as well 'beleif', 'greif', 'veiw', etc. In the final items in 'Volume the First', however, dated 1793, she occasionally uses the conventional spellings ('Manuscript', p. 236).

4 **a novel:** in *The Progress of Romance* (Colchester: W. Keymer, 1785), Clara Reeve distinguishes the term 'novel' from 'romance': 'The Romance is an heroic fable, which treats of fabulous persons

and things.—The Novel is a picture of real life and manners, and of the times in which it is written' (vol. 1, *Evening* vii). The distinction, however, was not yet a firm one, and despite its subtitle, 'Frederic and Elfrida' combines novel and romance elements.

5 **Elfrida:** the first of many examples in the juvenilia of esoteric, polysyllabic names, mocking the convention in contemporary fiction of avoiding everyday names. In the letter by 'Sophia Sentiment', possibly by JA (see Appendix D), the author of *The Loiterer* is advised that 'your hero and heroine must possess a great deal of feeling, and have very pretty names' (*Loiterer*, 9, p. 7). 'Elfrida' had been in disuse since the Norman Conquest. 'Frederick' (here spelled Frederic), in contrast, was a common name, used by JA for Frederic Gower, the hero of 'Evelyn', and in her novels for Frederick Tilney (*NA*) and Frederick Wentworth (*P*). The mock entry that the young JA made in the Steventon marriage register between herself and 'Henry Frederic Howard Fitzwilliam' (see frontispiece above) suggests that it was then among her favourite names.

6 **the Father's side:** Frederic and Elfrida thus have the same surname, Falknor, as Elfrida signs herself in her letter to Miss Drummond. Had they been cousins on the mother's side, their surnames would have been different. JA might have originally intended this, writing that Frederic's uncle was the 'Mother' of Elfrida before correcting the error to 'Father' (see textual notes). She meant, presumably, to write that 'they were first cousins by the Mother's side'.

7 **one school:** as improbable as the cousins being born on the same day, since children of their rank would have attended single-sex schools.

8 **wonderfull:** the suffix *full*, obsolete by the mid-eighteenth century, appears frequently, as Southam observes, in JA's earliest juvenilia, but not in the later items in 'Volume the First' or, generally, in the other two volumes ('Manuscript', p. 236).

9 **bare politeness:** marriages between first cousins were common in JA's time. In *MP*, Mrs Norris assures Sir Thomas Bertram that 'the only sure way of providing against' a marriage between his sons, Tom or Edmund, and their maternal cousin, Fanny Price, is 'to breed her up with them' (vol. 1, ch. 1).

10 **rules of Propriety . . . any one else:** such restraint on the part of
Frederic and Elfrida goes beyond conventional standards of propriety. Even Arabella, the excessively romantic heroine of Charlotte Lennox's satirical novel *The Female Quixote* (London: A.
Millar, 1752), criticizes a romance heroine 'who was so rigid and
austere, that she thought all Expressions of Love were criminal;
and was so far from granting any Person Permission to love her,
that she thought it a mortal Offence to be adored even in private' (book 2, ch. 9). JA heightens and complicates the comedy
by adding the phrase 'either to the object beloved'; in the original reading, the cousins' determination to conceal their love only
from others is more conventional.

11 **so much alike:** JA's satire of the romance convention that lovers
should resemble each other—here the two are utterly unlike—
recurs in 'A Collection of Letters', in which Lady Scudamore
assures Henrietta that she and her beloved Musgrove are 'born for
each other . . . your opinions and Sentiments so exactly coincide.
Nay, the colour of your Hair is not very different' (Letter the
fifth).

12 **Charlotte:** a popular name, following the marriage of Queen
Charlotte to George III in 1761. In *P&P* it is given to Sir William
Lucas' daughter, perhaps to mark the bestowal of his knighthood
and presentation at Court (vol. 1, ch. 5).

13 **fashionable Bonnet, to suit the Complexion:** in the 1770s, the
woman's cap became a large bonnet, a hat with a small brim, often
tied with a ribbon beneath the chin. The fashionable colour for
bonnets in the 1780s was pale, also the desirable colour for a
woman's complexion. As Lady Williams tells the unfortunately
flushed Alice in 'Jack and Alice', 'when a person has too great
a degree of red in their Complexion, it gives their face in my
opinion, too red a look' (ch. 3).

14 **Crankhumdunberry . . . sweet village:** echoing the first line of
Oliver Goldsmith's poem 'The Deserted Village' (1770): 'Sweet
Auburn, loveliest village of the plain'. 'Crankhumdunberry' is a
mock-Irish name, comparable to the mock-Welsh 'Pammydiddle' in 'Jack and Alice' and the mock-Irish 'Kilhoobery Park' in
'Sir William Mountague'. Part of the humour here is a pun, with
the last part of the proper name, 'berry', playing off against 'sweet'.

There is also a resemblance between the names Crankhumdunberry and Huncamunca, the gluttonous princess in Henry Fielding's burlesque comedy *Tom Thumb* (1730), which the Austen
family staged at Steventon on 22 March 1788.

15 **verdant Lawn . . . variegated flowers:** to enamel is 'to inlay; to
variegate with colours' (Johnson); the landscape here thus resembles an artefact, such as a painted box or vase.

16 **purling Stream . . . Valley of Tempé:** 'purling' (rippling or undu-
lating) streams are a clichéd feature of poetry, as William Wycherley notes in his 'To my Friend, Mr. Pope, on his Pastorals' (1709):

> So purling Streams with even Murmurs creep,
> And hush the heavy Hearers into Sleep.
>
> (lines 13–14)

JA's stream runs a most improbable underground course. Its
source is the valley in Greece between the mountains of Olym-
pus and Ossa, celebrated for its beauty and formerly a shrine to
Apollo. In *The Female Quixote*, Arabella compares the situation
of Bath, placed in a valley, with Tempé, of which her companions
have never heard (book 7, ch. 3).

17 **Damon:** a shepherd singer in Virgil's eighth eclogue, whose name
was adopted by English poets such as Milton and Marvell for rural
lovers.

18 **elegant dressing room . . . artificial flowers:** dressing rooms,
usually attached to bedrooms, were increasingly decorated as sitting rooms in the later eighteenth century, and used primarily by
women spending their mornings indoors. The decorations here
are ornamental carved woodwork in the shape of wreaths or gar-
lands of flowers. JA expresses her own preference for the dressing
room in a letter to Cassandra of 1 December 1798: 'I always feel
so much more elegant in it than in the parlour' (*L*, p. 24).

19 **Jezalinda:** a nonce name, combining the biblical Jezebel with
'Ethelinde', the name of the eponymous heroine of Charlotte
Smith's novel *Ethelinde, or the Recluse of the Lake* (1789). The
name 'Linda' was used only from the later nineteenth century.

20 **Rebecca:** an Old Testament name, popular in the seventeenth
century but unusual in JA's time. The only Rebecca in JA's novels
is the Prices' incompetent upper servant in *MP* (vol. 3, ch. 7).

21 **Lovely and too charming Fair one:** a possible allusion to an apostrophe by Arabella, 'too lovely, and unfortunate Fair-one', in *The Female Quixote* (book 6, ch. 11). In Arabella's case, the object of her concern is an imaginary woman, Philonice, invented by one of her suitors.

22 **greazy tresses and your swelling Back:** Rebecca's hair, as well as being unclean, is soaked in pomatum, an oil-based dressing; she is also apparently hunchbacked. JA's comic treatment of ugliness and physical deformity is a recurring feature of her juvenilia and of her correspondence.

23 **Indian and English Muslins:** muslin fabrics produced in English mills (often in Lancashire) were relatively inexpensive; those imported from India were more costly and generally considered superior. In 1774, the Imported Cottons Act helped protect the British muslin industry by placing taxes on imported materials.

24 **profound Curtesy:** a very low curtsy, as a sign of particular respect.

25 **From this period ... slightest provocation:** a striking example of JA's deflationary technique. The first two-thirds of the sentence, up to 'scruple to', employs the standard rhetoric of sentimental fiction, until 'kick one another out of the window' violently changes the tone. While kicking others out of the window is extraordinary, kicking someone down the stairs was relatively common. Men are kicked downstairs on two occasions in *The Loiterer:* one a creditor (4, p. 15) and one a tradesman (24, p. 10).

26 **ran off with the Coachman:** an outrageous lapse in gentility, even worse than eloping with the butler, as does Miss Dickins, the governess of the youthful Lady Williams in 'Jack and Alice'. In Sterne's *Tristram Shandy* (London: D. Lynch, 1759–67), the fact that Tristram's great-aunt Dinah 'about sixty years ago, was married and got with child by the coachman' is a subject so painfully embarrassing to her nephew Toby that 'the least hint of it was enough to make the blood fly into his face' (vol. 1, ch. 21).

27 **Buckinghamshire:** a county in the south of England, east of Oxfordshire and north of JA's native Hampshire.

28 **Rebecca ... little more than 63:** the disjunction between perception and chronological age is a recurring motif in JA's fiction. Elsewhere she varies the joke, with characters perceiving the relatively youthful as exceedingly aged. In 'The Three Sisters',

Miss Stanhope describes her suitor Mr Watts as 'quite an old Man, about two and thirty'. In *S&S*, Marianne Dashwood regards Colonel Brandon, at thirty-five, as 'an old bachelor' and declares that a woman of twenty-seven 'can never hope to feel or inspire affection again' (vol. 1, ch. 8).

29 **parents of Frederic proposed . . . between them:** it was not unusual for parents to propose a marriage of their child to the parents of a suitable partner, but a vital element is missing here: the consent of the parties themselves. This inverts the common predicament: agreement between the parties without parental consent being granted.

30 **the naming of the Day:** traditionally the woman's prerogative, and the only item in the various pre-marital arrangements entirely within her control.

31 **Patches, Powder, Pomatum and Paint:** echoing a line in Pope's *The Rape of the Lock* (1714): 'Puffs, Powders, Patches, Bibles, Billet-doux' (canto 1, line 138). JA originally wrote 'Rouge, Powder', etc.; in changing 'Rouge' to 'Patches' she created both the quadruple alliteration and the Pope allusion. In contrast to Pope's heroine Belinda, who makes good use of the battery on her dressing-table ('Now awful Beauty puts on all its Arms', line 139), plain Rebecca cannot be beautified by cosmetics. Black patches, made of velvet, were supposed to resemble beauty-spots, and remained fashionable until *c*. 1790. Powder was used for colouring hair; pomatum kept hair plastered in place. White paint was applied to the neck and red paint (rouge) to the cheeks, but the use of both colours declined in the 1780s, suggesting that Rebecca, like her name, is somewhat out of style. By the late eighteenth century there was less need for the thick white paint previously used to cover pits caused by smallpox, thanks to widespread inoculation.

32 **lovely vehicle:** JA's note, 'a post chaise', explains why Charlotte's carriage is 'lovely'; this was the most expensive and luxurious type of hired carriage. A post-chaise, using horses that were changed at posting stations, generally carried only two passengers and travelled rapidly, in contrast to the much cheaper and slower stage-wagon used by Captain Roger and Rebecca. JA very rarely adds notes to her writings; there is one in 'Lesley Castle' (Letter the first) and another in *NA* (vol. 1, ch. 3).

33 **postilion:** the driver, mounted on the 'near' (left) horse of the team drawing the post-chaise. Postilions also served as attendants during a journey. A larger carriage, such as Captain Roger's and Rebecca's stage-wagon, would have a driver mounted on a box at the front of the vehicle.

34 **Condescension:** 'voluntary submission to equality with inferiours' (Johnson): the term was thus used more positively than today.

35 **Portland Place:** a magnificently wide street, originally laid out by the Adam brothers, Robert and James, in 1778, and one of the most fashionable addresses in London. It was named after William Bentinck, the second Duke of Portland.

36 **seated . . . in one chair:** sitting two to a chair also features, more prominently, in JA's comedy 'The Visit' (Act 2, scene 1). Both scenes allude mockingly to an odd passage in Oliver Goldsmith's *The Vicar of Wakefield* (London: F. Newbery, 1766), in which the Vicar receives a visit from five ladies and gentlemen, including his landlord Mr Thornhill. In his account, 'We happened not to have chairs enough for the whole company; but Mr. Thornhill immediately proposed that every gentleman should sit in a lady's lap' (ch. 9).

37 **old pink Coat:** the colour of this foolish suitor's coat denotes his foppish character. In Smollett's *Roderick Random* (London: J. Osborn, 1748), the effete Captain Whiffle wears a coat of 'pink-coloured silk, lined with white' (ch. 34), and in *MP*, the obtuse Mr Rushworth is to wear a 'pink satin cloak' as Count Cassel in the performance of *Lovers' Vows* (vol. 1, ch. 15).

38 **new blue coat:** blue coats were the height of fashion for young men. The dark blue coat worn by the hero of Goethe's best-seller, *The Sorrow of Young Werther* (1774), helped to popularize the style. In 1788, George III made blue the colour of the domestic staff at Windsor Castle, and in 1790 a Russian visitor noted that it was 'the favourite colour of the English . . . of fifty persons whom one meets in the streets of London, at least twenty are dressed in dark blue coats' (Aileen Ribeiro, *The Art of Dress: Fashion in England and France 1750 to 1820* (New Haven: Yale University Press, 1995), p. 49). Blue was also a favourite colour of JA's. In *P&P*, Bingley wears a blue coat (vol. 1, ch. 3), while Lydia Bennet

hopes that 'dear Wickham' will 'be married in his blue coat' (vol. 3, ch. 9).

39 **something in the appearance . . . account for it:** the elaborate mystification satirizes a recurring debate in courtship protocol about whether 'person' or physical attractiveness ought to influence a modest girl in her choice of a husband. In Richardson's *Sir Charles Grandison* (London: C. Hitch, 1753–4), Harriet Byron's love for Sir Charles, although unrequited, is deemed worthy, since 'the *mind*, and not the *person*, is the principal object of [her] love' (vol. 2, letter 9). The topic recurs in 'The Three Sisters', in which Georgiana declares of her suitor Mr Watts: 'He is rather plain to be sure, but then what is Beauty in a Man' (pp. 78–9).

40 **Leveret:** a young, and therefore tender, hare.

41 **brace . . . Pheasants:** two partridges and three pheasants. The list combines scarce, prized game (pheasants and partridges) with common game (hares and pigeons). The numbers of each item mount precipitately: one, two, three, twelve. The total of seventeen birds and a hare makes a very large supper for two young women.

42 **double engagement:** a serious breach of propriety, though not, of course, as shocking an offence as Charlotte's suicidal response suggests. In *Sir Charles Grandison*, the hero must use all his agility not to become engaged to two women at the same time.

43 **deep stream . . . Portland Place:** the narrow town-houses of Portland Place did not possess 'pleasure Grounds', which would require extensive space, or a stream of any kind. Nearby Cavendish Square, however, had sheep grazing behind railings, in an attempt to bring pastoral delights into the city: a fashion condemned in 1771 by the author of *Critical Observations on the Buildings and Improvements of London* (Roy Porter, *London: A Social History* (London: Hamish Hamilton, 1994), p. 114).

44 **sweet lines, as pathetic as beautifull:** JA's comic self-praise here resembles advice to writers in *The Loiterer*, 59, by Henry Austen and the Reverend Benjamin Portal: 'When an author describes a scene which he wishes to be affecting, let him boldly pronounce it so himself' (p. 9).

45 **Reader . . . peruse them:** such addresses to the reader are common in novels of sensibility but rare in JA, either in the juvenilia or

in the novels. The logic resembles that of JA's remark on her readers, paraphrasing Scott's *Marmion*, in a letter to Cassandra of 29 January 1813: 'I do not write for such dull Elves / As have not a great deal of Ingenuity themselves' (*L*, p. 202).

46 **seven days . . . expired, together with the lovely Charlotte:** syllepsis, a form of zeugma in which a verb takes two different and incongruous objects (here 'days' and 'Charlotte'), is a favourite rhetorical device of the young JA. There are some famous examples in Pope's *The Rape of the Lock*, such as 'Or stain her Honour, or her new Brocade' (canto 2, line 107).

47 **smelling Bottle . . . dagger:** a parody of the traditional choice between dagger and bowl. In Joseph Addison's *Rosamond an Opera* (1707), Queen Elinor, wife of Henry II, gives her rival Rosamond the choice of committing suicide by drinking poison from a bowl or of being stabbed. Smelling bottles, small and ornamental, contained smelling-salts, hartshorn, etc., used as a restorative in case of faintness or headaches.

48 **terrible cold:** mocking the feigned reluctance with which singers or musicians, male and female, would typically respond to requests for a performance. The reluctance was designed to elicit further entreaties, as well as to excuse any imperfections.

49 **Corydon:** like Damon (ch. 1), a traditional name for a rustic lover in pastoral poetry, deriving from a shepherd so named in the *Idylls* of Theocritus and the *Eclogues* of Virgil. In her brief comedy 'The Mystery', JA gives the name to a character who speaks no more than the opening line. 'Bess', in contrast, is a thoroughly English, rustic name, a short form of Elizabeth.

50 **fess:** a dialect word from southern and south-western England for lively, gay, smart.

51 **Stage Waggon:** the cheapest, slowest and least comfortable form of public transport, and thus especially inappropriate for newly-weds. Passengers sat on benches in this very large conveyance, drawn by ten or more horses, which would proceed at walking pace.

52 **delicate frame of her mind . . . press her on the subject:** Elfrida's delicacy is presumably wounded by the prospect of sexual intercourse on her wedding night; hence she postpones the wedding indefinitely by refusing to name a day. Numerous heroines in

eighteenth-century fiction, including Richardson's *Pamela* and *Clarissa*, wish to postpone their wedding day as long as possible, but only Elfrida wishes the delay to be indefinite.

53 **Eleanor:** the name given to Eleanor Tilney in *NA* and, with different spelling, to Elinor Dashwood in *S and S*. Like Eleanor here, they are both attractive women with suitors.

54 **spluttered:** in use from the early eighteenth century, but Johnson prefers 'sputtered', terming 'splutter' a 'low word'.

55 **fainting fits . . . fell into another:** an exaggerated propensity to faint was a characteristic of the heroines of later eighteenth-century English novels. In JA's play 'Sir Charles Grandison', Sir Hargrave Pollexfen declares, 'I wish women were not quite so delicate, with all their faints and fits!' (Act 2).

56 **bold as brass . . . soft as cotton:** combining a proverbial simile with one, 'soft as cotton', created by JA.

57 **the dangerous way Elfrida was in:** perhaps alluding to this passage and to other humorous treatments of 'dying for love' in her juvenilia, JA wrote to Fanny Knight, speaking of a disappointed suitor, that 'it is no creed of mine, as you must well be aware, that such sort of Disappointments kill anybody' (18–20 November 1814, *L*, p. 281).

JACK AND ALICE

1 **Francis William Austen . . . Perseverance:** JA's fifth brother Francis (1774–1865), one year her elder, served on the ship *Perseverance* as a midshipman in the East Indies from December 1789 to November 1791, the earliest and latest possible dates for the dedication to this story, which Le Faye suggests was written 'early in 1790' (*FR*, p. 69). Claire Tomalin asserts, without evidence, that JA 'inscribed *Jack and Alice* to Francis more than a year after his departure' and conjectures that 'perhaps she and Francis had started on the story together before he went to sea' (*Jane Austen: A Life* (London: Viking, 1997), p. 61). Francis is also the dedicatee of a much briefer story, 'The Adventures of Mr Harley', in Volume the First. 'Esquire' was used as a courtesy title for gentlemen. Francis Austen was in his mid-teens when the dedication was written, but JA might have felt that his having left home and begun his naval career gave him the right to the title.

In a letter of 16 December 1816, JA congratulates her eighteen-year-old nephew James Edward on leaving Winchester College and addresses him as 'esquire' for the first time (*L*, p. 322). A midshipman is a rank between that of the crew and the lowest commissioned officer. In *MP*, William Price, although 'still only a midshipman', has enjoyed some of the privileges of the officers, being 'often taken on shore by the favour of his Captain' (vol. 2, ch. 6).

2 **Johnson:** perhaps alluding to the Reverend Augustus Johnson, who in 1791 became rector of Hamstall-Ridware, Staffordshire, a living that the Austens hoped to obtain for their own family.

3 **Masquerade:** a masked ball. Masquerades were frequently criticized for their excesses and for undermining the ordered structure of society. Eighteenth-century novelists had repeatedly depicted them in this manner: a recent example was the masquerade scene in Frances Burney's *Cecilia* (1782). Richardson's Sir Charles Grandison declares sententiously that masquerades 'are not creditable places for young ladies to be known to be *insulted* at them. They are diversions that fall not in with the genius of the English commonalty' (vol. 1, letter 27). In JA's comic dramatization of the novel, 'Sir Charles Grandison', Harriet Byron deplores 'these odious masquerades' (Act 3, scene 1). In proposing a masquerade for his children, rather than opposing their desire to attend one, Mr Johnson is a most unconventional father.

4 **tickets:** printed tickets were issued for public masquerades, but would be inappropriate for a small, private ball such as this. The 'ticket' here is probably a calling card, with an invitation written by hand.

5 **Charles Adams:** named after Sir Charles Grandison, to whom Charles Adams is a parodic counterpart.

6 **3 Miss Simpsons:** The first of many such sisterly trios in JA's juvenilia and novels, including Elinor, Marianne and their younger sister Margaret in *S&S*.

7 **neighbourhood of Pammydiddle:** the neighbourhood contains four families, in addition to the Johnsons, prefiguring JA's advice in a letter of 9 September 1814 to her niece Anna, a would-be novelist, that '3 or 4 Families in a Country Village is the very thing to work on' (*L*, p. 275). Pammydiddle, a

Welsh-sounding place name, is a portmanteau word, formed from 'pam', a card game, and 'diddle', to cheat or waste time (*Catharine*, p. 291).

8 **rather tall:** JA jokes about her own height in a letter to Cassandra of 25 January 1801, instructing her sister to buy two lengths of muslin for gowns for herself and her mother, 'but one longer than the other—it is for a tall woman. Seven yards for my mother, seven yards and a half for me' (*L*, p. 77). JA's nephew James Edward Austen-Leigh notes that 'her figure was rather tall and slender' (*Memoir*, p. 70). In general, height was held to be a sign of high rank. Thus when Rushworth, in *MP*, calls Henry Crawford 'an under-sized man' who 'is not five foot nine', he is suggesting that Crawford is of low birth (vol. 1, ch. 10). Much is made too in 'Lesley Castle' of the height of the Lesley sisters, in contrast to their short stepmother.

9 **passionate:** 'easily moved to anger' (Johnson).

10 **amiable:** an ambiguous word, meaning both 'lovely' or 'pleasing' and 'pretending' or 'shewing' love (Johnson). In *E*, Mr Knightley declares of Frank Churchill: 'No, Emma, your amiable young man can be amiable only in French, not in English. He may be very "aimable," have very good manners, and be very agreeable; but he can have no English delicacy towards the feelings of other people: nothing really amiable about him' (vol. 1, ch. 18).

11 **bewitching:** a polite term for Charles's sexual magnetism.

12 **none but Eagles . . . Face:** drawing on the traditional belief that only eagles could look at the sun. Charles's brilliant eyesight exceeds even that of Sir Charles Grandison, with his light-emitting gaze: 'a sun-beam from my brother's eye seemed to play upon his face, and dazle his eyes' (vol. 6, letter 51).

13 **Sukey:** a pet-form for Susan, itself a diminutive of Susannah. The Austens' washerwoman, Elizabeth Bushell, had a daughter (or granddaughter) named Sukey (*L*, p. 17), and, perhaps by association, the name here is given to the least attractive (and most unpleasant) of the Simpson sisters.

14 **Cecilia:** Burney's novel *Cecilia* (1782) brought the name into favour, but it is not used elsewhere in JA's fiction.

15 **Jointure:** 'Estate settled on a wife to be enjoyed after her husband's decease' (Johnson).

16 **Tho' Benevolent ... Entertaining:** although the sentence seems to be a model of Johnsonian symmetry, the three apparent antitheses are all false. 'Candid' is used in the eighteenth-century sense of 'free from malice; not desirous to find faults' (Johnson).

17 **family of Love:** alluding to a phrase used by Richardson, Henry Fielding and Sarah Fielding. The term derives from a pietistical sect, the 'Family of Love', founded by Henry Nicholas in 1540, but by the eighteenth century it was used without religious implications.

18 **addicted to the Bottle and the Dice:** metonymically, drinking and gambling. Excessive gambling created financial distress for many members of the leisured class, and excessive drinking was also common. In her letters, JA jokes about her own fondness for drink, telling Cassandra, on one occasion, 'I am put on the Sofa near the Fire & can drink as much wine as I like' (*L*, p. 251). The consequences of over-indulging in both alcohol and gambling are portrayed in the spectacular fate of Mr Harrel, one of the heroine's three guardians in *Cecilia* (book 5, ch. 12).

19 **Drawing Room:** during the eighteenth century drawing rooms, formerly attached to individual bedrooms, became important spaces, of about the same size as dining rooms. The dining room became established as primarily masculine; the drawing room as feminine.

20 **Sultana ... Masks:** oriental costumes, combining aspects of Turkish and Persian clothing, were very popular at masquerades, allowing their wearers to dress in exotic, flattering costumes, with gaudy displays of jewels. The Turkish dress of the Sultana—the wife or concubine of a Sultan—was a favourite among women. 'Masks' here are masqueraders with masks for disguise, worn on or held in front of the face, although JA also uses masks for the object itself in this story.

21 **Mask representing the Sun ... glorious Luminary:** mythological characters such as Apollo, the sun god and patron of music and poetry, were popular at masquerades. An Apollo also takes part in the masquerade in *Cecilia* (book 2, ch. 3).

22 **3 quarters of a mile ... breadth:** the preposterously outsized room is several times larger than the largest ones in Brobdingnag, in Swift's *Gulliver's Travels* (London: Benj. Motte, 1726), in which

a 'large Room' is said to be 'between three and four hundred Foot wide' (part 2, ch. 2). Johnson Court must thus be built on a far grander scale than any other edifice in England.

23 **concourse:** 'the confluence of many persons or things to one place'; 'the persons assembled' (Johnson).

24 **plain green Coat:** dark green was a fashionable colour for men's coats; in 1780, William Hickey, newly returned from India, was advised by his tailor to buy frock coats in dark green, dark brown and plain blue (Ribeiro, *Art of Dress*, p. 48). Pea-green, however, was out of fashion. In *The Loiterer*, 15, by James Austen, a young man wearing a 'handsome pea-green coat' is ridiculed by a group of style-conscious students (p. 8).

25 **Domino's:** that is, those wearing a domino, 'an all-enveloping gown, Venetian in origin, its serviceable shape ideal for intrigue, love adventures, conspiracy etc.; it was often, but not always, black and worn by both sexes' (Aileen Ribeiro, *The Dress Worn at Masquerades in England, 1730 to 1790* (New York: Garland, 1984), p. 29).

26 **in a horrible Passion:** in keeping with their 'passionate', quick-tempered characters.

27 **Flora:** the Roman goddess of flowers; hence, in poetical language, the personification of nature's power in producing flowers.

28 **in a studied attitude:** in the sort of pose adopted by an artist's model, as though she wished to be the subject of a painting.

29 **Caroline:** 'elegant but ambitious', she resembles her namesake, the snobbish Caroline Bingley in *P&P*. The name had been made fashionable by Queen Caroline (1683–1737), wife of George II, who acceded to the throne in 1727.

30 **3 Dominos:** five of the ten participants in the masquerade are thus dressed as dominos. This is too high a proportion for a well-balanced masquerade: 'when too many dominos appeared at a gathering, and too few of the more meaningful or picturesque dress types, connoisseurs were apt to complain of the dullness of the occasion' (Terry Castle, *Masquerade and Civilization: The Carnivalesque in Eighteenth-Century English Culture and Fiction* (Stanford: Stanford University Press, 1986), p. 59).

31 **Virtue:** abstractions such as Virtue, taken from Cesare Ripa's *Iconologia* (translated into English in 1709) and other printed

sources, were popular masquerade characters, as were Peace, Plenty, Hope, Fortune, Temperance, Liberty, etc.

32 **Envy . . . 3 Gamesters:** negative abstractions such as Envy were seldom adopted as masquerade figures, since they offered limited opportunities for attractive display. Envy here sits literally, rather than figuratively, on the foreheads of the three dominos, presumably causing them considerable discomfort.

33 **Entertainment:** 'treatment at the table' (Johnson); an elegant meal served to guests.

34 **For three months . . . Pammydiddle:** a parodic precursor of the conventional aftermath of a party in JA's novels.

35 **tout ensemble:** French for 'general effect'.

36 **Alice:** an old-fashioned, rustic name in JA's time. In the novels it is used only for a servant, Eleanor Tilney's maid in *NA* (vol. 2, ch. 13).

37 **so much her Junior:** JA's revision here from 'so much her inferior' produces a change in emphasis. Instead of feeling constrained by the convention that a woman should not marry a man of lower rank, Lady Williams feels bound by a different convention, that a woman should not marry a younger man.

38 **polite to all but partial to none:** echoing Pope's depiction of Belinda, the heroine of *The Rape of the Lock*: 'Favours to none, to all she Smiles extends' (canto 2, line 11). Like Charles, Belinda also has dazzling eyes: 'Bright as the Sun, her Eyes the Gazers strike' (line 13).

39 **insensible:** 'void of feeling' and 'void of emotion or affection' (Johnson). JA is playing with both senses of the term.

40 **like the great Sir Charles Grandison . . . at Home:** alluding to Harriet Byron's praise of Sir Charles for refusing to comply 'with fashions established by custom'. Sir Charles 'never, for instance, suffers his servants to deny him, when he is at home. If he is busy, he just finds time to say he is, to unexpected visiters' (book 4, letter 26). Conventionally, servants would use the phrase 'not at home' to mean not available to visitors.

41 **out of spirits:** punning deftly on 'spirits' in the sense of alcohol, as well as good cheer; Alice is 'out of spirits' despite drinking spirits.

42 **second attachment . . . serious consequences:** in *Sir Charles Grandison*, Lady G. deplores the romantic prejudice against

387

second loves: 'For how few of us are there, who have their first Loves? And indeed how few first Loves are fit to be encouraged' (book 7, ch. 43).

43 **Life and Adventures:** JA is mocking the convention of having characters tell their life stories: a recurring device in romances, taken over by eighteenth-century novelists such as Henry Fielding. Near the end of Charlotte Lennox's *The Female Quixote*, Arabella, as she has on several previous occasions, asks a new acquaintance, a countess, 'to favour her with the Recital of her Adventures' (book 8, ch. 7). She is told that her request, 'in the Style of Romance', is inappropriate: 'The Word Adventures carries in it so free and licentious a Sound in the Apprehensions of People at this Period of Time, that it can hardly with Propriety be apply'd to . . . the History of a Woman of Honour.'

44 **Berkshire:** a county to the west of London, south of Oxfordshire, where Windsor Castle is located.

45 **sending me to School . . . at Home:** the merits of home schooling for girls, with a governess, versus education at a school were frequently debated in the eighteenth century. Lady Catherine de Bourgh in *P&P* favours a governess, and is shocked to hear that the five Bennet daughters have been brought up at home without one (vol. 2, ch. 6). The Bertram sisters in *MP*, as well as the heroine of *E*, are also taught by governesses. JA herself, however, went to school for several years, and in general schooling for girls was becoming more common.

46 **Kitty:** a pet-form of Catherine, Lady Williams' first name. The heroine of 'Catharine' in 'Volume the Third' is likewise known as Kitty, as is the youngest of the Bennet daughters in *P&P*.

47 **t'ye:** dialect for 'to you'. Despite her supposed excellence as a governess, Miss Dickins does not speak standard English.

48 **Winter . . . in town:** fashionable people aspired to spend winter in a London townhouse, and summer at their country house. The London 'Season' lasted until 4 June, when the King celebrated his official birthday.

49 **too much colour:** either naturally, or from using too much rouge, or, as is the case with Alice Johnson, from excessive drinking. JA might have introduced the subject of red complexions here in response to number 25 of *The Loiterer*, by a correspondent

unknown to the editor James Austen. Writing in the persona of Omai, the Tahitian visitor to England, the author notes that in London women 'set off their complexions a little by rubbing something red upon their Cheeks', whereas in the country 'the Cheeks were naturally streaked with red, which made them exquisitely beautiful' (p. 7).

50 **red in their Complexion . . . red a look:** the irrefutable circular logic is the result of a deft revision by JA, changing 'too much colour' to 'too red a look'.

51 **"From Words she almost came to Blows":** adapting a line ('From words they almost came to blows') in James Merrick's poem 'The Camelion: A Fable after Monsieur De La Motte', in which a dispute arises over the colour of a chameleon. The poem is reprinted in volume five of Robert Dodsley's *A Collection of Poems* (1758), of which JA owned a copy.

52 **fracas:** 'a disturbance, noisy quarrel, "row", uproar' (*OED*), which gives 1727 as the date of first use.

53 **Claret:** red wine from Bordeaux, normally drunk by gentlemen; Alice's taste for claret is unusual.

54 **Citron Grove:** a grove of citrus trees, fruit trees that flourish in temperate and sub-tropical regions but not found in England. JA here establishes a comic link between Charles Adams and Adam, whose citron grove appears in Milton's *Paradise Lost*, book 5, line 22.

55 **pigstye . . . Horsepond:** two of the least picturesque parts of a country scene. Horseponds, used for watering and washing horses, were also traditionally used to duck offenders. JA places sty and pond in ludicrous juxtaposition with the exotic citron grove.

56 **sensible:** conscious, aware.

57 **what they may do:** Tomalin speculates that the sentence heavily deleted here, concerning the effects of drink on young women (see textual notes), 'sounds so like an older brother's piece of worldly wisdom that it is not surprising Jane crossed it out' (*Jane Austen: A Life*, p. 61).

58 **You seem . . . Life and adventures:** Doody and Murray note that Charlotte Smith's *Emmeline* (London: T. Cadell, 1788) 'seems to be one of JA's fictional sources here' (*Catharine*, p. 294). In Smith's novel, the heroine and her friend Mrs Stafford encounter

a young woman, Adelina, in obvious distress, who reluctantly agrees to explain her predicament. When she finally begins the account, she 'seemed to enter on her story with desperate and painful resolution, as if to get quickly and at once thro' a task which, however necessary, was extremely distressing' (vol. 2, ch. 11). The device of the reluctant young woman telling her life story to sympathetic listeners is also common in earlier novels, such as Sarah Fielding's *The Adventures of David Simple* (1744), in which Isabelle's story occupies five chapters (book 3, ch. 6–book 4, ch. 2).

59 **North Wales . . . capital Taylors:** North Wales was celebrated for the wildness of its mountain scenery and for its rustic peasantry. Tailors of any kind, let alone 'capital' ones, would be hard to find.

60 **breed me up at her own expence:** parents of large families welcomed opportunities such as this for one or more of their children to be adopted, formally or informally, into a wealthier household. Such was the case when Edward Austen, JA's third brother and one of eight children, was adopted by Thomas and Catherine Knight in 1783. Fanny Price in *MP*, the eldest daughter in a family of nine children, is adopted by Sir Thomas and Lady Bertram, and is later joined at Mansfield Park by her younger sister Susan. In *E*, Captain Weston's son Frank is adopted, after the death of his mother, by his uncle and aunt, Mr and Mrs Churchill, who had 'no children of their own, nor any other young creature of equal kindred to care for' (*E*, vol. 1, ch. 2)

61 **Dancing . . . Languages:** the focus on female 'accomplishments' at the expense of solid learning was the subject of much debate. In *The Loiterer*, 27, Henry Austen deplores this type of education, which teaches girls that their sole aim is matrimony (p. 10). John Gregory, however, recommended such 'elegant accomplishments, as dress, dancing, music, and drawing' to his daughters (*Father's Legacy*, pp. 19–20).

62 **receive the rents of the Estate:** for Charles to collect the rents from his Welsh estate in person would be shockingly vulgar, but 'receive' does not necessarily suggest that he does so. Rent collection was the task of an estate owner's steward; in *P&P*, Darcy's father had employed Wickham's father in this capacity.

63 **Mrs Susan:** a lower servant, and thus referred to by her first name. An upper female servant was normally known by her surname, together with the honorific 'Mrs'. Thus in Richardson's *Pamela*, the housekeepers Mrs Jervis and Mrs Jewkes are always so named, but the sixteen-year-old heroine is named either Pamela or Mrs Pamela, never Mrs Andrews.

64 **Place:** employment as a servant.

65 **pumping:** to pump someone is 'to examine artfully by sly interrogatories, so as to draw out any secrets or concealments' (Johnson).

66 **Youth . . . Money:** Charles Adams is still more exacting in his demands than Darcy, who complains of not 'knowing more than half a dozen' ladies who 'are really accomplished' (*P&P*, vol. 1, ch. 8). Elizabeth Bennet, mocking his exaggerated expectations, responds: 'I am no longer surprised at your knowing *only* six accomplished women. I rather wonder now at your knowing *any*.'

67 **wrote him a very kind letter . . . heart:** for a single woman to write a letter to a marriageable man, unless they were engaged, was in itself a breach of propriety. Proposing marriage to him compounded the offence. Lucy's proposal anticipates the behaviour of women in radical novels of the 1790s and early 1800s, who similarly flout conventions in their dealings with potential marriage partners.

68 **I pressed him again on the subject:** attributing the refusal of an offer of marriage to excessive female modesty was a familiar male response to rejection. After Elizabeth rejects Mr Collins's proposal in *P&P*, he tells her that he knows 'it is usual with young ladies to reject the addresses of the man whom they secretly mean to accept, when he first applies for their favour' (vol. 1, ch. 19). Lucy here plays the part of the obtuse male suitor.

69 **steel traps . . . gentlemen's grounds:** steel man-traps were placed on the grounds of private estates to catch trespassers, poachers, etc. In *The Loiterer*, 50, by James Austen, Humphry Discount has bought two steel traps to break the legs of youths 'of the lower ranks' who have been stealing from his garden (pp. 11–12).

70 **to wound the hearts and legs:** another witty use of syllepsis, one of the young JA's favourite rhetorical devices.

71 **After examining the fracture . . . such a one before:** in the tradition of women doing good works among the poor, epitomized by Lady Bountiful in George Farquhar's *The Beaux' Stratagem* (1707). Medical benevolence, however, was becoming rare in the late eighteenth century, with an increasing number of professional surgeons and doctors in practice. Lady Williams, moreover, is an extreme rarity: a female amateur surgeon. She has not yet set a broken leg, but she has apparently performed other operations.

72 **Lucy:** the name is also given to another 'considerable beauty', Lucy Steele, in *S&S* (vol. 1, ch. 21). Lane notes that JA uses it for girls 'struggling at the lowest reaches of gentility' (*Names*, p. 71).

73 **real defects:** JA's revision here (see textual notes) replaces a neutral remark by Lady Williams with one contributing to her characteristic flow of back-handed compliments and insults.

74 **Bath:** the famous spa town in Somerset, where JA herself would live with her family from 1801 to 1804, makes several appearances in her juvenilia, as well as in her novels. It was still at the height of fashion in the 1780s and 1790s. JA's earliest known visit to the spa was in November 1797, when she was almost 22, but as a child she was already well aware of its reputation. In 'Love and Freindship', Isabel warns Laura to 'beware of the unmeaning Luxuries of Bath' (Letter 4th), and in 'The Three Sisters', Mary Stanhope attempts to bargain for spending 'every Winter in Bath' (p. 83) as part of her marriage settlements.

75 **Jaunt:** 'Ramble; flight; excursion. It is commonly used ludicrously, but solemnly by *Milton*' (Johnson).

76 **the Hero of this Novel:** Jack Johnson, who is named only in the title and who lacks even a speaking part.

77 **my self unparalelled:** unlike Sir Charles Grandison, whose praises are repeatedly sung by others, Charles Adams delivers a eulogy on himself. He has a counterpart in *The Loiterer*, 2, by James Austen: a young politician, whose 'consciousness of his own superior abilities, information, and eloquence' compels him to 'bespeak the attention of the House for about five or six hours' (pp. 9–10). Adams prides himself on his appearance and accomplishments, but not on his good works. In *Sir Charles Grandison*, in contrast, the hero's sister Charlotte declares: 'My brother is

valued by those who know him best, not so much for being an handsome man; not so much for his birth and fortune; nor for this or that single worthiness; as for being, in the great and yet comprehensive sense of the word, a *good man*' (book 1, letter 36). In JA's 'Sir Charles Grandison', similarly, Charlotte tells Harriet Byron, 'My brother is a charming Man. I always catch him doing some good action' (Act 3, scene 1).

78 **One freind I have:** Mrs Susan, the cook. Friendship between a male employer and a female servant was, of course, highly irregular; for Susan to be Charles's mistress would be less surprising.

79 **Why do you hesitate . . . every day encreasing:** in *The Loiterer*, 19, James Austen also suggests that a young girl marrying a disagreeable but wealthy husband would be held to have married advantageously: 'Should a beautiful and accomplished girl, in the bloom of eighteen, make over her person for life, to a battered rake of family and fortune, with no good quality on earth to recommend him, and old enough to be her father; her female friends would not hesitate to pronounce her *well-married*' (p. 5). John Gregory, however, warns his daughters not to marry 'from vulgar and mercenary views', telling them 'you may be tired with insipidity and dulness; shocked with indelicacy, or mortified by indifference' (*Father's Legacy*, p. 47).

80 **credit . . . account:** punning on the economic and social connotations of the terms.

81 **the age of seventeen:** a critical age for girls, who were expected to 'come out' and take part in social activities in their late teens. Sukey murders Lucy just as she is establishing herself in society and receiving desirable offers of marriage.

82 **2 last:** originally '2 first'; the revision gives Miss Johnson and the Duke, rather than Lady Williams and Miss Johnson, a 'sincere regard' for Lucy, and thus implies that Lady Williams' affection is insincere.

83 **raised to the Gallows:** hanged: the punishment for murder, as well as many lesser offences. This is another example of JA's use of syllepsis: Sukey is 'raised' to the gallows shortly after her sister Caroline is 'raised' to the rank of a Duchess. In *The Loiterer*, 34, by an unknown contributor, the narrator similarly writes of

mounting four storeys to the lodgings of a hack, Mr Distich, when 'stopping to take a little breath' he 'had time to meditate with a heavy heart on the very elevated situation of my friend' (p. 7).

84 **some Prince . . . cheifly engaged:** alluding to the attachments of the Prince of Wales, later the Prince Regent (1811–20) and then George IV (1820–30), and of his younger brothers. George had secretly wedded Maria Fitzherbert, a widowed Catholic, in 1785. Frederick, Duke of York, was notorious for his many affairs, as were William, Duke of Clarence, and Edward, Duke of Kent. Three more princes—Ernest, Duke of Cumberland, Augustus, Duke of Sussex and Adolphus, Duke of Cambridge—were still in their teens when 'Jack and Alice' was written.

85 **great Mogul:** the European name for the emperor of Delhi. In becoming a Sultana, Cecilia assumes in life her sister Caroline's earlier masquerade role.

EDGAR AND EMMA

1 **a tale:** JA designates several of the shorter items in 'Volume the First' as tales, thus distinguishing them from the longer 'novels'. Johnson defines the tale dismissively as 'a slight or petty account of some trifling or fabulous incident'. 'Edgar and Emma' is also exceptional in having no dedicatee. Le Faye suggests that, with 'Amelia Webster', it is among the 'first of [JA's] efforts thought worthy of preservation' (*FR*, p. 66). Several of JA's revisions here are made in what seems to be a later hand, in darker ink.

2 **Godfrey:** a name associated with the Middle Ages, and rare in the eighteenth century.

3 **Market-town:** market-towns then as now would be full of life on market days, but likely to be moribund for the rest of the week.

4 **three pair of stairs high:** Sir Godfrey and Lady Marlow are living incongruously like merchants, who owned houses around the marketplace and had rooms above their shops. The best rooms in a town house were those on the ground and the first floor; those on the third floor were small, with narrow windows, and were normally used by servants or rented to impecunious lodgers.

5 **Consumption:** a virulent, rapidly progressing lung infection.

6 **Sussex:** a county on the south-east coast. The imaginary town of Evelyn in 'Evelyn' is situated there, as are the imaginary towns of Churchill in *LS* and the coastal town of Sanditon in JA's final novel.

7 **Marlhurst:** the Marlows' Sussex house, its name taken from the first syllable of their surname, with the addition of 'hurst', a wooded hillock.

8 **ninepence among the Ringers:** major events in a community were traditionally commemorated by a peal of the church bells. Since six or more ringers would be needed, the amount distributed is extremely small, about a penny per ringer: the Marlows are as parsimonious with others as with themselves. James Woodforde tipped the ringers in his village every Christmas, giving them 2s. 6d in 1786 (*All Things Austen*, p. 75).

9 **Villa:** a relatively small, newly built country house, normally situated near London. It was either the principal home of owners of moderate wealth, or the secondary home of those with a greater one elsewhere.

10 **the representative:** originally, 'a younger representative', but as such he would not have inherited his 'paternal Estate'.

11 **Mr Willmot . . . Lottery:** Despite coming from a 'very ancient Family', Mr Willmot is clearly nouveau riche. The sources and signs of his wealth are distinctly non-genteel: shares in a lead mine, which could provide substantial profits for its shareholders, and a ticket in the national lottery. The lottery, which was used throughout the eighteenth century to fund public works, was highly popular, and tickets could produce large dividends. Since tickets were expensive, they were often shared by a large number of purchasers: that Mr Willmot has sole possession of a ticket is a sign of his prosperity. The ticket, however, would of course be worthless unless it happened to bear one of the winning numbers.

12 **Children . . . particularly described:** in addition to the nine children visiting Marlhurst, we later hear of eleven more living away from home, as well as 'all the rest': the total is thus well over twenty. In *The Loiterer*, 29, James Austen wittily argues against marriages of affection, since they produce large families and a 'consequent increase of Population in a Country which cannot already support half its inhabitants' (p. 7).

13 **their Coach:** the coach somehow seats nine children and two adults, an impossibly large number for a private carriage. A group of this size would have travelled in at least two large carriages.

14 **Emma:** one of JA's favourite girls' names, used again in 'Volume the First' for the heroine of 'The Adventures of Mr Harley', as well as for Emma Watson, heroine of *W*, and Emma Woodhouse, heroine of *E*. The name was given to the heroines of many later eighteenth-century novels, perhaps in part because of the continuing popularity of Matthew Prior's poem 'Henry and Emma' (1709).

15 **Edgar:** an unusual name in the eighteenth century, not used elsewhere in JA's fiction.

16 **tremble:** originally 'fear'; the revision maintains Emma in a state of acute sensibility at this point in the chapter.

17 **Rodolphus:** this outlandish name stands out among the other conventional ones.

18 **sunk breathless on a Sopha:** the sofa, defined by Johnson as 'a splendid seat covered with carpets', became popular in the mid-eighteenth century. More comfortable and less formal than a settee, and supposedly of eastern origin, it made a suitable receptacle for fainting heroines. 'The Sofa', book one of William Cowper's *The Task*, was published in 1785, shortly before JA wrote 'Edgar and Emma'. The poem, a favourite of JA's, draws attention to the reclining position for ladies that the sofa permitted: the 'relaxation of the languid frame / By soft recumbency of outstretched limbs' (lines 81–2). In *MP*, Lady Bertram is 'a woman who spent her days in sitting nicely dressed on a sofa, doing some long piece of needle work, of little use and no beauty' (vol. 1, ch. 2).

19 **confidante:** with a pun on 'confidante', a style of sofa with angle seats at each end that was popular in the late eighteenth century. Thomas the footman is of the wrong gender and rank to be an appropriate confidant for Emma. John Gregory warns his daughters to 'beware of making confidants of your servants' which would 'spoil them, and debase yourselves' (*Father's Legacy*, p. 29).

20 **Parlour . . . social Manner:** the parlour, as well as the circular seating arrangement, is apparently of the old-fashioned, formal kind. Around 1780, as Mark Girouard notes, 'society was beginning to

revolt against the formal circle as the habitual form of social inter-course' (*Life in the English Country House: A Social and Architectural History* (New Haven: Yale University Press, 1978), p. 238). The term 'parlour' was itself becoming dated and gradually giving way to 'drawing room' in genteel society.

21 **Amy:** an unusual name in the eighteenth century, not used in JA's novels.

22 **Eton:** Eton College near Windsor, then as now the pre-eminent English public school. In *MP*, the wealthy Sir Thomas Bertram sends his sons Tom and Edmund there.

23 **Winchester:** Winchester College in Winchester, the cathedral town where JA died and is buried. The College is another major public school.

24 **Queens Square:** Queen Square, Bloomsbury, a fashionable part of London. Since the mid-eighteenth century, it had been home to a girls' school, known as the 'ladies' Eton', at which Kitty was presumably a pupil. Attended by Elizabeth Bridges, who became the wife of JA's brother Edward, and her sisters, it was 'run by the Misses Stevenson exclusively for the daughters of the nobility and the gentry' (*FR*, p. 70).

25 **Sam ... Patty:** Mrs Willmot refers to most of her children by pet-names: Sam for Samuel, Jem for James, Will for William, Kitty for Catherine, Ned for Edward, Hetty for Hester or Henrietta and Patty for Martha.

26 **convent at Brussells:** the Willmots are apparently a Catholic family, who have sent two of their daughters to a Belgian convent school. There were no convent schools in England.

27 **college:** probably a public school, such as Eton or Winchester College, rather than a college of Oxford or Cambridge, since Edgar does not seem to be of university age.

28 **at Nurse:** with a wet nurse, as an infant. Babies in even moderately wealthy families were routinely sent out to nurse, as were the Austen children.

29 **in tears the remainder of her Life:** a spectacular example of the follies of excessive sensibility. Marianne's grief over her betrayal by Willoughby in *S&S* is restrained in comparison to Emma Marlow's lifelong distress over the absence at college of Edgar Willmot.

HENRY AND ELIZA

1 **Henry and Eliza:** The title alludes to JA's fourth brother Henry (1771–1850) and her cousin Eliza de Feuillide, née Hancock (1761–1813), who had married a French soldier, Jean François Capot de Feuillide, in 1781, at the age of nineteen. As early as August 1788, five years before her husband was guillotined in Paris in 1794, Eliza was expressing an interest in Henry, then a seventeen-year-old student at Oxford. In a letter to her cousin Philadelphia, she wrote: 'I do not think You would know Henry with his Hair powdered & dressed in a very ton-ish style, besides he is at present taller than his Father' (Deirdre Le Faye, *Jane Austen's 'Outlandish Cousin': The Life and Letters of Eliza de Feuillide* (London: British Library, 2002), p. 89). In February 1789, Eliza noted that Henry had performed the leading role in an Austen family production of Isaac Bickerstaff's *The Sultan* (1775) during the Christmas holiday and was now 'taller than ever' (p. 96). Le Faye suggests that JA wrote 'Henry and Eliza' 'during this Christmas period', in late December 1788 or early January 1789 (*FR*, p. 67). Henry Austen and Eliza de Feuillide would eventually marry, in December 1797.

2 **Miss Cooper:** JA's cousin Jane Cooper (1771–98), who played the part of the lively heroine, Roxalana, in the Austen family production of *The Sultan* and also read the feminist epilogue by James, declaring that 'one good clever woman is fairly worth ten' men (David Selwyn (ed.), *The Complete Poems of James Austen* (Chawton: Jane Austen Society, 2003), p. 27). In December 1792, both JA and Cassandra Austen signed the Steventon marriage register as witnesses to Jane Cooper's wedding to Captain Williams (*FR*, p. 77).

3 **smiles of approbation:** in *S*, Mr Heywood also supervises his haymakers, but presumably rewards them with food and drink, rather than mere smiles. Doody and Murray note that in Shropshire in 1794, 'harvesters were daily given from 5 to 8 quarts of strong and small beer' (*Catharine*, p. 298). Haymakers were in high demand in harvest season and received relatively good salaries, as well as board and lodging (*All Things Austen*, p. 3).

4 **Haycock:** a conical heap of hay. 'Foliage', normally referring to leaves, is an odd term to apply to hay.

5 **stealing a banknote . . . inhuman Benefactors:** Eliza's adoptive parents have in fact been lenient; stealing a considerable sum of money, such as fifty pounds, was still a capital offence.

6 **M.:** supposedly an abbreviation for an actual market town. JA is playing with the convention in eighteenth-century fiction of disguising place names by their initials, as if to protect the identity of individuals living there. The names of characters, such as the 'Dutchess of F.' here, are also often disguised with initials or dashes, for the same purpose of mystification.

7 **the red Lion:** a common name for taverns and inns.

8 **Humble Companion:** normally a position for a destitute gentle-woman, employed to entertain another woman, such as a wealthy relative, in better circumstances.

9 **Willson:** changed from 'Jones', perhaps because there is a Mrs Jones in 'Jack and Alice'.

10 **Sarah:** never a genteel name in JA's fiction. There are servants named Sarah in *P&P* (vol. 3, ch. 13) and in *P* (vol. 2, ch. 1).

11 **reached the same Evening:** a duchess would not, of course, befriend an innkeeper, or travel to an inn to meet a potential employee.

12 **her Enmities, unconquerable:** the same characteristic that Elizabeth Bennet will condemn in Darcy, declaring '*That* is a failing indeed! . . . Implacable resentment *is* a shade in a character' (*P&P*, vol. 1, ch. 11).

13 **seat in Surry:** the duchess's estate in Surrey, the county south-west of London in which *W* and *E* are also set.

14 **a private union:** with a common licence from a bishop for a marriage in a church within his diocese, rather than after the publication of banns on three successive Sundays, as was otherwise required. Still more expensive was a licence to be married at a private house, which could be granted only by the Archbishop of Canterbury. Since the licences were costly, this form of marriage was considered prestigious, as Mrs Bennet's exclamations in *P&P* reveal (vol. 3, ch. 17).

15 **dutchess's chaplain:** a chaplain could not authorize a private marriage without a licence from a bishop. Since no such arrangement has been made here, the marriage is invalid.

16 **assembly:** a ball at the local Assembly rooms. Eliza, as a mere humble companion, has not been invited to attend.

17 **300 armed Men . . . few years Confinement:** with her private army and totalitarian powers, the duchess resembles a medieval monarch, rather than an eighteenth-century aristocrat.

18 **the Continent:** the mainland of Europe, but here signifying France, rather than the Continent in general.

19 **12,000 £ a year:** an enormous expenditure. The wealthiest character in JA's novels, Rushworth in *MP*, has an annual income of £12,000; next in line is Darcy in *P&P*, with £10,000. In revising the passage, JA increased Henry and Eliza's annual expenditure from £10,000 to £12,000.

20 **rather less than the twentieth part:** Henry Cecil's estate seems to be producing less than £600 per year. Henry and Eliza (like Eliza de Feuillide's improvident husband) have thus amassed huge debts, euphemistically termed a 'derangement in their affairs'.

21 **man of War of 55 Guns:** a fourth-rate warship, one carrying between fifty and sixty guns. A fourth-rate ship, which carried a complement of over 295 officers and crew, was an enormous size for a private vessel, and larger than Francis Austen's ship, the frigate *Perseverance*, which had thirty-six guns and a complement of 164 (Brian Southam, *Jane Austen and the Navy*, 2nd edn (Greenwich: National Maritime Museum, 2005), p. 28). The odd number of guns on JA's man of war is comically impossible: warships would carry an even number.

22 **stepped on Shore at Dover:** seventy miles south-east of London, Dover was the closest English port to the Continent and the most popular route to France.

23 **snug little Newgate:** a private dungeon, named after the famous London prison. The duchess's dungeon resembles the Gothic cell in which Catherine Morland supposes that General Tilney must have imprisoned his wife (*NA*, vol. 2, ch. 8).

24 **threw her Children after them:** several eighteenth-century novels, including Sarah Fielding's *Ophelia* (1760), have incarcerated heroines escaping by ladders from their imprisonment. JA might

also be echoing a scene in Susanna Centlivre's comedy *The Wonder—A Woman Keeps a Secret!* (1714), performed by the Austen family on 26 and 28 December 1787, with Eliza de Feuillide playing Violante, the leading female role. In the play, as Jon Spence notes, Violante's friend Isabella, 'jumps out a window and is caught in the arms of a man who happens to be passing—and who, of course, later marries her' (*Becoming Jane Austen: A Life* (London: Hambledon, 2003), p. 46).

25 **gold Watch for herself:** a gold watch was an expensive, luxury item: exchanging a costly wardrobe for an equally costly fashion accessory is hardly a 'fatal necessity'.

26 **walked 30 without stopping:** for an unaccompanied lady to walk any distance was considered improper. In *P&P*, Elizabeth Bennet defies convention by walking three miles to visit her ailing sister Jane, a feat condemned by Caroline Bingley as 'an abominable sort of conceited independence, a most country town indifference to decorum' (vol. 1, ch. 8). For Eliza to walk thirty miles is still worse.

27 **cold collation:** defined by Johnson as a 'treat less than a feast'; this assortment of cold meat, salads, etc., would not be sufficient for the Harcourts to 'regale themselves'.

28 **Junketings:** feasts, continuing the joke about feasting on inappropriate dishes. As elsewhere in the juvenilia, JA underlined the word to acknowledge its colloquial nature.

29 **receive some Charitable Gratuity:** an elegant euphemism; Eliza intends to beg from customers at the inn.

30 **give the Postilion . . . beauty of the prospect:** doubly ludicrous, since an inn-yard would offer little in the way of a picturesque prospect, and the postilion, mounted on one of the carriage horses, would be given no opportunity for such leisure activities.

31 **our real Child:** parodying the ending of many eighteenth-century novels, including Henry Fielding's *Joseph Andrews* and *Tom Jones* and Burney's *Evelina*, in which a foundling or orphan is found to be of noble birth. JA parodies the convention at greater length in Letter the 11th of 'Love and Freindship'.

32 **Polly:** a pet-name for Mary Anne, the first time that Lady Harcourt is named.

33 **raised an Army:** presumably one larger and more powerful than the '300 armed Men' employed by the duchess.

THE ADVENTURES OF MR HARLEY

1 **Francis William Austen ... Perseverance:** the dedication, resembling that to 'Jack and Alice', can also be dated between December 1789 and November 1791, when Francis served as a midshipman on the *Perseverance*. Le Faye suggests that both 'Jack and Alice' and 'Mr Harley' were written in early 1790 (*FR*, p. 69).

2 **Mr Harley:** the name of the hero of Henry Mackenzie's *The Man of Feeling* (1771), one of the sentimental novels parodied by JA in her juvenilia.

3 **Church ... Sea:** two of the acceptable professions for younger sons, who had to work for a living, the others being the army and the law. As a naval chaplain, Mr Harley combines the two Austen family professions: the Navy and the Church. Southam wonders whether his position 'catches some hint of a debate that arose at Steventon in the 1780s, when the boy's [Francis Austen's] career was under discussion' (*Jane Austen and the Navy*, p. 49). Naval chaplains were warrant officers, ranking lower than commissioned officers, and the position was not sought after (*All Things Austen*, p. 477).

4 **half a year:** an improbably brief period of naval service. Francis served for almost three years on the *Perseverance*, one as a cadet and two as a midshipman.

5 **sat-off:** JA uses both 'sat' and 'sate' as variants of 'set'.

6 **Stage Coach:** smaller, more rapid, and somewhat more genteel than the 'Stage Waggon' used by Captain Roger and Rebecca in 'Frederic and Elfrida' (ch. 5). It would normally be drawn by four horses and held up to six passengers: the number, including Mr Harley, listed here.

7 **Hogsworth Green:** presumably the country seat of Emma's father, rather than Emma, who at seventeen could possess no property of her own. The name is a farmyard joke, comparable to the reference to 'her Ladyship's pigstye' in 'Jack and Alice' (ch. 4).

8 **fine dark Eyes:** dark eyes are often associated with good looks in JA's novels. The beautiful Marianne Dashwood, for example,

has 'very dark' eyes (*S&S*, vol. 1, ch. 10), while Henry Tilney has 'dark eyes, and rather dark hair' (*NA*, vol. 1, ch. 6).

SIR WILLIAM MOUNTAGUE

1 **unfinished performance:** the term 'performance' is applied to no other item in the juvenilia. JA is possibly playing on Johnson's first definition of the word as the 'completion of something designed; execution of something promised'. Johnson's second definition, 'composition; work', fits more comfortably. The story might have been written in late 1788. Monday 1 September, one of the dates mentioned in the story, occurred in 1788 (*FR*, p. 66).

2 **Charles John Austen Esqre:** JA's brother (1779–1852), the youngest of the eight siblings and the only one younger than her, was about nine when this story was written. He would leave home in July 1791 to attend the Royal Naval Academy in Portsmouth. 'Esqre', an abbreviation of 'esquire', is a courtesy title properly applied to gentlemen, not to a young child.

3 **Sir Frederic Mountague:** the opening paragraph resembles an entry from a Baronetage, such as the *New Baronetage of England* (1769). *Persuasion*, similarly, begins with a mock-entry on the Elliots of Kellynch Hall, probably modelled on one from Debrett's *Baronetage of England* (1808).

4 **Park well stocked with Deer:** deer-parks were an important feature of most large country houses. The deer were kept both to be hunted for sport and to contribute to the elegance of the landscape.

5 **fell in Love with the 3 Miss Cliftons:** foreshadowing 'The Three Sisters', in which Mr Watts tells Mary Stanhope, to whom he has already proposed: 'as I am by no means guided by a particular preference to you above your Sisters it is equally the Same to me which I marry of the three' (p. 82). In *W*, similarly, the three Watson sisters receive equal attention from Tom Musgrave.

6 **Kilhoobery Park:** like 'Crankhumdunberry' in 'Frederic and Elfrida', a mock-Irish name, although the story is set in England.

7 **Dover:** the channel port that also plays a part in 'Henry and Eliza'.

8 **Monday . . . first of September:** 1 September marked the traditional opening of the partridge-shooting season. In *P&P*, Lydia is sure that her new husband Wickham 'would kill more birds on the first of September, than any body else in the country' (vol. 3, ch. 9).

9 **Shot:** that is, an expert in shooting: an early instance of this sense of the word. *OED* gives 1780 as the earliest use. In *The Loiterer*, 21, James Austen refers in the same way to a 'good Shot' (p. 9).

10 **even for such a Cause:** Sir William is so dedicated a sportsman that he sacrifices his impending marriage for a day of shooting. JA's target is the landed gentry and their obsession with shooting and hunting: a recurring topic in both her novels and letters.

11 **Brudenell . . . Stanhope:** both names recur in 'The Three Sisters', in which 'Stanhope' is the surname of the heroines and 'Brudenell' the name of a young man described by Georgiana Stanhope as 'the handsomest man I ever saw in my Life'.

12 **14s:** fourteen shillings, or £0.7; a ludicrously small amount to request as compensation for a murder.

13 **privately married:** the marriage would be legal only if Sir William had reached the age of 21 (he is 17 at the beginning of the story) and obtained a licence for a private marriage in London, which he could hardly have done in the brief time available.

14 **Chariot:** a light, closed, four-wheeled carriage, seating from one to three passengers.

15 **Brook Street:** a fashionable London street, running from Hanover Square to Grosvenor Square.

16 **free access:** the term associates Miss Wentworth with the deer in Sir William's park, to which, as the owner, he also had 'free access' for the purpose of hunting. The right to hunt was limited to landowners with a freehold worth at least £1,000 a year, a qualification that Sir William would easily meet. Miss Wentworth is depicted as his natural prey.

MEMOIRS OF MR CLIFFORD

1 **Charles John Austen Esqre . . . generous patronage:** this story, like 'Sir William Mountague', might have been written in late 1788, when JA's youngest brother was nine. 'Patronage' here suggests financial support, and perhaps alludes jokingly to Johnson's

famous definition of a patron: 'a wretch who supports with insolence, and is paid with flattery'.

2 **yr noble Family:** the Austen family was genteel but not, of course,
ennobled.

3 **that great Metropolis:** the population of London in 1801, when
the first census was taken, was just under a million, over eleven
times that of Liverpool, the second largest English city. It was
the world's largest city (with the possible exception of Tokyo) and
dominated English cultural, economic and political life.

4 **Coach and Four:** a large, closed carriage, drawn by four horses,
seating as many as six passengers.

5 **Chaise:** smaller and lighter than a coach, seating from one to
three passengers. The driver of a chaise was mounted on the near
horse, unlike the chariot, in which the driver was mounted on a
coach-box.

6 **Landeau:** that is, landau, a coach for four passengers, with a
folding top that could be opened in good weather; principally for
use in the country. With hoods at both the front and back, it
could be fully opened, half opened or used as a closed carriage. It
took its name from the German town in which it was invented
in 1757.

7 **Landeaulet:** that is, landaulet, a half landau, for two or three
rather than four passengers, with only one hood.

8 **Phaeton:** a light, four-wheeled chaise driven by the owner, seating two passengers. Phaetons were expensive carriages, built for
speed, and thus favoured by the wealthy for pleasure outings.
George Stubbs painted them in several paintings of the late 1780s
and early 1790s, such as 'Gentleman Driving a Lady in a Phaeton'
(1787) at the National Gallery, London.

9 **Gig:** a light, one-horse chaise, fashionable in the 1790s. As R. W.
Chapman notes, 'Admiral Croft, and almost all the young men,
from Darcy to Mr. Collins, drive gigs or curricles' ('On Carriages
and Travel', in Chapman (ed.), *Mansfield Park* (London: Oxford
University Press, 1973), p. 563).

10 **Whisky:** a very light, inexpensive one-horse chaise, named for
its speed in 'whisking' by larger carriages.

11 **italian Chair:** a light, one-horse carriage without a top, and thus
used only for short, pleasure excursions.

12 **Buggy:** a small carriage drawn by one horse, carrying a single passenger.

13 **Curricle:** a two-wheeled carriage, drawn by two horses abreast, and thus larger than a gig. The egregious John Thorpe, boasting of his gig to Catherine Morland, declares that it is 'Curricle-hung you see' (*NA*, vol. 1, ch. 7): that is, supposedly as good as the more expensive curricle.

14 **wheelbarrow:** any light, inexpensive one-horse carriage, although the modern sense of the term was already current and contributes to the humour of the passage.

15 **stud:** 'a collection of breeding horses and mares' (Johnson).

16 **Bays:** chestnut-coloured horses, with black manes and tails.

17 **poney:** pony, a small, inexpensive horse which could be used for drawing a small carriage or for carrying lightweight riders. At the age of seven, JA's brother Francis bought a pony 'for a guinea and a half; and after riding him with great success for two seasons, sold him for a guinea more' (*Memoir*, p. 36).

18 **Devizes:** a market town in Wiltshire, about twenty-two miles east of Bath and a popular stop on the coach road between Bath and London. Mr Clifford's coach and four, an especially rapid form of transport, could comfortably travel the 110 miles from Bath to London in two days. Instead, he takes eighteen hours to travel only twenty-two miles: at this rate, it would take him five days to get to London.

19 **Overton:** a town in Hampshire, three miles from Steventon, where JA's brother James became curate in April 1790. It is about fifty miles from Devizes, so Mr Clifford's progress has slowed to seventeen miles a day.

20 **celebrated Physician:** Robert Brookman, listed as Overton's apothecary in the *Universal British Directory* (1791). He was not, of course, 'celebrated' beyond Overton, and he was not a physician; JA inflates his title as well as his fame.

21 **Dean Gate:** the entry to Deane, three miles east of Overton. The Deane Gate Inn, just outside the village, still survives.

22 **Basingstoke:** five and a half miles east of Deane. Mr Clifford takes four days to make this short journey, averaging just over a mile per day.

23 **Clarkengreen:** Clarken Green, a village only half a mile east of Deane, so Mr Clifford's progress has slowed to a crawl.

24 **Worting:** a village two and a half miles east of Clarken Green.

25 **Mr Robins's:** Thomas Robins, landlord of the Crown Inn and Post House at Basingstoke.

THE BEAUTIFULL CASSANDRA

1 **Miss Austen:** Cassandra Elizabeth Austen (1773–1845), JA's elder sister, and as such known as 'Miss Austen'; Jane, the younger daughter, was styled 'Miss Jane Austen'. Le Faye suggests that an Austen family 'trip to Kent in July and August 1788, with its return via London, probably inspired the London setting of "The Beautifull Cassandra", as well as teasing Cassandra with a description of how she had *not* behaved whilst there' (*FR*, p. 66).

2 **Phoenix:** the bird that is supposed to rise with renewed youth from its own ashes; figuratively, 'a person (or thing) of unique excellence or of matchless beauty; a paragon' (*OED*).

3 **Cassandra:** JA does not use her sister's name elsewhere in her fiction, reserving it for the most indomitable of her heroines.

4 **Millener in Bond Street:** milliners sold caps and hats, made trimmings and accessories for dresses, and acted as arbiters of fashion. Their shops were located in fashionable parts of London, such as Bond Street (where Willoughby has rooms in *S&S*, vol. 2, ch. 7, and where Harriet's picture is framed in *E*, vol. 1, ch. 7).

5 **attained her 16th year:** also the age of Lydia Bennet, another character much taken with bonnets (*P&P*, vol. 2, ch. 16).

6 **fall in love with an elegant Bonnet:** JA's delight in bonnets is evident in her correspondence, which contains numerous detailed comments on women's headdresses. Styles for bonnets changed constantly; the one ordered here by the Countess of —— would be in the most recent fashion.

7 **Elegance and Beauty.** The Viscount is a Bond Street lounger: a gentleman at the height of fashion, with a distinctive manner of speech, walk and dress. In George Colman the Younger's comedy *The Heir at Law* (London: Longman, 1797), Dick Dowlass tells his father, Lord Duberly: 'A young fellow is nothing now

without the Bond-street roll, a tooth-pick between his teeth, and his knuckles crammed into his coat-pockets' (Act 3, scene 2).

8 **Pastry-cooks . . . six ices:** ice-cream and water ices, sold by pastry-cooks, as in *NA*, where several characters on an excursion to Clifton 'eat ice at a pastry-cook's' in the afternoon, before dining (vol. 1, ch. 15). Cassandra Austen seems to have alluded to the ices of this story in a letter (not extant) to her sister of September 1804. In her reply of 14 September, JA feigns horror at the report that no ice can be had in Weymouth, declaring that it 'is altogether a shocking place I perceive, without recommendation of any kind' (*L*, p. 92). In a later letter, written during a visit to her wealthy brother Edward, JA wrote to Cassandra about an elaborate dinner she would soon enjoy: 'I shall eat Ice & drink French wine, & be above Vulgar Economy' (*L*, p. 139). The expense involved in producing ices and keeping them cool, using ice stored throughout the year in ice-houses, made them a luxury item.

9 **Hackney Coach:** a coach available for hire, regulated by a central licensing office. A hackney-coach with two horses charged a shilling for one and a half miles.

10 **Hampstead:** an attractive, fashionable village, some four miles north of Bond Street, with fine views over London. Cassandra, far from admiring the prospect and taking the air, remains in her hired carriage. Austen's aunt Philadelphia Hancock would be buried there in March 1792, but had had no previous connection with Hampstead; see Le Faye, 'Jane Austen and her Hancock Relatives', *Review of English Studies*, new series, 30 (1979), 14.

11 **demanded his Pay:** about five shillings for the eight-mile round-trip to Hampstead.

12 **She placed her bonnet on his head:** not only in defiance of the coachman but also as a form of payment; the bonnet would have cost considerably more than the coach-fare. JA might be alluding here to Burney's heroine in *Cecilia*, who is driven to distraction when detained by a coachman and unable to pay the fare (book 10, ch. 7). Cassandra, in contrast, is perfectly unruffled.

13 **Bloomsbury Square:** the first of the great London squares, laid out in the early 1660s for Thomas Wriothesley, fourth Earl of Southampton.

14 **trembled, blushed, turned pale:** a display of the symptoms associated with extreme sensibility. Maria's surprise is mysterious,
but might stem partly from Cassandra's being outdoors without
a bonnet: women always covered their heads in public.

15 **her less window:** less large than the widow's head. The small-
ness of the window is a sign of the widow's indigence: she is in
an inexpensive upper-storey room, which would have narrower,
lower windows than one on a lower storey.

AMELIA WEBSTER

1 **Mrs Austen:** JA's mother, Cassandra Leigh Austen (1739–1827).
Le Faye suggests that 'Amelia Webster', which has no internal
indication of dating, is, with 'Edgar and Emma', one of JA's two
earliest surviving stories, written in 1787 (*FR*, p. 66).

2 **Letter the first:** this is the first of several examples in the juvenilia
of epistolary fiction, a form also used in *LS* but not in the published novels. The earliest version of *S&S*, 'Elinor and Marianne',
was written in epistolary form.

3 **Amelia:** perhaps named in honour of Princess Amelia (1783–
1810), the youngest of the six daughters of George III and Queen
Charlotte. Like the heroine of 'Amelia Webster', she was celebrated for her beauty. JA does not use the name in her novels.
Matilda's addressing Amelia by her first name is a sign of close
friendship between the two young women.

4 **Matilda:** a newly popular name in the late eighteenth century,
used on several occasions in JA's juvenilia but only once in her
novels, for the imaginary heroine of Henry Tilney's Gothic tale
in *NA* (vol. 2, ch. 5).

5 **Beverley:** men of equal rank habitually addressed each other, as
here, by their surnames alone.

6 **Maud:** an alternative form of 'Matilda'.

7 **two thousand Pounds:** a dowry yielding, at the usual 5% rate of
interest, £100 per annum. Since the amount is modest, Matilda's
brother George feels compelled to promote her charms, but the
phrase 'as much more as you can get' suggests that her intended
suitor Beverley will also bring little to the marriage.

8 **I have a thousand things to tell you:** In *NA*, similarly, Isabella
Thorpe assures Catherine, 'I have an hundred things to say to

you', but produces only the most vacuous comments (vol. 1, ch. 6).

9 **my paper will only permit me to add:** a trite excuse for ending a letter, which in this case contains only three lines.

10 **Miss S. Hervey:** the initial here distinguishes the younger from the elder sister, Matilda, who would be styled simply 'Miss Hervey'.

11 **Sally:** a pet-form of 'Sarah'. In *NA*, Catherine Morland's sister wishes to be known as Sarah, not Sally, 'for what young lady of common gentility will reach the age of sixteen without altering her name as far as she can?' (vol. 1, ch. 2). Sarah, however, is itself a servant's name in JA's fiction.

12 **old hollow oak:** drawing on a familiar convention in epistolary fiction of depositing letters in secret hiding-places. In Richardson's *Clarissa* (1747–8), Lovelace and Clarissa exchange letters illicitly by concealing them in a woodhouse, before he succeeds in persuading her to flee with him from Harlowe Place.

13 **private Correspondence:** her suitor's addressing Sally by her first name and maintaining a secret correspondence with her suggest that the couple are engaged to be married. In *S&S*, Elinor realizes that Marianne 'must then be writing to Willoughby, and the conclusion which as instantly followed was, that . . . they must be engaged (vol. 2, ch. 4).

14 **my Paper reminds me of concluding:** another formulaic closing, like 'my paper will only permit me to add': Amelia clearly has little to say to her supposedly intimate friend. Lucy Steele, similarly, ends her vacuous letter to Elinor Dashwood with 'My paper reminds me to conclude' (*S&S*, vol. 3, ch. 2).

15 **telescope:** advances in the design of telescopes in the late eighteenth century brought them into popular use for admiring landscapes, observing ships, etc. JA's device of having a character fall in love with a woman he spies through a telescope predates a similar scene in Maria Edgeworth's *Belinda* (London: J. Thomson, 1801). Here Lady Delacour is struck by Captain Sunderland's using a spyglass to admire the beauty of Virginia: 'For ought I know, he is the first knight or squire upon record, who ever fell in love with his mistress through a telescope' (ch. 31).

16 **Jack . . . Tom:** the two new correspondents, one of whom, Jack, writes nothing, are given the least distinctive of names: Tom, as in the phrase 'every Tom, Dick and Harry'; and Jack, a pet-name for John and the name given to the mute hero of 'Jack and Alice'.

THE VISIT

1 **the Revd James Austen:** JA's eldest brother (1765–1819), ordained as a priest at Oxford in June 1789. From 1782 to 1789, he directed a series of dramatic productions performed by the Austens at Steventon and wrote amusing prologues and epilogues for them: JA appropriately dedicates this comedy to her theatrically minded brother. Le Faye suggests that 'The Visit', like 'Henry and Eliza', was written in early 1789 (*FR*, pp. 67–8); the dedication could have been added later that year, after James became curate of Stoke Charity, near Winchester, in July. Paula Byrne speculates that 'The Visit' was performed by the Austen family as a burlesque afterpiece to their production of James Townley's farce *High Life Below Stairs* (London: J. Newbery, 1759) during the Christmas holiday, 1788–9 (*Jane Austen and the Theatre* (London: Hambledon, 2002), pp. 13–14).

2 **"The school for Jealousy" and "The travelled Man":** no eighteenth-century plays with these titles are recorded. They might be comedies written for Austen family performances, either by James or by JA herself. The latter possibility is strengthened by the correction from 'they' to 'it' in the manuscript: that is, from referring to the two earlier plays and the present one ('The Visit') to the present one alone. The deleted 'they' seems to acknowledge JA's authorship of the two lost plays; the inserted 'it' conceals her part. Southam suggests that 'the correction was perhaps necessary if Jane Austen wished to avoid any suggestion that the other plays had also been dedicated to James' ('Manuscript', p. 235). Byrne, who believes that the lost plays are by James, suggests that 'The travelled Man' derived from his recent travels abroad (*Jane Austen and the Theatre*, p. 21), but JA could also have used her brother's travels as the basis for a comedy. 'The school for Jealousy' might have been adapted from the libretto of an opera by Antonio Salieri, *La Scola de' Gelosi*, performed in London in March

1786. The titles also allude to celebrated comedies by Sheridan, *The School for Scandal* (1777), and Goldsmith, *The Good-Natur'd Man* (1768).

3 **Curate:** either of Stoke Charity or of Overton, the nearest town to Steventon, where James became curate in April 1790. A curate assisted a parish priest with his duties, or replaced him; Johnson defines a curate as 'a clergyman hired to perform the duties of another'.

4 **first composed:** suggesting that the dedication to James Austen was added after the play's first composition: perhaps over a year later, if JA wrote 'The Visit' in early 1789.

5 **Arthur:** The name was uncommon in the eighteenth century and JA had difficulty spelling it correctly; she originally wrote 'Authar', followed by 'Authur', before changing it to 'Arthur' throughout. She also gives the name to Arthur Parker in *S*.

6 **Stanly:** a surname. The use of 'Stanley' as a first name began in the late nineteenth century.

7 **Sophy:** the familiar form of Sophia. The contribution to *The Loiterer* by 'Sophia Sentiment', possibly a pseudonym for JA (see Appendix D), is dated 28 March 1789, about the time when JA wrote 'The Visit'. She also used the name for Sophia in 'Love and Freindship'.

8 **Cloe:** Chloe, a traditional name for women in pastoral fiction and poetry. JA's other Chloe, in 'The First Act of a Comedy', is a country dweller, accompanied by 'a chorus of ploughboys'.

9 **suiting all her Beds to her own length:** perhaps alluding to Procrustes, the brigand of Greek legend who gave hospitality to strangers before fastening them to a bed: mutilating them if they were too long for it, or stretching them if they were too short.

10 **The more free, the more Wellcome:** alluding to Townley's *High Life Below Stairs*, in which Kitty declares: 'Lady *Charlotte*, pray be free; the more free, the more welcome, as they say in my Country' (Act 2).

11 **discovered:** meaning 'revealed', a standard term in stage directions, indicating that the characters are in place when the curtain opens.

12 **Truth:** two sentences intensifying Miss Fitzgerald's praise of her brother are deleted here (see textual notes). JA presumably decided that they were redundant.

13 **Exeunt Severally:** another standard term in stage directions, indicating that characters leave the stage through different exits.

14 **Chairs set round in a row:** a sign of the old-fashioned formality of the domestic arrangements in Lord Fitzgerald's house: a formality undercut by the short bed, lack of chairs, etc.

15 **8 Chairs . . . pretty well:** developing the joke about sitting two to a chair in 'Frederic and Elfrida'.

16 **I beg . . . very light:** the ludicrous formality of this visit might have as its target a short play by Arnaud Berquin, 'Le Petit Joueur de violin', part of a twelve-volume collection entitled *L'ami des enfans* (1782–3), of which JA owned a copy (now at the Houghton Library, Harvard University). In Berquin's play, as Byrne notes, a social visit takes place in which the characters attempt to outdo one another in politeness (*Jane Austen and the Theatre*, p. 20).

17 **cherub . . . seraph:** two of the nine orders or 'choirs' of angels; together with thrones, cherubim and seraphim form the triad closest to God. JA makes no other allusion to the angelic orders in her fiction (*All Things Austen*, p. 13).

18 **hands:** escorts, leads by the hand.

19 **Miss Fitzgerald at top. Lord Fitzgerald at bottom:** as hosts, the Fitzgeralds are properly seated at the head and foot of the table, the lady of the house at the top and the master at the foot, where he would be expected to carve the meat. (In *E* (vol. 2, ch. 16), the frail Mr Woodhouse is nervous about carrying out this task.) The other guests would be seated in order of rank, with the highest ranking closest to the host and the lowest at the middle of the table.

20 **fried Cowheel and Onion:** a coarse dish consumed by labourers, like the tripe and suet pudding that follow. John Farley's *London Art of Cookery* (1783) contains a recipe for 'Fried Ox Feet', containing heels and onions (*All Things Austen*, p. 277). The dinner party ingeniously reverses the premise of Townley's *High Life Below Stairs*, in which servants live the life of aristocrats; here, aristocrats eat like servants.

21 **toss off a bumper:** drain a glass of wine filled to the brim, rather than sipping it in ladylike fashion.

22 **Elder wine or Mead:** cheap domestic alternatives to French wine, made, respectively, from elder berries and honey. They would be served by those of limited means and at rural entertainments, but never by people of fashion. JA's family, always financially constrained, drank home-made wine. In the same letter to Cassandra of 30 June 1808 in which she writes of eating ices at her brother Edward's house, JA contrasts the French wine of Godmersham Park with the home-made orange wine that the sisters and their mother would drink at their rented lodgings (*L*, p. 139).

23 **warm ale . . . nutmeg:** an invalid's drink, and thus especially inappropriate for the youthful and attractive Sophy Hampton.

24 **red herrings:** herrings preserved by being cured in smoke, considered inferior to fresh fish.

25 **Tripe . . . Crow:** the entrails and giblets of calves, pigs, etc.; food for the poor. William Ellis' *The Country Housewife's Family Companion* (1750) contains a recipe for frying 'liver and crow' together (*All Things Austen*, pp. 277–8).

26 **Suet pudding:** a pudding made of flour and suet (animal fat), usually boiled in a cloth; not, of course, a 'high' or rich dish.

27 **Desert:** dessert, consisting of fruit and nuts, served at the end of a dinner, after the pudding.

28 **Hothouse:** a heated greenhouse, in which fruits for dessert were cultivated: a much costlier and more prestigious structure than the 'receptacle for the Turkies' which replaces it. In *NA*, Catherine marvels at the 'village of hot-houses' owned by the epicurean General Tilney; her own father, in contrast, owns 'only one small hot-house', with 'a fire in it now and then' (vol. 2, ch. 7).

29 **Come Girls, let us circulate the Bottle:** the custom of passing a bottle of wine around a dinner table after the meal, normally among men only, after women have adjourned to the drawing room. John Gregory deplores the segregation of gentlemen from ladies, whose 'drawing-rooms are deserted, and after dinner and supper the gentlemen are impatient till they retire' (*Father's Legacy*, pp. 16–17). Here, in contrast, the women are hearty drinkers, while neither Stanly nor Sir Arthur 'touches wine'.

30 **Gooseberry Wine:** another simple, home-made wine, never served at a formal gathering. JA is probably alluding to Goldsmith's *The Vicar of Wakefield*, in which the vicar boasts of 'our gooseberry wine, for which we had great reputation' (vol. 1, ch. 1). The passage would have caught her eye, since the vicar professes 'with the veracity of an historian, that I never knew one of them [their visitors] find fault with it'. JA's 'History of England' in 'Volume the Second' takes issues with such professions of historical 'veracity'.

THE MYSTERY

1 **the Revd George Austen:** 'The Mystery' is the only one of the juvenilia dedicated to JA's father (1731–1805), rector of Steventon. The comedy might have been presented as an afterpiece at a 'private Theatrical exhibition' performed by the Austen family in 1788. James Austen's 'Prologue' to the main play performed on that occasion survives (*Poems of James Austen*, pp. 26–7), but the name of the play (possibly by James himself) and the month in which it was performed are unknown.

2 **Spangle:** 'any thing sparkling and shining' (Johnson): a comically inappropriate name for a character who does nothing but sleep.

3 **Humbug:** an imposter or fraud.

4 **Corydon:** a traditional name for a rustic lover in the pastoral tradition, also used in 'Frederic and Elfrida'.

5 **Fanny:** a pet-name for Frances, used repeatedly by JA in her novels: Fanny Dashwood (*S&S*), Fanny Price (*MP*), Fanny Harville (*P*), etc. There is also a Fanny in 'The Three Sisters'.

6 **Daphne:** a female equivalent of Corydon in the pastoral tradition, the name became common in England only in the early twentieth century.

7 **at work:** needlework, embroidery: a genteel occupation, suitable for ladies. John Gregory reminds his daughters that its usefulness 'is not on account of the intrinsic value of all you can do with your hands, which is trifling, but to enable you to judge more perfectly of that kind of work, and to direct the execution of it in others' (*Father's Legacy*, p. 21). It was, however, an important occupation for gentlewomen, with plenty of time on their hands,

and could include making family linen, embroidering fancy items and sewing or mending garments for the poor.

8 **whispers:** the stage whispering recalls a famous scene in the Duke of Buckingham's burlesque, *The Rehearsal* (1672). Here Bayes presents a play which 'instead of beginning with a Scene that discovers something of the Plot' does the opposite: 'I begin this Play with a whisper.' First a physician and then an usher whisper a series of secrets, concluding with the stage direction '*Exeunt Whispering*' (Act 2, scene 1).

9 **reclined in an elegant Attitude:** adopting the same affected pose as Caroline Simpson in 'Jack and Alice', with her 'studied attitude on a couch' (ch. 1).

10 **fast asleep:** such indolence had become the height of fashion for young men in the 1780s. It is personified in Burney's *Cecilia* by Mr Meadows, who is said to be 'at the head' of 'the present race of INSENSIBILISTS'. A 'man of the *Ton*', such as Meadows, 'must invariably be insipid, negligent, and selfish' (book 4, ch. 6). As an 'insensibilist', Sir Edward Spangle is the perfect recipient for the secret here: being asleep, he can be confided in safely.

THE THREE SISTERS

1 **Edward Austen Esqre:** JA's third brother (1767–1852), who had been taken into the home of the wealthy Thomas and Catherine Knight and then formally adopted in 1783. His engagement to Elizabeth Bridges was announced on 1 March 1791, and in the same year her elder sisters Fanny and Sophia also became engaged. JA probably wrote 'The Three Sisters' in 1791 to contrast 'the matrimonial plans of the Bridges girls' with 'those of three quarrelling sisters who had certainly never learned any good manners or social graces' (*FR*, p. 70). Edward Austen's wedding to Elizabeth Bridges took place on 27 December, together with that of Sophia Bridges. Noting that one of the three sisters of the story is called Sophia (with a friend named Fanny), Jon Spence suggests that the story was written as a wedding present (*Becoming Jane Austen*, p. 62). Edward's daughter Fanny, JA's first niece, was born on 23 January 1793.

2 **hardly know how to value it enough:** John Gregory warns his daughters that 'nothing . . . renders a woman more despicable, than her thinking it essential to happiness to be married' (*Father's Legacy*, p. 42).

3 **quite an old Man, about two and thirty:** three years younger than Colonel Brandon, whom Marianne finds 'exceedingly ancient' (*S&S*, vol. 1, ch. 8).

4 **Settlements:** property or money settled on the wife in the event of her husband's death. In this case, the amount of the settlement is devalued by the husband's good health; the longer he lives, the less useful his settlement will be.

5 **Georgiana:** an 'eighteenth-century female derivative of George (probably pronounced Jor-jane-a)' (*Names*, p. 65). It is also the name of a younger sister, Georgiana Darcy, in *P&P*.

6 **blue spotted with silver:** a ludicrously garish colour scheme for a carriage. The plain chocolate brown preferred by Mr Watts is far more orthodox.

7 **as low as his old one:** high carriages, which provided a better view, were fashionable and more expensive; low carriages were more stable, and thus favoured by the practical Mr Watts. In *The Loiterer*, 32, by Henry Austen, a young woman 'began talking of Equipage; she admired high Phaetons . . . to distraction' (p. 13).

8 **to chaprone:** from chaperone, a married or elderly woman who, for the sake of propriety, would accompany young unmarried women on their outings.

9 **Winter Balls:** either private parties or dances held at a town's public assembly rooms, during the winter season. In the summer, polite society retreated from towns to country estates; winter was thus the best time to hold dances, parties, etc.

10 **Women's always Staying at home:** in the tradition of jealous husbands. A well-known literary example is the aptly named Mr Pinchwife, in William Wycherley's comedy *The Country Wife* (1675). The play was rewritten by David Garrick as *The Country Girl* (1766), with the leading role played by Dorothy Jordan for fifteen seasons at Drury Lane, from 1785 to 1800.

11 **Mary Stanhope:** for this character, JA might have drawn on Nanny Johnson in Sarah Fielding's *The Adventures of David Simple* (vol. 1, ch. 5). Like Mary, Nanny is torn between her desire

for a wealthy husband and disgust with his person, and she too fears that if she does not marry him her sister will. Like Mary, she is especially interested in a new carriage and jewels.

12 **Law:** a colloquial euphemism for 'Lord', expressing surprise at being asked a question, used frequently by the vulgar Mrs Jennings in *S&S*.

13 **drinks Tea:** in the late afternoon, several hours after dinner had been served. It was followed by supper, a light evening meal, which in this case ended only at midnight. The late dining hours favoured in fashionable society meant late teas and still later suppers. In December 1798, JA wrote to Cassandra, then staying with the Knights at Godmersham Park, with apologies for the unfashionably early hours at Steventon: 'We dine now at half after Three, & have done dinner I suppose before you begin.— We drink tea at half after six.—I am afraid you will despise us' (*L*, p. 27).

14 **they should fight him:** Mary's exaggerated expectations of a duel resemble those of Mrs Malaprop in Sheridan's comedy *The Rivals* (1775), Act 5, scene 1, performed at Steventon in July 1784 with a prologue and epilogue by James Austen. Duelling was by now becoming obsolete. Earlier in the century, a gentleman would challenge another gentleman to a duel when his honour had been impugned; a father, however, would not challenge his daughter's suitor to a duel for changing his mind. JA returns to the topic in *P&P*, in which Mrs Bennet, after first fearing for her husband's safety in the event of a duel with Lydia's seducer Wickham, complains that he is not being belligerent enough: 'Who is to fight Wickham, and make him marry her, if he comes away?' (vol 3, ch. 6).

15 **his Countenance is very heavy:** he has a very dull or severe appearance.

16 **Three thousand a year:** a considerable income but not, as Georgiana observes, a vast one. It would, for instance, be too little for the expenses of a winter season in London, for which at least £5,000 a year was needed: in his negotiations with Mary, Mr Watts is acutely aware of the limitations of his own wealth.

17 **year:** in the deleted phrase that follows (see textual notes), JA specifies that Mr Watts currently drives a 'post-chaise and pair':

an oddity, since 'post' here implies that the chaise would be drawn by hired horses, not the pair that Mr Watts owns. The 'boot' is a compartment for luggage.

18 **your most obedient:** short for 'most obedient servant', a perfunctory form of greeting.

19 **pin money:** a small allowance paid to a woman during her husband's lifetime for personal expenses such as dress, free from any control on his part.

20 **Saddle horse:** a horse for riding, in addition to the four bay horses that would draw the carriage.

21 **suit of fine lace:** an expensive, formal dress of matching gown and petticoat. Lace, sold both by milliners and in specialist lace shops, was a much-desired material.

22 **out of number:** the jewels demanded would be far beyond Mr Watts's means. In a deleted passage, Mary asks for still more, specifying the fabulous jewels offered to the princess Badroulbadour in 'The Story of Aladdin, or the Wonderful Lamp': part of the *Arabian Nights Entertainments*, first translated into English *c*. 1706–21. Among the exotic jewels that Mary requests in this deleted passage are 'Turkey stones' (turquoises), 'Bugles' (tube-shaped glass beads) and 'Garnets' (gems formed from a deep-red crystal). In *E* (vol. 3, ch. 2), Miss Bates alludes to 'The Story of Aladdin' in one of her interminable monologues.

23 **Greenhouse:** 'a house in which tender plants are sheltered from the weather' (Johnson). They could be elaborate buildings, as John Dashwood's remarks in *S&S* reveal. Among the many drains on his resources of which he complains to Elinor is a greenhouse to be built for his wife Fanny: 'It will be a very fine object from many parts of the park, and the flower-garden will slope down just before it, and be exceedingly pretty' (vol. 2, ch. 11).

24 **every Winter in Bath, every Spring in Town:** Mary wants the best of all worlds, visiting Bath during the fashionable winter season and London at the most popular time, in Spring, but this would be ruinously expensive. Even the wealthiest families would not normally combine extended stays in London and Bath in the same year.

25 **taking some Tour:** either on the Continent or in some picturesque part of Britain, such as the Lake District (where the Gardiners originally plan to take Elizabeth Bennet in *P&P*) or the Peak District in Derbyshire (their eventual destination).

26 **Watering Place:** a spa, such as Tunbridge Wells, or a seaside resort, such as Brighton.

27 **Theatre to act Plays in:** at Steventon, the Austens used either their barn or the rectory dining room for family theatricals, from December 1782. A vogue for building private theatres in very large country houses began in the 1770s, but improvised arrangements were far more common. Thus in *MP*, the stage is erected in Sir Thomas Bertram's billiard-room, while his study is used as the green-room. Ecclesford, the Cornish seat of Lord Ravensford in *MP*, also has what seems to be a makeshift theatre, although a more elaborate one than that constructed at Mansfield Park (vol. 1, ch. 13).

28 **Which is the Man:** a comedy (1783) by Hannah Cowley, proposed by Eliza de Feuillide for performance by the Austens at Steventon at Christmas 1787, in their converted barn, but eventually rejected. Like Mary in 'The Three Sisters', Eliza had planned to take the part of the lively heroine, the widow Lady Bell Bloomer. The play seems to have been a favourite with JA, who also alludes to it in a letter to her nephew James Edward Austen of 16–17 December 1816 (*L*, p. 323).

29 **silver Border:** Doody and Murray (*Catharine*, p. 310) cite William Felton's *A Treatise on Carriages* (London: The author, 1796), according to which 'Nothing has ever been introduced with a better effect than . . . silver plating, which is now become so general, that almost every hackney carriage exhibits some portion of it' (vol. 1, p. 164).

30 **Writings:** that is, the Settlements, mentioned earlier in the story.

31 **Special Licence . . . Banns:** Mary wishes to obtain a special licence to avoid the reading of banns from a church pulpit on three successive Sundays.

32 **common Licence:** a licence granted by a bishop for marriage in a church within his diocese. It was a compromise between the reading of banns, the cheapest method, and marriage with a special licence, the most ostentatious.

33 **Stoneham:** probably an imaginary village. There is no other indication of the story's location.

34 **Leicestershire:** one of the counties in the Midlands, the central part of England. The deletion that follows (see textual notes) is the third substantial cancellation in the story, an unusually high number. JA might have found the riddle here too laboured and the address to the dedicatee, Edward Knight, too personal.

35 **appearance:** Mary's first public engagement as the newly married Mrs Watts.

36 **provision:** a sum of money left by the late Mr Stanhope to his daughter Mary, and presumably to his two younger daughters too. He left £500 per annum to his wife; the daughters would normally have been left a similar amount.

37 **Jemima:** an Old Testament name, unusual in JA's youth but becoming more popular in the early nineteenth century. It is also used in *P* for the Musgroves' nursery-maid.

38 **no occasion for it on the other:** comically prefiguring a remark by Catherine in *NA*: 'If there is a good fortune on one side, there can be no occasion for any on the other' (vol. 1, ch. 15). Catherine's observation is subversive, since partners were expected to bring similar fortunes to a marriage, but Mary's is outrageous, as the responses of the others indicate.

39 **chaprone her six Daughters:** Kitty is maliciously portraying Mary Stanhope as a governess or a school-teacher, chaperoning young ladies for pay, rather than as the elegant married woman she aspires to be.

40 **Entrée:** entrance, in the sense of a public entrance into a room. In a letter to Cassandra of 1 December 1798, JA uses the word to make fun of their mother: 'My mother made her *entrée* into the dressing-room through crowds of admiring spectators yesterday afternoon, and we all drank tea together for the first time these five weeks' (*L*, p. 23).

41 **Vixen:** 'the name of a she-fox; otherwise applied to a woman whose nature and condition is thereby compared to a she-fox' (Johnson); a fierce, ill-tempered woman.

42 **Blackguard:** 'a cant word amongst the vulgar; by which is implied a dirty fellow; of the meanest kind' (Johnson).

43 **Short and sweet:** proverbial since the sixteenth century.
44 **dressed:** dressed for dinner.

TO MISS JANE ANNA ELIZABETH AUSTEN

1 **Jane Anna Elizabeth Austen:** JA's niece Anna (1793–1872), the daughter of her brother James, born on 15 April 1793. Since the dedication is dated 2 June, she was not yet seven weeks old. The miscellaneous items dedicated to her might, of course, have been written well before the dedication. They are termed 'Detached pieces' in the list of contents for 'Volume the First', but not in the text itself.
2 **you will in time be older:** a long life was still uncommon for those born in the late eighteenth century, but Anna did live to be almost eighty.
3 **excellent Parents:** Anna's mother Anne, who married James Austen in 1792, died in May 1795, when her daughter was only two.
4 **Treatises for your Benefit:** alluding humorously to sententious works such as James Fordyce's *Sermons to Young Women* (1766), which Mr Collins is eager to read to the Bennet sisters in *P&P* (vol. 1, ch. 14). Other examples are John Gregory's *A Father's Legacy to His Daughters* (1774) and two treatises owned by JA: Ann Murry's *Memoria: or, The Young Ladies Instructor*, 2nd edn (1780) and Thomas Percival's *A Father's Instructions to his Children* (1775).

A FRAGMENT—WRITTEN TO INCULCATE THE PRACTICE OF VIRTUE

1 **Virtue:** this is the briefest of all the items in the three note-books and the only one with no apparent humour. JA deleted it (see textual notes), perhaps for this reason. It might also have been intended as a parody of treatises, such as Fordyce's *Sermons*, mentioned in the dedication to Anna.
2 **leave them unsupplied:** leave them without wants; satisfy their needs.

A BEAUTIFUL DESCRIPTION OF THE
DIFFERENT EFFECTS OF SENSIBILITY ON
DIFFERENT MINDS

1 **Melissa:** an unusual name in the eighteenth century, not used elsewhere in Austen's fiction.

2 **book muslin bedgown:** book-muslin is 'a fine kind of muslin owing its name to the book-like manner in which it is folded when sold in the piece' (*OED*). A bedgown is a house-dress, not necessarily worn for sleeping.

3 **chambray gauze shift:** an undergarment made of cambric, a fine white linen imported from Chambray in France. In 1808, JA wrote a poem in praise of cambric handkerchiefs, dedicated to her friend Catherine Bigg.

4 **french net nightcap:** a large, elaborate, indoor cap, fashionable in the 1770s and 1780s. Melissa's costume is carefully chosen to make her as 'affecting an object' as possible.

5 **five minutes every fortnight ... imperfect Slumber:** an extreme version of the traditional sleepless lover, Sir William personifies sensibility: his sympathy for Melissa keeps him at her bedside constantly.

6 **Town:** London.

7 **hashing up the remains of an old Duck:** not, of course, a 'little delicacy', but an economical way of using up the remains of a leftover meal. When Fanny Price returns to her impoverished family in Portsmouth, she finds 'Rebecca's hashes' difficult to endure (*MP*, vol. 3, ch. 11).

8 **toasting some cheese:** another cheap meal, not served in polite society.

9 **Curry:** a supposed invalid is given spicy food, requiring a sound digestive system. Curry was becoming popular in England in the eighteenth century, as India played an increasingly important role in the national economy.

10 **the punning Doctor:** other characters in JA's fiction also enjoy puns, including Mary Crawford with her much discussed play on 'Rears', and *Vices*' (*MP*, vol. 1, ch. 6).

11 **cordials:** 'a medicine that increases the force of the heart, or quickens the circulation' (Johnson).

423

THE GENEROUS CURATE

1 **moral Tale:** a term frequently used in the late eighteenth and early nineteenth century to describe didactic fiction written for children, such as Maria Edgeworth's *Moral Tales for Young People* (1801). The term 'tale' is used for other items in the juvenilia, but this is the only 'moral tale'.

2 **County of Warwick:** Warwickshire in central England. A branch of JA's mother's family, the Leighs, owned Stoneleigh Abbey, Warwickshire.

3 **Clergyman:** not the Curate of the title but a rector with a living of his own.

4 **living . . . about two hundred pound:** a living is the livelihood made by a clergyman of the Church of England, in the form of tithes paid by residents of his parish, income from the farming of land and a rent-free residence. This clergyman's living has about the same value as that of the two owned by JA's father: at Steventon, worth £100 per year, and at Deane, worth £110. It also has the same value as that presented to Edward Ferrars by Colonel Brandon, who regrets that it is 'but a small one' (*S&S*, vol. 3, ch. 3). Other livings in JA's novels are of greater value: Dr Grant's at Mansfield Park is worth a 'very little less than a thousand' pounds per year (*MP*, vol. 1, ch. 1).

5 **Royal Academy for Seamen at Portsmouth:** the Royal Naval Academy at Portsmouth, the navy's training college for officers, where both of JA's sailor brothers began their careers. Francis Austen entered the Academy in April 1786, just before his twelfth birthday, and Charles Austen shortly after his twelfth birthday, in July 1791. Tuition was free for the sons of naval officers, but George Austen had to pay some £75 per annum for tuition and expenses for Charles, a sum that would have placed a severe strain on Mr Williams' annual income of £200. The city and naval base of Portsmouth is about forty miles south of Steventon.

6 **small fleet . . . Newfoundland:** Newfoundland had been under British rule since the Treaty of Paris in 1763. Since its fisheries were valuable, the navy kept an active presence there during Britain's frequent wars with France, Spain and Holland.

7 **Newfoundland Dog:** dogs were shipped from Newfoundland to England from the late seventeenth century. Some were sent to Teignmouth in Devon, a major port for the Newfoundland fisheries. In her diary for 25 April 1773, Frances Burney's stepsister Maria Rishton, holidaying with her husband in Teignmouth, writes, 'we intend getting a very large Newfoundland dog before we leave this place' (Annie Raine Ellis (ed.), *Early Diary of Frances Burney, 1768–1778* (London: G. Bell, 1913), vol. I, p. 213). When Burney joined the Rishtons there in July, she met the 'Newfoundland Dog, Excellent for *Diving* in the Water, & which always goes with Mr Rishton to swim or Bathe' (Lars E. Troide (ed.), *Early Journals and Letters* (Oxford: Clarendon Press, 1988), vol. I, p. 279). JA seems to have shared the Rishtons' fondness for these dogs; Henry Tilney keeps a 'large Newfoundland puppy' at Woodston Parsonage (*NA*, vol. 2, ch. 11).

8 **every Month:** JA heightened the comedy here in changing 'Year' to 'Month', thus creating a steady stream of Newfoundland dogs bound for Warwick.

9 **adopted by a neighbouring Clergyman:** perhaps alluding to JA's elder brother Edward, who had been adopted by the Knights in 1783. Unlike Edward, however, adopted by a very wealthy childless couple, young Williams is mysteriously adopted by an impecunious couple with many children.

10 **Curacy of fifty pound a year:** the curate thus earns only a fourth as much as Williams' father.

11 **twopenny Dame's School:** a local elementary school for young children, run by a woman who would usually have little knowledge of the subjects she taught. With fees as low as twopence per week, it would be at the bottom end of the educational system. At eighteen, Williams is well beyond the appropriate age for such a school.

12 **genius:** not outstanding ability, but 'nature; disposition' (Johnson).

13 **brickbats:** fragments of brick, usually used as missiles. Young Williams is presumably expressing his resentment at having been adopted by a man who, for all his generosity, cannot support him.

ODE TO PITY

1 **Miss Austen:** JA's sister Cassandra.

2 **Ode to Pity:** alluding to the well-known 'Ode to Pity' (1746) by William Collins, which JA could have read in her copy of Robert Dodsley's *A Collection of Poems in Six Volumes by Several Hands* (London: R. and J. Dodsley, 1758). She sold the collection for ten shillings in May 1801 (*L*, p. 88). Despite their title, pity is strikingly absent from JA's verses.

3 **pitiful:** 'tender; compassionate' (Johnson).

4 **Myrtle:** a shrub traditionally used for victors' wreaths, sacred to the goddess of love. In Collins' Ode:

> There first the Wren thy Myrtles shed
> On gentlest *Otway*'s infant Head.
> (lines 19–20)

5 **Philomel:** in classical myth, the nightingale.

6 **brawling:** 'flowing with noise and commotion, as a brook' (*OED*). JA's 'Gently brawling' is an oxymoron.

7 **turnpike road:** a network of toll roads in which travellers were charged at toll gates, dating from the seventeenth century. The tolls were supposed to maintain the roads, which were often of poor quality. The prosaic word 'turnpike' is in ludicrous contrast to the 'Myrtle', 'Philomel', 'Dove', etc.

8 **Sweetly noisy:** another oxymoron. In Collins' Ode, in contrast, there is a 'Deserted Stream, and mute' (line 15).

9 **Gently brawling ... Silent Stream:** these two lines are a reworking of a sentence in 'Love and Freindship': 'Before us ran the murmuring brook and behind us ran the turnpike road' (Letter the 13th).

10 **Lovely Scenes:** the Gothic scenes revealed by the moon are, of course, far from 'Lovely'.

11 **hut:** alluding to Pity's 'Cell' (line 21) in Collins' Ode.

12 **Cot, the Grot:** a small, humble cottage; a grotto.

13 **eke:** also, likewise; a poeticism.

14 **Abbey too a mouldering heap:** abbeys, preferably in ruins, play a central role in Gothic fiction, which was becoming increasingly popular in the early 1790s. The 'mouldering' abbey

here foreshadows Catherine Morland's excited anticipation of Northanger Abbey, with 'its long, damp passages, its narrow cells and ruined chapel' (*NA*, vol. 2, ch. 2).

15 **Conceal'd by aged pines:** a stock feature of menacing houses. When Richardson's Pamela arrives as a prisoner at Mr B's Lincolnshire home, a 'large, old and lonely Mansion', she is struck by the 'brown nodding Horrors of lofty Elms and Pines about it' (Thomas Keymer and Alice Wakely (eds.), *Pamela* (Oxford: Oxford University Press, 2001), pp. 109–10).

16 **June 3d 1793:** a day later than the Dedication of the previous pieces to Anna Austen, and the latest date JA gives for any of her juvenilia.

VOLUME THE SECOND

1 **Ex dono mei Patris:** 'a gift from my father': one of the few Latin phrases in JA's fiction or letters. Le Faye suggests that she 'heard her father teaching Latin to his sons and pupils using Pote's *Eton Latin Grammar*' (*FR*, p. 58), as suggested by a remark in a letter to Cassandra of 24 January 1809: 'they seemed to me purely classical—just like Homer & Virgil, Ovid & Propria que Maribus' (*L*, p. 170). Here the Latin allusion is to one of the first lessons in Pote's grammar. George Austen probably gave JA the notebook in 1790, the date of the earliest items in 'Volume the Second'.

LOVE AND FREINDSHIP

1 **Madame La Comtesse De Feuillide:** Austen's cousin Eliza de Feuillide; see note 1 to 'Henry and Eliza'. Eliza was probably staying at Steventon in June 1790 (*FR*, p. 70), the date recorded at the end of 'Love and Freindship'. It is the only one of the juvenilia dedicated to her.

2 **Love and Freindship:** in addition to the epigraph, 'Deceived in Freindship and Betrayed in Love', there are several possible sources for this title. One is the Latin motto 'Amoris et Amicitiae' ('Of Love and Friendship'), inscribed on a miniature painting of Eliza de Feuillide, which Eliza presented to her cousin Philadelphia Walter in 1782 (Le Faye, *Jane Austen's 'Outlandish Cousin'*, pp. 55–6, 96). The phrase 'love and friendship' appears in a 1789

Loiterer essay by Henry Austen, in which 'every Girl who seeks for happiness' is advised to 'avoid love and friendship as she wishes to be admired and distinguished' (27, pp. 11–12). The most likely source, however, is Garrick's comedy *Bon Ton or High Life above Stairs* (London: T. Becket, 1775), performed by the Austen family at Steventon in 1788, with a prologue by James Austen and with Eliza playing the part of the heroine, Miss Tittup (Claire Tomalin, *Jane Austen: A Life*, pp. 55–6). In one of her first speeches, Miss Tittup declares: 'Love and Friendship are very fine names to be sure, but they are mere visiting acquaintances; we . . . let 'em knock at our doors, but we never let 'em in' (Act 1, scene 1).

3 **in a series of Letters:** a standard phrase on the title pages of epistolary novels, used by Richardson in *Sir Charles Grandison* and by Eliza Nugent Bromley, the author of one of JA's sources for 'Love and Freindship', *Laura and Augustus, An Authentic Story, in a Series of Letters, by a Young Lady* (1784). 'Amelia Webster' and 'The Three Sisters' in 'Volume the First' are also epistolary fictions, but neither uses the 'series of Letters' tag.

4 **"Deceived in Freindship and Betrayed in Love.":** the last line of an anonymous quatrain, published as a glee for three voices in *A Selection of Favourite Catches, Glees, &c. Sung at the Bath Harmonic Society* (Bath: The Booksellers in Bath, 1799):

> Welcome, the covert of these aged oaks;
> Welcome, each cavern of the horrid rocks;
> Far from the world's illusion let me rove,
> Deceiv'd in Friendship, and betray'd in Love.

A 'glee' is an unaccompanied song for three or more voices, in which each voice takes a different part.

5 **Isabel:** the original form of the newly popular name 'Isabella', given by JA to Isabella Thorpe in *NA* and to Emma's sister Isabella Knightley in *E*.

6 **Laura:** an unusual name earlier in the eighteenth century, but favoured by novelists in the 1780s and 1790s. A recent example was the heroine of Bromley's *Laura and Augustus*.

7 **detail . . . of your Life:** closely resembling the request, in 'Jack and Alice', made by Alice Johnson to Lady Williams, 'Will you favour me with your Life and Adventures' (ch. 2) and the same

request made by Alice and Lady Williams to Lucy, 'Will you favour us with your Life and adventures' (ch. 4).

8 **cruel Persecutions of obstinate Fathers:** fathers such as Mr Harlowe in Richardson's *Clarissa*, determined to marry his daughter to a man she abhors. In Bromley's *Laura and Augustus*, Laura declares: 'How have the joys of my youth been poisoned by the tyranny of a parent! from him have originated all my sorrows' (vol. 3, letter 47).

9 **Marianne:** the recipient of Laura's letters bears the same name as Marianne Dashwood in *S&S*, the personification of acute sensibility.

10 **natural:** illegitimate. Laura's mother thus could not take the surname of her aristocratic Scottish father.

11 **Opera-girl:** a dancer in the ballet, which was presented between the acts of an opera. They were usually attractive and scantily clad, and, like actresses, sought after as mistresses by wealthy gentlemen.

12 **My Father . . . Convent in France:** building on a passage in *Laura and Augustus* in which Eliza, who will later be found to be the illegitimate daughter of a duke, recounts her birth and upbringing: 'Fountainbleau was the place of my birth, and in giving me life my unfortunate mother expired. She was a native of Italy. I was educated at the convent of the Noblesse in Paris, and received every advantage which the attendance of the most renowned masters could give' (vol. 1, letter 4). JA is glancing at the fashion for using European settings in English fiction: a practice associated with the Gothic, but earlier developed by Richardson, who set large parts of *Sir Charles Grandison* in Italy and brought his Italian characters to England.

13 **romantic:** in the sense of 'full of wild scenery' (Johnson).

14 **Our mansion . . . Vale of Uske:** Usk, a picturesque river valley in south Wales; the river Usk flows north–south, through Monmouthshire. There would be few if any mansions in this remote region, and Laura will shortly describe her 'mansion' as a 'humble Cottage'.

15 **shortly surpassed my Masters:** echoing a sentence in Charlotte Smith's first novel *Emmeline* (London: T. Cadell, 1788), in which the heroine 'had a kind of intuitive knowledge; and

comprehended every thing with a facility that soon left her instructors behind her' (vol. 1, ch. 1).

16 **Rendez-vous:** The use of a newly fashionable French term contributes to Laura's affectations. JA originally explained the term with the phrase 'place of appointment', but then cancelled the apparently redundant explanation.

17 **tremblingly alive:** alluding to Pope's *An Essay on Man* (1733–4): 'Or Touch, if tremblingly alive all o'er, / To smart, and agonize at ev'ry pore' (epistle 1, lines 189–90). Burney uses the same phrase in *Cecilia*, noting 'how fearfully delicate, how "tremblingly alive" is the conscience of man!' (book 7, ch. 7).

18 **Minuet Dela Cour:** a court minuet; a formal dance, originally associated with the French court.

19 **neighbourhood was small . . . eoconomical motives:** JA might have read about another unpopulated Welsh neighbourhood in Sarah Fielding's *The History of Ophelia* (London: Robert Baldwin, 1760), reprinted in the *Novelist's Magazine* in 1785. Here the heroine is brought up by her aunt in a cottage 'situated above twenty Miles distant from any other House' (vol. 1, ch. 2). Another character in *Ophelia*, Captain Traverse, retires to Wales for the same 'oeconomical motives' that govern Marianne's mother, Isabel (vol. 1, ch. 28).

20 **first Boarding-schools in London:** such as the one on Queen Square, 'the ladies' Eton'; see note to 'Edgar and Emma', ch. 3.

21 **seen the World . . . Southampton:** unlike London and Bath, Southampton, a port and military town in Hampshire, on the south coast of England, had little claim to fashion. Dining there one evening (in contrast to spending two years in London) hardly adds to Isabel's having 'seen the World'. JA heightened the joke by changing 'slept' to 'supped': thus Isabel has not spent so much as a night in Southampton.

22 **Beware . . . the Metropolis of England:** JA makes a similar joke about the perils of London in a letter of 23 August 1796, in which she tells Cassandra: 'Here I am once more in this Scene of Dissipation & vice, and I begin already to find my Morals corrupted' (*L*, p. 5). Because of its size, and because so many went to London for its social life, entertainments, courtship, etc., the city was routinely depicted as a centre of vice and corruption.

23 **Stinking fish of Southampton:** the bad odours of Southampton were proverbial. In June 1811, for instance, Louis Simond found that 'Nothing can surpass the dirt and bad smells of the bye streets; the tide leaving putrescent quagmires all about the lower parts' (Christopher Hibbert (ed.), *An American in Regency England: The Journal of a Tour in 1810–1811* (London: Robert Maxwell, 1968), p. 150). JA's animus against Southampton probably stems from her own childhood. In summer 1783, with her sister Cassandra and her cousin Jane Cooper, she attended Ann Cawley's boarding school at Southampton, where she was infected with typhus. She and her aunt, Mrs Jane Cooper, became very ill with fever, which took Mrs Cooper's life (*FR*, p. 49). Typhus was brought to the town by troops who caught it at sea, rather than by 'Stinking fish'.

24 **social converse . . . rustic Cot:** pretentious and stilted terms to describe a family conversation in a rural cottage.

25 **We must not . . . partly convinced:** JA's substantial revision here (see textual notes) changes the tenor of the mock-solemn argument by Laura's father, delivered in formal debating style.

26 **Mary:** the most common name in JA's fiction and used for all ranks, 'from Earl's daughter to servant' (*Names*, p. 73)

27 **I long to know who it is:** the passage echoes a protracted comic scene in Sterne's *Tristram Shandy* (1760–7), book 1, ch. 21, continuing in book 2, ch. 6, in which Tristram's father and his uncle Toby dwell at length on the possible activities of their visitors: a parallel first noted by Annette Hopkins, ('Jane Austen's "Love and Freindship"', *South Atlantic Quarterly*, 34 (1925), 45–6). Another source might be Miss Tittup's lines on 'Love and Friendship' in Garrick's *Bon Ton:* we 'let 'em knock at our doors, but we never let 'em in' (Act 1, scene 1).

28 **the most beauteous . . . ever beheld:** Laura's delight in the visitor's beauty resembles that of the heroine in Sarah Fielding's *Ophelia* when a lost stranger—also a solitary Englishman, accompanied by his servant—arrives at her Welsh cottage: 'the Moon shone full upon him, and was bright enough to shew me a Face, which . . . seemed to me far more beautiful than my own' (vol. 1, ch. 3).

29 **The servant, She kept to herself:** a risqué remark from a female writer of fourteen.

30 **on him . . . must depend:** this insertion (see textual notes) emphasizes the artificial nature of Laura's passion, expressed in language learned from novels. The more spontaneous remark that it replaces is heavily deleted.

31 **Lindsay . . . Talbot:** mocking the convention in eighteenth-century novels of purporting to disguise characters' names with dashes, initials, etc. A further oddity is that the youth's surname, Lindsay, is a Scottish one, although his father is English; logically his name should be Talbot, disguised as Lindsay. JA is probably drawing on Sheridan's comedy *The Rivals* (1775), performed at Steventon in 1781. Here, as Peter Knox-Shaw observes, 'the heroine Lydia Languish, much addicted to novel-reading, causes her well-born and parentally sanctioned suitor to disguise himself as a half-pay Lieutenant, and take another name' (*Jane Austen and the Enlightenment* (Cambridge: Cambridge University Press, 2004), p. 55; *The Rivals*, Act 1, scene 1).

32 **Polydore . . . Claudia:** calling strangers by their Christian names is an outrageous breach of etiquette. Their names are also outlandish. 'Polydore' was confined to romances and dramas, and 'Claudia' was rare in the eighteenth century.

33 **Deluding Pomp of Title . . . Lady Dorothea:** as a baronet, ranking below the lowest grade of the peerage, Sir Edward Lindsay would welcome a marriage between his son and Lady Dorothea; as the style of her name reveals, she must be the daughter of a duke, marquess or earl.

34 **Never . . . obliged my Father:** conflicts between parents and children over the choice of marriage partner are commonplace in eighteenth-century fiction and drama: the heroines of Richardson's *Clarissa* and Fielding's *Tom Jones* are among many who refuse to marry the husband intended for them. Only in 'Love and Freindship', however, does a son defy a father who wishes him to marry the woman he loves.

35 **Gibberish:** 'the private language of rogues and gipsies; words without meaning' (Johnson).

36 **studying Novels I suspect:** reversing the standard criticism of women for their obsession with novels; here a male reader is the target. Sir Edward's scorn for novel-readers has a source in Bromley's *Laura and Augustus*, in which the young lovers are abused by

the wicked Benjamin Boswell for their love of prose fiction: 'This comes of people suffering their children to read those ridiculous books called novels' (vol. 1, letter 11).

37 **Bedfordshire…Middlesex:** Bedfordshire, a county to the north-west of London, is only some thirty miles north of Middle-sex. Instead of travelling this distance south to his aunt's house, Edward has travelled about one hundred miles west to the Vale of Usk.

38 **never taken orders … bred to the Church:** Laura's Irish father was presumably a Catholic, as she was educated in a French convent. Despite being 'bred to the Church', however, he cannot conduct marriages since he has not become a clergyman ('taken orders').

39 **Philippa:** a very unusual name in the eighteenth century.

40 **Augusta:** the name became fashionable after the birth of the second of George III's six daughters, Princess Augusta, in 1768.

41 **You are too ridiculous … to argue with:** the passage echoes one in Bromley's *Laura and Augustus* in which Laura's cruel father likewise ridicules her belief that love can sustain her and husband Augustus: 'take yourself off with your beggar's brat, and see if love will support you: you will find it, Madam heroine, I fancy damned slender diet' (vol. 2, letter 39).

42 **Augusta was one:** that is, Augusta was also one of 'that inferior order of Beings'. The word 'one' is a conjectural editorial emendation, replacing 'once', which leaves the sentence incomplete.

43 **Sophia:** although the name means wisdom, in her early fiction JA associates it with vacuous young women. Anne Thorpe's friend in *NA*, who had been one of her 'dear friends all the morning' (vol. 1, ch. 14), is named Sophia, as is Sophia Grey, the heiress whom Willoughby marries in *S&S*, 'a smart, stilish girl they say, but not handsome' (vol. 2, ch. 8). There is also a fickle Sophia, 'a Young lady crossed in Love', in the second of 'A Collection of Letters'.

44 **rather above the middle size:** in contrast to the merely middle-sized, and much less sympathetic, Augusta.

45 **most inward Secrets of our Hearts:** such instantaneous displays of intimacy, normally between young women, are a standard feature of sentimental novels and a recurring object of satire in JA's fiction. In 'Jack and Alice', Alice assures her new acquaintance

Lucy that, with the exception of 'a few dozen more of particular freinds, she loved her better than almost any other person in the world' (ch. 6).

46 **they flew into each other's arms:** expressions of friendship between heterosexual males could be less restrained in eighteenth-century England than today, but Edward and Augustus' 'affecting Scene' is comically exaggerated: 'my Soul' and 'My Adorable Angel' are terms normally reserved for lovers. The phrase 'flew into each other's arms' is also used a few lines earlier for the affecting meeting of Laura and Sophia, emphasizing the resemblance between male and female excesses of sensibility.

47 **pathetic:** 'affecting the passions; passionate; moving' (Johnson): a key term in the discourse of sensibility. The modern sense of arousing feelings of pity or sympathy was also becoming current.

48 **We fainted Alternately on a Sofa:** among the best-known lines in JA's juvenilia. The source is a stage-direction in the play-within-the play in Sheridan's burlesque drama, *The Critic* (London: T. Becket, 1781): 'They faint alternately in each others arms' (Act 3, scene 1). Sheridan, in turn, is parodying the discovery scene in the second act of John Home's tragedy *Douglas* (1756).

49 **the Same to the Same:** the lines deleted here (see textual notes) form the opening of letter the tenth. This suggests that JA, when copying an earlier draft into 'Volume the Second', accidentally skipped a letter before realizing her mistake.

50 **illiterate:** 'unlettered; untaught; unlearned; unenlightened by science' (Johnson). Laura evidently enjoys using the word, employing it later to denounce the 'illiterate villain' snoring in a stagecoach (Letter the 14th).

51 **Clandestine Marriage:** alluding to the title of a comedy by George Colman the elder and David Garrick, *The Clandestine Marriage* (1766).

52 **gracefully purloined:** a euphemism for 'stolen'.

53 **Escritoire:** a writing-desk with drawers.

54 **blushed at the idea of paying their Debts:** the satire is directed at the wealthy, who were apt to leave debts to merchants, tradesmen, etc. unpaid for lengthy periods of time, whereas 'debts of honour', incurred in gambling, would be paid at once. In *The Loiterer*, 4,

by James Austen, the 'Diary of a modern Oxford Man' records his contempt for commercial creditors, as well as for his father: 'Do think fathers are the greatest *Bores* in nature' (pp. 15–16).

55 **Execution in the House:** the seizure of goods, on the order of creditors; the goods would be sold and the proceeds used to pay outstanding debts. JA is punning on the word 'Execution', juxtaposing it with 'Barbarity'.

56 **Officers of Justice:** sheriff's officers, enforcing the execution of the creditors' writ.

57 **Holbourn:** Holborn, both a district of London and the name of a principal route by which travellers entered the city from the west. Laura has to look out for 'decent-looking' inhabitants, since Holborn was not favoured by fashionable residents. JA's original reading, 'Piccadilly', was the other principal route into London, but a much more salubrious area in the west end.

58 **Front Glasses:** carriage windows, which could be opened and closed.

59 **Newgate:** the notorious London prison, which features in many eighteenth-century novels.

60 **overpower my Sensibility:** unlike Sophia, with her exquisite sensibility, JA later visited a prison in Canterbury, with her brother Edward, a magistrate. She tells Cassandra, in a letter of 3 November 1813, that she was 'gratified' by the visit, '& went through all the feelings which People must go through I think in visiting such a Building' (*L*, p. 248).

61 **Annuity on their own Lives:** an annual return on capital, which ceased with the death of the recipients. In *S&S*, John Dashwood considers doing 'something of the annuity kind' for his mother before being discouraged by his wife, who believes that 'people always live for ever when there is any annuity to be paid them' (vol. 1, ch. 2).

62 **Marriage . . . Distant part of Ireland:** Ireland, in JA's fiction, is synonymous with the utterly remote; once characters remove to Ireland, they cannot be expected to be heard from again. In a letter of 18 August 1814, giving advice to her niece Anna on her novel in progress, JA writes: 'Let the Portmans go to Ireland, but as you know nothing of the Manners there, you had better not go with them' (*L*, p. 269).

63 **too long a Journey for the Horses:** a journey of some 300 miles, from London to the Scottish border, was far more than hired horses would travel. Instead, as the postilion recommends, the horses would be left at a staging post, where fresh horses would be supplied.

64 **travel Post:** a rapid but expensive means of transport. By changing horses at each stage the travellers could continue day and night, arriving in Scotland in about three days

65 **coroneted Coach and 4:** both the coronet and the four horses, rather than two, are status symbols. The coronet, an emblem on the carriage in the form of a crown, indicates that the owner is a peer. The ornaments surrounding the crown reveal his rank: four pearls for a baron, pearls above leaves for an earl, etc. Four horses make an ostentatious show of wealth; the hero of 'Memoirs of Mr Clifford' drives a coach and four, 'for he was a very rich young Man' (p. 51). A coach could also be drawn by six horses (a coach and six), but as fashionable carriages became lighter, the coach and six was becoming obsolete.

66 **Acknowledge thee!:** the recognition scene that follows is closely based on the famous scene in Burney's *Evelina* (London: T. Lowndes, 1778), in which the heroine is at last acknowledged by her father, Sir John Belmont. Like Laura, Evelina falls on her knees before her father, and like Laura's grandfather, Sir John exclaims 'Acknowledge thee' (vol. 3, letter 19).

67 **Yes dear resemblance of my Laurina:** echoing Sir John Belmont's interjection in Burney's recognition scene: 'Oh dear resemblance of thy murdered mother!'

68 **instinct of Nature whispered me:** echoing Laura's words, 'an instinctive Sympathy whispered to my Heart'. Both heroines discover their relationship to their grandfather instinctively, in keeping with current beliefs in the 'supposedly innate and "instinctive" affections that draw family members together' (*Catharine*, p. 317), although Sophia seems oddly confused about her grandfather's sex: 'whether Grandfathers, or Grandmothers, I could not pretend to determine'. In addition to the recognition scene in *Evelina*, JA is drawing here on the play-within-the-play in *The Critic*, in which the phrase 'whispers to my heart' occurs. As Byrne notes (*Jane Austen and the Theatre*, p. 80), an implausible

discovery scene there is swiftly followed a spectacular series of reunions:

> *I* am thy father, *here's* thy mother, *there*
> Thy uncle – this thy first cousin, and those
> Are all your near relations!
> (Act 3, scene 1)

69 **Youngest Daughter:** Laura's grandfather Lord St Clair, the Scottish peer first mentioned in letter the third, is thus found to have had four illegitimate daughters by Laurina, the Italian opera girl: Claudia, the mother of Laura; Matilda, the mother of Sophia; Bertha, the mother of Philander; and Agatha, the mother of Gustavus. All four daughters, as well as four children (except for Sophia), have unusual or outlandish names, scarcely used elsewhere by JA. Philander, 'a most beautifull Young Man', is given a type name suggesting his amorous prowesss; Gustavus, 'a Gracefull Youth', is given the name of the famous Swedish King, Gustavus Adolphus (1594–1632).

70 **have I any other Grand-Children in the House:** alluding to a passage in *Evelina* preceding the discovery scene, in which Sir John Belmont denies that Evelina is his child: 'I have already a daughter, to whom I owe every thing; and it is not three days since, that I had the pleasure of discovering a son; how many more sons and daughters may be brought to me, I am yet to learn, but I am, already, perfectly satisfied with the size of my family' (vol. 3, letter 17).

71 **Janetta the daughter of Macdonald:** Matilda, Lord St Clair's eldest daughter, married a Scotsman named Macdonald, the former owner of Macdonald-Hall. Their son, Sophia's cousin, is the current owner. In naming the younger Macdonald's daughter Janetta, JA is playing on her own name: Janetta is 'a manufactured, romanticized version of Janet, a Scottish form of Jane' (*Catharine*, p. 318). Aged fifteen, Janetta is only a few months older than JA, who was fourteen and a half according to the date at the end of 'Love and Freindship', 13 June 1790.

72 **never read the Sorrows of Werter:** Goethe's epistolary novel, *The Sorrows of Young Werther*, had been hugely popular and influential since its first publication in 1774. Its hero, hopelessly in love with

Lotte, who is engaged to another man, personifies sensibility and delicate feelings. Eventually, he commits suicide. Not reading *Werther* marks Graham as cold and unsympathetic. In Smith's *Emmeline*, Delemare recommends the novel enthusiastically to the heroine, so that she might learn 'the danger of trifling with violent and incurable passions' (vol. 2, ch. 7). In *The Loiterer*, 32, by Henry Austen, a young woman, Louisa, asks the narrator 'whether or no, I had ever read The Sorrows of Werter' (p. 12).

73 **Hair . . . auburn:** the absence of auburn hair is another sign of Graham's lack of elegance. There was a brief fashion for red hair in the 1780s; see C. Willett and Phillis Cunnington, *Handbook of English Costume in the Eighteenth Century*, rev. edn (London: Faber, 1972), p. 258. In *The Loiterer*, 15, by James Austen, a fashionable Oxford man has 'fine auburn hair', although it is 'tucked up in a plait, and concealed under a juckey [jockey] cap' (p. 10).

74 **Billet:** note.

75 **Gretna-Green:** a town in southern Scotland, just north of the border. Because Lord Hardwicke's Marriage Act of 1753, which required parental consent for marriages between those under 21, did not apply to Scotland, Gretna Green had become a favourite destination for eloping couples. It is, of course, ludicrous for Janetta and M'Kenzie to get married there, since they are already in Scotland and thus have no need to elope at all.

76 **at a considerable distance:** JA inserted this joke about travelling a long distance needlessly to replace two previous, less effective readings; see textual notes.

77 **we sate down . . . clear limpid stream:** Chapman suggests that this passage is 'a parody of Johnson's description of his sitting in Glen Shield in *A Journey to the Western Isles* (1775)', and that JA's Macdonald glances at Sir Alexander Macdonald, 'of whose sparing hospitality at Armadale in Skye both Johnson and Boswell complained' (*MW*, p. 459). Neither point is convincing, however: the two passages are dissimilar, and JA's Macdonald is inhospitable only in the eyes of his abusive guests. A more probable target is a scene in *Laura and Augustus*, in which the heroine sits down by a 'beautiful cascade' that 'lulls my soul into a kind of heavenly tranquillity' (vol. 1, letter 7); see Warren Derry, 'Sources of Jane

Austen's *Love and Freindship:* A Note', *Notes and Queries*, 235 (1990), 18–19. In 'Love and Freindship', Bromley's exotic 'hedge formed of lime, orange, and pomegranate' is bathetically replaced by elms and nettles.

78 **murmuring brook . . . turn-pike road:** the basis of two lines in 'Ode to Pity'; see 'Ode to Pity' note 9.

79 **if he is yet hung:** an exaggerated fear. If Augustus had been found guilty of stealing a 'considerable Sum of Money' (letter 9), he could have been hanged. He has, however, been arrested as a debtor, not as a thief; his creditors, not his father, have brought charges against him.

80 **Eastern Zephyr:** Laura's error, since 'Zephyr' is the west wind in classical mythology.

81 **He was like them, tall, magestic:** perhaps alluding to *Essays on Men and Manners* by the poet William Shenstone, who remarks that 'all trees have a character analogous to that of men'. Shenstone compares the 'manly character' to the 'majestic appearance' of the oak, whereas JA compares Augustus to a 'tall, magestic' elm (*The Works in Verse and Prose of William Shenstone* (London: R. and J. Dodsley, 1764), vol. 2, p. 134).

82 **blue Sattin Waistcoat striped with white:** striped waistcoats were fashionable in the 1780s, and blue was the colour made popular by *The Sorrows of Young Werther*. The hero's waistcoat also receives close attention in *Laura and Augustus:* 'his waistcoat and breeches are white lustring, the waistcoat wrought in rose-buds, and fastened with bunches of silver' (vol. 1, letter 10). In addition, there is a probable echo of a passage in *Tristram Shandy*, in which Susannah, on hearing that master Bobby is dead, finds her mind set upon 'a green sattin night-gown of my mother's' (vol. 5, ch. 7).

83 **apropos:** *à propos*; to the point, timely.

84 **road which ran murmuring behind us:** Laura here blends the 'murmuring brook', which lay before her and Sophia, with the turnpike road behind them.

85 **fashionably high Phaeton:** with their large wheels and high centres of gravity, gentlemen's phaetons were more readily overturned than other carriages. Since they were also favoured by young, fast drivers, they were especially likely to be involved in accidents. The

lower, more stable kind was favoured by ladies. Writing to her niece Elizabeth Bennet, Mrs Gardiner declares that for a carriage ride around Pemberley, 'A low phaeton, with a nice little pair of ponies, would be the very thing' (*P&P*, vol. 3, ch. 10).

86 **Life of Cardinal Wolsey ... thinking Mind:** Thomas Wolsey, the powerful cardinal and archbishop with papal aspirations during the reign of Henry VIII. His fall from favour and disgrace were frequently used to exemplify the dangers of pride. Shakespeare's Wolsey, in *King Henry VIII*, compares his downfall to a falling star:

> I shall fall
> Like a bright exhalation in the evening,
> And no man see me more.
> (Act 3, scene 2)

Knox-Shaw (*Jane Austen and the Enlightenment*, pp. 53–4) suggests that JA is also drawing on a passage in an essay by Hugh Blair. Recommending the judicious introduction of 'moral reflections' in tragedies, Blair cites Cardinal Wolsey's 'soliloquy upon his fall' in *King Henry VIII* as 'extremely natural' and 'at once instructive and affecting' (Blair, *Lectures on Rhetoric and Belles Lettres* (1783), ed. Harold F. Harding (Carbondale: Southern Illinois Press, 1965), vol. II, p. 512).

87 **horrid:** horrifying; a favourite term in Gothic fiction. Isabella Thorpe's reading, in *NA*, consists exclusively of 'horrid' novels (vol. 1, ch. 3).

88 **weltering in their blood:** lying prostrate, saturated with their own blood; a clichéd expression in Gothic and romantic fiction. The bloodshed normally derives from a duel, rather than a mundane carriage accident.

89 **sensible:** conscious; in possession of his senses.

90 **Cupid's Thunderbolts ... Shafts of Jupiter:** Laura is muddled in her madness. Cupid, the god of love, should have the shafts or arrows, and Jupiter the thunderbolts.

91 **Talk not ... Cucumber:** the Laura of Bromley's *Laura and Augustus* likewise has a mad speech, after her husband's death, in which she hears celestial music: 'hark! again do you not hear the music of the spheres! see how he rides on yonder cloud! how beautiful he

looks!' (vol. 3, letter 66). JA is also drawing on Tilburnia's mock mad scene in Sheridan's *The Critic*, which has a similar mixture of incongruous images:

> The wind whistles – the moon rises – see
> They have kill'd my squirrel in his cage!
> Is this a grasshopper! – Ha! no, it is my
> Whiskerandos – you shall not keep him –
> I know you have him in your pocket –
> An oyster may be cross'd in love! – Who says
> A whale's a bird?   (Act 3, scene 1)

Tilburnia's speech is in turn a parody of Ophelia's famous mad scene in *Hamlet* (Act 4, scene 5), while Chapman suggests that JA might also be parodying Lear's mad speeches on the heath in Act 3, scene 2 of *King Lear* (*MW*, p. 459). Only JA's Laura, however, reports her own ravings: part of the source of the comedy here.

92 **two Hours did I rave:** more sustained raving takes place in *Laura and Augustus* when the heroine hears of the death of husband, and 'for six hours, she was in successive fits' (vol. 3, letter 66).

93 **Seventeen . . . best of ages:** Cassandra Austen was then aged seventeen and five months, having celebrated her seventeenth birthday in January 1790.

94 **very plain . . . Bridget:** alluding to Richard Steele's *The Tender Husband* (London: Jacob Tonson, 1705), in which the heroine, Bridget Tipkin, finds her name objectionable. In place of Bridget, or its hated abbreviation Biddy, she favours 'a Name that glides through half a dozen tender Syllables, as *Elismonda*, *Clidamira*, *Deidamia*; that runs upon Vowels off the Tongue, not hissing through one's Teeth or breaking them with Consonants' (Act 2, scene 2).

95 **circulated and warmed my Blood:** knowingly learned medical discourse, drawing on theories of the circulation of the blood developed by William Harvey in the seventeenth century.

96 **galloping Consumption:** rapidly developing lung disease, or tuberculosis. It was a common fate for sensitive heroines, for whom it was considered appropriate, since it made its victims

pale and interesting, fading away rather than dying in a more unpleasant manner. In *Laura and Augustus*, the hero does succumb to a 'galloping consumption' (vol. 3, letter 49).

97 **It was so dark . . . Fellow-travellers:** drawing on the well-established novelistic convention by which travellers fail to recognize one another in the dark: a convention repeatedly used by both Henry and Sarah Fielding.

98 **Coach-box:** an elevated seat in front of the stage-coach, on which the driver sat; not intended for passengers.

99 **Basket:** the back compartment on the outside of a stage-coach, intended primarily for luggage. The coach is thus grossly over-loaded, with nine passengers in all, including five inside the coach and two beside the driver. It was designed to carry four to six people.

100 **Nymph . . . Swain:** poetical terms for a maiden and a country gallant or lover, highly inappropriate for the unpoetical Augusta and her deceased brother.

101 **Gilpin's Tour to the Highlands:** William Gilpin's recently pub-lished *Observations, Relative Chiefly to Picturesque Beauty, Made in the Year 1766, On Several Parts of Great Britain; Particularly the High-Lands of Scotland* (1789). JA names him humorously as one of the 'first of Men' in 'The History of England' (p. 182) and alludes to his theories of the picturesque elsewhere in her juve-nilia and her novels. That even the 'cold and insensible' Augusta is attracted to Scotland by Gilpin's enthusiasm for the wild-ness of its natural beauties indicates the persuasiveness of his writings.

102 **Stage . . . Acquaintance:** in turning his private coach into a public stagecoach, Philippa's husband ceases to be a gentleman and becomes a paid worker. Embarrassed by his changed cir-cumstances, he wishes to avoid his former friends.

103 **Edinburgh . . . Sterling:** Stirling, a town in central Scotland, is some thirty-six miles north-west of Edinburgh, the largest and most important Scottish city.

104 **visit the Highlands in a Postchaise:** improvements to roads and coaches made travel into the Highlands of Scotland increasingly popular in the later eighteenth century. A typical tour would include Loch Lomond and some of the great country seats, such

as Argyll at Inverary. In a post-chaise, travellers could choose their own itinerary and have exclusive possession of the carriage. Sir Edward, Lady Dorothea and Augusta, in contrast, are confined to the route between Edinburgh and Stirling; they can see only the unremarkable countryside between these two towns, and must share the crowded stagecoach with other passengers. In a letter of 23 August 1814, JA still had this ludicrous passage in her mind. Writing of a coach journey with various friends and relatives, she tells Cassandra: 'It put me in mind of my own Coach between Edinburgh & Sterling' (*L*, p. 270).

105 **desired me to step into the Basket:** the language suggests a conventional invitation to a drawing room, rather than a luggage compartment. Gustavus and Philander presumably avoid the inn where the other passengers alight because they cannot pay for any refreshment.

106 **Green tea:** tea roasted as soon as it has been gathered, and thus not allowed to ferment. Both the green tea and the 'buttered toast' of this breakfast reappear in *S*, in which Arthur Parker enjoys eating toast with 'a great dab' of butter (*MW*, p. 418). He also believes that green tea acts on him 'like Poison', so that 'the use of my right Side is entirely taken away for several hours!'.

107 **Sentimental:** not recorded in Johnson's Dictionary, this became a fashionable word in the mid-eighteenth century and a key part of the discourse of sensibility, emphasizing the importance of 'sentiments' (feelings and emotions), rather than rational thought.

108 **Staymaker:** a maker of women's corsets. JA has fun with the staymaker's name 'Staves': the wooden slats that surround a barrel.

109 **nine thousand Pounds . . . principal of it:** for illegitimate daughters, Bertha and Agatha were wealthy; Lord St Clair apparently endowed them with surprisingly large fortunes. They were imprudent to spend almost all of their capital; eighteenth-century practice was to live on the interest without touching the principal. The interest on £9,000 would have yielded the sisters £450 per year: enough to live in reasonable comfort, with two or three servants.

110 **common sitting Parlour:** a house of a reasonable size, including the Austens' rectory at Steventon, would typically contain two parlours: a common one, to which visitors would be admitted, and a private room reserved for family use. Unaware that this is a standard arrangement, Harriet Smith in *E* marvels at 'Mrs. Martin's having "*two* parlours, two very good parlours indeed"' (vol. 1, ch. 4).

111 **Silver Buckles:** expensive items for fastening shoes, worn by the wealthiest and most fashionable gentlemen. One hundred pounds, the sum that Philander and Gustavus assign to each category of their expenses, would buy about thirty pairs of silver buckles (*Catharine*, p. 321).

112 **strolling Company of Players:** a travelling group of actors, who presented often ill-rehearsed plays to local audiences.

113 **turn for the Stage:** punning deftly on the theatrical stage and the stagecoach, in which the two actors have just taken a 'turn'.

114 **Macbeth ... all the rest:** Gustavus and Philander thus contrive to play several characters who are on stage at the same time. Playing all three witches, Gustavus would have frequent conversations with himself, while Philander would play both Macbeth and those he plots to murder, such as Duncan and Macduff. JA might be drawing on *The Loiterer*, 12, by an anonymous contributor, in which a 'company of strolling players' inspires three daughters to rehearse the part of the witches in *Macbeth* (pp. 4–5).

115 **eclat:** *éclat*; French for flamboyance, conspicuousness.

116 **preferment:** advancement, employment.

117 **in their little Habitation:** again referring to the luggage compartment of the stagecoach as though it were a house.

118 **Covent Garden ... Lewis and Quick:** William Thomas Lewis (*c.* 1746–1811) and John Quick (1748–1831), two celebrated comic actors at Covent Garden, one of the two principal London theatres. They were at the height of their fame when 'Love and Freindship' was written.

119 **paid the Debt of Nature:** died, a clichéd euphemism.

120 **June 13th 1790:** the earliest date provided by JA in the juvenilia, although several items in 'Volume the First' were clearly written before 'Love and Freindship', some probably as early as 1787. JA

deleted the day, 'Sunday', before the date, 'June 13th', although 13 June was a Sunday in 1790.

LESLEY CASTLE

1 **Henry Thomas Austen Esqre:** JA's fourth brother (1771–1850), who completed his BA at Oxford in Spring 1792. Since the last of the letters in 'Lesley Castle' is dated 13 April 1792, JA might have dedicated it to Henry in honour of his graduation.

2 **Liberty . . . honoured me with:** as Southam notes, the wording here is ambiguous: JA could be referring to lost 'Novels' (juvenile fiction) by Henry that he had previously dedicated to her. Alternatively, she could be suggesting that she was now responding to a repeated request from Henry that she should write a piece for him. Or, the dedication could mean that she had already responded 'frequently' to his wish, and thus 'that a number of "Novels" dedicated to Henry have since disappeared' ('Jane Austen's Juvenilia: The Question of Completeness', *Notes and Queries*, 209 (1964), 181). The most probable explanation is that JA is referring to fiction of her own, not to be found in her manuscript notebooks or elsewhere.

3 **Messrs Demand . . . £105.0.0:** a mock-note, signed by Henry Austen, purportedly ordering his bank ('Messrs Demand and Co') to transfer to JA one hundred guineas (£105) in payment for her 'Lesley Castle'. Henry probably wrote this note at some time after he began his banking career in 1801. Southam suggests that the note might have been 'added by a member of the family' (*MW*, pp. 459–60), but it seems improbable that anyone other than Henry Austen himself would use his signature.

4 **My Brother:** Lesley, son of Sir George Lesley, is never given a first name. That JA relished his surname is suggested by a letter to her niece Anna of 18 September 1814, with remarks about Anna's novel in progress: 'I like the scene itself, the Miss Lesleys, Lady Anne, & the Music, very much.—Lesley *is* a noble name' (*L*, p. 275).

5 **Margaret:** JA also gives the name to Margaret Watson in *W* and to Margaret Dashwood, the youngest of the three Dashwood sisters in *S&S*.

6 **Aberdeen:** an ancient Scottish city, some 150 miles north of Edinburgh, on the north-east coast.

7 **Louisa:** a fashionable name in eighteenth-century fiction. In *NA*, Henry Tilney boasts of his 'knowledge of Julias and Louisas': the heroines of many of the hundreds of novels he has read (vol. 1, ch. 14).

8 **Rakehelly Dishonor Esqre:** the second of only two notes that JA added to her juvenilia. It turns 'dishonour' into a second male companion for the jilt Louisa, together with her lover Danvers, and thus jokingly augments the magnitude of her offence. Johnson defines 'Rakehelly' as 'wild; dissolute'; Rakehelly Dishonor is thus aptly named.

9 **stripling:** a youth.

10 **Perth:** another ancient Scottish city, in Perthshire, some fifty miles north of Edinburgh and 100 miles south of Aberdeen.

11 **old and Mouldering Castle . . . Rock:** JA is probably drawing here on the many descriptions of isolated, rock-bound castles in Samuel Johnson's *A Journey to the Western Islands of Scotland* (London: J. Pope, 1775). JA also took an interest in James Boswell's *Journal of a Tour to the Hebrides* (1785), telling Cassandra in a letter of 25 November 1798 that their father has bought a copy (*L*, p. 22). Boswell too describes the castles that he and Johnson visited during their tour, and JA's interest in Scotland was probably stimulated by both works.

12 **retired from almost all the World:** only two miles from Perth and regularly visiting ten nearby families, the Lesley sisters are not retired at all, and their castle is far less remote than Margaret claims.

13 **M'Leods . . . Macduffs:** most of the Scottish names here figure in Johnson's *Journey to the Western Islands of Scotland*. Three are bracketed together in Johnson's account of the Isle of Skye, which has lairds named Macdonald, Macleod and Mackinnon (p. 195). The last two names on JA's list, Macduff and Macbeth, are taken from Shakespeare's *Macbeth*, which Johnson mentions as well, when he encounters castles with *Macbeth* associations. *Macbeth* also figures in 'Love and Freindship' as the play acted by the travelling players, Gustavus and Philander (letter the fifteenth).

14 **bon-mot...repartée:** French for a clever or witty utterance and a 'smart reply' (Johnson). The use of fashionable French or Italian words and phrases in JA's fiction is usually a sign of a character's folly or duplicity.

15 **two first Letters in the Alphabet:** beginning to learn the alphabet at two, Louisa is indeed a prodigy. In the anonymous children's book *The History of Goody Two-Shoes*, the heroine teaches other children how to read by cutting letters out of pieces of wood. JA's signed copy of the book survives in private hands; see David Gilson, *A Bibliography of Jane Austen*, rev. edn (Winchester: St Paul's Bibliographies, 1997), p. 442. The alphabetical page is reproduced in Deirdre Le Faye, *Writers' Lives: Jane Austen* (London: British Library, 1998), p. 20.

16 **I live...Sussex:** almost at the opposite extremes of Great Britain, since Perthshire is in the east midlands of Scotland and Sussex on the south coast of England: the two counties are some five hundred miles apart.

17 **Tunbridge:** Tunbridge Wells; a spa town in Kent, not far from Charlotte Lutterell's home in Sussex. A lesser rival to Bath, it had reached its peak of popularity in the mid-eighteenth century.

18 **Glenford:** the name of the Lutterells' home in Sussex.

19 **Peggy:** a pet-form of Margaret. Charlotte can address her friend informally because they are old schoolfriends.

20 **Stewed Soup:** made stock for soup by simmering meat and bones in water.

21 **Whipt syllabub:** a cold dessert made with milk or cream, sherry, sugar and lemons, whisked (or 'whipt') together.

22 **Eloisa:** the only Eloisa in JA's fiction, she bears the name of the heroine of Pope's poem 'Eloisa to Abelard' (1717), whose love for Abelard also ended tragically.

23 **dressed:** prepared for the table.

24 **Physicians:** changed from 'Physician' to underline the Lutterells' wealth. A fashionable family would call in more than one physician in the case of a dangerous illness.

25 **Decline:** a wasting disease, such as tuberculosis. It was used as an all-purpose term when no precise diagnosis was possible.

26 **Bristol:** Bristol Hotwells; a spa with a pump-room just outside Bristol, a port and the largest city in the west of England. It

was a less fashionable but popular alternative to nearby Bath for pleasure-seekers and for invalids hoping to mend their health. Maggie Lane suggests that JA might have visited Bristol before writing 'Lesley Castle', noting that 'she seems aware of its customs' (*Jane Austen's England* (London: Robert Hale, 1986), p. 111).

27 **Mother-in-law:** stepmother.

28 **Matilda . . . Father's table:** as the elder sister, Martha took precedence over Margaret and would sit at the head of the table, with her father at the foot to carve. Susan Lesley, however, as the second wife, would take precedence over both sisters.

29 **Paris . . . Italy:** both form part of the classic Grand Tour of an English gentleman. The Tour was usually taken before marriage, as part of a man's education; here Lesley is taking it as a consolation for the end of his marriage.

30 **Cumberland:** a county in the north-west of England, bordering Scotland.

31 **Yorkshire:** a large county in the north-east of England, east of Cumberland.

32 **Estate near Aberdeen:** Lesley and his wife could live comfortably on the rents paid by the tenants of farms and cottages belonging to the estate. When he took 'the road to Aberdeen' at the beginning of the story, he was apparently returning to his estate briefly before setting off for Paris.

33 **Dunbeath:** probably the name of Lesley's estate near Aberdeen. There is also a fishing village named Dunbeath in the northern Highlands of Scotland, far from Aberdeen. Lesley's estate is presumably named after the village.

34 **one of the Universities there:** Chapman affirms that JA owed 'her knowledge of the two universities of Aberdeen' to Johnson's *Journey to the Western Islands*, while Southam finds this 'probably' her source (*MW*, p. 459; *VS*, p. 213). In his account of Aberdeen, Johnson describes King's College in Old Aberdeen and Marischal College in the new town, noting that they 'hold their sessions and confer degrees separately, with total independence of one on the other' (p. 27).

35 **I think and feel:** JA's underlining here suggests a literary allusion, which Chapman traces to Boswell's *Journal of a Tour to the Hebrides*

(*MW*, p. 460). In a footnote to his entry for 13 September 1773, Boswell refers to James II's grandson as Prince Charles Edward, rather than 'the Pretender', declaring that 'THE ONLY PERSON in the world who is intitled to be offended at this delicacy, "thinks and feels as I do"'. Explaining the quoted words, 'thinks and feels', L. F. Powell cites Boswell's journal for 15 June 1785, recording his conversation with George III on the subject of naming Charles Edward. At one point, according to Boswell, the King remarks, 'I think and feel as you do' (George Birkbeck Hill and L. F. Powell (eds.), *Boswell's Life of Johnson*, vol. v, *Journal of a Tour to the Hebrides* (Oxford: Clarendon, 1950), pp. 185–6, 531–2).

36 **Bristol-downs:** the hills around the city which, like the hotwells, were considered to have restorative properties. As the hotwells declined in popularity in the late eighteenth century, the downs and the elevated village of Clifton were becoming increasingly fashionable.

37 **Chairwomen:** charwomen; women 'hired accidentally for odd work, or single days' (Johnson). According to Swift's 'Directions to the Cook' in his ironic *Directions to Servants* (London: R. Dodsley, 1745), cited by Johnson to illustrate the word, they typically worked in the kitchen and were paid by the cook 'only with the broken Meat' (p. 41).

38 **Jellies:** leftover meat, preserved in jelly. All the items mentioned here are remains, transported to Bristol, of the enormous wedding dinner that Charlotte had prepared for her sister in Sussex.

39 **rouges a good deal:** applies red paint to her cheeks, like Rebecca in 'Frederic and Elfrida', although there JA changed 'Rouge' to 'Patches' (ch. 3). Since rouge was becoming unfashionable in the 1780s, Susan Lesley is displaying her characteristic bad taste.

40 **Brighthelmstone:** Brighton, an increasingly fashionable seaside resort on the Sussex coast, which since 1784 had been patronized by the dissolute Prince of Wales. JA gives several of her least admirable characters, beginning with Susan Lesley, a taste for Brighton. From Brighton, Lydia Bennet elopes with Wickham (*P&P*, vol. 2, ch. 16), and Maria Bertram goes there for her honeymoon (*MP*, vol. 2, ch. 3). The last word on Brighton in

JA's fiction is in *S*, in which Thomas Parker calls it one of 'your large, overgrown Places' (*MW*, p. 368).

41 **four thousand pounds ... places:** Susan Lesley's capital of £4,000 would yield £200 per annum at the usual 5 per cent interest. Charlotte believes that she will spend almost all of this on herself, so that her dowry will do nothing to mend Sir George's fortune.

42 **preside:** although both *MW* and *Catharine* replace 'preside' with 'reside', the manuscript clearly reads 'preside'. Doody and Murray add a note, suggesting that 'reside' would be 'ironically appropriate for Charlotte, who does reside at table' (*Catharine*, p. 324).

43 **so unfashionable a season of the year:** while the Bath season was at its height in February, the Bristol season traditionally ran from late March until the end of September. Lane cites a Bristol directory for 1793, advertising lodgings there for 'ten shillings a week for each room between 25 March and 29 September, and only half that sum during the other six months of the year' (*Jane Austen's England*, p. 111).

44 **set her cap at him:** attract him as her suitor. In *S&S*, the delicate Marianne Dashwood objects strongly to the expression as one 'which I particularly dislike. I abhor every common-place phrase by which wit is intended; and "setting one's cap at a man," or "making a conquest," are the most odious of all' (vol. 1, ch. 9). JA uses the same expression jokingly in a letter to Cassandra of 21 May 1801: 'I am prevented from setting my black cap at Mr Maitland by his having a wife & ten Children' (*L*, p. 88).

45 **London must be so gay:** the London season ran from late autumn until 4 June, when the King celebrated his official birthday. In March, the season was at its height, as the word 'giddy', which JA later changed to 'gay', suggests.

46 **more than four hundred miles:** Margaret Lesley's observation is accurate; Perth is some 450 miles north-west of London.

47 **Portman-Square:** a new, large, highly fashionable square on the western outskirts of London, begun in 1764 but not completed until the 1780s. Susan Lesley's enthusiasm for her 'charming House' there is another indication of her lack of taste: for JA, the most charming houses were not new ones.

48 **dismal old Weather-beaten Castle:** the disparaging depiction of Lesley Castle here contrasts with Johnson's praise for Boswell's ancestral estate of Auchinleck in *A Journey to the Western Islands*. Johnson admires 'the sullen dignity of the old castle', where he 'clambered with Mr. *Boswell* among the ruins, which afford striking images of ancient life'. Like Lesley Castle, it is 'built upon a point of rock' (p. 378).

49 **rigmerole:** rigmarole, an incoherent, long-winded, rambling account. This colloquial term, too recent to appear in Johnson's *Dictionary*, is aptly given to the fashionable Susan Lesley.

50 **Miss Somebody:** the disgraced Louisa Lesley, who has run away with 'Danvers and dishonour'.

51 **I hate everything Scotch:** Scottish melodies and songs ('Airs'), and poems by authors such as Allan Ramsay, James Thomson, James Macpherson and Robert Fergusson, were widely appreciated in England, and by 1792 Robert Burns (1759–96) was at the height of his fame. Scottish success in the arts, however, was also widely resented, and Susan Lesley voices popular prejudice. Scottish mountains were a favourite subject of landscape artists seeking for grandiose effects.

52 **at my toilett:** toilette or dressing table; hence, dressing, applying make-up, arranging hair, etc.

53 **Galleries and Antichambers:** long passages, typically used for hanging paintings (and for exercise in bad weather), and antechambers or withdrawing chambers, used as reception rooms by the occupants of adjoining bedchambers.

54 **Public-places:** London's numerous cultural pleasures, including theatres, concert halls, dances, artists' studios, picture galleries, museums, exhibitions and pleasure gardens, as well as churches.

55 **Vaux-hall:** Vauxhall gardens, the oldest of London's pleasure gardens. Its twelve acres, containing shrubbery, walks, statues and cascades, were located in Lambeth, south of the Thames from Westminster Abbey. In 1792, the price of admission was doubled from one to two shillings, in an attempt to reduce rowdy behaviour. The gardens remained popular until well into the nineteenth century.

56 **Beef there is cut so thin:** the extreme thinness of Vauxhall sliced meat was proverbial and constituted one of the pleasure garden's many attractions.

57 **Receipts:** recipes.

58 **drawing Pictures . . . drawing Pullets:** again using the device of syllepsis, a form of zeugma in which a verb takes two different and incongruous objects. Charlotte draws, or eviscerates, pullets, or young hens, as part of her food preparations, while her sister draws at an easel.

59 **even . . . She play'd:** Charlotte prides herself on her readiness to applaud even the simple music accompanying a country dance: an English dance of rural origin, in which couples stand face to face in two parallel lines.

60 **Malbrook:** a very popular eighteenth-century French nursery song, 'Malbrouck s'en va-t-en guerre' (Marlborough is off to battle), celebrating the military exploits of the Duke of Marlborough as leader of the coalition armies in the War of Spanish Succession (1702–13).

61 **Bravo . . . Poco presto:** a comic mixture of appropriate and inappropriate Italian musical terms. The first three are expressions of admiration: '*Bravo*' and '*Bravissimo*' meaning 'excellent' and 'outstanding', while '*Encora*' is the traditional demand for more music when an audience is especially pleased. The other terms, however, are all markings for instrumental performers. '*Da capo*' is an indication at the end of a piece to repeat from the beginning; '*allegretto*' calls for the tempo to be somewhat brisk, less brisk than '*allegro*', and '*con espressione*' for particular expression. The final term, '*Poco presto*', is a comic nonce phrase: to play '*presto*' is to play very fast, but to play '*Poco presto*' would be to play a little or somewhat very fast.

62 **Execution:** level of performance.

63 **Harpsichord:** as Patrick Piggott notes, by the early 1790s the pianoforte was replacing the harpsichord as the standard family instrument. The first mention of a pianoforte by JA is in 'Lady Susan' (Letter 17); see Piggott, *The Innocent Diversion: Music in the Life and Writings of Jane Austen* (London: Clover Hill Editions, 1979), pp. 32–7.

64 **satirical:** a voguish term, which JA returns to in *S&S*. There, Lady Middleton's dislike of Elinor and Marianne is explained: 'because they were fond of reading, she fancied them satirical: perhaps without exactly knowing what it was to be satirical; but *that* did not signify. It was censure in common use, and easily given' (vol. 2, ch. 14).

65 **languid:** another voguish term. Here it has the sense of sluggish and enfeebled.

66 **Grosvenor Street:** among the most prestigious addresses in London, with many notable residents: the Marlowes are obviously a wealthy family.

67 **Blooming Complexion:** apparently a euphemism, since Lady Lesley owes her 'bloom' to rouge.

68 **proper size for real Beauty:** the ideal height for a woman in JA's fiction seems to be between medium and tall, as exemplified by Jane Fairfax in *E*: 'Her height was pretty, just such as almost everybody would think tall, and nobody could think very tall' (vol. 2, ch. 2). Henry Austen's 'Biographical Notice' of 1818 describes JA's own stature as 'that of true elegance. It could not have been increased without exceeding the middle height' (*Memoir*, p. 139).

69 **Toad-eater:** a 'toady' or sycophant. The term derives from the practice, among mountebanks' assistants, of pretending to swallow a toad; the mountebank would then pretend to expel the poisons supposedly ingested. In Burney's *Evelina*, the heroine is distressed at being called 'a kind of toad-eater', a 'mortifying appellation': a charge stemming from her accompanying the wealthy Miss Mirvan in London (vol. 3, letter 4).

70 **a Journey of seven Days:** a reasonable rate of progress for a journey of some 450 miles: about 64 miles per day. Travellers could cover up to 100 miles per day with changes of horses, but the Lesleys are in no great hurry.

71 **in Papers, and in Printshops:** in newspapers and in prints bought in print-sellers' shops. Margaret Lesley, of course, is deluded. Public figures, famous beauties, etc., were the subjects of frequent gossip in newspapers and were often depicted in satirical prints, but an obscure visitor from Scotland would attract no such attention.

72 **Small-pox:** since Margaret Lesley has already had smallpox, she is immune to its disfiguring scars.

73 **Monday se'night:** seven nights ago; a week last Monday.

74 **Rout:** a fashionable gathering, reception or evening party.

75 **Mrs Kickabout's:** akin to a type name in Restoration and eighteenth-century drama. It apparently alludes to the lady's fondness for dancing, perhaps deriving from 'kickshaw', which Milton, writing 'kickshoe', 'used in contempt of dancing' (Johnson).

76 **From the first moment ... Life:** echoing Laura's words in 'Love and Freindship', at the end of Letter 5th: 'no sooner did I first behold him, than I felt that on him the happiness or Misery of my future Life must depend'. The lines in 'Love and Freind-ship' are a revision, and although the story is dated some two years earlier than 'Lesley Castle', it is possible that JA wrote them at the same time as or even after the passage in the later work.

77 **putting an end ... commenced:** the addition of the word 'never' here is a deft stylistic revision, turning Margaret's vexation about the interruption of a conversation into a much odder vexation about the interruption of a conversation that never takes place.

78 **Lady Flambeau:** another type name. The fashionable Lady Flambeau would make use of a 'flambeau', a lighted wax torch, in descending from her carriage at night.

79 **Pope's Bulls:** papal edicts. Since Lesley has 'turned Roman-catholic' and since his Protestant wife has committed adultery, he can obtain a papal affirmation that his marriage is no longer valid. He can thus marry again in Italy, but not in England, where the papal edict has no authority. JA is echoing the diffi-culties experienced by Richardson's Sir Charles Grandison, who is betrothed to an Italian Catholic but is romantically involved with an English Protestant.

80 **soon to be married:** like Lesley, Louisa can marry again in Italy, as her first marriage has been annulled. JA first wrote that Louisa 'obtained another of the Pope's Bulls for annulling'; she pre-sumably deleted this because the first edict would apply to both parties.

THE HISTORY OF ENGLAND

1 **Charles the 1st:** by beginning her account with Henry IV and concluding with the death of Charles I, JA can depict English history as the rise and fall of the Stuarts. She covers the earlier reigns briefly, presenting them primarily as paving the way for the House of Stuart: the House of Lancaster (Henry IV to Henry VI) being succeeded by the House of York (Edward IV to Richard III) and then by the House of Tudor (Henry VII to Elizabeth I), before culminating at last in the Stuart monarchy (James I to James II). JA's title is modelled on that of Oliver Goldsmith's four-volume *The History of England, from the Earliest Times to the Death of George II* (London: T. Davies, 1771). Her extensive marginalia on Goldsmith's volumes, probably written shortly before she wrote her own history, which is dated November 1791, are transcribed in Appendix B. JA might also have read Goldsmith's two-volume *An History of England in a Series of Letters from a Nobleman to His Son* (1764) and his popular digest of the 1771 history, *An Abridgement of the History of England* (1774). In addition to Goldsmith, JA's primary source, as she repeatedly acknowledges, is Shakespeare: the history plays from Richard II to Henry VIII.

2 **partial, prejudiced, and ignorant Historian:** alluding to the preface to Goldsmith's *History of England*, which concludes with the hope that 'the reader will admit my impartiality' (vol. 1, p. viii). JA also alludes to this in one of her marginalia on the *History*: 'Oh! Dr. Goldsmith Thou art as partial an Historian as myself!' (Appendix B, p. 337).

3 **To Miss Austen:** JA had previously dedicated 'The beautifull Cassandra' to her elder sister Cassandra. Here she is an especially appropriate dedicatee, since she illustrated the 'History' with thirteen medallion portraits, signing all but one 'C E Austen pinx': painted (*pinxit*) by Cassandra Elizabeth Austen. The portrait of Henry VIII is unsigned, probably through inadvertence.

4 **Revd George Austen:** the dedicatee of a comedy, 'The Mystery', in 'Volume the First', and now included in another dedication. JA thus associates him with her plays and her historical writing, rather than her short fiction.

5 **very few Dates in this History:** perhaps alluding to the first of Goldsmith's histories of England (1764), which, remarkably, contains no dates at all. JA, in contrast, does provide some dates, and even precise months and days for certain events. Goldsmith's four-volume history has numerous dates, but they are given in an unsystematic manner, which JA apparently found unhelpful. For her own list of dates in the first volume of the annotated Goldsmith, see Appendix B, pp. 318–19.

6 **Pomfret Castle:** Pontefract, a Norman castle in Yorkshire, southeast of Leeds. In *Richard II*, Shakespeare depicts the murder of the King at the behest of Henry IV, who afterwards declares: 'They love not poison that do poison need' (Act 5, scene 6).

7 **who was his Wife:** alluding to the absence of Henry IV's wives among the characters in Shakespeare's *Henry IV, Parts 1 and 2*. Henry was married twice; by his first wife, Mary Bohun, he had four sons and a daughter.

8 **long speech . . . still longer:** Henry IV's long speech is in *Henry IV, Part 2*, beginning 'Thy wish was father, Harry, to that thought' (Act 4, scene 5). The Prince's reply, which in fact is a few lines shorter, begins 'O, pardon me, my liege'.

9 **succeeded by his Son Henry:** in 1413.

10 **beat Sir William Gascoigne:** this incident is recounted by Goldsmith and dramatized by Shakespeare. In *Henry IV, Part 2*, William Gascoigne, the Lord Chief Justice, reminds Prince Harry of his offence: 'Your Highness pleased to forget my place . . . And strook me in my very seat of judgment' (Act 5, scene 2). JA's comic treatment of the incident seems indebted to that of her brother James, in *The Loiterer*, 43. Here, a correspondent named Bluster declares:

The brightest aeras of our History have been equally distinguished for Battles and Boxing Matches; for beating our Enemies abroad, and threshing our Friends at home. Henry the Vth, who afterwards gave the French so many *Cross-Buttocks*, first began practising against one of the Judges in England, and laid in a blow so neatly, that his Lordship, it seems, could neither *stop* nor *return* it. (p. 5)

11 **Henry the 5th:** Cassandra's portrait of Henry is copied from that of a soldier, in a blue uniform, in Henry Bunbury's satiric print 'Recruits' (1780); see Jan Fergus *et al.* (eds.), *The History of England* (Edmonton: Juvenilia Press, 1995), pp. ii, iv. The same print by Bunbury furnishes the portrait of Edward IV. This is the only portrait of a monarch in military dress, and the Battle of Agincourt is the only battle mentioned in the 'History'.

12 **forsaking all his dissipated Companions:** in the final scene of *Henry IV, Part 2*, the former Prince Harry, now Henry V, turns his back on Falstaff:

> I know thee not, old man, fall to thy prayers.
> How ill white hairs become a fool and jester!
> (Act 5, scene 5)

Goldsmith also recounts the King's renunciation of his former companions in his *History* (vol. 2, p. 176), although his account suggests that the King took their futures under consideration.

13 **Lord Cobham was burnt alive:** Lord Cobham, formerly Sir John Oldcastle, probably Shakespeare's model for Falstaff, was executed for heresy in 1417. Goldsmith lingers over his death with apparent relish: 'He was hung up with a chain by the middle; and thus at a slow fire burned, or rather roasted, alive' (vol. 2, p. 179). Here and elsewhere in her history, JA satirizes Goldsmith's fondness for such depicting such scenes.

14 **turned his thoughts to France:** as in Shakespeare's *Henry V*, where the King declares: 'For we have now no thought in us but France' (Act 1, scene 2).

15 **famous Battle of Agincourt:** a major part of Shakespeare's *Henry V* and of Goldsmith's *History*, in which it occupies several pages, but dismissed in a line by JA.

16 **Catherine . . . Shakespear's account:** Katherine, daughter of the French monarch Charles VI, is wooed by Henry in the final scene of *Henry V*. She is 'agreable' there in the sense of both likeable and, since she accepts Henry's hand in marriage, well disposed.

17 **succeeded by his son Henry:** in 1422, as a year-old infant.

18 **this Monarch's Sense:** drawing on Goldsmith's *History*. In his version, Henry fell into a 'distemper' in 1454, which 'so far encreased his natural imbecility that it even rendered him

incapable of maintaining the appearance of royalty' (vol. 2, p. 223).

19 **Lancastrian . . . right side:** as a 'partial' historian, JA champions the cause of the Yorkists against the Lancastrians in the War of the Roses (red rose Lancastrians versus white rose Yorkists). Henry VI was descended from John of Gaunt, Duke of Lancaster, the son of Edward III. His rival for the throne, the Duke of York, was descended from Edward III by John of Gaunt's elder brother: JA finds his claim superior.

20 **vent my Spleen:** give free expression to ill-humour, passion, etc. In the eighteenth century, the spleen was still regarded as an organ harbouring such emotions: 'it is supposed the seat of anger and melancholy' (Johnson).

21 **Margaret of Anjou . . . pity her:** the daughter of the Duke of Anjou, who married Henry VI in 1445. In Shakespeare's *Henry VI* trilogy, she is depicted as a scheming manipulator of the weak king and an enemy of the Duke of York.

22 **Joan of Arc:** the woman who inspired French forces to victories over the English in 1429. Captured by the English, she was tried, found guilty of treason and witchcraft and burned at the stake in 1431. Shakespeare depicts her unsympathetically in *Henry VI, Part 1.*

23 **row:** not a quarrel, as in modern usage, but a disturbance or commotion. JA uses a recently coined colloquial term to depict the historical event in a thoroughly casual fashion. In *The Loiterer*, 12, by an anonymous Oxonian, an Oxford student boasts that he will 'now and then kick up a *row* in the street' (p. 12).

24 **The King was murdered:** Shakespeare depicts both the murder of the deposed Henry VI and the banishment of Queen Margaret to France in *Henry VI, Part 3* (Act 5, scenes 6–7).

25 **Edward the 4th Ascended the Throne:** in 1461.

26 **Edward the 4th:** Cassandra's portrait of Edward IV is copied from that of an especially ill-dressed and unprepossessing recruit in Bunbury's caricature 'The Recruits', also her source for the portrait of Henry V. The illustration contrasts comically with JA's reference to Edward's 'Beauty and his Courage', taken from Goldsmith's *History*, which declares that 'his best qualities were courage and beauty' (vol. 2, p. 250).

27 **marrying ... engaged to another:** Edward was expected to marry Bona of Savoy, the sister-in-law of Louis XVI. Instead, he secretly married Elizabeth Woodville in 1464.

28 **confined in a Convent ... Henry the 7th:** Elizabeth was confined in Bermondsey Abbey by Henry VII. Since this event occurred after Edward's death, its inclusion here suggests a lack of memorable incidents in his unremarkable reign.

29 **play written about her:** Nicholas Rowe's *The Tragedy of Jane Shore: Written in Imitation of Shakespeare's Style* (1714). A success in its time, Rowe's play was still produced regularly in the 1780s and early 1790s.

30 **succeeded by his son:** Edward V, who succeeded his father in 1483, at the age of twelve, but was deposed only two months later.

31 **Edward the 5th ... picture:** despite JA's mock claim, Goldsmith's *History* has a portrait of Edward V. Although Cassandra did not provide an illustration, JA left space for one in the manuscript. She also wrote the words 'Edward the' below the space, presumably realizing, before completing the title, that no portrait of Edward V was to be provided.

32 **very respectable Man:** JA alludes to this sentence at the beginning of *NA*, declaring that Catherine Morland's father was 'a very respectable man, though his name was Richard' (vol. 1, ch. 1). She also seems to allude to Richard III in a letter to Cassandra of 15 September 1796, telling her sister that 'Mr Richard Harvey's match is put off, till he has got a Better Christian name, of which he has great Hopes' (*L*, p. 10).

33 **I am inclined to beleive true:** contradicting her previous remark that Edward V was 'murdered by his Uncle's Contrivance'. JA thus contrives to support both those who believed in Richard's guilt (including Shakespeare in *Richard III* and Goldsmith) and his defenders. His principal advocate was Horace Walpole, author of *Historic Doubts on the Life and Reign of Richard III* (1768), which provoked much discussion among eighteenth-century critics and historians. Ironically, Walpole came to disavow his own belief in Richard's innocence. In a Postscript to *Historic Doubts* dated February 1793, fifteen months later than JA's 'History', Walpole, disillusioned by Revolutionary terror, wrote: 'I must

now believe that any atrocity may have been attempted or practised by an ambitious prince of the blood aiming at the crown
in the fifteenth century' (*The Works of Horatio Walpole* (London:
G. G. and J. Robinson, 1798), vol. 2, p. 252*). In her marginalia on Goldsmith's *History*, JA wrote the word 'wretches' beside
his account of the death of the young princes, leaving open the
question of Richard's guilt or innocence (Appendix B, p. 319).
She returns to the subject again in 'Catharine', in which the
heroine engages in a 'historical dispute' with the unprincipled
Edward Stanley, who 'warmly defend[s]' Richard's character
(pp. 285, 286).

34 **kill his Wife:** both Shakespeare and Goldsmith also find Richard
III guilty of plotting the murder of his wife, Anne Neville.

35 **Perkin Warbeck:** an imposter, who during the reign of Henry
VII claimed to be Richard, Duke of York, son of Edward IV.

36 **Lambert Simnel:** another imposter during the reign of
Henry VII, who claimed to be Edward, Earl of Warwick, son of
Richard III's (and Edward IV's) brother, the Duke of Clarence.

37 **made a great fuss . . . Crown:** compressing the complex arguments over Henry, Earl of Richmond's claim to the throne,
which he derived from his mother, Margaret Beaufort, the great-
granddaughter of John of Gaunt (the third son of Edward III).
The first of the Tudor monarchs, Henry VII was the founder of
the line that culminated in the reign of Elizabeth I, the villainess
of JA's history.

38 **battle of Bosworth:** Richard III's defeat by Henry's forces and his
death at the battle of Bosworth, a town in Leicestershire, form
the climax of Shakespeare's *Richard III* (Act 5, scenes 3–5).

39 **succeeded to it:** in 1485.

40 **Henry the 7th:** Cassandra's portrait, depicting Henry in ragged
clothes, emphasizes his 'Avarice', briefly mentioned by JA in her
account of Edward IV.

41 **Princess Elizabeth of York:** in marrying Elizabeth, daughter of
the first of the Yorkist monarchs, Edward IV, Henry VII united
the houses of York and Lancaster.

42 **Characters in the World:** Margaret, the elder of Henry VII's two
daughters, married James IV of Scotland. Their granddaughter,
Mary Queen of Scots, is the heroine of JA's history.

43 **amiable young Woman . . . hunting:** following Goldsmith, who describes Lady Jane Grey as 'the wonder of her age' and gives an account of her 'reading Plato's works in Greek, while all the rest of the family were hunting in the Park' (vol. 3, p. 36). The great-granddaughter of Henry VII, Lady Jane acceded to the throne in July 1553, but was deposed by Queen Mary nine days later and executed in February 1554.

44 **taken into the King's Kitchen:** again following Goldsmith. Perkin Warbeck, after taking shelter in the monastery of Beaulieu in the New Forest, was eventually executed, while Simnel 'was pardoned, and made a scullion [a lowly dish washer and cleaner] in the king's kitchen' (vol. 2, p. 286).

45 **succeeded by his son Henry:** in 1509.

46 **Henry the 8th:** Cassandra's portrait ridicules Henry VIII by giving him a large moustache and a red nightcap (worn indoors as a morning cap), with a jaunty decorative tassel: a style popular in the 1780s. The cap might indicate that Henry was better suited to the interior of houses than to the field of battle.

47 **lay his bones among them:** JA mentions only the last days of Cardinal Wolsey (1475–1530). For many years a favourite of Henry VIII, Wolsey exercised remarkable powers in foreign and domestic policy. In disgrace at the end of his life, he was summoned to London but died on his way at Leicester Abbey. Goldsmith recounts his arrival at the abbey, where he declared: 'Father abbot, I am come to lay my bones among you' (vol. 2, p. 361).

48 **Anna Bullen:** the spelling used by both Shakespeare and Goldsmith for Henry's second wife, Anne Boleyn. Goldsmith, like JA, links Henry VIII's defiance of the Pope and his reformation of religion in England with his riding through the streets: 'to colour over his disobedience to the pope with an appearance of triumph, he passed with his beautiful bride through London, with a magnificence greater than had been ever known before' (vol. 2, p. 364).

49 **Crimes with which she was accused:** Anne Boleyn was charged with adultery, found guilty and executed in 1536, three years after her marriage to Henry VIII. Both Shakespeare and Goldsmith treat her sympathetically, as a victim falsely accused.

50 **6th of May:** Goldsmith transcribes a letter from Anne Boleyn to Henry VIII in which she proclaims her innocence. It concludes with the sentence 'From my doleful prison in the Tower, this sixth of May' (vol. 2, p. 384). JA is mocking Goldsmith for including the precise date but not, at this point, specifying the year, 1536.

51 **too numerous to be mentioned:** Henry's 'Crimes and Cruelties', including his brutal treatment of his wives, are recounted at length by Goldsmith.

52 **abolishing Religious Houses:** because of their opposition to Henry's breaking away from the Roman Church. According to Goldsmith, 'three hundred and seventy-six monasteries were suppressed' (vol. 2, p. 373).

53 **landscape of England in general:** alluding to eighteenth-century enthusiasm for medieval ruins, cultivated by the writers of Gothic fiction. In *NA*, Catherine Morland regrets the demolition of the ruined part of the Abbey, and 'could have raved at the hand which had swept away what must have been beyond the value of all the rest' (vol. 2, ch. 8).

54 **5th Wife…Marriage:** Catherine Howard, executed in 1542, less than two years after her marriage to Henry VIII. According to Goldsmith, she 'confessed her incontinence before marriage, but denied her having dishonoured the king's bed since their union' (vol. 2, p. 402).

55 **noble Duke of Norfolk:** the fourth Duke of Norfolk, grandson of the third Duke, whom JA has just mentioned. He wished to restore Catholicism to England, was a supporter and would-be suitor of Mary Queen of Scots and plotted against Elizabeth I. Found guilty of treason, he was executed in 1572. Southam suggests that there might be a 'sly allusion' here to Sophia Lee's historical novel *The Recess; or, A Tale of Other Times* (1785), in which 'a secret marriage takes place between Mary and Norfolk' (*VS*, p. 215). The modern editor of *The Recess*, April Alliston, likewise suggests that JA 'might be poking fun' at the novel 'by humorously exaggerating Lee's sympathy with Mary at the expense of Elizabeth' (*The Recess* (Lexington: University Press of Kentucky, 2000), p. xxi).

56 **The King's last wife:** Catherine Parr, who married Henry VIII in 1543, 'managed this capricious tyrant's temper with prudence

and success' (Goldsmith, *History*, vol. 2, p. 406). She survived Henry, who died in 1547, by a year.

57 **the Duke of Somerset:** Jane Seymour's brother Edward, designated Lord Protector when Edward acceded to the throne in 1547 and created Duke of Somerset.

58 **first of Men . . . Gilpin:** JA sings the praises of the 'noble and gallant' Earl of Essex in her section on Elizabeth I, comparing him to Frederic Delamere, the hero of Charlotte Smith's *Emmeline* (1788). William Gilpin, another of her favourites, shared some of her sympathy for Mary Queen of Scots. In his *Observations, Relative Chiefly to Picturesque Beauty* (London: R. Blamire, 1789), Gilpin refers to 'that unfortunate princess, Mary, queen of Scotts; whose beauty, and guilt have united pity, and detestation through every part of her history' (vol. 1, p. 92); see Darrel Mansell, 'Another Source of Jane Austen's "The History of England"', *Notes and Queries*, 212 (1967), 305.

59 **the Duke of Northumberland:** Goldsmith recounts the rivalry between the Dukes of Northumberland and of Somerset, with Northumberland prevailing. After the execution of Somerset, Northumberland arranged a marriage between his fourth son and Lady Jane Grey. He also persuaded Edward VI to make a settlement of the throne in favour of Lady Jane, excluding Henry VIII's elder daughter, Mary, and his younger daughter, Elizabeth, on the grounds of their supposed illegitimacy.

60 **the King died:** Edward VI died at the age of sixteen. The Duke of Northumberland was rumoured to have precipitated his death by dismissing the royal physicians attending him.

61 **vanity:** originally 'Cockylorum', JA's spelling of 'cockalorum', an early eighteenth-century colloquialism for a self-important little man.

62 **passing that way:** JA devotes half of her account of Edward VI to Lady Jane Grey, but does not give her a section of her own or an illustration by Cassandra. Goldsmith also incorporates his account of Lady Jane into his chapters on Edward VI and Mary, but his treatment of her death is at once more sensational and sympathetic than JA's. While she was being led to execution, according to Goldsmith, 'the officers of the Tower met her, bearing along the headless body of her husband streaming with blood,

in order to be interred in the Tower-chapel. She looked on the corpse for some time without any emotion; and then, with a sigh, desired them to proceed' (vol. 3, pp. 49–50). In her comic treatment of Lady Jane, JA appeals to contemporary prejudice against learned ladies, especially ladies knowing Greek.

63 **succeed her Brother:** in 1553. The daughter of Henry VIII and his first wife, Catherine of Aragon, Mary was half-sister to Edward VI. She proclaimed herself his successor, disavowing the brief reign of Queen Jane.

64 **Martyrs . . . a dozen:** a gross understatement. Goldsmith estimates that close to three hundred English men and women 'suffered by fire' during the religious persecutions of Mary's reign (vol. 3, p. 62).

65 **Philip . . . Armadas:** Mary married Philip, King of Spain, in 1554. Over thirty years later, in 1588, Philip's famous Armada—a fleet of warships carrying a large force of some 17,000 soldiers—set sail from Lisbon in an attempted invasion of England. It was defeated by the British navy, under the command of Sir Francis Drake.

66 **succeeded to the Throne:** the daughter of Henry VIII and his second wife, Anne Boleyn, Elizabeth succeeded Mary in 1558.

67 **Elizabeth:** Cassandra's portrait of Queen Elizabeth, facing one of Mary, Queen of Scots, depicts her as a crone, with a hooked nose and protruding chin. The chin seems to have initiated or been part of a family joke. In *P&P*, Lydia Bennet finds a waiter 'an ugly fellow' and declares, 'I never saw such a long chin in my life' (vol. 2, ch. 16). In a letter of 2–3 March 1814, JA tells Cassandra: 'I have seen nobody in London yet with such a long chin as Dr Syntax [William Combe]' (*L*, p. 256). The wording suggests that JA was looking out for chins of this kind. In his prologue to Susanna Centlivre's comedy *The Wonder*, performed at Steventon on 28–29 December 1787, Austen's brother James had also mocked Elizabeth's appearance:

> Distinguished both by ugliness & dress,
> First of the brilliant troop, march'd great Queen Bess.
> (lines 27–8)

68 **Lord Burleigh, Sir Francis Walshingham:** respectively Elizabeth's secretary of state and privy counsellor. The 'many people' who believed that Elizabeth was ably served include Goldsmith, who writes that she 'was indebted to her good fortune, that her ministers were excellent' (vol. 3, p. 152).

69 **Mr Whitaker ... Mrs Knight:** John Whitaker, author of *Mary Queen of Scots Vindicated* (1787); Anne Lefroy, wife of the rector of Ashe, near Steventon, a close friend of JA and her family; and Catherine Knight, wife of Thomas Knight, the childless couple who had adopted JA's brother Edward. Like JA in her 'History', Whitaker is both vehemently pro-Stuart and a fervent supporter of his subject. Mansell suggests that JA was led to Whitaker's vindication by a note in Gilpin's *Observations*; 'Another Source', p. 305. The note, documenting Gilpin's remark on Mary quoted above, observes that Whitaker 'hath given the public some new lights on the history of Mary; and thrown the guilt on Elizabeth' (vol. 1, p. 92). JA too, of course, has vigorously 'thrown the guilt on Elizabeth'. For JA's marginalia, in her copy of *Elegant Extracts*, on portraits of Mary and Elizabeth by William Robertson and David Hume, see Appendix C. JA's enthusiasm for Mary was noted by her niece Caroline Austen, who recalled that 'she always encouraged my youthful beleif in Mary Stuart's perfect innocence of all the crimes with which History has charged her memory' (*Memoir*, p. 173). JA's nephew James Edward Austen-Leigh, Caroline's elder brother, likewise recalled that she was a 'vehement defender' of Mary (*Memoir*, p. 71).

70 **abandoned by her Son:** James VI of Scotland (later James I of England), who succeeded Mary on the Scottish throne.

71 **Fotheringay Castle ... 1586:** a medieval castle in Nottinghamshire, in which Mary was imprisoned for nineteen years before her execution. JA gives the correct day and month, but the wrong year: 1586 in place of 1587.

72 **Sir Francis Drake ... round the World:** in an expedition financed by Elizabeth, Drake circumnavigated the globe in 1577.

73 **one who tho' now but young:** probably alluding to JA's brother Francis, then aged seventeen, who had left HMS *Perseverance* three weeks earlier, on 5 November, and was now serving on

HMS *Minerva*. He went on to become Admiral of the Fleet in 1863, at the age of eighty-nine, but as Southam notes, this position was not a reward for exceptional service but determined on the basis of seniority (*Jane Austen and the Navy*, p. 57). The allusion is more likely to be to Francis than to Charles Austen for several reasons. Francis Austen shared both Drake's first name and his piety: both were notably religious. Charles, then aged twelve, had joined the Royal Naval Academy in July 1791, but had not yet served aboard a ship; JA therefore had as yet less reason to boast about him than about his elder brother.

74 **Lord Essex . . . Delamere:** Goldsmith's *History* recounts the complex, quasi-romantic dealings between Elizabeth and Robert, Earl of Essex, who was long her favourite courtier. Like Frederic Delamare, the hero of Charlotte Smith's first novel *Emmeline* (1788), Essex was rash and impetuous. Since Emmeline breaks off her engagement to Delamere and marries another suitor, Godolphin, she could be said to torment him. Essex, however, who instigated a rebellion that led to his execution, is usually regarded as the torment of Elizabeth.

75 **25th of Febry:** JA gives the correct date for Essex's execution but fails to mention the year: 1601.

76 **hand on his Sword:** an incident recounted by Goldsmith. After Essex had discourteously turned his back on the queen, she gave him a box on the ear. Then, 'instead of recollecting himself . . . he clapped his hand to his sword' (vol. 3, p. 139).

77 **survive his loss:** Elizabeth died in March 1603, two years after Essex's execution.

78 **his Mother's death:** repeating the charge that Mary Queen of Scots 'was abandoned by her son'.

79 **Anne of Denmark:** James I married Anne of Denmark in 1589.

80 **died before his father:** Prince Henry died in 1612, at the age of eighteen; James I died in 1625; Henry's 'unfortunate Brother', Charles I, was executed in 1649.

81 **partial to the roman catholic religion:** reversing the position of almost all eighteenth-century English historians, including Goldsmith, who wrote with a Protestant bias.

82 **very uncivil . . . Lord Mounteagle:** alluding to, without naming, the Gunpowder Plot, by which Sir Henry Percy and other

Catholic conspirators planned to blow up 'the king and both houses of parliament at a blow' (Goldsmith, *History*, vol. 3, p. 164). The plot was brought to light, according to Goldsmith, by an anonymous letter from Percy to a parliamentarian, Lord Mounteagle, warning him to stay away on the day planned for the explosion.

83 **Sir Walter Raleigh . . . Hatton:** the famous courtier and explorer Raleigh flourished during the reign of Elizabeth I, but was imprisoned in the Tower of London for the first thirteen years of James I's reign. Released to lead an expedition in search of gold in South America, he was arrested on his return and executed in 1618. For Raleigh's freindship with Sir Christopher Hatton, who died in 1591, JA cites Sheridan's comedy *The Critic* (1779). Here Mr Puff's tragic play-within-a-play, entitled *The Spanish Armada*, features Raleigh and Hatton among the principal characters.

84 **keener penetration:** probably a risqué double entendre, glancing at James I's reputation for enjoying close friendships with young men. It is in the same vein as the joke about Lambert Simnel's being the widow of Richard III and as the remark about Sir Henry Percy confining his 'Attentions' to Lord Mounteagle, who, according to Goldsmith, was Percy's 'intimate friend and companion' (vol. 3, p. 167).

85 **Sharade:** charade, a riddle in which the syllables of a word are described (as here) or dramatically represented. They were popular in JA's family; charades survive by her mother, her sister, four of her brothers and JA herself.

86 **above-mentioned Sharade:** the charade depicts James I's favourite Sir Robert Carr as the king's 'pet', another probable double entendre alluding to homosexual behaviour.

87 **Duke of Buckingham:** the favourite who succeeded Carr. Goldsmith himself is more cautious in his treatment of James I's putative homosexuality than JA. Noting that Buckingham's 'beauty and fashionable manners . . . immediately caught the monarch's affections', he states that his sources do not 'insinuate any thing flagitious in these connexions' but impute James's 'attachment rather to a weakness of understanding, than to any perversion of appetite' (vol. 3, p. 178).

88 **Charles the 1st:** both Caroline Austen and James Edward Austen-Leigh recall their aunt's enthusiasm for Charles I. Caroline notes that 'she was a most loyal adherent', while James Edward terms her a 'vehement defender' (*Memoir*, pp. 173, 71).

89 **his lovely Grandmother:** Mary Queen of Scots.

90 **Laud . . . Ormond:** William Laud, Archbishop of Canterbury, executed in 1645; Sir Thomas Wentworth, Earl of Strafford, leader of the House of Commons, executed in 1641; Lucius Cary, Viscount Falkland (not 'Faulkland'), who died in 1643; and James Butler, first Duke of Ormonde, who died in 1688. JA had a family connection to Sir Thomas Wentworth, who was a remote ancestor of her mother, Cassandra Leigh. In her marginalia on Goldsmith's *History*, JA describes Falkland, who was killed in battle in the first campaign of the Civil War, as 'a great & noble Man' (Appendix B, p. 320).

91 **Cromwell . . . Pym:** JA's antipathy to Oliver Cromwell, Lord Protector from 1653 until his death in 1658, is revealed in a series of marginalia on Goldsmith's *History*, of which the strongest is 'Detestable Monster!' (Appendix B, p. 323). Thomas Fairfax was a prominent leader in Cromwell's army, as was John Hampden, who was killed in the same campaign as Lucius Cary. In her marginalia on Goldsmith, JA regrets that Cary's 'virtues shd be clouded by Republicanism!' (Appendix B, p. 320). John Pym, an influential member of Parliament, was one of Cromwell's key supporters. In his prologue to *The Wonder* (1787), James Austen had previously expressed his revulsion for Cromwell's government:

> Then came a set of men, with formal faces,
> Ranting quotations wild, with strange grimaces . . .
> For ten long years the nation groaned & sighed,
> And the men ranted while the women cried.
>
> (lines 31–8)

92 **my Attachment to the Scotch:** JA also expresses regret for the behaviour of the Scots in her marginalia on Goldsmith's *History*, writing 'What a pity!' beside Goldsmith's remark on the strength of the Scottish republican army (Appendix B, p. 321).

A COLLECTION OF LETTERS

1 **To Miss Cooper:** JA's cousin Jane Cooper, also the dedicatee of 'Henry and Eliza', who married Captain Williams in December 1792. The 'Collection' must predate her marriage, when she became Mrs Williams, and was 'probably written during the autumn of 1792 while she was staying at Steventon' (*FR*, p. 78), after the death of her father on 27 August. Southam, however, dates it as late 1791 or early 1792, 'certainly before "Lesley Castle"' (*Jane Austen's Literary Manuscripts* (Oxford: Oxford University Press, 1964), p. 31).

2 **Clime:** region, 'contracted from *climate* and therefore properly poetical' (Johnson).

3 **Curious:** in the sense of 'elegant' or 'exquisite'; a characteristic eighteenth-century use of the term.

4 **Comical Cousin:** in a letter of 9 February 1813, JA echoes this dedication, with its multiple alliteration on the letter 'c', telling Cassandra: 'you will be transported to Manydown — & then for Candour & Comfort & Coffee & Cribbage' (*L*, p. 205).

5 **appearance in the World:** taking their place in society, or 'coming out': a rite of passage for well-bred young women, typically taking place at sixteen or seventeen. Just before writing this, JA might have read Mary Wollstonecraft's thoughts on the subject, in *A Vindication of the Rights of Woman*, published early in 1792 (London: J. Johnson): 'what can be more indelicate than a girl's *coming out* in the fashionable world? Which, in other words, is to bring to market a marriageable miss' (ch. 12). In a discussion with Lady Catherine de Bourgh, Elizabeth Bennet tells her that all of her sisters are 'out', although the youngest, not yet sixteen, is perhaps 'full young to be much in company' (*P&P*, vol. 2, ch. 6). The subject is also debated in *MP*, in which Mary Crawford is unsure of the status of the eighteen-year-old Fanny Price: 'Pray, is she out, or is she not?' Edmund Bertram is similarly puzzled: 'My cousin is grown up . . . but the outs and not outs are beyond me' (vol. 1, ch. 5). In August 1814, JA was struck by a passage in her niece Anna Austen's novel in progress, 'Which is the Heroine?', remarking of one of Anna's characters that 'what he says about the madness of otherwise sensible Women, on the

subject of their Daughters coming out, is worth its' weight in gold' (*L*, p. 269).

6 **introduce them together into Public:** not exceptional, given their slight difference in age. The five Bennet sisters, aged from fifteen to twenty, are a much more unusual case, as Lady Catherine objects: 'What, all five out at once? Very odd!' (*P&P*, vol. 2, ch. 6).

7 **Morning-Visits:** short visits before dinner, which was served in the mid-afternoon. Several such visits could be made in the same day, over a period of about three hours, from midday until about three.

8 **Westbrook:** the name of a house.

9 **This mighty affair . . . out:** echoing the famous line in Richardson's *Clarissa* in which Lovelace tells Belford that he has carried out Clarissa's rape: 'The affair is over. Clarissa lives' (3rd edn, (London: John Osborn, 1751), vol. 5, letter 32).

10 **infancy:** 'Civil infancy, extended by the English law to one and twenty years' (Johnson). The girls' mother is referring to their late childhood and adolescence, as well as to their younger years.

11 **Warleigh:** presumably the name of Mrs Cope's house, although there is a village named Warleigh in Devonshire.

12 **Willoughby:** 'Letter the second' contains the surnames of several major characters in JA's novels: Willoughby and the Dashwood sisters in *S&S*, and the Crawfords in *MP*.

13 **Belle:** a diminutive of Arabella.

14 **Melancholy:** considered a disease of the nervous system and becoming a malady frequently suffered by fashionable women, as well as men. As Roy Porter notes, in Robert Burton's *Anatomy of Melancholy* (1621) and well after, melancholy was still considered a masculine disease. From the mid-eighteenth century, however, with its cult of sensibility, melancholy was increasingly feminized (*A Social History of Madness: The World Through the Eyes of the Insane* (London: Weidenfeld, 1987), p. 104).

15 **Sister:** sister-in-law

16 **advised to ride by my Physician:** riding was thought to be a valuable aid to good health. John Gregory recommends to his daughters 'those exercises that oblige you to be much abroad in the open air, such as walking and riding on horseback' (*Father's*

Legacy, p. 20). When Fanny Price loses 'her valued friend the old grey poney' in *MP*, her health suffers, and when deprived of the mare that Edmund buys for her, she becomes sickly again (vol. 1, chs. 4–8).

17 **Ride where you may . . . can:** deforming Alexander Pope's line in his *Essay on Man*: 'Laugh where we *must*, be candid where we *can*' (1, l. 15).

18 **fighting for his Country in America:** with the British army in America during the War for Independence, 1775–83.

19 **I dropt all thoughts of either:** in doing so, Miss Jane casts doubts on the validity of her marriage, as well as on her legitimacy. Her position resembles that of Burney's Evelina, who puzzles over what surname to use: that of her father, Sir John Belmont, who refuses to acknowledge her, or the invented surname 'Anville'. In writing to her guardian, she signs herself simply 'Evelina'.

20 **Lady Bridget became a Widow like myself:** Lady Bridget Dashwood is apparently a peer's daughter who married a commoner, Henry Dashwood's elder brother. On her marriage, she would have taken his surname but kept the style, 'Lady Bridget', that reveals her to be the daughter of a duke, marquess or earl.

21 **always loved each other . . . live together:** JA frequently satirizes instantaneous professions of friendship between young women, but this is an extreme case; Lady Bridget and Miss Jane become close friends before their first meeting.

22 **in her way:** on her way to the ball, without having to take a diversion. The 'honour' thus involves no difficulty for Lady Greville.

23 **sit forwards:** facing the direction of travel, the preferred position in a carriage.

24 **old striped one:** Lady Greville expects Maria to wear an everyday gown to a ball, rather than an evening gown bought for the occasion, and thus to advertise her poverty and inferior station. In this and much else she resembles Lady Catherine de Bourgh in *P&P*, of whom Mr Collins observes to Elizabeth: 'Lady Catherine will not think the worse of you for being simply dressed. She likes to have the distinction of rank preserved' (vol. 2, ch. 6).

25 **Miss Greville . . . felt for me:** Miss Greville is the elder of the two sisters; the sympathetic Ellen is the younger. JA changed the

latter's name from 'Fanny', one of her favourites, to 'Ellen', a name that she uses nowhere else in her juvenilia or her novels.

26 **Candles cost money:** beeswax candles were expensive. When Miss Bates enthuses over a ball in *E*, she declares: 'I never saw any thing equal to the comfort and style—Candles every where' (vol. 3, ch. 2). Wicks dipped in melted fat could be used as a cheap alternative to wax candles, but indicated the user's financial constraints.

27 **Bread and Cheese:** food associated with the poor. Cheese provided protein more cheaply than meat and did not require cooking.

28 **Ashburnham:** not a town (although there is an Ashburnham in Sussex) but a house named after its owner, Mr Ashburnham.

29 **too fashionable . . . to be punctual:** in addition to being fashionably late, Lady Greville can also take pleasure in inconveniencing others. Because of her rank, her daughter Miss Greville is expected to open the ball; no dancing can take place before their arrival. In *W*, the Osbornes are also fashionably late for a public ball, but there at least the dancing begins without them.

30 **white Gloves:** in his *Memoir*, JA's nephew James Edward Austen-Leigh notes that every ball began with a 'stately minuet', and that 'Gloves immaculately clean were considered requisite for its due performance' (pp. 32, 33). In *W*, the ten-year-old Charles Osborne is 'provided with his gloves & charged to keep them on' (*MW*, p. 331) when he dances with Emma at the public ball.

31 **cannot you get a partner?** a recurring problem in JA's novels, in which a series of young women—including Catherine Morland in *NA*, Elizabeth Bennet in *P&P* and Harriet Smith in *E*—suffer the indignity of being without, or appearing to be without, a dancing partner.

32 **hop:** a colloquial term for an informal dance or dancing party. By her choice of the slang word, Lady Greville is belittling Maria, suggesting that the ball is an insignificant affair.

33 **Grocer or a Bookbinder:** both tradesmen, and as such not part of polite society. In *P&P*, Mr Gardiner is 'a sensible, gentleman like man', but 'the Netherfield ladies would have had difficulty in believing that a man who lived by trade, and within view of

his own warehouses, could have been so well bred and agreeable' (vol. 2, ch. 2). One could be 'gentleman like' without being a gentleman.

34 **Wine Merchant:** since a merchant deals in large quantities, rather than selling to individual customers, Maria believes that her father's profession is superior to that of a mere tradesman. Lady Greville, however, is unimpressed by the distinction.

35 **broke:** became bankrupt.

36 **poor as a Rat:** proverbial since the seventeenth century. Lady Greville chooses the most offensive form of the proverb, rather than the more palatable 'poor as a church mouse'.

37 **Kings bench:** King's Bench prison, primarily a debtors' prison.

38 **too saucy:** JA made several revisions to this exchange between Lady Greville and Maria (see textual notes). Frances Beer suggests that she was 'working at letting Maria be spirited without quite being rude' (Beer (ed.), *The Juvenilia of Jane Austen and Charlotte Brontë* (London: Penguin, 1986), p. 373).

39 **high and very cold:** Charlotte Collins undergoes the same unpleasant experience in *P&P*, having to talk to Miss de Bourgh and her companion Mrs Jenkinson, who are comfortably seated in their phaeton. As Elizabeth Bennet remarks, 'she is abominably rude to keep Charlotte out of doors in all this wind' (vol. 2, ch. 5).

40 **umbrella:** since umbrellas were used by those who could not afford the expense of a carriage, this is another of Lady Greville's insults. Like parasols, which protected against the sun, they were used primarily by women, but unlike parasols, they were not considered a genteel accoutrement.

41 **your Complexion so ruddy and coarse:** a similar charge is made by Lady Williams in 'Jack and Alice' (ch. 3).

42 **shews your legs:** originally 'shews your Ancles'. The revision makes Lady Greville still more offensive.

43 **There will be no Moon:** travelling on foot or by carriage after dark without moonlight was avoided whenever possible. In 'Evelyn', Mr Gower fears his journey home 'with no light to direct him', even though there is a 'Moon almost full' (p. 240), but he is an exceptionally timid traveller. In a letter of 15 September 1797, JA tells Cassandra: 'We have been very gay since I wrote last; dining

at Nackington, returning by Moonlight, and everything quite in Stile' (*L*, p. 9).

44 **great curiosity . . . befallen her:** like her precursors in 'Jack and Alice' and 'Love and Freindship', the young lady here is eager for a stranger to recount her life story.

45 **a whispering Conversation:** as in JA's comedy 'The Mystery' (scene 2).

46 **Essex . . . Derbyshire . . . Suffolk:** Miss Grenville is surprised because Derbyshire is a county in the north midlands of England, some 150 miles from Essex. Suffolk, in contrast, is a neighbouring county to Essex, entailing a much shorter journey.

47 **dash:** a 'sudden stroke; blow' (Johnson).

48 **Stingy:** 'a low cant word' (Johnson).

49 **particular:** 'odd . . . commonly used in a sense of contempt' (Johnson).

50 **Sackville St.:** a fashionable street running off Piccadilly, with a mixture of shops and residences.

51 **you well know:** Musgrove has begun his letter in the third person, a very formal way of writing to one's beloved. Here he switches abruptly to the second person, and continues to alternate between the two incompatible systems for the remainder of the letter.

52 **toasted:** made the subject of amorous toasts, which could compromise a woman's reputation.

53 **Abandoned:** corrupted, dissolute, rather than forsaken, although both senses are possible here.

54 **improvable Estate:** capable of being more profitably cultivated or better managed, and thus yielding a higher revenue. This is a different kind of 'improvement' from the one that plays a large part in *MP*. There, James Rushworth wishes to change the appearance of his estate for aesthetic purposes, not to make more money from it.

55 **Amiable princess . . . humble Servt.:** Musgrove's ludicrously exaggerated complimentary closing lines are in the style favoured by Arabella, the heroine of Lennox's *The Female Quixote*.

56 **Musgrove:** JA here deleted a postscript (see textual notes), presumably because she felt that Musgrove's request for a prepaid reply was too crass, even for him.

57 **pattern for a Love-letter:** like the model letters found in compilations such as Samuel Richardson's *Letters Written to and For Particular Friends on the Most Important Occasions* (London: C. Rivington, 1741), which went through many editions. Love letters form a major part of Richardson's volume. A letter 'From a respectful Lover to his Mistress' is Richardson's 'pattern' for a man in Musgrove's position. Rather than boasting about his 'improvable Estate', Richardson's lover declares: 'What my Fortune is, is well known, and I am ready to stand the Test of the strictest Inquiry' (Letter 74).

58 **run mad:** echoing Sophia's dictum in 'Love and Freindship': 'Run mad as often as you chuse; but do not faint' (Letter the 14th).

59 **every day of my Life:** the heavily deleted lines that follow (see textual notes) are no bolder than the rest of Henrietta's letter. JA might simply have found them redundant.

60 **dab:** 'a man expert at something' (Johnson), who adds that 'this is not used in writing'.

61 **give a farthing for:** from the proverbial expression 'not worth a farthing', the smallest English coin, worth only a quarter of a penny.

62 **love at first sight:** echoing a couplet in Christopher Marlowe's *Hero and Leander* (London: Paule Linley, 1598):

> Where both deliberate, the love is slight:
> Who ever loved, that loved not at first sight?
> (sestiad 1, lines 175–6)

63 **Several hundreds an year:** a very small sum for a man seeking to marry an heiress. In *S&S*, Mrs Dashwood and her daughters must live on £500 a year. As Fanny Dashwood tells her husband, this means that 'they will have no carriage, no horses, and hardly any servants; they will keep no company; and can have no expences of any kind!' (vol. 1, ch. 2).

64 **Yes I'm in love ... undone me:** alluding to the first stanza of 'The je ne scai Quoi' by William Whitehead:

> Yes, I'm in love, I feel it now,
> And Caelia has undone me;
> And yet I'll swear I can't tell how
> The pleasing plague stole on me.

JA alludes to the same poem in *MP*, vol. 2, ch. 12. She could have read it in her copy of Robert Dodsley's *A Collection of Poems*, which also contains the poem by James Merrick quoted in 'Jack and Alice' (ch. 3).

65 **not in rhime:** Henrietta fails to recognize Whitehead's well-known stanza and is unperturbed by the lack of scansion in Musgrove's adaptation, with its unmetrical substitution of 'Henrietta Halton' for 'Caelia'. There are, of course, rhymes in Whitehead's quatrain, but none in the first two lines.

66 **my dear Tom:** the first and only occasion on which Musgrove's Christian name is given. He signs his letters 'T. Musgrove' and is otherwise addressed or referred to by his surname. JA first wrote 'my dear Cousin' here, before giving him a name by replacing 'Cousin' with 'Tom'.

67 **now and then:** in the phrase that originally followed (see textual notes), JA indicated that Henrietta had given a twopenny donation that morning: hardly a generous sum. She apparently found it more effective to leave Henrietta's constrained idea of charity to the reader's imagination.

68 **come and make the pies:** normally a task for the household cook, not for a young lady. This is apparently a sign of the stinginess and oddness in her uncle and aunt of which Henrietta has previously complained. In *P&P*, Mrs Bennet emphasizes the difference between Charlotte Lucas, who was 'wanted about the mince pies', and her own, more genteel daughters: 'For my part, Mr. Bingley, *I* always keep servants that can do their own work; *my* daughters are brought up differently' (vol. 1, ch. 9).

TO MISS FANNY CATHERINE AUSTEN

1 **Fanny Catherine Austen:** the eldest daughter of Edward and Elizabeth Austen, born on 23 January 1793, and JA's first niece. JA probably wrote this dedication shortly before the one in 'Volume the First' to her second niece, Jane Anna Elizabeth Austen, dated 2 June 1793 (p. 90). The items dedicated to Fanny are termed 'Scraps' in the list of contents for 'Volume the Second', but not in the text itself.

2 **Rowling and Steventon:** Rowling, in east Kent; a country house given to Edward and Elizabeth Austen by her parents

as a wedding gift. It was a two-day journey from Rowling to JA's home in Steventon, some 100 miles to the west in Hampshire.

3 **the conduct of Young Women:** as do the conduct books to which JA also alludes in her dedication to her other niece, Jane Anna Elizabeth Austen, describing her own writings as 'Treatises for your Benefit'.

THE FEMALE PHILOSOPHER

1 **female philosopher:** for JA an oxymoron, but not for others in the early 1790s. Mary Wollstonecraft describes herself as a philosopher in her *Vindication of the Rights of Woman* (1792), ch. 2.

2 **Sallies:** lively witticisms; a 'volatile or sprightly exertion' (Johnson).

3 **social Shake, and Cordial Kiss:** a handshake between two male friends was customary, but a 'cordial kiss' was typical of French, rather than English manners. Their behaviour, however, is restrained beside the raptures in 'Love and Freindship' of Edward and Augustus, who 'flew into each other's arms' (letter 8).

4 **amiable Moralist:** Julia's 'sensible reflections' resemble those of Mary Bennet in *P&P*. Both girls repeat commonplaces, rather than exercising independent thought. As the dry Mr Bennet remarks to Mary, 'you are a young lady of deep reflection I know, and read great books, and make extracts' (vol. 1, ch. 2).

5 **five or six months with us:** a ludicrously extended period for a visit. A visit even to the wealthiest and most generous of hosts would seldom last more than a month.

6 **her pride, and her folly:** the combination of praise and abuse here resembles that in the address to Rebecca in 'Frederic and Elfrida' (ch. 2), and in Lady Williams' account of Alice Johnson and her family in 'Jack and Alice' (ch. 6).

7 **Arabella:** a name becoming fashionable in the late eighteenth century. JA also gives it to one of Cecilia's 'lovely Sisters' in 'A Tale', the last of the pieces dedicated to Fanny Catherine Austen.

THE FIRST ACT OF A COMEDY

1 **the Lion:** the public rooms in the inn all have names: the Lion, the Moon and the Sun. The bedrooms, however, have numbers, as they would today.

2 **their Honours:** a title of respect; somewhat more deferential than 'the gentry'.

3 **bill of fare:** menu.

4 **wull:** dialect for 'will'.

5 **their Ladyships:** still more deferential than 'their Honours', implying that the occupants are titled.

6 **Popgun and Pistoletta:** both names perhaps inspired by that of Pistol in Shakespeare's *Henry IV*. 'Pistoletta' is JA's feminized version of 'pistolet', a small pistol. A popgun is a child's toy gun, and thus a ludicrous name for Pistoletta's father.

7 **Strephon:** a traditional name for a lover in pastoral poetry; his beloved is traditionally named Chloe.

8 **it wants seven Miles:** there are seven miles to go. Popgun's reply begins with much information needed by the audience but already well known to Pistoletta: JA is parodying a familiar dramatic convention.

9 **chorus of ploughboys:** the chorus identifies the play as a musical comedy or comic opera, a form becoming increasingly popular in the late eighteenth century. Byrne notes that JA 'satirises the artificiality of the comic opera, its spontaneous outbursts of songs, and distinctive lack of plot' (*Jane Austen and the Theatre*, p. 23). For her 'chorus of ploughboys', JA was probably indebted to Frances Brooke's often performed and reprinted ballad opera *Rosina* (1783), which features a 'Chorus of reapers'.

10 **Hounslow:** a town about fourteen miles west of London, not seven, as Popgun imagines.

11 **Stree-phon:** by hyphenating his name, JA emphasizes the absurdity of her rhyme: 'Stree-phon' and 'be fun'. The next rhyme on his name is still worse: 'Strephon' and 'tough one'.

12 **stinking partridge:** presumably stinking because it has been hung for a long time, to give it additional flavour. The usual term for well-hung birds is 'high'; 'stinking' suggests that the process has been carried too far.

13 **Staines:** a town about five miles west of Hounslow.

14 **marry Chloe:** Strephon is apparently unaware that Pistoletta intends to marry him, just as she seems unaware that he intends to marry Chloe.

15 **bad guinea:** a forgery of the gold coin worth twenty-one shillings. Forging coins was a capital offence; Strephon's plan to use his guinea in London is a dangerous one.

16 **undirected Letter:** a letter with no address. It would, of course, have no commercial value; the postilion is thus being remarkably generous in accepting it as security for his fee of eighteen pence (one shilling and sixpence).

A LETTER FROM A YOUNG LADY

1 **twelve Years:** in changing 'months' to 'Years', JA makes Anna Parker's perjuries, like her murders, begin at a 'very early period' of her life.

2 **forged my own Will:** an obvious impossibility, akin to forging one's own signature.

3 **Horseguards:** a cavalry brigade that protected the royal household; an elite regiment.

4 **eight Million:** this impossibly large amount would generate an annual income of £400,000 and make him by far the richest man in eighteenth-century Britain.

5 **his Small pittance:** £5,000 per year, the interest on his inheritance of £100,000. This makes him as wealthy as the very affluent Bingley in *P&P*, although only half as wealthy as Darcy.

6 **his illgotten Wealth:** in giving his eldest son the vast majority of his colossal fortune, the late Sir John Martin followed standard eighteenth-century practice: Sir Thomas' wealth is not 'illgotten'.

A TOUR THROUGH WALES

1 **on the ramble:** rambling. *OED* gives 1700 as the date of first use for the expression.

2 **last Monday Month:** a month ago last Monday.

3 **tour through Wales:** in the late eighteenth century, Wales was becoming increasingly fashionable for domestic tourists in search of the picturesque. Their interest was aroused by works such as William Gilpin's *Observations on the River Wye and Several Parts of South Wales* (1782), which described the beauties of the country, just as Gilpin's *Observations Relative Chiefly to Picturesque Beauty* (1789) inspires Augusta, in 'Love and Freindship' (ch. 14) to take a tour of the Scottish Highlands. Samuel Johnson travelled through north Wales in 1774, a year after his Scottish tour. He was accompanied by Hester Thrale, her husband and their daughter Queeney, and both Johnson and Mrs Thrale recorded their journey in unpublished diaries. Their tour lasted over two months, a month more than JA's fictional tour here.

4 **contiguous to England:** the style resembles that of a school geography book. Elizabeth Johnson writes as if Wales were unknown to her correspondent Clara, suggesting that the latter is a young child.

5 **Prince of Wales:** the current line of Princes of Wales goes back to 1301, when Edward of Caernarfon, the future Edward II, was invested with the title. Since the investiture of Edward, the Black Prince, as Prince of Wales in 1343, the eldest son of the monarch has normally held the title. George III's son had been created Prince of Wales as an infant in 1762 and retained the title until he acceded as George IV in 1820.

6 **on horseback:** an implausible way for unaccompanied women to travel together. Worse still, they have only one pony among the three of them.

7 **Drawings of the Country:** tourists would typically be equipped with both notebooks for recording their impressions and sketchbooks in which to draw the scenery. Amateur artists, such as Fanny here, were naturally attracted to the spectacular Welsh landscapes.

8 **capped and heelpeiced:** repaired with new toe coverings and new heels.

9 **Carmarthen:** a town in south-west Wales.

10 **blue Sattin Slippers:** formal evening shoes, suitable neither for walking nor for hopping. In the 1790s, they would have broad, flat heels and long, pointed toes.

11 **hopped home from Hereford:** more alliteration to complement that in the dedication. Hereford, the last place visited on this tour, is a cathedral town near the Welsh border.

A TALE

1 **I shall conceal:** a familiar device in the eighteenth-century novel, used to suggest that a real-life character is the subject.

2 **Pembrokeshire:** a county in south-west Wales, bordering the sea. Many cottages were built there in the late eighteenth and nineteenth century, for use by both locals and visitors.

3 **Closet:** a small room, often adjoining a bedroom.

4 **Wilhelminus:** a Latin version of the German name Wilhelm; an outlandish name for an English gentleman.

5 **advertisement in a Newspaper:** in August 1788, the Austens, seeking a tenant for the vacant Deane parsonage, had placed an advertisement in the *Reading Mercury*. As Le Faye notes, the advertisement, describing the parsonage as a 'neat brick dwelling-house', 'made it sound far more desirable than the later family memories of a "low damp place with inconvenient rooms"' (*FR*, p. 68). In 'A Tale', the cottage is advertised for rent, but we are told at the outset that Wilhelminus has bought, rather than rented it. We do not, however, see the transaction take place; Wilhelminus simply 'take[s] possession' of the cottage.

6 **Robertus:** a Latin version of Robert; as outlandish as 'Wilhelminus'.

7 **three days and Six Nights without Stopping:** a journey from southern England to west Wales might take three days and three nights without stopping. Three days and six nights is odd, but possible if they rested during three of the days.

8 **pair of Stairs:** a flight of stairs.

9 **Marina:** an unusual name, probably derived from the Latin '*marinus*' (of the sea) and thus appropriate for this story.

10 **attached:** the syntax leaves it unclear whether Wilhelminus is attached to both 'lovely Sisters' or to Marina alone.

11 **Genius:** not outstanding talent, but 'nature; disposition' (Johnson).

12 **two noble Tents:** such tents would, of course, be made from materials more costly and durable than ' a couple of old blankets'

and 'four sticks'. Wilhelminus' tents are makeshift ones, of the kind used in children's games.

VOLUME THE THIRD

1 **May 6th 1792:** a puzzling date, since the dedication to 'Catharine' is dated August 1792. JA might have signed and dated the volume at the same time that she wrote the contents page and transcribed 'Evelyn', transcribing and dedicating 'Catharine' some three months later. During those three months, she would have changed the title of 'Catharine', and the name of the heroine, from the 'Kitty' of the contents page. Le Faye suggests that 'Evelyn' was written immediately after 'The History of England', which is dated 26 November 1791 (*FR*, p. 74).

2 **Kitty:** although JA changed her heroine's name to 'Catherine' on most occasions in the text, she did not revise the title 'Kitty' on her contents page.

EVELYN

1 **Miss Mary Lloyd:** Mary Lloyd (1771–1843), a friend and neighbour of JA, the younger sister of Martha Lloyd, to whom 'Frederic and Elfrida' is dedicated. Martha and Mary, with another sister Eliza and their newly widowed mother, had rented Deane parsonage since Spring 1789, but were forced to leave it before James Austen became curate at Deane in 1792, after his marriage in March of that year. There are obvious connections between the subject of 'Evelyn'—the hero's acquisition of a new house and a new bride—and James Austen's real-life acquisition of both Deane parsonage and his new bride, Anne Mathew. In addition to dedicating 'Evelyn' to Mary Lloyd, JA presented her with a sewing bag containing a poem, 'This little bag', dated January 1792.

2 **Evelyn:** an imaginary village.

3 **about twenty years ago:** this sets the action in about 1772, some three years before JA's birth in 1775.

4 **Alehouse:** a public house, 'distinguished from a tavern, where they sell wine' (Johnson).

5 **to be lett:** the title of the newspaper advertisement in 'A Tale', the final item in 'Volume the Second'.

6 **Parish:** a subdivision of an English county, with its own church.

7 **Landlady:** the hostess of the alehouse.

8 **sash:** a sash window, which could be raised and lowered. Sash windows became popular in the late eighteenth century, letting in more light and air than the leaded casement windows they replaced.

9 **their house:** the original reading, 'the remainder of their Lease', suggests that the Webbs rented, rather than owned, their house, making it a less desirable possession for Gower.

10 **circular paddock:** 'a small inclosure for deer or other animals' (Johnson). Circularity was associated with the landscape gardening of Lancelot ('Capability') Brown (1715–83), who would surround the park of a country house with a border of trees and provide a walk around the estate.

11 **paling:** a fence made of pales, pointed lengths of wood driven into the ground.

12 **Lombardy poplars:** a tall, narrow columnar variety of poplar, originating in Lombardy in northern Italy and brought to Britain in the eighteenth century. While not an indigenous tree, it was used by Brown and other landscape gardeners to delineate property limits. No gardener, however, would have planted tall poplar trees and bushy spruce trees around a house in the middle of a 'small paddock', blocking out the light. At Cleveland, the Palmers' home in *S&S*, the same combination of trees is used to better effect: 'the house itself was under the guardianship of the fir, the mountain-ash, and the acacia, and a thick screen of them altogether, interspersed with tall Lombardy poplars, shut out the offices' (vol. 3, ch. 6).

13 **alternately placed in three rows:** alluding to tree-planting at Grandison Hall in Richardson's *Sir Charles Grandison*, undertaken by Sir Thomas Grandison 'in his days of fancy'. There the orchard is bordered 'with three rows of trees, at proper distances from each other; one of pines; one of cedars; one of Scotch firs, in the like semicircular order' (vol. 7, letter 5). Sir Thomas' plantation, however, was designed to afford 'shady walks in the summer' and to 'defend the orchard from the cold and blighting winds'; it did not obstruct the view from his house.

14 **Shrubbery:** a plantation of shrubs, with paths for walking and admiring views. It was a prized part of the eighteenth-century country house, and a necessary addition when improvements were being made. As Lady Bertram tells Mr Rushworth in *MP*, 'if I were you, I would have a very pretty shrubbery. One likes to get out into a shrubbery in fine weather' (vol. 1, ch. 6). Walks through shrubberies, however, were winding and irregular; a straight gravel walk that 'ran through' would be an oddity. Fanny Price, in *MP*, enjoys Mrs Grant's shrubbery, in which she 'sauntered about' and admired its 'growth and beauty' (vol. 2, ch. 4).

15 **four white Cows . . . from each other:** defying the advice of William Gilpin, whose 'doctrine of grouping *larger cattle*' insists on three as the perfect number:

> *Two* will hardly combine . . . But with *three*, you are almost sure of a good group, except indeed they all stand in the same attitude, and at equal distances . . . *Four* introduce a new difficulty in grouping. *Separate* they would have a bad effect . . . The only way, in which they will group well, is to *unite three* . . . and to *remove the fourth*.
>
> (*Observations, Relative Chiefly to Picturesque Beauty . . . on several parts of England* (London: R. Blamire, 1786), vol. 2, 'Explanation of the Prints', pp. xii–xiii)

The grouping of the cows in 'Evelyn' is thus thoroughly unpicturesque: both in their number and in their 'equal distances from each other'.

16 **without any turn or interruption:** like the walks in a shrubbery, the road leading to a country house would be winding, rather than straight. In *P&P*, Elizabeth and the Gardiners 'gradually ascended for half a mile' until 'the eye was instantly caught by Pemberley House, situated on the opposite side of a valley, into which the road with some abruptness wound' (vol. 3, ch. 1). On a more modest scale, in *S&S*, Cleveland is approached 'by a road of smooth gravel', which 'winding round a plantation, led to the front' (vol. 3, ch. 6).

17 **Webb:** an appropriate surname for a family who live like spiders in the middle of a web, in their 'small circular paddock'.

18 **best of Men:** the phrase repeatedly applied to the superlatively generous and proficient hero of *Sir Charles Grandison*. When Mr Gower first meets Mrs Willis at her alehouse, he likewise addresses her as 'best of Women'.

19 **Chocolate:** a drink of hot chocolate, a luxury item. It was made by dissolving cocoa—a paste or cake of ground and roasted cacao seeds—into milk, sweetened with vanilla and other substances. Elsewhere in JA's novels, cocoa (made without milk), not hot chocolate, is drunk. General Tilney has cocoa for breakfast with his newspaper in *NA* (vol. 2, ch. 10), while Arthur Parker in *S* is a cocoa connoisseur, 'coddling and cooking it to his own satisfaction' before pouring it out 'in a very fine, dark coloured stream' (*MW*, pp. 416, 417).

20 **venison pasty:** a pie made from the flesh of deer, another luxury dish.

21 **sandwiches . . . Jellies and Cakes:** a bizarre mixture of items normally served at different times of the day and at different stages of a meal, here served as a vast hors d'oeuvre before dinner. Sandwiches are a mid-eighteenth-century creation, 'said to be named after John Montagu, 4th Earl of Sandwich (1718–1792), who once spent twenty-four hours at the gaming table without other refreshment than some slices of cold beef placed between slices of toast' (*OED*, which gives 1762 as the date of first use). Austen refers to eating 'sandwiches all over mustard' at Oakley Hall, in a letter to Cassandra of 25 October 1800 (*L*, p. 49).

22 **handsome portion:** a large dowry.

23 **but ten thousand pounds:** not 'too small a sum' but a dowry that makes Miss Webb one of JA's wealthiest female characters. At the beginning of *MP*, we learn that Maria Ward, 'with only seven thousand pounds, had the good luck to captivate Sir Thomas Bertram, of Mansfield Park'. She is, her uncle believes, 'at least three thousand pounds short of any equitable claim' to such a marriage. Thus with ten thousand pounds, Miss Webb might expect to marry a wealthy gentleman, with a large house.

24 **next day, the nuptials . . . were celebrated:** no banns have been read, no special licence obtained and no clergyman officiates: this is thus another of the many invalid marriages in JA's juvenilia.

25 **cultivate his acquaintance with Mrs Willis:** the sexual innu-
endo here is picked up in James Edward Austen's conclusion to
'Evelyn' (see Appendix E), in which Mr Gower and Mrs Willis
are married, again at a day's notice and again illicitly.

26 **rose tree . . . pleasing variety:** a rose bush. As with the grazing cows, the arrangement of the rosebushes in a group of four
contradicts Gilpin's recommendations and provides monotonous
regularity, rather than a 'pleasing variety'.

27 **high rank . . . desirable to theirs:** strong objections by noble or
genteel families to alliances with commoners occur in several of
JA's novels. The haughtiest of her aristocrats, the earl's daughter Lady Catherine de Bourgh, declares memorably to Elizabeth Bennet that, should she marry Darcy, 'You will be censured,
slighted, and despised, by every one connected with him. Your
alliance will be a disgrace; your name will never even be mentioned by any of us' (*P&P*, vol. 3, ch. 14).

28 **Carlisle:** a city in Cumberland in the north-west of England,
near the Scottish border, some 350 miles from Sussex.

29 **Family Chaplain:** a sign of the family's exceptional wealth and
their adherence to tradition. Chapels had been a standard part
of the English country house, but by the late eighteenth century
even the largest houses seldom had their own functioning chapel
and officiating chaplain. In *MP*, Mrs Rushworth tells her visitors
that a domestic chaplain presided over Sotherton's chapel until
the time of her late husband. Fanny Price regrets that the practice
has been abandoned: 'There is something in a chapel and chaplain
so much in character with a great house, with one's idea of what
such a household should be!' (vol. 1, ch. 9).

30 **Isle of Wight . . . foreign Country:** not, of course, a foreign country but a small island off the coast of Hampshire, separated from
the mainland by the Solent estuary and visible from Portsmouth.
The ill-educated Fanny Price, recently arrived at Mansfield Park,
makes a poor impression on her cousins by her ignorance of the
Isle of Wight's location: 'she thinks of nothing but the Isle of
Wight, and she calls it *the Island*, as if there were no other island
in the world' (*MP*, vol. 1, ch. 2).

31 **Rosa:** a Latinized version of 'Rose', coined only in the late eighteenth century.

32 **wrecked on the coast of Calshot:** the channel between the mainland and the Isle of Wight is very narrow, and not known for
storms of any kind. Calshot Castle, overlooking the Solent, was
built by Henry VIII in 1539 as part of a chain of coastal defences
against the French and Spanish.

33 **great distance . . . would admit of:** since 1784, mail had been carried in special, rapid stagecoaches, which travelled at an average
speed of about ten miles per hour. Here, the letter from Evelyn
takes three days to travel the 350 miles to Carlisle: a reasonable
rate of progress.

34 **dead these six weeks:** As the thirteenth Gower daughter, Rose is
proverbially unfortunate.

35 **fit of the gout:** an inflammatory disease associated with excessive
eating and drinking, and thus an appropriate ailment for Mr
Gower, who has displayed a prodigious appetite at Evelyn while
drinking 'the most exquisite wines'.

36 **that favourite character . . . a nurse:** another allusion to the hero
of *Sir Charles Grandison*, among whose numerous accomplishments is expertise at tending the injured and sick. His patients
include the badly wounded Jeronymo della Porretta and, near
the end of the novel, his own newly wed wife, the former Harriet Byron, who exclaims: 'Every cordial, every medicine, did he
administer to me with his own hands' (vol. 7, letter 48). Despite
his prowess, however, Sir Charles much prefers female to male
nurses, telling his uncle, Lord W., 'Male nurses are unnatural
creatures! . . . Womens sphere is the house, and their shining-
place the sick chamber, in which they can exert all their amiable,
and, shall I say, lenient qualities' (vol. 3, letter 11).

37 **enliven the structure:** placing the treeless, flat circular paddock
of Evelyn lodge beside the craggy castle would create a startling
incongruity. The slope of the grounds and the profusion of trees,
in contrast, which Gower finds 'illsuited to the stile of the Castle',
provide the irregularity and ruggedness favoured by theorists of
the picturesque such as Gilpin.

38 **its' winding approach:** in approved picturesque style, unlike the
straight gravel road leading to Evelyn lodge.

39 **universal tremor . . . whole frame:** trembling of his entire
body.

40 **in the day, as nine o'clock:** darkness would have set in by 9pm in August, but few travellers other than Gower would have objected to the light of an almost full moon and twinkling stars. JA is caricaturing the plight of a type figure in Gothic fiction, the benighted rider; see A.D. McKillop, 'Allusions to Prose Fiction in Jane Austen's "Volume the Third"', *Notes and Queries*, 196 (1951), 428.

41 **Gipsies:** a nomadic people without nationality, regarded as pariahs in eighteenth-century England. Here, the alliterative 'Gipsies or Ghosts' points to the irrationality of Gower's fears. In *E*, however, a group of real, not imaginary, gipsies presents a threat to the terrified Harriet Smith, 'she trembling and conditioning, they loud and insolent' (vol. 3, ch. 3).

42 **gallop all the way:** JA's 'Evelyn' ends abruptly here. For the later continuations by James Edward Austen-Leigh and Anna Lefroy, see Appendix E.

CATHARINE

1 **Miss Austen:** JA's sister Cassandra, the dedicatee of 'The beautifull Cassandra' and 'The History of England'. In June 1793, ten months after writing her dedication to 'Catharine', JA would also dedicate the 'Ode to Pity' to her.

2 **threescore Editions:** even the most popular works of fiction, such as Defoe's *Robinson Crusoe* or Richardson's *Pamela*, went through many fewer than sixty editions in the eighteenth century. JA's juvenilia, which remained in manuscript, were of course known only to her family and close friends.

3 **Catharine:** originally 'Kitty'. JA changed her name to 'Catharine' on most but not all instances, and occasionally used the spelling 'Catherine'. In expanding the name, JA gives her heroine greater dignity, using 'Kitty' instead for Kitty Bennet of *P&P*. Lane notes that the forms 'Kitty' and 'Lizzy', as Elizabeth Bennet is known to her family, 'were rapidly becoming dated and before long would be associated only with old women' (*Names*, p. 70).

4 **Bower:** 'an arbour; a sheltered place covered with green trees, twined and bent' (Johnson). Edmund Spenser's Bower of Bliss in *The Faerie Queene*, Book II, plays a substantial intertextual role in 'Catharine'; see Clara Tuite, *Romantic Austen: Sexual Politics*

and the Literary Canon (Cambridge: Cambridge University Press, 2002), pp. 40–9. Book II of *The Fairie Queene* relates the exploits of Sir Guyon, the Knight of Temperance, who captures Acrasia and destroys her Bower of Bliss. Austen creates various comic links between Guyon and Catharine's Aunt Percival, as well as between Acrasia and the heroine.

5 **infantine:** 'not mature' (Johnson), rather than literally in infancy.

6 **tenure:** tenor.

7 **enthousiastic:** by the 1790s, the term 'enthusiastic' was being used more positively than earlier in the century, when it was associated primarily with excessive religious 'enthusiasm', defined by Johnson as 'a vain belief of private revelation; a vain confidence of divine favour or communication'. Johnson also, however, defines enthusiasm as 'elevation of fancy; exaltation of ideas', the qualities possessed by Catharine here. In a letter to Anna Austen of 18 August 1814, JA regretted that her young niece's novel in progress would no longer be called 'Enthusiasm': 'I like the name "Which is the Heroine?" very well . . . but "Enthusiasm" was something so very superior that every common title must appear to disadvantage' (*L*, p. 267). Anna might have made the change because of the use of 'Enthusiasm' in the titles of previous novels, such as Charles Brockden Brown's *Philip Stanley; or, the Enthusiasm of Love* (1807).

8 **Miss Wynnes:** presumably finding it redundant, JA here deleted a sentence describing Catharine's friendship with the Miss Wynnes in more detail; see textual notes.

9 **equip her for the East Indies:** young women had excellent prospects of finding a husband in India, where numerous single Englishmen were employed by the East India Company. Equipment for the voyage included light clothing for the hot climate, linen, medicines, etc.

10 **Bengal:** a province in north-east India, where the East India Company was based.

11 **double her own age . . . respectable:** the passage is informed by the experiences of JA's aunt Philadelphia Austen, who set sail from England to India in January 1752, reached Madras in August and married Tysoe Saul Hancock, an East India Company surgeon, six months later, in February 1753. Hancock was only seven

years older than his wife, but 'a melancholy man—unhappy in his
medical profession, frequently ill and given to harping upon his
fast-approaching decrepitude' (Le Faye, *Jane Austen's 'Outlandish
Cousin'*, pp. 12–13).

12 **Dowager:** a widow in possession of a title or property inherited
from her late husband.

13 **companion:** the same position that Eliza holds as 'humble companion' to the Duchess of F. in 'Henry and Eliza'.

14 **Chetwynde:** a village in Gloucestershire, the county in which
General Tilney's home, Northanger Abbey, is located. This imaginary Chetwynde, however, is in Devonshire, as JA indicates later
in the story.

15 **Mrs Percival:** despite being a 'Maiden Aunt', Mrs Percival is so
titled as a sign of respect for her age. In changing her name from
'Peterson' to 'Percival' (although not consistently), JA might have
been prompted by Mrs Percival's fondness for conduct-book dicta
of the kind found in Thomas Percival's *A Father's Instructions to his
children: consisting of Tales, Fables, and Reflections* (1775–1800). In
a letter of 7–9 October 1808, she tells Cassandra that 'we have got
a new Physician, a Dr Percival, the son of the famous Dr Percival
of Manchester, who wrote Moral Tales for Edward to give to
me' (*L*, p. 145). JA's brother Edward seems, from this, to have
given her a copy of Percival's book; the change from 'Peterson' to
'Percival' might have been made at about the same time.

16 **Dudley . . . very noble Family:** the family name of the Earl of
Leicester, the first of Queen Elizabeth's favourites. Mr Dudley
here is presumably a member of the same 'very noble Family'.
The Dudleys' 'Pride' and quarrelsome nature are in keeping with
their family association with Queen Elizabeth, whom JA con-
demns in her 'History of England'. JA's dislike of the Dudley
family might also have stemmed from her own family history:
her maternal ancestor Alice Leigh married the Earl of Leicester's son, Robert Dudley, who then deserted his wife for a mistress, Elizabeth Southwell; see George Holbert Tucker, *A Goodly
Heritage: A History of Jane Austen's Family* (Manchester: Carcanet
New Press, 1983), p. 56.

17 **tythes:** or tithes (tenths); taxes amounting to one tenth of a farm's
annual production, supposed to be paid by landowners to the

rector of a parish. Rather than paying the rector in kind, however, landowners would in practice make fixed payments. Iniquities caused by the payment of tithes were a subject of debate throughout JA's life. In a letter of *c.* 21 December 1815, James Stanier Clarke urged her to write a novel depicting 'an English Clergyman after *your* fancy', showing 'what good would be done if Tythes were taken away entirely' (*L*, p. 307). In her burlesque 'Plan of a Novel', probably written in 1816, JA did create such a clergyman, who opines on 'the Benefits to result from Tythes being done away' with (*MW*, p. 429).

18 **parade:** ostentatious display.

19 **on his travels:** taking the Grand Tour of France and, normally, of other countries in Europe. JA's brother Edward had returned from his Grand Tour in 1790 after an absence of four years, having visited Switzerland, Dresden and Rome.

20 **Stanley:** like Percival, the name has Elizabethan associations. Henry Stanley, fourth Earl of Derby, took part in the trial of Mary, Queen of Scots.

21 **Working:** undertaking needlework, such as embroidery: a genteel occupation for a young lady.

22 **Establishment:** the domestic staff, responsible for running household affairs and providing for the reception of visitors.

23 **sweep:** a curved carriage drive, leading to a house. The earliest example in *OED* is from the final chapter of *S&S* (1811).

24 **Italian Opera . . . hight of Enjoyment:** In Burney's *Cecilia*, a chapter (vol. 1, ch. 8) is devoted to a rehearsal of an opera at the King's Theatre in the Haymarket, which held some 3,000 spectators. Cecilia is delighted by the performance of Pietro Metastasio's *Artaserse*, featuring the castrato singer Gasparo Pacchierotti, and soon returns to the King's Theatre to hear Pacchierotti again.

25 **half the Year in Town:** a Member of Parliament would remain in London during the winter season, from the New Year until 4 June, when the King's official birthday was celebrated. He would spend the remainder of the year at his country seat.

26 **was:** JA here deleted a phrase indicating that Miss Stanley was 'about Kitty's age'.

27 **great reader . . . not a very deep one:** Catharine personifies a new type of reader in the late eighteenth century, in which

a shift from 'intensive' to 'extensive' reading took place. Modern readers, with access to a much larger number of books, wished, as the bluestocking Frances Boscawen noted, 'not to read strictly, but *feuiller* [browse]'; see John Brewer, *The Pleasures of the Imagination: English Culture in the Eighteenth Century* (London: HarperCollins, 1997), p. 169.

28 **well read in Modern history:** like JA herself, who had completed her own 'History of England' in November 1791, nine months before writing her dedication to 'Catharine'.

29 **Mrs Smith's Novels:** Charlotte Smith (1749–1806) had published four novels by August 1792, the date of 'Catharine': *Emmeline, the Orphan of the Castle* (1788), *Ethelinde, or the Recluse of the Lake* (1789), *Celestina* (1791) and *Desmond* (1792). Smith's subsequent novels are *The Old Manor House* (1793), *The Wanderings of Warwick* (1794), *The Banished Man* (1794), *Montalbert* (1795), *Marchmont* (1796) and *The Young Philosopher* (1798).

30 **Emmeline:** Smith's first novel seems also to have been JA's favourite. She alludes to its hero, Delamere, in both her 'History of England' (p. 185) and her marginalia to Goldsmith's *History of England* (Appendix B, p. 334).

31 **Ethelinde is so long:** *Ethelinde* was published in five volumes; *Emmeline* and *Celestina* were four-volume novels; *Desmond*, the shortest of the four, was published in three. A review of *Ethelinde* in the *Critical Review* likewise complained of its excessive length: 'in the third and fourth volumes, the conversations are too numerous, the same sentiments frequently repeated, and . . . the story is scarcely progressive' (new series, 3 (September 1789), 57).

32 **Descriptions of Grasmere:** a small, picturesque lake in the Lake District, in the north-west of England, a favourite destination for tourists. The opening chapters of *Ethelinde* are set on the shores of Grasmere, which Smith depicts in idyllic fashion. From 1799, William Wordsworth lived at Grasmere, in Dove Cottage.

33 **the Lakes:** the Lake District is also, in *P&P*, the intended destination of Elizabeth Bennet and the Gardiners for their 'tour of pleasure' (vol. 2, ch. 4), and Elizabeth's raptures at the prospect resemble Catharine's: 'What are men to rocks and mountains? Oh! what hours of transport we shall spend!' In his *Observations*,

Relative to Picturesque Beauty (1786), William Gilpin had celebrated the beauties of the region.

34 **Devereux:** another name with Elizabethan associations. Robert
Devereux, Earl of Essex, was Elizabeth's favourite courtier, until
his rebellion against her in 1601. In her 'History of England', JA
writes that he was 'equally conspicuous in the Character of an
Earl, as Drake was in that of a *Sailor*' (p. 185).

35 **travelling Dress:** probably a riding habit, comprising jacket,
waistcoat and petticoat, worn not only for riding but 'as an ordinary day- or travelling-dress' (Cunnington, *Handbook of English
Costume*, p. 305).

36 **races:** horse races, a popular site for matchmaking. Spectators,
male and female, would wear their finest clothes; Camilla here
intends to buy elaborate outfits for special occasions, such as race
meetings.

37 **Matlock:** a town in the Peak District of Derbyshire, also visited
by Elizabeth and the Gardiners in *P&P* (vol. 2, ch. 19).

38 **Scarborough:** a seaside resort in Yorkshire, on the east coast.
Stopping at Matlock en route to the Lake District was practicable,
but going via Scarborough would entail a lengthy detour.

39 **know nor care:** Camilla is doubly confused: she is unaware that
Matlock is in the county of Derbyshire, or that Scarborough is
in Yorkshire. Elizabeth Bennet, in contrast, insists that in her
tour, 'We *will* know where we have gone—we *will* recollect what
we have seen. Lakes, mountains, and rivers, shall not be jumbled
together in our imagination' (*P&P*, vol. 2, ch. 4).

40 **all order was destroyed . . . five in the Morning:** alluding to
the early stages of reaction in England against the threat of sedi-
tion inspired by the French Revolution. Mrs Percival's sentiments
are a comically debased version of those of Edmund Burke in
Reflections on the Revolution in France (1790), with its strident
warnings of the dangers that the Revolution posed to English
society.

41 **said her Neice:** JA here deletes part of Catharine's reply, 'I beleive
you have as good a chance of it as any one else', and thus softens
her character.

42 **good old Age . . . very Clever Woman:** Queen Elizabeth (1533–
1603) died at the age of sixty-nine. In her 'History of England',

JA describes her as 'that disgrace to humanity, that pest of society . . . the destroyer of all comfort, the deceitful Betrayer of trust reposed in her' (p. 183).

43 **Politics:** Camilla's ignorance of politics resembles that of the naive Catherine Morland in *NA*, in which Henry Tilney holds forth on property rights to the heroine and his sister: 'he shortly found himself arrived at politics; and from politics, it was an easy step to silence' (vol. 1, ch. 14).

44 **Harpsichord:** as in letter the seventh of 'Lesley Castle', the harpsichord has not yet been replaced by the more modern and fashionable pianoforte.

45 **sweetest Creature in the world:** in *The Loiterer*, 52, James Austen likewise mocks such affected language. Here a letter-writer, Cecilia, meets her cousin for the first time: 'before she had been in the house three days, I gave it as my opinion, that she was the sweetest woman in the world' (p. 7). A similar declaration is made in *NA* by Isabella Thorpe, who tells Catherine Morland about 'a particular friend of mine, a Miss Andrews, a sweet girl, one of the sweetest creatures in the world', who is making herself 'the sweetest cloak you can conceive' (vol. 1, ch. 6).

46 **in Public:** at public places, such as churches, theatres, ballrooms, etc.

47 **blue hat:** one of JA's favourite colours; see note 38 to 'Frederic and Elfrida'. The rear-view portrait of JA by Cassandra, a watercolour sketch dated 1804, depicts her in a blue bonnet and gown.

48 **Brook Street:** the fashionable London street in which Sir William Mountague falls in love with a 'charming young Woman entering a Chariot' (p. 49).

49 **find her in Cloathes:** supply clothes for her.

50 **two or three Curacies:** in addition to his living at Chetwynde, Mr Wynne has other livings, or curacies, at which he employs curates to take over his clerical duties.

51 **Cheltenham:** a fashionable spa resort in Gloucestershire.

52 **got into the Army:** originally 'sent to Sea'. With two brothers in the navy, JA presumably revised the phrase to make the Bishop's patronage of one of the sons seem less appealing; military service was not as attractive as naval service in her eyes.

53 **School somewhere in Wales:** attending a Welsh boarding school was a dubious privilege. Welsh schools were cheaper and less well equipped than their English counterparts. Their remoteness was a disadvantage for the boarders, but useful for patrons who wished their charges to remain at a distance.

54 **Ranelagh:** Ranelagh Gardens, a pleasure garden in Chelsea, opened in 1742 after the death of Lord Ranelagh, when his grounds were bought by an investment syndicate. It was a more expensive and ambitious rival to the older Vauxhall Gardens, with a large rotunda at the centre containing an orchestra and boxes for taking refreshments. Paintings, sculptures, lighting effects and fireworks were among its attractions.

55 **Bengal or Barbadoes:** both British colonies, but Barbados, a sugar-producing island in the West Indies, is very distant from Bengal in the East Indies, where Miss Wynne has been sent.

56 **nice:** in the sense of 'fastidious; squeamish' (Johnson).

57 **lent it to:** JA again deletes a retort by Catharine (see textual notes) in order to make her less censorious.

58 **Draws in Oils:** paints or sketches in oils, considered a higher achievement than working with watercolour or crayon.

59 **have one:** another sharp reply by Catharine is here deleted; see textual notes.

60 **to sea:** previously changed to 'into the Army'; JA apparently forgot to make the second alteration.

61 **Gold Net:** a cap with a hairnet made of golden thread, fashionable in the 1790s. 'Gold Net' is an insertion, indicating JA's interest in the latest fashions.

62 **longing for the pattern:** commercially printed patterns were scarce and much sought after. The *Lady's Magazine* (1770–1819) contained fold-out patterns in many issues, but these were usually removed by readers and are missing from surviving copies. In a letter to Cassandra of 2 June 1799, JA writes: 'I am quite pleased with Martha [Lloyd] & Mrs Lefroy for wanting the pattern of our Caps, but I am not so well pleased with Your giving it to them' (*L*, p. 43).

63 **receipt book:** a printed or manuscript collection of home remedies and prescriptions for ailments, including toothache.

64 **have a tooth drawn:** since extraction would take place without anaesthetic, Camilla's fears are understandable. The operation could be performed by a tooth-drawer, using a pair of forceps, or by a more specialized and expensive dentist, using a dental key (*All Things Austen*, p. 661). JA returns to the subject in *Sandi-ton*, in which Diana Parker prescribes tooth extraction as a rem-edy for her sister's headaches: 'being convinced on examination that much of the Evil lay in her Gum, I persuaded her to attack the disorder there. She has accordingly had 3 Teeth drawn, & is decidedly better' (*MW*, p. 387). In a letter of 16 September 1813, JA writes to Cassandra about her young niece Marianne Knight's sufferings at the hands of a London dentist. Marianne had to have two back teeth extracted, and 'when her doom was fixed . . . we heard each of the two sharp hasty Screams' (*L*, p. 223).

65 **pull it all down:** alluding to Guyon's destruction of the Bower of Bliss in Spenser's *The Faerie Queene*:

> But all those pleasant bowres and Pallace brave,
> Guyon broke downe, with rigour pitilesse.
> (Book 2, canto 12, 83)

66 **Regency walking dress:** an insertion that must have been made after February 1811, when the Regency Act proclaimed that the Prince of Wales would reign in place of his incapacitated father, George III. The Regency lasted until the death of George III in 1820. A walking dress, used for day and outdoor wear, had a skirt shorter than that of an evening dress.

67 **Pelisse:** defined by Mary Delany, in a letter of 20 January 1755 cited in *OED*, as 'a long cloak made of satin or velvet, black or any colour; lined or trimmed with silk, satin, or fur, according to the fancy'. In *MP*, Fanny Price, despite 'coming from a Baronet's family', offends the young ladies of Portsmouth: 'for as she nei-ther played on the pianoforte nor wore fine pelisses, they could, on farther observation, admit no right of superiority' (vol. 3, ch. 9).

68 **so flourishing and prosperous a state:** Stanley is a member of the Whig government of William Pitt the Younger, who had been

Prime Minister since 1783. Pitt was far more popular than his predecessor, Lord North, who was Prime Minister during the War of American Independence (1775–83). Under Pitt, confidence in the government was restored, especially in the first ten years of his leadership.

69 **at sixes and sevens:** in a state of disorder and confusion; an expression repeatedly used by Mrs Percival. The phrase, proverbial since the fourteenth century, derives from dicing, and originally denoted the hazard of one's entire fortune. Johnson terms it, in a sentence added to the fourth edition of the *Dictionary*, 'a ludicrous expression that has been long in use'.

70 **scotch Steps:** Scottish steps were incorporated into English country dances, but Scottish reels were considered too lively for dancing in public places. When Darcy asks Elizabeth Bennet to dance a reel it is at Bingley's private house, and Elizabeth takes the request as an insult: 'You wanted me, I know, to say "Yes," that you might have the pleasure of despising my taste' (*P&P*, vol. 1, ch. 10).

71 **gone an hour . . . in another hour:** originally half an hour and an hour and a half respectively (see textual notes). The changes give Catharine more time to write a 'long account' in her letter, and make her able to dress more quickly.

72 **dress:** JA here deleted a phrase, 'and providing herself with Lavender water'. Made from water and crushed lavender leaves, lavender water was used as a perfume and drunk as a stimulant.

73 **Chaise and four:** a light carriage drawn by four horses, and thus an exceptionally dashing form of transport. In *NA*, JA refers jestingly to 'three villains in horsemen's great coats, by whom [Catherine] will hereafter be forced into a travelling-chaise and four, which will drive off with incredible speed' (vol. 2, ch. 1).

74 **hair is just done up:** Tom the footman has had his hair elaborately arranged, as was customary in a fashionable household; the footman would wear a splendid uniform and was expected to make a fine appearance.

75 **Apron:** a working apron, made of coarse linen, not a decorative lady's apron. JA deleted a phrase explaining why the apron was needed: 'because you know Ma'am I am all over powder'. Anne

(originally given the more familiar diminutive form 'Nanny') has been powdering Catharine's hair.

76 **such a litter:** untidiness associated with feminine disorder. Johnson defines 'litter' as 'any number of things thrown sluttishly about'.

77 **Livery:** the uniform worn by a servant; its quality would signify the wealth and importance of the servant's employer.

78 **hack horses:** hackney horses, hired from a stable. Lacking servants and horses of his own, the visitor is of questionable social status. He has apparently hired four horses in an attempt to enhance his appearance.

79 **Glass:** mirror. Since Catharine is in her dressing room, the mirror is probably one mounted on a dressing table.

80 **Devonshire:** a county in the south-west of England. We later learn that Edward Stanley has travelled there from Brampton, the Stanleys' country seat. Since no location is provided for Brampton, it is unclear how far Stanley and his four horses have travelled.

81 **shocking:** the same fashionably hyperbolic term used by Camilla to describe Sir Peter, who is 'such a horrid Creature' and 'quite Shocking' (p. 250). In *NA*, Catherine Morland's misuse of the word, 'I have heard that something very shocking indeed, will soon come out in London', confuses her friend Eleanor Tilney (vol. 1, ch. 14).

82 **go to the door . . . comes:** Catherine is insisting on her genteel status, since answering the door was a servant's responsibility and she is displeased at having been mistaken for 'the prettiest little waiting maid'.

83 **smart:** smartly dressed.

84 **all your Devonshire Beaux:** Johnson defines a beau as 'a man of dress; a man whose great care is to deck his person'. Stanley, as usual, is exaggerating; a rural county, remote from London, Devonshire would have few beaux.

85 **travelling apparel:** probably a riding outfit, including boots and overcoat; most inappropriate for a ball, at which both men and women would wear their finest clothes.

86 **powder:** hair powder, usually white or grey, was still used by men of fashion in the 1790s, but became less common after 1795

when a tax of a guinea was imposed on its users. JA seems to have disliked it. In a letter to Cassandra of 21 January 1799, she notes that her brother Charles appeared 'to far more advantage' when he was 'neither oppressed by a pain in his face or powder in his hair' (*L*, p. 37).

87 **pair of Shoes:** flat leather shoes, with decorative buckles or shoe-strings, fit for the ballroom.

88 **Lyons:** a large city in central eastern France, Lyons was a popular destination on the Grand Tour. From Lyons, tourists could travel by ship on the river Rhône to the south of France.

89 **linen:** shirts, made of linen.

90 **Mr Stanley's dressing room:** the Stanleys have been given a large visitor's apartment, with a bedroom and two dressing rooms. The arrangement, like the footman's attire, suggests the size and importance of Mrs Percival's house.

91 **gone by eight:** in letter the third of 'A Collection of Letters', Mr Ashburnham expects the guests at his ball to arrive at eight thirty, although Lady Greville arrives fashionably late, at ten. Kitty here is even tardier, only getting into her carriage after ten.

92 **monthly Ball:** a public ball, with an entrance fee, as opposed to the private ball given by Mr Dudley. Stanley apparently prefers to envisage it as a public ball to cover the awkwardness of his not having received an invitation.

93 **Dignity of a Hall:** a substantial entrance hall was still a standard feature of country houses, allowing for the reception of a large number of guests, but they were gradually being replaced by smaller vestibules. Mr Dudley has fitted out his vestibule in the style of a hall, but it is clearly insufficient for the purpose. The 'younger son of a very noble family', he is trying to turn his parsonage into a stately home.

94 **upper end of the room:** where the musicians were placed, at the end opposite to the door through which guests entered.

95 **playing at Cards:** a room with card tables was a standard feature of a ball, providing entertainment for those, such as Mrs Stanley, who did not dance, or for those resting from dancing.

96 **Hunter:** a horse used for hunting. They were often thoroughbreds and thus expensive.

97 **Express:** a messenger, sent to deliver news as rapidly as possible.

98 **Brampton:** the name of the Stanleys' country seat, where they spend their summers when Parliament is not sitting.

99 **led her to the top of the room:** dancers at the top of the room lead the way in the dance, and therefore occupy the place of honour. For Stanley to take this place with Catharine is a double breach of propriety: neither he nor his partner has the rank or social standing to justify the move.

100 **only a tradesman:** Catharine's father is, in fact, a merchant, an important distinction, since tradesmen were considerably lower on the social scale. In the third of 'A Collection of Letters', Maria insists on the distinction.

101 **Mr Pitt or the Lord Chancellor:** two of the most powerful men in Britain, after the monarch, George III. William Pitt the Younger (1759–1806) was Prime Minister in 1783–1801, and 1804–6; when 'Catharine' was written he had been in power for nine years. The Lord Chancellor's responsibilities include presiding over the House of Lords and the judiciary. From 1778, the office was filled by the overbearing Edward, Lord Thurlow (1731–1806), until his dismissal by Pitt in June 1792: after JA wrote 'Catharine' but two months before she transcribed it into 'Volume the Third'.

102 **her partner during the greatest part of it:** a breach of etiquette; dancing with the same partner for more than two consecutive dances was considered impolite.

103 **Address:** 'manner of addressing another; as, we say, *a man of an happy or a pleasing address; a man of an aukward address*' (Johnson).

104 **come out:** out in society, the subject of the first of 'A Collection of Letters'.

105 **impudent:** utterly immodest. This is a serious charge, implying the 'intimacies with Young Men' that Mrs Percival deplores in the deleted sentence that follows.

106 **ever existed:** JA here deleted a sentence in which Mrs Percival denounces Catherine's 'intimacies with Young Men' as 'abominable'; see textual notes.

107 **tremblingly alive:** the same quotation from Pope's *An Essay on Man* used by Laura to characterize her sensibility in letter the third of 'Love and Freindship': 'Or Touch, if tremblingly alive

all o'er, / To smart and agonize at ev'ry pore' (epistle 1, lines 197–8). It is here applied ironically to Mrs Percival's alarms and apprehensions.

108 **calculated:** fitted, suited.

109 **temper:** 'Calmness of mind; moderation' (Johnson).

110 **Richard the 3d ... warmly defending:** in her 'History of England', JA notes that Richard's character 'has been in general very severely treated by Historians', but expresses her doubts about his guilt: 'as he was a *York*, I am rather inclined to suppose him a very respectable Man' (p. 179). In 'warmly defending' Richard, Stanley goes considerably further.

111 **pressed it passionately to his lips:** a kiss calculated to enrage Mrs Percival, for whom it would be a further sign of Catharine's 'impudence'. Kissing a lady's hand could be mere gallantry, but kissing it 'passionately' was a gesture of excessive intimacy.

112 **Profligate:** 'Abandoned; lost to virtue and decency; shameless' (Johnson), who also defines a profligate as 'an abandoned shameless wretch'.

113 **Blair's Sermons:** the Reverend Hugh Blair (1718–1800), Professor of Rhetoric at Edinburgh University, published his much admired sermons in five volumes between 1777 and 1801. Even Mary Crawford, no reader of theology, alludes to them in *MP* (vol. 1, ch. 9). Although Blair was a Presbyterian, not an Anglican, his sermons were a safe choice for Catharine's edification, expressing thoughts on the necessity for modesty and filial obedience similar to those of Mrs Percival.

114 **Coelebs in Search of a Wife:** a didactic novel of 1809 by Hannah More. JA originally wrote 'Seccar's explanation of the Catechism', alluding to *Lectures on the Catechism of the Church of England* (1769) by Archbishop Thomas Secker. Secker's work was popular in its time, but JA might have found it dated by the early 1800s. More's novel, about a bachelor in search of the perfect wife (his name derives from *caelebs*, Latin for unmarried), caught JA's attention as soon as it was published. In a letter to Cassandra of 24 January 1809, she writes that 'my disinclination for it before was affected, but now it is real; I do not like the Evangelicals'. A week later, she added that in the name 'Coelebs, there is pedantry & affection.—Is it written only to

Classical Scholars?' (*L*, pp. 170, 172). JA's dislike of the book, which developed ideas propounded in More's *Strictures on the Modern System of Female Education* (1799), made it a fit work for Mrs Percival's collection.

115 **key to my own Library:** probably the key to a locked bookcase containing Mrs Percival's library, rather than the key to a room. A woman's collection of books was seldom large enough to fill a room, and a library would also be unlikely to be locked.

116 **overthrow the establishment of the kingdom:** a rare allusion by JA to the threats posed to England by the French Revolution. Catharine suggests that the country faces greater dangers than those posed by her flirtation with Stanley. For her aunt, however, as for various conservative writers in the 1790s and early 1800s, female modesty and chastity formed an essential part of national stability.

117 **Oh ... how unreasonable:** Catharine seems to be recalling, and inverting, Hamlet's famous speech: 'What a piece of work is a man! How noble in reason, how infinite in faculty!' (*Hamlet*, Act 2, scene 2).

118 **nice Girl:** Stanley is using the word in the new sense that Henry Tilney deplores in *NA*: 'Oh! it is a very nice word indeed!—it does for every thing. Originally perhaps it was applied only to express neatness, propriety, delicacy, or refinement ... But now every commendation on every subject is comprised in that one word' (vol. 1, ch. 14).